CHRISTMAS DELIVERY

Christmas...
It's for *children*—every child knows that.

But then, think about the mistletoe.
Christmas is for *lovers*, too!

Maybe Christmas is for being together
with *all* the people you love—
young and old alike.

Yes, that's it!
Christmas is for *families*.
And families always have room for one more,
don't they?

Especially at *Christmas*.

CHRISTMAS DELIVERY

Relive the romance...

By Request™

Three complete novels by
your favorite authors!

DALLAS SCHULZE

The bestselling author of almost forty books, Dallas sold her first book when she was twenty-four, and is eternally grateful to the publishing world for saving her from having to find a "real" job. Dallas has been the recipient of numerous awards, including the Lifetime Achievement Award from *Romantic Times* and two bestselling book awards from Waldenbooks.

MARGARET ST. GEORGE

The talented author of over thirty novels, Margaret has fans worldwide for her novels that range from historical to mystery to contemporary romantic romps. A past president of Romance Writers of America, this award-winning author makes her home in Colorado.

MARGOT DALTON

A top-selling and award-winning author, Margot has written more than twenty contemporary romance novels. Of course, she started writing at a very early age—in fact, she completed her first book at the age of eleven! Margot's Superromance novel *Another Woman* was recently made into a television movie and aired by CBS.

CHRISTMAS DELIVERY

DALLAS SCHULZE
MARGARET ST. GEORGE
MARGOT DALTON

Harlequin Books

TORONTO • NEW YORK • LONDON
AMSTERDAM • PARIS • SYDNEY • HAMBURG
STOCKHOLM • ATHENS • TOKYO • MILAN
MADRID • WARSAW • BUDAPEST • AUCKLAND

HARLEQUIN BOOKS

by Request—CHRISTMAS DELIVERY

ISBN 0-373-20141-9

This edition published by arrangement with Harlequin Books S.A.

Printed in U.S.A.

CONTENTS

She allowed herself one night in his arms. But that one night only made her want him more.... As a lover—and now as the father of her baby!

A CHRISTMAS MARRIAGE

Dallas Schulze

Chapter One

They'd had a Christmas wedding and a Halloween divorce. That was what Tess Armstrong always said if the subject of her brief marriage came up. It was a light, breezy answer, perfectly suited to turning away any probing questions. Not that very many people would have asked probing questions anyway, not in Southern California. If there was one thing Southern Californians understood besides how to get the perfect tan, it was how to mind their own business.

But on the off chance that the questioner was too new to the area to understand the unwritten social laws that governed the famous laid-back life-style, Tess's casual reply made it sound as if the subject of her marriage was simply not interesting enough to pursue.

Sometimes, she almost managed to convince herself that the five years that had passed since the divorce had put her marriage in the distant and nearly forgotten past. Weeks would go by when she didn't even think about her ex-husband. If asked about him, she might even have taken a moment to recall his face.

Tess was proud of the distance she'd managed to put between herself and her youthful marriage. It had taken her years to achieve that indifference.

It only took a moment to show her just how thin a facade it really was.

AS USUAL, FRAN invited twice as many people as her house could accommodate, on the theory that most of them wouldn't show up. As usual, most of them showed up. Fran and Charlie McKenzie's parties were always worth attending, for the spectacular views from their hilltop home and for the interesting mix of guests. You could find yourself talking to anyone from a state senator to a garbage collector who just happened to do watercolors that Fran admired. And if smog obscured the lights of the city or the guests happened to be a dull batch, there was always the food.

Fran's Food was generally acknowledged to be one of the city's best catering services. And Fran always catered her own parties. "It's good for business," she said, whenever someone suggested that she worked as hard on her own parties as she did on her clients'. "Besides, I can hardly hire the competition, now can I?"

She might not hire the competition, but she was perfectly capable of inviting them to the party, along with anyone else who happened to catch her endlessly roving eye.

Tess leaned against the balcony railing and watched the ebb and flow of people moving through the open balcony doors. Half-shielded by a potted ficus tree that towered over her head, she was free to observe without being noticed, which suited her just fine. It was August and the temperature still hovered at seventy, despite the fact that the sun had set a couple of hours before. In typical fashion, the party had expanded onto the balcony and into the gardens beyond. Guests strolled along strategically lit pathways and sat on cushioned wrought-iron benches, balancing plates of food on their knees.

Tess had already nibbled to her heart's content and now she was indulging in one of her favorite entertainments—people watching. And she could always count on Fran to provide plenty of interesting people to watch.

The woman stepping through the balcony doors, for example. From the top of her artfully tousled, pseudo sun-streaked hair to the tips of her three-inch scarlet pumps, she was the picture of casual sophistication. She looked like an actress or perhaps a model. Nothing else could justify that exquisitely lean body and the taut skin that owed as much to a scalpel as it did to genes. As it happened, Tess recognized her. The woman owned a construction company, one she'd built from the ground up, and she was just as comfortable with a hammer in her hand as she was cradling a wineglass.

Behind her was a perennial loser in the political sweepstakes. He was a candidate in every election and he consistently lost by a landslide. Tess had never been able to decide whether she admired his determination or deplored his inability to take a hint.

And standing just behind him...

Tess's fingers clenched around the stem of her wineglass as shock washed over her.

Nick.

It didn't matter that she could see only the thick wave of dark blond hair and the angle of his jaw. She would have known him anywhere, even if all she could see was the back of his head. No one else stood like that, feet slightly apart, broad shoulders squared, one hand hidden in the pocket of his tailored gray trousers. She'd once teased him, saying that he looked as if he were standing on the bridge of a ship, feet braced against the motion of the water, shoulders braced against any gale that might blow.

He'd laughed and called her "my pretty" as he swept her into his arms. With a comic leer, he'd said that of all the booty he'd captured, she was the prize piece. The scene had ended in bed, which was the one place their marriage had never had a problem.

Tess swallowed hard and forced the memories away, shifting her eyes from Nick's back at the same time. She hadn't seen him since the divorce, hadn't thought of him in months. Yet all it took was a glimpse of him to bring the memories tumbling back.

Why hadn't Fran warned her?

Because she knew Tess wouldn't have come if she'd been told Nick was to be there.

Out of the corner of her eye, she saw him turning toward the balcony doors. On a surge of pure panic, Tess turned and pretended absorption in the sprawl of glowing lights that was Los Angeles. *Idiot.* What was the matter with her? She was hiding from Nick as if he were the bogeyman. She eased closer to the ficus, wishing there were a nice, dense hedge she could hide behind.

It was just the shock of seeing him after so long, she told herself. As soon as she recovered her balance, she would turn and act like the mature adult she was. With luck, Nick wouldn't even notice her as she scuttled for the door.

"Tess?" The low voice stroked over her skin, as if he'd trailed fingers the length of her spine, most of which was left bare by the halter dress she wore.

For a split second, she considered the possibility of diving over the railing into the shrubbery beneath, but she was sure that didn't appear in any handbooks about how to react to seeing your ex-husband. Instead, she drew a deep breath, and forced her mouth to curve in a smile as she turned to face the man she'd once loved more than life.

"Nick! What a surprise." The tone was a little too hearty but her voice was steady. "I didn't see you," she added, just in case he thought his presence had anything to do with her position behind the ficus. Casually she edged away from the sheltering foliage.

"I just got here a few minutes ago. I bumped into Charlie at the airport and he insisted on dragging me home with him. Said Fran was throwing a party. He brings home stray puppies, too, I understand."

Tess laughed at the small joke, even as she was thinking that Nick Masters had about as much in common with a stray puppy as a cougar did with a calico kitten.

Was it possible he'd gotten even handsomer in the last five years? Or was it just that she'd managed to convince herself that he wasn't as impossibly good-looking as she'd remembered?

"How have you been?" he asked. "You look terrific."

Tess told herself that his look of masculine approval had absolutely no affect on her. The goose bumps popping up on her shoulders must have been caused by a stray breeze.

"Thank you. You look good yourself."

"Good" was an anemic description. "Good" didn't begin to describe the way the light caught in the heavy gold of his thick hair. Tess's fingers tightened around her wineglass.

"Thanks." Nick's smile softened, his eyes warm. "How are you, Tess?"

"I'm fine." Her voice sounded too tight and she took a quick sip of wine. Damn him! Why did he have to look just as she'd remembered? Why couldn't he have gone bald and developed a potbelly? Better yet, why couldn't he have gotten glasses? They might have helped to conceal those emerald green eyes that had always seemed to look right into her soul.

"I hear your shop is doing well," Nick said, when it became clear she wasn't going to say anything more.

"From whom?" The words came out sharper than she'd intended. She saw Nick's eyes widen in surprise and felt a flush come up in her cheeks. "I wouldn't think you'd have much interest in a tiny little place like mine," she added, lifting one shoulder in a half shrug.

"I was always interested in what you did," he reminded her quietly.

And he had been, Tess admitted to herself. He hadn't been one of those men who talked about what happened at work and never thought to ask how their wives had spent their day. Nick had always asked. The problem was, she'd never had anything to tell him.

"The shop is fine," she said, sidestepping the question of his interest. "I've been lucky."

"I doubt luck had much to do with it. Small businesses don't succeed on luck."

"Well, I've put in a lot of hours," she admitted, wishing she didn't feel such a response to the admiration in his eyes. "How is the architecture business these days? Still traveling all over the country?"

Nick was the star architect in the firm his grandfather had founded. Masters Architectural designed everything from office buildings to private homes. During their brief marriage, he'd spent two weeks of every month away from home, meeting with clients, supervising projects, examining building sites, doing all the things that went along with maintaining the firm's reputation for quality.

She'd traveled with him at first, but after a few months, the novelty of life in a series of hotel rooms had worn thin and she'd started staying home when he left.

"I'm doing a lot less traveling these days," Nick said. "Hope joined the firm two years ago and she does quite a bit of the traveling."

"I thought Hope was determined to do noble deeds. Wasn't she thinking about joining the Peace Corps or something like that?"

"She gave that idea up when she found out she might have to live without flush toilets."

Tess chuckled, trying to imagine the exquisite Hope Masters roughing it in the bush. "I guess nobility only goes so far."

"Well, she hasn't given up entirely. She talked my father into taking on several low-income housing projects. I think it makes her feel less of a traitor when she finds herself working on a ten-thousand-square-foot mansion."

"How are your parents? And Annie and Sara?" His family was a safe topic—and she was groping for one, desperately trying not to let her eyes linger on her ex-husband's face. Anyway, she'd been fond of her in-laws and she'd honestly missed them after the divorce. She felt her face flush with heat. There was only one other thing she missed more....

NICK WAS WILLING to give her updates on his family if that was what she wanted. The tension had eased from her face, her eyes didn't look quite so panicked.

Five years, he thought, his eyes going over her. She'd been only twenty when they separated. She'd been pretty then, with a youthful softness that had brought out his protective instincts. In the past few years she'd lost the last traces of girlishness and matured into a beautiful woman.

The changes were subtle. At twenty-five, her skin was still smooth as silk, all sun-warmed peach tones that glowed against the sapphire blue of her dress. The halter-style top revealed most of her shoulders and he found himself wanting to trace his fingers over the delicate line of her collarbone, wanting to see if that light touch would make her tremble the way it once had.

Her hair was coiled into a smooth chignon at the back of her head. Raven's-wing black, it was thick and straight. He remembered it tumbled over her shoulders, the morning sun picking out blue highlights, her neck arched with pleasure as they made love. Had she cut it or did it still fall to her waist in a shining black curtain?

He glanced away, swallowing hard against the sudden wave of hunger that swept over him. It was a good thing he was wearing loosely tailored trousers and not tight jeans, he thought ruefully. It had been a long time since he'd become aroused just looking at a woman. Since the divorce, he thought. Since the last time he'd seen Tess.

One of the other guests had joined them and was asking Tess something about her shop. Nick let his mind drift from the conversation and his eyes drift over his ex-wife. God, but she looked good. How could he have forgotten how beautiful she was? How desirable? He had only to look at her to find himself growing hard. It had always been like that. From the first moment he'd seen her, he'd wanted her.

They'd met at a Halloween party. Tess had been dressed as a black cat. Wearing a black leotard, a ridiculous black velvet tail, with penciled whiskers on her cheeks and a headband with ears on her head, she'd looked at once sensuous and innocent. And Nick had wanted her more than he'd ever wanted a woman in his life.

It had taken him less than a week to convince her to sleep with him and no one had been more surprised than he was when he found himself proposing the next morning. Tess had refused, telling him that he was just feeling guilty because he'd been her first lover. But it hadn't been guilt he'd felt. It had been a soul-deep hunger, a need to tie her to him as solidly as he could, to make her his in every way possible. Making love to her wasn't enough.

It had taken him almost two months to convince her to

marry him and he was willing to admit that he hadn't played completely fair. He hadn't hesitated to use sex as a persuader, tumbling her into bed whenever she started to argue about how little time they'd known each other.

After they were married, their sex life had been everything he'd fantasized it would be. That was one place they'd never had any problems with their marriage. No matter what else had gone wrong, *that* had been right—more right than it had been either before or since.

And in the last five years, he thought, he'd almost managed to make himself forget just how right it had been.

"It's good to see you, Tess," he said abruptly, as soon as the guest had taken her leave. He saw her eyes widen, saw surprise and some other emotion he couldn't identify, and then her lashes lowered, concealing the sapphire blue of her eyes.

"It's good to see you, too, Nick." But her tone made the words nothing more than a polite response, telling him nothing of how she really felt.

That had been one of the most frustrating aspects of their marriage—the way she had of concealing what she was feeling, of saying what she thought he wanted to hear, not what she really thought. And he'd learned then that the harder he pushed, the deeper she retreated into that polite little shell. It had gotten to the point where he'd had to fight the urge to grab her and shake her until the shell cracked, revealing the emotions inside.

"I've missed you." The words tumbled out before he could censor them.

The startled way her eyes swept up to his made him wish the words unsaid. He was going too fast. Again. Just as he'd done when he met her, sweeping her into marriage without giving her a chance to think about it. Hadn't he learned his lesson then?

He scrambled to cover up his blunt remark. "I haven't had a decent apple pie in five years," he said, and added a sly grin.

The subtle tension in her eyes seemed to ease and her mouth curved in a smile. "You always did have a sweet tooth."

"It's still there."

An awkward silence fell between them. Nick thought of half a dozen things he wanted to ask. He wanted to know if she ever thought about the time they'd had together, if she ever regretted the divorce. Was there still an empty place inside her when she thought about him? Was she dating? Did she have a lover?

His chest felt tight and hard at the thought of Tess in bed with another man. Not jealousy, certainly. He was long past the stage where he was jealous of her. But he was willing to admit to a certain possessiveness, a foolish male reluctance to share something that had once been his.

"I think Fran needs some help," she said suddenly, looking past his shoulder.

Nick didn't bother to turn. He knew as well as she did that Fran's parties always ran like clockwork. He also knew that Fran would rather tap-dance nude down Wilshire Boulevard than ask one of her guests to help.

"Maybe we could get together and have a cup of coffee somewhere," he said, reluctant to let her walk away. Nostalgia, he told himself. He was just feeling nostalgic.

The suggestion brought Tess's eyes back to his face. For just an instant, he thought he saw something there, a look that said his words had touched some chord of response. But then it was gone, her expression shuttered against him.

"I don't think that's a good idea, Nick." Her eyes met his for an instant before sliding away. "It was nice to see you," she murmured. She slipped past him without waiting for his response.

Nick didn't try to stop her. He stayed where she'd left him, one hand cradling an untouched glass of Scotch, his eyes on the spectacular view of the city. But he wasn't seeing the sprawl of lights. He was seeing a pair of sapphire blue eyes. And wondering if he'd imagined that brief moment when they seemed to reflect an emptiness that matched his own.

TESS RESISTED THE URGE to walk away from Nick and straight out the front door. That would look as if she was running away. And even though that was exactly what she wanted to do, pride demanded she stay at least long enough to show she'd taken the meeting in stride.

She chatted with casual acquaintances, laughed at the right times and tried not to be too obvious about keeping tabs on Nick's whereabouts. Since Fran's house sprawled over the hillside and the party spilled not only into every room but out into the gardens, it was all but impossible to keep track of any one person, especially while trying to appear completely disinterested.

But she did see Nick several times. He seemed to be having a great time, she thought resentfully. Watching him talk to a long-legged busty blonde, she found herself wondering if he even remembered that his ex-wife was here. The blonde leaned forward to say something to him, practically nibbling his ear in the process, her breast pressed intimately against the sleeve of his dark jacket. Nick didn't appear to have any objections to having a strange woman all but plaster herself to his side.

Of course, maybe she wasn't a stranger. The thought created an odd pinched sensation in Tess's chest and she turned away. Who was or wasn't a stranger to Nick was not her concern anymore. When she'd asked for a divorce, she'd given up the right to feel jealous because another woman had her hand on his arm.

IT WAS ALMOST ELEVEN before Tess decided she could leave without anyone being able to say her departure had anything to do with her ex-husband. She located Fran and said her farewells, thankful that Fran was occupied with her duties as hostess and didn't have time to offer more than a token protest at Tess's somewhat early departure.

As she headed for the door, Tess looked for Nick, uncertain whether she hoped to see him or not. Part of her craved another glimpse of him, while another more cautious part suggested it would be better if she didn't see him.

He was not in sight and she tried to feel relieved. She'd said her goodbyes five years ago. There was no need to say them again.

Since the McKenzie home was perched on a hilltop, the driveway to it was steep. There were no stairs leading down to the street. As Fran put it, this way they knew that anyone who made the climb *really* wanted to see them. Tess hesitated at the top of the slope and then reached down to slip off her high-heeled sandals, glad she'd decided against wearing hose.

The concrete held a day's accumulation of sun and it felt warm against her bare feet. Her shoes dangling from her fingers, she made her way down the drive, grateful for the soft illumination provided by the low lamps that lined the drive. Her car was parked at the bottom of the hill, a pale blue compact wedged between a silver Mercedes and a rusty pickup truck. She smiled, thinking that the three cars were a perfect metaphor for Fran's eclectic guest list.

She had just pulled her keys from her purse when she heard someone call her name. Her fingers tightened over the keys.

Nick.

She turned reluctantly toward the sound of his voice, watching him negotiate the steep drive at a speed far greater than her own cautious descent.

"I'm glad I caught you," he said, as he reached the street level and started toward her.

"Why?" Despite herself, Tess felt her pulse pick up speed. Half a dozen possibilities flashed through her mind, ranging from he wanted to beg her to come back to him to he wanted to tell her he was getting married again.

"Could you give me a lift home?"

"Home?" She stared at him blankly for a moment. Home to the house they'd shared for eighteen months? The house he'd given her in the settlement? The one that still occasionally reminded her of him so strongly that she sometimes thought it would be better to sell it to finally escape the memories?

"My condo," Nick clarified. "I caught a ride from the airport with Charlie and I hate to ask him to leave his own party to take me home. It's not far out of your way."

"I don't know, Nick...." Her voice trailed off as she sought, and failed to find, a good reason for refusing his request.

"I'm not asking for a loan, Tess. Just a ride." Nick's tone gently chided her hesitation, making her feel foolish.

"Sure." Her agreement sounded anything but gracious. Was it because she resented feeling manipulated...or because she resented the quick flare of pleasure that came with the thought of spending more time with her ex-husband?

Tess didn't care to answer.

Chapter Two

Nick folded his long legs into the passenger seat, guiltily aware of the car keys in his pocket. He'd never been a man inclined to easy lies, whether in business or in his personal life. But when he'd seen Tess leaving the party, he'd had the sudden feeling that he couldn't just let her walk out.

He'd watched her all evening without seeming to do so. The memories of the girl who'd been his wife were already blurred by the reality of the woman she'd become. He found himself wanting the woman she was even more than he'd wanted her before. The deep hunger he remembered seemed sharper, more demanding than it had been five years ago. He simply couldn't let her walk away.

So he'd left the party without bothering to say good-night to his hosts, followed his ex-wife and lied shamelessly to her. Glancing sideways, he saw her profile against the window—long forehead, short straight nose, the soft pout of her mouth.

And he felt no regret at his prevarication.

TESS WAS VIVIDLY AWARE of Nick's large presence. She'd thought he was too close at Fran's party but the compact car made them positively cozy. Why hadn't she bought a van? Or better yet, a bus? A nice, big bus where Nick could have been seated at least twenty feet away.

He shifted, trying to find a more comfortable position. The little car hadn't been designed with a man of his size in mind.

His leg was only inches from hers. In the pale blue light from the dashboard, she could see the way the crease in his trouser leg flattened over his bent knee. Nick had been a runner when she knew him and she'd sometimes teased him that he had better legs than she did. She didn't have to close her eyes to remember what he looked like in running shorts.

Or what he looked like without them. Tess swallowed hard and forced her thoughts in other, safer, directions. But she felt her breath catch when his hand settled on the back of her seat. He was just trying to get comfortable, she told herself. The fact that his fingers were nearly touching her hair was pure coincidence. It didn't mean he was remembering the way he'd always pulled the pins from her hair so it would spill over his hands, or the way he'd tangle his fingers in it when they made love, holding her head beneath his, his eyes intent on her face, watching her response.

"So, you bought a condo." The words were abrupt, a little forced, her voice higher than normal. Too revealing, she thought, too obvious that she wanted—needed—to break the silence.

"Yeah. I didn't feel like getting a house, not just for myself."

His words brought the memories flooding back—the two of them looking at the old house in Pasadena for the first time, Nick pointing out that it needed a lot of work, her wrapping her hands around his upper arm and telling him to stop looking with his mind, and listen with his heart. The house *needed* them. It needed someone to buy it and take care of it, restore it to its former glory. Besides, there was a huge sycamore in the backyard that practically cried out to have a bench set under it. Nick had muttered that the tree cried out to have a chain saw taken to it, but he'd given in and admitted that the place *did* have some possibilities.

She didn't have to look at him to know he was remembering the same things: the midnight wallpapering sessions, the miles of trim they'd stripped by hand, removing nearly a hundred years' worth of paint to reveal the beautiful wood beneath.

"You could have had the house," Tess said into the silence.

"No. It meant a lot to you. You're still there?"

"Yes." She flipped on a turn signal and eased her way off the freeway. She didn't add anything to the flat statement. She certainly couldn't tell him that there were still moments when she turned, half expecting to see him in a doorway, his thick blond hair spattered with paint, demanding that she come and help him with some task. After all, he'd say, she was the one who'd wanted this white elephant. As if he hadn't wanted the place too, the moment he saw it.

The remainder of the drive was silent, broken only by Nick's quiet directions. Strangely, it wasn't an uncomfortable silence. The sharing of memories, even if unacknowledged, seemed to have eased the tension. Maybe it was the idea that something concrete had come from their marriage, even if it was only the restoration of an old house.

TESS PULLED THE CAR to a stop in front of the building Nick indicated. In the darkness, the row of condos was visible only as sharply angled rooflines against the night sky. When Nick didn't move to get out of the car, she shut the engine off. The sudden silence was almost deafening.

"Come in for a nightcap," Nick said, turning his head to look at her.

Tess shook her head, even as she felt a little leap of something that could have been—but wasn't—anticipation.

"I'm driving."

"Then come in for a cup of coffee."

"It's late."

"Decaffeinated."

"I shouldn't."

"Fresh ground," he coaxed, sensing she was weakening.

"Really, I shouldn't." It wasn't the coffee that tempted her, fresh ground or otherwise. And that was why she couldn't take him up on his offer. The last thing she needed was to let Nick Masters back into her life, even just the tiny bit necessary to share a cup of coffee with him.

"I'm not going to bite, Tess." The trace of amusement in his voice brought her chin up a fraction.

"I'm not afraid of you," she said. *Only of myself.*

"Then come in for coffee. Please, Tess. I'd like to talk to you." His hand still lay on her seat and he shifted it now, brushing the back of his fingers against her cheek.

Tess felt the light touch all the way to her toes. She kept her gaze lowered, not wanting Nick to see her reaction, knowing he'd already sensed it. It had always been like that between them, the awareness that needed only the barest touch to spring to life. *That* was why she wasn't going to accept his invitation. *That* was why she was going to issue a polite refusal, see him out of her car and drive away without a backward glance. It had taken her five years to put her life back together. She wasn't going to let Nick Masters back into it, not even by the smallest amount.

"A cup of coffee does sound good."

THE CONDOMINIUMS WERE SET against the foothills above Glendale. The view drew a murmur of appreciation from Tess when Nick pulled open the drapes in the living room.

"It's not as spectacular as the view Fran and Charlie have, but it's not bad," Nick commented as he tugged open the sliding glass door and gestured her through onto the narrow balcony. "The whole building really should be turned about ten degrees for the best advantage," he added critically.

"Obviously it's not a Masters design. A Masters design would have been perfect." The teasing comment surprised Tess even as she said it.

"Actually, it *isn't* one of ours." Nick leaned one hip against the redwood railing. "*I* would have found a way to take advantage of the view." The tuck in his cheek made a joke of his haughty tone.

"Naturally." Tess set her hands on the railing and settled her gaze on the sparkling lights below. It seemed like a hundred years ago that she'd been looking at a similar view from Fran's balcony. Before she'd known Nick was at the party, before she'd had reason to remember the way he could make her tingle all over with just a look.

Nick cocked his head as the kettle began to whistle. He'd

found the coffee and set the water to boil before showing her the view.

"The water's ready. I'll go pour it over the grounds."

Tess nodded. She closed her eyes as he went back into the living room. This was crazy. What was she doing in Nick's condo, pretending to admire the view? The only view she could see at the moment was emerald green eyes and a pair of shoulders where she'd once rested her head.

She opened her eyes and turned restlessly away from the view, moving back into the living room. A heavy pottery lamp cast a circle of light onto the thick black carpet and lit one side of the curved gray sofa. The black-and-gray color scheme was softened by splashes of mauve. It was a sophisticated look. A bachelor's look, she thought and then told herself she didn't feel a stab of pain when she thought of Nick as a bachelor.

"Jamaican Blue Mountain. Freshly ground, with just a spoonful of cream." At Nick's words, Tess turned toward him.

Her breath caught in her throat in involuntary reaction. He'd discarded his suit jacket and tie. The sleeves of his pearl gray Egyptian cotton shirt were rolled up to reveal his muscled forearms and the top two buttons were undone, allowing a glimpse of the mat of dark blond hair that covered his chest.

Tess's palms tingled with the memory of how that crisp hair felt against her fingers, under her palm. She could see the ripple of muscle under the fine cotton and she felt an answering ripple of response in the pit of her stomach.

"Tess?" She blinked and dragged her eyes from Nick's chest to his face. "Something wrong?"

"No." Her voice was hardly more than a whisper and she cleared her throat and tried again. "No. My mind was just wandering."

"No law against it." She was grateful he didn't question just where her mind might have wandered. But as she took the cup from him, their eyes met and she had the uneasy feeling he knew exactly where her thoughts had gone.

The coffee was smooth and rich. Nick was the one who'd taught her that coffee could be something to be savored rather than merely consumed. After the divorce, she'd gone back to instant and she'd nearly forgotten just how good coffee could taste.

"You could have bought a grinder," Nick responded when she said as much. "If I'd known you were going to go back to swill, I'd have left mine."

"Swill seems a bit extreme," she protested, obeying his gestured suggestion to sit on the sofa. As she sank into the thick gray leather, it occurred to her that she'd never imagined the time would come when either of them would be able to make casual references to their divorce, to the painful process of dividing their lives.

"Trust me, swill is a compliment."

Tess's fingers tightened around her cup as Nick sank onto the sofa. She'd expected him to take one of the chairs, where he'd be at a nice, safe distance. But the sofa was placed to offer a good view of the city lights, so it didn't seem unreasonable that Nick should choose to sit there.

What did seem unreasonable was the way her pulse accelerated at his nearness. It was the same reaction he'd always inspired in her, the reason she'd let him seduce her into his bed, the reason she'd married him. But it wasn't enough to build a relationship on, she reminded herself. Her pulse ignored her, continuing to beat too quickly.

"It really is a beautiful view," she said, trying to distract herself from the direction her thoughts were going.

"I like it."

But when she glanced at Nick, he wasn't looking at the view. His gaze was on her, searching, questioning. Tess reached up to touch her hair in a self-conscious gesture.

"Is my hair coming down or do I have a smudge on my nose?"

"Sorry. I didn't mean to stare." But he didn't look away. "I was just thinking that you've changed."

"It's been five years. Most people change in five years." Needing something to do with her hands, she reached out to set her cup down on the low glass table that sat in front of the sofa.

"Most people don't get more beautiful."

The husky words made Tess's eyes jerk to his. And what she read there ended any hope she had of making her pulse behave.

"Nick..."

"When I saw you at the party, all I could think of was that you'd become even more beautiful than you were five years ago."

"Nick..." His hand came up, his fingers delving into the soft chignon.

She was going to move away, Tess told herself. She was going to stand up and tell him that she hadn't come here to be seduced by him. She was going to walk out with her pride—not to mention her virtue—intact.

He pulled the pins out and her hair spilled over his hand like heavy black silk.

"You didn't cut it," he whispered, watching it ripple past her waist.

"No." Tess swallowed hard, her skin flushing at the look in his eyes. It was that remembered look—the remembered hunger—that had stopped her every time she decided to get her hair cut into some short-and-sassy style.

"I used to dream about the way you looked," Nick said softly. He curled his fingers deeper into her hair as his eyes lifted to hers. "After the divorce, I wanted to forget you. But at night, when I closed my eyes, I'd remember the way you'd look when we made love, wearing nothing but that black cape of hair. And me."

Tess couldn't drag her eyes from his. She was going to put an end to this scene. She was going to walk away before she did something incredibly stupid. Like let herself be seduced by the look in her ex-husband's eyes.

Nick's thumb brushed over the sensitive skin beneath her ear and she forgot how to breathe.

"Nick..." She started to twist her head away from his touch and found herself leaning into it instead.

"You used to say my name just that way when we made love. All breathless and hungry."

When had he gotten so close? She could see the faint gold lines that radiated out from his pupils, giving depth to the dark green. The hunger in his eyes made it hard to breathe, made it impossible to think.

"I can't," she whispered, shivering as he trailed his fingers down the length of her throat.

"This was inevitable, Tess. You know it. I know it. It has to happen."

"We're divorced." He was tracing the edge of her halter top, his fingertips almost touching the side of her breast. Tess felt her breast swell in anticipation of that touch. If he looked, she knew Nick would be able to see the shameless invitation of her nipple thrusting against the soft silk of her dress.

"I want you, Tess. And you want me." Without taking his eyes from her, he cupped her breast in one wide palm. Shock dried Tess's mouth. Hunger made her eyes dilate. With just that light touch, he'd rolled back the clock. *This* was what she'd spent five years forgetting. *This* was what she'd never be able to forget.

"We can't." Her fingers closed around his wrist but her strength ended there. She couldn't find the will to push him away.

"We can." Nick's thumb brushed over her swollen nipple and this time she knew he felt the shiver that ran through her. He brought his free hand up, his fingers circling her wrist as he carried her hand to his chest. He pressed her hand flat against his shirt and Tess could feel the heavy beat of his heart beneath her palm. The rhythm was quick and hard, matching her own pulse.

"This isn't what I came here for," she whispered, lifting her eyes to his face.

"Isn't it?" he asked huskily. "Admit it, Tess. You want this as much as I do. Don't turn away from it. I need you."

The three words struck deep. He needed her. He'd always needed her in this way. The tragedy had been that he hadn't needed her on any other level. But that didn't stop her visceral response to that simple declaration.

"Oh, Nick." The words were half protest and all surrender.

"Tess." Her name was a caress. His hand shifted, sliding beneath the silk of her halter-style bodice.

Tess was helpless to stop the soft moan that escaped her, betraying her need. His hand was warm and hard. Nick was as likely to be found with a hammer in his hand as he was a drafting tool and his callused skin abraded her tender flesh in a way that made breathing require a conscious effort.

He caught her nipple between thumb and forefinger, and she swayed toward him like a flower bending in the wind. Her fingertips flexed against his chest and her eyelids half closed as she savored the feel of him touching her, holding her.

It had been so long. She must have murmured the words aloud or perhaps Nick read her mind.

'Too long, Tess. Much too long." Without moving his hand from her breast, he set his other hand on the back of her neck, drawing her closer.

Tess told herself she was going to tell him this had to stop. Here and now. Before they did something she was going to regret. They were opening a door that had been closed a long time, and behind that door lay a great deal of pain. But so much pleasure, too, she thought, her eyes closing as Nick's mouth hovered over hers.

There was nothing tentative in his kiss. He was a man kissing a woman with whom he'd been intimate, a woman who'd shared his bed for nearly two years. He knew her, knew her responses as intimately as he knew his own. His tongue traced the softness of her lower lip before sliding past the barrier of her teeth and into the honeyed sweetness of her mouth. Tess could taste the smoky darkness of coffee on his tongue. Or was it on hers? It didn't matter. It wasn't possible to tell where one began and the other ended. There was only the two of them, joined together, just the way they were meant to be.

NICK TASTED HER SURRENDER in the way her fingers clutched his shirt in pleading little handfuls, in the ripe swell of her breast in his hand, in the eager way her tongue met his, teasing him deeper.

He hadn't consciously planned this when he'd asked her to

come in for coffee. He'd told himself he only wanted to talk to her, perhaps to find some footing between them besides the old hurts they shared. But looking at her in the shadowy lamplight, her eyes deep, mysterious pools, her mouth full and soft, all he'd been able to think about was how desperately he wanted her. There'd never been another woman who'd made him ache the way he did for Tess.

Kissing her, he felt like a man dying of thirst who'd just been given a drink of cool, clear water. Only there was nothing cool about the way she made him feel. He felt the way he'd always felt with her, hot and hungry and in danger of forgetting that he was a man of thirty-eight, not a randy teenager.

He fumbled at the back of her neck, finding the soft bow that held her bodice up and tugging it loose. Tess gasped something against his mouth—a protest, approval—he didn't know which. And then the peacock blue silk slipped to her waist.

Nick dragged his mouth from hers to look down at the treasure he'd uncovered. Tess murmured an embarrassed protest, her hands shifting as if to cover herself. He caught her wrists.

"You're so beautiful, Tess. So damned beautiful." He released his hold on her wrists and Tess shivered as his hands came up to cup her full breasts, lifting them. Unable to resist the temptation they presented, he bent his head over her, taking one swollen nipple into his mouth, tasting her.

TESS FELT THE STRENGTH drain from her legs as he sucked strongly at her breast. She felt the pressure deep inside, a burning need that hovered on the knife-edge of pain.

God, it had been so long. So very long.

Her fingers delved into the heavy gold of his hair, pulling him closer as she arched her back to offer herself to him. From the moment she'd seen Nick, she'd known this was how the evening had to end. Not consciously, but on some visceral level she hadn't wanted to acknowledge, she'd known.

She'd been running from the knowledge when she left the party early, denying it when she refused his invitation to come in for coffee. But she was tired of running, no longer interested in denial.

"Nick." His name was a moan. A plea. An admission of hunger.

Nick's mouth abandoned her breast but only to capture her sweet whimper of protest. His tongue stabbed into her mouth, claiming it as his own. His palm flattened against her spine, pulling her closer.

But it wasn't enough. He needed her laid out beneath him, her slender body molded to his, every inch of her bared to his touch.

Tess's eyes opened in dazed surprise as Nick dragged his mouth from hers and rose from the sofa. For an instant, he loomed over her, big and powerful, making her feel small and fragile and a little helpless. Before the feeling could overwhelm the sensual daze, he bent and scooped her off the sofa, lifting her against his chest as if her weight were nothing to him.

His mouth caught hers, smothering her gasp of surprise. And if Tess had thought to offer a protest, it was burned away by the heat of his kiss. He carried her across the living room and into a short hallway illuminated by a wall sconce that sent a splash of light upward against the plaster. Without taking his mouth from hers, Nick kicked open a lacquered black door and carried her into a dimly lit bedroom.

When he set her on her feet beside the bed, Tess's knees threatened to buckle beneath her. She clung to him, pressing her forehead against his chest, feeling the ragged rise and fall of his breathing. The unevenness of his pulse was oddly reassuring. It told her that she wasn't the only one slipping out of control.

"Tess." Her name was a husky whisper, Nick's breath stirring the soft tendrils of hair that lay on her forehead.

She lifted her head to look up at him, her eyes wide and uncertain. The room was dimly lit by a black porcelain lamp that sat on the sleek built-in dresser, but there was enough light to let her see the green fire that burned in Nick's eyes.

"If this isn't what you want, tell me now." The words were

clearly not offered without cost. She could feel the hunger in him. It was the same hunger she felt, the same need.

She should tell him to let her go, she thought dimly. Sanity demanded the words. She was only going to end up hurt again. But that hurt seemed a distant, unimportant thing when compared to the ache she felt now. To the need that burned in both of them.

Her hands slid up to his shoulders. She let her body sway into his, her bare breasts pressing against the thin fabric of his shirt.

"You talk too much," she whispered, tilting her head to trail teasing kisses along the hard line of his jaw.

With a laugh that was half a groan, Nick wrapped his arms around her, lifting her off her feet, crushing her so close that not even a shadow could have come between them. His mouth caught hers, telling her without words how much he wanted her.

With that kiss, Tess consciously blocked out everything but the here and now. Nothing mattered beyond this. The future would come and she might pay a price for tonight, but she wasn't going to think about that now. She refused to think of anything but the pleasure of Nick's hands on her body, the sweet torment of need that throbbed in the pit of her stomach.

Her zipper slid downward without a protest. Nick set his hands on her hips, sweeping the dress down, taking her panties with it. Her shoes had vanished somewhere in the living room and she now stood before him completely naked. Any self-consciousness she might have felt was burned away by the green fire of his gaze as it swept over her, devouring her, telling her without words how much he wanted her.

NICK FELT THE IMPACT of Tess's beauty strike deep in his gut. *This* was the image he'd never been able to forget. The hunger he'd never completely lost.

He reached out and caught a handful of her hair, pulling it over her shoulder so that it draped over her breast. The contrast of her black hair against the ivory of her skin was another thing he'd never forgotten.

"You are so beautiful."

"And you are overdressed." Her fingers were trembling as she unbuttoned his shirt. Nick tugged it loose from his pants and shrugged it off, tossing it behind him. His hands closed over her waist, pulling her forward until the taut peaks of her breasts brushed against the hair-roughened surface of his chest. At the contact, a soft moan tore from her. The sound went straight to Nick's gut, tearing away the last fragile layer of patience to expose the raw hunger beneath.

Tess gasped as she was swept up in his arms and set on the bed. The cool linen sheets did nothing to cool her heated skin. She watched from beneath heavy lids as Nick jerked open his belt. The rasp of his zipper being lowered shivered over her skin like a physical touch. He shoved his trousers down over his lean hips, taking the plain white cotton briefs with them. Looking up at him, Tess felt her breath catch.

Stripped of the veneer of clothing, he looked powerfully male. Six feet two inches of corded muscle and tanned skin. He was all hard angles and hunger, and his arousal was blatant.

"Doubts, Tess?" The question brought her eyes to his face. All she had to do was say yes and he'd back away. He'd leave her alone in his bed. Alone, where she'd been for five long years. Tonight, she didn't want to be alone.

"No doubts." She lifted her arms and he came to her.

The heavy weight of him was familiar. Familiar and welcome. Her legs opened to him, her breath catching in a quiet moan as she felt his hips slide between her thighs, felt the hard, silken pressure of him against her.

"Tess." Her name was a whisper, a command. "Look at me," he ordered huskily. She forced her eyelids up as Nick levered himself up on his arms. His eyes burned down into hers, fierce and demanding. "I want to watch you. I want to watch your eyes as you take me inside you."

She wanted to close her eyes, turn her head away. She was afraid of what he might see, what she might reveal at that moment of vulnerability. But she was helpless to turn away from the demand of his gaze.

His look holding hers, Nick let his hips sink against hers.

Her eyes widened endlessly as her body accepted his. She'd thought she'd forgotten but she discovered the memories were there. This was how it had always been, should have been forever. There was no past, no future, only Nick and the feel of his body above her, within her. This was what it was to feel complete.

Her fingers dug into the hard muscles of his hips as she pulled him to her, arching her back to take him deeper. It had been so long, she thought feverishly. He withdrew and then filled her again. The breath that exploded from her was half a sob. God, she'd forgotten how it felt, forgotten how he filled her, body and soul.

Her eyelids fell shut as she pressed the back of her head into the pillow, her heels digging into the bed as she sought to take him still farther into herself, so deep that nothing could ever separate them.

Nick groaned and lowered his body to hers, sliding his arms under her back and hooking his hands over her shoulders, holding her for the driving thrusts of his body. She met him, matching her movements to his, her breath coming in sobbing little pants that added to his arousal.

Tess could feel the burning pleasure building up inside her, could feel her skin flush with it. She was so close. Completion hovered just beyond her fingertips, drifting out of reach as the pleasure built and built until she was sure she would shatter into a million pieces.

And then she did shatter. And found what she'd sought.

She cried out, her body arching against Nick's, her fingers digging into the sweat-dampened muscles in his back. Nick felt the trembling convulsions that rippled over her and ground his teeth against the urge to follow her. He didn't want it to end. Not now. Not ever. But then her delicate contractions took him, caressing him, sending him tumbling headlong into pleasure.

Tess heard his guttural groan and tightened her arms around him, holding him, letting the powerful pulse of his climax carry her still higher.

For the first time in five years, she was whole, the emptiness in her soul filled.

IT WAS SEVERAL MINUTES before Nick found the energy to move. Several minutes after that before either of them spoke.

"Are you all right?"

All right? Lying with her head on his shoulder, his arms cradling her, Tess thought "all right" hardly captured how she felt. But she nodded without lifting her head from his shoulder. "I'm fine."

Except for the fact that reality was trying to intrude, reminding her this was a moment out of time, a slice of pretend before real life continued. A real life that didn't include Nick anymore.

Frowning, she pushed the thought away and shifted closer to him, easing her leg across his thighs. She'd only intended to cuddle close enough to keep the future at bay. But when she felt the solid pressure of him against her thigh, she was caught off guard by an answering response in the pit of her belly.

She moved her leg again and Nick groaned. Catching her around the waist, he slid her over him until she straddled his hips. Lifting herself, she took him inside, their soft moans echoing in the quiet room.

Reality—and the future—could be ignored for at least a little while longer.

Chapter Three

It felt so natural to wake in Nick's arms, so completely right, that it took Tess several minutes to start wondering what she was doing there. Opening her eyes, she found her field of vision filled by a muscled expanse of chest. Nick lay on his side, facing her, her head on his arm, his forearm resting in the curve of her waist.

For a moment, it was almost as if the last five years had never happened. She could pretend the divorce had been nothing but a bad dream. If she didn't look at the sleek, modern room, it might have been the bed they'd shared in the house they'd worked so hard to turn into a home.

She turned a deaf ear to the little voice that tried to point out that the last five years *had* happened and that this *wasn't* their old room. Just a little while longer, she pleaded with her conscience. Just a little more time to pretend. Last night had been wonderful. Magical. She didn't want to give up that magic just yet.

"Good morning." Nick's voice was sleep rough, the huskiness stroking over Tess's skin like a warm cloth. She'd been so absorbed in inner argument that she hadn't noticed when he opened his eyes.

"Good morning." She wondered if there was some protocol on how to behave when one found oneself in bed with one's ex-husband.

"I thought I'd dreamed you but you feel pretty real." She

felt her cheeks flush at the look of sleepy hunger in Nick's eyes.

"I do?" At the moment, nothing about this situation felt real. And she wanted to keep it that way for just a little while longer.

"Very real." Nick's hand flattened against her lower back, shifting her closer. He took her mouth in a slow, thorough kiss. There was none of last night's urgency in this morning's embrace. Yet Tess found herself trembling, her skin almost painfully sensitized to his touch as his hand moved downward to flatten against her bottom and crush her gently to him. Feeling his arousal, Tess moaned softly against his mouth, her fingers flexing on his chest.

It was just the way she remembered it, she thought dimly. How many mornings had they awakened just this way? It didn't matter that they'd made love several times the night before, the hunger between them was always there, needing only a touch to turn a spark into fire.

This morning, it was a slow burn. Long, stroking touches, and soft whispers. There was an unspoken but mutual need to make it last forever. The completion was, if anything, more powerful for the leisurely climb to reach it. Tess arched into Nick's body as wave after wave of sensation rolled over her. Nick shuddered in her arms, his big body taut and hard as fulfillment took him.

He collapsed against her, a welcome weight on her trembling body. Tess held him, feeling tears burn the backs of her eyes. It had been so long since she'd felt this complete, this sense of wholeness. For five years she'd been telling herself she'd made her peace with her failed marriage, with her life without Nick. It had taken less than twelve hours to show her how wrong she'd been.

Nick started to shift to the side and Tess tightened her hold on him, suddenly afraid.

"I'm too heavy, honey," Nick murmured, forcing her to loosen her arms enough to allow him to roll from her. His arm slid under her, immediately pulling her to his side, but the closeness was not enough to reassure Tess. She closed her eyes, pushing back the fear.

"I've missed you, Tess." Nick's husky admission brought tears to her eyes and she blinked them back, pressing her cheek against his chest, savoring the way the matted hair felt against her skin.

"I've spent five years convincing myself it wasn't as good between us as I'd remembered." Nick's fingers sifted through the heavy black cape of her hair, arranging it so that it draped over her bare shoulder and onto his flat stomach. "I think I always knew I was lying to myself."

Tess said nothing. She wasn't sure she could force her voice out past the lump in her throat. It felt so wonderfully, terribly right to lie here in Nick's bed, in his arms. This wasn't the way it should be, she thought. It shouldn't feel like coming home to be here, like this, with her ex-husband.

"We need to talk, Tess."

The words sent a bolt of pure panic through her. She wasn't ready to talk about what had happened. She didn't even understand what had happened. The last thing she wanted to do was talk about it. Not until she felt a little less like she was standing on shifting ground.

"Not now."

"We can't put it off forever." His tone was gentle but implacable.

"I know." She tilted her head to smile up at him, hoping the morning light that filtered through the heavy black drapes was dim enough to conceal the panic that must be visible in her eyes. "But we don't have to talk right this minute, do we?"

"Why not?"

Because I'm scared to death of what you're going to say. Of what I might say. It's all happened too fast, Nick. I need time, time to figure out what I've done. And why.

"Because I'm starving," she told him apologetically.

"You're hungry?" Nick seemed surprised, as if he hadn't been expecting such a prosaic response.

"It's been a long time since Fran's party." His eyes

searched her face, as if seeking some sign that she was being less than truthful. "You don't plan on starving me, do you?" she asked, thrusting out her lower lip in the merest hint of a pout.

The doubt vanished from Nick's expression and his mouth curved in a grin that went straight to her heart—her damned, traitorous heart.

"I suppose I could be persuaded to feed you." He frowned, thinking. "I don't have anything here, though. I cleaned the kitchen out before I went to Virginia last month. We'll have to go out."

"That's okay." Tess tried not to sound too eager. Out. That was exactly where she wanted to be. Out of this bed, out of this apartment, somewhere nice and neutral. Someplace where she could gather her thoughts without feeling as if she was surrounded by Nick.

"Okay." It was obvious that Nick didn't share her feelings, but since there was no food in the house, he couldn't argue. "The bathroom's through there." He nodded to a lacquered door opposite. "I'll shower down the hall. I'd suggest saving water and showering with a friend but I have a feeling you wouldn't get fed today."

Tess flushed and bit the inside of her lip to hold back the words that would have had them sharing a shower—and would have put off talking about what had happened between them. Nick seemed to be waiting for something but when she said nothing, he sighed and eased his arm out from under her before swinging his legs over the side of the bed and sitting up. He cast a last look over his shoulder at her slender body and stood up.

Tess felt her breath catch at the sheer, male beauty of him. Broad shoulders tapered to a narrow waist and sleek hips. He'd always worked out, getting up at dawn to run, going to the gym at lunch. With Nick, it was less a matter of vanity than it was a desire to feel his best. He'd always claimed that he was basically one of the laziest people in the world, he just worked hard to conceal it.

She watched him cross to the door with long, lazy strides.

Her mouth was suddenly dry and she wondered at her own sanity. How could she let him out of her sight?

Nick turned at the door and caught her staring. Her expression must have revealed something of her thoughts because his smile was pure, masculine satisfaction, his eyes gleaming.

"Don't take forever in the shower, like you usually do. Anything over thirty minutes and I'm coming in after you." Grinning, he turned and disappeared into the hall. A moment later, Tess heard a door close.

Don't take forever in the shower, like you usually do.

Just as if they'd been sharing a house, as if the past five years had never happened.

Shivering, Tess closed her eyes. It wasn't that easy. It couldn't be. They weren't married anymore. And that had been largely her choice. She couldn't just fall back into the same old patterns. She couldn't just let five years of her life disappear as if they'd never happened. She drew a deep breath, inhaling the warm fragrance of Nick, the musky scent of their lovemaking.

She opened her eyes and looked at the sleek, modern decor, reminding herself that the last five years had really happened. This wasn't the cozy bedroom she and Nick had shared in the house they'd worked to restore. She was no longer a girl of twenty. She was a woman of twenty-five. A woman who was running a successful business of her own. She'd worked hard for that success, worked hard to convince herself that she was capable of having a life without Nick.

And last night, she'd walked—eyes wide open—into Nick's arms, into his bed. She heard the sound of water running and knew Nick must be showering. No doubt he assumed that she was doing the same. And that, when he came out, they'd go somewhere for breakfast and discuss... Discuss what? What did he think they needed to talk about?

Shivering, Tess slid off the bed and gathered up her clothing. There wasn't much, just her panties and her dress. Next time she went to a party where she was going to see her ex-husband, she was going to wear a great deal more clothing, she told herself, so distraught that the vow seemed sensible.

She darted into the bathroom and splashed water on her face, trying not to look at her reflection as she scrambled into her clothes. Her fingers patted ineffectually at her tangled hair. There was a comb in her purse. She'd worry about her hair when she'd reached the marginal safety of her car.

Because she wasn't going to wait for Nick to get out of the shower. She didn't know what he wanted to say, but she knew she wasn't up to hearing it. Not now. Not until she could figure out how she felt about last night. About him.

Tess crept across the bedroom with all the caution of a sneak thief and as much guilt. Since the water was still running, she felt reasonably safe, but there was no sense in taking chances. Once in the hallway, she ran across the living room, pausing just long enough to grab her shoes and purse.

At the door, she threw a last look over her shoulder, torn between the instinct that screamed at her to get while the getting was good and the deep, visceral urge to run back to the bedroom, back to Nick. With a muffled sob, she wrenched open the door and dashed out into the warm summer sunshine.

HE WASN'T GOING TO RUSH her this time. He would give her all the time she could possibly want. More even. Nick frowned at the tiled wall, letting the hot water sluice over his body as he repeated the vows to himself. He had another chance with Tess, a chance he hadn't even realized he wanted. But he had it and he wanted it and he wasn't going to blow it.

He shut the shower off and pushed open the glass door of the cubicle. He dried himself with a thick, blue towel. In this bathroom and the guest room, a soft colonial blue replaced the black-and-gray that accented the rest of the condo. When he'd bought the place, he'd been glad that the decorating was so diametrically opposed to the cozy, country Victorian look of the house he'd shared with Tess. But this morning, the black and gray, lacquer and leather all looked hard and cold and slightly pretentious.

Wrapping one towel around his hips, he rubbed a second one over his hair with a vigor that reflected his inner tension more than his desire for dry hair. This time was going to be different. This time, he was going to give her room. Time. In that last, awful conversation when Tess had told him she wanted a divorce, she'd said she felt as if she was suffocating in his shadow, that she wasn't even a person anymore, only his wife.

Nick frowned at his blurred reflection in the steamed-over mirror. He was sure it would never win him any awards for non-sexist thinking, but his first reaction had been to question why being his wife wasn't enough. His mother had always been happy being his father's wife. Before he could think better of it, he'd said as much, and he'd seen something die in Tess's eyes. Hope, perhaps?

He'd had five years to consider her words. He still didn't entirely understand what she'd meant. After all, he'd never asked her to stay home, never believed that a woman's place was strictly in the home. If she'd wanted something more, something like this shop she'd started, no one would have been more supportive than he. But Tess obviously hadn't believed that and that was one of the things that was going to have to change.

He was going to have to show her that he wasn't the chauvinist she imagined, that he could be as enlightened and supportive as the next man—or woman. And he wasn't going to rush her. They were going to start out by having a nice, quiet breakfast together, talking about what had happened, talking about the future. All nice and civilized.

And he was going to resist the urge to kidnap her and take her to Las Vegas and make her his wife before midnight. He could wait until at least noon tomorrow.

A rueful smile acknowledged that patience was not one of his strong suits. Especially not when it came to something he wanted as badly as he wanted Tess. But he wanted to keep her this time, and that meant doing things her way.

Looking more determined than patient, Nick left the bathroom and walked down the hall to his bedroom. It was empty, the rumpled covers silent witness to what had gone on there the night before. Cocking his head, Nick listened for the sound of the shower. He grinned when he heard only silence. Tess must be really hungry if she'd managed to take a shower in less than twenty minutes.

Opening the closet door, he pulled out a pair of jeans and a shirt. Tossing them on the tousled sheets, he got briefs from the dresser and stepped into them. By the time he had tugged the jeans over his hips and was buttoning them, it had begun to sink in that there was no noise coming from the bathroom.

Leaving the last button undone, Nick moved over to the black door and tapped lightly.

"Tess? Are you all right?"

There was no response. He stared at the sleek door for the space of several heartbeats, feeling a sudden tightness in his chest. He was almost surprised to see that his hand was steady as he reached out and pushed the door open.

The room was empty, the shiny black tile dry. The only sign that Tess had used the room at all was the fact that one towel had been draped crookedly over the rack.

His face expressionless, Nick turned and crossed the bedroom, going into the hall. It wasn't really necessary but he searched the entire condo, even looking in the utility room off the kitchen and stepping onto the balcony as if Tess might be hiding behind one of the potted plants. The way she'd been hiding behind that damned tree last night at the McKenzies'.

Nick's hands clenched over the balcony railing. The view that had sparkled with magic last night was gray and tired this morning. The classic Los Angeles mixture of haze and smog obscured the city.

She was gone.

He couldn't quite make the thought sink in. Any more than he'd been able to make it sink in when she'd told him she wanted a divorce. The comparison brought a wave of anger so fierce, he could feel his hands start to tremble. Spinning away from the rail, Nick strode into the living room. Without thinking, he swept through the condo again, as if he had to confirm that Tess was really gone.

He ended his search in the bedroom, standing in the middle of the floor, his fingers curled into fists at his sides, his eyes brilliant green with anger. She was gone, leaving nothing to show for her presence but a cup of cold coffee in the living room and the love-rumpled sheets.

With an inarticulate sound that was nearly a growl, he bent and ripped the sheets from the mattress. Carrying them through the living room and into the kitchen, he stuffed them in the trash, jamming them down until they were crushed into the container and then letting the lid bang down with a metallic clang.

Stepping back, his breath coming too quickly, he stared at the square black container. But he couldn't throw the memories away with the sheets.

Tess's eyes when she'd turned to look at him at the party last night. The feel of her skin under his hands, the way it heated at his touch, until she almost seemed to be melting into him.

"Not this time, Tess," he said aloud. "Not this time."

Spinning on one heel, he stalked out of the kitchen. Entering the bedroom again, he found the shirt he'd gotten out earlier lying on the floor. Yanking it over his head, he picked up the trousers he'd discarded the night before, emptying the pockets with quick efficiency and stuffing wallet, cash and car keys into the pockets of his jeans. The rental car was still at the McKenzies' but it was just going to have to wait.

When the phone rang a third time, he cursed but moved to answer it. Snatching the receiver off the hook, he barked a hello into it.

"Nick?" A small voice sounded in his ear, shaken and on the verge of tears.

"Sara?" At her tone, he felt his anger toward Tess quickly drain, replaced by concern for his sister. "What's wrong?" he asked. "Are you all right?"

"It's...it's Dad," she said on a sob. "He's had a heart attack...and it doesn't look good."

No, it couldn't be. Bill Masters was as tough as they came. Nick's words reassured Sara as he tried to reassure himself with his thoughts. Their father was only sixty, he said, still young enough to recover from something like this.

"Don't worry, Sara. I'm leaving right now."

But by the time he set the receiver down, Nick was aware that his hand was not quite steady. His father was in the hospital. Possibly dying. It was inconceivable. Bill Masters was built like an oak tree and twice as strong.

He turned away from the phone, thrusting his fingers through his damp hair, destroying the dubious order it had held. His eyes lit on the stripped bed, and he closed them. He couldn't bear the sight of it.

Tess.

He couldn't go after her now. That was going to have to wait. *He* was going to have to wait. He'd waited five years for an explanation. He supposed another day or two wouldn't really matter.

But now or a week from now, he was going to have an explanation.

Chapter Four

"The shipment from Crafthouse got here Friday. The kits are on the wall across from the register." Tess glanced up from her clipboard to make sure her companion had heard her.

"Just at child height, I suppose." Josie lifted her eyes from the skein of floss she was untangling, the result of a bored four-year-old's inquisitive fingers.

"They're sealed in plastic," Tess offered soothingly.

"It won't matter." Josie refused to be soothed. The gloomy expression sat oddly on her round features. "The little darlings will find a way to destroy them."

"You're just upset because Mrs. Levine's grandchildren got into the floss drawers last week."

"Mrs. Levine's grandchildren should only be allowed out on a leash."

Tess grinned but didn't comment. Dealing with a customer's ill-behaved offspring was just one of the things a retailer had to deal with. Despite her grumpy expression, Josie coped better than most. Tess made a note on the clipboard before setting it on the overcrowded desk that was wedged into the tiny room she somewhat grandiloquently called her office. It was as much a storeroom as it was an office, the walls lined with boxes of floss and needlework kits awaiting their turn on the shelves and racks in the front of the store.

She'd started the shop with money obtained by mortgaging the Victorian Nick had insisted she take in the divorce settlement. Friends had told her she was crazy to risk her house. Didn't she know the statistics about how many small businesses failed in the first year? And a needlework shop? What kind of business was that?

But Needles & Pins hadn't failed. It had prospered. This year, for the first time, Tess was going to be able to take out not only living expenses, but enough to start putting money in the bank. And it was a good thing, too, she thought. This year she was going to need it. She sighed and reached for her cup of herbal tea.

Josie worked the last knot loose from the floss and began winding the bright green thread around her hand. It couldn't be sold, of course, but one of them was sure to find a use for it in their own needlework projects.

Tess cradled the teacup between her hands and told herself that she had too much to do to be sitting here doing absolutely nothing. She should tackle some of the paperwork that was covering her desk. She should prepare for the Christmas rush that was sure to descend on them now that it was late November. Or she could go out and make sure everything was ready for the shop to open in twenty minutes. But she didn't move. It felt good to just sit here, watching Josie start on another tangled skein, and thinking about nothing in particular.

"I suppose I should get up and go dust the counter or something." Since she hadn't bothered to take her feet off the box on which they were propped, Tess's comment was clearly an idle threat.

"I'll dust the counter." Josie busily worked another knot loose. "You should stay off your feet."

"I'm all but over the cold," Tess said.

"It's not the cold I'm worried about," Josie said, giving her friend a stern look from under her pale lashes.

"I'm fine." Tess swung her feet to the floor and stood up to prove it.

"Have you heard from Nick?"

The question caught Tess off guard, causing a sharp little ache in her chest.

"There's no reason I should," she said, proud to hear that her voice was level.

"Hah." Josie's snort was eloquent if not particularly polite. "He's a jerk."

"No, he's not. What happened between us was as much my doing as it was his. Maybe he thinks I should be the one to call him."

"Well, you should." Josie didn't seem to think there was anything odd in her abrupt about-face. She rested her hands on the table and tilted her head to fix Tess with a stern look. "You should have called him months ago."

"We've gone over this before." Tess's thinning patience was audible. "I'm not going to call Nick. We slept together. It happens all the time between ex-husbands and wives. It was just one of those things."

She shrugged to show how completely she'd put the incident behind her. She could only hope the older woman couldn't see the effort that casual gesture took.

"If you think I believe that it meant nothing to you, then you must think I'm a whole lot stupider than I look. I saw the way you watched the phone and I know how much you want to tell Nick—"

"Enough." Tess's sharp tone cut Josie off in midstream. She drew a deep breath and continued more quietly. "I don't want to talk about it anymore, Josie. I've made my decision, and obviously Nick has made his. It was just a stupid encounter and it's over." She lifted her hand when Josie drew breath to interrupt. "I don't want to hear another word about it."

Josie's mouth shut with a snap, her soft chin set with annoyance. Seeing that she'd made her point, Tess drew a relieved breath. Not that she was foolish enough to think that it was the last she'd hear on the subject. A romantic to the core, Josie simply couldn't believe that everybody didn't get the sort of happy ending she felt they should have.

Tess wished now that she hadn't told Josie what had happened that night. But she'd needed someone to talk to and Josie was not just her employee, but her best friend. But for the last three months, she'd put up with more lectures than she could count.

"I'm going to make sure everything is in order," Tess said again, forcing the lingering irritation from her voice.

"Just don't overdo it." Her concern made Tess feel guilty for snapping at her.

"I run a needlework shop. I'm not a stevedore. I don't think lifting a few skeins of yarn is going to do any harm."

"As long as that's all you lift," Josie warned her.

"Yes, Mother. If anyone asks for more than two skeins of yarn at a time, I'll call you."

"See that you do," Josie said calmly.

"I'm going to go unlock the front door, if you don't think that'll be overdoing it," Tess said with heavy sarcasm.

Josie appeared to consider and then nodded, setting her sandy hair swinging. "I think that should be all right."

"Remind me to fire you after Christmas."

"I'll make a note of it."

Tess was shaking her head as she left the tiny office. There were certainly advantages to being friends with someone who worked for you. But there were also disadvantages, like Josie's tendency to fuss over her like a mother hen. Still, there was something rather sweet about the concern. Without Josie's friendship, her life would be a lot emptier.

Her eyes skimmed the crowded walls as she moved through the store. Even after four years, it still amazed her to look at the shop and know that it was hers. Something she'd built with her own drive and hard work. No matter what other mistakes she made, *this* was something she'd done right.

She slid the key in the front door lock but she didn't turn it immediately. She looked out at the sunshine pouring over the sidewalk just beyond the blue-and-white striped awning that shielded the front windows. This morning, the weatherman had cheerfully announced that it was going to be seventy-five degrees and sunny today, with the same for the foreseeable future. It was hard to believe it was barely four weeks until Christmas.

She sighed and twisted the key in the lock, officially opening the shop for the day. Lingering by the window, she tried to imagine the street outside covered in snow, but the brightly colored poppies blooming in the flower beds that lined the sidewalk made the image difficult to capture.

The holidays were her least favorite time of year. And the Southern California sunshine didn't make her like them any more. She remembered her parents, both now gone. Her father had been career army and he'd always been eager for any transfer that might advance his career. Since he was also a difficult man to get along with, his superior officers had had no hesitation about transferring him as often as he liked.

He'd simply come home and tell Tess and her mother to start packing. They were on the road again. They'd seldom lived in one place for more than a year. And for Tess, a little girl who didn't make friends easily, the holidays had generally served to emphasize her loneliness, and she had learned to endure rather than enjoy them.

Until she met Nick.

Her mouth curved in a half smile, remembering that first Christmas with him. Her first Christmas as his wife, though just barely. They'd been married on Christmas Eve in a tiny chapel in Burbank. Nick had paid an outrageous fee to convince the woman to marry them, insisting they had to spend their first Christmas together as husband and wife. The first of many, he'd said.

Only it hadn't been. Tess's smile faded. They'd only had one more holiday together. But those two Christmases stood out in her memory as the only times she'd really understood the holiday spirit. Since then, the memories had become just one more regret to haunt her during the last few weeks of the year. And this year, there was more reason than ever for regrets.

Though she'd been staring out the window, she was so wrapped up in her thoughts that when the bell over the door rang, announcing the day's first customer, she was startled.

"I need another skein of Christmas red floss," the woman announced as soon as she saw Tess. Her tone hovered on the edge of panic and Tess gave her a soothing smile.

"Do you have the color number?" she asked, as she led the way to the oak cabinet that held the floss.

Ten minutes later, the bell jingled again as the door closed behind the woman. She'd left in a calmer state than she arrived, the floss tucked carefully in her purse. Tess felt her melancholy mood lift. There was something very satisfying about being able to give a customer just what she wanted, even when it was something as simple as a skein of floss.

She had to stop dwelling on the past, she reminded herself as she dusted the cash register keys unnecessarily. Whether it was her marriage or the night she'd spent with Nick after Fran McKenzie's party. Both were over and done and if she'd been so foolish as to think that night might have meant something to Nick, then his silence over the last few months had told her just how wrong she was.

You were the one who ran out on him.

Yes, but he could have called.

Why should he? Maybe he thought this was the way you wanted it. A one-night stand. No entanglements. No regrets.

He knows me better than that. Doesn't he?

Tess frowned at the Christmas kits that hung on the wall opposite the register. *Did* Nick know her better than that?

"Why don't I handle things out front this morning?" Josie's words preceded her. Tess blinked and forced her thoughts into focus on the present, pushing aside unanswerable questions about the past.

"Okay." She moved out from behind the glass-fronted desk. "I've got a bunch of paperwork to catch up on."

She retreated to her office and shut the door. Despite the clutter, the little room had become a sort of haven since she opened the shop. Here, she was surrounded by the evidence of what she'd accomplished. There were no old memories to disturb her. Except that lately, the memories seemed to follow her wherever she went.

"It's just that it's Christmas," she muttered, frowning at the row of brightly colored cards Josie had hung on a string draped over the door.

And it had been three months since Fran's party—and still

not a word from Nick. But she wasn't going to think about that, she reminded herself briskly. The future was what was important and she had plenty of reason to look forward rather than back. From now on the past was going to stay where it belonged—in the past.

And she might as well start by keeping busy. She tilted her head as she heard the soft jingle of the front door. Maybe waiting on customers was just what she needed today. The paperwork could wait. Distraction was what she needed now.

She walked out of the office, a friendly smile firmly in place. The past she'd just decided to forget was standing in her shop.

"Nick."

His name was hardly more than a breath. He couldn't possibly have heard her. Yet his eyes slid past Josie, focusing on Tess's frozen figure. Tess felt the impact of that look all the way to her toes.

It wasn't possible that he was here, in her shop. Yet there he stood, the light catching in the heavy gold of his hair, his vivid green eyes locked on her.

Tess felt a wild tangle of emotions. She was trembling with relief—he hadn't forgotten, hadn't simply let her vanish from his life. She was furious—what had taken him so long? She was resentful—how dare he intrude on the one place that wasn't already filled with memories of him? And there was that odd little clench of hunger in the pit of her stomach—the one she always felt when she saw Nick. That never changed. Until the day she died, she knew she'd feel that same hunger, that same need.

"Tess."

The sound of her name released her frozen limbs, making it possible for her to step forward.

"Nick. What a surprise." If the greeting fell short of the casual tone she'd have liked, at least her voice was steady. The same could not be said of her fingers. She slipped her hands into the pockets of her floral cotton jumper and summoned what she hoped was a Mona Lisa-like smile. "What brings you to this neighborhood?"

"I wanted to see you."

"Oh, really?" Tess stopped at the end of the counter and leaned unobtrusively against it, half-afraid that her knees might betray her and deposit her unceremoniously on the floor at his feet. "What for?"

"I think we should talk." Nick glanced at Josie, who was making no secret of her interest in the conversation, her eyes going from Nick to Tess as if she were watching a tennis match.

"About what?" Couldn't she manage something more than a two-word sentence?

"About us," he said bluntly and Tess leaned more heavily against the counter, feeling her knees start to tremble.

"Us?" she managed. God, now she was reduced to one-word sentences. What did he mean by "us?" They'd ceased to be "us" five years ago.

Hadn't they?

NICK WATCHED COLOR flood her cheeks and then recede, leaving her skin the color of pale porcelain. He'd intended to approach things more subtly: start a light conversation, ask about the shop, then move on from there. But his first glimpse of Tess had brought such a welter of emotion roiling up inside him that he'd found himself incapable of anything but the most direct approach.

He wanted to snatch her into his arms and kiss her senseless. He wanted to grab her and shake her for walking out on him—again. And he wanted to just hold her and feel her against him, where she belonged.

"I'm not sure there's anything to talk about," Tess said at last, her voice thin and uncertain.

"I disagree. I think we have a great deal to talk about." Nick didn't bother to disguise the iron hand beneath the polite tone. He'd had three months to think about this meeting and the time had done nothing to soften his determination to understand why she'd run away from him—again.

"I can't really spare the time, Nick." Tess turned and began busily straightening the magazine rack at her elbow. ''I have a shop to run. Christmas is a very busy time.''

''You could spare a few minutes for a cup of coffee, couldn't you?'' The words were a question but the tone was a demand and he didn't care who heard it, whether it was Tess or the middle-aged woman who was watching their exchange with open interest. He and Tess were going to talk. And if he had to come back every day for the next year, that's what he'd do.

''I have a lot to do,'' Tess said. ''This is a busy time of year for retailers, you know.''

''So I see.'' Nick glanced pointedly around the shop, empty but for the three of them. Tess flushed and set her chin.

''I have a great deal of paperwork to do. I can't just run off anytime I want.''

''The papers aren't going to go anywhere,'' Josie commented, to no one in particular. ''You've been putting them off for a week now. A couple more hours won't matter.''

''I've already put them off long enough,'' Tess said, giving Josie a warning look.

''I can take care of things out here.'' Josie ignored the warning.

''Thank you.'' Nick turned the full force of his smile on her and Tess was unsurprised to see Josie blink, looking as dazed as a deer caught in a car's headlights.

IT WOULD SERVE HER right if Nick broke her heart, too, Tess thought, with unaccustomed malice. What kind of a friend was she, anyway? It was obvious to everyone that she didn't want to go anywhere with her ex-husband. The odd trembly feeling in her stomach was annoyance, not excitement. Just because she'd spent the last three months wondering why he hadn't tried to see her, it didn't mean that she'd *wanted* to see him. If he turned and walked out the door right now, it would be fine with her.

Liar. Her conscience nudged her sharply. The fact was, just being in the same room with Nick made her feel alive in a way she hadn't felt in months—three months, to be exact. And even if he hadn't had the ability to make her feel tinglingly alive, there were still plenty of reasons why she should talk to him.

"I guess the place won't fall apart if I'm not around for an hour," she said, trying to sound as if she weren't being railroaded into a decision.

"Of course it won't," Josie said, her tone so hearty that Tess wanted to hit her. "We won't start getting really busy till mid-afternoon," she added, directing the comment to Nick, as if giving him permission to keep Tess until then.

"I'll certainly be back long before that," Tess said quickly, cutting off any reply Nick might have made. They were just going to go have a quick cup of coffee and settle a few things. The last thing she wanted was to spend the afternoon with her ex-husband.

And if she repeated that a few hundred times, she might come to believe it.

Chapter Five

At Tess's suggestion, they walked down the street to the small Fifties-style café that had opened a few months ago and had been doing a brisk business ever since. Walking next to Nick, Tess was vividly aware of the sheer size of him. At six foot two, Nick loomed over her own height of five foot nothing. She found herself wishing she were wearing three-inch heels instead of the comfortable flats she had on. But she knew it would take more than high heels to make her feel on an equal footing with her ex-husband.

Nick held the door for her when they arrived at the café and Tess murmured her thanks as she entered. She caught a faint whiff of his after-shave as she brushed by him. The familiar scent brought an equally familiar response—a little flutter in her stomach, a slightly breathless feeling that she well remembered. It had been that same breathless feeling that had made her ignore her common sense three months ago.

She couldn't do this, she thought. She couldn't sit across a table from Nick and calmly discuss their relationship. She hadn't been able to do it five years ago, or for that matter three months ago, and nothing had changed.

She was hovering on the edge of full-blown panic when she felt Nick move up behind her. In a ridiculous about-face, she immediately felt reassured by his presence. He'd always done that—made her feel safe and secure, made it seem as if he could take care of any problem that might crop up. Even when he *was* the problem.

She bit back a slightly hysterical giggle. *I'm losing my mind,* she thought. That was the only possible explanation for the way her mood was seesawing between panic and excitement, between wanting to run from Nick and wanting to cling to him. Insanity was the obvious answer. At least, it was the only answer she wanted to consider at the moment.

IT WAS TOO LATE for breakfast and too early for lunch and the café was nearly empty. The waitress, clad in bobby socks and a pink poodle skirt, showed them to a red vinyl booth. There was a box next to the window for selecting songs to be played on the vintage jukebox near the counter, and bright plastic holders for the cone-shaped paper water cups the waitress filled for them.

"Two coffees," Nick told the girl, waving away the menus she was offering.

"Make mine a decaf," Tess said quickly.

"Since when are you drinking decaf?" he asked as the waitress left. "I thought you couldn't live without your daily doses of caffeine."

"I'm trying to cut back." She shrugged, dismissing the change.

He looked as if he might have pursued the topic, but the waitress reappeared promptly, setting a pair of thick white mugs on the table. Tess was grateful for the interruption, though she was sure anything he'd have said would have been nothing more than idle conversation. Lots of people decided to cut back on caffeine, she reminded herself.

Nick pushed the cream pitcher toward her automatically and reached for the sugar for himself. Watching him pour two heaping spoonfuls of sugar into his cup, Tess felt the backs of her eyelids sting. Nick's love of sweets had always seemed an endearing trait, a touch of boyishness that had made him a little less intimidating. She lowered her eyes to her cup, not wanting to remember the other things she'd found endearing about him.

NICK FELT THE SILENCE stretching and found his mind suddenly gone blank. He'd had three months to think of all the things he wanted to say to Tess, all the questions he wanted to ask. Clever phrases had tripped through his thoughts. But now that he had Tess in front of him, more or less a captive audience, they showed no sign of tripping from his lips.

He stared at the swags of plastic holly that decorated the edges of the booth. The red ribbon bows that adorned it had a vaguely disarrayed look to them, as if they'd seen one too many holiday seasons.

Christmas. It hardly seemed possible that it was less than a month away. Last week's Thanksgiving celebration should have been a clue, he supposed. But it still hadn't prepared him for the holiday now rushing toward him.

And still the silence stretched.

Nick slid his eyes back to Tess. She was staring intently out the window, as if fascinated by the traffic in the street. He allowed his gaze to linger. She looked as good as he remembered—better even.

Her hair was pulled back from her face and caught at the nape of her neck with a big bow. The bow was the same soft blue as the cotton shirt she wore under her loose jumper. There was something slightly girlish about the outfit, but the curve of her mouth and the outlines of her figure were all woman.

He shifted uncomfortably in the booth and looked away from her. Answers. That was what he was here for. It wouldn't do to let himself get distracted by noticing how beautiful she was. Heaven knew, she was beautiful enough to distract a saint, which he was far from being, but he had to remember why he was here. So he plunged in without preamble.

"Why did you run off without a word?"

THE SUDDEN QUESTION made Tess jump. She'd expected it, of course. She'd been expecting it for three months. And she still didn't know how to answer.

"I didn't think a postmortem was necessary," she said, knowing that it was neither the truth nor an answer that would satisfy him. But she couldn't even begin to explain the wave of panic that had sent her running from his bedroom. He'd never understand. She didn't understand it completely herself.

"Bull." The blunt rejection startled her. Her eyes jerked to his face.

"Excuse me?"

"You heard me." Nick leaned forward, pinning her to the booth with his gaze. "That's a bull excuse and you and I both know it."

"I don't know what you mean," Tess said. She twisted her coffee cup nervously between her hands. This conversation was not starting out at all the way she'd envisioned.

"It wasn't a postmortem you were afraid of, Tess. You weren't afraid of going over a relationship that was already dead. You were afraid we might find that there was still quite a bit of life in it. Which there obviously is or you wouldn't have been in my bed to start with."

"Sleeping with someone doesn't necessarily imply a commitment, Nick." Tess lowered her hands to her lap to conceal their trembling.

"It does for you. You forget how well I know you."

"*Knew* me, Nick. You *knew* me five years ago. I've changed."

"Not that much."

He looked so sure, so...male. Tess felt anger start to burn away her nervousness. How dare he wait three months to contact her and then sit there looking so smug? So full of answers about how she'd felt, what she'd thought?

"I could have had several lovers since the divorce."

"But you didn't. In fact, I'd be willing to bet that you haven't had *any* lovers since we broke up."

"What makes you so sure?" she snapped. Her fingers curled into palms that tingled with the urge to smack the confidence from his annoyingly handsome face.

"Because it was like making love to a virgin again." Nick leaned toward her, his voice low and intimate. "And I know exactly how that felt. Remember, Tess?"

Remember? Tess felt her face flame. As if she could possibly forget that he'd been her first lover, her *only* lover, damn him. She wished she could throw half a dozen other men in his face.

"What's your point?" she asked, sidestepping his question.

"The point is that it was not a casual one-night stand for you."

Now how was she supposed to argue with that? She had no desire to claim she made a habit of one-night stands, even if he'd believe her, which he obviously wouldn't. On the other hand, she wasn't ready to admit to Nick that the night she'd spent with him three months ago had meant as much to her as it had. The man was arrogant enough as it was.

In the face of uncertainty, Tess settled for the one completely safe response. She shrugged. Nick drew in a quick breath as if her noncommittal response had annoyed him. She was slightly shocked by the pleasure that thought gave her. It was childish but she couldn't summon up any sincere regret.

"Tess, it wasn't a one-night stand for me, either," Nick said at last, his tone struggling for equanimity. "I've thought about you a lot since that night."

"And you've had *plenty* of time to think," Tess snapped. She immediately wished the words unspoken. The last thing she'd wanted to do was reveal how much his three months of silence had stung.

The flare of pleasure in Nick's eyes told her he knew exactly what her words meant. Cursing her quick tongue, she lifted her coffee cup and took a drink, trying to look indifferent.

"I started to come after you," Nick said, making it clear that her casual air fooled no one.

"Car trouble?" she asked sweetly, abandoning pretense.

"I was on my way out the door that morning when Sara called and told me that Dad had just had a heart attack."

"Oh, no!" The anger Tess had nursed for three months disappeared in an instant. "Oh, Nick, I didn't know. How is he?"

"He's going to make it. If the family can keep him from trying to work himself to death." Nick wondered if she was even aware of having reached across the table to touch the back of his hand. He turned his hand, closing his fingers over hers.

"He's very strong," she said reassuringly. "I can't imagine anything keeping him down for long."

"He was giving orders from his hospital bed," he said, smiling at the memory.

"I'm not surprised." Tess's smile was soft as she thought of her former father-in-law. It had always been easy to see where Nick had gotten his drive and determination. But Bill Masters had never made her feel as if she might be swallowed up in his shadow. Of course, maybe that was because she hadn't been head over heels in love with him.

"Dad was in the midst of several projects and I've spent the last three months keeping things on track and browbeating him into obeying his doctor's orders."

Which explained why he hadn't tried to see her before now. So all these months of hurt, of building anger—even when she'd known that anger wasn't quite fair—had been for no reason. The realization left Tess with a hollow feeling inside. She hadn't realized how much she'd been clinging to the anger and hurt. Or maybe what she'd really been doing was hiding behind it. But there was nothing to hide behind now and she felt as if she'd been stripped of a shield, leaving her exposed. Vulnerable.

"Did you think I was just ignoring what had happened?" Nick asked. He ran his thumb absently over the back of her hand, sending shivers of awareness down her spine. Tess hadn't even realized that he held her hand until that moment. The feel of his fingers around hers felt disturbingly right. Uneasily aware of a reluctance to do so, she drew her fingers from his and cupped them around her coffee cup.

"I didn't know." She shrugged. "You didn't call. I thought you might want to forget it had happened. Maybe that's what we both should have done."

"Do you hate seeing me so much that you'd rather I'd forgotten?" Nick's tone was completely neutral, denying her any hint of what he was thinking, giving no clue as to what her answer meant to him, if anything.

"I don't hate you," she said at last. "And I'm glad you didn't forget."

Now why had she added that? Why reveal that it mattered to her one way or another?

Because it was Nick and he mattered more than she wanted to admit, even to herself. He always had. And that night had only drawn the ties tighter. Of course, she didn't have to admit as much to him. Well, it was too late to take the words back. They probably didn't mean anything to him, anyway.

NICK HADN'T REALIZED how tautly he was holding himself until he heard Tess's words and felt the tension leave his shoulders. Over the past weeks, his time had been more than filled with trying to keep the business and his family on an even keel. There'd been little time for personal reflection. But in the back of his mind had been the knowledge that, as soon as he could manage to redistribute some of the responsibilities that had fallen his way, he was going to find Tess and get the explanation he wanted—needed.

Yet now, sitting across the table from her, he found himself less interested in explanations than in the way the light caught in her hair. He couldn't help but notice the tiny golden flecks that made her dark eyes so warm. Or the coral tint of her mouth. Was it just his overheated imagination or had she actually managed to grow even more beautiful in the last three months? There seemed to be a glow about her, an inner illumination he'd never noticed before.

He looked away, aware that he was becoming aroused. Worse than a teenager on a Friday night date, he thought in disgust. But then, Tess had always had the ability to do that to him, to make him lose his control in a way no other woman had ever done.

"The phone rings both ways, you know. Why didn't you call me?"

WHY HADN'T SHE CALLED him? There was no one answer to that question. The answers had changed as the weeks slid by.

Tess's eyes slid to his and then away. She turned her coffee cup between her hands, focusing her gaze on the aimless motion, afraid of what Nick might read in her expression.

"I guess I should have," she said finally, when it became clear that he was waiting for her response.

"So, why didn't you?"

"I don't know." She lifted one shoulder in a half shrug and slanted a quick look at him. "I felt bad about running out like the heroine in a gothic novel fleeing a turreted mansion."

"I didn't even show you my turrets," Nick protested.

Tess smiled, grateful to him for trying to lighten the atmosphere. Her smile faded with his next question.

"Why did you run out, Tess?"

Another question to which she could only give half an answer. She couldn't possibly try to explain the tangled reasoning that had made running away seem like such an obvious choice. The waitress arrived just then to refill their cups, giving Tess a few seconds to consider the best answer.

When the woman had gone, Tess picked up the cream and poured some into her cup before lifting her spoon. Watching the pale swirl blend with the dark brew, she was aware of Nick's eyes on her, aware that she owed him the truth, even if it wasn't all the truth.

"Everything had moved so quickly." She set her spoon down and lifted her eyes to his face. "I hadn't expected to see you at Fran's. I hadn't thought of you in ages," she said bluntly. "If someone had asked me, I would have said I didn't feel anything but indifference toward you."

"Please, Tess, you'll make my head swell." Nick's ironic tone and pained expression drew a half smile from her.

"Sorry, but you wanted an answer." The lightness faded quickly, however. "It just happened so fast, Nick. One minute, you were part of my past. The next we were in bed together. And then you said we needed to talk."

"It seemed like a pretty obvious next step," Nick said.

"It was. Of course we needed to talk. But I didn't know what I was supposed to say and I was scared to death of what you might say."

"What did you *think* I was going to say?" he asked, frowning.

"I don't know." Tess looked away. She couldn't explain that she'd been afraid he would say he didn't want to see her again and equally terrified that he might suggest the opposite.

"It wasn't a logical reaction," she admitted. "It was emotional. I got dressed and left without thinking it out clearly, I guess. I panicked and acted like an idiot."

Nick didn't say anything for several seconds, letting the silence stretch while he considered her words. Tess took a sip of her coffee and glanced at the street outside, half-surprised to see the bright sunshine. This didn't seem like the kind of conversation that should be taking place in daylight. If this were a movie, the scene would have been a quiet table in an intimate café, perhaps with soft music playing in the background. It definitely would not be filmed with the two of them sitting in a red vinyl booth decorated with sagging holly swags, sunlight spilling in through the window beside them and Bobby Darin singing "Splish, Splash" as accompaniment. Which all went to prove that life didn't always imitate art, she supposed.

Tess lifted her coffee cup and took a drink. She felt oddly calm. Nick was right. They *had* needed to talk. The question was: Now that they'd straightened out some of the misunderstanding, where did they go from here? Now that Nick had the explanation he'd wanted, was that the end of it? Was he going to walk away with a polite handshake?

Could she let him walk away without telling him the whole truth?

Her conscience had been jabbing her for weeks and she'd silenced it by pointing to his obvious indifference. But it hadn't been indifference that had kept him away. What would she tell her conscience now?

"I have to admit that it's the first time I've been the cause of a panic attack," Nick said at last.

"It wasn't you, Nick. It was me. Everything happened so fast, there was no time to think. And when I had a few minutes to think, I panicked."

"Remind me not to leave you alone while I shower next time," he said lightly.

The implication that there might be a next time was enough to make Tess's mouth go dry. Her eyes dropped from his face to the speckled surface of the table. Did she want a next time? She shied away from the answer.

"Where do we go from here, Tess?" The quiet question brought her attention back to his face.

Why couldn't his eyes be a nice muddy color instead of clear, piercing green? How was a woman supposed to think intelligently with those eyes on her? How was she supposed to think intelligently when her pulse beat too quickly and all she could think about was the words next time?

"I don't know," she said slowly.

"Do you regret that night?"

Regret? It had changed her life forever, changed it in ways Nick knew nothing about. But did she regret it? Why did he keep asking her questions she didn't want to answer?

"I should."

HEARING THE TACIT admission, Nick had to suppress a smile. She might not be willing to say the words, but she didn't regret that night any more than he did. It wasn't much, but it was a start. He reached across the table and took her hand, holding it despite her automatic attempt to withdraw.

"Tess, I think we've both got to admit that there's still something between us." Startled blue eyes swept to his face and her fingers went still. She said nothing, and try as he might, Nick couldn't read her expression.

Setting his jaw, he continued, knowing that for his own peace of mind, the words had to be said. She could pitch him out of her life if she wanted, but he wasn't going without saying what he'd come to say.

"I want to see you again."

TESS'S HAND JUMPED in his, as if the flat statement had a physical impact. If her life had depended on it, she couldn't have looked away from him. She could only stare at him, frozen and silent with shock.

He wanted to see her again. Not once since he'd shown up this morning had she let that thought cross her mind.

She felt a tiny shiver run down her spine. She wished she could attribute it to cold winter weather, but not in Southern California. No, she had to be honest—with herself if no one else—and admit that the shiver was born of pure anticipation. To be seeing Nick again. Their brief courtship stood out in her memory as the happiest time of her life.

But he hadn't said anything about a courtship, she reminded herself.

"Why?"

If the blunt question surprised him, he didn't allow it to show.

"There's something between us, Tess. You can't deny it, even if you want to."

He paused, as if anticipating an argument, but she said nothing. There was more between them than even he knew.

"What happened between us that night of Fran's party made it pretty obvious that whatever caused you to ask me for a divorce five years ago, it didn't kill the attraction between us."

"There's more to a relationship than a physical attraction." Tess stirred restlessly against the vinyl booth. She tried to pull her hand from his, but Nick refused to allow it, his fingers tightening over hers.

"It's more than physical attraction, Tess, and we both know it."

"Maybe it's nothing more than nostalgia. We used to be married and a lot of the old feelings are still there," she suggested, knowing she'd be devastated if he accepted the glib explanation.

"Is that what you think it is?" Nick's eyes demanded nothing less than the truth.

"No," she whispered, shaking her head.

"Neither do I." He stroked his thumb absently over the back of her hand, the rhythmic gesture making it almost impossible for her to gather her thoughts into a coherent pattern.

"I want to see you, Tess. No expectations, no promises. I just don't want to walk away from what we have. Whatever it is."

Tess hesitated, torn between a desperate need to say yes and the impulse to run. Yes, she wanted to see him. Yes, she wanted to find out what still lay between them. Almost equally strong was the old fear that she'd find herself swallowed up by his shadow, that Tess Armstrong would cease to exist, becoming nothing more than an unimportant extension of Nick Masters.

"We wouldn't rush things?" Her voice was hardly more than a whisper.

Sensing her surrender, Nick's fingers tightened over her hand.

"We'll take it as slow as you like," he promised.

It was such a risk, she thought. But there were more reasons to agree than even Nick knew about.

"No expectations?" As if her heart wasn't already swelling with expectation.

"Not a one."

"If it doesn't work out, no regrets?" Only over the death of a dream she hardly dared admit to having.

"No regrets."

"No sex?" Sleeping with him would only make it impossible to think clearly.

"No sex." Nick hesitated a moment over that one, his mouth twisting a little ruefully. "It's more than sex. I'll admit we're a pretty combustible combination, but there's more to it than that. You and I both know it."

She couldn't deny it but she didn't have to admit it, either, she thought, feeling a little defiant. Not that it would make a difference if she did. Nick would know she was lying.

"Are we agreed? We're going to see where this goes?"

"Agreed."

And heaven help her.

Chapter Six

"You're seeing *who* again!"

Nick winced as his youngest sister's voice rose perilously close to a shout, threatening both the health of his eardrums and the studied peacefulness of his decorous office at Masters Architectural. At that decibel level, soon every one of his employees would know about his love life.

"You heard me."

"I heard you but I can't believe I did." Hope fixed her brother with a look that held equal parts outrage and pleading. "Tell me you're not seeing Tess again."

"I'm not seeing Tess again," Nick parroted obediently.

"How could you, Nick? After the way she walked out on you five years ago." Hope's eyes, the same brilliant green as her brother's, were filled with reproach.

"You make it sound like she disappeared into the night, taking the family silver and my faithful hound with her."

Hope refused to be humored out of her mood. "That's practically what she did. Disappear into the night, I mean."

"Don't be dramatic, Hope. We had a perfectly civilized divorce." Nick leaned back against the supple leather of his desk chair and looked at his youngest, and though he rarely admitted as much, his most loved sister.

Of all his family, he knew Hope would be the toughest one to sell on the idea of him renewing old ties with his ex-wife. Not that he was doing that, at least not exactly. He wasn't ready to put a label on what was happening between him and Tess. Were they renewing old ties, making new ones or just wasting their time? All he knew was that, whatever had drawn them together in the first place, divorce and a five-year separation hadn't been strong enough to destroy.

"Now there's an interesting phrase: a civilized divorce. There was nothing civilized about it and you and I both know it."

"Well, it certainly wasn't *War of the Roses,*" Nick said.

"You can't tell me you weren't upset," she snapped.

"Of course I was upset. No one wants to watch their marriage break up." *Especially when you aren't quite sure just why it's breaking up,* he thought. But he wasn't going to say as much to Hope. It would probably just set her off again.

Tess and Hope were only a year apart in age and the moment he'd introduced the two of them, they'd hit it off. A friendship had developed that had little to do with the fact they were related by marriage. The relationship hadn't survived the divorce.

Hope, at twenty-one, had been completely unable to understand or to forgive what she saw as Tess's betrayal of Nick. He'd done his best to convince her that he and Tess getting a divorce didn't mean she had to sever her friendship with his soon-to-be ex-wife. But Hope hadn't been interested in his calm assurances. Maybe she'd sensed how rocky he was under the cool facade he'd assumed. Maybe she'd seen Tess's decision as a personal blow.

Whatever it had been, he'd known she wouldn't be thrilled at the thought of him seeing Tess again. On the other hand, she was his sister—his baby sister at that—and she was just going to have to learn to live with the idea.

"There's no sense in you getting in a snit, Hope." Nick stood up and came around his desk.

"What a chauvinist you are, Nick. I'm not in a snit. I'm concerned to see you doing something really dumb. You'd feel the same way if it were me." She eyed him without much favor as he sank onto the wide black leather sofa next to her.

"I'm your older brother. I'm supposed to be a chauvinist

where you're concerned. It's part of the job description. You, on the other hand, are the younger sister.'' He reached out to tug a lock of her silky blond hair. "You are supposed to look up to me with admiring eyes and agree with everything I say.''

"Garbage.'' Hope pulled her head back, forcing him to release her hair. The lock promptly curled back into the neat pageboy that fell just to chin level, its obedience a testament to the skill—and price—of her hairdresser. "I'm long past the age of thinking you're God, Nicky.''

The childhood name weakened the impact of her words. She seemed to realize it and fixed him with stern green eyes to show she intended to be taken seriously.

"A pity,'' Nick said. "You were much easier to deal with when you thought I was God.''

"The point is that you're walking right back into a situation where you're likely to get hurt,'' Hope said, ignoring his comment.

"I may not get hurt.''

"Why take the risk?''

"Life's a risk, Hope. Didn't anyone ever tell you that?'' His attempt at levity did nothing to lighten her expression. He sighed, his eyes suddenly serious. "Look, I don't know what Tess and I have, but it's something I've never experienced with anyone else.''

"Typical man. Putting sex at the top of your priority list. It takes more than sex to build a relationship, Nick. You must have told me that a million times when I was a teenager.''

"More like two million.'' He leaned his head back on the sofa and stared at the thick walnut paneling on the opposite wall without seeing it. "It's not just sex, Hope. There's something there—a connection of some kind. When I saw her at Fran McKenzie's party, it was…'' His voice trailed off and he shook his head. "I don't know what the hell it was. But I want to find out.''

There was a brief silence while Hope digested his words. "Did she tell you why she divorced you?''

"I didn't ask.''

"Are you still in love with her?''

From the quick way she delivered the question, it was obvious Hope was trying to surprise some hidden truth out of him. But the question was hardly a new one to Nick. It was one he'd asked himself—more than once. He could only give her the same answer he'd come up with on his own.

"I don't know."

"You don't know?" Hope's tone was disbelieving. "How can you not know whether or not you're in love?"

"It's not all that hard." Nick's mouth twisted ruefully. It was obvious Hope had never been in love, he thought. "All I know is that I need to find out, once and for all, what the link is between us. And I don't want to hear a lot of flack from anyone in the family about it."

"So you called me in separately?" she questioned, raising her eyebrows.

"I know you're the one most likely to give me grief," he told her bluntly. "I'm not asking your permission, Hope. I'm just doing you the courtesy of letting you know what's going on."

She was silent a moment, digesting his words and the flat, matter-of-fact tone. "Well, I guess that puts me firmly in my place."

"You wouldn't know your place if it bit you on the nose."

"I hope this works out the way you want, Nicky," she said, her eyes suddenly turning serious. "I really do."

"Thanks, kid." Nick brushed his knuckles over her cheek, feeling a rush of affection.

"Well, even if I think you're doing something stupid—and I do—I want you to be happy."

"Thanks for the vote of confidence," Nick said dryly.

"You're welcome." Hope glanced at her watch and grimaced. "I've got a meeting with Ben Sinclair in half an hour and I need to go over my notes."

She stood up, smoothing her skirt into place. Nick eyed the length of leg exposed by the narrow black skirt with an older brother's disapproval but restrained the urge to comment. He had to admit, reluctantly, she had the legs for it.

"Don't let Sinclair buffalo you into lowering the bid. He

tries it every time. To tell the truth, I think he'd be disappointed if he won."

"I can handle him." She said it with such confidence that Nick felt a swell of brotherly pride. Sometimes it was hard to remember that the cool, elegant professional he worked with was the same little girl who'd come to him with skinned knees and boyfriend troubles.

He walked to the door with her. Her hand on the knob, Hope hesitated.

"This thing with Tess is really important to you, isn't it, Nicky?"

"I don't know yet," Nick said, knowing that wasn't really true. It had been important enough for him to seek Tess out, even after three months. He wasn't sure he really wanted to look at just how important it might be. The look in Hope's eyes told him she recognized his hedging for exactly what it was.

"Don't rush her," she said abruptly. "If you want a chance to make things work, don't push too hard."

"Are you trying to tell me I'm normally pushy?" Nick asked, raising his brows.

"No. At least, not obnoxiously so." There was friendly spite in her smile but it soon faded. "I sometimes got the feeling from Tess that she felt a little overwhelmed by you. Maybe by the family, too. Tess wasn't inclined to open up much, at least not to me."

Nor to me, Nick thought, remembering old frustrations.

"But she said something once about all of us knowing where we were going," Hope continued. "That we all managed to be ourselves without disappearing in each other's shadows. I got the feeling that maybe she thought she disappeared in your shadow."

Hope's words lingered in Nick's mind after she'd gone. He sank into the chair behind his desk but he didn't reach for any of the paperwork that was waiting for him. Since his father's heart attack, he'd had plenty of opportunities to hone a natural talent for ignoring reports. Now, he put that talent to work, turning his chair to face the floor-to-ceiling windows behind his desk.

The Santa Ana winds had blown most of the night before, leaving the sky over Los Angeles a pale, clear blue. The temperature hovered in the mid-seventies. Hardly traditional Christmas weather, unless you were a native Angeleno.

Nick was only peripherally aware of the view spread out before him as he considered the idea that Tess might have felt overwhelmed by him. That had certainly never been his intention, not now and not five years ago.

Don't rush her, Hope had said. Well, maybe he had done that when they'd first met. But this time, he was determined to take things more slowly, to explore what, if anything, remained of the ties between them. No rushing into anything this time, he thought.

One day at a time and they'd see where it led them.

"TELL ME EVERYTHING." Josie punctuated the command by plopping her purse onto the floor next to her chair. Her pale blue eyes pinned Tess to her seat. "We were so busy when you got back yesterday and then I had to leave early. You didn't get a chance to tell me how your meeting with your ex-husband went."

"You mean you didn't get a chance to grill me," Tess corrected.

She dropped the catalog she'd been perusing onto the desk. She'd worry about ordering more crewel kits after the holidays when she had a better idea of what her inventory looked like. It had nothing to do with the fact that she hadn't been able to concentrate on anything since her meeting with Nick the day before.

"Grill has such a harsh sound," Josie said. "I prefer friendly interest."

"Let's face it, Josie, all you need is a rubber hose and a bright light for atmosphere." Tess reached for her cup of herbal tea.

"I resent the implication, Tess. You'd think I was nosy or something."

"You *are* nosy." Tess said it without malice. The truth was, Josie was the nosiest person she'd ever known. She wanted to know everything about everything and she rarely hesitated to ask personal questions. But her curiosity was backed by a genuine concern that made it impossible to take offense.

Josie tried to look indignant but the twinkle of laughter in her eyes ruined the attempt. "I'm not at all nosy. So what happened between you and Nick?"

The blatant contradiction drew a laugh out of Tess. "You're incorrigible, Josie, and I should fire you."

"You can't fire me. Union rules."

"What union?"

"The one I started. Now, talk to me. Did you tell him?"

"No." When Josie gave her a disapproving look, Tess raised her chin. "It's too soon."

"Not if you ask me." Josie got up and poured herself a cup of coffee from the pot Tess had made for her. Tess sniffed wistfully at the rich smell of it before sipping her own herbal brew.

"I didn't ask you," she said as Josie sat down again. "I'll tell Nick when the time seems right."

"So you're going to see him again?" Josie asked, catching the implication in Tess's words.

"Yes. We decided that, since there's obviously something between us—"

"More than he knows."

"—that we should see each other a little more," Tess continued, ignoring Josie's muttered comment.

"So you're going to start dating."

"Not dating," Tess denied. "Not really. We're just going to go out a few times. You know, get to know each other again, see how we feel."

"So when's the first date?"

Tess started to protest and then decided not to waste her breath. After all, on the surface, it did seem as if she and Nick were going to be dating. It would be impossible to explain to Josie how it differed. She couldn't even explain it to herself.

She just knew she wasn't ready to put that term to what was happening between her and Nick.

Dating implied things. Things like beginnings and possibilities for the future. Scary things she didn't want to think about quite yet.

"Nick's picking me up tonight. He has tickets to see a performance of *A Christmas Carol* in Pasadena."

"Sounds like fun," Josie said. She glanced at the clock and stood up. "You look comfortable. Let me open up this morning." She lifted the keys off the hook where Tess kept them. "I think things are going to work out just fine for the two of you. I liked the look of your Nick."

Tess opened her mouth to say that he wasn't "her" Nick. Not anymore. But Josie was already out of the office. No doubt she'd planned her departure to leave no time to respond, Tess thought, mildly annoyed. If it wasn't for the fact that the older woman was her best friend, she'd be sorely tempted to fire her.

Her Nick.

He wasn't hers at all, she thought, reaching for an invoice. She wasn't sure he ever had been.

In fact, she'd always felt more like she belonged to him.

No, Josie had the wrong idea. She thought that Nick had come back into her life and that everything was going to work out the way it would in the movies. But life seldom imitated film. She knew that from personal experience.

They were just going to take things one day at a time and see where they went.

No promises. No expectations.

Just one day at a time.

THE SUNSHINE THAT had been bathing L.A. for the last three weeks of November had not made its usual appearance that morning. Instead, the sky had been overcast with clouds that threatened rain. The temperature had dropped and Southern Californians broke out their heavy coats to deal with the chilly, fifty-degree weather.

Nick was oblivious to the chill in the air. If it had suddenly snowed and delivered them a white Christmas season, he wouldn't have noticed.

He stood on the walkway in front of Tess's house—the house that had once been theirs—and had the odd sensation of time shifting around him.

Nothing seemed to have changed. The shutters and trim were still colonial blue, standing out against the barely yellow siding. They'd painted it themselves, though he could have afforded to hire professionals. But this had been their home, their first together, and they'd wanted to do the work themselves. It had taken days, but when they'd stood back to admire the results of their labors, it had been worth every aching muscle and paint-spattered shrub.

"Of course it's the same color," he muttered aloud now, hoping to release himself from his memory's spell. "Tess picked it. Why wouldn't she keep the same scheme?"

He continued up the walkway, resisting the elusive whisper of old memories, old dreams. The rosebushes Tess had planted that first spring were thick and bushy, some of them nearly as high as his head. A few late roses still clung to the canes, the pale colors standing out against the darkness like muted globes of light.

Stepping up onto the porch, he saw the old-fashioned swing in the corner and felt sweet remembrance pierce him. He'd hung the swing the first summer they were here. They'd spent a lot of lazy hours there, Tess's head on his shoulder, his arm holding her close as they rocked.

Odd, he didn't remember spending much time there after that first summer. He'd started traveling more for the firm that fall. When he was home, there always seemed to be so much to do, there just hadn't been much time for quiet pursuits like sitting on a porch swing. Maybe he should have made a point of making time.

A huge wreath of fresh evergreen boughs with a festive red bow hung on the door, giving off a crisp pine smell that he immediately associated with Christmas. The Christmas they'd spent together, right here in this Victorian. The house had been decorated inside and out, gaily proclaiming the holiday that they anticipated sharing.

He shook his head, as if to dispel the memories. What was it Tess had said to him earlier? Oh, yeah. This wasn't the time for postmortems.

No past. No future. Only today.

It felt strange to be ringing the doorbell when he used to walk freely in and out of this same door. There was a short pause and then Tess was pulling open the door and Nick felt his pulse accelerate in a way that had nothing to do with the casually friendly attitude he'd determined to take.

"Nick." Just his name, certainly nothing to make him want to drag her into his arms and kiss her breathless. Nick forced down just that urge and smiled.

"TESS."

Tess's fingers curled over the door. How was it possible that just hearing her ex-husband say her name could make her pulse beat faster? Though if she were completely truthful, she wasn't sure her pulse had been completely normal since seeing him yesterday.

The porch light turned his hair to pale gold and cast his eyes in shadow, emphasizing the chiseled line of his jaw. He looked like nothing so much as a Viking warrior, come to claim a prize won in battle. For a moment, she wished that it were really that simple.

Wouldn't it be wonderful to be the helpless heroine in an old Errol Flynn movie, with Nick in the role of swashbuckling hero? He could sweep her up over his shoulder and carry her off and she wouldn't have to worry about whether it was a good idea. It wouldn't matter if she found herself disappearing in his shadow because the movie would end before it became important.

"Tess."

She blinked and found herself staring into Nick's puzzled eyes. A slow flush crawled up from her neck and suffused her cheeks. She must have been standing there staring at him as if she'd been struck dumb.

"Sorry. I didn't mean to space out on you."

Thank heavens he couldn't possibly know what had been going through her mind. He'd think she was nuts. And he'd probably be right.

"No problem. I feel like that after work sometimes. Rough day?"

She shrugged. "Christmas is busy for everyone."

"True. But it must be good for business."

"Yes."

There was a pause. Tess stared at Nick, racking her brain for something intelligent to say. But she seemed to have momentarily depleted her store of intelligent conversation.

"Can I come in?"

Nick's quizzical tone brought the color rushing into her cheeks again. She hadn't even realized they were still standing in the doorway.

"Of course. I'm sorry. I don't know where my brain is today."

Tess backed away so quickly, she stumbled over the throw rug that lay in the center of the entryway. Nick's hand shot out automatically, catching her elbow to steady her as he stepped inside.

"Thanks," she said, pulling away from his light hold. The breathlessness of her voice was only partially caused by her near fall. Her skin tingled where Nick's fingers had been.

"That rug always was a hazard," he commented. He pushed the door shut behind him, closing them in together.

"I suppose I should move it." Tess eased a little away, feeling as if the spacious entry had suddenly gotten much smaller.

"You've been saying that ever since we put it down," Nick said, grinning.

"Well, it looks nice there," she said defensively.

"You've been saying that, too."

"You just have no appreciation for aesthetics." She looked up at him, her eyes gleaming with laughter.

"And you have no understanding of practicalities."

"Plebeian."

"Romantic."

They grinned at each other, each swept up in the warm familiarity of the old argument, one they'd had often during their marriage. Then, as now, the point had never been for either of them to win or even to come to any solution. It had been a game they played, a way of confirming their closeness by perversely emphasizing their differences.

Of course, five years ago, the argument would have ended with a kiss. Tess's smile faded abruptly as she read the same awareness in Nick's eyes. She'd been uncertain about having him pick her up at home but it had seemed ridiculous to suggest meeting him somewhere else. But this was exactly what she'd been afraid of.

Here, in this house, where they'd built so many dreams—albeit on too fragile a foundation—it was all too easy to remember only the dreams and forget their ending. It was easy to forget there'd *been* an ending.

"It brings back a lot of memories, doesn't it?" Nick said softly. He'd read the haunting thoughts in her mind. "The two of us together in this house."

"Yes." Tess slipped her hands into the pockets of her pale gray slacks to conceal the fact that they weren't quite steady. "I almost suggested meeting you at the theater," she confessed, surprising herself.

"I almost suggested the same thing."

Nick's admission jerked her eyes back to his face.

"You did?"

"I was nervous about picking you up here. I haven't seen the place since the divorce. I wasn't sure which would be worse—to find everything the way I remembered or to see everything changed."

"I guess I didn't change it all that much," Tess said, only just then realizing how little she *had* changed.

"I noticed."

"Does it bother you?" It was the first time she'd considered the idea that Nick might feel some of the same uncertainties she did.

He took his time answering, glancing around the entry hall,

at the wallpaper they'd picked out together, at the gilded mirror they'd bought at the Rose Bowl swap meet and restored. Tess tried to see it through his eyes, wondering what it would be like to walk into a place that had once been your home and see the physical surroundings almost as they had been, even though the circumstances had changed completely.

"I like it," he said at last, his eyes coming back to hers.

Tess returned his smile and for some reason, the tension that had been between them since his arrival was suddenly eased. It was as if acknowledging the awkwardness they both felt had made it disappear. She wondered if the time would ever come when she was completely at ease with him again.

"It's going to take some time," Nick said, again reading her thoughts just the way she remembered.

"I know."

"It's worth it, Tess." He reached out to cup her cheek with one broad hand. "We can't walk away from this again."

"No." For reasons he couldn't even begin to guess, she thought.

"Maybe we can make it work this time," he said, his thumb brushing across her soft skin. It was perilously close to breaking their agreement that there would be no promises, no expectations, but Tess didn't protest.

She leaned her face into his hand, half closing her eyes. She wanted to believe they could make it work. More than he could possibly know.

Chapter Seven

Tess had had five years to forget how much fun her ex-husband could be. When she'd thought of Nick, she'd tended to focus on the negative: his traveling, the way she'd always felt overwhelmed by his drive, by his mere presence. At first, it had made it hurt less to think only of the bad things. After a while, it had become such a habit that she'd almost managed to convince herself that there hadn't been very many good things.

But it took less than two weeks to show her she'd been lying to herself. She'd forgotten Nick's ability to make her laugh, the way he never hesitated to laugh at himself.

She'd also concentrated so much on the way she'd often felt overwhelmed when he was around that she'd forgotten that she had also never felt safer or more cared for than when she was with him. It was a feeling to which she could easily grow accustomed.

What scared her was that it would be even easier to get accustomed to having the man himself around.

THEY HADN'T DISCUSSED the specifics of their tentative new relationship; things like how often they'd see each other had not been mentioned. Vaguely, Tess had thought that "taking it slow" might mean getting together once a week, maybe less considering the holidays.

Nick's idea of slow was altogether different.

On Thursday they went to see *A Christmas Carol*. On Saturday, they went to see a new animated Christmas movie in the company of what seemed like a thousand children. Watching Nick waiting in line at the snack bar, children eddying around him like windblown grass around an oak tree, Tess felt a pang. If they'd stayed married, would they have had kids of their own by now? What kind of a father would Nick be? Did he even want children? She realized she didn't even know.

They'd only discussed having a baby once during their marriage. Nick had said that he wanted to wait, to have some time for just the two of them before they expanded their family. Tess had agreed. After all, there was plenty of time to think about having a child. All the time in the world—or so she'd thought.

When their marriage hadn't worked out, she'd been doubly glad that they'd waited. The divorce had been hard enough without adding a child to the mix.

As Tess watched, a little girl tugged at the knee of Nick's jeans to get his attention. He bent down, listening with careful attention to whatever she was saying. When she opened her palm to display a handful of crumpled bills, it wasn't hard to guess that she wanted to know whether she had enough money to buy whatever candy she'd set her heart on.

The child's hair was almost the same color of golden blonde as Nick's. Anyone seeing them together would have assumed she was his daughter.

Seeing the picture the man and child made, Tess felt the sting of tears at the back of her eyes. Without conscious thought, her hand shifted, her palm flattening over her stomach.

Maybe…

No. She shook her head as if she could literally shake the disturbing questions from her mind. Not yet. It was too soon. Maybe after New Year's. If they were still seeing each other, maybe then.

"I WANT POPCORN and chocolate raisins and Milk Duds and a big Coke."

"That's an awful lot for such a little girl," Nick cautioned his small companion.

"Mama said I could order whatever I wanted while she was in the bathroom with Billy. He's my baby brother and she has to change his diapers all the time." A grimace accompanied this announcement, making her opinion of diapers—and maybe of baby brothers in general—perfectly clear. "Anythin' I want," she added, as if he might not have understood the first time.

Nick bit back a smile. Those serious eyes made it clear that a smile would not be appreciated at this point. He was no expert on children, but he guessed she couldn't have been much more than five. An adorable five, he added to himself. Big blue eyes, flaxen hair caught back from her face with a pair of lavender barrettes that just matched her dress, she could have persuaded the most confirmed child hater to soften his opinion.

He and Tess could have had a daughter this age, he thought suddenly. And she might have looked like this little girl, with his blond hair, her mother's eyes.

Odd that the thought should pop into his head now. They were a long way from thinking about children—if they were ever going to reach that point.

"Have I got enough?" the girl questioned him again, showing a touch of impatience with his apparent slow-wittedness.

Nick counted the crumpled bills in her hand. She had enough, but he couldn't help but wonder if her mother had intended for her to spend it all. Still, it wasn't his concern, and from the determined set of the child's chin, he doubted he could talk her out of her candy.

"You've got enough," he told her.

He was rewarded with a wide grin that revealed a matched pair of dimples and a set of pearly white teeth. He grinned back at her, feeling an odd little catch of emotion in his chest. God, what a feeling it would be to be responsible for a little charmer like this one, he thought. To watch her grow and learn. To catch a glimpse of the world through her eyes.

He straightened, his gaze seeking out Tess. Their eyes met

and locked and Nick thought he saw something of his own thoughts reflected in her face. Did she ever think about the fact that they might have had a child about the same age as this girl? Did Tess wonder if their lives might have turned out differently if they hadn't decided to postpone having a family?

Did she care?

ON SUNDAY, Nick brought a picnic and they went to Griffith Park. Tuesday, he just happened to have tickets to see *The Nutcracker* performed at The Dorothy Chandler Pavilion. Wednesday, Tess insisted she had paperwork. It was the truth, though there was nothing she couldn't have put off another day or two. But she had the feeling she'd been caught up in a whirlwind, her life spinning out of her control. She had to take time to catch her breath.

But once she had the time, she found herself staring at the phone and thinking about calling Nick to tell him she'd changed her mind and wanted to have dinner with him after all. Pride kept her from picking up the receiver but pride couldn't prevent her thoughts from drifting in his direction. The paperwork sat on her desk, unnoticed and undone.

When Nick picked her up at the shop Thursday at closing time, it was to go on a tree-shopping expedition. Tess hadn't bothered putting up a Christmas tree since the divorce, thinking it would only serve to make her feel more alone.

"But it isn't Christmas without a tree," Nick announced, looking shocked.

Tess agreed. That suited her just fine. If it weren't for the brisk business that Christmas brought to her shop, she would be just as glad to avoid the holidays altogether. They held too many memories.

But somehow, Nick had convinced her that a tree was absolutely essential, and in no time Tess had found herself laughing and agreeing that the corner of the front room was indeed the perfect place for one.

An hour after Nick picked her up, he was struggling through the front door with an eight-foot Douglas fir that had no interest in compressing itself to fit through a doorway.

Tess wasn't sure how her "small" tree had grown so big, anymore than she could have said just why she'd agreed to having a tree in the first place. The only thing she was sure of was that she couldn't remember the last time she'd had so much fun.

THE SUNSHINE FOR WHICH Southern California was so justly famous had disappeared again at the beginning of the week. Temperatures dropped and heavy gray clouds blanketed the sky, promising rain but delivering little more than an occasional drizzle. Rain or no, the chill was enough to make a fire the perfect accompaniment to an evening spent trimming the Christmas tree.

Once Nick had muscled the tree into the stand, he piled wood into the grate and lit a fire. The flames were just starting to lick up over the logs when Tess brought in a tray of cocoa and cookies. She'd baked them the night before when she should have been doing the paperwork that was still piled on her desk.

Nick had been crouched in front of the fire but he stood up as she entered the room, turning toward her. He looked so right there, as if he belonged, as if the room needed his presence to be complete.

Like her life?

The thought slipped in so quietly that it was a moment before Tess felt its impact. The tray settled onto the coffee table with more force than she'd intended as her fingers seemed to weaken abruptly.

"You should have asked me to bring that in for you," Nick said, stepping forward and bending to slide the tray farther onto the table.

"It's not heavy," Tess said automatically. The scent of his after-shave didn't make it any easier to clear her unaccountably confused thinking. She straightened, hoping even that small distance would put everything into better perspective.

Her eyes fell on the way the gold of Nick's hair contrasted with the green of the sweater he was wearing, a green that matched his eyes to sinful perfection. The thin cashmere clung to the muscles of his back. Tess's fingers curled into her palms at the memory of the way those muscles felt under her hands.

"Cookies!" Nick's voice held unabashed greed. His eyes smiled in delight.

Tess blinked and dragged her thoughts to more acceptable paths.

"I thought they'd be nice with the cocoa," she said.

She watched as Nick's strong teeth bit into the soft sugar cookie shaped like a toy soldier. He chewed and swallowed, his expression as serious as that of an oenophile testing a fine cabernet.

"Fantastic," he pronounced.

"Thanks." Tess told herself the fact that it came from Nick didn't make the compliment any more important than it would have been from someone else. But the quick lecture didn't stem the warm tide of pleasure that washed over her.

Nick finished the first cookie with obvious relish and bent to take another one. "I haven't had cookies like this in years."

"If it's my baking you missed, I could give you the recipes," she said lightly.

"I missed more than your cooking."

"That's what they all say." She reached for her cocoa, only to have Nick's hand close over hers. Startled, Tess's eyes flew to his face.

"I didn't spend the last three months thinking about your apple pie, Tess." His tone was light, but there was nothing light about the look in his eyes.

"I believe you," she whispered, finding her voice nearly choked off by the sudden tightness in her throat. Believing that he was interested in more than her cooking skills wasn't the problem.

It was determining what he *was* interested in that had her tied in knots.

NICK WATCHED Tess's face, wishing he could read what she was thinking. But those beautiful blue eyes hid so much more than they revealed, just as they'd always done. He knew she didn't seriously believe he was only interested in her cooking, and he was becoming impatient with this game they were playing.

He didn't want to be Tess's friend. Or at least, that wasn't all he wanted. He wanted to be her lover. He wanted to feel he had some claim to her besides the extremely tenuous one of being her ex-husband. He didn't want to be her ex-anything. He wanted his presence in her life to be based on more than past connections.

Tess tugged on her hand and he released it. He watched as she picked up her cocoa mug, though he doubted she had any real interest in the steaming drink.

Patience, he reminded himself as her eyes flickered to his face and then away. It had been barely a week since he'd pushed his way back into her life. He couldn't expect to make up for five years in a few days.

"So, are we going to decorate this thing or leave it *au naturel?*"

He saw the tension ease from Tess as his light tone put them back on safe ground. It was like dealing with a half-wild kitten. She drew close only to dart away if he tried to tighten the fragile ties that bound them together.

Patience. A quality of which he'd never possessed any great quantity. But he was going to have to cultivate it if he wanted Tess back. And that *was* what he wanted.

Watching her open boxes of ornaments—ornaments they'd bought together, stored in the attic since the divorce—Nick determined that this was going to be only the first of many Christmases spent together. He still didn't know what had gone wrong before, why she'd wanted a divorce, but whatever it had been, this time they'd find a way to work it out.

He wasn't giving her up again.

"BE CAREFUL, NICK." Tess watched anxiously as Nick, perched on a stepladder, leaned over to slip the angel into her place on top of the tree.

"I'm not going to break my neck. Not after all this work." He leaned a little farther and set the angel in place.

"Actually, I was afraid you might fall into the tree and ruin it."

"Thanks for your underwhelming concern for my safety and well-being," he said dryly.

"Anytime."

Seeing the tuck in her cheek and the sparkle in her eyes, Nick wondered if it would be rushing things to drag her into his arms and kiss the smile from her mouth. Probably, he decided with an inward sigh. He folded up the stepladder and carried it to the back porch. When he returned, Tess was just clicking off the last lamp, leaving only the flickering firelight to light the room.

"Are you ready?" She hovered next to the outlet where the tree lights were to be plugged in.

"For someone who didn't want a tree at all, you sure are impatient."

Tess ignored his teasing remark and plugged the cord in. She stood up and backed away, coming to a stop beside Nick. They stared at the tree in silence. The colorful lights sparkled off the tinsel and were reflected in the ornaments. Nick had placed a single white lamp on the branch just below the angel and its pure light was reflected upward, giving her porcelain face a lifelike glow.

"It's beautiful." Tess's voice was hushed. She liked to think she was immune to the holidays, and yet, she couldn't pretend to be unaffected by the hope and promise that the glittering tree seemed to represent.

Or was it the hope and promise of Nick's presence that she felt?

"Not bad for two people who haven't decorated a tree in years," Nick commented.

"Not bad at all," Tess agreed softly. She could feel something dissolving inside, a hard knot that she hadn't even known was there until now.

It occurred to her that this past week had been one of the happiest she'd ever known. She'd divorced Nick because she'd been afraid she'd never be complete as long as she was in his shadow. Yet, with him gone from her life, there'd been a part of her missing.

"I think this calls for a toast." Nick picked up their cocoa mugs, which Tess had refilled just before they added the final touches to the tree.

"To Christmas," he said, his eyes holding hers.

"To Christmas," she whispered, knowing that neither one of them was thinking about Christmas.

She barely tasted the warm chocolaty drink. The room, which had always seemed quite spacious, was suddenly much smaller. The soft mutter of the fire wrapped them in intimacy, reminding her that they were alone.

They'd only spent one Christmas together in this house but the moment seemed filled with memories. Of all the Christmases they'd planned to spend together? Tess wasn't sure what it was, but she knew she hadn't felt this sense of rightness—of completion—in a long time.

Perhaps Nick read the feelings in her eyes, because he reached out to take her cocoa and set both cups on the coffee table. When he turned back to her, there was no mistaking the look in his eyes. Hunger. Need. And a question he didn't have to voice.

Nor did she have to give him her answer. At least, not in words.

NICK READ WHAT WAS in Tess's eyes and felt his heart start to pound in a heavy rhythm. He'd schooled himself to patience, promised himself he'd give her all the time she could possibly want. But her eyes were telling him that patience and time weren't what she wanted now.

His fingers found the red Christmas bow with which she'd tied back her hair, and tugged it loose. The ribbon drifted to the floor, a bright spot of color on the gray carpet. Loosened from its confinement, her hair fell in a heavy black curtain down her back.

"I used to dream about seeing you wearing nothing but your hair," Nick said quietly. He pulled a handful forward, letting it drape across the ivory linen of her blouse.

His hand came up to cup her cheek. His thumb brushed over her mouth and her lips parted in an invitation that echoed the look in her eyes.

"If I kiss you, Tess, I'm not going to want to stop," he whispered, his mouth only a heartbeat away.

"I'm not going to ask you to."

Nick's lips touched hers and the world was suddenly reduced to a space no bigger than the room that held them. Tess's mouth opened to him, her breath leaving her on a soft sigh as his tongue traced the soft line of her lower lip. Her hands came up to rest against his chest as she leaned into his strength.

As always, passion lay waiting between them, like kindling that needed only a match to set it ablaze. Nick flattened his hand against her spine, drawing her closer as his mouth hardened over hers.

Tess let herself melt against him, her fingers curling into his sweater, feeling the ripple of muscles beneath the fine cashmere. His tongue swept into her mouth, tasting her surrender. She gave him everything he asked and more, her body pliant in his arms, her tongue dueling with his in a battle neither wanted to win.

The hunger they had been trying to deny suddenly smoldered. It needed only a kiss to flare, and quickly the fire blazed out of control. Tess didn't care anymore. Just like it had been three months ago, there was only this man, this moment. And the knowledge deep inside her that this was right, that this was what had to happen.

No more regrets. No more pretending. Nick was the other half of her soul. She could no longer deny herself. Nor could she deny him.

In all her life, she'd only known true completion in this man's arms. For years she'd lived without it. Tonight, she was going to taste that completion again.

Heaven knew, the consequences could hardly have more impact on her life than those of that hot summer night.

NICK WAS NOT THINKING about consequences. He couldn't think beyond the soft miracle of having Tess in his arms again, of feeling her body bend to his, her hunger burning bright and hot to match his.

He'd wanted her so long. Like a starving man suddenly presented with a banquet, Nick was torn between conflicting urges. He wanted to drag every moment out, to savor each sigh, every touch. Yet he ached to sheathe himself in her and know the completion that he could find only with her.

Tess's hands slid up his shoulders, her slender fingers burying themselves in his thick gold hair at the nape of his neck as she rose on her toes, pressing herself closer, arching her body to his. Nick flattened his hand against her buttocks, letting her feel the aching ridge of his arousal. Her soft moan unraveled the fragile thread holding his control. With a groan, he crushed her to him, needing to feel her with every fiber of his being.

There was no question of right or wrong, no concern about future regrets. There was only the two of them, at this moment, in this place. Only the two of them and the hunger and need that had always drawn them together.

Clothes whispered to the floor. Neither of them could bear the time it would take to go upstairs to a bed. The thick carpet was bed enough. Nick's sweater provided a pillow for Tess. Her hair spilled over it, black against jade.

"You're so beautiful." Nick's voice was hushed as he looked at her. The firelight flickered over her skin, painting golden shadows on soft curves, teasing him by concealing even as it revealed.

"Don't make me wait, Nick." Tess's husky plea shivered over him, making him ache.

"Tess." Her name was almost a prayer.

His hips settled into the cradle of her thighs. Tess reached between them, her slim fingers closing over his arousal. Nick shuddered at the sweet torture of her touch as she guided him to her.

At the very threshold of paradise, he hesitated. Bracing himself on his arms, he looked down at her. Her face was flushed with passion, her eyes almost black with need. He could feel the moist welcome of her body, feel her hunger in the way her hands clutched at his hips, urging him to complete the union that lay only a heartbeat away.

Nick didn't doubt that her hunger burned as hot as his. But he wanted more than her passion. *That* had always been his. He wanted something more lasting, a promise toward the future.

"No regrets, Tess?" he asked, his voice husky. "No more running away?"

Her restless little movements stilled, her eyes locking on his. For a moment, the silence was so complete that the soft crackle of the fire seemed almost deafening.

Nick waited. Though it would damn near kill him to do it, he'd end this here and now unless she was as sure of the rightness of it as he was.

"No regrets, Nick." Her words were little more than a whisper but they were clear and steady. "And no more running away. Not anymore."

Nick felt relief wash over him. This wasn't the way he'd planned it. This was hardly a prime example of patience. But maybe patience wasn't what she needed, after all.

"Come to me, Nick," she whispered softly. "Make me whole again."

The invitation in her voice and the hunger in her eyes shredded the last ounce of his control.

"Tess." He sank against her with a slow thrust, feeling her heated dampness enfold him in the sweetest of embraces.

It was like coming home. It was completion. Wholeness. It was everything he'd remembered and so much more.

Tess shuddered under the impact of his entry. She'd asked him to make her whole again and he had. He'd filled her emptiness, made her complete. It was as if a part of her was his alone and she could only be complete in his arms.

In contrast to the urgency that had gone before, their lovemaking was slow and drugging. Nick set the pace—long, slow thrusts that drove the passion ever higher. The flames that crackled in the fireplace next to them were as nothing compared to the fire that burned between them.

He lowered his weight to his elbows, his broad chest gently crushing her breasts. Tess moaned as she felt his chest hair abrade her swollen nipples. Her hands slid up and down the length of his back, seeking something to cling to as the world spun madly around her.

It was too much, she thought feverishly. She would surely shatter in another moment. Yet she drew her knees up against his hips, taking him deeper still, needing to feel him in her very soul.

Nick wrapped his hands in her hair, holding her head still as his mouth devoured hers. His tongue thrust into her mouth, mimicking the rhythm of his deeper, more powerful thrusts. Tess whimpered against his mouth, her tongue twining hungrily with his.

The tension spiraled tighter and tighter, coiling low in her body until her entire being seemed focused on their joining. Her nails dug into his muscled back as she tore her mouth from his, her neck arching as the tension grew to unbearable proportions.

"Nick!"

His name was a plea. She was begging him to end the nearly painful sensations and yet praying they would never end.

Nick drew his head back, watching her face as he shifted the angle of his entry. He saw her eyes fly open, read the ecstasy there as the wave of completion caught her. And then she was melting against him.

His own climax was only a pulse beat after hers. The feel of her body tightening around him, caressing him in the most intimate of ways, sent him tumbling headlong into his own fulfillment.

Tess's pleasure was magnified a hundredfold by the feel of him shuddering inside her.

It was a long time before Nick gathered the energy to move from her. He hushed Tess's murmured protest with a kiss, his mouth lingering on hers. She didn't protest again when he slid an arm beneath her, tucking her head against his shoulder and drawing her to his side.

There were things to be said, but neither of them wanted to

break the silence. Lying there, with the firelight flickering over their bodies and the soft glow of the Christmas tree in the corner, both were content to savor the moment. The questions could wait.

This was enough for now.

Chapter Eight

The Santa Anas began during the night, and by morning, the clouds that had hung over the L.A. basin for the past few days had dissipated, leaving clear blue skies and the promise of seventy-degree weather.

When Nick woke, sunshine was spilling through the light curtains, painting bright patterns on the polished oak floor and then tumbling over the pastel fabrics of the patchwork quilt that lay across the footboard.

The room hadn't changed a great deal since the days when he had shared it with Tess. The curtains were new but the wallpaper was the same ivory-and-blue floral stripe. The oak dresser still sat under the window but the bed in which they lay was no longer the huge oak frame he'd dragged up the stairs. Tess had never liked the bed and she'd replaced it with a brass frame that added a jaunty spark to the big bedroom.

It was the first time he'd awakened in this room in five years, yet it felt completely natural to be here. It was almost as if he'd been gone on a long business trip and had come home to find that Tess had rearranged the furniture. The differences were so minor that they hardly impinged on his consciousness.

Or maybe it was just that any bed would feel natural if Tess were in it, too.

Nick rolled onto his side and rose on one elbow, moving slowly to avoid disturbing her. She seemed to be deeply asleep, her breathing light and even. He couldn't resist the opportunity to look at her with all the barriers down between them.

Her lashes lay in dark crescents against her cheeks, a contrast to her sleep-flushed skin. Her mouth was soft and relaxed, her full lower lip tempting him to wake her with a kiss. Instead he feasted his eyes on the pure feminine beauty of her.

Her skin seemed to hold a gentle inner glow that he didn't remember from when they'd been married, as if she were lit from within. Her hair was scattered over the pillow beneath her, jet black against pristine white linen.

Nick traced his fingertip down one silken lock where it trailed over her shoulder, curving across the upper swell of her breast. From there, the temptation was irresistible. He nudged the sheet aside, exposing one dusky rose nipple. Tess stirred slightly, murmuring something unintelligible as he brushed his thumb over the soft bud, which puckered magically under the gentle touch.

He was tempted to lower his head and taste the response he'd elicited but he wasn't quite ready to have her awake. It had been a long time since she'd been his to look at and touch. He wanted to savor the moment.

At his urging the sheet slid down her slender body, baring her to the early-morning sunlight. He wasn't satisfied until the fabric had been banished to thigh level, leaving him an uninterrupted view.

God, but she was exquisite. From the tousled black satin of her hair his eyes trailed over each delicate feature. The winged darkness of her brows, the inviting fullness of her mouth, the fragile line of her collarbone. The fullness of her breasts had always seemed a delightful surprise on a woman of her slender proportions. They seemed even fuller than he remembered, a delicate tracery of blue veins just visible beneath her ivory skin.

Her waist was not as slender as he'd remembered either, and there was a gentle swell to her stomach that he'd never noticed. In his mind, he'd pictured her as being so slender that she hovered on the edge of being too thin. Nick half smiled, thinking that time distorted even the memories he'd thought most sharp.

By the time his gaze had reached the dark triangle of curling hair that marked the top of her thighs, a slow but intense arousal was building in him. Though they'd made love again after he carried her to bed the night before, his body obviously couldn't get enough of hers.

He cupped his palm around one soft breast, teasing the nipple to hardness with his thumb. Tess stirred but seemed reluctant to wake. Smiling, Nick bent to take her nipple into his mouth, nibbling gently until he heard her moan and felt the restless shifting of her legs. He lifted his head and looked down into her face, watching her lashes flicker once or twice before slowly lifting.

"Wake up, sleepyhead."

"Nick?" His name was a question, as if she couldn't quite believe he was really there.

"In the flesh." He grinned and dropped a quick, hard kiss on her mouth. "And I must say, Ms. Armstrong, that you have very nice flesh indeed. I was just admiring it."

"Admiring what?" she asked, her eyes still sleepy.

"Your flesh. Every beautiful inch of it." He swept one hand from her shoulder to her thigh before letting it come to rest on the softness of her belly. "Daylight becomes you, Tess." She smiled, her lashes starting to drift downward as if sleep was still beckoning. Nick grinned, thinking that waking her up could prove to be a most rewarding activity. But he didn't get a chance to find out.

Tess's eyes suddenly flew open, her pupils dilated, something akin to panic in their depths. She sat up so suddenly that if Nick hadn't jerked out of the way, she would have banged her head into his. Oblivious to the near collision, she grabbed for the covers, snatching them up over her breasts and clutching them there as if her life depended on keeping them securely in place.

"Whoa!" Nick sat up beside her, rubbing one hand over his forehead as if half expecting to find a bruise. "What was that about?"

"Nothing."

"Nothing? You damned near concussed yourself on my head."

"I'm sorry." Tess's cheeks were deeply flushed, her eyes still showing traces of an inexplicable fear.

"I *have* seen you naked before," Nick said, eyeing her quizzically. "Just a few hours ago, if memory doesn't fail me."

"I know. I'm sorry." Her flush deepened, her eyes shifting away from his. "I guess it was just the idea that you'd been watching me while I slept."

"Sorry. It was irresistible." He grinned at her. "You look just as good as you did five years ago. Better, even. You've gained a little weight. It suits you. You always were on the thin side."

"Weight?" The color on her cheeks receded, leaving her suddenly pale.

"I think it looks great."

Nick wondered if he shouldn't have mentioned it. He wouldn't have if she hadn't thrown him so off balance. He was sincere in saying he thought the weight suited her, but you never could tell about women. They could be so touchy about their weight, turning five pounds into fifty in the mirror.

"I mean it," he said, when Tess didn't speak. "I think it looks good. You're even more beautiful than I remember."

Tess stared at him. "Thank you," she whispered.

There was a brief silence while Nick tried to think of something more to say. Tess sat there, clutching the sheet to her breasts, one hand pressed over her stomach as if to conceal the slight thickness there.

The way she was acting, you'd think he'd caught her in a lie, Nick thought. Or that she had something to hide. Some reason to fear what he might see, what he might learn.

Afterward, he'd never know where the thought had come from. There seemed no reason to think Tess's sudden skittishness was caused by anything more than the fact that, just as she'd said, it had startled her to think he'd been watching her while she slept.

No reason to think anything else.

But he was suddenly thinking about that almost luminous glow she seemed to have. About the slight thickening in her waist. About the new heaviness in her breasts and how sensitive they'd been last night when they were making love, his lightest touch sending shudders through her.

And about the fact that Tess—who'd always sworn she couldn't survive without caffeine to keep her going—was suddenly drinking decaffeinated coffee. And refusing even half a glass of wine, he remembered.

All the signs of pregnancy.

It was absurd. Maybe she was just cutting out caffeine for health reasons. And lots of people gained weight in the stomach. Half the men he worked with had guts and he'd never jumped to the conclusion that any of them were pregnant.

Yet the thought grabbed him by the throat and refused to let go. While logic told him he'd never had a stupider thought, every instinct was shouting that, logic or no, he was right. Tess was pregnant.

Feeling as if someone had slammed a fist into his gut, he dragged his eyes from that protective hand pressed to her stomach to her face.

And her eyes gave him the answer to the question he'd hardly managed to form in his mind.

She was carrying a baby. His baby.

TESS SAW THE KNOWLEDGE in Nick's eyes. He didn't have to say anything, any more than she'd had to tell him the truth. He knew. Without a word exchanged, he knew.

In a sudden flurry of panic, she started to swing her legs off the bed. She wasn't sure where she was going. Certainly there'd be no avoiding Nick, no pretending that he didn't know. There'd be questions she'd have to answer. But not right now, she thought. Later, when she'd magically come up with all the right answers. Then they could talk. But not now. Not right now.

As if she really had an option.

Nick's hand closed over her shoulder before she could get

her feet untangled from the sheet. Tess tensed but she didn't try to resist the solid strength that pressed her inexorably back down onto the bed.

She did make a futile effort to retain her white-knuckled grip on the sheet when Nick started to pull it away, but he yanked it from her grasp, stripping it down, leaving her exposed to the emerald heat of his eyes. Totally vulnerable.

His palm flattened over her belly, testing the gentle swell, exploring it with a softness at odds with the emotions that hardened his jaw.

"It's true, isn't it?"

Her response was an instinctive, and foolish, attempt to put off the inevitable. "What's true?"

Nick's eyes swept to her face, burning with angry fire. "Don't lie to me, Tess. Not now. You're pregnant, aren't you? And it's my baby."

Tess opened her mouth to deny it, her only thought that she couldn't deal with this now. Not coming so quickly on the heels of last night's near paradise. She would have told him, she thought despairingly. Just not now. And certainly not this way. Just a few more days. Hours even. She just needed a little time to regain her equilibrium.

But it was clear that she'd run out of time.

"It's true." Her whispered confirmation seemed to echo, as if she'd shouted it.

"My God." The impact on Nick could not have been more powerful if her words had had actual, physical strength. He'd known, even before she said it. He wouldn't have believed the denial he knew she wanted to give him. Yet hearing her actually admit it left him without words.

He stared at her, the anger momentarily replaced by stunned disbelief. Illogically, he denied the truth he'd insisted she confess. "You can't be pregnant."

"Tell my doctor that," she snapped.

This time, he didn't try to stop her when she swung her legs off the bed. Tess glanced over her shoulder as she stood up but Nick didn't even seem aware of her departure. His eyes were focused on empty space, his features slack with shock.

Tess took advantage of his shock to grab her robe from the closet and pull it on. She felt a little less vulnerable with her body concealed from him, a little more capable of coping.

"When we were married, you were on the Pill," Nick said, still sounding as if he'd been hit with a baseball bat. He stared at her without really seeing her. "I didn't think... It seemed so much like old times...."

Tess closed her eyes, trying not to remember just how much like old times it had seemed. She didn't blame Nick for not thinking of birth control. She hadn't given it a moment's consideration herself. Like him, all she'd thought about was how right it felt, how much like coming home.

"I quit taking the Pill after the divorce," she told him.

Reluctantly, yet knowing she had no choice, she turned to face Nick. He still sat on the bed, one knee drawn up, the other leg bent beneath him. He seemed unconcerned with his own nudity. Tess wished it were as easy for her to ignore.

"How long have you known?" He sounded dazed, the reality of what she'd told him not quite sunk in. He didn't wait for her to answer but continued. "It's been three months. You must have known for weeks now."

Anger rose in his eyes, driving out the shocked disbelief. "You must have known for weeks," he said again.

Tess's teeth worried her lower lip, her eyes shifting away from his. She could hardly lie to him, tell him she'd just found out. Yet she couldn't bring herself to confirm the knowledge in his eyes—the realization that she'd known she was carrying his child and had chosen not to tell him.

"When were you going to tell me, Tess? When were you going to tell me about the baby?"

She tightened her belt unnecessarily and kept her eyes on the floor. What should she tell him? That she didn't know the answer to that question? That she didn't know the answer to any of the questions he had a perfect right to ask?

"When were you going to tell me you were pregnant, Tess?" His voice roughened. "Or had you decided not to tell me at all?"

Her eyes met his for a fleeting moment before she half

turned from him, lifting one shoulder in an uncertain shrug. Another question to which she had no answer. She didn't *know* what she'd planned, hardly knew what she'd thought.

She heard Nick's bare feet hit the oak floor an instant before she felt his fingers close over her shoulder, turning her to face him. If it hadn't been Nick standing before her, Tess might have felt actual fear. The anger that blazed in his eyes and hardened his jaw to iron made him more than a little intimidating.

"*Were* you going to tell me, Tess?"

She met his eyes. She refused to cower, no matter how justifiable his anger.

"I was going to wait until after the holidays and see where we stood then." It had seemed so reasonable when she'd made the decision. Now, saying it out loud, it sounded weak and selfish.

"And what if things weren't going well between us? Were you just going to keep it from me?" Nick stopped, his fingers tightening on her arm as a new thought occurred to him. "You've known this for weeks already. What if I hadn't come to find you? Would you have called me to let me know I was about to become a father?"

"I don't know," she told him, giving him the honesty she should have given him in the beginning. "I don't know."

Nick's hand dropped from her arm as if she'd suddenly become too hot to touch. His eyes were filled with a sort of angry hurt that tore at Tess's heart.

"My God, what did I do to you that you'd keep something like this from me?" he asked hoarsely.

There was so much pain in the question that she reached out to him, wanting to take away the hurt she'd unthinkingly inflicted. He jerked away before her hand reached him as if her touch were acid, and gave her a look in which rage and pain were mixed in equal measure.

"It wasn't anything you did, Nick." Tess let her hand fall to her side, telling herself he had a right to his anger. "I just didn't know how to tell you."

"A phone call would have done nicely." Nick turned and

grabbed his pants from the pile of clothes that they'd brought up with them the night before. Tess's blouse was tangled with them and he tossed it carelessly to the floor.

He stepped into the faded jeans and jerked them up over his hips, his mind spinning with what he'd learned.

Tess was pregnant.

That night three months ago they had created a child.

She'd known for weeks and hadn't told him.

He was going to be a father.

Each fact seemed separate and distinct, as if they had nothing to do with each other. He simply couldn't get his mind to grasp the reality of it. Neither the idea that she was having his baby, nor the fact that she'd chosen not to tell him about it. None of it seemed real.

"I thought about calling," Tess said.

Nick spun to face her, his face tight with fierce anger. "Is that what you were going to tell our child when he got old enough to ask why his father never came around? 'Gee, I meant to call and tell him. I just never got around to it.'"

Despite her determination not to cry, Tess felt her eyes sting with tears at Nick's savage tone.

"I don't know what I would have said."

"Maybe you figured you'd just let him think I don't give a damn about him. That would probably have been a lot easier for you. Fewer questions to answer."

"I wouldn't have done that," she cried. "I would never have let him think that."

"You'll forgive me if I don't take your word on that," Nick said, his icy tone as sharp as a knife.

"I wouldn't have let your son or daughter think you didn't care, Nick. You have to believe me."

"I don't believe you," he said coldly. "Lying to a man is not one of the best ways to gain his trust." Nick reached for his sweater and jerked it over his head.

"I didn't lie." Tess regretted the words the moment they were out. It was a weak defense and she knew it. The look Nick cut her told her he knew it, too.

"All right, so maybe I should have told you," she admitted.

"*Maybe,* Tess?" Nick's left brow disappeared into the heavy gold hair that lay on his forehead. "*Maybe* you should have told me?"

Nick saw the quick little gesture as she brushed away a tear and thought vaguely that he should be moved by her distress, that her regret should be enough to mollify his anger. Perhaps later, when he'd come to terms with the monumental changes in his life, then maybe he'd be more sympathetic.

At the moment, all he could think of was wanting to shake her until her teeth rattled. Along with that urge came another, just as strong. That was to hold her close and put his hand on her stomach, to feel the miracle of life growing inside her, the child they'd created together.

But she'd taken from him the right to do that, the right to share the miracle of it. All he could do was stand there and look at her through a veil of anger and hurt that was so thick, he wasn't sure it would ever dissipate.

"I'm sorry, Nick. I didn't mean to hurt you."

"For someone who wasn't trying, you did a bang-up job."

He wasn't giving an inch. Not now. Not yet. Maybe not ever.

"I was afraid," she whispered, her fingers twisting restlessly around the end of her belt, crushing the soft velour and then smoothing it out again.

"Of me?" he asked incredulously.

"Not exactly."

"Then of what?"

"I don't know," she admitted.

"There seems to be a hell of a lot you don't know," Nick snapped. "Is there anything you *do* know?"

"I know I didn't mean to hurt you."

He didn't need the tears that shimmered in her eyes to tell him that she meant it. He felt a tiny crack in the wall of anger he'd thrown up between them. But he was not yet ready to let the crack widen into forgiveness.

He wasn't sure he'd ever be ready.

"I have to go." The flat statement was the only response he could give her.

Tess's head came up, her eyes wide and startled. "Aren't we going to talk?"

"Coming from you, that's an interesting question." But the sarcasm was softened by a deep weariness. "We should have been talking weeks ago."

"I admitted I was wrong. I said I was sorry."

"Sometimes, sorry isn't enough, Tess." He looked away from her, glancing around the quiet room, his eyes lingering on the sleep-tousled bed. It didn't seem possible that less than thirty minutes ago, he'd awakened in that bed, feeling as if the world—his world—was getting back on track.

He thrust his fingers through his hair before sliding his hand to the back of his neck and squeezing the knotted muscles there. Tess stood there looking at him, her eyes wide and uncertain. He wanted to reassure her, to tell her they'd work everything out. But at the moment, he didn't know if that was going to happen.

"I'll be in touch," he said at last, knowing it wasn't enough. But it was all he could offer with any honesty. And God knew, honesty was one thing they needed right now.

"All right." Tess wanted to press him for something more definite. *When* would he be in touch? Where did they go from here? Did last night's intensity mean anything in the face of this morning's debacle?

She bit her tongue, holding back the questions. She'd have to wait and see what happened. Maybe that was to be her punishment.

Nick stared at her, obviously looking for something else to say. Perhaps he was as reluctant to end on such an unsatisfying note as she was.

"I'll be in touch," he said again, at a loss for anything more profound.

"I'll be here." She could hardly force her voice above a whisper but she was proud of its steadiness. At least, if she never saw him again, he wouldn't remember her as a sniveling child.

Tess thought he hesitated for a moment as he walked past her. For a wild moment, she thought he might take her in his arms and say that nothing mattered but that they'd created a baby together. But then he continued, the hesitation—if it had existed at all—gone.

She stayed where she was, listening as the bedroom door closed behind him. A minute later, she heard the front door close and then the sound of his car starting.

It wasn't until the engine's whine had faded completely that she moved. Feeling as if she were a hundred years old, she sank down on the edge of the bed. The faint musky scent of their lovemaking lingered on the sheets, rising up in a ghostly reminder of last night's passion. She closed her eyes against the acute pain that stabbed through her.

Against her closed eyelids, she could see Nick's face, hurt and angry. Her eyes snapped open, banishing the image. Staring at the wall opposite, she pressed one hand flat against the slight swell of her abdomen.

"What have I done?" she whispered.

But there was no answer.

Chapter Nine

The Christmas tree sparkled with light and color. Red and blue, green and gold, shiny silver from the strands of tinsel, the gleam of lights, and above it all, the serene porcelain face of the angel. It was a beauty that dazzled even as it soothed, excited even as it comforted.

"Tess."

Hearing her name, she turned, feeling a rush of joy and happiness when she saw Nick walk into the room.

"Nick."

"She wanted to see the lights," he said, looking down.

It was only then that Tess saw the infant he held cradled in his arms. She was wrapped in a gossamer-fine blanket of purest white. As Tess moved closer, seeming almost to float over the floor, the edge of the blanket fell back.

"Oh." The hushed exclamation was all she could manage. She had never seen a more exquisite baby in her life. Her beautifully shaped skull was covered by downy curls of a familiar gold and when she opened her eyes, Tess saw they were a pure clear green, seeming to hold a knowledge far beyond her tender age.

"She's beautiful," she whispered, reaching out to stroke one finger across the baby's cheek.

"Of course she is. She's ours. How could she be anything but beautiful?" Nick's voice was full of pride.

"She's ours?" Tess was filled with wonder. This *was the*

child she'd carried under her heart? The child she'd dreamed of holding in her arms?

"Would you like to hold her?" As always, he seemed able to read her thoughts.

Tess nodded, holding out her arms to take the baby from him. The weight of her seemed to fill an emptiness she hadn't known existed until just that moment. The baby looked up at her with eyes just the color of her father's, eyes that were calm and steady.

"We did a good job on the tree."

At Nick's comment, Tess turned, looking up. The tree seemed, if possible, even more beautiful than it had a few minutes ago, as if having Nick and the baby there added something to its beauty.

"It's a wonderful tree," she said, feeling as if her world was absolutely perfect.

"I'm so glad the three of us are together." Nick put his arm around her shoulders, drawing her against his side in an embrace that encompassed both her and the baby. "It means so much to me, Tess, to be here like this."

"Where else would you be?" She tilted her head to look up at him, puzzled by his words. In the back of her mind, something stirred, a vague uneasiness that she couldn't quite put her finger on.

"Families should be together for the holidays," he said. "Fathers should be there."

"Yes."

She felt the weight of his arm easing from her shoulders as he stepped back. Or was she the one who'd moved?

"I want to know my child, Tess."

"Nick?" He seemed to be moving farther away.

"A child should have a father."

It was hard to distinguish his outline against the lights of the Christmas tree, which were suddenly glaring in her eyes.

"Nick?" She heard the fear in her voice. She wanted to reach out to him but she couldn't move her hands from the baby. She wanted to run after him but her feet seemed rooted to the floor. "Nick?"

"Don't tell her that I didn't care, Tess."

"I won't." She could no longer see him. She couldn't see anything but the harsh glitter of the tree, a mad swirl of colors and lights that loomed in her field of vision.

"Don't tell her I didn't care." The words were a whisper, rife with pain.

"Nick!"

There was no response. He was gone. And she knew he wouldn't be back.

Feeling as if there was only emptiness where her heart had been, Tess looked down at the baby she still held. The weight of her seemed less substantial, as if, with her father's disappearance, she'd lost something. The green eyes that looked up at Tess held a question.

"I didn't mean to hurt him," Tess whispered. "I didn't mean it."

But the question in those eyes had become an accusation and Tess knew she'd never be able to explain, never be able to make her understand.

Just like Nick would never understand....

TESS WOKE WITH A START. She sat bolt upright, her eyes flashed open and her heart pounded furiously. It was several seconds before her eyes took in her surroundings, the familiar surroundings of her bedroom. She was lying in her own bed, illuminated only by a soft pool of light from the bedside lamp.

It was just a dream, she told herself. *Just a dream....*

Her hand settled on the bulge of her belly and she squeezed her eyes shut, trying to force back the tears that burned at the backs of her eyes.

But all she saw emblazoned there was the burning image of Nick and the stark hurt on his face when he accused her of hiding her pregnancy. The absolute wonder in his eyes when he touched her stomach. The total disappointment when he walked out the door three days ago.

Unable to sleep, she got up and walked into the living room, as if drawn there. Moonlight streamed in through the open drapes and was caught and refracted over and over again by the strands of tinsel, making the tree shimmer with a life of its own. She felt oddly compelled to plug in the lights, and soon the tree was aglow with the colorful bulbs.

She and Nick had had so much fun decorating the tree. Laughter and the inevitable arguments about where to hang the lights had reminded her of the good times they'd once had. And hinted at what they could have again.

But in her dream Nick didn't hang around long enough. Like a spectre, he was suddenly gone, leaving her calling out to him, leaving the baby looking up at her with accusing eyes.

But it was just a dream, she told herself again.

She couldn't answer when the niggling voice inside her head asked, *Wasn't it?*

BY THE AFTERNOON, Tess was no closer to answering that question. She'd forced herself to eat something, knowing the growing baby needed nourishment, and she'd just finished mixing the ingredients for a batch of Christmas cookies. During December she made it a point to keep the shop stocked with fresh coffee and cookies. Usually she bought them, but today baking seemed a good antidote to the blues that threatened her. But her heart simply wasn't in it.

When the doorbell rang, she was almost grateful for the interruption. She set down the mixing spoon and wiped her hands on a towel as she went to the door. It was probably the elderly woman next door dropping in for a chat, as she often did. Tess pulled the door open without confirming her guess. When she saw who was on the other side, her welcoming smile vanished and her eyes widened with sudden uncertainty.

"Nick."

"HELLO, TESS." The flat greeting was all Nick could force out.

On the way over, he had wondered what he would feel when he saw her again. A deep anger still boiled in his gut, an anger like he'd never felt before.

But seeing her now, his first thought was not of how angry

he was with her. It was of how beautiful she was. And how in awe he was of the miracle they'd created together. He wanted to press his hand to her stomach, to feel his child growing within her. But they were a long way from that moment, if they were ever to reach it at all.

The mixture of feelings made his voice flat, his tone cooler than he'd intended.

"How are you?"

"I'm fine." She brushed a tendril of hair back from her forehead, looking uncertain. "Would you like to come in?"

"Thank you." Nick stepped past her and into the entryway. He felt the same welcome from the house that he'd felt the day they'd first seen it. It seemed that no matter what passed between them, this house still felt like home. He pushed that thought aside and turned to face Tess.

"Would you like a cup of coffee?" she asked.

"Is that good for the baby?" The question came out sharper than he'd intended, sounding accusatory.

Tess raised her chin, her dark blue eyes showing a touch of annoyance. "I haven't had coffee since I found out I was pregnant. But the fumes are hardly likely to be a problem if I make some for you."

"Sorry. I didn't mean to sound pushy. I guess this whole idea has thrown me off balance."

"Babies have a tendency to do that," Tess told him, trying to regain a polite tone. "You get used to it after a while."

"Do you? I haven't had time to find that out."

The cool reminder extinguished her tentative smile like water thrown on a lit match.

"I suppose you haven't," she said expressionlessly.

There was a tense silence and then Nick exhaled abruptly. "I'm sorry, Tess. I shouldn't have said that."

"It was the truth."

"Maybe, but we're not going to get anywhere by beating a dead horse."

"Are we going to get anywhere if we don't beat it?" she asked carefully.

The second the words were spoken she regretted them. Why

had she asked him that? It wasn't the time for talk of the future. She remembered the tiny life growing inside her belly and thought maybe it was too late.

Nick looked at her, his eyes brooding. All he said was "I don't know."

Tess started to say something but he shook his head, stopping her. "I don't want to talk about it right now. I just came over because I said I'd put up the lights."

"Lights?" Tess stared at him blankly, unable to follow him. "What lights?"

"The outdoor Christmas lights. I said I'd put them up for you."

"You came over to put up the Christmas lights?"

"I said I would," he repeated doggedly.

"I haven't had lights in years, Nick." It was not so much a protest as an expression of bewilderment. After the way they parted three days ago, the last thing she'd expected was to have Nick show up to hang Christmas lights. "You really don't need to go to all that trouble."

"It's no trouble."

Looking at the determined set of his jaw, Tess decided to give up the argument. For whatever reason, Nick had made up his mind that the house was going to be decorated for Christmas. If this was what he'd chosen as the first step toward them working out their problems, then it was easy enough to accommodate him.

"The lights are in the attic."

"Is the ladder still in the garage?" Some of the tension seemed to go out of him, as if he was relieved at her acquiescence.

"On the rafters." *Where you left it five years ago.* But she didn't say that out loud. The balance stretching between them was too fragile.

THOUGH TESS WOULDN'T have believed it possible, the afternoon passed pleasantly enough. She returned to her cookie baking while Nick clambered over the outside of the house, putting up lights. He even climbed up on the roof and set up the plastic Santa and all his reindeer that had graced the house the one Christmas they'd spent here together.

"Where'd you dig those things up?" Tess called to him on the roof when she went out to check his progress. "I'd even forgotten we had them."

Nick swung around toward her voice, almost losing his footing.

"I'm sorry," she said, knowing she'd startled him. "I didn't mean to intrude. I just came out to see if you wanted anything."

Even from up on the roof, his eyes bore into hers. "No, I'm fine" was all he said, and he turned back to the Santa.

On the way back into the kitchen, Tess could still feel those eyes on her.

She turned on the radio, which was playing the inevitable Christmas melodies, and started rolling out another batch of sugar-cookie dough on the counter. The occasional thump of the ladder against the side of the house reminded her of Nick's presence, and she was aware of a fragile feeling of contentment.

As she cut out reindeers and angels and chubby Santas, Tess thought about the baby she carried and how wonderful it would be if her child—their child—were to grow up in a home with two parents who loved each other. Just like her dream last night.

Not that she was ready to say she loved Nick, she told herself hastily. It hadn't even been two weeks since he'd come back into her life. It was premature to start thinking about love.

You fell in love with him quicker than that the first time, a sly voice whispered in her mind.

"And look where that ended," she said aloud.

Did *it end? Did you* ever *stop loving him?*

But that was a question she wasn't prepared to answer for anyone, not even herself.

BY THE TIME the sun started to sink toward the Pacific, Tess had baked half a dozen batches of cookies, enough to keep even the most voracious hordes of Christmas shoppers at bay for a day or two. She was just sliding the last sheet of cookies out of the oven, when the overhead light went out with a pop.

"Damn." She set the tray on top of the stove and shut the oven door. The only light in the room came from the fluorescents beneath the upper cupboards, and what little the setting sun cast through the west window.

Knowing it was silly, Tess wiggled the switch up and down a few times. The light remained off and her kitchen remained in gloom. Muttering under her breath, she got a light bulb out of the cupboard and dragged a chair under the fixture.

She had just reached up to unscrew the old bulb when she heard the back door open. Twisting her head to look behind her, she saw Nick step into the kitchen. Saw, also, the look of horror on his face.

"What the hell are you doing?" His tone could only be described as a bellow. He didn't bother to give Tess time to respond. He crossed the kitchen in three long strides and swept her off the chair.

Tess cried out, startled, and threw her arms around his neck. The bulb she held in her hand smacked into Nick's ear.

There was a moment of silence where Tess could hear the accelerated beat of her pulse. Or was it that she could feel Nick's heartbeat where she lay against his chest?

"What were you trying to do?" The bellow had become a growl but his displeasure was obvious.

"I was trying to change a light bulb," she said deadpan.

Tess pushed against him in a silent demand to be released. He seemed to hesitate for a moment, as if not sure she was safe to be allowed on her own. She drew her head back, glaring at him in the dim light, annoyed with him because he'd frightened her. Annoyed with herself because she didn't really want to leave his arms.

Reluctantly, Nick lowered the arm beneath her knees, bending to set her on the floor. Even then, he kept his arm behind her back, as if prepared to sweep her up again should she show any signs of toppling over.

"I realize that. What I meant was, what were you doing on that chair?"

"I was changing a light bulb," Tess said again, tugging her shirt back into place, smoothing it over her jeans.

"You were standing on a chair." He made it sound as if she'd been doing acrobatics.

"That's how I reach the old light bulb so that I can replace it with the new one." She held up the new bulb for emphasis.

"You shouldn't be standing on a chair."

"Well, it's easier than leaping up there and clinging to the fixture by my teeth while I change the bulb," she said with an insultingly sweet smile.

"You could have fallen." His scowl told her that her sarcasm was not appreciated.

"I've been changing light bulbs my whole life and I haven't fallen yet."

"You haven't been pregnant your whole life, either," he snapped.

There. He'd said it. The subject they'd tiptoed around all afternoon.

Dead silence hung between them as they faced each other in the darkened room. Their eyes were locked, as if each was trying to gauge the other's reaction.

"I'd make the record books if I had been," Tess said finally. "I don't think even elephants are pregnant that long."

Nick's smile came reluctantly but it *was* a smile. "That wasn't exactly what I meant."

"That's what it sounded like."

"I guess it did."

The momentary humor faded but it had served to break the finely drawn tension that had been between them all afternoon. There was a pause and then Nick's hand came out to flatten against her stomach in an almost convulsive gesture. Tess caught her breath at the touch but she didn't move away.

"God, Tess, I can't believe we're going to have a baby."

The breath she'd been holding all day came out on a sigh. "I thought maybe you'd forgotten," she said. She felt shaken to the core by his touch and the look of wonder in his face.

"It's all I've thought about." He didn't lift his eyes from

her stomach, his fingers moving caressingly, as if touching the infant she carried. "Have you felt him move yet?"

"It's a little early for that. And it could be a her, you know."

"Either way. As long as she's healthy." Nick raised his eyes to hers. "What does it feel like, to know that you're carrying another life?" His hunger to share this with her was obvious.

Tess felt a pang of guilt. She'd been so wrong.

"It feels like a miracle," she said softly. Her eyes stung with tears as she set her hand over his. "I'm sorry, Nick. I should have told you about the baby. I'm so sorry."

"Why didn't you?"

There was no anger in the question, only a genuine need to understand. Here in the dimly lit kitchen, filled with the homey scent of baking, there didn't seem to be any place for anger. The time for anger was past. What each sought was to understand the other.

"I'm not sure," Tess said slowly. She tried to remember why it had all seemed so clear at the time. "At first, I was hurt that you hadn't called or come to see me. I know that was stupid." She gave him a shaky smile. "I was the one who ran away. I should have been the one to call. I guess I'm not as liberated as I like to think."

"No one said emotions are logical." Nick shrugged.

The movement seemed to remind him he was still touching her. His hand fell from her stomach and he stepped back.

Tess felt a deep sense of loss, as if he'd taken away a part of her. At the same time, she was grateful for the extra bit of distance between them. Her thought processes had never been at their best when Nick was too close.

"I can understand that maybe, when you thought I was ignoring what had happened between us," he said slowly, obviously not at all sure he believed what he was saying but trying to be generous. "But what about later, when you knew about my father? When you knew what kept me away? Why didn't you tell me then, Tess?"

She hesitated, knowing she could never make him understand how much it had frightened her to think of letting him back into her life. It was something she only partially understood herself. So she offered him a partial truth.

"I guess I wasn't sure you'd be interested."

"Not interested!" Nick stared at her in disbelief. "What kind of man wouldn't be interested in his own child?"

"My father." She hadn't intended to say the words out loud but there they were, hanging in the air between them. Nick's eyes widened in surprise and then a look of understanding came into them. She looked away, annoyed with herself for revealing something she'd tried very hard to forget.

"I'm not your father, Tess," Nick said quietly. "I could never ignore my child. Don't you know me better than that?"

"Yes, I do. I guess I just wasn't thinking very clearly. One day we were divorced and out of each other's lives and the next I was carrying your baby—and somehow we skipped all the steps in between."

"All those steps in between aren't always necessary, Tess. Sometimes, you know what's right without them."

Maybe he knew, but all she was sure of was that, when it came to Nick Masters, she'd made a habit of going from point A to point Z without making any stops. And each time she arrived at the end she was out of breath and wondering if she'd made a mistake.

"I'm sorry I hurt you, Nick. That was never my intention."

"What's done is done." Nick shrugged and gave her a half smile. "I'll recover. What's important now is, where do we go from here?"

It was meant as a rhetorical question. He was thinking out loud. But Tess chose to answer it.

"I don't now. Where do you think we should go?"

Well, that was putting the ball squarely back in his court, Nick thought. The problem was that he wasn't quite sure what to do with it. Where *did* he think they should go from here?

"I want to be part of my child's life," he said slowly.

"But not of mine?" Tess lifted her chin, as if bracing for a blow.

"That's not what I meant." Nick thrust his fingers through

his hair, trying to articulate feelings he hadn't yet clarified in his own mind. "My feelings for you haven't changed. I don't like what you did but I don't hate you for it, either. I...care about you."

The phrase was hopelessly inadequate. An anemic word like "care" didn't even begin to describe what he felt about her. But it was the best he could come up with at the moment.

"I care about you, too," Tess said, her voice hardly more than a whisper.

They looked at each other, each grateful for the poor light that concealed their own expressions while regretting that it hid the other's.

The air was pregnant with things unsaid, only half-understood. Nick wanted to pull her into his arms and hold her close. But it was too soon for that, for both of them. They needed time.

It was Nick who looked away first, glancing up at the dark light fixture.

"Why don't I change that bulb for you?" The prosaic offer was just what was needed to ease the tension before it became uncomfortable.

He stepped up on the chair and unscrewed the old bulb, handing it down to Tess and taking the new one from her.

"Thank you," she said as he jumped to the floor. "But I really would have been just fine."

"Maybe. But I'd rather you didn't go climbing on chairs, at least not as long as I'm around to do the climbing for you."

But you won't always be around. Tess didn't say the words out loud. She didn't have to. The same thought was in Nick's eyes.

For a moment, she thought he was going to say something and she held her breath, hoping for— What? She didn't even know what she wanted him to say.

But he turned away without speaking, leaving her with an indefinable feeling of something lost.

But you can't lose something you don't really have, she told herself.

Nick flipped the wall switch, and the kitchen was bathed in

light. Painfully bright light. Tess blinked and looked around the room as if seeing it for the first time. The racks of cookies cooling on the counter, the canisters and mixing bowls beside them, all seemed to be part of someone else's life. It seemed like hours since she'd taken the last cookie sheet out of the oven, though a glance at the clock showed her it had been only a few minutes.

"That's better," Nick said, letting his hand drop from the switch.

"Is it?" Tess wasn't referring to the light.

"Yes." The strength of Nick's answer told her he knew what she was talking about. "We'll just go back to where we were."

"I don't think that's possible." She shook her head slowly. "I don't see how we can go back and pretend." Her doubt was painfully obvious.

"We don't have to pretend. We'll just do what we planned to do in the first place. We'll take things one day at a time and see where it goes from there."

"All right." It was, after all, the only choice. The baby linked them even without whatever it was that kept drawing them together.

"There's more drawing us together than the baby, Tess." Her flush revealed just how accurately he'd read her mind.

There might be more than a baby drawing them together, but there'd always seemed to be just as much pushing them apart. Tess brushed a tendril of hair back from her forehead, suddenly achingly tired.

Looking at her porcelain pale skin and seeing the subtle slump of her shoulders, Nick wanted to cross the room and take her in his arms and tell her everything was going to be all right.

"I'd better get going." He glanced at his watch as if just remembering somewhere he had to be. The truth was, the only appointment he had was with a TV dinner and a book.

"Of course." Tess straightened her shoulders with a visible effort. "Thanks for putting up the lights."

"You're welcome." They both knew the lights had merely provided him with the excuse he'd needed to come over.

There was an awkward little silence. They looked at each other across a few feet of polished oak floor that might as well have been the Grand Canyon. The distance was proving as uncrossable.

After a moment, Nick moved toward the door. Tess followed him into the front entry, not sure which she wanted more: to throw her arms around him and beg him not to go, or to see the door close behind him so that she could crawl up to bed and collapse.

Luckily for her muddled state of mind, she didn't have to make the choice. Nick paused before opening the door and turned to look at her.

"I'll call you."

"Okay."

He reached behind him for the doorknob but didn't immediately open it. "You'll be all right alone?"

"I'll be fine." She could have pointed out that she'd been alone for years, but there seemed no point to it.

"Try not to worry. We'll work it all out."

"Yes." It was easier to agree than to argue.

"I'll see you soon."

As if he couldn't stop himself, he reached out, brushing his fingers over her cheek in a caress so fleeting, she almost thought she'd dreamed it. Before she could respond, he'd pulled open the door and left, leaving her staring at the blank panel.

It wasn't until she'd heard his car pull away from the curb that she gathered the energy to move.

She was sure there were all sorts of things she should think about. Things to do with her and Nick, things to do with her and Nick and the baby. But at the moment, all she wanted was a warm shower, a soft nightgown and a firm mattress.

Like Scarlett, she'd think about everything else tomorrow.

Chapter Ten

"Can you give me a hand?"

The question came from behind him. Nick turned, not sure it had been addressed to him. A middle-aged man smiled at him from the bed of a battered pickup. Seeing that the request *had* been directed at him, Nick walked toward the truck.

At this point, any distraction was welcome. He'd been standing across the street from Tess's shop for five minutes, debating the wisdom of going in. The two days since he'd seen her last seemed like two weeks. He found himself wondering if her pregnancy had become any more obvious, even though it seemed unlikely that two days would make an enormous difference.

"If you could just take that end of it, I'll get this one."

Nick looked into the bed of the pickup at a stack of plywood that had been painted red, with thin black lines drawn on it to indicate bricks.

"What is it?" he asked, as he slid his hand under the sheets of wood.

"Santa's house." The old man lifted the other end of the stack and walked the length of the bed with it. He set it on the tailgate and jumped into the street before picking it up again.

"Santa's moving to a warmer climate?" Nick questioned, following the other man's lead as they rounded the corner of the stationery store.

"Just making a visit. Here. Lean it against that lamp pole."

Nick followed his instructions and set the house-to-be down. Stepping back, he dusted his hands together and turned a critical eye on his companion.

"Don't tell me you're one of the elves? You don't look a thing like I expected."

"Not an elf." Blue eyes laughed at him from under dark brows liberally sprinkled with gray. "I'm Santa himself."

"You're Santa?" Nick eyes went automatically to the man's nearly nonexistent hairline before giving his clean-shaven features and slight build a doubtful look. "You're not what I expected, either."

"The wonders of makeup," he was told with a laugh. "Thanks for the help."

"You're welcome."

For lack of anything better to do and because it gave him a legitimate excuse to delay making a decision about seeing Tess, Nick followed him back to the pickup. If the man was surprised, he didn't reveal it. He merely gestured to a big wooden chair and lifted a box himself.

"You play Santa for the kids?" Nick asked as they carried the chair and the box to where they'd set the plywood.

"Sure do. I've been the Santa on this corner for eight years now."

He began assembling the little wooden shack that would be Santa's house for the next couple of weeks. It was obvious he'd done this so many times that he didn't need assistance. Still, Nick lingered.

"You like working with the kids?"

"Most of the time. Like anything, there's an occasional bad day where all the little ones do is cry and all the older ones want to do is pull your beard off to see if you're really Santa Claus."

Nick laughed with him but his eyes drifted across the street to the colorfully decorated front windows of Needles & Pins. Would Tess be glad to see him?

"Any kids of your own?" The friendly question drew Nick's attention back to Santa.

"We're expecting our first," he said slowly.

"Now that's a scary time. Exciting but scary, too." He unfolded the sides of the building, which were attached to the back with hinges. Nick helped him balance the little shack while he eased the supports into place.

"You have children?" Nick asked.

"Two. And one grandchild, born last spring. She's cute as the dickens but I don't envy my son and his wife a bit. It's a tougher world out there than it was when my two were little. Everybody expects so much of everybody else. And of themselves."

"Yeah." Nick's attention had drifted across the street again and he missed the shrewd look his companion gave him as he positioned Santa's chair in front of the plywood house.

"I wouldn't worry too much. I guess people have raised kids in tougher times. Not that it does much good to know that. You still worry yourself to death. Especially with the first one. You're not quite as bad with those that come after."

At the moment, Nick's only concern was the first one. And his or her mother. And where he was going to stand with both of them. He sure wasn't going to get any closer to finding out by lurking across the street from Tess's shop.

He said his farewells to his new acquaintance and started across the street, uncertain whether he felt like Sherman marching to conquer Atlanta or Napoleon about to meet Wellington.

TESS LOOKED UP as the bell over the door jangled and felt the familiar catch in her heartbeat when she saw Nick enter the shop. It took a considerable effort to return her attention to the customer in front of her.

"I wish I could help you, but it's just not possible to get a pillow finished for you in time for Christmas." She turned and gestured to the cross-stitched sign that announced the schedule for sending items out for professional finishing. "The end of October was the last possible date."

"But I just got the top done," the woman protested, as if

that should be the only consideration. She tapped her fingers on the needlepoint canvas spread out on the counter.

"I'm sorry." Tess's smile was regretful but firm.

"It's an original. I painted the canvas myself."

"It's lovely," Tess said, hoping her nose wouldn't grow from telling such a lie. She glanced at Nick, who'd stood close enough to listen to the conversation, and saw his brows go up as he looked at the needlepoint picture of a naked woman holding a bunch of grapes. The colors were garish and the stitching was sloppy. But Tess wasn't in business to tell her customers to find another hobby.

"Perhaps you could have this finished as a Valentine's gift?"

The suggestion made the woman's frown ease. A few more minutes of discussion and lamentation over the unreasonableness of people who couldn't drop what they were doing to finish an obvious masterpiece and she'd agreed that maybe Valentine's would be better after all.

Tess filled out the paperwork and carefully rolled the canvas under the woman's eagle eye. Another promise that it would be ready by the first week in February and the customer departed.

"Who's she giving it to? A madam?"

Nick's dry question made Tess grin. "Her son and daughter-in-law."

"You're kidding."

"No. She says it will be perfect for their decor."

"Early American bordello?"

"Could be," she said with a laugh. She finished putting a tag on the canvas and set it on a shelf behind the counter before turning back to Nick. What would she say to him?

"I know I said I'd call you," Nick said, breaking the silence before it could stretch too far. "But I happened to be in the area and thought I'd drop by instead. I hope you don't mind."

"Not at all. Are you on your way to a construction site?"

"How'd you know?"

"I assume you don't dress like that to go to the office," she said, gesturing to his black jeans and work boots. He wore a green-and-black buffalo plaid shirt with them. His golden hair was tousled just enough to make her fingers curl with the urge to tidy it. He looked, as he always did, devastatingly handsome.

Tess smoothed a hand over her hair, wishing she'd done something more elaborate with it and her clothes, too.

"I'm on my way to a project up near Angeles Crest," Nick was saying. "The client wanted a mansion built into the side of a mountain. Worst building site I've seen in years. Makes me glad I only have to design the things, not try to build them."

"But I bet you managed to design something spectacular *and* buildable," she said, knowing it was no more than the truth.

"I don't know about spectacular, but I came up with a modest little seven-thousand-square-foot cottage that seemed acceptable."

"*Only* seven thousand square feet?" Tess raised one dark brow in disdain. "Paltry."

Nick shared her smile, wondering if she had any idea how lovely she looked. She was wearing another of those loose jumpers, this one in a soft yellow that made him think of daffodils and springtime. Her hair lay over her shoulder in a thick black braid. His fingers tingled with the urge to loosen it from its confines and see it tumble over his hands.

But now was not the time for that. They were supposed to be taking things slow, finding out where they could go from here. And while going straight to bed held a definite appeal, it was hardly the answer.

"Actually, I'm glad you dropped by," Tess said. "I was thinking about calling you."

"That would be a change." But there was no anger in Nick's dry comment.

"I have a doctor's appointment tomorrow afternoon and I thought you might want to come along."

"Is something wrong?" Nick's hands gripped the counter as he leaned toward her, his features suddenly taut with worry.

"No. It's just a checkup. I know Dr. Kildare wouldn't mind if you came along."

"Dr. who?" Nick's tone made it clear that he thought he was hearing things.

"Dr. Kildare," Tess repeated, lifting her chin. "She happens to be an excellent ob/gyn. There *are* people named Kildare, you know."

"But not doctors," Nick said, laughing. "Why doesn't she change her name to Hossenfeffer or Geizendorfer? Something nice and normal."

Tess laughed reluctantly. "I admit I had my doubts but she's really very good."

"I'll take your word for it. I don't have much experience with ob/gyns."

"I guess not."

"What time is the appointment?"

"Five o'clock. Don't feel like you have to come just because I asked," she added quickly. "I just didn't want to shut you out."

Like I did before lay unspoken between them.

"I'd like to be there. If it won't bother you."

"No. That's fine. Just fine." Tess let her voice trail off, thinking that they sounded more like strangers than like two people who'd once been married, two people who were expecting a child together.

NICK WAS THINKING much the same thing as he left the shop, after having arranged to pick Tess up there the next day. She'd catch a ride in with Josie and then he could take her home after the appointment.

Crossing the street, he paused near the little red plywood shack that had somehow, magically, been transformed into Santa's house. Children were already lined up waiting to speak to Santa.

Nick studied them and their parents. No one seemed to find anything at all incongruous about a man in a red suit and the bright sunshine that poured down out of the clear blue sky. To them, this *was* Christmas weather.

Nick, too, had spent all his childhood Christmases in Southern California sunshine. He never thought twice about it—until, when he got older, his parents packed up the family and escaped to Tahoe for the holiday. Nick relished the snow and cold. Somehow, nothing was quite like twinkling snowflakes making lacy patterns on an icy window, or a cozy fire to warm you when you came inside. Even last year, when he got snowed in on a design job up in the Sierras, he loved it.

But there was no snow here. And hard as he tried, he could see no resemblance between the thin, balding man he'd met and the plump, white-haired figure who now sat in the big wooden chair, a little Oriental girl on his knee.

He leaned down, listening as she lispingly itemized her Christmas list, which seemed to include every toy advertised. Nick smiled at the innocent greed she displayed, remembering the days when he'd thought that life as he knew it couldn't possibly continue unless he had the latest battery-operated whizbang gadget he'd seen on television.

In a few years, he and Tess would be bringing their own son or daughter to talk to Santa, and no doubt he or she would have the same ridiculous urge to own everything. He hoped that it was something he and Tess would be doing together.

He was going to do his damnedest to see that it worked out that way. But it would only happen if it was what Tess wanted, too.

He laughed. Somehow, he never would've thought the first stop in rebuilding their relationship would be at an ob/gyn.

DR. KILDARE BORE no resemblance to Richard Chamberlain. She was a slender black woman in her forties, with a voice that seemed too deep for her build and eyes that inspired instant confidence.

Tess wasn't sure what she'd expected from Nick. A vague but uninformed interest at best. Boredom, at worst.

But he was showing no sign of boredom. Instead, he listened attentively as the doctor discussed the changes Tess could expect in the next month. At first Tess was acutely uncomfortable at finding herself in the midst of a very personal discussion of her body with Nick in the room. Not that he didn't know her body intimately, she reminded herself. But there was a difference.

This was a new level of intimacy. She'd never really thought about how closely entwined a man and woman became with the creation of a child. A part of Nick now dwelt inside her. It hadn't been quite real until the two of them sat down with the doctor and discussed the progress of that new life.

"Is everything going the way it's supposed to?" Nick asked.

"Tess and the baby are in good shape." Dr. Kildare's smile was understanding. She'd dealt with plenty of anxious fathers in her time. In fact, she preferred them to the ones who felt their duty ended at conception.

"There's nothing to be concerned about?" Nick probed, wanting to be sure. "Tess is awfully small, don't you think?"

Tess looked at him, startled by his obvious concern. She'd thought he'd be more concerned with the baby than with her, but that didn't seem to be the case.

"She's small but her pelvis is fairly wide. As the baby grows, we'll keep an eye on things. If there's any reason to be concerned, either for Tess's sake or for the baby's, we can always opt for a cesarean delivery. But I don't think it will be necessary."

Nick looked unconvinced but he didn't press the point. As they talked on, Tess hugged that concern close, feeling a warm glow in her chest.

And the concern didn't end when they left the doctor's office. Nick matter-of-factly told her she needed to get some solid food into her stomach and drove her over to dinner at Marie Callendar's. They got there early enough to beat the dinner crowd and were seated in a high-backed booth that provided an illusion of intimacy.

Their conversation ranged from disposable diapers—to which they both were opposed—to the possibility of world peace in their lifetimes—for which they both prayed.

Though Tess would never have believed it possible two

days ago, when they left the restaurant she was pleasantly relaxed. She didn't even hesitate when Nick suggested taking the long way home so they could see the Christmas lights decorating people's homes.

"Want to check out the competition?" Tess teased him.

"I *have* no competition," Nick responded arrogantly.

Tess just rolled her eyes and laughed.

Days ago, she'd thought she might never see Nick again. Yet here she was, in the dark intimacy of his car, laughing with him.

But maybe she shouldn't be so surprised, she thought. The changes in her relationship with Nick had always come suddenly. From marriage to divorce to parenthood—none of it had been done at a reasonable pace. There had never been any time to stop and catch a breath.

They drove up and down the residential streets for almost an hour, admiring the decorations. It didn't matter whether it was just one long string of lights along the roofline or if the entire property was aglow from twinkling bulbs, they admired each and every one.

It was after nine when Nick pulled up to the curb in front of Tess's house. He walked her to the door, and went inside with her to flip on lights and make sure everything was all right. Tess was touched by his concern. Strangely, she'd missed that feeling of being protected.

"Would you like a cup of cocoa?" she asked, as she walked to the door with him. Since the question was followed by a yawn, it was hardly surprising that Nick shook his head.

"You need your sleep."

She wanted to argue but her body was telling her that he was right.

"I feel like Rip van Winkle," she grumbled, forcing back another yawn.

"You're much prettier than he was," Nick teased.

"Gee, thanks."

"Good night, Tess." His smile faded and he reached out almost compulsively, brushing his fingertips over the curve of her cheek. "Thanks for letting me go with you to the doctor's."

"You're welcome." Tess leaned her face into his hand, enjoying the faint roughness of his callused palm against her cheek. "I don't want to shut you out again. This is your baby, too."

"And a beautiful baby it's going to be." Nick's other hand settled on her stomach, his touch light through the fabric of her dress.

Tess felt his touch all the way to her core. It was always that way between the two of them. As if a fire lay waiting, ever ready to spring to crackling life.

"I want to kiss you, Tess." The words were not quite a question but Tess answered anyway.

"I want to kiss you, too." She leaned into his touch, her hands coming up to rest on his chest.

"Just a kiss. No more," Nick whispered, his mouth hovering over hers. "We're not going to rush into anything."

"No. We're not going to rush." Dimly she was aware of how foolish it was to say it when she could already feel the blood rushing through her veins, speeding her pulse.

Nick's hand slid from her face to cup the back of her neck as his mouth came down on hers. He might have intended the kiss to be only a warm good-night, a promise of what the future might hold for them. But the moment Tess responded, her slender body bending into his, her fingers sliding up his shoulders to tunnel into the thick blond hair at the back of his head, his intentions flew out the window.

His tongue swept the full line of her lower lip before dipping into her mouth, tasting the honeyed sweetness of her response. It was impossible to say that one was the match and the other tinder. The heat simply flowed between them, threatening to blaze out of control at any moment.

Nick's hand flattened over her spine, pressing her close to his hard frame as if he wanted to absorb her into himself. Tess could feel his arousal pressed against her stomach. The feel of it added to her own hunger.

She wasn't thinking about taking things slow. She wasn't

thinking about anything but how right it felt to be in Nick's arms.

It was Nick who recognized the danger in what was happening. A dimly heard warning bell rang in his mind, far away but insistent. Wasn't this exactly what had caused them trouble in the past? It would be so easy to sweep Tess up in his arms, to carry her up the stairs and into the bedroom. She wouldn't offer a whisper of protest.

They both wanted it, he thought defiantly. They were consenting adults. Where was the harm?

The harm was in the inevitable regrets, afterward. It was in the feeling that they kept trying to build a relationship based on the undeniable sexual attraction between them. If he couldn't restrain himself even once, how could he expect Tess to believe him when he said that his feelings for her were more than physical?

But he wanted her and she wanted him.

His arms tightened around her but it wasn't enough to keep his thoughts at bay. Every instinct told him that to make love to Tess now would be a mistake—maybe the last one he'd get to make with her.

With a smothered groan, he dragged his mouth from hers. Setting his hands on her shoulders, he put her away from him, though he couldn't stop his fingers from caressing her arms.

Tess blinked up at him, her eyes all invitation. Nick ground his teeth together, feeling as if he were literally holding on to his willpower by the skin of his teeth.

"I don't want to screw things up this time, Tess," he said huskily.

Tess stared at him, her skin flushing as she realized how close she'd been to ending up in bed with Nick. Again. When she'd sworn not to. Again. And it hadn't been *her* common sense that had intervened.

She pressed her fingertips against her warm cheeks.

"Don't." Nick pulled her hands down, forcing her to meet his eyes. "Don't be embarrassed. I want you just as much as you want me. I can't hide how much I want you," he admitted ruefully.

Tess's eyes automatically dropped down his body, her cheeks flushing anew before she jerked her eyes away. But he'd succeeded in distracting her from her own feelings of embarrassment.

"There'll be other nights," he said, making the words a promise. "When we're sure."

He didn't wait for her response but drew her forward to press a quick, undemanding kiss on her mouth. Before Tess could respond, he was gone, the door closing quietly behind him.

Moving slowly, Tess twisted the dead bolt into place and then turned to lean against the heavy door. She stared into space.

She loved him.

The thought slipped in so quietly that she felt no real surprise when she realized it was there. Of course she loved him. She'd loved him from the moment they'd met. She'd never really stopped loving him, not even when she'd asked him for a divorce. It hadn't been Nick she'd doubted then. It had been herself.

Now, she'd proved she didn't need to doubt herself; she could survive on her own, succeed on her own. She didn't have to stand in anybody's shadow anymore. And now Nick had come back into her life.

She set one hand on her stomach, her fingers caressing the still-subtle bulge. Nick. A baby. A home for the three of them. Her business. Was it possible that she was going to be one of the lucky ones who had it all?

Of course, it was one thing for her to know she loved Nick. It was something else to know whether he loved her.

There could be no question he wanted her. But that wasn't love. There could be no question he wanted things to work out between them. But that was because of the baby.

No. Tess didn't want him to come to her because of the baby or because of an undeniable physical hunger. She wanted him to come to her because he loved her as much as she was finally willing to admit she loved him.

He'd loved her once. Was it possible he could love her again?

Chapter Eleven

"How do you feel about becoming an aunt?"

Hope Masters looked up from the salad she'd ordered, her startled green eyes meeting her brother's contained look.

"An aunt? What kind of aunt?"

"Are there different kinds?" Nick asked, amused.

Hope set her fork down and gave the question her full attention.

"Well, there's the adoptive sort of aunt—the ones who aren't related by blood. And there's the sort of ant that lives in holes in the ground and steals food at picnics. And then there's the sort of aunt that you become when your brother or sister has a child. I sincerely hope you're not talking about the last one."

"Sorry." Nick neither looked nor sounded apologetic. After last night, he wasn't sorry about anything. He was going to be a father and he and Tess were on the right track. This time, they were going to make it work. He could feel it in his bones. And he didn't think it would be very long before Tess knew it, too.

"Tess?"

"Who else?"

"She's pregnant?"

"That's what it usually takes for someone to become an aunt."

"Oh, Nick." Hope sat back against her seat, oblivious to

the lunchtime crowd in the restaurant as she looked at her brother.

"You sound like I just told you that I have a fatal disease," Nick commented, not in the least disturbed by her reaction.

"Are you sure?"

"That I have a fatal disease?" he asked, raising his brows.

"That Tess is pregnant?" Hope brushed aside his attempt at humor.

"Absolutely. I'll be a father in May."

She started to speak, thought better of it and closed her mouth without saying a word. Nick sliced off a bite-size piece of chicken breast and put it in his mouth, giving his sister time to digest the news he'd just given her.

He'd finished that bite and was starting on another before Hope spoke again.

"Are you happy about this, Nicky?"

"Very. I didn't know I wanted to be a father until I found out I was about to become one. But now that I know, I couldn't be happier."

"Then I'm happy for you," she said, her tone more fitted to pronouncing death sentences.

"You certainly sound it," Nick commented dryly.

"I'm sorry." She picked up her fork and poked at her Chinese chicken salad without much interest. "I don't mean to sound gloomy. This has all been so sudden," she said fretfully. "I mean, one minute Tess has been out of your life for years. The next, you tell me you're seeing her again. And now she's expecting a baby."

"You sound just like Tess, complaining that things are going too fast."

"Well, much as I hate to agree with her, she's right."

"Sometimes things just happen that way," he said. "There's no rule about relationships having to take a certain amount of time to work."

"I didn't say there was, but I still think you're rushing things. I mean, a baby, Nick. You and Tess haven't even worked out the problems between you and you're going to have a baby. And after all the lectures you gave me about safe sex.''

To his surprise, Nick felt his color mount. ''I'm a little old for lectures, Hope.''

''Apparently not. Really, Nick, how could you be so careless?''

''I don't have to justify my sex life to you,'' he snapped loudly. There was a momentary pause in the buzz of conversation near their table. Glancing around, Nick found himself the recipient of several discreet but interested looks. His flush deepened. He glared at Hope, laying the blame squarely at her feet.

She grinned heartlessly, amused to see her unflappable older brother blushing like a schoolboy caught in a misdemeanor.

''Before you were born, Bill MacDougal offered to trade me his brand-new bicycle for you, sight unseen. He thought having a baby sister would be fun. I should have traded you,'' he said regretfully.

''The bike would have worn out by now,'' Hope pointed out, unconcerned.

''Maybe. But it wouldn't have caused me near as much trouble before it did.''

''It wouldn't have been half as much fun. And don't think that all this talk of Billy McNugget and bicycles is going to distract me from the subject.''

''Billy MacDougal,'' he corrected. ''And I know you well enough to know that nothing short of a nuclear blast could distract you once you sink your teeth into something.''

''Thank you.'' Hope took this as a compliment, though his tone made it difficult to be sure he'd meant it as such. She bit into a snow pea and chewed thoughtfully.

''Are you and Tess going to get married again?''

''I don't know. I hope so but we haven't talked about it yet.''

''Do you love her, Nick?''

She'd asked him that question once before and he'd told her that he didn't know the answer. Deep in his heart, he'd known he was lying even then. This time, he felt no such uncertainty.

"Yes. I do."

"Does she love you?"

Trust Hope to ask a difficult question, Nick thought ruefully. "I think she does. I'm not sure she knows it yet."

"Have you told her how you feel?"

"I don't think she's ready to hear it right now. I think she's as worried as you are about moving too quickly."

Hope pushed away her uneaten salad and fixed him with a worried look. "You know I want nothing more than to see you happy, Nicky. If Tess can make you happy, then I'll welcome her back with open arms. But if she makes you miserable again, I'm going to scratch her eyes out."

"Thanks. It's nice to know there's someone available to defend my honor."

"Anytime, Nick."

Nick glanced at the ticket the waiter had left and put enough bills on the tray to cover meal and tip. Hope slid out of the booth as he stood up. Slipping her arm through his, she pressed her head against his shoulder.

"Good luck, Nick. One way or another, you know Sara and Annie and I will make the best aunts any kid ever had."

NICK THOUGHT ABOUT her good-luck wishes a few hours later as he parked his car in the lot behind Tess's shop. Good luck. Did he need it? Was it gross overconfidence that made him think that Tess loved him as much as he loved her?

He'd seen her every day for the past week. They'd gone Christmas shopping together, wrapped gifts, picked out a small tree for Nick's condo. He knew it wasn't his imagination that they'd been some of the best times the two of them had ever had together. They'd talked and laughed and drawn closer together. Several times, he'd looked at Tess and seen love in her eyes.

Or had he only seen a reflection of his feelings for her?

Damn. Why did life have to be so complex?

Well, he certainly wasn't going to simplify it by sitting in his car, staring at her shop. He turned up his coat collar and stepped out into the drizzling rain—as close as L.A. ever got to a white Christmas.

Though it was after normal closing hours, the back door was unlocked. Tess had told him the shop would be open late and she'd explained why. But that hadn't been enough to prepare Nick for the shock of walking into Needles & Pins at nine-thirty in the evening and finding it full of customers. All male.

A men-only shopping night was an idea Tess had gotten from listening to her customers' complaints about the gifts their husbands picked out for them. It wasn't simply that men were inconsiderate louts who thought buying their wives a new food processor was the ultimate in thoughtful gift giving, though there were women who considered that a strong possibility. But part of the problem was that many of the things they really wanted were the sort of things that most men felt incapable of picking out.

So Tess had come up with the idea of a gift registry. It worked on the same principle as a bridal registry. Weeks before Christmas, women selected the items they wanted and wrote them on file cards. Tess kept the cards in the shop and the week before Christmas, Needles & Pins stayed open late one night—only to men.

Nick lingered in the back of the store, taking stock of the clientele. What had seemed at first to be a veritable horde reduced itself to fewer than a dozen men. But in the shop's narrow confines, that was enough of a crowd. It seemed to be a mixed bag. Wing tips mingled with construction boots. Brooks Brothers brushed shoulders with Levi's.

As Nick watched, Tess appeared from behind a rack of crewel kits. She was holding a white file card and talking to a burly construction worker who hung on her every word.

Nick shifted position slightly so he could keep an eye on things without drawing attention to himself. He enjoyed watching Tess work. He couldn't hear her but that didn't lessen the pleasure of watching her and knowing she was his. More or less his, anyway.

From the number of purchases Josie was ringing up, it was a safe bet that Tess's men-only night was a successful, and profitable, idea. It was also a tiring one, he thought, as he watched yet another customer approach Tess for help. Nick had been standing here for twenty minutes and she hadn't paused once.

"Do you know anything about needlework?" The question came from Nick's left, forcing him to drag his attention from Tess and turn it toward the man who'd spoken.

"Not much," Nick admitted.

"I don't know anything about it." He was about five foot eight and something less than twenty-five years old. From the way his shoulders filled his purple sweatshirt, it was a safe bet he was a weight lifter. In fact, he looked like nothing so much as a refrigerator with a head.

"Didn't your wife write down what she wanted?" Nick asked, glancing at the card the man was clutching.

"My mother," the younger man corrected gloomily. "She wrote down half a dozen things. How'm I supposed to know which one she wants?"

"Well, I'd guess if she wrote down more than one thing, any one of them would do."

But Refrigerator was already shaking his head. "Not my mother. I know her. There's five things here that she hates and only one she really wants. And if I don't pick the right one, then I don't love her."

A deep tuck appeared in Nick's cheek as he tried to suppress a smile he was sure would be unappreciated.

"What kind of needlework does she do?" Maybe they could narrow it down to the right technique and go from there.

"I don't know. She does stuff with yarn." He moved to a rack and stared gloomily at an array of counted cross-stitch charts. "She's always got something she's making. I don't know what she does with all of it. I mean, how many pillows can one house hold?"

Nick couldn't answer the plaintive question so he settled for nodding in a way that he hoped would look sympathetic.

"You have a mother?" Refrigerator asked, deep in gloom.

"Yes. But she plays golf and gardens."

"Lucky for you. What about your wife? She do this needle stuff?"

"My wife owns this shop," Nick said, his tone full of pride.

"Yeah?" For a moment, the cloud seemed to lift as he glanced around at the brightly lit shop. "That's impressive."

"She's an impressive woman."

The momentary distraction faded and Refrigerator turned back to the crumpled card. "At least you don't have to worry about buying her any of this stuff." With a sigh, he moved off to continue a quest he'd already deemed hopeless.

While they'd talked, they'd moved closer to the front of the store, and when Nick turned, he found himself face-to-face with Tess, who'd been standing right behind him. There was something in her eyes, a kind of surprised pleasure he didn't understand. He started to question it but Josie called her name. Tess gave him a quick smile and turned to answer and the moment was gone. But the look lingered in his mind.

IT WAS ALMOST eleven o'clock before Tess could close the shop. She hadn't had even one minute all night to talk to Nick.

The evening's drizzle had turned to a downpour and Tess didn't argue when Nick said he'd drive her home. The next day was Sunday and the shop was closed, so she wouldn't need her car first thing in the morning. Nick could bring her back to get it sometime during the day.

They didn't talk much on the drive home. Nick accepted her invitation to come in and share a cup of hot cocoa.

"Not the most exciting nightcap," Tess commented as she poured steaming milk over the mixture of cocoa and sugar she'd already measured into the cups.

"I've never had a better offer."

"I doubt that." The smile Tess threw him was tired but happy. "I've got marshmallows or whipped cream. Choose your poison."

"I think I'll have mine straight up."

"A purist. I guess I'll do the same."

She led the way into the living room and sank onto the sofa

with a sigh. She took a sip from her cup. She'd always loved to drink cocoa around the holidays, regardless of the fact that the temperature rarely dipped below freezing. Tonight, though, it seemed the perfect drink to keep the chill and rain at bay.

Nick set his cup down on the coffee table and went to the Christmas tree. Reaching behind it, he plugged the lights in, bringing the tree to sparkling life.

"How about a fire?"

Tess hesitated only a moment, remembering what had happened the last time he'd built a fire. She nodded slowly. "That would be nice."

She watched as he crouched on the hearth and crumpled newspaper to use as a base for the kindling. He'd discarded his suit jacket and tie. His sleeves were rolled up to his elbows and his shirt was open at the throat. If she narrowed her eyes just a little, it wasn't hard to imagine that the cozy house was a log cabin they'd built themselves. The rain outside became a raging blizzard. They were snowbound till Christmas, isolated in the wilderness, with only themselves to depend on.

And she'd have felt every bit as safe and cared for under those circumstances as she did now, Tess thought. There was never a doubt about Nick's ability to cope under any and all conditions. He'd keep her dry and warm, and present her with a Christmas she'd never forget. Without being overbearing about it, Nick believed in protecting what was his. There was a part of her that was still uneasy in the face of his strength, but she was starting to believe that he could be strong without swallowing her up completely.

When the flames were licking up around the logs, Nick slid the screen into place and stood up, staring down into the fire for a moment before moving to join her on the sofa.

"Thanks for the help tonight," Tess said.

"Getting a box of bags out of the storeroom hardly constitutes a major contribution."

"Well, it was one thing Josie and I didn't have to do. Besides, I think just having you standing around looking calm helped some of the men. They tend to get nervous."

"It was easy for me to look calm. I didn't have to worry

about choosing the right gift. You'd think with the choice narrowed down for them, it would make it simpler.'' Nick grinned at the memory of mangled cards and otherwise-competent men looking completely helpless.

''I think it's sweet that they care enough to worry,'' Tess said.

''If they worried less and trusted their instincts more, they'd have a lot less trouble making decisions.''

Tess slanted him a sideways glance, acknowledging that it was probably difficult for him to understand that most people didn't trust their instincts the way he did. Nick believed in going with what his gut told him was right, whether it was buying a gift or marrying a woman he'd known for barely two months.

''That man you were talking to,'' she said slowly. ''The one who was trying to find something for his mother.''

''The one who looked like a refrigerator with a head?''

The description startled a smile out of Tess but it faded quickly.

''You told him that your wife owned the shop.''

''Should I have said *ex*-wife?'' he asked, turning to lay his arm along the back of the sofa, drawing his leg up on the cushion so that he faced her. ''I didn't see any point in getting into semantics.''

''It's not that.'' Tess waved one hand dismissively. ''You said I'd done a good job with the shop.''

''I said you were an impressive woman,'' Nick corrected her. Again, he saw that odd look of surprise come into her eyes.

''Do you really think that?'' she asked tentatively. ''You sounded almost...proud.''

Nick's brows came together. ''I *am* proud. You've done a hell of a job with that place. Most small businesses fail in the first year. You made it—and in spite of a soft economy. Of course I'm proud of you.''

Tess looked down but not before he'd caught the sheen of tears in her eyes. He reached out and set his hand under her chin, tilting her face back up to his.

"Would you rather I wasn't proud of you?" he asked, bewildered by her reaction.

"No. Of course not." She sniffed back the tears. "I guess I never expected to do something that you'd be proud of."

"I was always proud of you," Nick said, his voice deepening.

"For what? Baking a good apple pie and needlepointing a pretty pillow?" Her tone scoffed at the possibility that she'd done anything to be proud of.

"Among other things." Nick had the feeling there was something important going on here, that he was on the verge of finding some of the answers he'd wanted five years ago. "You didn't have to do anything specific for me to be proud of you, Tess. You just had to be you. Sweet and giving and strong."

"But I never *did* anything," she said, seeming to think that explained everything.

"You didn't have to do anything. I loved you."

"But you were always doing things." She stood up, too agitated to remain seated. Nick rose more slowly, watching as she moved to stand next to the glittering tree. "Your whole family did things."

"Like what?" Nick couldn't remember anybody in the family doing anything extraordinary five years ago.

"You all had careers. You were going places and doing things."

"Mom's never worked in her life."

"But she's on every charitable committee in the state."

"If you wanted to do volunteer work, I'm sure she would have been happy to put you to work."

"You don't understand." She twisted her hands together, frustrated by her inability to make him see what she meant.

Nick caught her hands in his, stilled their restless movements. "Then make me understand, Tess."

She looked up at him looming over her and felt a totally illogical anger that he couldn't understand what was so obvious to her.

"You're so damned big," she burst out finally.

Nick's brows shot up. "I'm what?"

"You're big. You loom over me," she said crossly.

"Is that why you divorced me? Because I was too big?"

"Don't be stupid," she snapped. "Of course that wasn't why."

Completely bewildered, Nick stared at her, afraid to even guess at what she meant.

Tess sighed and tightened her fingers around his. "Look." Nick obediently lowered his gaze to their linked hands. "Look at the way your hand swallows mine."

"There's not a whole lot I can do about my size, Tess." But he was starting to get a glimmer of an idea as to what she was getting at.

"All my life, I watched my mother disappear in my father's shadow. Everything in her life revolved around him and his career. She was a pretty, intelligent woman, and when I was little she wrote poetry. Then my father told her that it was a waste of time and suggested that, if she wanted to write, she should try to do something for the base newspaper. Nothing controversial or too exciting. Officers' wives weren't supposed to be exciting. She threw her poems away, Nick."

Tess was unaware of the tears that had slipped from the corners of her eyes and were tracing silvery paths down her cheeks.

"She threw them in the trash and started writing a little column on household tips for the base newspaper. I was ten. When I asked her why she didn't write poems just for herself, she said that my father was right and that she'd been wasting her time.

"But he wasn't right," she said fiercely. "She had a right to have something for herself, to be something besides just his wife. I watched her let go of every one of her dreams for him. And he neither knew nor cared. He just accepted it as the way things should be."

"And you thought that you might do the same thing?" Nick questioned slowly. "That you might give up your dreams for me?"

"I swore I wouldn't be like my mother. I promised myself I'd never live in someone else's shadow."

"Who asked you to?"

The question startled her. Looking up at him, she was surprised to see genuine anger etching his features.

"I've got news for you, Tess," he continued without giving her a chance to answer him. "There isn't room for anyone in my shadow but me."

"You don't understand—" she began but Nick cut her off.

"I understand just fine. You're the one who's a little slow-witted about this." His fingers tightened over hers, refusing to let her withdraw. "Five years ago, you asked me for a divorce and I gave it to you because I knew you were unhappy. You didn't give me a decent explanation and I spent a lot of time wondering what I'd done. Now, I find out it had nothing to do with us at all. You were just trying to protect yourself from something that couldn't possibly happen."

"You don't know that," she protested.

"I've told you before, Tess, I'm not your father. And you're not your mother." He paused to let that idea sink in. "You took something that happened between two completely different people and applied it to us, twisting our relationship in your mind to make it fit your fears."

"It wasn't like that," she cried, reeling from the impact of his words.

"It was exactly like that," he said, his voice gentling at the shocked look in her eyes. "Tess, what happened between your parents had nothing to do with us. You didn't have to go off and make a success of your shop just to prove something to me. I already believed in you. What did you think I'd do if you told me you wanted to start your own business?"

"I...don't know." She was shocked to realize that she'd never really thought about it.

"So you just decided it would be safer to ask for a divorce?"

"I was scared," she admitted.

"So you ran. And we lost five years together." There was

a wealth of sadness in his voice and Tess felt tears sting her eyes.

She stared at his shirtfront, trying to absorb the possibility that he was right, that her fears had cost them years of happiness and accomplished little else.

"I love you, Tess."

The quiet words brought her head up and her eyes met his in startled question. Nick released one of her hands, and his fingers brushed a soft tendril of dark hair back from her face.

"I loved you five years ago. I don't think I ever stopped loving you."

"Oh, Nick." The choked exclamation was all she could manage.

One small step brought her to him. His arms closed convulsively tight around her, drawing her closer still, holding her as if he'd never let her go.

"It's all right," he said. His lips brushed over her forehead. "We've got it straightened out now."

"Nick." Her hands clung to his shoulders as she tilted her head back. His mouth closed over hers, smothering anything else she might have said.

How was it possible that she'd lived so long without his touch? As his hand moved up and down the length of her spine, Tess thought vaguely that it was only in Nick's arms that she felt whole, only with his touch that she came alive.

Her mouth opened to him, her tongue coming up to twine with his. Her hands slid upward, her fingers delving into the thick gold hair at the back of his head as she rose on her toes, pressing herself to his broad frame.

She felt as if she needed to be so close that she was a part of him, so close that nothing and no one could ever pull them apart again. Tasting her hunger, Nick groaned low in his throat. One hand swept down her back, his fingers splaying over her firm derriere, crushing her to him.

Tess whimpered softly as she felt the hard ridge of him against her belly. Her head fell back, offering him free access to the slender length of her throat.

It was an invitation Nick didn't hesitate to take. His mouth slid downward, tracing the taut line of her throat with lips and tongue, sending shockwaves of pleasure throughout her body.

"Nick."

His name was a moan, a plea, an aching need.

He bent, one arm catching her behind the knees as he swept her off her feet and into his arms. Tess looped her arms around his neck, lowering her head to his shoulder as he carried her from the room.

He took the stairs as if her weight were nothing to him. Shouldering open the bedroom door, he carried her inside and stopped beside the bed before letting her slide slowly to her feet, the brush of her body on his a delicious torture.

Clothing whispered to the floor. Each touch, each caress was a promise for the future, a future they'd almost given up. Both felt conflicting urges—the need to rush to fulfillment contrasted with an equally strong need to savor every moment of this coming together.

Nick reached behind Tess and pulled down the covers before lifting her onto the bed. Light from the hallway splashed across the room, creating soft patterns of light and darkness.

Kneeling beside the bed, Nick set his hands on Tess's stomach, cradling the barely visible swell that marked where his child lay. His touch was tender, reverent, and Tess felt tears come to her eyes. How could she have thought to keep the knowledge of his child from him? How could she have failed to see how cruel it had been?

When he lifted his head to look at her, she raised her arms to him. He rose to lie beside her, keeping one hand on her stomach.

"God, Tess, I can't believe we're going to have a baby."

"I know. It seems like a miracle, doesn't it?"

"The miracle is having you back in my arms," he said, reaching up to brush her hair back from her forehead.

"It's being able to touch you like this again."

He bent to kiss her collarbone, stirring the fires to life.

"It's knowing you're mine."

Tess moaned as his palm closed over her breast.

"It's knowing you'll always be mine."

His mouth closed over hers, smothering anything she might have said. Tess's arms came up to circle his shoulders, her palms flattening on his back as he rose above her, his legs sliding between hers.

"I love you, Tess," Nick whispered against her throat. "I love you."

Tess caught her breath on a gasp of pleasure as he sank into her. She wanted to tell him she loved him, that she'd be his forever. But the words caught in her throat, drowned in a rising tide of pleasure.

But hadn't they always communicated best on this level? Maybe words weren't necessary, after all.

Chapter Twelve

"How about Ermingarde if it's a girl and Reginald if it's a boy?" Nick was leaning on the counter, watching Tess roll out pie crust for a mince pie.

"How about you don't try to publish a book of names for baby?"

"Okay, if you don't like Ermingarde and Reginald, what about Ophelia for a girl and Opie for a boy?"

"Opie? You want to name a child after Ron Howard?"

"No. I want to name a child Opie. I always liked that character. Little old ladies were always sneaking him ice-cream cones." Nick sounded wistful.

"Not Opie. And not Ophelia."

"Fine. Let's hear some of your brilliant ideas," he challenged.

Tess draped the crust over the rolling pin and carefully unrolled it over the filled pie pan. "How about Mickey for a boy and Minnie for a girl?"

"You laugh at my suggestions and then you want to name my son or daughter after a mouse?"

"Very successful mice." She slapped his hand as he tried to slip it under the crust to snatch some filling. "There's not going to be pie if you keep sneaking bites."

"But I love mince pie and nobody ever makes it except at Christmas. Besides," he said in a whiny tone, "I'm hungry."

Tess took one look at his fretful expression and burst out laughing. He looked so ridiculous wearing that petulant scowl.

"Laugh at me, will you?" Nick hooked his arm around her waist, swinging her off her feet and up against his chest. "You're a cruel, heartless wench."

"And you're too old to whine."

"Well, at least I don't have flour on my face."

"Where?" She wiped her hand over her face and saw Nick's eyes gleam with laughter as her flour-covered fingers spread a liberal dusting of white powder over her cheeks. Before he could duck, she wiped her hand over his chin, leaving a white trail.

"Brat."

"Fiend."

With each name they hurled at each other, they drew closer, until their mouths were only a breath apart. Once his lips touched hers, all game playing was abandoned. If Tess hadn't remembered the pie, Nick might have carried her upstairs immediately. He delayed only long enough for her to slide the pie into the oven.

The pie ended up with a charred crust. Nick could hardly complain since, as Tess pointed out primly, it was entirely his fault for distracting her.

"And," she said smugly, "you'll have to wait a whole year till next Christmas for me to make another one."

AFTER LUNCH THEY SLICED the pie and Nick consumed two large pieces, pronouncing it the best he'd ever eaten, char and all.

Outside, rain continued unabated. Inside, Nick had built a fire in the fireplace and they were settled in the living room with the glitter of the Christmas tree and the crackle of the fire holding the gloom at bay.

Nick was stretched out on the sofa, his head pillowed in Tess's lap. She stroked her fingers through his hair, watching the fire with dreamy eyes. It was hard to believe how everything had changed. Four months ago, she'd thought Nick was out of her life forever. Four months ago, the idea of having a baby had been a distant thing, postponed to the nebulous "someday."

"How did you feel when you found out you were pregnant?" Nick asked, seeming to read her mind.

"Happy. Scared. Confused."

"Happy?" He picked that emotion to question. "You were happy to be carrying my baby? Even then?"

"Yes."

The simple answer seemed enough to satisfy him. He turned his head so that his cheek rested against her stomach.

"Do you want a boy or a girl?"

"I don't care. As long as it's healthy."

"Me, too. Though I have to confess that a little girl who looked like her mother would be nice."

"No nicer than a little boy who looked like his father."

"Maybe we'll get one of each."

"Bite your tongue." She tugged a lock of golden hair. "One will do quite nicely, thank you."

Nick grinned but didn't bother to open his eyes.

Looking down at him, Tess was almost overwhelmed by a feeling of love. She couldn't imagine a more perfect moment than right now. Snuggled warmly in front of a fire with the man she loved next to her and his baby growing inside her. Tess knew nothing could ruin this moment.

"Mom's got a golfing buddy who's a justice of the peace," Nick said out of the blue. "I bet she could talk her into marrying us on Thursday."

Nothing could ruin this moment...except that.

Suddenly Tess felt her perfect moment shatter into a million pieces.

"What?" She struggled to keep her voice even.

"You know, she could pull a few strings for us by Thursday."

"Thursday?" The word stuck in her throat.

"Christmas Eve. Our old anniversary, remember?"

"I remember." She wasn't likely to forget her own wedding day. "Isn't that awfully soon?"

"It would be a rush," Nick said, mistaking her meaning.

He opened his eyes and frowned up at the ceiling. "There wouldn't be time for anything fancy, but we'd be spending Christmas together as husband and wife."

Tess felt as if a hand had been clamped around her throat, threatening to cut off her air. This was Sunday and Nick was talking about getting married on Thursday. Four days. It was too soon. She hadn't had time to think, time to absorb all the changes.

She said nothing but Nick must have sensed something. He looked at her, his eyes searching. She didn't know what he read there but it was enough to cause his jaw to tighten. He sat up and swung around to face her.

"What's wrong?"

"It's awfully sudden, isn't it?"

"There doesn't seem much reason to wait, does there? I love you. You love me. At least, I assume you love me?" He made it a question and Tess suddenly realized that she hadn't said the words. Not last night and not this morning.

"Of course I love you, Nick." She reached out and he caught her hand in his. "With all my heart."

"Then why wait?" he asked. "I want to go into the new year with you as my wife, Tess. I want—I *need* to know that we're solidly together. I thought you'd want the same thing."

"It's not that. It's just...so sudden." She looked away. "Couldn't we wait?"

"How long?" His voice sounded restrained.

"I don't know. A few months, maybe?" She slid a quick look at him, reading his rejection even before he said anything.

"Tess, the baby will be born in a few months. Call me old-fashioned and hopelessly outdated but I'd like to be married to my child's mother before he or she is born."

"A few weeks, then."

"Why wait?"

Why indeed? She stared at him, unable to come up with a single reason except the same old fears.

He must have read her answer in her eyes. His fingers tightened around hers for a moment and then released them.

"Please, Nick. Just give me a little more time."

"No." There was no give in him. "You either love me enough to trust me not to become like your father or you don't."

"I do love you!"

"But you don't trust me."

"It's not that."

"It's exactly that."

"I'm just not sure about getting married right away."

"When will you be sure?"

"I don't know," she cried, frustrated by her inability to explain the panic she felt.

Nick's jaw set to iron hardness. He stood up and peered down at her with eyes that were suddenly a bleak and wintry green.

"I'm not your father, Tess." Before she could utter the words on her tongue, he cut her off. "Maybe you should consider that it takes two people to make a marriage, good or bad. Your mother made her choices, too. Just like you have to make yours." He turned toward the door.

Tess jumped up. "Where are you going?"

"I'm going home. I can't force you to trust me, Tess. If you decide you can, let me know and we'll go from there."

He walked out before she could frame a single sentence. Tess sank back down onto the sofa, staring at the door through which he'd disappeared.

"What happened?" she whispered aloud.

But the only reply was the crackle of the fire and the soft hiss of the falling rain.

TESS SAT THERE without moving, trying to absorb the rapid change in her life. It didn't seem possible that Nick had gone, that he'd walked out.

It had all been a misunderstanding. She'd only asked him for some more time. He couldn't have understood or he wouldn't have gotten so upset. It wasn't a matter of trust. It wasn't. She just needed a little time to adjust to the changes, time to be sure she was making the right choice.

The movement was so subtle at first that she almost didn't

notice it, a tiny flutter, hardly stronger than the stroke of a butterfly's wing. It came again and she lifted her hand to her stomach, pressing her palm flat.

There it was again.

Her breath caught as she suddenly realized what was happening.

The baby was moving.

In the space of a breath, Tess's entire world shifted.

Her baby had just moved. The tiny life that was only just beginning to seem real had just made its presence known. There was a person inside her, a new life.

Tears burned her eyes but her mouth stretched in a foolish smile. She was having a baby. The statement was suddenly new and different. In a few months, there was going to be a new person in the world, someone completely different from either her or Nick.

Nick.

He should have been here. He should have been here to put his hand on her belly and feel this first tentative stirring.

The movement came again and Tess caught her breath on a half sob.

The realization struck her suddenly. What a fool she'd been. Nick had been right all along. It *had* been about trust, as much as it was about love.

She hadn't wanted to get married so soon because she hadn't really believed in him, hadn't really believed they could make it work. She had been trying to protect herself from being hurt by keeping a little distance between them.

She'd been looking to the past instead of to the future. But you couldn't feel the miracle of a new life stirring inside you without realizing that the future was all that really mattered.

And she'd just thrown it away.

SHE CALLED NICK'S apartment to tell him what a fool she'd been, but he didn't answer and she couldn't bring herself to leave a message on his answering machine. She kept calling until midnight but, if Nick was there, he wasn't picking up the phone.

By Monday morning, she'd convinced herself that he would never forgive her. He'd been hurt by her lack of trust and he'd never get past that. Oh, maybe he'd be civil enough. After all, there was still the baby to think about.

Unless he was so disgusted that he didn't want anything to do with her at all.

A healthy bout of tears accomplished nothing more than plugging up her nose and making her eyes water.

Reminding herself that she had a business to run, Tess mopped up the damage as best as she could and went in to open the shop, grateful that Josie wasn't coming in until after noon. By then, she'd have pulled herself together. She hoped.

It was just after eleven when the bell over the door rang, announcing the arrival of yet another customer. Tess looked up without much interest. The way she felt right now, she didn't particularly care whether she ever sold another skein of floss in her life. But she was interested in *this* customer.

Hope Masters.

Tess hadn't seen Nick's youngest sister in five years but there was no mistaking that tall, slim figure or that thick fall of pale gold hair.

"Hope. What a surprise." The banal greeting was all Tess could manage.

"You know, there was a time when I admired you, Tess," Hope began without preamble. "I thought Nick was lucky to have found you. And then you divorced him without a word of explanation to anybody and for a while, I actually hated you for hurting him."

She stopped and planted her hands, palms down, on the glass countertop. Everything about her stance was combative. Especially her eyes, dazzling with green fire.

"When Nicky told me he was seeing you again, I told him he was taking a big chance but I wished him luck. And when he told me about the baby and how he hoped to marry you again, I told him I'd welcome you back into the family, as long as you made him happy." Hope leaned over the counter, drawing her face just inches from Tess. "I also told him that, if you hurt him again, I would scratch your eyes out."

"Is that what you're planning on doing?" Tess asked, when Hope had to pause to draw breath. Tess held her ground, refusing to back away from the woman's hostile presence.

"I'd like to," Hope admitted bluntly. "But what I came here to do was to tell you that I think you're the blindest, stupidest woman on the face of the earth." She tapped a finger on the counter for emphasis. "Nick Masters is a terrific guy—and not just because he's my brother. Any woman can see what a great guy he is."

"I agree."

"Any woman would be lucky to have a man like Nick in love with her," Hope continued, oblivious of Tess's remark.

"I agree."

"Nick loves you and you used to love him."

"I still do."

"Nick—" Hope stopped mid-sentence and glared at her.

Tess's words had finally sunk in. Hope shook her head. "Then what the hell happened? How come Nick spent last night at my apartment, watching terrible old movies on cable and refusing to say anything except that I had a right to say that I'd told him so?"

"I'm the blindest, stupidest woman on earth," Tess said simply. "Just like you said."

Hope opened her mouth to argue, registered what Tess had said and closed it again. Her eyes reflected her confusion.

"You want to run that by me again?"

"I'm agreeing with you. I'm an idiot. Nick asked me to marry him again yesterday and I panicked for some stupid reason. He walked out before I realized how stupid I'd been. I called his apartment last night but I didn't get him. Now I know why."

"You admit you were wrong?" Hope asked, wanting everything clear.

"Absolutely. I love your brother more than anything on earth. I was going to go to his apartment tonight and see if he'd talk to me."

"You're too late," Hope said. "Nick left for San Francisco this morning to check on a project up there."

Tess felt tears sting her eyes. She'd been hoping—no, praying—that Nick could still pull those strings and arrange a Christmas Eve wedding.

"When will he be back?" she asked in a tiny voice.

"Christmas Eve."

Tess felt the words drive a knife through her heart. Christmas Eve—what would have been her second wedding day.

"I don't recall Nick mentioning anything about a San Francisco project." Tess was amazed she could even force words around the tightness that had formed in her throat.

Hope shook her head. "It's somebody else's design. Nick just wanted to get out. Said he needed a change of scenery."

Yes, Tess thought, *and I'm the scenery he wanted to change.*

"Look," Hope interrupted her thoughts. "You want to marry him, right?"

"More than anything." Tess forced a smile through the tears that now were spilling down her cheeks. "He wanted us to get married on Christmas Eve again. It seemed so quick." She shrugged. "Like I said, I panicked. I don't know if he'll be able to forgive me."

"Christmas Eve." Hope pinched her lower lip between thumb and forefinger, her eyes narrowed in thought. "It's just possible," she murmured.

"What is?"

"I've got to make some calls," Hope said abruptly, glancing at her watch. "Are you sure you love Nick?"

"Positive."

"And you'll do your best to make him happy?"

"Absolutely." Her sincerity must have been convincing because Hope suddenly smiled and it was like the sun breaking through storm clouds.

"Then I only have two things to say to you, Tess. One—you better dig out your wedding dress. And two—welcome back to the family."

And with that, Hope was gone in a swirl of poppy red slicker.

Tess had the feeling she'd been caught up in a tornado, spun around a few times and deposited in a foreign land.

She could only guess what Hope had in mind.

Whatever it was, she prayed it would be enough to convince Nick just how much she loved him.

NICK'S FLIGHT HAD BEEN delayed in San Francisco and he'd spent almost an hour sitting on the runway in an airplane packed full of people anxious to get home for the holiday. Ordinarily, he had as much Christmas spirit as the next man, but this year he could only wish the holidays over and done with. When some cheerful soul convinced the passengers that singing Christmas carols would help pass the time, Nick glowered out the window, feeling Scrooge-like and ill-tempered.

By the time his plane landed at LAX, he'd had all the good cheer and comradery he could stand. He wanted a stiff drink, a hot shower and a really terrifying horror novel, preferably one in which carolers were subjected to dreadful torments.

Hope had said she'd meet him and for once she was on time. Or maybe it was just that the flight had been late enough. Not even the sight of her smiling face did anything to lift his spirits.

"Merry Christmas Eve, Nicky." She threw her arms around him and gave him a hug. Nick returned the embrace but he couldn't manage much more than a grunt in response to the greeting.

"How was the trip?"

Discussion of the San Francisco job served to fill the time until they reached Hope's car. Nick was grateful for long-legged sisters who bought cars that didn't require a contortionist's skill to get into the seats. He slid onto the Cadillac's wide leather seat and dropped his head back with a sigh.

"Everyone's waiting for us," Hope said cheerfully.

Nick groaned. "Can't you just take me home and tell them my plane is missing somewhere over the Sierras?"

"Don't be a grouch, Nick. It's Christmas Eve."

As if he could forget, he thought, staring glumly out the window. He and Tess should have been getting married right about now.

"Thinking about Tess?" Hope asked, slanting him a sharp look.

"I shouldn't have rushed her," he said abruptly. "I should have given her the time she needed."

"Well, maybe you'll be able to straighten things out after the holidays," she said.

Nick threw her an annoyed look at her callous disregard for his feelings and then turned to look out the window. He subsided into brooding silence.

They didn't speak again until Hope pulled the car into the driveway of their parents' big home. Nick looked up at the sparkling Christmas lights and brightly lit windows and wondered how he could possibly get through the evening even pretending good cheer.

"Nick." Hope's tone was urgent and she caught his arm when he started to get out of the car. "You do love Tess, don't you?"

"For God's sake, Hope, leave it alone," he snapped.

"Do you love her?"

"Yes, dammit. Now I don't want to hear another word about her."

He stalked up to the front door, wondering what on earth was the matter with Hope. She wasn't usually so completely insensitive. When he pushed open the front door and stepped into the tiled entryway, the first thing that struck him was that the place was ablaze with lights. The second was that his entire family was gathered in the hallway, along with the minister from the church his parents attended and...Josie?

Nick felt his pulse start to beat a little faster. Behind him he heard Hope shut the door, then her soft murmur as she slipped past him to join the family. "Merry Christmas, Nicky."

He barely heard her. His eyes had been drawn upward. There was a woman descending the staircase. A woman wearing a tea-length ivory dress that he well remembered. She'd worn it seven years ago. He'd thought she looked like an angel then and the same thought occurred to him now.

"Tess."

As if walking in a dream, he moved toward her, meeting her at the foot of the stairs. She didn't descend the final step, so her eyes were level with his.

She swallowed, her eyes dark with uncertainty. "It's Christmas Eve."

"So it is."

"It's our anniversary."

"Yes."

She swallowed again. "I'm sorry for panicking."

"I'm sorry I was so pushy."

"Do you still want to marry me?"

"Only as much as I want to keep breathing."

He reached up, brushing his fingers through her hair, which she'd left down. "I love you, Tess."

"Oh, Nick. I love you, too. I felt the baby move and it made me realize what a fool I'd been."

"She moved?" His hand dropped to her stomach, pressing against the soft mound that held his child. In his eyes she could read his regret that he hadn't been there to share in the miracle. Tears stung her eyes and her smile shook around the edges.

"There'll be other times." She pressed her hand over his. "When I felt her move, it made me realize that I was looking only at the past when I should have been looking only at the future."

"Our future," he said.

"Our future. I trust you, Nick. I trust you with my heart. I trust you with our child. I trust you with my future."

"Without you, there is no future." He smiled slowly into her eyes and leaned forward, sealing their words with a kiss.

In a moment they'd exchange their vows and seal those with another kiss. But these were the first and most important promises they'd exchanged this night.

Tess put her arms around his neck, knowing she'd come home at last.

Families are *supposed* to be together.
Amy and Flash know that, even if their parents don't. So the kids take matters to a higher court—they write a letter to Santa!

DEAR SANTA

Margaret St. George

Chapter One

The frosty air turned Penny Martin's cheeks pink as she stood in the open door, holding a bowl of candy against her swollen waist, blinking incredulously at the man standing under the porch light.

She had to be hallucinating. It couldn't be him.

Some events were too shocking to immediately assimilate. Such as a letter from the IRS. Or missing a period. Or finding one's soon-to-be ex-husband standing on the front porch when he should be two thousand miles away.

"I thought you were a trick-or-treater," she whispered. The jolt of seeing him robbed her of her voice. Four of the six children who lived in the rural subdivision had been to her door. When she answered the bell, she had expected the last two. Instead, John Martin stood before her, staring at her with an expression as stunned as her own.

"Good God," he murmured, briefly closing his eyes.

Penny could guess what he was thinking as surely as if his thoughts were stamped on his forehead. Drawing a deep breath, she looked past him to the Porsche parked in the driveway under the yard light. A small U-Haul trailer was hitched to the back of the car, an incongruity that reminded her of one of those captions: What's wrong with this picture?

Giving him a moment to recover, feeling the intensity of his shocked stare, she raised her eyes to the cold dark sky. Because the mountain air was thinner and without competition from city lights, she could see the Milky Way carpeting the sky with glittering brilliance. Smoke curled from the chimneys of several houses in the valley and the pleasant smell of woodsmoke permeated the night air.

A puff of silvery vapor formed in front of John's lips as he swore softly. He collapsed against the doorjamb, then with obvious effort forced his eyes up from her waist. "Tell me you're wearing a Halloween costume, Penny. Tell me this is a joke."

"Amy and Flash told you, didn't they?" Irritation deepened the pink in her cheeks. She had spoken to Amy and Flash individually and together and made them promise on their scout's honor not to tell. Her irritation vanished as quickly as it had come, ending as a sigh. Some secrets were too big for eight- and six-year-olds to keep.

"You're pregnant!" He returned his stare to her middle with wide dazed eyes. "I thought Flash and Amy were joking, I didn't believe them. No, that's isn't true, I believed them, I just didn't..."

Deep inside she really hadn't believed the kids could keep the evidence of a new baby secret. But she had hoped they wouldn't blurt it out until she was ready to tell John herself.

"Penny...you...you are *pregnant*!"

"I know."

"I..." He rubbed a hand across his face. "How far along are you?"

"Beginning the eighth month." Immediately, she sensed his mind racing, thinking back to the previous March and what seemed in retrospect to be a foolish attempt at a reconciliation.

When he opened his eyes, he gave her a thin smile. "It seems we have a lot to talk about. Are you going to invite me inside? It's cold out here."

"Yes, of course." A blush of embarrassment tinted her cheeks. She wasn't thinking straight. "I'm sorry, come in."

When he stepped forward, close to her, the sudden moment of awkwardness caused Penny to frown and bite her lip. What was the etiquette in situations like this? Did they kiss as they would have less than a year ago? Did they politely embrace?

Shake hands? For a moment they looked at each other, then both turned aside abruptly and cleared their throats.

Stepping backward, Penny gestured to the pegs along the entry wall and watched John hang up his coat and driving cap. She couldn't believe he was really here, in Aspen Springs. Then she gave herself a small shake and waved the candy bowl toward the stairs leading up to the living room, kitchen and bedrooms. "The other set of stairs go down to the recreation room and the kid's rooms. Mom and I have the upstairs bedrooms. Amy and Flash wanted to be downstairs. They call it their apartment."

She was babbling, stalling while she wondered what on earth they would say to each other. They would discuss her pregnancy, of course. And John's work. The upcoming divorce. She flicked a glance at him from beneath her lashes. Of course. That was why he was here. Most likely he wanted to discuss the divorce settlement. Maybe he was regretting his generosity and wanted to renegotiate.

"Nice place," he murmured automatically at the top of the stairs, after a cursory glance toward the rock fireplace and floor-to-ceiling windows. Penny was aware he hadn't looked away from her stomach for more than two seconds.

"I forgot. You haven't been to Mother's house." She hadn't forgotten, but it was a sore subject. When they were living together, she had tried several times to persuade John to visit Colorado, but somehow it had never worked out. In the early years they hadn't had the money; later, they hadn't had the time. Instead, Penny's mother visited them in Los Angeles.

After putting the bowl on the counter and self-consciously brushing imaginary crumbs from her smock, Penny lifted a hand. "The view is spectacular. I don't know if you can tell in the darkness, but the house sits on the side of a hill overlooking the valley. We can see the Blue River, and there's a breathtaking view of the back range. A month ago, when the aspens turned color, it was absolutely—"

"Penny. You and I have to talk."

He spoke from directly behind her. When Penny realized

how close he was standing, she drew a sharp breath. For an instant she responded to his solid warmth, to the familiar lingering scent of his spicy after-shave. It would have been so easy simply to turn into John's arms and rest her head against the hollow of his shoulder, that special place she had once thought of as being fashioned just for her.

But she didn't, of course. A woman didn't cuddle up to a man she was divorcing. Instead, she stepped around the counter into the kitchen and managed to smile across the counter. "Coffee? It's a fresh pot."

"First the kids. I'd like to see them. Are they here?"

Penny looked at him for a long moment, thinking uncharitable thoughts. John had been very good about phoning Amy and Flash regularly, but he had not been good at actually seeing them. He had been too involved with work to take them for the summer, too busy to fly out for a weekend. If she had not taken the children to L.A. last March during spring break, he wouldn't have seen them then, either. Of course, if she hadn't taken the children to L.A. over spring break, she would not now be pregnant. Before she had realized a reconciliation was impossible things had gotten out of hand.

"Mom took the children to the Halloween carnival at school." Aside from a tremor in her fingers, the normalcy of the conversation amazed her. "They plan to do a little trick-or-treating in town afterward. I expect them home about nine o'clock."

It was seven now. They had two hours of privacy. A new thought occurred and she looked up at him. "John, did the kids know you were coming?"

"Not really. I told them I'd try to make it for Christmas. But..." He ran a hand through hair as ash blond as Amy's. "I'm sorry to keep staring, but...Penny, we're going to have a baby!"

"I've noticed." His expression was much as her own must have been the day Dr. Adler confirmed her condition. Now her smile was wry but genuine. "Believe me, a woman who is approaching her eighth month of pregnancy knows it."

"I expected this." His eyes dropped again to her rounded

smock. "But seeing you makes it very, very real. How can you be so calm about it?"

"I've had time to get used to the idea." As much as that was possible. Being pregnant at this particular point in her life was one of fate's little jokes. And not very humorous.

Since her stomach got in the way of getting close to the counter, Penny approached the coffeepot sideways and poured two cups. Responding to habit, she added sugar to John's cup, milk to hers, then pushed his cup across the counter.

"It's not French Roast, and not made from freshly ground beans," she murmured, then wondered why she was apologizing. She hadn't expected John; he hadn't been invited. Even if she had expected him, she probably wouldn't have found the time to buy French Roast coffee beans, his favorite.

Beginning the conversation by getting defensive about her brand of coffee did not strike her as a good sign. Determined to keep their discussion civil, she stepped past John and entered the living room, choosing the sofa, because it was the firmest place in the room. Her mother's chairs were deep and inviting, but at Penny's stage of pregnancy soft, upholstered furniture was a trap just waiting to snare her.

She sat on one end of the sofa and John sat on the other.

"Good coffee," he said politely, taking a sip, then looking toward the fire crackling in the fireplace.

His comment indicated he was as nervous as she was. John was particular about his coffee. According to her soon-to-be ex-husband, the absolutely right way to make coffee required grinding precisely measured beans seconds before brewing. In his opinion, this method assured the richest, most flavorful taste. Once upon a time, Penny had agreed.

Now she wasn't sure if she could tell the difference between coffee from a can and coffee from freshly ground beans. Suppressing a sigh, she admitted there were a lot of things she wasn't sure of anymore.

"I don't know where to start," John said after a moment, looking at the mound where her waist used to be.

Penny glanced at the clock over the television set. If he was here to renegotiate the divorce settlement, then they had a lot of ground to cover and not much time before her mother and the children returned.

"Did you receive the latest packet from my lawyer?" she asked, opening the conversation, struggling to keep her voice carefully polite and neutral.

Suddenly she felt as if she must be dreaming. This could not be real. She and John—her John—were sitting here discussing a divorce. It was crazy. Impossible. So far everything had been handled long-distance through the attorneys or the mail. Until now she had not been forced to directly face what was happening.

Blinking at the heat behind her eyes, Penny looked at him, sitting where she had imagined him a hundred times. Finally John was here, but it was too late. In ninety days she would walk into a courtroom and a few minutes later their marriage would be dissolved. How was that possible? she thought in bewilderment. How had they arrived at this point?

"I heard from your lawyer, and I want to talk about it, but first..." Placing his elbows on his knees, John leaned forward over his coffee mug, then turned his head to look at her. "Penny, for God's sake, why didn't you tell me you were pregnant?"

His dark eyes seemed darker in the firelight, his California tan more deeply golden. He was as handsome now as the day she had met him, maybe more so, Penny thought. Dressed in a cashmere sweater and wool slacks, the firelight glowing in his golden hair, he might have stepped from an ad depicting the smart set enjoying themselves before a cheery fire on a cold Colorado night. The realization made her feel very bulky and very unfashionable. The maternity smock and slacks she wore was a set she had purchased when she was carrying Flash. That was six years and a hundred washings ago. And the outfit hadn't been particularly fashionable even then.

It occurred to Penny that she had never seen a fashionable maternity outfit. There was no such breed. Granted, there were designers who tried, who gave it their best. But the result was always the same. You ended looking like a lump wearing fashionably padded shoulders. Or a lump sporting evening sequins.

Or a lump wearing beautiful material but with a peculiar hemline that hiked up in front and dipped in back. It was rather like putting a head and limbs on a basketball than draping it stylishly. It could not be done. No matter how well-intentioned, you ended as a lump wearing a tent.

And while the mother-to-be was getting lumpier by the minute, her husband remained slim and great looking. There was no justice.

"Penny?"

She pushed a hand through her hair. "Being pregnant doesn't change anything."

"The hell it doesn't." Anger darkened his eyes.

"Let me put it this way. It shouldn't change anything. At least not for you."

"I'll let that comment pass for the moment. I want to know why you didn't tell me you were pregnant. Asking the kids to do it seems small and irresponsible."

"I intended to tell you. And I asked the kids *not* to say anything." Crimson flamed on her cheeks. "But the right moment just didn't arrive." She met his eyes. "Plus, I thought you might be tempted to make some kind of heroic gesture if you knew. I thought you might decide to quit your job, and move here. You and I talked about moving to a small town with small-town values from the beginning of our marriage. But I wanted you to make the move for the right reasons. Because this was where you wanted to be. Not because you felt pressured, not because you felt you had to be here or that the decision was not your own."

"Did you—"

"Get pregnant on purpose? No. When I took the kids to L.A. during spring break, I had no idea you and I would get carried away." Crimson again flared on her cheeks. "If I had anticipated what would happen, I would have taken precautions."

"That isn't what I was going to ask." He was controlling the anger she identified in his steady gaze, but it was there. "Did you stop to think that I had a right to know? This is my baby, too. When were you planning to tell me? When the baby was a year old? Ten? Ready to start college?"

Suddenly Penny felt tired. Lately she had been trying to juggle too many balls at once, and the effort was beginning to show.

"The truth?" she asked, leaning back against the sofa cushions. "I don't know." Closing her eyes, she rested her coffee cup against her stomach, feeling the warmth through her smock. "When I first learned I was pregnant, I was stunned. I didn't want to accept it. Then I got depressed thinking how hard it was going to be: trying to make it as a divorced mother with three children, one of them an infant. I felt overwhelmed. I've been taking it one day at a time, not thinking too far into the future. I guess I would have told you about the baby after the divorce was final."

"That's big of you." When he realized what he had said, a humorless smile lifted his mouth. "But you know damned well you don't have to worry about making it on your own. If there's one thing that isn't a factor in this mess, it's money."

"Isn't it?" Penny asked quietly, then looked toward the steps as the doorbell rang. After a minute John offered to take the Halloween candy to the door, but Penny shook her head and struggled to rise from the sofa. "That will be the Galloway kids, and—"

"You want to see their costumes," John finished, his expression softening. "Remember the year before Amy was born? You and I dressed up like clowns and went trick-or-treating in our apartment building?"

"We put ice cubes in a couple of glasses and went trick-or-treating for booze."

"We were too poor to buy decent liquor, remember?"

"I remember we kept collecting people, and we were all getting giggly and having a great time. That was the night we met Betty and Fred. We ended up in their apartment with a collection of adult trick-or-treaters we'd picked up along the way."

They smiled at each other.

Then Penny cleared her throat as the doorbell rang again.

"Well. Excuse me a minute." After getting the candy bowl, she descended the short flight of stairs to the foyer, opened the door and exclaimed over the Galloway kids. "Oh dear, who could this be? A pirate and Darth Vader. Pretty scary."

Susan Galloway waited at the end of the porch. When she caught Penny's attention, she lifted her head from her coat collar and tilted a nod toward the Porsche gleaming under the yard light, then raised a questioning eyebrow. Penny shook her head, indicating they would talk about it later.

She remained in the frosty doorway, watching the Galloway kids run back to the car. Susan waved, then backed out of the driveway and onto the dirt road that looped through the subdivision. The word subdivision was a misnomer, more of an optimistic forecast than an actuality. So far there were only eight homes, and four of them belonged to summer or weekend people. On long nights when Penny couldn't sleep and had the lonely feeling that she was the only person in the world, it was good to look out the window toward the Galloways' yard light and know that other people were only half a mile away. It was a measure of how much she had changed that she could consider a half-mile distance as close.

But it was a nice change. She could no longer imagine living as she had before, in a condominium with people above and below her and on both sides, packed in like upscale ants living in a luxury anthill. The solitude and quiet of country living appealed to something basic. No matter how tired she was, no matter the turmoil of the day, she had only to gaze toward the snow-capped peaks to calm her thoughts.

When she returned to the living room, John had lit candles in the jack-o'-lanterns. They grinned at her now from the kitchen counter, the hearth, the top of the low bookcase that ran along the north wall. The pungent scent of heated smoke against damp pumpkin filled the room. It was a scent Penny liked, an autumn scent, a scent that conjured memories of her own childhood.

"So," she said a little too brightly, "tell me about you." After placing the candy bowl on the counter, she returned to the sofa, lowered herself carefully onto the cushion, then shifted to smile at John. "Are you on vacation? How long will you be staying? Do you have a telephone number where the kids can reach you?"

When she had reappeared at the top of the stairs, fresh shock filled his eyes at the sight of her.

"We haven't finished talking about the baby."

"If you don't mind, let's put that subject aside for a little while. We'll come back to it." They needed some time to adjust to the idea of being together again.

Although he obviously disagreed, John made an effort to do as she asked. "Okay. One thing at a time." Dropping back on the sofa, he turned to face her. She noticed he had refilled their coffee cups. "I've taken a leave of absence until the baby is born. I guess I'm on vacation."

"Now I'm staring," Penny said. "That doesn't sound like you. Are you sure Blackman Brothers can function without you?" Immediately, she regretted her sarcasm. She wanted to handle this encounter in a civilized manner. But old wounds lay close to the surface.

"Maybe I deserve that crack," John said quietly, "but is it so hard to believe that I want to share the holidays with the kids? Also, I was present at Amy's and Flash's birth, I'd like to be present for the birth of this one."

"Look, I'm sorry." She felt a flush of discomfort. "I'm just surprised that anything could drag you away from Blackman Brothers." And not sure how she felt about having him nearby until the baby was born. A silenced opened.

Leaning forward, he propped his elbows on his knees again and looked into the fire. "The timing is perfect, actually. I built up enough vacation days to cover four months away from the office at full pay." When she winced, he managed a smile. "I know you hate reminders that I rarely took vacations." Before she could comment, he turned his gaze back to the fire. "After you and the kids left, I promised myself I'd wrap up the Claxon Cat Food takeover, then resign and follow you."

"Oh, John. You've been promising you would resign after one deal or another since Amy was born."

He nodded, still without looking at her. "You probably

won't believe this, but I thought I'd go crazy after you left. I discovered I didn't just lose a wife, I lost my best friend." Now he looked at her, a glance and then away. "Anyway, to fill the time, to keep from thinking about you and the kids, I worked harder."

"I can see what's coming," Penny said with a sigh. "Working harder meant you were always in the middle of one deal or another."

"Right." He turned to look at her. "The problem is, I like what I do. At least most of the time. After all, investment banking has been pretty good to us, Penny. It's what allows us to support two households comfortably, drive new cars—"

"I think I've heard this song before," Penny commented. The bitterness had crept back. Biting her tongue, she dropped her head and moved her coffee cup in circles on top of her stomach.

She knew how addictive investment banking could be, how seductive. There was no high on earth as exhilarating as guessing right and winning. She would never forget the first time *she* had made a million dollars for a client.

From then on she had been as committed, as addicted, as John. She ate, drank, slept and breathed the market. Her conversations were liberally peppered with references to greenmail, mergers, buy-outs, hostile or friendly takeovers. Then she had gotten pregnant with Amy and her perspective had changed abruptly. A sense of balance had returned to her life. She had continued working part-time, but working was no longer the be-all and end-all.

"If only you could have agreed to three more years in L.A., investment banking would have made us wealthy."

"We're already wealthy."

"Have you forgotten the crash of October '87? No one is ever as secure as they think."

"I can't figure it out," Penny said, frowning. "You're a huge success in one of the highest-risk businesses in the world, but you won't take a risk in your personal life."

"By moving here? Come on, Penny. Where's the opportunity in Aspen Springs?"

The had been together less than an hour and already voices were rising and expressions tightening.

"Why on earth do you need opportunity? Why do you think you have to amass another million or so before you can risk making a move?" They were both getting angry. Penny felt the tension growing in her chest, could see it in John's expression.

"I simply can't grasp why you won't see the enormity of what you're asking." Leaning forward, he pushed a hand through his hair in a gesture of frustration. "You want me to abandon a successful career and all the perks that go with it, give up the security of an extremely lucrative profession, and spend the next forty years sitting on my thumbs going crazy with boredom!"

"I'm not as stupid as you make me sound!"

"Dammit, Penny, I've never said you were stupid. I said it's hard to understand why you can't see—"

"People do make changes, John. I have. I'm not sitting on my thumbs bored to death. Other people in this town have found something productive to do with themselves. The point is, the pace of life is slower and better! What I can't grasp is why you prefer an artificial high-octane life where people aren't judged by who they are inside, but by what they're wearing, eating, or driving and by the status of their job title or bank account!"

"That's how it is. Like it or not, Penny, the people who run this world don't live in small towns, no matter how terrific you think those small towns are. Taking risks has nothing to do with it. Lack of opportunity has to do with it. Living in a backwater has to do with it. Being out of the mainstream. Can't you understand that?"

"I understand this conversation is going nowhere," Penny said between her teeth.

"Look," he said after a minute. "I didn't mean for us to say hello then start fighting. I apologize for losing my temper." He gave her the smile that once had melted her toes. "Let's not push things. We'll have plenty of time to discuss all this."

"There's nothing to discuss, isn't that obvious?" She bit her lip and looked away from his determined smile. "You and I are never going to agree. You want the run-run-run excitement of a big city. I want a relaxed pace and the solid value system small towns are famed for."

Straightening against the sofa, he extended his arm along the back cushions and studied her with a curious expression. "Is that how it's working out? Is moving to Small Town, Colorado, everything you thought it would be?"

Penny didn't respond immediately, though the question was one she had pondered frequently.

"I'm not sure," she admitted finally. Then her chin lifted. "Mostly the answer is yes. But nothing is perfect. I didn't expect that. There are problems here, too."

"Such as?"

"I'm still looking for a slower pace to allow me to spend more time with Amy and Flash, more time to pursue all the things I put off during the busy years." The words emerged slowly. "Somehow it hasn't happened yet. I'm confident it will, but it just hasn't yet. But then I'm still getting established," she added. To her surprise, she sounded defensive. "Once I feel solid in my job, I'll—"

"Your job? You're working?"

She nodded. "I'm an assistant manager at Santa's Village."

Santa's Village was not Aspen Spring's primary attraction—that was skiing—but it ranked near the top. As the name suggested, Santa's Village was a park built around a Christmas theme. There were rides in the summer, sledding and ice-skating in the winter. A small theater ran holiday movies, a dozen gift shops featured toys and ornaments and Christmas-related gifts. There was a bi-weekly newspaper that printed the letters to Santa collected in the mailboxes located around the park, and Santa's workshop, and games galore. And Santa, of course, available all year around to hear the hundreds of daily requests.

John listened in silence to the description, studying her expression as she spoke.

"Penny, why are you working? Wasn't the whole point of

this move to escape the corporate grind? To spend more time with the kids? Am I sending too little money? Is that the problem?''

Fresh color rushed into her cheeks. ''You've been very generous. But I don't want to be one of those women who remains solely dependent on her ex-husband.'' She spread her hands. ''I need to feel I'm taking charge of my own life.'' When his expression stiffened and turned stormy, she added, ''this has nothing to do with you. I worked and carried my part during our marriage. I don't want to become dead weight now that we're divorced.''

''We aren't divorced yet.''

''I need to start rebuilding my life, John, and a job is part of that process.''

After a moment of uncomfortable silence, John leaned forward, staring at her intently. Before he spoke they both heard the front door bang open.

Alice Sage, Penny's mother, called from the entry in a cheery voice, ''Does the Porsche with the California plates mean we have company?'' The lack of surprise in her voice brought a frown of suspicion to Penny's brow. ''Wait a minute.'' Now Alice was calling to the kids. ''The surprise I mentioned will keep until you've hung up your coats.''

Penny turned angry blue eyes toward John. ''You arranged this visit with my mother!''

''I figured I'd have better luck with Alice.'' He grinned. ''You would have said no.'' When her glare deepened, he spread his hands. ''Will it make you feel better if I tell you I brought your dining room set in the U-Haul, and the boxes of stuff you'd left under the staircase?''

The kids reached the top of the stairs and stopped in their tracks, their mouths dropping, their eyes wide.

''Daddy!''

''It's Daddy!''

A miniature Rambo and a fairy princess flew across the living room and hurled themselves on John. His laughter was as eager and delighted as theirs as he swung Flash up on his shoulder, tucked Amy under one arm.

"Be careful with my crown, Daddy."

"We got lots of candy. Do you want to see?"

"I sure do. But first, let me say hello to Grandma."

After setting the children on their feet in a whirl of excitement, he hugged Alice and kissed her cheek. "You look wonderful." Then he lifted an eyebrow. "You didn't tell me how cold it is in Colorado."

"No comment," Alice said, smiling. "It's good to see you, John." Her cheeks were pink with cold, her blue eyes sparkled. Firelight glowed in her short white curls.

Penny scowled at her.

Mothers never stopped mothering. They always believed they knew what was best, no matter how old their children were, Penny thought. The recognition diminished her anger and wrested a sigh from her lips. Alice—she had always called her mother Alice—had joined in the secret of John's arrival because Alice hoped for a reconciliation. She had made her feelings known from the beginning. Alice encouraged Penny and the kids to remain with her and discouraged Penny from seeking a place of her own because, despite everything Penny said to the contrary, Alice insisted the separation was only temporary.

"Isn't this a nice surprise?" she said to Penny, her face bright and falsely innocent.

"It's certainly a surprise," Penny answered with a look that said, We'll discuss this later. Both she and her mother watched the kids spill their cache of candy over the kitchen counter for John's inspection.

Amy tossed a braid over her shoulder and turned pleading eyes toward Penny. "Can we eat some now, Mom? Please, please?"

"Right before bedtime? I don't know…" Penny said, teasing, knowing she would relent.

"Please, Mom?" Flash's sticky mouth and cheeks indicated he had already enjoyed a liberal sampling of the night's plunder.

"Please, Mom?" John said, smiling at her. "Halloween only comes once a year…"

"All right," Penny decided, ignoring him. "Choose three things. Then it's time for your baths and bed."

They protested.

"Can we have five pieces?"

"Can we stay up late? We want to talk to Daddy."

"Four pieces," Alice said, leaning over the kitchen counter to *ooh* and *ah* over the collected goodies.

Penny decided it was time to take charge. Pushing against the sofa cushions, she heaved herself up and moved to the counter. "Three," she said firmly, frowning at Alice. She didn't remember her mother being this indulgent when she was six or eight.

"Do I have to have a bath?" Flash asked, looking up at her with John's mischievous dark eyes. His reddish gold hair resisted taming by the Rambolike bandanna twisted over his forehead and tied in back. An unconscious smile curved Penny's lips. She didn't recall that Rambo had freckles. Or the mustache Flash had insisted she draw with her eyebrow pencil. And she suspected it would have diminished some of Rambo's macho appeal to have chocolate laced around his mouth and chin.

"Yes, you have to have a bath."

Amy grabbed her hand. "But we can stay up late, can't we, Mommy?" She gave her father a radiant smile. "Daddy's here!"

"You can see Daddy tomorrow. Maybe he'll pick you up from school..." She glanced at John for confirmation and addressed her next question to him. "Where are you staying?"

Amy looked astonished. "He's staying with us. Aren't you, Daddy?"

"Of course he is," Alice said quickly, stepping into the sudden silence.

"Mother!"

"Let's see. I'll put you in my room unless you and Penny..." She examined Penny's thunderous expression, then smiled and shrugged. "I guess not. So, you take my room, John, and I'll sleep in Amy's room."

"This is crazy," Penny protested hotly. She was being railroaded. "It's bad enough we've taken over your house and your hospitality without us putting you out of your bedroom. I won't hear of it. John? Say something."

The something she wanted him to say was that he would find a hotel room.

"Penny's right, Alice." He dropped an arm around Alice's shoulders and gave her a hug. "Thanks, but I wouldn't feel right taking your room. How about I sleep with Gordon?"

They all looked at him.

"Gordon?" Amy asked, puzzled.

"He means me," Flash said proudly. It was only in the past two months, since beginning first grade, that he had learned Gordon was his real name. After two days of agonizing indecision, he had decided to stay with Flash. Flash sounded cooler than Gordon.

"Why don't you sleep with Mommy, like always?" Amy asked. She and Flash gazed at them, bewildered by the conversation.

John flicked a look at Penny from the side of his eyes, hesitating, waiting to hear her response. Penny didn't look at him or at her mother.

"Now, Amy, you and Flash remember what we discussed. Mommy and Daddy don't live together anymore." It was more painful to say it in front of John that it had been when she'd first told the children. She drew a deep breath and made herself smile. "People who aren't married don't sleep together." Not quite true, but suitable for the discussion of the moment. Alice cleared her throat, lifted an eyebrow, but said nothing.

"But Daddy's here now," Amy insisted. "That means you're married again, doesn't it?"

Her children's hopeful expressions tugged Penny's heart and she glanced away.

Finally John spoke. "Are you trying to get rid of me? Kick me upstairs to Mommy's room?" He grinned at them. "I want to see this apartment of yours."

The excitement of having him to themselves displaced Amy's and Flash's concern about the sleeping arrangements.

"You could stay in my room," Amy suggested, pulling on his hand. Immediately Flash protested and an argument erupted.

"Flash's room it is," Penny said, ending the bickering. Flash beamed; Amy's small face puckered with disappointment.

"Okay, kids. Off we go. Bath time," Alice said, herding them toward the stairs. "I'm sure Mommy and Daddy have some things to talk about." Ignoring the flood of protests, she followed them downstairs. "You'll have plenty of time to talk to Daddy. He'll be along in a few minutes."

When they had gone, John leaned on the kitchen counter and asked softly, "Angry?"

"Angry and feeling steamrolled," Penny said, her expression grim. Plus bewildered and confused. And suddenly very tired. "I can see you're right. We need to talk further." But this wasn't the moment. The kids were waiting for him, and she felt exhausted, assaulted by too many conflicting emotions. "What are you doing?" she asked after a minute, watching him spill Flash's and Amy's trick-or-treat sacks onto the counter.

"Checking the candy."

Carefully he set aside the apples and oranges, and all pieces of candy that weren't store wrapped.

Penny's eyebrow lifted, then she touched his wrist as he prepared to sweep the isolated pieces into the waste can he'd removed from under Alice's sink. "That isn't necessary."

Her comment surprised him. "Better safe than sorry. There's no way to know what might have been done to this fruit and candy. Last Halloween the papers were filled with stories about crazies putting razor blades in apples or poisoning soft candy, or injecting it with drugs."

She stared. "John, for heaven's sake. This is Aspen Springs. The people who gave the kids treats are people Alice has known all her life. People I grew up with. They aren't monsters."

"Come on, Penny. It's a nasty world out there. You can't trust anyone." He swept the candy and fruit into the trash.

Silently Penny watched him replace the waste can then push the remaining candy back into the kids' trick-or-treat bags.

"What happened to us?" she asked softly, genuinely bewildered. "We didn't used to think the world was a nasty place. Or look at life with a cynical eye. Or believe we couldn't trust anyone." The use of *we* was an effort to be polite. She didn't feel those things. To her the world was a nice place and she couldn't imagine living without trust.

"We grew up," John said, as if that explained everything. As if the world and the people in it had always been threatening and unpleasant, but they had been too young and too naive to notice.

"I don't believe that," Penny said, shaking her head.

But there was a time when she had started to. That was when she had understood she couldn't wait any longer for John to resign; when she had to leave the big city and return to her roots and a positive value system. They had always planned to leave Los Angeles when they began a family. They had promised they would raise their children in a small town, if not Aspen Springs then another much like it. It had been important to them both to raise their children in a place where people weren't afraid to walk alone or in a strange neighborhood. Where people knew their neighbors and knew they could rely on them in an emergency. Where a man's handshake was as good as a contract.

"Small towns can't be that different," John said.

"So you've said." Every time she pointed out that the children were growing and they were still in Los Angeles. "But you're wrong, John. It is different here." She met his eyes, saw he didn't believe her.

"Not different. Just smaller and slower."

Before they resumed an argument they had already had a hundred times before, she smoothed her hands over her stomach and managed a thin smile. "I'm very tired, and the shock of finding you on the doorstep... If you'll excuse me, I think I'll have a bath and turn in early."

Another awkward moment opened between them. Their eyes met and held, then Penny cleared her throat self-consciously. "When you see Alice, would you tell her I'd like a word with her?"

"Good night," he said quietly. "Penny, I—"

Before he could say more, she lifted a hand. "Good night, John." Turning, she fled toward the staircase.

Chapter Two

John stood at the kitchen counter watching Penny walk toward the stairs leading to the upstairs bedrooms. Her beauty took his breath away. As she had with Amy and Flash, she carried her pregnancy with quiet pride and a stately dignity, which she probably didn't recognize. For reasons he had never comprehended, Penny believed she was bulky and clumsy when she was pregnant. She was not.

Her skin glowed with radiant health. The golden hair, tied back in a ribbon, was rich and shining with warm red highlights. The serenity he associated with her earlier pregnancies was missing from her expression, but he attributed that to the shock of his unexpected arrival. With very little effort, he could imagine her naked. Her breasts would be full and firm, the faint bluish veins visible through her translucent skin. Her stomach would be taut and rounded and lovely, though she had never believed him when he told her so.

He unwraped a piece of taffy and put the candy in his mouth, shifting his gaze to one of the grinning jack-o'-lanterns. The thing he most regretted was that the impending divorce was largely his fault. Penny had been more patient than he'd had any right to expect. She had waited eight years for him to honor the promise they had given to each other on their wedding night.

For a time their life together had worked out as planned. During the early years they had both worked for Blackman

Brothers. They had joked about seeing each other on the run, about sleeping together but not really living together. The situation had been tolerable, because they were building toward a future in which there would be a lifetime of evenings and weekends together.

But he'd kept delaying the move to Small Town, America. Finding reasons to do it later. Amy was born, then Flash, and then John had been offered a partnership in the firm, which prompted the most serious argument of their marriage. Penny realized if he accepted the partnership, they would never leave Los Angeles. He had accused her of being unsupportive, of resenting his success. She had accused him of letting his ambition obscure his values. They had argued into the night, then she had accused him of breaking his promise. He'd had no answer for that one. The truth was he thrived on life in Los Angeles. He liked the big city, liked his job, their friends, all of it. The idea of moving no longer had appeal. He wasn't really sure it ever had.

Three months later Penny and the kids were gone.

Tilting his head, he listened to Amy and Flash laughing and shouting downstairs as they put on their pajamas, listened to the sound of Penny's bath running. God, he had missed these homey noises. Nothing was more silent than a bachelor apartment.

Standing in front of the fire, he inhaled the pleasant pungent smoke of the candles burning inside the jack-o'-lanterns, anticipated the good soapy scent of his children fresh from their baths. The faint sweet smell of Ivory and flannel pajamas and damp curls. The minty scent of toothpaste hiding candy breath. He smiled.

From where he stood, he could see into the kitchen, could see the refrigerator door plastered with crayoned portraits of witches and goblins. One of Flash's battered sneakers peeked from beneath the sofa. Amy had left her crown and wand on one of the stools beneath the counter. A stack of schoolbooks sat on top of the bookcase. These were the sights and scents of family and home. His chest constricted with the familiar pain of missing them.

During the drive to Colorado he had decided to test Penny's decision not to return to Los Angeles. He needed his family; he wanted them back. Learning about the new baby increased his determination. He didn't want his children growing up without him, didn't want to watch them mature in yearly increments.

Alice's smile appeared at the top of the stairs. "Two wild Indians are waiting for you," she announced, nodding toward the basement. "I made up the bunk bed in Flash's room. If you need extra blankets, you'll find some on the shelf in the closet."

"Bunk bed?" He groaned and rolled his eyes. "What have I let myself in for?"

"It gets worse," Alice said, returning his grin. "You get the top one." John lifted his hands in mock despair. "Young Rambo longs to sleep on top, but he's afraid of falling out."

"So am I." As he headed toward the steps, he stopped and pressed Alice's arm. "Thank's for having me, Alice. I appreciate all you've done and everything you're doing."

She kissed his cheek. "I've loved having everyone here—it hasn't been any trouble. I hope you and Penny get things worked out."

The water was shut off upstairs and he looked toward the upper staircase, and the silence that followed. It felt strange and wrong to be going downstairs when Penny was upstairs. "Well," he said, turning to the steps leading to the basement. "I'm off to the North Pole."

"The North Pole?"

"About as far away from anything soft and warm that a man can get."

Alice laughed and waved good-night. A few minutes later she rapped on Penny's bathroom door, then poked her head inside. "May I come in? John said you wanted to talk to me."

Penny sat in a tub full of bubbles, her hands laced together over her stomach. She stared straight ahead at the steamy tiles.

"Playing innocent, Alice, isn't going to work." She bit her lip. "I've been sitting here trying to think what to say to you."

"I brought a peace offering." Alice set a glass of white

wine on the side of the tub, then sat on the lid of the commode and sipped from a glass of her own. "An amusing little wine," she said, parodying Penny's Los Angeles friends. Usually Penny laughed. Tonight she didn't.

"How could you?" After hesitating, Penny tasted the wine then raised blue eyes dark with anger. "How could you conspire against your own daughter? You should have told me he was coming!"

"I thought about it," Alice agreed, nodding. She looked at herself in the mirror on the other side of the tub, pushed at her tousled white curls. "But I figured you would object."

"Thanks for the wine—it's just what I needed. And damned right I would have objected."

"Now Penelope, you can't have it both ways. You can't castigate John for being too busy to see the kids, then refuse him when he misses them so much he drives twelve hundred miles to be with them."

"Of course you're right." Penny glared at her wineglass, then a huge intake of breath lifted her stomach above the bubbles. "Do you think that's what his sudden appearance means?" she asked softly. "He's missing Amy and Flash?" She didn't ask the obvious question—if John had mentioned anything about missing her.

"What did he tell you?"

"I didn't ask. What did he tell *you*? When the two of you were hatching this plot?"

Alice peered more closely at the mirror. "The steam in here is wrecking my hair." Standing, she finished her wine, then made a show of glancing at her watch. She covered an exaggerated yawn. "Do you want me to get you anything before I turn in?"

"You're avoiding an answer."

"Right." Alice laughed and patted Penny's head. "I admit I like to meddle, but only to a point. I've done my part. The rest is up to you and John."

Lifting her chin from the moat of bubbles between her throat and her stomach, Penny studied her mother. Alice Sage was a youthful fifty-six. Regular exercise kept her figure slim and attractive, and the wrinkles deepening around her mouth and eyes reflected a sunny nature and decades of smiles and easy laughter. The fashionable slacks and angora sweater subtly stated Alice's pride in her contemporary outlook. No old-fashioned attitudes for her.

"Mom...I heard it again last night."

"Uh-oh," Alice said at the door. "When you call me Mom, something serious is coming."

"Did you hear anything?"

"Hear what?"

"A car in the driveway. About two o'clock."

"Good heavens." Alice blinked. "What are you doing awake at two in the morning?"

"I woke up worrying whether I'd ordered enough star ornaments for the Holly Shop." Penny shifted in the tub. "I could swear I heard tires on the gravel. Then a scratching noise against the side of the house." She frowned. "I looked outside, but it was too dark to see anything. No moon, and there were heavy clouds."

"With any luck we'll get some snow. Jim Anderson said they'll start making snow in the ski areas if we don't get a base started by next week."

Penny raised her hands. "Alice, we are talking about people driving up to the house in the middle of the night!"

"I wouldn't worry about it, honey. You know how sound travels in the country, especially at night. I heard that Mort Cantrell is working the night shift at the Henderson Mine. Maybe you heard Mort come home. Sometimes when conditions are just right, you can hear Mort and Mildred waxing their skis." She smiled.

"You're probably right," Penny said reluctantly, as she always did when they had this conversation, then added as she always did, "But it sounds like a car in *our* driveway. And I swear something is bumping against the outside wall."

"There's a trellis on that side of the house. Maybe the wind is bumping it against the siding."

"I can't believe you haven't heard anything. This has been happening off and on since I arrived."

"Well, you know me. Out like a light the minute my head touches the pillow. Speaking of which..."

After Alice left, Penny continued to think about the odd sounds because she didn't want to think about John. The first time she had awakened to the sound of a car in the driveway—about a week after she and the kids arrived—it had frightened her badly. She was certain something sinister was afoot. But following the equally peculiar bumping noise on the side of the house, silence had returned and nothing further had happened. That had been the pattern since. Every few days she awoke to the sound of a car in the driveway, a bumping, then silence.

She supposed Alice was right. What she was hearing was Mort Cantrell coming home from work. The sounds no longer frightened her—this was Aspen Springs, after all—but they continued to puzzle her.

Putting the small mystery out of her mind, she opened the drain, then heaved her swollen body up and out, noting the task was becoming more difficult with each passing day. After toweling and patting herself with baby powder because she liked the scent of it, Penny dropped a singularly shapeless flannel nightgown over her head. For a moment she stared at her reflection in the mirror against the back wall of the tub.

"We call this creation Lump in Flannel," she murmured, striking a pose. "Note the gathered yoke, ladies and gentlemen, the very gathered yoke. Once baby has arrived, an enterprising mother can dismantle this creation and use the flannel to make pajamas for all the children of India, with enough material left over to upholster New York City."

Then her thoughts changed abruptly. John was downstairs with the children. A few feet away. Never before had they been in the same house and slept apart. It didn't feel right.

Don't think about it, she told herself.

It was hard not to. And it was a hell of a thing to encounter one's almost ex-husband looking the way she did. Squinting her eyes, she studied herself in the mirror and tried to remember what she had looked like when she had a waist. Pressing her hands to the approximate site, she caught the billowing yards of flannel and tamed them against her sides. Squinting until her image was a blur, she tried to see the barest suggestion of a waist. There was none. Her waist and hips had vanished.

Was John thinking about her? Or was he reading Amy and Flash a bedtime story?

Don't think about it. Keep the hurt at arm's length.

Since her body was hopeless, she turned her attention to her face, leaning close to the mirror over the sink and studying her skin with an unforgiving eye.

But there was nothing to forgive. Pregnancy did great things for her skin and breasts. Seen in the warm light from the heat lamp overhead, her skin looked creamy and flawless, still dewy from her bath.

As for her breasts... One of the really great things about pregnancy was what it did to one's breasts. Normally she was small-breasted with a small-breasted woman's secret envy of full-figured women. All through high school and college she had yearned to look down and see a crease. She had longed to walk into a lingerie department and nonchalantly say, "I'll take the D cup, please."

Now, for a brief time, she had been granted a lifelong wish and wore an adult size C cup, but no one could tell because her stomach had expanded to size Z. Her figure was lost in a slope that began beneath her throat and ended near her thighs. Right now she didn't want to even think about her thighs.

Switching off the bathroom light, she turned into her room, the one she had as a child, and climbed into bed. After Penny finished college and married John, Alice had converted Penny's room into a guestroom. The canopied four-poster had been moved to the basement and a queen-sized bed had appeared in its place.

Penny touched the empty pillow beside her. And thought of John downstairs. She closed her eyes. John had always liked her small breasts. It had taken him three years to convince her that he was telling the truth. If he was. Hollywood and Hugh Hefner had cast permanent doubt on the issue.

She thought about the U-Haul parked behind the Porsche

and what a pain it must have been to pull a trailer twelve hundred miles. When she first saw it, her heart had jumped. She had thought perhaps he was moving to Aspen Springs. Maybe with the idea of a reconciliation.

Anger and hurt constricted her chest. When *she* wanted to attempt a reconciliation, John hadn't budged an inch. If anything, he had become more entrenched, more insistent that he was being a realist and she was just kidding herself that they could build a life in a small town and find something they couldn't find in Los Angeles.

It infuriated her that he believed he was being realistic and she was not. Anyone could see how phony and superficial their life in California had been. Except John.

If he had the faintest hope that she would return there, he could forget it. She knew who the realist in the Martin family was. Enough of a realist to know a reconciliation was out of the question.

But it hurt. It hurt so much. Penny turned her face into the pillow and pressed the cool material against the tears standing in her eyes.

BECAUSE HIS INNER CLOCK was still ticking on Los Angeles time, John rose an hour earlier than anyone else. After making coffee—out of a can—he sat at the kitchen table, which was placed before floor-to-ceiling windows that extended into the living room. Entranced by the view, he watched a rising sun drape the snow-capped peaks in shades of pink and gold.

He had awakened filled with a familiar cramping anxiety, forgetting for a moment where he was and that he didn't have to rush to the office. When he remembered, he studied the narrow configuration of the bunk bed and smiled, listening to his son roll over below him. Then he thought about the rush-hour traffic he wouldn't have to fight today, about the shrill phones he wouldn't have to answer, about the lonely sterile condo he wouldn't be going home to. All this sounded unpleasant, and much of it was, but there was also the exhilaration of the city, the steel mountains to climb.

The hectic pace Penny objected to suited him well. Rush

hour didn't annoy him; he'd had some of his best ideas while stalled in traffic. Ringing phones meant something was happening. Others could claim the rush and bustle of big cities created an artificial excitement, but to him the excitement was genuine.

Penny couldn't accept that he honestly valued their life in the city. To her, their entire problem centered on his ambition. Yes, he was ambitious, but he didn't see it as a crippling fault. Lacking ambition, man would still be living in caves eating dinosaur burgers.

Now, sipping his morning coffee and watching the sunlight on the mountains, listening as the house began to stir, his thoughts shot toward Blackman Brothers. Already he missed work, wondered what was happening to his accounts. It frustrated him to read yesterday's quotes in the morning paper instead of being on top of things as they occurred.

He was on vacation, he reminded himself, hoping to resolve his personal life. But he decided to phone the office later, just to keep in touch. For the moment, it surprised him to realize that looking at the mountains relaxed him. As he generally equated relaxing with slothfulness, the realization brought him immediately to his feet.

Because he knew how frantic mornings with the kids could be, he explored the kitchen, deciding to make himself useful. The pans he found were home size, not restaurant size as he preferred, but serviceable. The stove was the right height for most women, a bit awkward for a man. Penny had always laughed when he insisted their dream house would have his and her stoves and restaurant-size utensils. He wondered if she still had the file of dream-house clippings and drawings they had started to collect shortly after they were married.

Whistling, he heated a skillet, cut a chunk of country butter into it, and started bacon in another skillet while he waited for the butter to melt. Enjoying himself, he stirred up a batch of hotcakes, pouring juice for the kids, placed a bowl of eggs on the stove top ready to go the minute someone appeared.

"Good grief!" Alice exclaimed, following the scent of coffee and bacon into the kitchen.

"Scrambled or sunny-side up?"

"Plus hotcakes? You have enough food to feed the whole county." Smiling, she poured a cup of coffee. "Over easy. And thanks. This is a treat."

"You look wonderful." Alice wore a green wool skirt, a Paisley blouse and fashionable knee-high boots.

"I volunteer at the library three days a week. Keeps me busy and I get first shot at the new books. Do you need any help?"

"Nope. Everything's done."

Amy and Flash ran up the stairs and slid into their chairs. They watched their father moving about the kitchen with the kind of astonishment they might feel if they had just discovered he could step off the balcony and fly.

"I didn't know you could cook," Amy said. Her blue eyes widened as if she wasn't certain this new side of Daddy was a good thing.

"A lot of men are terrific cooks," John said, smiling. "I'm one of them."

"I want Fruit Loops," Flash announced.

"Tough," Alice told him with a grin. "Today you get eggs and/or hotcakes. Your daddy has gone to a lot of trouble to make you a great breakfast, and you are going to eat it, mister."

Flash pulled up on his knees and leaned on the back of the chair so he could watch John cooking his egg. "Grandma likes to sound mean, Daddy," he explained. "But she isn't. She just likes to sound that way."

Alice rolled her eyes. "Listen, Rambo. I'm plenty mean and don't you forget it." Both the children giggled.

"Look, Mommy," Amy shouted when Penny appeared in the kitchen. "Daddy can cook!"

"You're still pregnant," John said, staring. "I thought maybe I'd dreamed it."

Penny smiled and accepted a cup of coffee with a nod of thanks. "As a matter of fact, your daddy is a better cook than I am. His degree is in Hotel and Restaurant Management, even though he decided to be a broker instead." She gave John a quizzical look. "Now that I think of it, this is a surprise. I don't recall that you've done any cooking in years, have you?"

"I thought you did deals, Daddy."

"I do deals when I'm not on vacation." Draping a kitchen towel over his arm like a waiter, he inclined his head to Penny in a half bow. "What would the very pregnant *madame* like for breakfast? Eggs and hotcakes? One or the other?"

"Just coffee and vitamin pills." She glanced at her watch, resisting his charm. "I'm running late. Alice, can you drop the kids at school? They're going to miss the bus."

"No problem."

John frowned. "You should eat some breakfast." He cast a pointed glance at the soft gray plaid stretching over her swollen stomach. The blue stripe matched her eyes. She was every man's private vision of a mother-to-be. Radiant, healthy, fragile and lovely. Looking at her, he experienced a caveman urge to protect her.

"Eating for two is an old wives' tale. Eating right is better. Where on earth did I leave my car keys?"

Flash spilled his milk, which dripped on Amy's slacks and raised a howl of blame and protest. Alice shouted, while John dived for a roll of paper towels.

"Eating right is coffee and vitamins?" he called over his shoulder as he mopped the table, Amy's slacks, Flash's jeans.

Grinning, Penny watched the scene, overcoming an impulse to jump in and take charge. "You can't guess how many times I have imagined you coping with the morning madness." In the frenzy of mopping up and jumping out of the way, someone knocked over Amy's milk. Penny's grin widened as John tore off more paper towels and tried to catch the stream of milk flowing toward the table edge and the floor. Naturally he would fail. The first law of physics stated that milk could run faster than parents.

"Gotta go," she said, grabbing the kids long enough to plant a kiss on top of their heads. "Don't forget your homework." She wiggled her fingers at John, still grinning. Milk was streaming off the table edge, dripping onto the floor.

"Penny, wait. Will you have lunch with me?" John asked.

"I have a pretty crowded schedule," she said, hesitating. The commotion over the spilled milk magically quieted.

"We need to talk," John said.

Three heads nodded. One white, two small and gold.

"Can't argue with that," she said lightly, feeling outnumbered. Clearly she was the victim of a conspiracy. "How about twelve noon at Santa's Village? I'll meet you at Mrs. Claus's Kitchen." After glancing at her watch again, she edged toward the stairs. "Take Highway 9 through town, the entrance to the Village is about two miles further south. You can't miss it. 'Bye, everyone. See you tonight."

"Tonight?" John asked Alice when Penny had gone. Soggy paper towels littered the table and counter.

"This is the busiest time for Santa's Village, from now until Christmas," Alice explained after sending Flash and Amy off to brush their teeth. "The staff arrives at eight. The park closes at nine at night, and sometimes Penny doesn't get home until ten. Hours are supposed to be staggered, but it doesn't always work that way."

"That's an appalling schedule! Can't they see the woman is pregnant?"

"A blind man could see Penny is pregnant." Alice laughed.

A thought occurred to him as he poured a cup of coffee. The mess could wait. "What time do the kids get home from school?"

"Not to worry. I'm here when the bus arrives. It works out nicely." She saw the clock over the stove and started. "Good grief. Kids? Hurry up! We're all going to be late."

A flurry of confusion ensued. Coats and caps had to be found, Flash needed some Halloween candy for his pockets, Amy wanted to stay home with Daddy. There were goodbye kisses. The door opened and closed, then opened as Amy dashed back inside for her homework. She left, then Alice ran inside waving a rubber-banded stack of mail.

"John, would you drop these bills by the post office on your way to lunch? I'm not going to have time."

"I'd be glad to."

"Oh, dear, I feel like I'm forgetting something. Well, never mind. 'Bye. Sorry to leave you with the cleanup."

He heard Alice's car crunch across the frost-coated gravel, then he stepped outside onto the balcony and waved as the car passed below, on the road looping through the subdivision.

When he came back into the kitchen he stopped short and smiled. Penny was right when she teased him that men dirtied more dishes than women. It looked to him like every dish and pan in the house was on the stove and table. Soggy paper towels littered every surface.

Reminding himself there was no reason to hurry, he poured another cup of coffee and sat down at the table. Already he was beginning to feel slightly proprietory about Buffalo Mountain, the rounded peak framed in the window. He suspected that staring at mountains might be as conducive to thinking as being stalled in traffic.

He really should jump up and clean the kitchen, then unhitch the U-Haul and unpack Penny's table and boxes.

The thought passed through his mind, then evaporated like the wisps of cloud floating about the top of Buffalo Mountain. For the first time in years he had a morning with absolutely nothing pressing to do and hours in which to do it. A guilty feeling of laziness stole over him as he sipped his coffee and watched the clouds flirting with Buffalo Mountain.

He thought about the kids spilling their milk and the confusion of getting everyone out the door and on their way, and he laughed. It was good to be home.

HELEN SCRANSKY, Penny's secretary, was already at her desk when Penny hurried into the office. Looking up from her typewriter, Helen pointed to the hallway leading to the manager's office. "The department heads just left."

"Damn!" Running late made her crazy. She had a feeling she would be a step behind all day. "Is Lydie there?" Helen nodded and gave her a sympathetic look. After tossing her coat inside her office, Penny ran down the hallway toward Allenby's door. Waddled was more the word. Pregnant women didn't run; they did a fast waddle.

It was no secret that both she and Lydie Severin were being considered to replace Ian Allenby. Allenby's promotion to corporate headquarters would take effect after the first of the year. His replacement had not yet been named, but he had let it be known the choice was between Penny and Lydie Severin.

She knocked once then stepped inside Allenby's office and dropped into the seat beside Lydie. "Sorry to be late," she murmured. "Have I missed much?"

"Is everything all right?" Lydie asked, her warm eyes dark with concern.

"Fine. I'll tell you about it later."

The rivalry between them was more a fabrication by the staff than genuine. Lydie Severin was a good friend.

"We're discussing the inventory problems at International House," Ian Allenby said. "Only half the Swiss angels survived shipping."

"There's no problem securing credit for the broken items," Lydie added.

"Except Helga will delay filling out the forms until it does become a problem," Penny finished. Ian and Lydie nodded. "I'll talk to her again. Part of the problem may be lack of help. Helga could use another clerk, especially between now and Christmas."

They discussed personnel problems, inventory warehousing, anticipated delays from the snow-removal crews, extending the parking lot, the print runs for the Village newspaper; then Ian asked if Penny had received the new cut of *Mary Poppins* for the theater. She gave him a blank look.

"Our copy is getting scratchy. You ordered a new cut, remember?"

"Oh, Lord." She pushed a hand through her hair. "I'm sorry, Ian, I spaced it out."

"You didn't put in the order?" He straightened behind his desk and looked at her. "Will you take care of it immediately, please? Perhaps you can put a rush on it."

"Of course. I'll see what I can do to speed things along."

After the meeting Lydie followed her back to her office for a quick cup of coffee. "Tough break about the *Mary Poppins* flick." She perched on the edge of Penny's desk. "Allenby's keeping score on screw-ups."

"Don't I know it." A teasing smile curved her lips. "But I figure I've still got an edge on you. Forgetting to hire a replacement Santa when Kurt Pausch went on vacation did you in. I mean, what's Santa's Village without Santa?"

Lydie laughed. "I'm never going to live that one down. You're right. You can forget to order a lot of movies and still not equal one missing Santa." They drank their coffee in companionable silence, listening to the Christmas carols piped through the park and into all the offices.

Penny leaned back in her chair and touched her fingertips to her forehead. "There's just the two of us here, Lydie, no one to overhear...."

"Uh-oh."

"So tell me the truth. Do you have days when you think if you hear one more version of 'Rudolph the Red-Nosed Reindeer' you're going to scream and rip the speaker off the wall?" Lydie laughed and nodded. "Or that you can't bear to look at this candy-cane wallpaper for one more second?"

All the administration offices were papered in green wallpaper with vertical red stripes. Hundreds of tiny candy canes marched down the space between the stripes. The first time Penny had seen the wallpaper, she had thought it charming, if a bit overwhelming. Recently it had begun to lean more to overwhelming and less toward charming.

"It's the bowls of ornaments that get me when I'm feeling stressed out," Lydie confided. Beribboned baskets of shiny glass ornaments decorated every desk, every table in the reception area and were scattered throughout the park. "Do you ever want to tuck one of those baskets under your arm, then run after Allenby and see if you can hit his bald spot with a glass ball?"

Penny grinned. "Right now I'd like to take after Helga. Maybe if she knew she was going to be bombed with ornaments, she'd make an effort to fill out the damned forms."

"Possible, but doubtful," Lydie said. "Helga considers paperwork the scourge of the earth. So," she said, studying

Penny, "how are you feeling? Is the baby still scheduled to arrive *after* Christmas, please, God?"

"I'm feeling great, and everything's on schedule as far as I know."

"You look tired." Tilting her dark head back, Lydie smiled at the ceiling and remembered. "Let's see. Right about now it feels like you have Muhammed Ali in your tummy and he's using you as a punching bag. Am I right?" Penny laughed, nodding. "You have to go to the bathroom all the time, and I mean all the time. It feels like you have to go even when you don't have to go. You feel like you have a twenty-pound bowling ball strapped to your stomach and there is absolutely no comfortable sleeping position. Am I close?"

"Right on the money."

"You hate your clothes, hate your figure, hate your exercises, hate stuffed furniture. You haven't seen your feet in so long you couldn't say for certain if you're wearing matching shoes. You want the whole thing to be over."

"Don't I ever!"

"You run into things, drive with your arms out stiff to reach the steering wheel, try to convince yourself it's all water weight and you're going to look great five minutes after the baby's born. You wish the guy who did this to you could get pregnant so he'd appreciate what he's done."

Penny laughed, then her expression grew more serious as she told Lydie about John's appearing on her doorstep.

"No kidding? He's in town?" Interest gleamed in Lydie's dark eyes. "Does this mean a reconciliation?"

"What you're really asking is, does this mean I'm out of the race for the manager's position?"

"Well, does it?"

Penny threw up her hands. "I keep telling you I don't want the promotion."

"Right."

"Honestly, Lydie. I don't want to get sucked into the corporate game any more than I already am. This is enough," she said, tapping the brass plate that identified her as assistant manager. "Curiosity is the only reason I haven't withdrawn my name from consideration. I'd like to know if I could have gotten it. And staying in the race has nothing to do with beating you. It's strictly a personal thing."

"If I believed you I'd understand, because that's how I'd feel in your place." Lydie smiled. "Meanwhile, back to the original question. Is a reconciliation in the wind?"

Penny picked up a pencil and frowned at it. "John is here to spend the holidays with the kids, that's all there is to it."

"You're sure? I mean, it isn't the usual thing to invite a man you're divorcing as a houseguest. Would it be pushy to inquire about the sleeping arrangements?"

"Very pushy," Penny said, feeling a rush of pink tint her cheeks. "But if you have to know, he's sleeping with Flash in the basement. He's going to move to a hotel."

"If he can find one. 'Tis the season, kiddo. There isn't a room to be had." Lydie finished her coffee and stood. "Need I say that I hope your ex sweeps you off your feet and carries you away from all this?" She waved at the candy-cane wallpaper and grinned. "Ambition has made me shameless. But, in case it doesn't work that way and you're still in the running, I'd better get to work."

Penny groaned. "What do I have to say to convince you? If Allenby offered me the promotion, I'd turn it down."

"Sure. And I'm the Christmas fairy. Don't forget to order *Mary Poppins*," Lydie called as she left. Penny envied her brisk step.

She looked at her phone messages and the paperwork hiding her desk, then glanced at the wall speaker as "Rudolph the Red-Nosed Reindeer" filled her office.

A person could get to hate Christmas, she thought with a sigh. She wondered at what point overkill set in.

THE POST OFFICE was unbelievable. For an instant John wondered if the real post office was somewhere else and this one was a Chamber of Commerce project created to charm tourists.

First, it was smaller and more attractive than any post office he had ever seen. Second, there were no long lines in front of the clerk's windows. Third, everyone present seemed to know each other. He had watched this scene in a dozen movies about small towns and had never quite believed it. People greeted each other by name as they passed in and out, chatted as they opened their postal boxes. Although the weather was definitely on the cold side, two old guys sat on a bench outside the front door, talking to everyone who passed. It was Small Town, U.S.A.

"That your car, son?" one of the old guys said to John when he came outside after mailing Alice's letters. "The one with the California plates?" He pronounced it calee-forn-i-a.

Ordinarily John would have ignored an overture made by a stranger, but it occurred to him that Alice and Penny might know this man. Effecting a compromise, he didn't ignore the inquiry, but didn't fully respond. He nodded, then waited to hear the pitch. There was always a pitch; everyone wanted something. Strangers didn't instigate a conversation for no reason.

"Nice piece of machinery," the old man said. Looking away from the Porsche, he smiled at John's driving cap. John waited. "Enjoy your vacation, son. Should have some snow for you by the end of the week. Probably not enough to ski on, though." Turning, he waved to a man emerging from the post office. "Mornin' to you, Tim. How's the missus feeling? Any better?"

It was a moment before John realized that was it. When he understood he was standing like a fool still waiting for the old man to ask for a handout or push some printed material into his hands, a rush of heat warmed his cheeks. Turning on his heel, he strode to the car, unlocked it and slid inside. After watching the old man for a minute, he put the car in gear and backed out of the space.

People weren't friendly to other people for no reason. The world didn't operate that way.

After deciding he'd steer clear of the old man if he came to the post office again, he put the incident out of his mind and drove slowly through Aspen Springs.

Small was the word that came immediately to mind. But he supposed some people might consider Main Street charming in a rustic sort of way. Historic buildings mixed with new construction built to resemble the older shops. As in most resort towns, the shops featured a display of goods ranging from the definitely upscale to more modestly priced souvenirs. The restaurants looked surprisingly top row.

Aspen Springs definitely possessed a laid-back atmosphere. A man draping the street lamps with chains of holiday greenery seemed more interested in artistic effect than in speed. No one leaned on the car horn when the town's three traffic lights turned red. The noise level was so low it was nearly nonexistent.

How did people stand it here? he thought, passing the town square slowly, turning south when he reached the pond at the bottom of Main Street. What on earth did they do to get the adrenaline going? Watch the lights on the old-fashioned barber pole? Taking his time, he explored the side streets, located the courthouse and the school, drove past rows of sturdy pine-and aspen-framed houses built to look as if they dated from the Victorian period.

On the outskirts of town he found houses more like Alice's, built of wood and stone and glass, mountain chalets, rows of condominiums, many of which were positioned to enjoy a view of Aspen Lake. The dock was deserted now, the lake covered by a thin layer of ice, which would be thick enough to drive on before Christmas.

All this was snuggled in a valley that offered spectacular views. A shrewd investor could make a fortune on those condominiums, he thought, parking on the side of the lake road. John looked back at the town, feeling a sense of déjà vu. He'd seen this town in a dozen Disney movies. Too good to be true. Or maybe he was thinking of the town in *The Stepford Wives.*

As he pulled back onto the road and continued south on Highway 9, he found himself wishing for a breath of good old smog to remind himself who he was. There was nothing like a powerful dose of exhaust fumes to put a man's perspective right.

The entrance to Santa's Village was through an arch formed by two interlocking candy canes that opened to a large parking lot. After staring at the giant candy canes a moment, he drove inside, parked and locked the car. Speakers at the end of each row played "Frosty the Snowman," and fluorescent sleigh tracks led to an admissions booth manned by an elf.

John paid the park fee, then entered a village that Charles Dickens would have recognized. Or maybe it was only a fantasy of the Dickens era. It didn't matter. The village appealed to a nostalgic sense of how Christmas ought to look.

Before he let the kid in him run away with his thoughts, he reminded himself why he was here. He was here to test the waters, which so far appeared as icy as the lake he had driven past. Equally as troubling, was the possibility of losing his children. But beyond that... He glanced down the main street of Santa's Village, then walked toward Mrs. Claus's Kitchen.

Chapter Three

The morning passed quickly until Penny noticed it was eleven o'clock. Then time sagged and seemed to move forward in slow motion. Her ability to concentrate evaporated, and she found herself gazing out the window thinking about her upcoming lunch with John and dreading it. What irritated her most was recognizing the chemistry that still flashed between them. Realizing she was still drawn to him flipped her thoughts into chaos. She didn't want this emotional upheaval, especially now when the demands of her job were greatest and she was uncomfortable physically. She wished John had remained in California.

At twelve o'clock she straightened her desk, then walked to Mrs. Claus's Kitchen. While she waited for John at a table by the window, she observed the restuarant's smooth operation with a critical eye. The waiters were dressed in black slacks and red velvet jackets; the waitresses wore red velvet jumpers over crisp white blouses. The menu offered a holiday feast, or, in smaller print, conventional burgers for those who might prefer them to turkey and plum pudding. At the end of the meal each diner received a tiny gift package containing a truffle.

Mrs. Claus's Kitchen was the main restaurant on the premises. The Village also offered a cafeteria, three soda shops, a pastry shop, two candy stores, a specialty fudge shop, and a cheese-and-sausage shop. Turn-of-the-century carts positioned along cobbled lanes offered roasted chestnuts, hot chocolate, hot dogs, and hot pretzels. No one went hungry at Santa's Village.

She spotted John the moment he appeared on the platform beyond the admissions booth.

It gave her an odd feeling to watch him when he didn't know, almost as if she were spying. But she couldn't help herself.

John Martin was catch-your-breath handsome, the type of man all women looked at twice. His driving cap and tailored overcoat marked him as a tourist; a local would have been wearing jeans and a jean jacket. But he was heartachingly handsome. It was no wonder they had such great-looking kids, Penny thought with a small sigh.

And his smile. It had been a long time since she had seen him smile like that. Open and genuinely delighted. It was a smile Penny noticed hundreds of times a day, when people saw Santa's Village for the first time. But it had been a very long time since she had seen that particular smile on John's lips. As she watched, his smile faded and was replaced by a look of loss, then determination.

For a moment she felt like crying, felt the sting of sudden tears behind her eyes. The tears weren't caused by John or their situation, she told herself. She was merely experiencing one of the hormonal swings caused by pregnancy.

Knowing that the staff at Mrs. Claus's Kitchen was very aware of her presence and that they continually glanced in her direction, she blinked the tears back and self-consciously smoothed the plaid smock over her stomach. It wouldn't do to turn sloppy over lunch. Ian Allenby would hear about it even before she left the restaurant.

She swallowed and forced a smile as John was shown to her table and seated with a flourish.

"The park is wonderful!" John said, taking the chair that faced her across the table linen. His dark eyes swept the gaily decorated restaurant. "It even smells like Christmas. How do you manage that? And do I get a tour after lunch?"

"If you like." Mentally she reviewed her appointment calendar, did a quick reshuffle. Lydie had agreed to take her one o'clock appointment if the lunch stretched into overtime. "So, what have you been doing all morning?" she asked, hoping he would answer that he had booked a hotel.

He told her about exploring Aspen Springs, told her about stopping by the post office and the old man on the bench.

"That would be Wesley Pierce," Penny explained with a smile of affection. "That's his bench. I don't mean he has it staked out—it's truly his bench. He bought it and installed it."

"You're kidding? Some guy bought a park bench and set it up on government property?"

Penny nodded. "Wes Pierce is one of the men who developed Vail. During the war, he and a small group trained in this area for cold-weather operations. They fell in love with the mountains. When the war ended, each man in the group bought land here. Several years later they decided to share their discovery by developing the area for skiing." She shrugged. "The rest is history."

"That old man on the bench in front of the post office is wealthy?" John looked astonished.

Penny smiled. "About as wealthy as they come. But I doubt Wes Pierce thinks about it very often. People are important to him, and community. You could say Wes Pierce is the town crier, so to speak. If you need something, you'll get quicker results by mentioning it to Wes than if you took out a classified ad."

"The man who developed Vail is a busybody?"

"Not exactly," she said, watching him curiously. "More like an information pipeline. By this time tomorrow everyone will know who you are." When John made a face, she added, "Does that bother you?"

"Anonymity is one of the blessings of a big city."

"No one is anonymous here. There aren't many secrets in a small town." They paused to give their order to the waitress. "That can be annoying sometimes—if there's something you want to hide—but it can be a comfort, too."

"Really? Frankly, that's hard to imagine."

She shrugged. "I like knowing everyone in town knows

Amy and Flash. If one of them needed help, they could go to any house in town and the owner would know who to call.'' Her eyes twinkled. ''And I kinda like knowing that Bobby Willis is meeting Jeannie Groton out behind the Elks Club. Or that Martha James changed her will again. To me, being involved with other people is what being part of a community means.''

''I wouldn't like everyone knowing my business.''

''No man is an island, John. People need people.''

He met her eyes. ''What about us, Penny? Do we still need each other?''

He said it quietly, but the impact was the same as if he had shouted.

''I think the time for that question is long past,'' she answered finally, feeling a twinge of resentment that he had opened a door they had agreed to close.

''We had something good for a lot of years.''

For a long moment Penny stared at him. ''What are you trying to say, John?''

''I'm not really sure.'' He turned toward the window. ''Maybe I'm taking stock. Trying to discover how things stand now that we've had some time apart.''

A cramp of anger tightened Penny's stomach. It wasn't fair for John to reappear in her life now. Now, when she had finally accepted the wreckage of their dreams, had finally and painfully accepted that it was over.

''If you're asking if a reconciliation is possible—''

''I didn't say that,'' he said quickly.

''—the answer is no.'' Drawing a breath, she waited until she could speak without sounding so harsh, until she could handle the pain of what she was saying. ''Last March it might have been. That's why I flew to L.A. I was missing you so much and I hoped...'' The words came in a rush bringing with them the same sense of rejection she had felt then, when her hopes had come to nothing. ''But now I've accepted our situation. I'm rebuilding my life, and all in all, it's okay.'' Maybe that was stretching the truth a little, but not by much.

''You honestly don't feel the new baby changes anything?''

"Like what?" She spread her hands. "If anything, having another child confirms my decision. Aspen Springs is where I want my children to grow up."

He nodded, moved his coffee cup in circles on the table top, then looked up at her. "The change in my life will be significant. I'll have a child I'll never know. Is that fair, Penny?"

Of course it wasn't fair. It also wasn't fair to make her feel guilty about it.

"The choice was yours as much as mine," she snapped.

She wished they weren't seated in a public restaurant. The urge to slam doors and shout was almost as overwhelming as the tension clamping her chest. She wished John had stayed in California. She didn't want this.

"I guess what I'm trying to say, what I was thinking about during the drive here, is that perhaps we should use this time before the new baby arrives as a period of reassessment. We owe our children that much. And ourselves."

"Look, I'm genuinely sorry you'll have a child you won't know as well as you might have. But you're a little late with this line of thinking, aren't you?" Bitterness crept into her tone and her gaze. She would have given the world to hear him say these things a year ago. Now it was too late.

"My thinking hasn't changed," he answered sharply. Her tone of voice had triggered a flash of anger. "I never wanted to lose my family."

"You could have stopped it."

"So could you," he said, making a deliberate effort to keep his voice level.

When the silence became uncomfortable Penny lifted a wary gaze. "This reassessment you're suggesting, what exactly do you want to reassess?"

"I think we should consider whether it's possible to set aside our personal differences for the sake of our children."

"I've never believed in people living together just for the sake of their children."

"Neither have I. But maybe it's something we should reconsider. Maybe that belief is still valid, maybe it's not. All

I'm suggesting is that we reexamine our positions during the next few weeks and make absolutely certain they still apply."

"I think I've made my feelings clear." As clear as she could, considering she was riding a hormonal roller-coaster that swept her up one day, down the next. At this point she couldn't take a stand on anything with any certainty. Except this. On this issue, she knew how she felt. "And I thought I understood your feelings. Are you saying you've changed your mind about the divorce?"

The anger receded from his gaze, and he pushed his coffee cup away. "The truth? I honestly don't know. I guess the answer is yes and no." He met her eyes. "I hate the thought of having a child I won't know and who won't know me. I miss you and the kids. Sometimes missing you is so painful that..." He looked away from her. "I imagine it's fair to assume there are occasions when you miss me." When he paused, she nodded in reluctant agreement. "On the other hand, I know we can both build a life without each other—we're doing that now. And I imagine you're discovering as I am that there are some benefits to living alone. The bottom-line questions are, is a life apart better than a life together and is that the best thing for our children?"

"We've already made those decisions."

"Agreed. But the situation has changed." He nodded toward her stomach. "We've been given a chance to take one last hard look at what we're doing. All I'm asking is that we agree to take a second look." He smiled. "We made a lot of major decisions in a very heated emotional climate, Penny. I realize there's still a lot of anger on both sides, but we're no longer in the eye of the storm. I'm suggesting we use this period to take a calmer look, that's all. Make sure we're doing the right thing."

"Suppose we decided, for the children's sake, to try again," she said after a lengthy pause, watching his face. "Would you expect us to return to Los Angeles to live?"

Surprise lifted his eyebrows. "Of course."

A bubble of hysterical laughter formed in her chest and

pressed against her rib cage. Shaking her head, she pushed her plate aside, her appetite gone.

"Penny? What's wrong?"

"Me. You. Everything." Her shoulders dropped. "For one stupid moment I thought you were saying you would consider living in Aspen Springs. I was sitting here arguing the morality of that because obviously your willingness to reconsider came about solely because of the new baby. All the time you were talking about Los Angeles."

"That's where we live. That's where my job is." He lifted a hand. "I know what you're thinking. But I grew up in L.A. and it didn't scar me. Kids can learn a decent value system in big cities, too. Millions of them do."

"I should have known where this conversation was leading," she said angrily. "John, we agreed. We said we would raise our children here. In a small town."

"We weren't being realistic. Time has proven we were wrong to lock into such a promise. One of the mistakes we made was not accepting each other as we are. I'm a big-city kid. Always have been, probably always will be. Additionally, if we're honest, we both knew taking jobs with Blackman Brothers meant a long term commitment. You knew you were getting a big-city banker when we married, Penny."

"I have a longer memory than you appear to." She was leaning forward, her hands clenched on the table. When she remembered people were watching, she hastily thrust her hands into her lap. "When we made the decision to get married, you were about to get your degree in Hotel and Restaurant Management. Your dream was to manage and someday own a luxury hotel with a world-class restaurant. That dream was not incompatible with raising children in a small town. Aspen Springs has half a dozen excellent hotels catering to the ski crowd with restaurants as fine as you'll find anywhere in the world!"

"Whose managers are starving to death on less than thirty thousand a year! That isn't what we wanted, Penny. We wanted a shot at the brass ring. And we got it."

"Yes, we caught the brass ring. Now it's time to cash it in

and start thinking about our children and about slowing down and about the rest of our lives."

Her voice had risen and people at the next table turned to glance at them. Embarrassed, Penny gestured to the waitress to remove their plates.

When the waitress had gone, she released a long breath. "Look. Let's stop this. We've fought this battle a thousand times. Neither of us can win. It's hopeless. All we're doing is making each other furious."

John was as visibly upset as she was. When he reached for his coffee, his fingers were shaking. Seeing the tremble surprised her, for it was so unlike him.

Then her shoulders stiffened. No, she was not wrong to insist on her point of view. It was as valid as his.

"All I'm asking is that we take a second look at everything," he said finally, struggling to keep his voice level. "That's all."

"Too many things have been said, John. There've been too many hurts, too many heartaches."

"On both sides. And maybe neither of us can forgive and forget. That's something else to consider. For Flash and Amy's sake I'm willing to make that effort. Are you?"

Blinking rapidly, wishing she were anywhere but here, she looked at her wristwatch. "Good heavens, I didn't realize what time it was. I'll have to ask for a rain check on that tour. I have an appointment and I'm already late." Pushing to her feet, she fumbled for her purse, found it hanging from her shoulder.

Standing when she did, John stepped close to her and touched her cheek, brushing his thumb gently across the dampness beneath her eye. Penny stifled a gasp. His touch was electrifying, explosive with memory.

"All I'm suggesting is that we consider the future with an open mind. We have too much shared history to throw it away without taking a hard second look."

They had discussed second chances last March; it hadn't gotten them anywhere then and it wouldn't now. She lifted an expression that mixed resentment and anger. "Do you really think anything is going to change?"

He shrugged. His face was carefully expressionless. "I just want both of us to be very sure."

"Why does it always have to be on your terms?"

"If you're referring to location, there's no investment bank or brokerage house in Aspen Springs."

There was no rebuttal to that one. Penny clamped her lips together. Outside the restaurant, she glanced down the Main Street of the Village, automatically checking the traffic flow, then feeling the bite of the frosty air, wrapped her arms around her upper body.

Looking up, John extended his hand, palm upwards with a blink of exaggerated surprise. "Good Lord, what's this?"

One of the things she had loved about him was his ability to ease a tense situation. Penny smiled and felt the tightness ease in her shoulders. "Around here, stranger, we call that snow."

"So, this is what it looks like." He grinned down at her.

"Not much of that stuff in California. But here, we get about twelve to twenty feet of it every winter."

A mock shudder convulsed his body. "A horrible place to live. You have to agree even Eskimos have it better," he said with a wink.

"Afraid not," she answered lightly. "If you were a skier, you'd think Aspen Springs was heaven."

"Maybe I'll take some lessons while I'm here."

They looked at each other and an awkward moment opened. In the past they had always made a point of ending arguments with an embrace. It was their way of offering comfort and saying all was forgiven. Penny moved backward a step and rubbed her arms vigorously.

"It's getting cold."

"I've heard that happens when it snows," he said, still smiling.

"John...I really have to insist that you find a hotel." The words emerged in a blurted rush. "It would be easier on all of us."

"I don't agree," he said after a minute. "I have a lot of time to make up with Amy and Flash." His gaze reminded her there might not be another chance. "And I'd rather not disrupt their usual routine to do it. Unless the situation is absolutely intolerable, I'd like to accept Alice's invitation and stay at the house."

"It isn't absolutely intolerable," she admitted finally, wondering if that was really true. One thing was certain, she resented him for dismissing her feelings in favor of his own. It wasn't her fault he had been too busy to take the kids over the summer, hadn't spent as much time with them as he wanted. "I'm not convinced that having you stay with us is the best thing for the kids." When she saw she had hurt him, she touched his sleeve briefly, the gesture instinctive. "I'm sorry, but this is going to make it very tough on Amy and Flash. You can see that, can't you? Think how hard it will be on them to say goodbye again. We're sending them mixed signals."

"I hear what you're saying, and I regret any confusion this arrangement might cause. But would pushing and pulling the kids between their home and a hotel be better for them? Part of their things would be at my hotel. Their friends and part of their things would be at your house. You and I would be placed in a position of competing for the kids' time and attention..."

Everyone involved would hate it, Penny conceded with a frown. "Staying with us places complex pressures on a situation that's already complicated."

"I'm willing to do whatever you think is best, Penny. You decide."

"Dammit." Chewing her lip, she wrapped her arms around herself again, hating this, and looked down the Village's Main Street. He was right, of course. The kids' lives would be less disrupted if he remained at Alice's. It would be easier, more convenient, for everyone except her. "All right," she said finally, unhappily. "You can stay."

"Thank you."

He leaned forward as if to kiss her cheek and she hastily

stepped backward and raised a hand. "Don't," she said quietly. "Please, John. If we're going to live in the same house for the next few weeks, we need some rules. The first one is...don't push. I'm not part of the deal, okay?" The snow was falling thicker now. She brushed at her shoulders, shook the flakes from her hair.

"Sorry, some habits are hard to break," he apologized. His dark eyes centered on her mouth and a shiver that had nothing to do with the cold trembled through her body.

"Please don't let it happen again."

He raised both hands and smiled. "Not a chance, ma'am. You could beg me to kiss you and I wouldn't do it. Me? Kiss my wife? No way. Not if you dragged me out of the North Pole and threw yourself on me."

"The North Pole?"

"A euphemism for a bunk bed in the basement."

She smiled in spite of herself. "The North Pole, huh?"

"Just out of curiosity, how long should I not kiss you? Is there a time limit on this? Suppose I run into you in a shopping mall ten years from now. You say, 'Well hello, John Martin, isn't it?' and I say 'If it isn't ole what's-her-name,' do we exchange a polite kiss then? Or how about this—we come out of the divorce court, smile and given each other a peck to show we're civilized people handling our troubles in a mature manner. Is that allowed? Suppose we run into each other some New Year's Eve, do we hide in the host's basement at the midnight hour or do we exchange a kiss for old time's sake?"

Penny smiled. "Let's agree to cross those bridges when we come to them." She tilted her head. "You're pushing and you agreed not to."

"Is cheek kissing allowed?" he continued, grinning.

"No."

"Shaking hands?"

"No."

"I'm merely trying to locate the perimeters. How about waving?"

She laughed and threw up her hands. "This is crazy. John, we're in the middle of a divorce. The court date is set. It's what we both want.'' Then her gaze dropped to his lips and she felt her mouth go dry. It had been a very long time—since March, to be exact—since she had been kissed. And John Gordon Martin was a world-class kisser.

''I know. I'm sorry things worked out as they did,'' he said softly, looking down at her.

''I am, too.'' Snow drifted between them, falling softly on his cap and on the top of her stomach.

''Well.'' He cleared his throat. ''You need to get inside. It's cold out here.''

''Yes.'' She moved backward a step. ''I...I'll see you tonight.''

The words rang in her head the rest of the day. The next weeks were going to be the longest in her life.

''And it's your fault, Whosit,'' she murmured, pushing back from her desk to place her hand on her rounded stomach. She suspected this child was going to be a handful. He or she was already causing complications she wouldn't have believed.

PENNY PLACED her cafeteria tray on the table, then sat down across from Lydie. ''Why are we both scheduled to work late tonight? I thought the whole point of having two assistant managers was to stagger the workload and the closing schedules.''

''It's your night to close. But I don't want to talk about work. I suggested coffee and pie for the sole brazen purpose of learning every gossipy detail about your lunch with John. He is one gorgeous guy, by the way.''

Penny looked up. ''You saw him?''

''Everyone in the Village saw him. A straw poll says you're an idiot to divorce that guy. He's great looking, has a smile to swoon for, drives a Porsche and he looks at you like he's crazy about you.''

''That's ridiculous! We agreed to keep our behavior as amiable as possible for the sake of the children. Believe me, Lydie, John is as much in favor of the divorce as I am. You're mistaking civility for something more.''

''If you say so. Remind me why you're divorcing this guy,

will you? And it better be something worse than leaving whiskers in the sink.''

Penny laughed. ''John's a workaholic.''

''A good provider.''

''The best. Except the work he's addicted to is in L.A. He's a big-city boy and I'm a small-town girl. Plus, he'd be a workaholic no matter where he lived. I'd rather have a husband in the house instead of all the latest appliances. There's a downside to living with a good provider.''

''If I had a choice between my ex-husband and a microwave, I'd take the microwave any day.''

''Then you don't regret the divorce?'' Penny asked curiously.

Lydie frowned, pushed the whipped cream off her pie. ''I suppose there are always regrets when a marriage crumbles. How about you?''

Not really hungry, Penny pushed her pie aside and looked up at the ceiling. ''I hate the feeling of failure. And guilt. My father died when I was eleven. I know a little about growing up without a father, and I can't bear to think about Amy and Flash and little Whosit not having a father.'' She lifted her gaze. ''The problem is, they didn't really have a father when John and I were married. We didn't have time to do the family things. So which is worse? Not having a father and no father expectations? Or having a father who continually disappoints you by not having time to be there?''

''Look, Penny, you haven't asked my advice...''

''But you're going to give it anyway, right?''

Lydie grinned. ''Right.'' Her smile faded while she thought about what she wanted to say. ''What the kids think is important. So are their expectations, I'm not saying it isn't.''

''But?''

''But the foundation of any marriage is the wife and husband, not the kids. You can't beat yourself with guilt about the kids if you and John can't be happy together. Kids are resilient—they'll cope. We adults are less resilient. You can't live your life based on what you might think is best for your children. Even that one,'' she said, nodding to Penny's stomach. "You have to marry or divorce based on your own feelings and expectations."

"I've always thought that, but lately..." The lunch with John had made a greater impact than she had realized. Frowning, she thought out loud. "Actually marriage is a family affair. Amy and Flash have a stake in this decision, too."

"If that's how you feel, then you're in for some tough times ahead." When Penny lifted an eyebrow, Lydie spread her hands. "Think about it. If you really see marriage as a family affair, then every family event that comes along when you're divorced is going to be agonizing. Because part of that equation is missing."

"Like the holidays," Penny said slowly.

"Kiddo, you haven't suffered until you've spent your first Christmas alone," Lydie commented grimly.

Penny raised her head and looked around the cafeteria at the beribboned wreaths, the strings of bright ornaments, the gaily wrapped packages under the cafeteria's Christmas tree. She frowned.

"Trust me," Lydie said, pushing away her plate and reaching for her coffee. "Christmas is for kids. And what they want most is a complete family. If you see a family as incomplete without a man to carve the turkey, you're in for a rough time of it."

Oddly, she hadn't thought about this year's upcoming holidays. She was surrounded by Christmas every day, but she hadn't let herself think about spending a real Christmas without John. Or about Christmas future.

JOHN PICKED UP THE KIDS from school, the first time he had ever done so. When the final bell sounded and a stream of children poured out the school doors, he watched them with a critical eye. In short order, he decided his were definitely the best-looking kids in the Aspen Springs school system. Glancing at the other parents waiting in the line of cars, he felt sorry for them, having to make do with ordinary children, hoped they didn't envy him too much when the best of the bunch jumped in his car and gave him excited kisses.

"It's snowing, Daddy!"

"Then it's probably too cold for ice cream, right?"

They grinned and assured him it was never too cold for ice cream. Since he happened to agree, they drove to Ye Olde Ice Cream Shoppe and spent fifteen minutes picking out flavors for double dippers, then they sat in front of the steamy windows and licked their cones, each claiming their flavors were the best.

He needn't have worried what they would talk about. Amy told him about her best friend, Diedre, and Flash showed him a page of large-figured arithmetic. They argued about who had the best teacher. Everyone, including him, dripped ice cream on their clothes and didn't care. Amy said she wanted to be a famous ice skater when she grew up. Flash said that was dumb; he wanted to cook eggs and hotcakes when he grew up.

"Like you, Daddy," he said, wiping at a chocolate mustache. "I want to be just like you."

John's heart lurched and melted, and he had to look away. "Got something in my eye," he muttered gruffly and reached for a napkin.

"Now who's being dumb," Amy said indignantly. "Daddy doesn't cook eggs and hotcakes for a living. He does deals." Her small brow furrowed and she tossed a braid over her shoulder. "Don't you, Daddy?"

"Then I want to do deals," Flash announced.

"You'd be good at it," John said. Leaning forward, he dabbed Flash's mouth with a fresh napkin. Some of the chocolate came away, but most of it looked like it was there to stay. He wondered if women knew some trick that he didn't. "Right now I'm on vacation."

"I know what you can do. You can stay home and take care of us and Mommy and Grandma Alice." Having disposed of his vacation time, Amy applied herself to licking the drips from her fingers.

"I'll think on that while I get a cup of coffee," he said, finishing his cone. While he was at the counter, he remembered to ask where he could buy coffee beans.

"You could try City Market," the man behind the counter said, pouring John's coffee. "I think they carry coffee beans."

"That's the only place?"

"As far as I know."

He would have expected a specialty shop in a resort town. Most groceries carried a limited selection and the beans weren't always fresh. Someone was missing a great business opportunity by not recognizing a market.

The kids looked up at him when he returned to their table, then looked at each other.

"Okay. What's going on with you two?" he asked, smiling.

"Do you still love Mommy?" Amy asked, speaking for them both. They clutched their ice-cream cones and looked at him, waiting.

Oh boy. How did he answer that one? "Love changes sometimes," he answered. "People change."

"But do you love Mommy?" Flash asked.

"Does that mean you stopped loving us, too?" Amy whispered.

Oh, my God! "No, no, honey, I'll always love you and Flash. Always!" The crucial thing was to reassure them. He drew a quick breath. "And I'll always love Mommy. It's just a different kind of love now."

"If you love us, why didn't you come with us to Colorado?"

He should have anticipated these questions, but he hadn't. "It's a long story…" They waited. "Well, the place where I do deals is in California—"

"Are you and Mommy going to get a divorce?" Flash asked.

"Diedre's mommy and daddy are divorced and she says it's okay. Sorta. Except her mommy and her stepmommy fight on the telephone and she misses her real daddy. Her stepdaddy is okay, but she says her real daddy is better. Her real daddy gives her lots of stuff, but most of it is for little kids, so she only pretends to really like it. She spends two weeks in the summer with her real daddy and her stepmommy and a week after Christmas." Amy's eyes were very round, very blue and very brave. "We don't want you to divorce us, Daddy, but if you do we want to know if we can spend the whole summer with you instead of just two weeks."

"Oh, God," John whispered.

"How many steps will we have?" Flash asked, pulling his knees up under him on the chair.

"Steps?"

"He means stepdaddys and stepmommys and stepAlice's and stepbrothers and stepsisters. Diedre even has a stepaunt."

"Look," John said, swallowing. His chest and throat were tight. Their faces devastated him. "It appears that Mommy and I will get a divorce." They looked at him with big eyes. "I'm sure she told you."

"Yeah."

"Yeah."

"It's important you understand that both Mommy and I love you. The divorce has nothing to do with you." But it would have an enormous impact on them. Guilt and regret clamped his teeth together. "Mommy and I both love you very much. We both wish we could all stay together. But sometimes mommys and daddys just can't live together anymore."

"Like Diedre's mommy and daddy."

He nodded, hating this. "Mommy and I have some problems we don't seem able to work out."

"Did we make you mad, Daddy?" Flash asked, licking at his cone, trying to present a six-year-old's version of cool and casual. He looked at his lap. "We don't want you to divorce us."

Us. There it was again. For a moment John closed his eyes against the pain. Penny had been coping with this from the beginning. How had she endured it? Each word was like a dagger to the heart.

"No, honey. You and Amy didn't do anything wrong," A thousand-pound weight pressed against his chest. "This is strictly a problem between Mommy and me. It's terribly important you understand the divorce is not your fault. It has nothing to do with you."

For the first time he noticed an older woman sitting at the

next table, facing him. A flush of discomfort darkened his cheeks as he realized she had overheard the conversation.

When she stood up to leave, she smiled at him. "You're Alice Sage's son-in-law, aren't you?"

"Yes," he said, standing.

"I'm Winnie Greene. Greene's Antiques, just up Main Street." She pressed his sleeve. "Take my advice, John."

He blinked. She knew his name.

"This divorce is a big mistake. Forget about it and concentrate on winning Penny back."

"I beg your pardon?"

"You should romance her. Pregnant women need romance, too. Some candy and flowers wouldn't hurt. Right?" she asked the children. "Flash Martin, look at your face." She bent over Flash, and when she straightened, the chocolate mustache had disappeared. "Romance." She leaned near his ear. "You should bend a little. You've made a killing in the market, so you can afford to retire from that hotshot job and start over here. Stop being so stubborn."

His mouth dropped and he stared after her as she stepped through the door into the swirling snow.

ALICE LAUGHED when he told her about it. "That's Winnie for you. The woman doesn't have a shy bone in her body.'

"Alice, you're missing the point. This Winnie Whoever—"

"Greene. Greene's Antiques. It's at the end of—"

"Main Street. Yes, I know. The point is, she knew our private business." Anger flashed in his eyes.

"Now, John." Alice sat forward on the sofa and patted his hand. "Winnie has known Penny all her life. She means well."

"Does everyone in Aspen Springs know about Penny and me?" Taking Alice's wineglass, he carried it into the kitchen and poured refills for them both. For the hundredth time he checked the wall clock, starting to worry.

"Probably," Alice admitted. "There may be a couple of tourists who haven't heard yet," she said smiling.

He stopped at the windows and peered into the darkness, trying to see past the falling snow. "What time—"

"She'll be here any minute. Stop worrying. Penny grew up driving on snowy roads. She's a careful driver."

The drank their wine in front of the fire, listening as the wind picked up.

"Alice, how often does Penny get home after the kids are asleep?"

"More often than she would like," Alice said lightly. "She's trying to carve a niche for herself. Things should ease up for her after the first of the year. At least, that's the plan."

"You're not convinced."

Alice hesitated. "Frankly, I'm worried about Penny. Leaving you has been very hard on her. I know what she's doing, of course. I did the same thing after Marshall died. She's keeping herself too busy to grieve, too busy to hurt. If she works until she's exhausted, then she'll sleep at night. She won't have to think about being alone or being lonely. She thinks she's working this hard to provide for the future, but…I think what she's really doing is running away from the present."

Knots formed in his jawline. "The present isn't too pleasant right now."

"John, I don't mean to meddle, but is there any way you two can work things out? If I ever saw two people who were made for each other…"

"I don't know." He frowned, thinking about his conversation with Amy and Flash. "You happen to have a very stubborn daughter."

Alice looked at him with affection. "And a stubborn son-in-law," she added mildly.

They heard a car in the driveway and John's face relaxed. He glanced at his watch. "A pregnant woman shouldn't be out on icy roads at this time of night."

A blast of snow and frosty air filled the entryway, then Penny appeared at the top of the stairs. Snow dusted her cap and the fur collar turned up around her face. Below the fur she resembled a wool ball.

She looked at them, at the wineglasses and the crackling fire, then burst into tears.

Alice took her coat and cap, John led her to the sofa before the fire, then knelt in front of her and rubbed her hands.

"Penny, honey, what's wrong? Are you all right? Are you hurt?"

"Don't 'honey' me!" The tears kept rolling down her cheeks, infuriating her.

"Sorry, it just slipped out."

She dashed at the idiotic tears with an angry motion. "I'm not crying."

"You are crying," Alice said, leaning down to stare at her.

"No, I'm not!" She was behaving like a pregnant woman, whose hormones were out of whack and running emotionally amuck. Which was exactly what was happening.

"Can I get you something?" John asked anxiously. He lifted a hand as if to smooth back her hair.

She slapped at his fingers. "No. I'm fine. It's just..."

Raising her hands, she pressed the heels of her palms against her eyelids, deeply embarrassed. "It took forever to close tonight, and then when I got out to the parking lot I discovered I had a flat tire. I couldn't find anybody to help, then I finally did, but...and all the time I wanted some lemon custard ice cream in the worst way."

"You craved lemon custard ice cream when you were pregnant with Amy." Standing, John started for the door. "I'll get you some."

"You can't. Ye Old Ice Creame Shoppe is closed. I drove by on the way home."

"Then I'll drive to Vail or Denver and get some."

"John, that's crazy. It's seventy miles to Denver. One way."

Alice stood. "We don't have a problem here. I have some lemon custard in the freezer."

"I don't want it now," Penny said, knowing how contrary she sounded and hating it. Alice sighed and sat back down. "It's snowing and I had to drive slowly, and I knew the kids were already asleep and the baby is kicking up a storm and I'm exhausted and I missed the turnoff and..."

And then she had hauled herself up the stairs and found Alice and John drinking wine and chatting before the fire, and they looked so comfortable and relaxed while she was feeling bulky and exhausted. She had taken one look at them and she had fallen apart.

"Honey...Penny. You don't need this job. Any job that makes you this upset and keeps you out this—"

"It's not the job, dammit!" Pushing her hands against the sofa cushions, she tried to thrust herself up. "It was just a bad day, okay?" The sofa cushion had turned vicious. Having gotten a grip on her, it refused to let go. She leaned over her stomach and tried to rock forward. "I forgot to order *Mary Poppins* again. And, in case you haven't noticed, I am very, very pregnant!"

The rocking wasn't working, and she was digging herself deeper into the sofa cushion. She could feel the soft upholstery closing over her like the arms of a woolen trap. Planting her feet beneath her, she slid forward, hoping to balance the bulk of her weight over her feet.

"Of course you're pregnant," said John. "And there's going to be emotional swings—"

"Don't be condescending!" Sliding forward had been a big, big mistake. Her feet slipped out from under her and now most of her weight was perched precariously on the outer edge of the sofa cushion. Seeking balance, she tilted backward. Too far backward. Her head slid down the back cushion. It occurred to her that she must look like a plaid whale wallowing helplessly on an upholstered beach. "And don't blame everything on my being pregnant. You used to do that and it made me crazy!"

Her head slipped further. Now she was talking to the ceiling. Frantically, she tried to find something firm to push against, but the evil sofa cushion swallowed her fists as easily as it had swallowed her body. Her stomach began a forward roll heading toward the sofa edge. Her hair pulled up along the back cushion as her head slipped down.

In an effort to halt the forward slide, she spread her legs and pushed her heels into the carpet. God only knew what she looked like, spraddle-legged, talking to the ceiling while her skirt slid up toward her thighs and she slid off the sofa.

"I hate this," she said to the overhead beams.

John reached for her, then changed his mind, afraid she would get upset if he touched her.

Her knees were doing the splits. She tried harder to dig her heels into the carpet in a last attempt to save herself. In her mind she pictured a plaid ball going over the side of a Herculean cliff.

"I really hate this." She sighed at her helplessness, felt like the world's biggest, bulkiest, clumsiest fool. "Are you going to help me or just let me fall on the floor?" she said, glaring, giving up.

John caught her under the arms a split second before she plopped onto the floor, then lifted her back onto the sofa. Immediately she felt the cushion grab her again.

"Up," she said between her teeth. "Clear up." Her voice was shrill. Once John set her on her feet, she straightened her skirt then lifted cheeks flaming with embarrassment and mustered what dignity she could before she waddled toward the stairs leading to her bedroom.

When she turned at the staircase, Alice and John were staring.

"I know what you're thinking. You're thinking the job is getting to me. You're thinking I'm working too hard and too long. Well you're wrong. It's not the job." After mounting the short staircase, she turned around and went back down. "And it's not because I'm pregnant, either!"

"Then what is it, dear?" Alice asked.

"It's just..." Appalled, she realized she was going to cry again. "I'm just upset. All right? Everyone has a bad day occasionally."

But she didn't usually cry about it. Welcome to the world of pregnant women. Last week she had wept over a TV toilet-tissue commercial.

"Listen," she said to them, her voice spiraling upward. "If

you had an ex-husband who was sleeping in your basement, you'd cry, too! Whoever heard of such a thing?'' Having delivered what was clearly an exit line, she tossed her head and did a fast waddle up the stairs to her bedroom.

John and Alice looked at each other.

''Did any of that make sense?'' Alice asked after a moment.

''I'm not sure. Did she mean she's crying because I'm sleeping in the basement instead of with her? Or did she mean she's crying because I'm here in the first place?''

''I have no idea.''

''Maybe I should talk to her.''

''It's up to you of course, but…''

''Bad idea?''

Alice nodded. They heard doors slamming upstairs. Half an hour later Penny came back down the stairs. This time she was wearing a voluminous orange robe and she had cold cream on her face. Her hair was piled on top of her head.

She stopped at the bottom of the stairs, her expression furious. ''Okay, John, you've got me feeling guilty as hell about the kids. I don't think it will change a damned thing, but I agree to your stupid reassessment!''

John rose to his feet. ''I appreciate that.''

''Just don't push, okay?'' She glared at him.

''I won't. I promise.''

''And don't be charming!''

''Whatever you want. No charm.''

''Don't patronize me!'' She placed her fists where her waist used to be and scowled. ''I have to know this. Are you just being amiable like we agreed, or do you still feel something toward me?''

''Of course I still care about you. You're the mother of my children. We were married—happily, I thought—for a lot of years. Maybe I don't love you like—''

''If you laugh, John Martin, I'll never forgive you!''

''I swear, I'm not laughing,'' he said. But his voice sounded peculiar.

She narrowed her eyes. ''You have that funny look like you're trying not to laugh!''

"Maybe it's the cold cream, but you look—" Hastily he spread his hands. "I'm not laughing."

"Okay. That's all I wanted to say." Turning, she took hold of the banister, then glared back over her shoulder.

"Honestly, I'm not laughing."

"This reassessment is a waste of time, it's too late. You have to understand that."

"I'm sure you're right. I just think we should be very certain about what we're doing."

She looked at him. Her face was shiny with cold cream; the orange robe fell around her like the folds of a parachute. She looked vulnerable and adorable. And she would have flown into a fury if he had said so.

"Okay, as long as you understand how it is. We care about each other, but we don't love each other. If it wasn't for our children we would be one hundred percent sure of the divorce. Before we go our separate ways, we're going to take one last hard look."

"That's how I see it."

"All right. Good night."

When he heard her bedroom door slam, he returned to the sofa and grinned at Alice. "No doubt about it...the woman's crazy about me."

Alice laughed then clapped a hand over her mouth and shot a look toward the staircase. "You're both crazy."

Chapter Four

Each morning, John ticked items off the list from the day before and compiled a list for the current day. Since the list of things he actually had to do was shockingly brief he added such things as: fix breakfast—a task he had relegated to himself—phone office, go to the post office—there was no mail delivery in Alice's subdivision—read trade journals, pick kids up from school, check closing market quotes, stop by grocery if needed.

Dull stuff, he thought, as he drove to the post office one afternoon to mail his comments on Emil Blackman's client report. Not that Emil had solicited his comments, he thought sourly. Out of sight, out of mind had never been truer. Every time he phoned in, his office pretended to have forgotten his name, made a joke out of reminding him that he was on vacation.

He mailed his comments, then paused before the bulletin board mounted near the post office door. The Optimist Club announced it would host a pancake supper on Saturday night to benefit the Syshell family whose home had burned. Miss Applesham's subject for the Wednesday Garden Club was edible mountain plants. The Sax Act, a rock and roll group, was opening at the Holiday Lounge. Mike at Peak Five offered free Labrador puppies to anyone who would give them a good home.

Surprising himself, he wondered idly who was organizing

the pancake supper, not that he would have recognized anyone's name. Organizing a pancake supper sounded kind of fun, figuring the ingredients, stirring up vats of batter. It reminded him of college.

"Good Lord," he muttered when he realized what he was thinking. Talk about small-town boredom. To the best of his memory, he had never attended a pancake supper in his life, let alone organized one. Yet for a minute there...

"How do, John," Wes Pierce called when he stepped outside. "Have yourself a seat. The show's about to start."

"What show?" It was absurd to feel flattered that this old man had invited him to share a bench. But Penny insisted Wes Pierce didn't invite just anybody to sit on his bench. Thrusting his hands into his pockets, he hesitated, wondering what had prompted the invitation.

"Jim Anderson hired that Ute Indian fella to do a snow dance."

"You're kidding!"

Sure enough, when he turned in the direction of Wes's nod, John saw a man in full feathered regalia sitting cross-legged in the center of the town square. Despite the frigid temperature, he was bare chested. For all the notice he took of the cold he might have been sitting in the heart of Los Angeles. He wore a feathered headdress, doeskin britches, and moccasins. At the moment, he appeared to be in a trance, sitting before a long feathered pipe resting in a pipe stand.

After conceding he didn't have anything pressing to do, John decided he could spare a minute or two. He sat beside Wes Pierce on the bench and pushed his driving cap back on his hair.

"Do you people really think that guy can make snow?"

Wes Pierce shifted to look at him. "Who knows? Can you say for sure that he can't?" When John smiled and shrugged, Wes turned back to the Indian. "God knows we need something. The ski areas have already delayed opening twice. What little snow we're getting isn't sticking and the machine-made snow just isn't the same as the real thing."

As they watched, the Indian reverently lifted the pipe from

the stand and raised it toward the cold blue sky. After pushing himself to his feet, he offered the pipe to the four directions. No one in the crowd understood what this meant, but everyone murmured approval. A round of applause erupted when he returned the pipe to its stand and picked up a drum. Beating his palm against the drum in a slow commanding cadence, the Indian dipped his feathered headdress and began to sing and dance in a circle, which narrowed into a series of intricate patterns too complex to follow.

"He's loud," Wes Pierce noted with approval. "You got to be loud or it isn't any good." With the snow dance satisfactorily under way, he turned his full attention to John. "Now then, son. How's the romance coming? You making any progress?"

John couldn't believe it. This noisy old man wanted details of his personal life. Anger stiffened his response. "I'd say that isn't any of your business."

"Not good, huh?" Wes shook his head and made a clucking noise. "Too bad. First thing you have to do, you have to get yourself out of the basement." He raised a hand to stop John's outburst. "I know, I know. Penny's mighty pregnant. But that doesn't mean you can't cuddle. Women like to cuddle. You aren't going to get anywhere with this romance while you're still in the basement, take my word for it. Now if you ask me—"

John stood abruptly. "I'm not asking you, Mr. Pierce. I don't appreciate this kind of interference. Not from you, not from anyone."

"Prickly fella, aren't you?" Wes Pierce narrowed his eyes and pushed back his baseball cap to look up at John.

"No offense, but when I want your advice, I'll ask for it. Okay?"

"Sounds to me like you could use a bit of advice, son. How long you been here? Two weeks? And you're still sleeping in a bunk bed? That doesn't sound like much progress to me. It's time to get on with it."

Exasperated, John stepped away, feeling the indignation tensing his shoulders. "Look, Wes. Let's make a deal. You don't help me. I won't help you. Agreed? We'll both live and let live."

"Stubborn and prideful. Just like a city boy." Shaking his head, Wes looked at the ground before he lifted his head. "Son, I'd say there wasn't much hope for you except I noticed this time you didn't lock your car when you went inside. I guess that's progress of a sort."

"What?" Horrified, he spun to look at his Porsche. As far as he could tell no one had broken into it.

Wes smiled at his expression. "It's not likely someone is going to steal it during the five minutes you're inside, and with me sitting here watching." Removing his baseball cap, he ran his fingers through a thatch of iron-gray hair. "This isn't by way of helping out, you understand, but I heard you were looking for coffee beans. Auntie Maud's carries coffee beans. Down by the pond." After waving to someone in the crowd watching the snow dance, he settled back on his bench and spoke without looking up. "If I were you, I'd hang up that tweed cap and get me a good pair of Levi's at the store up in Leadville, and while I was at it, I'd get me a fleece-lined jean jacket so I wouldn't look like a dumb tourist."

For an instant John was too flabbergasted to do anything but stare. Then he turned on his heel, clamped his lips together and strode toward the Porsche. He couldn't believe he'd been so careless as to leave it unlocked while he was inside the post office. A quick check confirmed nothing was missing. All his tapes were accounted for. His camera was still on the seat.

After looking toward Wes Pierce's bench, he swore, then slapped the car in gear. Since he still had a hour before he was scheduled to pick up Amy from Brownie Scouts, he cruised Main, seething over the encounter with Wes Pierce. Was there anyone in this damned town who didn't know every intimate detail of his life? Down to the sleeping arrangements at Alice Sage's house?

Did they also know that he ached for Penny every night? And hated himself for it? Did they know that his emotions were in a conflicting mess? That he was afraid he would lose his children just as he was finding them again?

What he needed was a cup of coffee. With a grimace of annoyance he found himself parked in front of Auntie Maud's, debating if he should go inside. When he recognized he was stubbornly resisting solely because Wes Pierce had made the suggestion, he got out of the car, locked it and opened the glass door to Auntie Maud's.

The shop was patterned along the lines of an old-fashioned general store. A pot-bellied stove glowed on the back wall. He inhaled the salty tang from the pickle barrels and the sweet aroma from a row of tobacco jars. A glass case filled with penny candy—now selling for a dime—occupied the space near the door. There were shelves of various dry goods, racks of parkas and ski clothing. The jars of coffee beans were behind the cash register.

"Can I help you?"

"I thought this was a restaurant," he said, feeling foolish. "I was looking for a cup of coffee."

"Got some right here." The smiling woman behind the counter poured coffee into a paper cup from a thermos she kept under the counter.

"I didn't mean... Well, thank you," he said, accepting the paper cup. "How much do I owe you?"

"No charge. Compliments of Auntie Maud's." The woman's gaze flicked to his driving cap. "You're Alice Sage's son-in-law, aren't you?"

Finally he understood. It was his driving cap. That's how they were recognizing him. Maybe that's what Wes Pierce had been trying to tell him. Before the woman behind the counter could advise him on his love life, he inquired about the coffee.

"You're drinking plain ole Folger's. I carry the beans for bulk buyers, but for personal use I just buy a can at City Market. Less trouble."

Though the selection was limited, he bought a pound of French Roast and a pound of vanilla-flavored beans, then he selected a couple of sticks of penny candy for the kids. Deliberately he kept the conversation focused firmly on coffee.

"Aspen Springs could use a good coffee shop," the woman agreed. Her name was Jennifer Woodly. "Art Friedy was talking about putting in a coffee place last year, but then he and Jean moved to Phoenix because their little boy had asthma so bad. So nothing came of it, but—"

"Thank you very much," he interrupted, making a show of consulting his watch. "I have to run."

"Right. Brownies should be letting out any time now."

It wasn't until he was parked in front of the Scout leader's house that he realized Jennifer Woodly had guessed where he was going.

"Dammit," he muttered. He didn't know how Penny and Alice tolerated the whole damn town's knowing their every move. First thing tomorrow, he would buy a pair of jeans, a jean jacket, and a baseball cap or a ski cap. Maybe if he looked like a local, people wouldn't notice him.

One thing was certain. The easiest job in Aspen Springs had to belong to the sheriff. Tracking down a suspect's moves would be as simple as following a string.

"Hi, Daddy!" Amy's braids fell forward as she rushed up to the car window. Penny had tied the ends with little bows to match Amy's Brownie uniform. "I got a new badge!"

Leaning, he opened the door for her and made a production of inspecting the new badge. "Not bad. What did you have to do to earn this?"

He listened carefully as Amy explained in excruciating detail exactly how she had earned the badge. Her excitement and expression were like nectar for the spirit. How many small wonderful events had he missed in the past because he had been too busy? Looking at his daughter, he realized how quickly she was growing. One day the golden braids would be swept into prom curls. Her figure would blossom and her legs lengthen. She would start talking about boys and college and a career and a home of her own.

He hoped to God he would be there to see the changes as they occurred, to share in her triumphs and disappointments. The very real possibility that he wouldn't be turned his expression grim.

"YOU LOOK TIRED," Dr. Adler said, raising a silvery eyebrow. "Are you getting enough rest?"

"I haven't been sleeping well," Penny admitted, swinging her legs over the side of the examining table.

"Are you sleeping on your side? One leg straight, the other bent?"

"If I don't know the routine by now, I never will," she answered, smiling.

"So what's the problem?" Dr. Adler asked, leaning back against the sink. "Are you worrying about John? Work? The kids?"

"All of the above." She touched her fingertips to her forehead and sighed. "It seems everyone wants to tell me how I should run my life."

"What do you want to do?"

"I don't know," she said, looking at him between her fingers. Doctor William Adler was a handsome man approaching sixty. Silvery white hair and mustache, a tall quiet bearing. Thirty-two years ago, he had delivered her. "John couldn't have come at a worse time. We're approaching record crowds at Santa's Village and it's only going to get worse. I just don't need any distractions right now."

"How are the kids coping?"

"Better than I am." Amy and Flash had swiftly adjusted to having John back in their lives. They adored sharing their basement quarters with him. She heard them in the mornings laughing and shouting; heard them romping together when she arrived home early enough in the evenings. At times she had an uncomfortable feeling that she was becoming an outsider. The family had subtly shifted into a different configuration.

"They seem to think everything is solved and John is here to stay. Alice is no better. Everything she says indicates she assumes John and I will get back together." Tilting her head, she stared at the ceiling. "I'm feeling pressured on all fronts. Pressured to make a decision I thought was already made. Pressured to compromise. Pressured to give in. Pressured at work. Pressured at home."

"We can remove one of those pressures. I'd like you to stop working about the third week in December."

Her head snapped down and she stared. "Not possible. I can't. That's going to be our busiest time at the Village. Lydie would kill me if I took a leave then. Allenby would go into cardiac arrest. I'd be letting everyone down." Sliding from the table, she reached for her coat. "Is it dangerous for me to continue working?"

"No," Dr. Adler said slowly. "You're healthy, the baby's healthy. I suppose you could continue working right up to the moment John drives you to the hospital. But if you can manage it, I'd advise you to consider taking a leave of absence a couple of weeks before your due date. The rest will do you good."

"Maybe after Christmas," she said to appease him. More likely she would continue to work up to the moment baby Whosit started knocking at the door. The week between Christmas and New Year's was traditionally the Village's busiest week.

Alice stood when Penny emerged from the examining room and smiled at Dr. Adler. "Well, Bill, does she get a clean bill of health?"

"Clean as a new whistle. This girl should have ten children. She makes it look easy," he said, smiling. "You look especially nice today, Alice."

Penny looked up from the counter where she was writing a check. Alice did look especially nice. Her hair was softly curled, and her makeup had been applied with special care. She wore a jersey dress the same energetic color as her eyes. But there was something peculiar about her today. She seemed to have developed a tic in her left eye, which made it look as if she were winking. And she was making strange gestures with her hands, until she saw Penny was watching. Then she brought her hands up to her face and studied her fingernails.

"Alice, are you feeling all right?" Penny asked as they walked to the car.

"Never better. Why?"

"You've been acting a little strange lately."

"Good heavens! I can't think what you mean."

"You seem distracted, like your mind is a thousand miles away. Remember last week when you put your car keys in the freezer? And a few minutes ago, you were winking like crazy. If I didn't know better, I'd swear you were flirting with Dr. Adler," she teased.

"Take my arm. I don't want you to fall."

"For heaven's sake, the pavement is dry as a desert. I'm not going to fall."

"Your exercise class is tonight, isn't it?"

"You're changing the subject, but yes. Why?"

"Oh, nothing. Just that John mentioned he would like to go with you..."

"What?" She stopped in her tracks. "I begged him to go with me when I was pregnant with Amy. Asked him when I was pregnant with Flash. He was always working. Now he wants to go?"

"That's what he said."

Her eyes narrowed. "Did you suggest it?"

"Haven't you noticed John's been reading your pregnancy books?"

She hadn't. "I don't think John has read anything except the *Wall Street Journal* in years. As far as I know, the only thing he knows about pregnancy is how women get that way. This has to indicate a new level of boredom."

"Or a new high of interest."

They slid into the car and Penny switched on the ignition. "I'm not being fair," she said with a sigh. "John's always been interested in my pregnancies. He just didn't have time to pursue it. But he insisted on being in the delivery room when Amy and Flash were born. And he was wonderful." She bit her lip.

"He's trying, Penny."

Another sigh compressed her chest. "I know," she whispered.

"I DON'T KNOW if it's a good idea to have dinner with you," she said, intending the comment as a mild tease. "Look what happened to me the last time we did this.''

Immediately she regretted the reference, as memories assailed her. She remembered soft candlelight and a twinkling view of Los Angeles. Remembered long looks over the candle's flame, a brush of fingertips that set her skin on fire. Then the mad dash back to her hotel room and the urgency of their lovemaking. Their hunger had surprised them both. It seemed they could not get enough of one another. A rush of crimson stained her cheeks as the images flashed through her memory.

''It was a beautiful night,'' John said in a low voice, guessing what she was thinking. ''You were so lovely. You wore a green silk dress, remember?''

She remembered, but she was astonished that he did. ''Good heavens,'' she murmured, staring at him. ''Is it possible I was married to a romantic all those years and didn't know it?''

A groan accompanied his smile. ''Ouch. I'm wounded. Do you mean to say you've forgotten the notes I used to leave you?''

Whenever he departed for work before she did, he'd left a note on the counter by the coffeepot where she would find it first thing when she came downstairs for her morning coffee. Usually the notes were brief, a quick ''I love you,'' followed by what time he expected to be home that evening. Maybe a request to pick up the cleaning or a reminder that they were having dinner out. Sometimes the notes apologized for an argument, sometimes they gave rave reviews of the night before. But always they ended with ''I love you.'' During all the years of their marriage, he had never once forgotten to leave her a note.

The first morning she'd awakened in Aspen Springs without a note had devastated her. She had stared at the spot in front of the coffeepot where the note should have been, then her knees had collapsed. She'd sat at the kitchen table, buried her head in her hands and wept.

Clearing her throat now, she poked at her pizza. ''Odd, but I never thought of the notes as romantic. I considered them a thoughtful gesture. In retrospect, you're right. It was romantic.'' It seemed so obvious now. Now that she had no notes and no romance in her life.

The waiter appeared with coffee and removed the pizza tray.

''Penny, everyone in this crazy town wants to know if I'm making progress with you.'' Reaching across the checkered tablecloth, he took her hand in his. ''Where do things stand? Is it time to have another serious talk?''

She hesitated. ''No matter what happens between us, you're going to stay until the baby is born, aren't you?''

''Of course.'' One eyebrow tilted in surprise. ''I was there for Amy's and Flash's births. I don't want to miss this one.''

Her instinct was to ask him to reconsider. But in some secret part of her heart she wasn't sure if that was really what she wanted. The thought of going through labor and delivery alone overwhelmed her.

''Penny?'' Lowering his head, he tried to see her face. ''Have you been thinking about things? About us?''

''It isn't that I don't care about you, John,'' she whispered.

''Thank God. I was worried that—''

''But loving someone isn't enough.'' She raised her head and met his eyes. ''Maybe love solves everything in the storybooks, but in real life it doesn't work that way.''

''It's a good starting place.''

''We've shared a lot of ups and downs. You're the father of my children. And I'll always love you for that, but...''

''I love you for the same reasons, Penny, and there's nothing wrong with those reasons. Maybe neither of us is sure right now exactly what they're feeling. But love based on habit and history isn't such a bad thing. It's a start.''

''John, we grew apart. We're not the same people we were back when. You and I want very different things out of life. Loving each other isn't going to change our personal goals or make our differences easier to live with.'' Dropping her head, she pulled her hand from his and twisted her wedding ring on her finger. ''Look. You have a right to live wherever you please and work until you collapse, if that's what you want to do. I have that right, too. But I've reached the conclusion that neither of us has the right to inflict our wants and needs on the other."

"Surely two people who care about each other can find a compromise..."

The tenderness in his gaze wounded her. "We tried. And we failed. There's no compromise on this issue. All there can be is surrender. One of us gives up entirely. And that's not fair to either of us."

"The stakes are high, Penny. If we proceed with the divorce, I lose my children. I can't stand the thought of losing Amy and Flash."

They stared at each other across the table. "Every time you say something like that," Penny whispered, "I feel so guilty I want to cry. That isn't fair, John. We're both to blame for things going wrong."

"I'm not blaming you for anything. Please believe that. But the truth is the stakes are higher for me than for you. If we proceed with the divorce, you lose a husband. I lose a wife and my children. Penny, I can't stand the thought of losing Amy and Flash."

"I don't know what to say. I...I'm sorry it has to be that way."

"Well," he said after a lengthy silence. "At least you've admitted you still care about me."

"Please John. Remember what I said. Love isn't enough. Love isn't going to dissolve our obstacles or make them easier to bear. That's the tragedy of this whole mess." The ever present tears that seemed to plague her lately stung her eyelids. "I think we're going to be one of those couples who love each other, but who can't live together."

"I hope not. That sounds terrible," he said quietly.

She drew a breath and swallowed the tight lump in her throat. "We're going to be late for class." Pressing her hands on the table edge, she struggled up from her seat and blinked at her watch. "Are you sure you want to do this?"

Smiling, he helped her on with her coat. "I can't imagine you doing a workout. Jogging, yes. One, two, three, kick—no."

"You can say that again," she said, making herself return his smile. "I am definitely a runner. I run to work, run around Santa's Village, run here, run there." A sigh accompanied her smile. "Running has become my sport."

The exercise class was held in a meeting room above Dr. Adler's clinic. Nearly everyone had arrived when Penny began introducing John to the other prospective parents.

"You're just the man I've been hoping to meet," Dan Driver said, shaking John's hand. "I'm the President of the Optimists Club. We're hosting a pancake supper Saturday. The reason I've been eager to meet you is that I have it on good authority—your daughter to my daughter—that you're quite the cook. Is that true?"

"Not since college," John said. Immediately he liked Dan Driver. Driver reminded him of a Viking, tall and golden, fierce-looking until he smiled. "Actually, I'm a banker."

"Dammit, just my luck." Driver groaned. "We're short-handed in the kitchen for Saturday and I was hoping to coerce you into lending a hand. No one else is a cook, either. God knows what those pancakes are going to taste like."

"Actually…I'd be glad to help out," he heard himself say. He turned his head in time to see Penny's look of astonishment. It was no greater than his own. He could not believe what he had just done. As if Dan Driver suspected he was about to withdraw the impulsive offer, Driver backed away toward his wife.

"Great! I'll call you tomorrow with the details."

"I can't believe I did that," John marveled as he followed Penny to the exercise mat and helped her sit down.

"I can't, either. You must be bored out of your mind."

"You're right about that."

Except he wasn't. Not exactly. At first he had thought he was bored. Bored with Aspen Springs and a pace a snail would consider too slow. But he had thought about it carefully last night when he couldn't sleep, and he realized it wasn't the town or the pace he found boring as much as the inactivity. When he examined that realization, he had to admit the fault did not lie with Aspen Springs as much as with himself. His constant phone calls to his office and creating make-work projects to fill the day were forcing him to realize that Penny was probably right about his being a workaholic. He needed something constructive to do.

"Good evening, class. Everyone feeling okay?" Greta Ecklund, the instructor, bustled into the room and tossed her coat on a table. "Doing your exercises at home?"

"Are you?" John whispered, looking down at Penny. She lay on her back on the mat, her reddish-gold hair spread around her head like a halo.

She gazed up at him. "Yes. Alice helps me."

"Okay, class. You know the drill. Let's hop to a few knee thrusts."

Doing as the other fathers-to-be did, John moved forward on the mat to kneel in front of Penny's feet as she pulled her legs up. "What am I supposed to do?"

"Place your hands on the outsides of my knees. When I push my knees apart, you're supposed to provide a little resistance."

If she hadn't been eight months pregnant, her position on the mat would have been intensely sexual. She was lying back, her knees drawn up, her eyes closed and her lips parted. He stared at her soft expression, at the graceful arch of her throat, and thought she was the most beautiful woman he had ever seen.

When he placed his hands against her knees, it was a caress, not the resistance she had requested.

Her knees flopped apart easily and she lifted her head to glare at him. The moment she saw his expression, her own expression altered. For a moment their eyes held, then she lowered her head and closed her lashes. "Let's try it again," she murmured in a throaty voice.

He could feel the warmth of her skin beneath her sweat pants as he pressed his hands firmly to her knees. Tiny beads of sweat appeared on Penny's temples as they continued the exercise. He felt sweat appear on his own brow, but not for the same reason.

"Okay, class. Good. Now we're going to practise breathing

and working with labor discomfort. Fathers, pay attention, please. Some women enjoy stroking during the phase before delivery. They find it calming and relaxing. Other women can't bear to be touched. Right now there is no way to predict which your wife will prefer. So we're going to practice stroking so you'll know how to do it."

"Oh boy," Penny groaned. "I forgot about this part."

"This is the part I think I'm going to like," John whispered back, smiling down at her. Her face was moist from exercising, the way it usually was after lovemaking. Her fingers trembled slightly until she laced them together over her stomach.

"All right, ladies. Begin your breathing routine. Gentlemen, we're going to start at her shoulders and work our way down."

Watching what the other fathers did, John leaned over Penny and gently massaged her shoulder, feeling the tension beneath his fingertips. "Is that too hard?" he asked her. It was an old joke between them.

"It's never too hard," she whispered, smiling beneath closed lashes. "Feels good."

When he felt the tension relax in her shoulder, he stroked her arm. Because he felt an urgency to touch her skin, he opened the cuff at her wrist and slid his hand up the inside of her sleeve—and drew a breath at the remembered soft touch of her. Penny opened her eyes and gave him a drowsy look midway between pleasure and a frown.

Next, still following the other fathers' lead, he ran his hand from her throat to her thigh, barely touching her, tracing the curving outline of her body with his palm.

She drew a breath, almost a gasp, and opened her eyes.

"That's right," Greta Ecklund said above them, startling them. "Make love to her. Gently, softly." She grinned. "I can see how you two got pregnant. Keep breathing, Penny. Slow, even. Do the count."

When Greta moved on to the next couple, John placed his hands on Penny's thighs and stroked down to her calves. He wasn't certain if she was trembling or if the tremble was in his own fingers. Moving to her feet, he slipped off her canvas shoes and gently worked her foot between his hands. He placed that foot against his stomach and took the other. Penny made a small sound and he looked up to see her bite her lip and turn her head.

Reappearing, Greta Ecklund knelt beside John and gestured him up between Penny's legs. She took his hands and placed them gently but firmly on Penny's stomach. "Move with the contractions. In and down. Stroke her, relax her."

"Oh, my God," he gasped, his eyes widening. "The baby moved!" He blinked at Greta, then turned his astonishment to Penny. "It moved! Did you feel that?"

She laughed and threw out her hands. "This baby has a dozen fists and feet. You bet I felt it."

"What does it feel like from your side?" he asked, his hands on her rounded stomach. He had forgotten the stroking in the wonder of the tiny thrust against his palm. He could have remained like this, frozen, his hands on her taut flesh all night, waiting for the next sign of a miracle.

"It feels like...I can't explain it...like a tiny spinning pinwheel, maybe. Or maybe, less romantically, like gas." She smiled up at him, enjoying his wonder. "Too bad we can't trade places."

"It did it again!" His dark eyes widened. "Good Lord, Penny." He stared at her. "We're going to have a baby!"

"One of us is," she said, smiling. "And she needs to breathe."

After class they drove home in comfortable silence, enclosed within the dark warmth of the car. Underlying the comfort and silence was a deep awareness of each other. In other circumstances, the intense awareness would have expressed itself sexually. Now the sexual electricity transmuted to tenderness and a deeply shared sense of intimacy that extended beyond any need for words. It was the nicest moment they had shared since John's arrival, and he treasured it.

When he opened the door to help her out of the car, he regretted the end of the drive.

"It's getting frosty," she said. Lifting her chin from the collar of her coat, she looked at him, then slipped past and hurried toward the porch.

"Well, I'll be damned." Tonight was made for marvels. A swirl of snowflakes danced out of the black sky and eddied through the light shining from the yard pole. "The Indian did it!"

Alice was waiting when they came up the stairs. She had changed into a pair of designer jeans and a creamy sweater, which struck Penny as peculiar. Usually by this time of night, Alice was wearing her robe and slippers. "Shhh," Alice said, placing a finger across her lips. "The kids are finally asleep, I think. They wanted to wait up for you. Anyone ready for a drink or some coffee?"

Penny hesitated, then glanced at John and shook her head. "Thanks, but I'll pass. I think I'll turn in early."

He felt the same. He didn't want anything to interfere with the warmth he was feeling right now, he wanted to hold it close as long as he could. Taking her hands, he looked down into her face, her soft blue eyes.

"Thank you for tonight," he said, meaning it. They had shared something very special.

Then, wonder of wonders, she raised her arms and embraced him wordlessly. That is, she tried to. Her fingertips reached his shoulders, the curve of her stomach pressed against his abdomen.

"That's about as close as I can get," she said, smiling. "Thank you, John. It was a nice evening."

She could have gotten closer for a better hug, she thought as she undressed and creamed her face. But it would have meant leaning forward at an awkward angle and pushing out her fanny. Not a pretty sight from Alice's interested viewpoint.

It had probably been a mistake to hug John at all. But the moment had felt right. It would have been wrong not to end the evening with an embrace.

Once in bed, she touched the empty pillow next to hers and tried not to think of his hands stroking, caressing her. Not easy for a woman who had not been kissed in eight months.

God, she missed him. The situation was impossible.

AFTER SAYING GOOD-NIGHT to Alice, John descended the stairs into the hushed basement. First he looked in on Amy and pulled up her blankets against the cold night. Light from the doorway gleamed on her braids and turned them the color of spun gold. The faint scent of Ivory soap lingered on her cheek when he bent to kiss her.

"Did you and Mommy have a good time?" she whispered as her arms stole around his neck.

"The best. What are you doing still awake?"

"We wanted to see if the snow dance worked."

He tucked her in, smoothed back her bangs. "Sure did. It's snowing now."

"I knew the dance would work," she murmured drowsily. "I love you, Daddy."

"I love you, too," he whispered.

When he entered the room he shared with Flash, he stood beside the bed for a moment looking down at his son's freckled cheeks, the tousled gold hair so like Penny's. *My cup runneth over,* he thought, feeling his throat tighten.

Then he raised his eyes to the top bunk and a rueful smile touched his lips. As long as he was sleeping in a bunk bed, his cup didn't quite runneth over, after all.

After stripping off his clothes, he climbed the rungs at the end of the bed, pulled back the covers, then, shivering, he crawled inside.

Then he swore and leapt out of bed as if he had been shot.

Jumping to the floor, he grabbed his pants and stepped into them, then flipped on the light and stared at his son who was trying hard to feign sleep.

"Okay, Flash. I know you're awake. What's going on here?" Anger firmed his voice. He tossed back the blankets on the top bunk and ran a hand over the sheets. "Flash? I want an explanation."

His bed was wet from the pillow to the center. Thoroughly wet. Soaking wet and cold.

"Gee, Daddy, what's wrong? I don't know anything about any water." Sitting up, Flash blinked at him.

Amy appeared in the doorway, rubbing her eyes with an exaggerated movement. "What's all the noise?"

He looked at them. Innocence in flannel. "All right. What happened here. Why is my bed soaked?"

"Soaked?" They both looked at his bunk with dumbstruck expressions, which he didn't believe for a minute. "We don't know how it happened, Daddy."

"That bed didn't get soaked by itself."

Flash looked at Amy. Amy looked at Flash. Then they said in unison. "I guess you'll have to sleep with Mommy."

Now he understood. A breath of air rushed from his lungs and his anger vanished as quickly as it had come. He didn't know whether to give in to the laugh building in his chest or the sorrow constricting his throat.

"Listen, fellas," he said finally, sitting on the edge of Flash's bed. He opened his arm for Amy. "I understand what you're trying to do, and I love you for it." The warmth of their small bodies pressed against his sides, and he wondered how he could ever have let them go. "I know you're trying to help, but this is something Mommy and I have to work out alone."

"You aren't going to sleep with Mommy?" Amy's voice was heavy with disappointment.

"No, I'll take the sofa tonight." He pressed her close. "Sleeping with Mommy is a decision she and I will have to make together. Understand?" He looked at each of them, knowing they didn't, couldn't understand.

"I'm sorry," Flash said.

"Me, too."

"It's okay. All's forgiven." Standing, he tucked Flash's covers beneath his chin. "Just no more water in my bed. Don't do it again, all right?"

"Okay." Flash kissed him. "Did all the ice cubes melt?"

"Ice cubes? Good grief."

After tucking Amy in, he found the extra blankets on the closet shelf and headed for the lumpy-looking basement sofa. He had believed nothing could be worse than being banished to a bunk bed at the North Pole.

He had been wrong. A wet bunk bed was worse. And the sofa was almost as bad.

Because he couldn't find a comfortable spot, he kept waking through the night. Sometime around three in the morning, he could have sworn he heard a car in the driveway followed by a bump on the side of the house. Sitting up in the darkness, he waited, straining to hear. When nothing further happened and he heard only the silence of a deep snowy night, he lay down again and thought about Penny sleeping in a dry warm bed upstairs. Alone. For one crazy instant he thought about…

No. Patience was the key here. Lifting himself up on an elbow, he dug one of Flash's toy cars out of the cushions and dropped it on the floor, then sought a comfortable position. If there was one, he didn't find it.

Chapter Five

Dear Santa,
Please bring me a million bucks then I'll buy my own toys and it won't be so heavy for you to carry. I also want a savings account and a machine gun that makes noise.

Be good,
Winston B. Tarkington II

Smiling, Penny placed the letter in the pile she was setting aside to be printed in the Village newsletter.

Dear Santa,
If you're real then you already know what I want for Christmas. You also know who this is from.

That one went into the undecided pile.

Dear Santa,
Please bring me a six-pack of valium and a quart of aspirin.

Desperately,
Dennis's mother

Penny laughed out loud. Every mother had "valium days" as Lydie called them. Days when she looked at her kids and wished someone had told her that adorable little babies grew into occasional Excedrin headaches. Deciding that she wasn't stalwart enough to shatter illusions, Penny placed the letter from Dennis's mother in the Do Not Print file.

Dear Santa,
My name is Jimmy Asquith and I live at 347 Lariat Loop Drive in the second house. I am eight and a half and I have two sisters. Please bring me lots of good stuff. How is Rudolph? You don't have to bring my sisters any stuff. Ha. Ha. I want a rocket racer and a space-ship the most. Say hi to Rudolph and Frosty.

Jimmy Asquith

This one also went to the print pile.

Dear Santa,
If you can please bring me a warm coat and some shoes for Billy and pills for mama and if you can please bring us a daddy because we need one awful bad we don't mind if you can't come this year either that's okay but it would be nice if you did and if you wanted to leave us some tuna or Spam that would be nice too but I like soup better I hope that doesn't make you mad.

Love,
Mary Sealy

The last was the kind of letter that wrenched her heart. She never got used to them; they were always a shock. After reaching her secretary on the intercom, she asked Helen to add Mary Sealy's name to the list of people they would try to locate. Usually it wasn't difficult, for the elf at the admissions booth asked everyone to sign in with an address. But occasionally a letter like Mary Sealy's came through and they couldn't track her down. Penny hoped they would find Mary Sealy and that Mary's mother would allow Santa's Village to give the Sealy family a merry Christmas.

"Hi," Lydie said, poking her head in the door. "Ready for the walk-around?"

"Yes." Penny looked up and dropped her fingers from her temple.

"Doing the Santa letters?" Lydie asked with sympathy.

"Some of them rip your heart out." After rolling her chair back, Penny placed her palms on her desk and hoisted herself up.

Lydie stared. "Am I imagining it or are you swelling up by the minute? I swear you look twice as big as you did last week! That's an awning you're wearing, isn't it?"

"Fashions from Seaworld," Penny said, smiling. "We whales are into wool and plaid this season." She pressed a hand to the small of her back and suppressed a groan. "Let me dash into the bathroom, then I'll be ready."

"I can make the rounds alone if your back is aching."

"And let you score points with Allenby? Not a chance. Just give me a minute." Logic told her she didn't need to go to the bathroom; she had been there five minutes earlier. But at this stage, she never knew if the sense of urgency was real or a false alarm. The situation did nothing for her confidence.

"And you keep saying you don't want the promotion," Lydie said when Penny emerged and slipped into her coat. "If that's true, then I'm the Church Lady."

"You, the Church Lady?" Penny grinned. "Not likely. But I'm too tired and pregnant to argue."

They passed through the administration offices and stepped out onto Main Street. It was still snowing, creating a Christmas idyll. The Village resembled a scene on a Victorian Christmas card. Penny frowned at the cobbled streets. "One of us needs to speak to the snow-removal supervisor. We don't need any icy patches."

Lydie tightened a scarf around her throat. "Someone should find that crazy Indian and make him do a dance to stop this. It's snowed thirteen inches in the last four days. Enough is enough."

"The ski people are ecstatic."

They paused in front of the sled runs and listened to the

whoops of laughter darting down the hill. Bright parkas flashed over the new snow.

"Did I see Amy and Flash and your ex here earlier today?" Lydia asked as they turned toward the ice-skating rink.

"John brought the kids over for the works. Sledding, skating, games and lunch with Daddy."

"How's that going?" When she realized her attempt to sound casual had failed, Lydie laughed. "Okay, it's none of my business. But I want to know."

Penny ducked her head and watched for ice patches. "I don't know, Lydie. I'm so confused I can't think anymore."

"Have you talked to your attorney?"

"If you're asking if I've stopped the divorce proceedings, no, I haven't."

"Maybe you haven't noticed, kiddo, but it looks like John is here to stay. Next Thursday is Thanksgiving. He's been here three weeks."

"Thanksgiving already?" Where did the time go? Now that she thought about it she remembered noticing crayoned Pilgrims and turkeys clamped to the refrigerator door. It seemed only yesterday the door had been plastered with pumpkins and witches.

They stepped inside the North Pole and inspected the lines of eager children waiting to climb onto Santa's lap and whisper secrets in his ear.

"Kurt has started drinking again," Lydie mentioned quietly.

"Oh, no," Penny groaned. Narrowing her eyes, she stared at Santa, looking for signs of anything out of the ordinary.

"He seems okay today. But last night he smelled heavily of bourbon and mouthwash." Lydie shrugged. "Much as I hate it, I thing we're going to have to start looking for a new Santa."

"Has Allenby talked to him?"

"A hundred times. As you know, Kurt's the greatest Santa a kid could wish for. He's terrific from January to Thanksgiving. Then he starts drinking. He's one of those people who gets depressed about the real Christmas."

"This is the first time I've ever understood getting depressed at Christmas,'' Penny said, making a face. ''I don't know how I'm going to find time for it.''

''Speaking of which, a huge shipment of toys came in this morning for the Toy Factory. Allenby wants everybody to work late tonight. We've got to inventory the stuff and get it on the shelves.''

''Tonight?'' Penny stopped at the door. ''John's helping out at the Optimist's pancake supper. We were all going to go.''

''Tell them to bring you a doggie bag. If we get out of here before ten o'clock, I'll be amazed.''

IT WAS A QUARTER TO ELEVEN when Penny got home. The car slid in the driveway and plowed into the snowdrift that had formed across the front of the garage. Common sense demanded she put the car in reverse and rock it out of the drift so she wouldn't be stuck the next day. But she was too exhausted to make the effort.

''I'm home,'' she called as she hung her cap and coat on the entry-hall pegs, speaking softly so she wouldn't disturb Amy and Flash. But they were still awake.

Amy ran to the stairs as Penny gripped the banister and pulled herself up. ''Mommy, Mommy! You should have seen Daddy!''

Flash caught her free hand. His dark eyes sparkled up at her. ''Daddy tossed the pancakes in the air! One of them stuck on the ceiling!''

''Lulu Henner ate so many pancakes, she threw up! You should have been there, Mommy. It was great!''

''I wish I could have been.'' John and Alice were drinking coffee in the kitchen. Amy and Flash climbed on their chairs in front of milk and cookies as Penny took a cup from the hook and poured a coffee. With a sigh, she sat down and pressed her aching back against the wooden rungs of the chair. Summoning a smile, she looked at John. ''I gather the pancake supper was a success?''

''It was terrific.''

She wouldn't have known it from his expression.

''John was the hit of the evening,'' Alice said quickly. ''I didn't know how talented your husband is. He flipped pancakes behind his back, over his shoulder. Put on quite a show. How much did the Optimists raise, John?"

"About eighteen hundred dollars."

Alice beamed. "Gladys Syshell was in tears. She hugged everyone, especially John, and said the money would help tide them over until their house can be rebuilt."

"I'm glad it was a success," Penny said uncertainly. She didn't understand why John looked so glum. "It's way past the kids' bedtime, isn't it?"

"They wanted to see their mother," he said, meeting her eyes. "I thought it would be nice if you tucked them in for a change. None of us realized you would be this late."

His voice was carefully neutral, but the implied criticism stung. "I'm sorry, but this is the busiest time of year at the Village. If I could have gotten home earlier I would have."

"Exactly when was the last time you were home in time to tuck the kids in?" John's voice remained even, but she saw the accusation in his steady gaze.

"Oh, wait a minute." Leaning forward, she narrowed her eyes and clenched her fists. "Don't talk to me about not being there. You wrote the book on the subject." He flinched, then his mouth tightened. "I'm doing the best I can, okay? This is a temporary situation. I don't like it, either, but there's not much I can do about it right now."

Her feet hurt, her back hurt, she had to go to the bathroom, and pain throbbed behind her temples. She didn't need a case of the guilts. But of course that was what she was feeling. And she had felt it long before John said anything. But surely he didn't think she preferred this killer schedule. Did he imagine she enjoyed bending over boxes, marking prices, arranging displays? Didn't he realize she would far rather have been with her family at the pancake supper?

"There are people here who need you, too," John said sharply.

"That's not fair!"

"Please don't fight," Amy begged. Tears welled in her

large blue eyes. Flash lowered his glass, leaving a milk mustache behind. He looked at them with a stricken expression.

Oh, Lord. Fresh barbs of guilt pierced Penny's heart. Reaching, she smoothed Flash's hair and drew Amy to her side.

"We're not fighting," she lied. "Look, fellas, I'm sorry I've been gone so much lately," she murmured against the top of Amy's head. "Things will slow down soon, then we'll see more of each other."

"It's okay," Amy said, laying her head against Penny's stomach. "Daddy's a real good tucker-inner. We don't mind."

Flash nodded solemnly, his dark eyes large above the mustache.

Their loyalty constricted Penny's throat. Ignoring her aching back and pounding head, she stood and took her children's hands. "Come on, you two. Let's brush teeth and put on jammies, and I'll read you a story before you to go to sleep."

"Great!"

Ignoring the silence from John and Alice, she led the children downstairs. And she tried to ignore the hurt when Flash or Amy told her she wasn't reading the story right. Daddy growled in this place, or Daddy tickled them in that place, and Daddy made faces and funny voices. After turning off the lights, she paused, listening to the warm silence. She would be very glad when the December push ended and life returned to normal.

When she emerged upstairs it was after midnight. Alice had tactfully called it a night and had gone to bed, but John was waiting.

"Can we talk a minute?" he asked.

Marching past him, she entered the kitchen and poured a glass of juice, then leveled a steady look over the counter top. "I don't want this to happen again, John. Please don't start an argument in front of the kids."

"I apologize. I was wrong to bring it up in front of Amy and Flash. But the point is valid." Taking one of the counter stools, he sat down and folded his arms. Choosing his words, he continued, "Believe it or not, I understand your position. As you pointed out, I've been there."

Biting her lower lip, she turned toward the dark window.

"Since I've been in Aspen Springs, our positions have reversed. We've been given an opportunity to see each other's perspective. What I'm starting to see is that everything you used to say about my hours was right on target. What I don't understand is why you're putting yourself through this. Wasn't the whole point of moving here to slow down? To spend more time with the kids?"

"What are you suggesting, John? That a woman's place is in the home?"

"Come on, Penny, you know better than that. I've never objected to your working."

"Really?" Her gaze narrowed. "You could fool me. It seems you don't miss an opportunity to make some remark about me rushing off to work or getting home late. If you're not objecting to my job, then what exactly are you trying to say?"

His eyes darkened. "It seems to me this particular job makes excessive demands on your time that doesn't fit your original goals, not as you explained them to me."

"What I can't seem to make you understand is the present situation is temporary." She thrust a hand through her hair and wondered if it would appear she was dodging the argument if she dashed to the bathroom. "The demands on my time will slow abruptly after the first of the year."

"Really? I doubt that. Especially if you win the promotion Alice says you're hoping for."

"I hope Alice also told you I don't plan to accept the promotion if it's offered. I've kept my name in the running solely to discover if I could have had the promotion if I wanted it."

It was obvious he didn't fully believe her, but he chose not to pursue the issue. "There's something I'd like you to think about, Penny." Standing, he moved toward the basement stairs. "If you're going to continue this pace and this lifestyle, it's a waste to do it here. Come home to Los Angeles and let's do it together. Emil would love to have you back at Blackman Brothers."

"The present pace is *not* going to continue!" she called to the top of his head as he disappeared down the stairs. "This is only *temporary*!"

There was no way to know if he heard. With the children and her mother in the house, the argument had been conducted in whispers.

Tense with frustration, Penny stomped up the stairs and into her bedroom. She was beginning to understand why divorced women got a mad gleam in their eyes when they talked about their ex-husbands. Some men heard only what they wanted to hear.

IT AMUSED JOHN TO REALIZE what he had said to Penny was true. They had switched traditional roles. Every morning she rushed off to work, while he called his office, then worked through a list of domestic chores to keep himself from going bananas. On the days Alice worked at the library, he cleaned up the breakfast mess, made the beds—except Penny's—tossed some laundry into the washing machine and ran the vacuum if the carpet looked as if it needed going over. He picked the kids up from school, supervised their homework, made them clean up their supper plates, monitored their TV watching. Gradually he had taken over the household errands. He took in the cleaning, did the shopping.

Now, as he pushed his grocery cart up and down the aisles of City Market shopping for Thanksgiving dinner, he admitted he enjoyed taking an active role in family life, but he also felt a little itchy. He craved the stimulation of a good old hostile takeover. Or did he? Was that really true? Frowning, he wondered if he was genuinely missing Blackman Brothers, or if his restlessness stemmed solely from a lack of challenging activity.

Reaching for a bag of prepared stuffing, he examined the label, then replaced the bag on the shelf. He would make the stuffing from scratch.

Actually, he wasn't entirely inactive. He was keeping up with his client list, checking in every day. Staying current with the news and the markets. Reading the journals. He made the daily post office run. But it wasn't enough. He missed working.

At odds with this realization was an uncomfortable suspicion that he had reached a crossroad in his career. After this vacation he would return to the same frenzied pace, the same unrelenting emphasis on the bottom line, the same cynical attitudes. Dog eat dog. Oddly, he hadn't looked at it that way before. Maybe it was time to consider shifting departments.

"Hi, John. Heard you were a smash at the pancake supper."

Looking up from the cranberry bin, he discovered Jennifer Woodly smiling at him from the lettuce display.

"It was fun." He was glad he'd purchased jeans and had hung up his driving cap. Sneaking a look behind him, he noticed several tourist types, flocking into Aspen Springs to take advantage of the new snow. The man behind him, speaking in a heavy Oklahoma accent, wore wool plaid slacks and a driving cap very like John's. Absurdly, he felt a bit superior. He was a quasi-local, whereas the Oklahoman was a tourist.

Jennifer Woodly sidled up to him and spoke from the corner of her mouth. "I know we're all dependent on the tourist trade, but will you look at the coat that guy's wife is wearing?"

John snuck a look behind him, pretending to examine a bin of oranges. The gorgeous woman on the Oklahoman's arm was wearing a calf-length black mink.

"If she wears a coat like that to the grocery store, what do you suppose she wears when she's dressing up to go out?" Jennifer giggled into her hand and nudged John with her shoulder. "Oh, I almost forgot. I ordered the Parisian Cinnamon coffee beans you wanted. They'll be here tomorrow, in time for Thanksgiving. By the way, the crust on my pumpkin pie doesn't brown properly. Any suggestions?"

"Brush the edges with egg white," he said, pleased she had asked his opinion. After double-checking his list, he pushed his cart to the checkout line and found himself parked behind Susan Galloway, who lived on the road below Alice's house.

"Glad I ran into you," Susan said as she placed her grocery items in front of the cashier. "I was going to call today and thank you for picking the boys up from school yesterday."

"It wasn't any trouble. They're nice kids."

She glanced at his cart. "Are you doing the Thanksgiving cooking?"

Smiling, he lifted his hands in innocence. "I'm not a cook, honest. I've done more cooking in the past two weeks than in the past ten years. In real life I'm a banker."

Susan Galloway laughed. "Not in the eyes of this town. Gladys Syshell is spreading the word far and wide that you are the best cook ever seen in these parts. You're one of us now, a dyed-in-the-wool local."

His stock had risen a hundredfold since the pancake supper. Even without his driving cap, people recognized him and insisted on stopping him for a word. The good news was, only a few wanted to discuss his love life; most just thanked him for helping the Syshells. The thanks embarrassed him, but it was better than discussing the sleeping arrangements at Alice's house.

As he loaded the groceries into the Porsche and drove to the post office, he thought how pleasant it was to run into people he knew at the grocery store. The thought brought him up short. First, that he knew enough people in Aspen Springs with whom to exchange greetings, and second, that he found the experience enjoyable.

Worse, he glumly acknowledged he was forming a relationship of sorts with Wes Pierce. When he emerged from the post office, he did so slowly, waiting for Wes to invite him to sit a spell.

Wes eyed him up and down, approving the jeans and fleece-lined jacket. "Looks too spanking new, but better." He nodded at the bench beside him. "If you wash those jeans in bleach a few times, you won't look like such a dude. That's not helping out, mind you, just a comment."

Grinning, John crossed an ankle over his knee and leaned back against the bench, looking out at the snowy square. "Good. I believe we agreed not to interfere, that is, help each other. I'm holding up my end of the deal."

"Heard you put on some razzle-dazzle at the pancake supper. I would have been there, but the missus forgot about it and fixed her famous sauerbraten. Sorry I missed your performance. Heard it was something to see."

"It wasn't that big a thing."

"Yes, it was, son. Nobody expected you to agree to help out. Especially me. Wouldn't have blamed you if you'd taken a pass." He slid a look toward John. "It said a lot that you showed up."

Uncomfortable, John glanced toward the Porsche. He had tied the trunk down over the groceries. What was a wonderful car in the city was wildly impractical in the mountains. One more point in favor of big-city living.

"So. How's the romance coming?"

Though he was glad to change the subject, exasperation brought a frown to John's brow. "I thought we agreed my personal life is strictly my business."

"You agreed. I didn't. I got my reasons for being interested."

One eyebrow lifted. "Really? Mind sharing those reasons?"

"Yep, I do. At this point it doesn't concern you except at the edges."

Straightening, John stared. "Let me understand this. You want to know the intimate details of my personal life, and you have some reason for thinking it's your business to know, but I'm not permitted to learn that reason?"

Wes Pierce grinned. "That's about the size of it, son."

"Does that sound fair to you?"

"Didn't say it was fair. Didn't even say I agreed with it. All I'm saying is this town has its reasons for being interested in what happens between you and Penny."

"The whole town?"

"If you don't mind my saying so, you being the prickly sort, some of us think you're losing ground." Tilting his head, Wes pursed his lips in a speculative gesture. "Maybe you should rethink your tactics, son. Penny was in here yesterday and she did not look like a happy camper. She didn't have that romancy glow, if you take my meaning."

"I don't believe this!" What he didn't believe was his own stupidity in thinking he could sit five minutes with Wes Pierce without getting hot under the collar. "Look, I don't give a damn why this town thinks my business is their business. But you can tell anyone who asks that what goes on between my wife and myself is none of their damned concern!"

"Now that's where you're wrong. But I can understand why you don't see it. And right now you're not supposed to. That's the point."

Because he didn't think he could say another word without losing his temper, John stood up, strode to the Porsche and spun it out of the post office lot.

No one knew better than he that everything came with a price tag. The price tag for knowing enough people with whom to exchange a friendly greeting in the grocery was also knowing people like Wes Pierce, who seemed to believe they had some kind of crazy right to know other people's personal business.

Leaning forward, he patted the dashboard. "Hang in there, old girl. We'll be going home in a month or so."

A month or so. He groaned aloud. A couple of more weeks and everyone in Aspen Springs would know his shoe size and which side of the bed he slept on.

A goldfish had more privacy than the residents of a small town.

ANXIETY GRABBED PENNY when she awoke and saw the bedside clock. Good Lord, she had overslept badly. Throwing back the blankets, she pressed her hands to her stomach and heaved herself sideways. Then she remembered.

It was Thanksgiving. She had the day off. Dropping back to the pillows, she released a blissful sigh and stretched languorously.

"You're awake, too?" she murmured, smiling at a series of small thrusts against her nightgown. Placing her hands against the rising swell of her stomach, she stroked the flannel. Whether or not the motion was soothing to little Whosit, she didn't know, but she liked to think it was.

Each pregnancy was different from the last. With Amy, she had been consumed with every tiny detail. She had read everything she could get her hands on about pregnancy, had poured over books of names, had been unable to talk or think about anything except her impending motherhood. She had started wearing maternity clothes in the third month, before she even had much of a tummy.

When Amy was born, she had fussed like any first-time mother. She had scrubbed walls with disinfectant, given away the cat, sterilized the entire condominium, made John put on a boiled smock before he held the baby.

This lasted until she discovered Amy cheerfully eating a dust bunny Penny's eagle eye had missed. When Amy didn't immediately require emergency treatment, she had wondered if she was overdoing things a bit. Then one day she had tiptoed into the nursery toward the end of Amy's nap and found that her daughter had discovered the contents of her diaper along with an artistic bent. The diaper contents were painted on the crib headboard and on Amy herself. At that point, Penny decided babies were sturdier creatures than she had realized.

She was more relaxed with Flash. She had stopped sterilizing visitors before the end of the first week. The boiled smock had vanished and she made no effort to replace it. Flash ate dust bunnies on a regular basis and thrived.

She peered at her stomach and smiled. "Poor baby. By the time we get to you, I'll be borrowing other people's dust bunnies for your midmorning snack."

Most likely her more relaxed attitude toward this pregnancy was the natural outcome of having been through it before. Not to mention the really lousy timing.

Although she had started by not wanting this baby, she had reconciled herself to the idea. For the most part, anyway. Having a baby at this time in her life was going to complicate things enormously.

It already had. If she hadn't been pregnant, John would have spent a week with the kids, then he would have been on his way back to Los Angeles. He wouldn't be camped in the basement, pressuring for unconditional surrender, and running her emotions through a shredder.

Plus, if she hadn't been pregnant, the possibility of a promotion might have looked different. Certainly, she would have felt more prepared for the hectic schedule between now and the first of the year.

"Poor baby," she said again, stroking her stomach gently. "You're getting shortchanged in this deal."

Unlike her other pregnancies, she hadn't devoted a lot of hours thinking about the new baby. There just hadn't been time. Not with the upheaval of moving to Colorado, filing for divorce, finding and settling into a new job, and all the attendant et ceteras. By this time with Amy and Flash, she had chosen names, had fantasized what they would look like. But this baby didn't seem real. The difference lay in seeing oneself as pregnant or seeing oneself as a mother-to-be. Penny saw herself as pregnant. She couldn't see past that point.

But she definitely saw herself as pregnant, she thought, as she rummaged through her closet seeking something attractive to wear. The rose tent or the green parachute—which was it to be? The striped awning or the plaid sofa cover? Sighing, she eyed a row of belts. Oh, to wear a belt again. Something at the waist that was not elastic. After a spasm of indecision, she chose a pair of cream-colored slacks and a matching sweater that cupped under her tummy.

"That is ghastly," she pronounced, staring at herself in the mirror. "You look like Tweedledum." With emphasis on the dumb. Why hadn't she behaved herself that night in Los Angeles last March?

Because she loved him.

But love wasn't enough. Once she would have argued with anyone who claimed love wasn't enough. Now she knew the truth of it. And the truth hurt.

After a moment she opened her eyes, pulled her hair back and tied it with a green ribbon, threw an emerald-colored scarf around her shoulders, then followed the wonderful aroma wafting from the kitchen.

"Sorry I'm late. I overslept," she said guiltily when she saw preparations for the feast were under way.

"Exactly what we wanted you to do," Alice answered

cheerfully, pouring her a cup of coffee. "We sent Amy in to turn off your alarm. Thought you could use a sleep-in day."

"What can I do to help?"

"Not a thing, madam," John said. Throwing open the oven door with a flourish, he allowed her a peek. "The turkey is stuffed and roasting, the pies are coming along nicely. That wonderful smell is the giblets, slow cooking for gravy."

"Good coffee," she murmured after praising the rich warm scents filling the kitchen.

"Freshly ground." His smile removed any hint of the ongoing coffee-beans-versus-can argument.

"Daddy's doing all the cooking, Mommy," Amy said proudly.

"So what am I?" Alice demanded, hands on her apron-clad hips. "Chopped liver?"

The kids giggled as Alice winked at Penny.

"Actually they're mostly right. John has taken over."

"Good heavens," Penny blinked and smiled. "Send a guy to one pancake supper and he goes berserk."

Laughing, John nodded. Putting on a show for the kids, he did some fancy work over the chopping block, cutting apples for a Waldorf salad. Amy and Flash watched in awed fascination.

"To tell the truth, I'm enjoying this." Scooping the apples into a bowl, he squirted lemon juice over the pieces. "I'd forgotten why I wanted to go into the restaurant business all those years ago. Part of the reason is because I like to cook."

"Hey, you get no argument from me," Penny said, smiling over her coffee cup. "I just wish you'd displayed some of this creative cookery a few years earlier. When I think of all the dinner parties I slaved over, when you make it look so easy."

Pleased by the compliment, he looked up and grinned.

"Mommy, you look like a snowman," Flash observed. "Can I touch your tummy?"

A snowman. No more all-white ensembles. "Sure, honey. Come say hello to Whosit." Both kids placed their palms against her sweater.

Alice wiped her hands on her apron. "If we have everything

under control here, I think I'll set the table. Where did I put the place cards? Penny, do you think I should put Dr. Adler next to Winnie Greene, or should I put Winnie next to John?''

John groaned. ''You've been worrying about this since dawn.''

''You have?'' Penny asked, surprised. Alice wasn't usually the type of woman to come unglued over something as inconsequential as place cards.

''I vote for Dr. Adler,'' John said. ''If you put Winnie Greene next to me, she'll spend an hour telling me how to woo my wife.''

''Your—'' Penny bit her tongue. She had been about to say *your ex-wife.* But she looked at the children and changed her mind. The mood was close and warm; she didn't want to spoil it with technicalities. And then, she realized, that technically they were still husband and wife. ''You're probably right,'' she amended. ''Put Winnie at my end of the table.''

''Good idea,'' Alice agreed. But she continued to look flustered and uncertain.

When everyone arrived and the time came to be seated, however, Penny discovered Winnie had been placed at the head of the table and her own card was next to John's.

She and John exchanged a glance, then they both looked at Amy and Flash who were begging Dr. Adler to make quarters appear out their ears. Both children steadfastly avoided their parent's lifted eyebrows.

''It's Thanksgiving,'' John whispered in her ear as he seated her. ''What the heck.''

After a moment Penny capitulated. Every holiday had its special memories. This would go down as the Thanksgiving dinner that Winnie Greene presided in the hostess's chair. Winnie looked a bit startled, then flattered. Then she gazed fondly at John and Penny and gave them a knowing wink.

''Do you get the feeling this whole town is in collusion about you and me?'' she asked when John had carved a perfect bird and filled the plates. She knew she wasn't imagining it. Winnie, Dr. Adler and Alice continued to glance at her and John with encouraging little nods.

"You've noticed, too?" He seemed genuinely surprised. "I assumed I was the only one getting advice."

"I can't stop at a traffic light without someone pulling up next to me wanting to know how you and I are getting along." Frowning, she stared at her plate. It looked like a photo from a gourmet magazine.

"What do you tell them?"

Lifting her head in the sudden hush, Penny leveled a mock glare at the table. "You're all shameless, do you know that?"

"Yes, yes, dear, we know," Winnie said, leaning forward. "But what do you tell them?"

"I don't answer," Penny said, smiling sweetly.

Dr. Adler laughed. "And right you are." He lifted his wineglass. "I'd like to propose a toast to the cooks, John and Alice. And to a lovely table and a wonderful dinner. Thank you all for sharing this holiday with friends. And to Winnie and Penny whose beauty and grace compliment the event."

"What about us?" Flash demanded.

"And to Flash and Amy whose suspected creativity is to be commended."

"What does that mean?" Flash asked, his freckles twisting into a frown.

Penny managed a weak smile in the burst of general laughter. "It means your handiwork with the place cards."

Flash's dark eyes swung toward Amy and they both giggled, then applied themselves to their heaping plates.

"Everyone is right, John," Penny said. "Your dinner is wonderful."

His eyes, filled with warmth and pride, held hers for a long moment. "Thank you."

When she finally looked away, Penny thought of what Lydie had said about spending holidays alone. Listening to John's deep laughter and the flow of conversation, she could not imagine this dinner without him. It would have been dismal.

As if Alice had guessed her thoughts, she looked down the table at Penny and raised her wineglass in a silent toast. Penny wasn't entirely sure what they were toasting, but it was a nice moment of accord. Then Alice turned to Dr. Adler and the moment passed.

Looking about the table at her friends and family, Penny decided she had a lot to be thankful for. Then tears brimmed on her lashes as she thought ahead to next Thanksgiving. It was going to be so hard facing the holidays alone.

"What are you thinking?" John asked, pouring more wine into her glass.

"I was thinking how complex the human mind is. How we can want something and reject it at the same time."

Lifting her head, she looked at him, so handsome, so relaxed. His tan had begun to fade making his eyes seem especially dark and seductive.

She had to talk to him very soon and tell him she had done all the reassessment possible and had made her final decision. But not today.

Chapter Six

When the phone rang, Penny dismissed the snow-removal supervisor, Frank Spats, and reached for the receiver. Lydie's voice erupted in her ear.

"We've got a problem. King size."

"What's happened?" Frowning, Penny stared at the loudspeaker mounted near the ceiling of her office. "Rudolph the Red-Nosed Reindeer" was playing for the millionth time. The melody set her teeth on edge. She had begun hearing it in her dreams. "Come on Dasher and Dancer and Prancer and Vixen, Comet and Cupid and..."

"Kurt Pausch is dead drunk in his dressing room. It looks like he didn't go home last night—he's still wearing his Santa suit." A sniff of distaste sounded over the phone wire. "Need I mention the suit is a little the worse for wear?"

"Did you phone the evening-shift Santa? What's his name? George Hanson."

"I called George immediately, but his wife said he's in Denver for the day. Then I called everyone on our emergency list. No luck. And that, my fat pregnant friend, is the problem. We don't have a Santa and I can't find one."

Penny covered her eyes with her hand. "We've got five busloads of kids coming up from Denver today. Plus the usual crowd."

Lydie groaned. "That's right. The Police Association is bringing up a new group of underprivileged kids. They're more disadvantaged than they know. They don't even get a Santa.''

''Lydie, we can't let that happen. There must be someone we can grab on short notice.'' Eyeing the loudspeaker, she considered hurling the bowl of ornaments at it. Who could think with ''Rudolph the Red-Nosed Reindeer'' playing cheerily in the background?

''I've hit a wall, Penny. I even called your doctor. But your mother said he'd just left for the hospital in Vail. One of his patients went into labor.''

''My mother? You must be mistaken. What would Alice be doing at Dr. Adler's? She's at the library this morning.''

''It sounded like Alice. Never mind that, what are we going to do? If you've got any magic rabbits in your hat, Ms. Martin, now is the time to pull one out.''

Penny couldn't think of a soul. ''Wait a minute.'' No, it would be asking to much. ''I could try John. He'd planned to go skiing this morning...'' She darted a glance at the wall clock. Hands shaped like Christmas trees edged toward eight o'clock. ''I could try him. Maybe he hasn't left yet.''

''Call him! Fast.'' Lydie hung up.

Biting her lip, Penny looked at the telephone and hesitated. Then she thought of the busloads of kids the Police Association were bringing to Santa's Village. This might be the only Christmas treat those kids would have. They deserved a Santa.

She dialed home and listened to the phone ring and ring, her heart sinking. Who else could they ask?

''Hello,'' John said after the sixth ring. ''You just caught me. I was in the garage when I heard the telephone. What's up?''

She came at it the long way. She told him about Kurt Pausch getting depressed at Christmas, about his drinking problem and how he was now passed out in Santa's dressing room. She informed him of the busloads of underprivileged kids. She explained that Lydie had called every replacement Santa they could think of and they had drawn a blank.

''Penny, is this leading where I think it is? You want me to play Santa?''

"I know it's an imposition. I know you planned to ski today. But I don't know where else to turn. If you'd lend us a hand, John, we'd really appreciate it."

A silence stretched over the phone pressed to her ear. Then he laughed and her shoulders relaxed.

"Why not? How soon do you need me?"

"An hour ago. The park opens in thirty minutes. How quickly can you get here?"

"I'm on my way. Oh, would you phone Alice at the library and ask her to pick the kids up from school? I assume I'll be ho-ho-hoing all day."

"I'm afraid so—the shift ends at five. I'll phone Alice right now." She drew a breath. "John? Thank you."

Keeping the phone to her ear, she disconnected then dialed the library. "May I speak to Alice Sage, please?"

"I'm sorry, Mrs. Sage isn't here. Can I help you?"

Penny frowned. Alice had left at the usual time this morning, dressed for work. "This is her daughter—"

"Oh, Penny. I didn't recognize your voice. Do you want to leave a message for Alice?"

"I thought she would be there. Well, when she comes in, would you tell her..."

After hanging up, she considered the telephone for a moment, wondering where Alice was and if she should be worried. Then Allenby stuck his head in her office door and asked about yesterday's gate receipts; then Helen relayed a message concerning a contretemps among the kitchen staff at Mrs. Claus's Kitchen. Twenty minutes later the elf at the gate phoned to inform her that John had arrived.

"Tell him to meet me at the North Pole."

When she arrived, Lydie was showing John the baskets of lollipops and candy canes beside Santa's throne. "You get a coffee and pottie break once in the morning and once in the afternoon. An hour for lunch, but Allenby prefers you eat in your dressing room. He doesn't want any of the kids seeing Santa wolfing down an ordinary cheeseburger."

It annoyed Penny to realize that Lydie was flirting with

John. It also aggravated her that Lydie had a waist and wore a soft clinging jersey dress that showed it off.

"This way," she said crisply, beckoning John toward the dressing room. A row of Santa suits hung in the closet along with the requisite padding and false beards. Penny stared at the figure sprawled across the cot against the wall, then swung her gaze to Lydie. "You just left him here?"

Lydie shrugged. "I didn't know what to do with him."

Kurt Pausch opened one bleary eye and looked at John. "You the replacement Santa?" John nodded. "Don't let the little buggers bite you."

"They bite?"

"They spit, too." His eyelids sank, then rose with difficulty. "They're just showing off, that's all. Or they're scared. Or mad about something. 'Fraid they won't get what they want. Or maybe they're 'fraid they will."

As they watched, Kurt gave them a dreamy smile. Then his eyes closed and his head fell backward. A moist snore rattled his chest.

"Yo-ho-ho and a bottle of rum," Penny murmured. A sad expression crossed her features. "I'll check the records and find out where Kurt lives. Lydie, will you scare up somebody to drive him home?"

"Will do." Lydie had seated herself at the makeup table and showed no sign of leaving any time soon. Smiling at John through a sweep of dark lashes, she crossed one nylon-clad leg over the other.

A flash of jealously tightened Penny's lips and she stepped closer to John. The feeling surprised and irritated her. For the first time it occurred to her that after the divorce John would probably date other women. The thought brought an unpleasant taste to her mouth.

"I think you should get moving on it immediately," she said to Lydie. "Hopefully we can get Kurt out of here before the park opens. Too late," she added, glancing at her watch. "Well, do what you can to make sure none of the kids sees Santa being carried out to a car."

"If anyone sees, I'll tell them he was run over by a reindeer."

When John laughed, Penny glared at him. "After you," she said to Lydie, opening the door. With a last look at John, Lydie sighed and stepped outside. Penny's glare intensified. "Hurry up, will you?" she snapped at John.

"Is something wrong?" He glanced at her over the beard he was holding to his chin. Even with a flowing beard, he looked heartachingly handsome.

"You aren't here to flirt with the staff. You're here for the kids. The North Pole was supposed to open fifteen minutes ago!"

"Flirt with the staff? What are you talking about?"

"You know perfectly well what I'm talking about, John Martin!" Lifting her nose in the air, she did an about-face, then sailed, stomach first, out the door and slammed it behind her.

But not before she heard him say, "Well, I'll be damned," then laugh.

Crimson burned on her cheeks. She hoped one of the little buggers bit him.

IAN ALLENBY STOOD beside her at the entrance to the North Pole, his hands clasped behind his back. They examined the lines of children peering past each other to stare wide-eyed at Santa while they waited their turn.

"Your husband is a natural," Allenby commented, pleased. "I don't suppose..."

Penny smiled. "No. John's just filling in for today. I believe Lydie has found someone to replace Kurt through January. The new Santa will arrive this afternoon to observe the evening shift."

They watched John cuddle a three-year-old for the photographer. The flash popped, then he reached into the basket beside him and presented the little girl with a bright candy cane as he whispered something in her ear. The tiny girl smiled, then wrapped her arms around John's neck in a quick shy hug. The photographer gave the girl's mother a Polaroid print just as a little boy ran up the steps and hurled himself into John's padded lap.

After checking the animated figures, Ian Allenby took Penny's arm and turned her toward the street outside. He helped her into one of the horse-drawn sleighs and asked the driver to take them to the administration building.

"Are you sure we can count on you to be here until the first of the year?" he asked, lifting an eyebrow in the direction of the coat buttons straining over her stomach.

Dr. Adler's voice echoed in her ear, but she pushed it aside. "Absolutely. But after the first..." She smiled and shrugged.

"How long do you anticipate being absent?"

It was a loaded question. Village policy offered six weeks maternity leave. Therefore, the question Allenby was really asking addressed attitude and commitment.

"Barring anything unforeseen, I plan to return to work a month after the baby is born."

He nodded. "Penny, Santa's Village has been very pleased with your performance. I believe you know that." Turning his head, he automatically checked the hot-chestnut carts, the flow of people passing in and out of the shops. "What problems do you foresee regarding meshing your work schedule with the demands of an infant?"

Another loaded question. Penny drew a breath and held the frosty air for a moment. "I don't anticipate any difficulties. I believe I mentioned I live with my mother, and she's willing to care for the baby until I get settled in my own place and hire a nursemaid."

"If you're chosen as my replacement, your hours will increase."

"I'm aware of that." It was a bridge she would cross later.

He cleared his throat with an uncomfortable sound. "I dislike prying into people's personal lives, however I think you'll understand when I say it doesn't make sense from the company's standpoint to hire and train someone who may be planning to move out of the area. For that reason, much as I hate to ask, I feel I must inquire as to the status of your marriage.

Are you planning to return with your husband to Los Angeles?''

''No,'' she said very quietly after a brief hesitation. ''I am not.'' She plucked at the button pulling across her stomach.

''I didn't hear?''

''No,'' she said in a firmer voice. ''My home is in Aspen Springs. My children attend school here. This is where I plan to live and stay.''

''Future promotions could require relocation,'' Allenby said as he helped her to the cobbled street. After glancing toward a leaden sky, he looked at her again. ''You're aware of that, naturally.''

Another problem to be faced later. ''Of course.''

''Well, then.'' He opened the heavy glass door leading into the administration building and followed her inside. Before he turned down the corridor to his office, he asked her to thank John for filling in as Santa.

''I will.''

Once inside her own office, she leaned back from her desk, chewed on a pencil and tried to assess the conversation. Did it mean the powers that be were edging toward a decision?

Helen buzzed on the intercom and told her that Mrs. Johnson, the head seamstress, needed to see her immediately.

''Tell her I'm on my way.''

Rising, she glanced around her office, at the candy-cane wallpaper, her overflowing desk. Her gaze lingered on the photos of Amy and Flash positioned beside the basket of ornaments.

All questions regarding the possible promotion were moot. Nothing for her to waste time thinking about. For a moment Penny felt ashamed for having forgotten even for a moment. ''I don't want the promotion. I won't accept it if it's offered,'' she said aloud. And she meant it, she really did.

When she arrived at the costume department, she found John bent over at the waist and Mrs. Johnson kneeling behind him, patching a tear in the seat of of his Santa suit.

''There's justice, after all,'' Penny remarked, grinning. ''One of them bit you on the butt?''

He turned his head to look at her and smiled. "Nothing that dramatic. The kids have been wonderful."

"What then? Did Lydie grab you?" An acid edge appeared in her voice.

Before he answered, Mrs. Johnson spoke around a mouthful of pins. "That's why I called you, Mrs. Martin. Apparently there's a nail coming up on the Santa throne. Maintenance should have a look at it. Don't want some child gouging his leg or getting scratched. Never mind your husband's, uh, behind."

"You couldn't pound down a loose nail?" she asked John.

One eyebrow lifted and he looked at her curiously. "I offered to take care of it, but Jim—he's the photographer—"

"I know."

"—said the union wouldn't approve. He said you've got a union guy around here dressed like an elf who does minor repairs."

She absolutely was not being fair and she knew it. Which made her angrier. "It still seems to me you could have given it a whack," she snapped, hating herself. It wasn't like her to be so unreasonable.

"Penny—"

"Never mind, I'll phone the union elf." The sooner she got out of the tailoring department the better. She knew she was behaving badly, but seemed unable to stop herself. And there was no way she was going to admit her snappishness had anything to do with jealousy. It was just too ridiculous.

John caught up with her in the corridor. "Wait a minute." He cupped her shoulders between his hands. "Honey, what's wrong? Why are you so upset?"

"Please, John. I've asked you not to call me honey."

"You weren't this testy the last time you were pregnant."

Her eyes narrowed. "Why does everyone insist I'm being unreasonable because I'm pregnant? You, Lydie, my secretary, even Alice, has made some remark."

He grinned. "Well, then, why are you being so unreasonable?"

"Dammit, I am *not* being unreasonable!" Yes, she was. She

bit her lips and stepped back from the warmth of his hands. "I'm sorry," she murmured, pushing a hand through her hair. "I guess I am a little out of sorts today. Allenby talked to me about the promotion. No, he didn't offer it," she added when she saw John's expression. "And Alice isn't where she's supposed to be. So I'm worrying if she received the message to pick up Amy and Flash. I have a dozen phone memos on my desk that I don't have time to return. It looks like a late night again tonight, and...well, you get the picture."

"How late do you think you'll be? I'd like to talk to you."

He looked so damned appealing, standing there in the chunky Santa suit, his eyes like melted chocolate above the white beard. Penny swallowed and took another step backward.

"We both look pregnant," she said, trying for a smile to ease the moment. Then she made a show of glancing at her watch. "I don't think I'll make it home before ten," she said. "And I already know I'm not going to feel up to a serious talk. But soon, John. We'll talk soon."

"I don't have anything serious in mind," he said, leaning against the candy-cane wallpaper. "I'd like to discuss Christmas. Our Christmas."

"Oh. Well, that shouldn't take too long."

"Okay, it's a date."

She wished he hadn't phrased it that way. But it was her fault. He didn't know yet what she had decided. She definitely had to find the right time for a serious talk. No matter how much she dreaded it.

PENNY'S MOOD had not improved by the time she arrived home. As she hung her coat and cap in the entryway, she promised herself that she would apologize to Lydie first thing in the morning. She had been sulky through dinner, rebuffing Lydie's attempts at conversation. Whether Lydie had actually flirted with John or whether Penny had only imagined it, the implications of being bothered by either circumstance made her head ache. The bottom line was that she had behaved unfairly toward Lydie. It didn't help her feeling of guilt that Lydie seemed to understand.

"You look tired, dear," Alice said, glancing up from her knitting. A fire crackled in the fireplace, and the news was ending on TV.

"I am," she said as John offered a cup of hot mulled wine. After casting a suspicious eye over the furniture, all of which was wickedly soft, she lowered herself onto the raised hearth and let the fire warm her back.

John switched off the TV, then sat on the sofa where he could see her. "Alice and I have been talking. If you agree, we'd like to make this a real old-fashioned Christmas for the kids."

"I like the idea so far," Penny said with false brightness, too fatigued to feel genuine enthusiasm. "What are you planning?" And how much time would it require?

Excitement sparkled in John's eyes. "For starters, I was thinking we could cut our own tree this year. And instead of buying gifts for friends, we could give them a basket of homemade cookies."

Penny blinked, her mind racing. Cutting a tree would require the better part of an afternoon. Baking Christmas cookies was an all-day project.

"John, our resident cook, has volunteered for the cookie patrol," Alice offered, reading her daughter's thoughts.

John leaned forward, speaking earnestly. "The thing that struck me while I was playing Santa is how commercial Christmas has become. How would you feel if we agreed that everyone has to give each other at least one homemade gift?"

"Is that what this flurry of knitting is all about?" Penny asked, nodding toward the yarn in Alice's lap, stalling while she marshaled her energy. "By the way, where were you today?"

"I was at the library, of course."

"You weren't there when I phoned. I was worried about you."

Alice waved a knitting needle. "Nothing to be worried

about. I'm a big girl, for heaven's sake. I had breakfast with a friend, then ran a couple of errands before I went in."

"What do you think, Penny? The kids could string popcorn and cranberries for the tree—"

"Popcorn and cranberries is probably not a good idea," Alice interrupted. "I'm old enough to remember how hard that is. How about a modification? Paper chains and strings of macaroni."

"Great! Well, Penny?"

"I love the idea," she conceded slowly. It sounded wonderful. Exactly the sort of Christmas she had imagined they would have in Aspen Springs. Except…there just were not enough hours in the day to do all the things she wanted to do.

"Good. It's settled then." Leaning back, John smiled broadly. "I'll get the tree permit tomorrow."

Penny sighed. "Great," she said finally, mustering a smile. "The kids will love it."

THERE JUST WEREN'T enough hours in the day.

After tightening the belt of her bathrobe, Penny frowned and leaned against the freezer. She adjusted the beam of the flashlight to shine on the carton of ice cream she was struggling to open. Good. By sheer luck she had managed to locate the lemon custard. Midnight cravings were a pain in the neck, but what was a pregnant lady to do?

For a moment she considered turning on the garage light so that she could see what she was doing, then rejected the idea. If one of the Galloways couldn't sleep, either he or she might look up the hill and notice the light and wonder if something was wrong. All she needed to cap another long day was to have Bill Galloway pounding at the door and waking everyone at three in the morning.

Leaning against the freezer, she spooned a bite of lemon custard into her mouth and held it on her tongue, savoring the flavor, feeling foolish to be shivering in the garage at three in the morning for the sake of some ice cream, of all things. It was so cold she could see her breath between bites.

After swallowing another spoonful of lemon custard, she

tightened the collar of her bathrobe around her throat and swept a glance over the darkened shapes filling the third bay of the big garage. The furniture she had brought with her from Los Angeles, covered now with sheets and moving pads, waited for the time she found her own house. The sight of her broken household was too sad to bear thinking about, so she turned her gaze to the hood ornament on her car and ate another gazillion calories of lemon custard.

Where was she going to find the time to do everything she was committed to do? A sigh lifted the ice-cream carton propped against her stomach. She loved Christmas. At least she used to, back in the days before listening to ''Rudolph the Red-Nosed Reindeer'' had become a teeth-grinding experience. Before the thought of making homemade gifts caused her eyes to glaze over and her throat to tighten in panic. Where would she find the time? Or the creative energy? Whenever she tried to think of something she could make for Amy and Flash, her mind went blank.

Covering her eyes with one hand, she drew a long breath. Something had to go. She could not continue at this pace and hope to enjoy the holidays. But what? She didn't immediately see which responsibility she could set aside.

A sweep of headlights flashed across the garage windows just then, curved over the wall and across Penny's startled face, then cut to blackness.

For an instant she froze. Then she set the ice-cream carton on the lid of the freezer and hurried between her car and John's toward the garage windows. Holding her breath, she peered outside.

She saw nothing unusual. The only car in the driveway was Alice's, parked in the usual place beneath the yard light. Frowning, Penny pressed her cheek to the frosty glass, straining to see beyond Alice's car.

When the bump sounded against the house, she jumped, even though she realized she had been half expecting the noise.

The bump was faint enough that Penny could almost persuade herself that she had imagined it. But the sweep of headlights had been very real. And they proved she was not imagining someone in the driveway even though the car had seemingly vanished.

Maybe the driver had not.

This frightening, confused thought raised the hair on the back of her neck, and she quickly backed away from the row of garage windows. Responding instinctively, she rushed inside the house and headed down the basement stairs. Not pausing to question that she automatically turned to John, she tiptoed into Flash's bedroom then reached to the upper bunk and shook John awake.

"John," she whispered urgently when he rose on an elbow and blinked at her. "Someone's in the yard! I heard a car and saw headlights."

Instantly, he threw back the blankets and swung his legs over the edge of the bunk before he dropped to the floor beside her. A flash of nakedness skimmed her gaze before she hastily averted her eyes. But she felt her cheeks burning in the darkness. It wasn't that she had forgotten he slept naked; she had forgotten she wasn't supposed to look at or appreciate what a wonderful body he had. Gradually she was deciphering the etiquette for divorced partners, and staring at one's naked soon-to-be ex-husband was probably not the accepted thing. Judging by her response, it was definitely not a wise move.

Outside Flash's bedroom, she pushed aside any thoughts of firm naked bodies and leaned to John's ear. Speaking in a low voice, she told him what had happened.

But her thoughts were not focused as sharply as they should have been. Aside from the electric jolt of seeing him naked, she felt a growing embarrassment that she had come to him at all. They were estranged; she should have handled the problem herself instead of responding to habit and running to John. She didn't like the underlying thought that she still needed him.

A frown drew his brow as he listened. "I know what you're describing. I heard the same noises a couple of weeks ago." His lips pressed together and he glanced toward the basement stairs. "Do you have a flashlight?"

She pushed it into his hands, then followed him up the staircase. "All I could see from the garage window was Alice's car. It's her turn to park outside."

"Wait here."

Cupping her hands around her face, she leaned to the window beside the door and watched the flashlight bob over the snow toward Alice's car. He circled Alice's Subaru, then disappeared around the corner of the garage.

When he returned inside, John shook his head. "I've been all around the house and there's no one there," he said, hanging up his coat. "I can't tell if any of the tracks are fresh or left from yesterday. You're sure you saw headlights?"

"Positive." They stared at one another. "The only way headlights would sweep the garage is if a car were actually in the driveway. It couldn't have just vanished." She thought a moment. "Maybe it doused its lights and drove away while I was downstairs waking you."

"Obviously that's what must have happened. Maybe one of your neighbors has a drinking problem, came home late and turned into the wrong driveway."

"Why not just back out and go on home? Why the mystery? And, John, this isn't the first time this has happened."

"Maybe the person has a persistent drinking problem and persistently turns into the wrong driveway. He cuts the lights because he doesn't want to wake anyone, or maybe because he's embarrassed about making a mistake and doesn't want to be identified."

He didn't sound entirely satisfied with this explanation and neither was she, but nothing else sprang to mind. "Maybe," she said doubtfully.

"You know," John said, looking at her, "it just occurred to me—why were you in the garage at three-thirty in the morning?"

She gave him a sheepish shrug. "The freezer is in the garage. I wanted some lemon custard ice cream."

He didn't smile as she expected him to. Instead, he raised a hand still cold from the night air and touched her cheek. "Couldn't sleep?" he asked softly.

"I've had a lot on my mind." His touch paralyzed her. Then a rush of heat warmed her cheeks and she stepped back away from his hand. Dammit, it was over between them. She wasn't supposed to react like this.

"Want to talk about it?"

"Now?" she asked, surprised.

"Why not? I have an idea neither of us is going to go back to sleep. Come on. I'll put on a pot of decaf. It'll be like old times."

Silently she followed him upstairs, seated herself at the kitchen counter and watched as he made coffee. There had been a time early in their marriage when sleep hadn't seemed to matter much. Too excited by work or by each other, too wound up to sleep, they had raided the fridge at two or three in the morning, laughing and whispering in the darkness like teenagers. She pressed her lips together and looked away from him, feeling an ache deep inside. So much of her personal history revolved around John.

"Come sit beside me on the sofa," he suggested when the coffee finished perking. "I'll help you up later."

"I'd better stay where I am," she said in a low voice. And she stopped him when he moved to turn on a table lamp. This was as good a time as any for the serious talk she had been avoiding. And it would be easier to say what she had to say in the darkness. She didn't want to see his expression.

"You've made up your mind," he said quietly when the silence between them had grown uncomfortable.

The pain of what was coming clamped her body like a vice.

Chapter Seven

"I've thought about everything, done the reassessment you asked, and I've realized nothing has changed. I won't go back to Los Angeles, John. It isn't what I want for myself or the children. I think...a divorce is the right thing."

Because she couldn't bear his awful silence, she continued talking, speaking above the vice that had tightened by a notch around her chest. "I didn't reach this decision lightly or without difficulty. I've given it careful thought." That was the understatement of her life. She had scarcely been able to think of anything else. And the pain of the decision was with her always. A long sigh collapsed her shoulders and she lowered her head to look unseeing into her coffee cup. "I'm sorry, John."

"I thought we agreed we care about each other. I thought we were getting to know one another again. Putting things back right."

Sudden tears blurred the darkness. "As I mentioned earlier, loving isn't enough. I wish it was, John, but it isn't. And the John Martin you are now isn't the same John Martin who lives and works in L.A. This John Martin is on vacation. More relaxed than I've seen him in years." She shook her head. "You're right. These weeks have been more easygoing than any we've experienced in years. And maybe we're seeing different sides of each other. But once you return to Los Angeles and work, the regular routine..."

"Is that why you won't return to Los Angeles? You resent my job?"

"Look, John. If I had to describe you in one word, the word I would choose is ambitious. And you're a workaholic. I don't resent Blackman Brothers. If it wasn't Blackman Brothers, it would be something else equally as demanding." She spread her hands. "Another rat race. Another treadmill. Whatever job you have, you'll throw yourself into it one hundred percent. Don't you think I've noticed how hard it is for you to relax? You can't. At least not for long. People pay thousands of dollars to vacation in Aspen Springs, but all you've done since you arrived is look for something to do. How many times have you skied? Twice? Three times? Sure, you've taken the kids sledding and snowmobiling on the weekends. But during the week, you're phoning your office a couple of times a day, doing work you receive through the mail, reading mounds of reports and journals. And the rest of the time... Can you honestly tell me you aren't going crazy with boredom?"

"You're being unreasonable, Penny. I didn't quit Blackman Brothers, I took a vacation. I have to keep up with what's going on or I'll be lost when I return." Leaning forward, he placed his elbows on his knees and looked at her across the dark room. "As for being a workaholic, I admit it. I've never fought you on that point. What I've objected to is your opinion that being a workaholic is negative. I saw it as a positive, as an extra source of fuel, maybe, that would get us where we wanted faster. What you need to understand is that I've taken a hard look at my work habits since coming here. Frankly, my reassessment was prompted by watching you."

"What is that supposed to mean?" she asked sharply.

"You are as much a workaholic as I am."

"That is utterly ridiculous!"

"Observing you these past weeks has given me an opportunity to see myself more clearly. And every objection you ever voiced was valid. The workaholic surrenders the best of his personal life and causes inconvenience and frustration to those around him."

Penny leaned forward angrily. "Are you accusing me of

sacrificing my personal life and disrupting the lives of those around me?''

''Yes. Exactly as I did all the years we were married. The point I want to make is that I've finally seen the light. I'm not ready to retire as you seem to want me to—''

''Which you think is an irresponsible attitude on my part!''

''Frankly, I do. I'm thirty-five, Penny, too young to be put out to pasture. I'll continue to work because work is satisfying to me. But I won't continue at the same pace as before. I won't do that to myself anymore, or to the people I love. You have my word on that.''

''Your word is several years too late!'' She was practically sputtering. Drawing a deep breath, she held it until she felt her blood pressure return to normal. ''I know you believe that now, John, but that's not how it will work out. Something drives you. From one point of view, that's a wonderful quality. From my point of view it means never seeing you, never spending as much time alone with you as I'd like. It means taking second or third place in your life.''

''Penny—''

''I know exactly what would happen. You'd have all the best intentions in the world. At first you would work nine to five. Then it would be one night a week, then two. Then an occasional weekend. Very soon everything would be just like it was. We'd be seeing each other at parties, or late at night, and talking on the telephone instead of in person. We'd be right back trying to convince ourselves that spending a lot of time with our children isn't as important as making that time 'quality' time. Well, quality time is a lie designed to ease a parent's guilt, John. Ask any kid. Ask any wife. Children and wives need more than an hour or two a week, even if that hour or two is utterly fantastic!''

''Penny, will you just listen for a minute? I—''

''The difference is that my situation is temporary. It's not a habit or a way of life. With you, it is.''

''Was. Not is. Something happened to me after you left. I woke up and realized I had sacrificed everything important in my life.'' After a pause, he continued, ''One night I came home early and the condo was too silent, too empty without you and the kids. I had to get out of there, so I decided to call someone and meet for a drink. But there was no one to call. I was surrounded by millions of people and there was no one I really wanted to see or be with. It wasn't a drink I wanted, I wanted you and Flash and Amy."

"On your terms," Penny said sharply. "When you had a night off."

"I understand that now. And I intend to change it." He looked at her, his face a pale blur in the darkness. "I know no career is going to consume my life ever again. It's been a tough lesson to learn and I've hurt a lot of people. But now I know what's important and what I want. I want you and my family. I don't want my kids growing up with 'steps,' as Flash puts it. I don't want you working a murderous schedule because you're worried about money. I've enjoyed the kids tremendously these past few weeks, and I've learned how much I missed by not being there all those years. I don't want to miss anything else, especially our new baby."

Sudden tears wet her lashes. She heard his sincerity, knew he believed what he was telling her. But she also knew John. And she couldn't believe he could change that much. Tigers didn't change their stripes.

"Is it possible you're mistaking loneliness for something else?" she asked, trying to put her doubts in a tactful manner.

"Of course I'm lonely. Aren't you, Penny? I don't like sleeping in the North Pole while you're sleeping a million miles away. I miss lying in bed with the lights out, sharing the day's events. I miss waking up and finding you smiling at me. I even miss trying to shave over your head while you're putting on your makeup. I hate it that we're so carefully polite with each other, that we don't really talk. You're afraid to tell me what you're feeling because I might misconstrue what you're saying and think you're making some kind of commitment. I'm afraid to tell you what I'm feeling because you might think I'm pressuring you. And on we go. But I don't want you back because I'm lonely, if that's what you're thinking. I want you back because I love you and because I believe in us. I think you do, too."

"Not anymore." They were the hardest two words she had ever spoken. "There's too much water under the bridge."

"Come on, Penny." Now she heard anger enter his voice. "Are you so afraid of loving that you won't look at the truth? For instance, you're sitting here raking me over the coals for being ambitious, for being a workaholic, but what about you?"

"I've explained it over and over again. My present work situation is temporary."

"If you believe that, Penny, you're deceiving yourself, and that isn't like you. The day I played Santa, I had a look around the Village. And I kept my ears open. Other employees aren't killing themselves, working till they're exhausted." He stared. "Did you know the supervisory staff resents the pace you and Lydie Severin are setting? The two of you are competing so hard for Allenby's position that you're establishing expectations of perfection that no one can meet. You're both asking too much of your employees and yourselves so you can look good."

Penny gasped. "That's not true!"

"It is true. You're driving yourself and your staff beyond what's reasonable. Everyone around you sees it. Why can't you?"

"Because that's not what's happening," she snapped. "I have responsibilities, I have—"

"Look, I'm the first person to understand what you're doing. And I certainly don't fault you for having ambition and wanting to move up the ladder."

"I do not want that promotion! I just—"

"I know. You just want to know if you can win it." He lifted his head and looked at her, but the darkness was too thick to read his expression. "We've heard that one before, haven't we? Only it was me speaking the words. Me involved in the self-deception."

"You are so wrong, John."

"If I'm wrong, then show me. Take yourself out of the

running. Take a hard look at your priorities, Penny. Is this what you wanted to do when you moved to Aspen Springs? Work yourself into exhaustion? Ambition isn't a bad thing. It's a quality we share. But it's something that's a problem for both of us. If we work together on it, maybe we can find a solution we can live with. But first, you have to admit ambition is driving you, too."

White-faced, she slid from the counter stool and pulled the collar of her bathrobe to her throat. "Somehow you've managed to shift this conversation to make me the bad guy."

"I'm not trying to make anyone a bad guy. I'm trying to point out how easy it is to fall into the trap. And under different circumstances there would be nothing wrong with that. But it isn't what we decided we want right now. Not for either of us. We decided we wanted a slower pace and more time with our kids."

"There's nothing like a recent convert when it comes to preaching, is there?" she said sharply. Then she added in a defensive tone, "Besides, I am spending time with the kids. It's—"

"Quality time?"

Crimson flooded her cheeks and she was glad he couldn't see her expression in the darkness.

"Penny, you were right about quality time. First, there's never enough quality time, and second, it isn't really quality. I suspect you're doing what I used to do. Thinking about inventory and gate receipts while you're reading bedtime stories, for instance. Were you really watching the Disney feature last Sunday, or were you worrying about replacement Santas and removing the snow from the Village ice rink?"

The crimson intensified in her cheeks. "I know what you're doing, John," she said finally, her voice tight. "The best defense is offense, right?"

He was silent for a moment. "Maybe that's part of it," he finally admitted. "I don't think it's fair for you to give up on us. Especially not when you're doing what you're accusing me of."

"Maybe that's how you see it, but that's not how it is."

"I think you're fooling yourself. It looks to me like we're both at a career crossroads. Me, willing to gear down. You, preparing to gear up."

"I didn't tear up my life and the lives of our children to move here and fall into the same old trap. You have it wrong." She moved toward the upper staircase feeling like an angry basketball in motion. It was difficult to effect dignity when her stomach preceded her. "It's time we ended this discussion."

"Penny—"

"No, John. All we're doing is rehashing an old argument." She drew a breath. "You're welcome to stay until the baby is born. I...I'll be glad to have you with me. Then we'll go our separate ways." She drew another tight breath and blinked at the tears scalding her eyelids. "I'm sorry it has to end like this. I know you are, too. But that's how it is. We'll make a nice Christmas for Amy and Flash, then you and I are finished. And that's final, John." Before either of them could say another word, she hurried up the staircase and away from him.

THERE WAS NO POINT returning to the bunk bed. Sleep would be impossible tonight. Instead, John seated himself at the kitchen table, drinking the rest of the decaf, thinking and watching the sky lighten toward a gray cloudy dawn.

After silently reviewing the conversation, he reached the same conclusion. Penny was deceiving herself. He didn't blame her. No one understood what she was doing any better than he. He had played the same scene often enough in the past. Eventually the promotion would be offered or it wouldn't, then she would have to confront what was going on inside.

Because he knew her and because he believed in her, he trusted she would not flinch from the confrontation. In the end, her basic values would assert themselves and the deception would fall away. What she did then would measure the depth of her commitment to the ideal that Aspen Springs represented.

Whatever happened, it would happen here. Not in Los Angeles. Penny was not coming home. He had recognized the conviction in her tone.

He drank his coffee and thought about that.

Actually he should have anticipated her decision. Aspen Springs had always been the dream.

It was a quiet group who gathered for the breakfast he prepared. Penny looked as if she hadn't slept; her eyes were pale and red-rimmed. A fresh pot of Hawaiian ground coffee beans was not enough to prevent Alice's yawns. Even the kids seemed subdued this morning.

"Your shirt is buttoned wrong," Amy said to Flash, her tone ripe with an older sister's scorn. It was a provoking statement and she knew it, though her heart didn't seem to be in it.

"Is not," Flash replied, gulping his milk.

"Is too."

"Amy, your braids need redoing," Alice said. But she didn't volunteer for the task. Instead, she turned sleepy eyes to the window. "Overcast but not snowing," she announced to no one in particular.

"Good. Maybe my flight won't be too bumpy," John said.

Penny's head jerked up from her coffee cup. "What flight?"

He cleared his throat and turned to pour more coffee. "I'm returning to Los Angeles. My flight leaves Denver at noon."

They stared at him. Tears welled in Flash's eyes; Amy's lower lip trembled and her shoulders sagged.

"Hey, guys. It's just for a couple of days."

"When did you...?"

He looked at Penny and thought how lovely she was even with faint circles bruising her eyes. He had never known another woman with that particular shade of reddish-gold hair or eyes as blue as the Mediterranean. How had they ever been so foolish as to let things reach this point?

"I called early this morning for a flight. The reservation desks are open twenty-four hours a day."

"You are coming back, aren't you?" Alice asked, looking

wide awake now. A frown deepened the lines between her eyes.

"Something has come up that has to be taken care of in person," he replied, adding sugar to his coffee. "It shouldn't take too long. I'll be back Friday night in time for the town's tree-lighting ceremony." He smiled at Amy and Flash. "And guess what we're going to do Saturday afternoon? We're going to find the perfect Christmas tree!"

They fell on him with hugs and kisses before they ran for their coats and caps and schoolbooks. Alice discreetly found something to do upstairs. Standing, Penny moved around the counter and placed her fingertips on his sleeve.

"John, are you leaving because..."

Briefly he touched her cheek, then let his hand drop. "I think we need a little time apart." His gaze swept the rounded swell of her stomach beneath a wool smock. "I'll be back in a couple of days. You said I'm welcome to stay until the baby comes, and I plan to take you up on that."

"I didn't intend to drive you away."

"You haven't." A humorless smile brushed his mouth. "This is a damned peculiar conversation for two soon-to-be-divorced people to be having, isn't it? Seems like you should be glad I'm leaving."

She frowned and her hands moved. He thought he saw a struggle ensuing behind her eyes, then she shrugged and gave him a helpless smile. "This whole mess is confusing, isn't it?"

"Yes," he said, watching her walk away from him.

HIS EYES BEGAN TO STING the minute he stepped off the airplane, which impressed him as odd, for he didn't usually notice Los Angeles's infamous smog. Six weeks of crisp clean mountain air had apparently stripped away his immunity.

After renting a sedan at the Hertz counter, he found his way out of the rental-car parking lot and turned left onto the highway. If he was lucky the Santa Monica Freeway wouldn't be too crowded and he'd have a straight shot to Harbor and Wilshire.

Maneuvering skillfully through the heavy traffic whizzing along the freeway, he started to relax, enjoying the warm temperature, the green plantings, and the feeling of being home. No one in the next lane was going to roll down a window and shout advice or questions about his relationship with his wife. Anonymity was the name of the game here. A man became anonymous the minute he stepped outside his usual perimeters. He became just another face in the crowd.

John frowned. He had never thought of it in those terms before—losing one's identity. But of course it was true. The people driving the cars enclosing his had no meaningful identity, not to him. He didn't care about them; they didn't care about him. He would never see them again.

The same could be said about the people he sat near in the Grand Avenue Bar, or at Perino's, one of his favorite restaurants. If by chance he made an ass of himself, he didn't have to suffer jokes about it the following day from people who had been sitting at the next table. They were strangers. Los Angeles, like any huge metropolis, was populated by strangers, by people who brushed the periphery of one's life, then moved on, having left no appreciable effect.

Frowning, he gripped the steering wheel and edged into the ramp lane. The man driving the car he cut in front of shouted out his window and made a rude gesture. The fast lane had its minor disadvantages, John thought with a mirthless smile.

Somehow it didn't surprise him when Jason, the doorman at the Blackman building, gazed at him without a flicker of recognition. The blank look lasted only a moment, then Jason's face broke into a grin. It was Christmas, after all, a time when doormen were remembered. "Mr. Martin, nice to see you," he said, beaming. "You've been gone a few days, haven't you?"

"Six weeks."

"Has it been that long?" Jason shook his head, unsure how to proceed. From his expression, it was a fair guess he assumed John no longer worked at Blackman Brothers.

John pressed an envelope into Jason's gloved hand. "Merry Christmas," he said, feeling foolish. Outside the air-conditioned lobby, it was a balmy seventy-seven degrees. Despite the plastic holly garlands draping the lobby and the plastic tree near the bank of elevators, the humid heat made Christmas seem impossibly distant.

"Thank you, Mr. Martin." Jason lifted his cap and smiled broadly as he escorted John to the elevators.

The first thing he saw when he stepped onto the twenty-second floor was the bowl of ornaments decorating Marla Simpson's receptionist desk. It reminded him of Santa's Village. Except Marla wasn't wearing winter wool; she was dressed in crisp lime-colored linen.

She blinked when she saw him, then grinned and flipped through a bowl of paper slips, withdrawing one. "We have an office pool betting on how soon you'd return." Her smile widened. "Walt Hanson in corporate finance wins." She waved the slip of paper. "He predicted you'd be back before Christmas."

John smiled. "Don't pay off yet. This is merely a visit. Is Emil in?"

Emil Blackman shook his hand when he was shown into the senior partner's plush office. "John! I wish I could say this is a surprise, but it really isn't." He smiled broadly. "In fact I understand there's an office pool..."

Emil continued speaking, but John wasn't listening. Instead, he studied the office he had coveted as long as he could remember. The mauve carpet was thick and rich; the furnishings were upholstered in buttery soft leather. There was a scattering of polished glass tables. Museum-quality paintings adorned the cherry-wood walls. A spectacular view of the bay opened behind Emil's oversize desk. In recognition of the holidays, Emil's secretary had installed and decorated a small artificial tree on top of a side table. A few gifts wrapped in distinctive Rodeo Drive paper lay beneath the branches.

John's office was down the corridor, a smaller, less lavish version of Emil's. Briefly he closed his eyes.

This is what he had sacrificed his wife and children to gain. A thick carpet, company paintings, a great view, and his name on the door in discreet gold letters. For this he had traded warmth and love. A smiling face on the pillow next to his. Small arms and sticky kisses.

"Emil," he said, interrupting. "We have to talk."

AFTER LEAVING Blackman Brothers, he drove to the condo he and Penny had bought almost eight years earlier. During the drive, he rolled down the car window, letting the warm breeze rush over his face. Palm trees and oleander lined the freeway. The day was humid and overcast. People in the cars flashing past him were in summer pastels.

In Aspen Springs Amy's scout troop would be ice-skating on the pond today. The ski slopes would be crowded. The temperature would hover at a chilly twenty-eight degrees. Wes Pierce would be sitting on his bench in front of the post office warming his face in the steam from a thermos of hot chocolate.

A person had to be crazy to trade palm trees and sunny beaches for freezing weather and snowdrifts.

In the lobby, he distributed Christmas envelopes to the doorman, the maintenance super and the head of housekeeping. He left envelopes for the paperboy and the maid service with the doorman, then rode the elevator to the eighth floor.

With half the furniture in Colorado, his living room looked spartan. The condo smelled dusty and hot, unused. After throwing apart the curtains, he opened the balcony doors to let the California light and air in to the rooms. Stepping onto the balcony, John glanced at his watch, then leaned on the railing and looked down to the swimming pool below.

Amy and Flash would be home from school by now, telling Alice about their day, doing their homework under her supervision. He wondered if Amy had done well on her math test, if Flash had had a good time at Billy Galloway's birthday party.

Turning back inside, he walked down the corridor to their rooms, standing for a moment in the doorways. Penny had taken the kids' furniture to Aspen Springs, and their rooms were empty. Idly he noticed the walls needed a coat of paint. A box of outgrown clothing sat forgotten in Flash's closet; Amy had left her swim fins behind.

Because he found the silence oppressive, he returned to the living room and snapped on the TV, tuning to CNN. When the national weather came on, he carried a cold beer into the living room and listened as America was informed that a cold front was sweeping toward the Rockies from Canada.

When the forecast ended, he finished his beer and slowly walked through the condo, seeing Penny in every room. He remembered the night of her thirtieth birthday, the day they had brought Flash home from the hospital, the afternoon Amy swallowed the bottle cap, the night they had celebrated a quarter-of-a-million-dollar commission.

Suddenly the silent condominium on Moss Morency Drive seemed the loneliest place on God's earth.

"DO YOU THINK Daddy misses us?" Flash asked for the hundredth time, looking up from the strips of paper he was coloring with fat crayon stubs.

"I'm sure he is," Penny said in an expressionless voice. After checking to make sure Flash wasn't also coloring the tablecloth, she added, "Right now Daddy's probably having dinner with friends."

A woman friend? It wasn't any of her business, she reminded herself with a frown. But they probably should have talked about it. She should have mentioned he was free to date if he wanted to. The thought made her feel light-headed. He didn't need her permission, for heaven's sake. The divorce papers could be considered an official invitation to the dating game.

Amy brushed white paste over the ends of Flash's crayoned strips and pressed them together, adding to the growing paper chain that twisted across the kitchen floor.

"Do you think Daddy will call us?" she asked.

"Tonight?" Penny asked, glancing at the stove clock. "He probably won't get home until after you're in bed. But I know he's thinking about you."

Ha. Like hell he was. Right now, John was probably calling for more champagne, leaning across a candlelit table to gaze deeply into the eyes of his dinner date. And the longer Penny thought about John taking some bimbo out to dinner, the angrier she became. He could at least have waited until the divorce was final before he started acting like some romance-crazed teenager, hitting on every available woman who crossed his path.

She could just see it. He had probably taken the bimbo to the Spice Shack and was sitting with her in Penny's favorite booth. Mario would have given the bimbo a fresh daisy at the door, raising his thick eyebrows when he saw John was not with Penny.

The bimbo would slide into Penny's place in Penny's booth. She would be wearing something low cut in black silk or satin, and she was probably braless, because that's how bimbos were; it was in the bimbo rule book. You could not be a bimbo unless you had big breasts and went braless. And it was a given that bimbos turned up their noses at panty hose. They wore only black garter belts and smoke-colored stockings—rule number two. And every man alive knew it.

The bimbo would be raven-haired and look like a young Joan Collins—Penny was certain. Her eyelashes would be as long as the tines on a garden rake, as sultry as a Johnny Mathis recording at midnight. Her fingernails would be perfectly manicured, painted crimson and made for scratching a man's naked back. Her seductive voice would purr as she uttered inanities that would bore any intelligent man to tears. Except she would be wearing a perfume so provocative it wiped out a man's intelligence quicker than an erase key on a computer board.

John didn't have a chance. The bimbo would have him wrapped around her crimson-lacquered finger before the salad was served.

"Penny?" Alice looked up from the macaroni she was stringing on a needle and frowned. "Are you all right? You have the most peculiar look on your face—"

"How could he!" Penny flared, her cheeks as red as the bimbo's lips and nails. "The divorce isn't even final and…and it's Christmas!"

Amy and Flash looked up at her.

"It just isn't fair!" Slapping a bag of unopened macaroni on the kitchen counter, Penny scowled at it. "I'm home for dinner for the first time in weeks, and is he here to notice? No! He's in California having dinner with some painted bimbo who has a waist!" She placed her hands on her swollen stomach in the vicinity of the hips she used to have. "Well, I'll tell you this. He's not the only one who's free to date!"

They stared at her.

"Alice? You asked what I wanted for Christmas? I want a black lace garter belt and a pair of smoke-colored stockings!"

"Really?"

But who in the world was going to ask an eight-and-half-month pregnant woman for a date? And if, by some miracle, such a crazy man appeared, would she really want to to go out with him? She didn't remember how to date. What did strangers talk about? What if he tried to kiss her good night? The idea of kissing anyone other than John made her shudder. Ugh.

And where would they go? Dancing? Right. Skiing? Oh, sure. In her condition about the only choice was a movie, and then only if her date agreed to pull her out of the seat afterward.

Then there was the problem of how her date would introduce her to his friends. "This is Penny Martin, my date. I didn't do that to her. Ha, ha." Or, "Yes, she's pregnant, but she's still a sexy exciting woman." Wink, wink.

Oh, God.

"I don't want to date," she said, spreading her hands. Her voice sounded suspiciously like a wail. "It just wouldn't work out and I don't want to, anyway."

When she saw Alice, Amy and Flash staring at her as if she had lost her mind, she burst into tears, spun and did a fast waddle out of the room.

"What's a bimbo?" Flash asked Alice, his dark eyes wide.

"What's a garter belt?"

"Why is Mommy crying?"

Alice sighed, frowning after her daughter. "Well, kids. Your mother has a rich fantasy life, you see. And generally that's a good thing." Lifting a piece of macaroni, she sighted through it, then pushed it over the needle. "And she's pregnant. Being pregnant messes up a woman's metabolism." Amy and Flash looked at each other, then back at her. "Metabolism? Well, never mind. We have to be understanding during this difficult time for your mother, okay? Now, how are you progressing on that paper chain?"

Penny swept back into the kitchen. Her eyes were a bit red and her hands weren't as steady as she'd have liked as she dumped the bag of macaroni into a bowl. "The paper chain looks very nice," she said, her voice artificially bright. "Now who's going to help me string this macaroni?"

"Mommy, what's a bimbo?"

"Ask your father," she said grimly, squinting at the needle and string.

THE DAYS PASSED in a busy blur, then suddenly, it seemed, it was Friday. The tree-lighting ceremony was almost finished by the time Penny arrived at the pond. Before dashing out of her car, she cut the headlights, then paused to catch her breath and peer through the windshield at the group gathered on the ice.

Mayor Windell had already pressed the official lighting switch. A thirty-foot Christmas tree lit the center of the frozen pond with brightly colored twinkling lights. Skaters flashed across the ice, cutting through the light from the torches and the red and green shadows cast by the Christmas tree. Myrna Gordon led the carol singing.

As Penny stepped out of the car and drew on her gloves and pulled her cap over her ears, she spotted her family standing near the front of the group. Dr. Adler and Alice shared a song sheet; Flash and Amy were pressed against John. Penny imagined she could hear his clear baritone rising above the other voices.

Biting her lips and holding her arms out for balance, she placed each boot carefully in the snow and made her way down to the pond.

She was late again, and slightly embarrassed by how glad

she was to see John. In the back of her mind she had half expected to receive a phone call telling her he had changed his plans and would be remaining in Los Angeles for the holidays. Also, she was angry with herself for being so consumed by curiosity. What had he done in Los Angeles? Who had he seen? Where had he gone?

A flush of pink heated her cold cheeks as she remembered how her imagination had run away with her a few nights before.

The idiotic part of it was that she hadn't felt particularly jealous when they were married. She had been secure enough in herself and in their marriage that even when John worked late, as he usually did, it had never occurred to her to question it. Her imagination had not soared into overdrive and tormented her with jealousy-provoking suspicions. So why was she behaving so badly now? It didn't make any sense.

When he saw her, John's face lit with a smile of genuine pleasure, and her heart turned over in her chest. Knowing she would regret it later, she moved into the arm he opened for her and stood close to him, bending her cap over the song sheet.

"'Joy to the world, the lord is come...'"

When she had regained her equilibrium, Penny smiled and waved at Alice and Dr. Adler. Colored Christmas lights blinked across the faces of Alice and John and her children as they sang. Amy, her cheeks tinted from the cold, looked radiant in her joy of the moment; Flash gripped John's hand and happily sang off-key in a loud boyish soprano. Alice had moved to link arms with Dr. Adler and sang in a clear bright voice, harmonizing with the doctor.

Silvery breath rose in front of the carolers. The exuberant swish of skates sounded on the ice.

Suddenly Penny remembered Christmases past, standing in this same spot, her hair braided like Amy's, her small hand clasped in Alice's. Even then she had sensed that some day she would be standing here with a family of her own, gazing in joy and wonder at the bright star blazing atop the tree while carolers filled the night with song.

Myrna Gordon's strong vibrant voice rose above the others. "'Oh holy night, the stars are brightly shining...'"

Penny's throat closed and the bright Christmas lights shimmered behind a moist film. It was so beautiful. The star shining from atop the tree, the frosty night, Myrna's joyful voice soaring, and John's arm warm around her shoulders. The faces of her children. The tension falling away like snow melting down a window pane.

This was Christmas. This was what it was intended to be. Joy and fellowship and family. Voices raised in celebration. This was the way she had remembered Christmas all those years when she was so far from home. This is what she had wanted for her children.

And for John.

Chapter Eight

"'Hi ho, hi ho, it's off to work we go,'" John sang. After glancing back to grin at the kids, he adjusted a small ax on the shoulder of his parka and led the march from Penny's car to the area flagged by the forest service.

Other families had also driven up the mountain to search for the perfect Christmas tree. Voices called across the snowy mountainside, shouting greetings, calling Merry Christmas.

"Watch out for the stubs," John called over his shoulder to Flash.

Stumps of trees stuck out from the carpet of snow, evidence of the previous year's Christmas harvest. Flash manfully maneuvered his sled around them, happily singing "'Hi ho, hi ho,'" at the top of his voice whenever John did.

Penny and Amy brought up the rear, calling and waving to friends, trying to keep up with Flash and John.

"What do you think, sport?" John stepped back in the snow to squint at a perfectly shaped spruce.

"It isn't big enough, Daddy," Flash protested. Amy agreed.

"I believe you're right. We need a big one. How are you holding up?" he asked Penny. To her surprise, he seemed to be in his element, thoroughly enjoying the outing.

"Fine," she lied, pausing to catch her breath. Women as pregnant as she was had no business hauling themselves through a snowy pine forest. Granted, the slope was gentle, but she was so bulky and awkward that even flat land presented a problem.

"I wish you'd agree to wait in the car."

"I know you're thinking of my welfare, and I appreciate it, but I've dreamed about cutting our own tree for years. How much it would mean to the kids. And I want to be part of it, okay? Will you please stop fussing over me? Just let me do this at my own pace and I'll be fine."

"Okay," he said, raising his gloves in surrender. "But if—"

"John!"

"Just don't be stubborn, all right? If it gets to be too much, I'll take you back to the car."

Maybe it was a dumb idea to insist on sharing the experience, but she was determined to see it through. And, she thought grimly, she was determined to enjoy it.

The sky was a brilliant cobalt blue, and winter sunlight cast a sparkle of diamonds across the snow. If the cold hadn't been so intense, it would have been a fabulous day. But it seemed to Penny that she inhaled icy needles with each breath. As no one else appeared to notice the cold, Penny pulled her cap more firmly over her ears and summoned a cheerful smile. She made a vow not to spoil the outing by focusing on her discomfort or dwelling on how difficult it was to hike through knee-high snow while baby Whosit did somersaults inside her stomach. She told herself for the hundredth time in the past five minutes that she absolutely did not have to go to the bathroom. But she eyed the forest, looking for a wide-based tree just in case.

"Anybody want to rub my tummy for luck?" she joked, trying to take her mind off the cold.

"Our resident Buddha," John said grinning. They all patted her tummy, then John led them deeper into the forest. "Is this the perfect one?" he asked, stopping in front of a snow-tipped pine.

"It doesn't have enough branches," Amy commented doubtfully.

"Right you are. Okay, how about that one? Is that the perfect tree, or am I seeing things?"

Penny struggled after them, hoisting her boots over the drifts or breaking through them. "This is fun," she told herself grimly. Fighting up slopes through knee-high drifts was a great family outing. Everyone should cut their own tree. "Wouldn't have missed it for the world," she muttered.

At this point she could have sworn she had been pregnant, bulky and longing for a nap, most of her adult life. Among other things, she could no longer recall the convenience of bending from the waist. Since she could no longer bend, John had had to push her snow boots on her feet and lace them for her. And as if she wasn't bulky enough, the layers of woolen underwear and heavy clothing made her feel like a cartoon character, one of those with so much padding that his arms stuck straight out at his sides.

Panting from the exertion of climbing through drifts of wind-sculpted snow, she finally caught up to the others, who were waiting for her with expectant faces.

"Look, Mommy! I found the perfect tree!" Grabbing her hand, Flash eagerly pulled her forward.

Penny eyed his sled enviously, wishing pride would allow her to let someone pull her back to the car.

"Looks terrific to me," she enthused, guiltily aware she would have said the same thing if the tree under discussion had been an anemic specimen with only three branches. It seemed as if they had been fighting the deep snow and walking for hours. Days. Everyone's cheeks were bright pink from the cold. Eyes sparkled and silvery vapor puffed in front of each mouth.

"Okay, guys, now that Mommy's given the official approval, here we go." John applied himself with the ax and in a moment the tree was down. Laughing at Flash and Amy's efforts to help, he tied the tree to the sled, then straightened and smiled at Penny. "You know, I've always wanted to do this." Pushing back his cap, he looked at the sky, inhaled the heavy pine scent perfuming the frosty air. "Buying a tree from a lot will never be the same."

This was no time to rhapsodize. Not when one-fourth of the tree-cutting party was freezing, exhausted, and had to go to the bathroom in the worst way. *It's all in your mind,* Penny told herself.

"Wagons ho," she called, leading the long waddle back to the car.

By the time they returned home and Alice had served marshmallow-capped cups of steaming hot chocolate, Penny felt like a truck had rolled over her.

"I'm pooped," she said, dropping onto a stool in front of the counter.

Alice nodded, understanding. "I remember the final month when I was pregnant with you. It seemed to last forever. All I wanted to do was sleep. The least little thing wore me out."

John emerged from the basement carrying the carton of ornaments and Christmas decorations.

"We're going to decorate now?" Penny groaned. Being surrounded by Christmas every day at work had diminished any need for an immediate display of Christmas decorations. Then she saw the excitement lighting the kids' faces and she bit her tongue.

"Look, Grandma Alice!" Amy clasped her hands together and stared at the tree John was fitting into the stand, her eyes shining. "Isn't it the best Christmas tree you ever saw?"

"The very best," Alice agreed, smiling.

"I found it," Flash claimed proudly, crawling under the branches to help John.

Penny watched with a tired smile. She didn't recall John's having so much patience in the past, but he didn't complain as Amy and Flash continually got in his way in their efforts to help. He seemed to be enjoying himself, and he praised the kids when they managed to actually assist, more by accident than anything else.

"Do you need help with the lights?" Penny asked when the tree was secured in the stand. She hoped he would say no. She wasn't sure she had the energy to do anything more than watch.

"I don't think you can get close enough to the tree to do

much good,'' John said, smiling. ''Alice? Can you give me a hand?''

''I'll do it,'' Flash insisted.

''You're too short, sport. Maybe next year.''

Sitting at the counter, unreasonably feeling left out, Penny sipped her chocolate and watched the lights wind around the tree, then the strings of macaroni and the paper chains. When she saw the pride in Amy's and Flash's expressions, she realized the macaroni and the paper chains had been a wonderful idea.

''Penny, you look absolutely exhausted,'' Alice commented, looking up from the box of ornaments she was opening. ''Darling, why don't you pop yourself into a nice hot tub? Relax for a while. I'll call you for dinner.''

A sudden overwhelming case of the guilts overtook her. She was too pooped, too pregnant to participate in the tree trimming. And she hadn't even thought about offering to help with dinner. The tree reminded her that she hadn't started her Christmas shopping, hadn't give a thought to the homemade gifts she had agreed to. She should have phoned Lydie an hour ago to see how things were going at Santa's Village. She should have paid bills last night. Tomorrow or the next night was Amy's and Flash's Christmas program at school. Vaguely she remembered promising to bring a plate of cookies. Where would she find the time?

''Thanks for the suggestion. I think I'll do that,'' she said to Alice, sliding from the stool. John and Amy were singing along with the carols playing on the radio and happily selecting silver and red ornaments from the boxes. Flash shouted and laughed and flung handfuls of tinsel at the lower branches.

It didn't seem to Penny as if they would miss her.

Leaving the scent of pine behind her and the familiar sound of carols, she climbed the stairs to her bedroom, entered the bathroom and turned on the water in the tub. For a moment she inspected herself in the mirror tiles, seeing the pink wind burn across her cheeks, the fatigue dulling her eyes. Alice was right. She looked ready to fall over.

Maybe John was also right. Maybe she was keeping too

hectic a pace. But it was only temporary, dammit. A frown drew her brows together as she discovered that her bottle of bubble bath was empty. Amy must have borrowed it again. After dropping the empty bottle into the waste can, she added shampoo to the bath water and nodded as bubbles foamed across the surface of the water.

She locked the bathroom door, symbolically shutting out the world, then stepped into the hot water with a sigh of pleasure and carefully lowered herself into the bubbles.

But she couldn't lock away her thoughts.

This was the Christmas she had dreamed of all those years in Los Angeles. She could remember standing on the condo balcony on Christmas Day last year, looking down at people splashing in the swimming pool below, and longing for a good old-fashioned snowy Christmas in Aspen Springs. She had felt almost a physical craving for the clean cold softness of new snow on her cheeks, for the scent of freshly cut pine. Something in her heart had rejected the sight of Christmas lights wound through palm trees and jacaranda shrubs, had protested Santas dressed in red bermudas and short sleeves. She had yearned for a real Christmas. A Charles Dickens Christmas, with frost lacing the windowpanes and fat snowflakes tumbling out of the sky. With the cinnamon smell of home-baked cookies and the tang of green pine boughs and holly wreaths.

Now that she had what she longed for, but she wasn't enjoying it as she had thought she would.

For one thing, it was difficult to be enthusiastic about all the Christmas trimmings when she was surrounded by them every day at work. For another, it was hard to enjoy much of anything when she felt so tired all the time.

And she felt left out.

It was her own fault, of course, but she felt the sorrow and regret just the same. She was running as fast as she could, but the tree-lighting ceremony had begun without her. Naturally. She couldn't go ice-skating or snowmobiling with John and the kids on weekends because she had to work or catch up around the house. Of course. It was the busiest time of year at Santa's Village. It seemed that all she had done today was struggle to keep up, arriving at one tree, panting and gasping, just as the others were moving on to the next. Now her family was enjoying the warmth and camaraderie of decorating the tree. And she was too pooped to take part. She was a quart low on Christmas spirit.

Christmas was turning into one big headache.

Folding her hands over her stomach, Penny sighed and pushed her toes against the water spigot.

The night she had told John she would not return to Los Angeles, he had said she was afraid of loving. In addition to everything else she had to think and worry about, she had been thinking about that.

She was not afraid of loving; she was afraid of the pain when the loving was no longer enough. She did love him. Covering her face with one sudsy hand, she drew a long breath. She loved him so much it hurt.

The John Martin who had arrived on her doorstep was the John Martin they had both lost sight of. If he could be like this all the time—wonderful with the children, tender and loving toward her. With no distracted frowns, no late nights and weekends at work. And if he could do it here, in Aspen Springs. If, if, if.

She scrubbed her hand across her forehead. It was going to be terrible for Amy and Flash when John returned to Los Angeles. As terrible as leaving him the first time. Maybe worse, because he had spent so much time with them, had genuinely gotten to know them and let them know him.

It would also be terrible for her. Already she felt hints of the renewed pain of missing him.

The new baby would help, she thought, gently tracing her fingertips over her stomach. And she had her job to keep her busy. But still…there were the nights. The long lonely nights.

This line of thinking was taking her nowhere and was only upsetting her. She would wrap herself in a warm robe and join the others.

Because she couldn't bend forward to reach the drain, she opened it with her toes. The water receded around her and she waited until she thought she could push herself up without splashing the floor.

Then she pressed her heels against the bottom of the tub and pushed her hands against the sides. Her heels shot out from under her, and before she could catch herself, she slid awkwardly down the back of the tub until she was lying flat on her back as the last of the water gurgled down the drain.

Feeling foolish, thankful there was no one to see, Penny pushed her feet against the base of the tub. Her shoulders rose up along the back curve, but she immediately slid down flat the moment she moved her feet.

It was the shampoo, she realized. Unlike her usual bubble bath, the shampoo had left a slippery residue. The tub was as slick as oiled porcelain. There was nothing on which to get a grip.

"This is nutty," she muttered, flat on her back on the bottom of the tub. She tried to bend forward to sit up, but it was like trying to fold a beach ball.

Lying flat, she stared up at the heat lamp, wishing she had turned it on. "Now, think about this," she told herself. After a moment, she decided to try a sideways maneuver. She would roll on her side, draw her feet up, then, wedged on her side with something solid to press against, she could pull herself up.

Rolling sideways was a mistake. When she tried to draw her legs up, all that happened was that she slid toward the drain and had less control than she seemed to have on her back. Plus, she saw that she would not fit sideways in the tub.

Now she was beginning to get cold. Doubling her efforts, she slid and slipped around the tub, pushing herself up the back curve, sliding back down. She began to feel frantic.

There was only one thing to do if she ever hoped to get out of this rotten tub, and she hated the thought.

"Help," she whispered, closing her eyes and imagining what she looked like. A naked wet hippo wallowing in a shampoo-slick trap.

"Help!" Would they hear her over the carols on the radio and their voices?

"Help!" she shouted.

John paused beside the tree, an ornament in his hand. "Was that your mother?" he asked Flash.

"I thought I heard something, too," Alice said, glancing up from the pot of chili she was stirring on the stove. "Amy, honey, run upstairs and see if your mother wants something."

When Amy returned, her blue eyes were wide. "Mommy's stuck in the bathtub. She can't get out."

"What?" John stared at her.

"She wants you to come, Daddy."

They all went. John tried the bathroom door. "Penny? The door's locked."

"I know," she answered in an embarrassed voice. "I can't reach it."

"Is there a key?" he asked Alice.

Alice shook her head. "If there is, it disappeared years ago. But I'll search. The bathroom lock is a push button. It works from the bathroom side of the door."

"Penny? Are you all right?"

A silence ensued. "I'm getting cold," she finally called out. "I can't reach the towels." There was another silence while John stared at the door. "Are the kids out there with you?" Penny asked.

"I think I'll have to break down the door."

"Good heavens," Alice murmured. She straightened her shoulders. "Come along, children. Let's…let's finish the tinsel, then you can set the table."

"I want to watch Daddy break down the door," Flash begged. His dark eyes sparkled with excitement.

"Me, too! We can, can't we, Daddy? We can stay and watch?" Both children looked at him with awed eyes.

"I don't think your mother would like that."

"Your Daddy's right," Alice interjected hastily, eyeing the door. "Let's go."

The dragged their feet, faces long with disappointment. John studied the door until Alice and the children had gone. He had seen this done on TV a hundred times. How hard could it be?

"Penny? I'm going to break it down." Actually, it looked pretty sturdy. "Stay out of the way."

"John, I can't get in the way! I'm stuck in the tub."

Moving back a step, he contemplated the door, deciding where he would hit it. "Don't worry, honey. I'm coming to get you."

"Be careful!"

There was enough room to take three running steps. His shoulder hit the door and he bounced back, landing on the floor. Rubbing his shoulder, he swore between his teeth.

"What happened?" Penny called anxiously.

He pushed himself to his feet and narrowed his eyes on the door with a look of grudging respect. It was built to last. But they broke down doors on *Miami Vice*. They did it on *Wiseguy* and the *Equalizer*. Tom Selleck had built a career around breaking down doors. Television made it look easy. According to those guys, there was nothing to it. He rubbed his sore shoulder and stared at the door.

"John? Are you okay?"

"Tom Selleck is a fraud. Did you know that?"

"What?"

"Stay out of the way."

"John, I told you..."

This time, knowing what he was up against, he bunched up, imagined he was a tank and hurled himself at the door, hitting it with all his strength. The door hurled him back. Pain ran up his shoulder in a hot pulsing current. Sprawled on the floor, he rubbed his shoulder and cursed through a clenched jaw.

"What the hell is this door made of? Steel?"

"It's solid oak," Penny called from the other side. He groaned. "John? I don't mean to rush you along, but...but it's cold..."

"Okay. Hold on, I'm coming. I'm going to kick in the lock." His shoulder felt like it was on fire. The lock looked as sturdy as the rest of the door. But by God, he was going to rescue his lady. "Stand back."

"Listen, if you say stand back one more time—"

"Here goes."

The Karate Kid he was not. His heel struck, then slid off the doorknob, and he crashed to the floor, convinced he had sprained his back. For a moment he lay there, staring up at the closed door, swearing mightily. First he was going to get a blowtorch and open that damned door if it was the last thing he ever did. Then he was going to hurl the TV set off the balcony. It wasn't only kids who watched too much television. Then he was going to write an acid letter to Tom Selleck and Don Johnson, telling them exactly what he thought of their door-breaking scenes.

Alice walked into the bedroom and stared down at him. "Are you all right?"

"Do I look all right?" he asked sourly, getting to his feet. Groaning, he placed a hand at the small of his back. "At present it's three for the door, zip for the home team. Do you own a blowtorch?"

"Something better," she said, opening her hand. The key to the bathroom door lay in her palm. "I found it."

"Thank God."

"I'll be downstairs," Alice murmured, discreetly withdrawing as John bent to fit the key into the lock.

Penny looked pitiful. She was laying flat on her back on the bottom of the tub, her knees drawn up, her hair wet on her bare shoulders. She was shivering and her teeth were chattering.

"Penny, honey, I'll have you out of there in a flash," he said, flipping on the heat lamp before he bent over her.

Tears of embarrassment and frustration formed in the corner of her eyes. "I was out of bubble bath, so I put shampoo in the water, but it's so slick! Then, after I drained—"

"I know, darling. Here, let me get you under the arms."

"—the water, it was like the drain was pulling me down too, and—"

The angle was excruciatingly awkward. Once he got his arms around her, he was leaning too far over the tub to exert any upward strength.

"—every time I tried to get out, I kept slipping back down."

When he saw he wasn't going to succeed, he released her. She gasped, then slipped down the back curve of the tub again. She lay on the bottom of the tub, staring up at him.

"Was that supposed to be funny?" she asked in an expressionless voice.

"This is more difficult than I thought. I don't want to risk dropping you or having you fall."

The heat lamp spread a rosy glow over her naked body. If it hadn't been for the goose bumps, she would have been ripely beautiful. Lush and dewy. He hadn't seen her naked in, well, in almost nine months. Exerting massive self-control, he kept his gaze focused on her face, but he could still see her magnificent breasts from the corners of his eyes. He swallowed.

"I know that look, John Martin," she said in an accusing tone, narrowing her lashes. "And believe me, this is not the time! I'm trapped and cold and I need to get out of this tub! Please, do something."

"Okay." He shook his head, shaking free of the hypnotizing sight of her. The rose-tipped breasts, the golden triangle. "Let's try it sideways."

She pointed to her stomach. "I won't fit sideways."

"All right, can you kinda lean sideways then, at least enough so I can get a firm hold under your arms?"

Her breasts were sensational. Her skin glowed. With her golden hair wet on her shoulders, with that radiant skin, she looked like a pregnant Venus. The touch of her reminded him of cool smooth ivory.

When he had his hands under her arms, trying not to think about touching her, he leaned near her face, his eyes lingering on her mouth. "This is what we're going to do. I'll lift you to a sitting position on the edge of the tub, all right? And I'll hold you steady while you swing your legs around to the floor."

"Okay." The trust in her eyes steadied his hold.

"On the count of three."

Penny pushed; he pulled. When he had her sitting on the edge of the tub, he chanced to glance at the mirror tiles on the back side of the tub and caught a quick breath. She was splendid, beautiful. Radiant in impending motherhood. He stared at her image, hypnotized. Reuben would have killed to paint skin tones like hers.

Finally she was standing, shivering, her forehead pressed to his shoulder. "Thank you," she whispered.

Grabbing a towel, he rubbed her body briskly, restoring the warmth to her glorious skin.

He supposed there were men who were turned off by their wife's pregnancy, but he was not one of them. In his opinion, Penny never looked lovelier than when she was pregnant. Something wonderful happened to her skin. It became like satin, creamy and smooth, almost luminous. He wanted to touch her, stroke her, wanted to shape his hands around the firm swell of his child, wanted to cup her heavy breasts in his palms. The feeling was reverential, but it was sexual, too.

"Right now I wish you weren't pregnant," he murmured against her hair, his voice husky. He held her against his warmth while he toweled her back.

"Me, too," she whispered.

Before he could decide if she meant she was weary of being pregnant or if she meant she wanted him, too, she stepped away from him and wrapped herself in the voluminous orange robe.

"I don't know what I would have done if you hadn't been here," she said, bending slightly to wrap her hair in a towel. "Thank you, John."

"Actually, I didn't do much of anything." Now he was beginning to feel the ache in his shoulder. It was going to be sore for days. "Alice found the key. She's the heroine of the day."

They looked at each other across the small space, Penny leaning against the sink, him standing with his hands in his pockets.

Finally Penny dropped her eyes and plucked at her robe. A blush rose on her cheeks. "The chili smells good, doesn't it?" she whispered.

He cleared his throat. The moment passed. "Ready for something to eat?"

"Starving."

When she stepped past him, he caught the scent of shampoo and soap and baby powder and the scent that was uniquely Penny's. After a moment, he sighed and followed her. She tried to open the bedroom door and frowned.

"That's odd," she said. "The door will only open a crack." Placing her eye to the crack, she looked down at the knob. Amy's jump rope had been tied around the handle. By shifting position, Penny could see the other end of the rope tied to the handle of the guest-bathroom door. "You won't believe this! We're tied in."

She banged her fist on the door. "Kids? Amy and Flash? Let us out of here right now!"

John groaned. "Amy's last Brownie badge was for knots."

Carols blasted on the other side of the door. Amy or Flash had turned up the radio until it was loud enough to rock the house. And drown out any cries for help.

John glanced at Penny's bed, then smiled at her. "Right idea, wrong methods."

She gave him a weak smile, then returned to beating on the door.

When Alice finally came to see what was keeping them—and unlocked the door—she found Penny napping in the bed and John sitting in the chair next to her pretending to read.

"I DON'T GET IT," Lydie Severin said, tucking her chin into the scarf wound about her throat. Thick snowflakes swirled out of the evening sky and danced in the light shining beneath the Victorian lamps lining Main Street.

"What don't you get?" Penny asked, as they stepped into the employee cafeteria bringing a blast of cold air with them. At a dozen good-natured protests, they quickly shut the door. Then they hung up their coats, took trays from the rack and started down the cafeteria line.

"When you talk about John, you get a mushy look in your eye. It's like you're still in love with him." Lydie leaned over the glass counter then pointed to the chicken-fried steak. "I'll take the chicken-fried, please. Yet you aren't stopping the divorce."

"I do love him," Penny admitted. She ordered a fruit salad, thinking about the weight she had gained. "But love isn't enough. Unfortunately."

"You're kidding," Lydie commented when they had settled themselves at a table away from the door. She flicked her napkin across her lap. "A job certainly isn't enough. Try snuggling up to a title or a paycheck. Kids aren't enough. They're terrific, sure, but what do you do after they go to bed?"

"Come on, Lydie. You know what I'm saying."

"No, I don't. Hey, look at the sign behind you—Christmas Is Love. In my opinion, *life* is love. That's what it's all about. The whole ball of wax. What else is there that counts for anything?"

"I'm not saying love isn't important. I'm just saying other things are important, too." Penny looked at the fruit salad and decided she wasn't hungry, after all.

"Not a chance. I think you're nuts."

"Come on, Lydie, give me a break. Lately it seems like you're always on my case. I thought you were my friend."

"I am your friend, dummy. I'm trying to understand what you're thinking. You have this terrific guy you love and who loves you. But you say love isn't enough. You'd rather have a job that's wearing you to a frazzle, and raise three, count 'em, three, kids by yourself, not to mention sleeping alone. Does it strike you that possibly there is a flaw in your thinking? That just maybe you're making a bad bargain?"

"Love shouldn't mean one person has to surrender everything that's important."

"Hey, it's not a perfect world. But think about what you just said. Where does it end, Penny? Once you start saying, I'm not the one who's going to give in…then what you're doing is placing conditions on love. How do you get off that trip?"

"What are you talking about?" Penny asked, frowning.

"Isn't that what you're doing? Aren't you saying to John

that you'll love him if he'll give up his career, move to Aspen Springs and live your life-style?''

''That's what he's saying to *me*. But I don't think either of us should have to give up our ideals.''

''Giving each other up is better? Look, suppose John gave in and did it your way. What happens next? What's the next condition? You'll love him if he's home for dinner every night? You'll love him if—'' she spread her hands, searching for words ''—he never mentions business after five o'clock or takes a business call at home? If you ask me, this whole thing sounds like a power play.''

''I don't recall asking you,'' Penny replied coldly. The bright color had intensified in her cheeks.

''Listen Penny, you won't believe this right now, but what I'm going to tell you is true.'' Lydie pushed her chicken-fried steak to one side. ''Three months after your divorce is final, you'll be looking for another man. You'll join the ranks of the single and the recently divorced. And we're all looking for the same thing. Love. We aren't looking for a man who is geographically convenient, or a man who will promise to spend every single weekend at home, or a man who is as wealthy as Midas. We aren't thinking about conditions. We're looking for a man we can love and who will love us in return. Those are the criteria. Look around you. Take a look at Helga.'' She nodded toward the next table. ''What do you think Helga wants from Santa?''

Penny didn't answer.

''Love. That's what Helga wants. It's what we all want. Dear Santa, please bring me someone to love who will love me in return. Penny, love is damned hard to find. You're one of the lucky ones, but you're too confused right now to recognize it.''

''Look Lydie, I know you mean well, but I don't want to discuss my personal life. Okay?''

''Suit yourself. I just think you're making a big mistake, that's all.''

Penny poked her fruit salad. ''And if I pack up and return

to Los Angeles, you get the promotion. That wouldn't be influencing your advice, would it?''

''That isn't fair, Penny.'' Lydie's shoulders straightened and her expression stiffened. ''Since you've said you won't take the promotion even if it's offered, I'll get it anyway.'' She paused. ''Unless you aren't shooting straight with me and you do want the promotion.''

Suddenly Penny remembered John saying, ''Show me. If you don't want the promotion, then take yourself out of the running.''

Frowning, she turned her coffee cup in the saucer. Until now she hadn't taken time to realize that it was possible she was building her ego at the expense of Lydie's. If she did indeed win a promotion that she didn't plan to accept, she would have the ego stroke of knowing she had won. But Lydie would be left with the knowledge that she was second choice.

''If my circumstances were different, I would want the promotion,'' she admitted slowly, working it out in her mind. Sometimes when she couldn't sleep, she thought about the changes she would make at Santa's Village if things had been different and she could seriously consider accepting the promotion. Even knowing it was a waste of time, she couldn't help thinking about it.

''Then I wish your circumstances were different,'' Lydie said, looking at her across the table. ''I wish this was an honest competition.''

''It is honest, but it's just...'' There was no point in going over it again. She drew a breath and shifted the topic. ''Some of our employees feel we're pushing them too hard because we're both competing so strenuously for Allenby's approval,'' Penny said quietly. ''Some of the staff believe we're asking too much of them and of ourselves.''

''Maybe we are,'' Lydie conceded after a moment. ''I blew up at Don Compton yesterday over some little thing that didn't really merit such a strong reaction.'' After a pause, she added, ''I'll be glad when the choice is made and the suspense is over.''

Penny noticed that Lydie looked tired, too. ''Oh, Lydie, do

you really think I've been deceiving you? That I'd change my mind and accept the promotion if Allenby offered me the job?'' she asked in a soft voice.

Lydie studied her friend. ''Honestly? I don't know, Penny. It's difficult to believe you'd drive yourself this hard if part of you didn't want it.''

The observation was distressing. Long after Lydie had departed for the day, Penny thought about their conversation. She was still thinking about it when she turned out the lights in her office and walked through the park to the deserted parking lot.

It was ten o'clock at night, her children were asleep, her back ached, she was hungry enough to wish she had eaten the fruit salad, and she couldn't wait to fall into bed.

''Dear Santa,'' she said as she scraped snow and ice off her windshield. ''Please bring me three extra hours a day. And give the promotion to Lydie. It would make things so much simpler.''

Simpler? What could be simpler than saying no? But it wouldn't be simple, because deep down she admitted she wanted the promotion. At least she wanted to know she could have had it if her circumstances had been different.

And, Santa, she added after a moment, if you can manage it, please bring me a solution to John. Because she wanted him, too.

It looked like this would be the year Santa didn't bring anything on her list.

Chapter Nine

A brightly lit Christmas tree occupied one side of the school stage. A manger scene crowded the other. Wes Pierce, dressed as Santa Claus, sat in a rocking chair beside the tree, beaming and ho-hoing and presenting gifts to the kindergartners and first graders, who were dressed in pajamas and holding teddy bears in their arms.

Sitting in the darkened audience, Penny leaned over her stomach when it was Flash's turn to recite his poem. She held her breath and smiled encouragement. Beside her, John and Alice leaned forward, too, silently mouthing the first words of the poem.

Flash gripped his teddy bear and approached the front edge of the stage. He stood there, not speaking and squinting at the audience as the silence lengthened. A whisper prompted from the wings, but Flash ignored it, saying nothing.

Penny raised her hand above the heads in the audience so that Flash could spot his family. A broad smile pleated his freckles, and he leaned forward from the waist and bellowed his poem.

"Santa, Santa, Santa dear/ Here's my wants, I hope you hear/ Bring us peace and bring us health/ Bring Mama rest and Daddy wealth..."

"I coached him," John whispered as the audience chuckled. He gave Penny's hand a proud squeeze.

"...and a train for me!" Flash finished, shouting the words.

The Flash Martin school of performing equated loud with excellence. The audience laughed and applauded, then Dr. Adler's granddaughter stepped to the front of the stage to recite the next Christmas poem.

Like a wave passing over the audience, one set of parents strained forward to mouth words as another set leaned back in their seats, beaming with pride and relief.

Penny, John and Alice leaned forward again when Amy, dressed as a shepherdess, followed the Wise Men onto the stage. Possibly there were other speaking parts, but they heard only Amy as she waved her crook over the manger and said to the audience, ''Oh, what a beautiful baby!''

''Oh, dear,'' Penny murmured when Amy's part was over. She gripped John's arm in alarm. ''I was supposed to bring a plate of cookies, but I forgot until this minute!''

''Don't worry,'' John whispered, covering her hand with his. ''Alice remembered. I baked cookies this afternoon and she brought some with us. The Martin family honor has not been tarnished.'' He grinned.

''You baked them?''

In all likelihood, if Penny had remembered the cookies, she would have stopped at Santa's Village Bake Shoppe and bought a bag. An edge of panic sharpened her nerves. There was too much to do and not enough time. She couldn't keep up with it all. There was Amy's Brownie party and Flash's class party; was she supposed to furnish cookies for them? She needed to organize an office party for her staff, and she recalled seeing a couple of holiday invitations in the mail. And when was she going to address cards?

She suppressed a groan at the thought of all the letters she needed to write to enclose with her cards. Maybe this was the year for the Christmas letter, that generic impersonal enclosure she had always professed to dislike. What she hated most about the ''Dear Friends'' Christmas letter was its relentlessly cheerful tone. No one ever wrote a ''Dear Friends'' Christmas letter that said: ''I'm pregnant and I don't want to be, but I've left my husband anyway and here I am living in a small town in my mother's house and working too many hours to get a promotion I don't plan to accept. I'm exhausted, thirty pounds overweight, confused and upset. But I hope you have a nice Christmas."

Nope, this was not the year to send out a Christmas letter. And now was not the proper time to start making mental lists of all she needed to do tomorrow and everything she had forgotten to do today.

As she forced herself to relax and focus on enjoying the remainder of the Christmas program, Penny gradually realized this was another of those close moments with John that she had begun to love and to dread. She was very aware of his presence beside her. With each breath, she inhaled the expensive spiced scent of the cologne he wore, could sense his genuine pleasure in the shared moment, at watching their children perform. His arm lay across the back of her seat, possessive, near enough that she felt his solid warmth enclosing her.

Suddenly a rush of longing overwhelmed her. She experienced an urgent disconcerting need to rest her head against his shoulder and deepen the emotional sharing to some physical expression. They were as one in their pride in their children; at the moment she longed to close the circle and reach for him.

Swallowing hard, Penny clasped her hands tightly over her stomach. She fixed her eyes on the stage and leaned slightly away from the warmth brushing her shoulders.

The divorce had been her idea; she wanted it. Nothing had changed. They were still entrenched in their positions.

But the divorce was not working out as she had envisioned. Because her job demanded more time and energy than she had anticipated, she was not spending as much time with Flash and Amy as she wanted and as she had planned. She had been in Aspen Springs nearly a year, but she was still living with Alice; she didn't have a home of her own. Consequently she didn't really feel settled. Finally, she hadn't dreamed how much she would miss John. Naively, she had believed that once the decision to divorce was made, the confusion and the ache would end. She had been wrong. That's when it began.

She darted a look at him from the corners of her eyes, wondering what he was thinking right now. Unquestionably, he was the most handsome man in the audience. Intense, golden, a beautiful man. When he noticed she was staring, she quickly looked back at the stage.

What if she agreed to return to Los Angeles? This wasn't the first time she had asked herself that disturbing question, but it was the first time she hadn't shouted a silent *no!* Did this mean her resistance was crumbling?

And actually, was Los Angeles really so terrible? Of course it wasn't. But it wasn't Aspen Springs, either, and something inside her needed a small community. As well, she had to admit Aspen Springs wasn't working out as she had hoped. The pace of her life hadn't slowed; the values she sought to regain seemed to hover just out of reach. And what if Lydie was right? What if—eventually, in a few years—she decided she wanted to date or remarry? What were her chances of finding Mr. Right in a small town like Aspen Springs? Frankly, the opportunities would be slim.

Especially when Mr. Right was sitting beside her now, beaming at the stage. She bit her lip. John was so right in so many, many ways. But so wrong in the areas she considered vitally important.

"You look like you're about to cry," Alice said to her as the lights came up and the stage curtains swished shut for the final time. "Christmas makes me cry, too," she said, dabbing her eyes with the cuff of a Liz Claiborne sweater. "It's so lovely."

"This is what Christmas is all about," John commented, still looking toward the stage. "Children singing carols, demonstrating their faith and their belief in a better and peaceful world."

"Can't argue with that," Dr. Adler agreed, appearing beside them. Smiling, he shook John's hand, then Penny's. "How are you feeling?"

"Tired most of the time. Ready to get this show on the road." Dr. Adler smiled with understanding as Penny smoothed a hand over a festive smock. "This one is going to be an athlete. He danced to every carol."

Dr. Adler chuckled, then linked arms with Alice. "Mrs. Sage, I wonder if I might have a word with you?"

Amy and Flash ran into the audience as Dr. Adler led Alice toward the tables of punch and cookies.

"Did you see me, Mommy?" Amy called, catching Penny's hand.

"I was the loudest, wasn't I?" Flash demanded, looking up at John.

John laughed and swung Flash up on his shoulder. "Absolutely, sport. They could hear you in Denver. I predict the birth of a star. And you," he said to Amy, giving her braid an affectionate tug, "were fabulous. You put those other kids to shame!"

All over the auditorium parents were praising their children. Here and there Penny noticed a family with one of the spouses missing. Next year she would be among them, trying to speak with two voices, trying to make up for John's absence. A shudder constricted her shoulders and she ducked her head.

"Are you cold?" John asked. When she shook her head, he set Flash on his feet and gave both children a hug. "Let's find those cookies, shall we? I'll bet acting makes a guy hungry for cookies." As they passed Wes Pierce dressed in his Santa suit, John grinned and murmured, "Suits you."

"Ho, ho, ho. And what do you want Santa to bring you, son?" Wes asked, clapping John on the back.

"A bit of privacy."

Wes chuckled and patted Penny's arm. "Guess we know what you want," he said, winking at her stomach. "Are we hoping for a boy or a girl?"

"No preference," Penny answered, smiling.

"Looks like the buzzer could go off any day now," Wes noticed.

"Bite your tongue!" Penny said with an exaggerated groan. "I don't have time to have a baby right now. Lydie and Ian Allenby would have a fit if I took off during our busiest season. I've promised to wait until after the first of the year."

"Last I heard, babies don't take much account of their parents' wishes in the matter. They show up when they're darn good and ready and never mind if it's a convenient time for the parents. So what's this little critter's name going to be?"

Penny didn't look at John. "We haven't decided yet."

Wes grinned. "Better start thinking about it. Soon."

John hung behind as Penny caught the children's hands and started toward the refreshment table. He found himself following Wes Pierce backstage, leaning in the doorway as Wes changed out of his Santa suit.

"The scenery was great," Wes said, stripping off his fake beard. "Didn't know you were handy with a hammer."

John shrugged. "I thought you knew everything." But the compliment pleased him. Now that he wasn't phoning Blackman Brothers every day and his mail had all but stopped, he had expected to find time dragging. But it hadn't worked out that way. His morning list was a long as it ever had been, but the emphasis was different. Now it included such items as building stage scenery.

"Tell me something, Wes," he said casually. "You have money. You could live anywhere in the world. Why did you choose Aspen Springs?"

Wes unbuckled his Santa's suit. "Let me ask you a question, son. Do you think you could run for mayor of Los Angeles and have a chance of winning?"

"I doubt it. It would take years and a small fortune to build name recognition, then a vigorous campaign, and the results would still be up in the air." He lifted a curious eyebrow. "Have you ever been mayor?"

Wes nodded. "Served three terms here in Aspen Springs. Every man ought to be mayor at least once in his life just to understand the meaning of the word *aggravation*. My point, son, is that here you can do it. Hell, you could throw your hat into the ring next fall and have as good a chance as anyone of winning. In a town like Aspen Springs, you can make a difference. One man has a chance to change the things he doesn't like, a chance to make life a little better for his community and his family." He stepped into a pair of corduroy pants then looked up at John and grinned. "Take a guy like you. You start out cooking pancakes for a benefit supper, then you move up to building scenery for a school play, and before you know it, you're looking at the potholes thinking maybe you'll sit for a position on the town board, and you can do it. That's what community is all about, John, and it feels good. Helping others, and getting help when it's your turn to need a hand."

John shook his head. He had too much pride to ask anyone for help. It was an admission of failure. "Why Aspen Springs specifically?"

"Why not?" Wes shrugged. "The scenery is spectacular, the people congenial. It's a nice little town. I like it." He snapped off the light and dropped an arm around John's shoulders. "I guess you heard I made a lot of money when Vail was developed. You've made a lot of money, too. But think about that baby in the manger scene we saw tonight and the man he grew up to be. Some day we're all going to be standing before him having a little talk about our lives. I don't think he's going to say: 'Wes Pierce, how much money did you make in your lifetime?' I think he's going to say: 'Wes, how did you treat the people in your life? Did you enjoy the life you were given?'"

"Interesting point of view."

"Sure there are lots of places to live. Good places. But for me, I enjoy life best right here. And every now and again I have a chance to help someone. Keeps life interesting."

"Have you ever asked for help?" John inquired.

Wes's iron-gray brows lifted in surprise. "Sure. Lots of times." He paused in the doorway and looked out at the crowded auditorium. "It's easy to give help, son. Nothing to it and you walk away feeling good about yourself. What's hard is to accept help." He transferred his gaze to John. "But no man is truly part of a community until he's asked for help. Once he's done it, he's never the same. A man doesn't truly understand that humanity is one big family until he draws on that family for help and learns it's there for him. I guess you could say it's a growth step."

"Isn't it also a risk?"

"What isn't? But you have to trust in community and in

yourself." He patted John's shoulder and his arm fell away. "And I'd say that's a good bet."

The conversation was hard to shake off, and there were points he wanted to argue, but John placed it on the back burner when he rejoined Penny. "So. What do you think about Scott Eliot Martin?" he asked after accepting a cup of punch and a paper plate of cookies. "I've always liked the name Scott."

"But...Eliot? I don't know. What if it's a girl?"

"How about Penelope Anne Martin?"

"I don't like juniors. Two Penelopes is one too many, don't you think?" Pushing back her sleeve, she glanced at her watch. "If we can find Alice, we should think about leaving. I have some inventory forms to review tonight."

A distance appeared in John's gaze. "Let's not rush the kids, okay? This is their night. It's not every day they get to be stars." Turning away from her, he looked toward Flash and Amy who were standing with their friends, basking in the afterglow of their performances.

Penny pressed her lips together. Of course he was right. "Talk about role reversal," she murmured with a sigh, trying to make a joke out of it. In the past it had been she who had to admonish John about not hurrying away from somewhere. John gave her a thin smile but said nothing.

By the time they returned home, it was nearly midnight, and she was too tired to review the inventory forms.

And too confused. All the things she had believed settled still weren't. Least of all her own feelings.

"Mommy," Amy said when Penny tucked her in and leaned to kiss her good night. "The Brownie party is Tuesday after school. You said you'd come."

"I will, honey."

Amy beamed. "You promise?"

"I promise. You were terrific tonight. I was so proud of you!"

Amy's eyes closed. "I knew you'd be there. Flash said you wouldn't, but I knew you would. I love you, Mommy."

Penny stared at her daughter in shock. Did Amy really believe she would have let anything cause her to miss the school program? Apparently, Amy did.

Deeply troubled, she tiptoed from the room.

"GOOD HEAVENS!" Penny gasped, halting at the top of the stairs. She stared toward the kitchen. The air was fragrant with the warm scent of cinnamon and heavy spices, but she had never seen such a mess.

Cooling cookies crowded the counter top; broken pieces covered what empty space remained. Crumbs and splotches of raw dough littered the floor tiles. It seemed that every bowl and every pan Alice owned was dirty and stacked in whatever available space could be found. As Penny walked slowly toward the counter, she noticed that Flash had cookie dough clumped in his hair; cinnamon and melted chocolate stained Amy's new blouse. Both children were painted like Indians, their cheeks artistically streaked with food coloring.

"Hi," John called cheerfully, looking up from the bowl of dough he was kneading. "You're home early. Did you have a good day?"

"Busy," Penny said.

"We're making cookies and cakes," Amy explained. After giving Penny a sticky kiss, she returned to her chair at the table to position red-hot buttons down the fronts of a row of gingerbread men.

"I can see that," Penny said. Frosting dribbled from the front of the stove and down the lower cabinets. As Penny's eyes widened, Alice stepped on a gumdrop and lifted her foot to glare at the bottom of her shoe. "You guys are making a spectacular mess."

"It'll clean up," John said, dismissing the dough zone with admirable unconcern. Opening the oven with a flourish, he removed a golden coffee cake. "The coffee cake and puff pastry are for us. Wait until you taste this!" He placed the coffee cake on a rack above the cutting board. "But not until it cools and is frosted. Okay, Flash, what happened to the white icing?"

"I colored it red, Daddy," Flash explained, waving an empty bottle. "Red frosting is the best."

"Can I eat another chocolate-chip cookie?" Amy asked.

Alice fell into a chair and waved a napkin before her flushed face. She directed a weary smile toward Penny. "We've been at this all day. When it comes to baking, John is indefatigable. The man doesn't know the word quit."

"You have enough cookies and cakes to feed most of China," Penny smiled, inspecting the cellophane-wrapped packages covering the kitchen table.

"Gifts," Alice explained. "Remember? We have a baked gift for everyone we know, have ever known, or will ever know in the future."

John grinned and pushed at a lock of hair with the back of his hand, leaving a streak of flour across his forehead. "It's great, isn't it?"

"Some of this is pretty exotic," Penny noticed after she poured a cup of eggnog. "Linzer Schnitten? Date Lebkuchen? Spitzbuben and nut meringues? I am impressed!" Then she noticed the pans of fudge, and creamy fondant. "Candy, too? And...are these homemade croissants?"

An explosion of powdered sugar erupted at the end of the counter, and Amy and Flash doubled over in giggles at the sight of each other. Faces, hair, hands, they were covered with powdered sugar.

"Don't worry about it," John said, placing a hand on Penny's arm. "We have plenty of sugar. They're making frosting. They know how to do it."

"So I see," Penny said, raising an eyebrow. Powdered sugar drifted toward the floor and over the cabinets. The thought of cleaning up this mess staggered her. "You couldn't have made do with a pan of fudge and a few popcorn balls?"

"Nope." After greasing a pan, John began shaping almond crescents onto the surface. "This is too much fun. Too bad you had to work," he added, without looking at her. "You missed the action—we're about finished. But you can help with the taffy tomorrow."

Penny's eyes widened and her lips formed a circle. Speculating on what two kids could do with warm taffy was enough to buckle her knees, and she sat abruptly at the table across from Alice.

"There's no stopping him," Alice said with a shrug.

Slowly Penny looked about her, examining the devastation wrought on Alice's kitchen. It was spectacular and total. "This time I think it's you who should have a long soak in the tub. I'll clean this up." While releasing a long breath, she wondered what it was going to take to get the dough and powdered sugar out of Amy's braids.

"You don't mind?" Alice asked gratefully. "It doesn't seem fair for you to do the cleaning—"

"I don't mind. Honestly. I want to contribute something to this project."

"In that case, I think I'll escape before you come to your senses and change your mind." Alice wiggled her fingers in a wave and almost ran toward the stairs leading up to the tub.

"Well, that does it for today," John said with satisfaction, removing the last pan of cookies from the oven. He wiped his hands on Alice's ruffled apron. "By the way, I've been meaning to ask you, who supplies the baked goods for the bake shop at Santa's Village?" When she hesitated, he smiled. "I know, you executives would like the customers to think everything is baked in-house. But when I was playing Santa that day, I ducked into the bake shop for a doughnut and noticed they don't have the kitchen facilities to produce the variety and amounts shown in the cases. Your bake shop can do cakes and pies, but not much else. They must be buying the rest—the pastry items."

"You caught us." After telling him the name of the Denver supplier, she tilted her head curiously. "Why do you ask?"

"I just wondered. Why doesn't Santa's Village use a local supplier?"

Penny spread her hands. "We would, but there isn't one."

"That's what I thought." After a glance at the wrecked kitchen, he untied Alice's apron and dropped it across the counter. "It's really nice of you to volunteer for the cleanup," he said, patting Penny's shoulder with a distracted gesture. "Come on, kids. Let's head for the showers."

Her eyebrows shot up as she watched them go, leaving her to a mess that would have done credit to a dozen chimpanzees. Then she smiled. What the heck. Cleaning up was a small price to pay for having all these cellophane-wrapped Christmas gifts. It was one less thing to worry about.

Whistling under her breath, she tied John's discarded apron around her waist and started loading the bowls and pans into the dishwasher. The almond crescent cookies were terrific and she ate half a dozen as she worked, feeling good that she was participating.

Of course, she didn't realize that devastating Alice's kitchen was destined to become a daily occurrence.

JOHN MADE TAFFY Sunday morning. Despite Penny's misgivings, the event was fun, and they finished with a minimum of mess. In the afternoon, while Amy and Flash played with the Galloway kids in the basement and Penny and Alice watched the Bronco game and twisted the lumps of taffy into colored paper wrapping, John made cheesecakes.

"What do you think?" he asked, handing them each a sample at half-time.

"Another cheesecake? How many did you make?" Penny asked, blinking at the plate in her hand.

"This is an Amaretto cheesecake. The others are strawberry and pineapple. Is the Amaretto taste too strong? It seems a little strong to me."

"John, what are we going to do with three cheesecakes?"

"If I eat another piece," Alice moaned, staring at her plate, "I'm going to look like Penny. Each slice must have eight thousand calories in it."

"We'll send one home with the Galloway kids. Alice can take one to the library tomorrow. What do you think? Too much Amaretto?"

"No, it's perfect." Perfect was too mild a word. The cheesecake was fabulous. "By the way, what is this coffee? It's wonderful."

"Kenya roast. Nothing fancy, but if you blend it with the Viennese mint it creates something interesting, don't you think?"

Penny watched him return to the kitchen, then she blinked at Alice. "Does it strike you that something's wrong here? Isn't it John who should be watching the football game and one of us working in the kitchen?"

"I can't believe a daughter of mine would make such a sexist remark. Will you look at that? Elway got sacked again. When is Reeves going to get a decent offensive line?"

"Alice, I'm serious. What's going on here? John is acting like a new bride who's just discovered cookbooks." She stared into the kitchen. He was leaning on the counter, eating a slice of cheesecake and studying a stack of recipe cards.

MONDAY MORNING, after everyone left for school or work, John poured another cup of coffee and studied his notebook. His lists had outgrown the scratch pad he had been using and were now relegated to the back of a notebook containing market studies, financial breakdowns, sample menus, price lists and sales targets. He added Santa's Village to the growing list of sales targets, then leaned back in his chair, chewed the end of his pencil, and studied the winter sunlight glittering atop Buffalo Mountain.

The first possible obstacle had been overcome. When the idea initially occurred to him, he wondered if he could recover his enthusiasm for baking, or if large-scale cookery was a dead passion from his past. It wasn't. Baking satisfied a creative urge that numbers never had. Every morning he bounced out of bed, looking forward to the day and the excitement of a new discovery.

It reminded him of the good old days, except he had never thought of them as the good old days until recently. Those days of building from scratch, of taking risks, of dreaming and planning. The days when he and Penny had squeezed every nickel, had gone trick-or-treating for a splash of scotch because they couldn't afford to buy their own.

He saw now that having success wasn't nearly as exciting

as getting it. The early years had been the best of times. The dreams, the excitement, the sheer adventure of stepping into life and shaping it into what one wanted it to be. He was beginning to see how lucky he was to have this chance at a second career, at seizing excitement and challenge all over again.

It was funny how things worked out. He had resigned from Blackman Brothers and moved to Aspen Springs because Penny believed the divorce was inevitable. But he refused to lose his children. Living here, he would be near them and could share their lives. He hadn't expected, however, to find an exciting work opportunity in Aspen Springs. Something he genuinely wanted to do. He had expected to drift awhile, then eventually settle into a dull job, probably with one of the commercial banks.

Yes, he was a lucky man in many respects. He only wished Penny could share in this beginning as she had shared in the dreams of the past. But she had made her feelings clear. No compromise. The divorce would go through.

Soon, he thought, adding it to his lists, he would have to find a place of his own. The thought was wrenching.

To take his mind off living without Penny, he reached for his jean jacket, found his car keys and consulted his list of today's activities. The first stop was the post office. Maybe the restaurant supply catalogue had arrived, or a response to his letter requesting an appointment with Denver's largest supplier of coffee beans.

"Don't you ever get cold sitting out here?" John asked Wes Pierce after discovering the restaurant supply catalog had arrived and the coffee-bean rep would be in Aspen Springs next week to meet with him. Not even the leaden sky, dark with snow-swollen clouds, could diminish his good mood.

"Thermal underwear, that's the secret." Wes nodded an invitation for John to sit for a spell. They leaned against the bench, watching the locals and tourists moving in and out of the shops facing the town square.

"Penny and Alice sent this for you and your wife," John said, placing a cellophane package on the bench between them.

Though he didn't admit it, not even to himself, bringing the package to Wes was the real purpose for his visit to the post office today.

"That's right nice of Penny and Alice," Wes said with a smile. "I heard someone up at Alice's place was doing a lot of Christmas baking." When John didn't comment, his smile widened. "Also heard you were nosing around over at the jeep dealer's." He nodded his cap toward John's Porsche. "Thinking about a trade?"

"Maybe."

"The way I see it, a Porsche isn't much good for mountain driving. And a jeep isn't too impressive on a California freeway. So?"

"So?"

Wes laughed. "So, some of us hereabouts figure this means something. You dyed-in-the-wool Yuppies don't trade in a Porsche for no reason.... Are you still sleeping in the North Pole, son?"

John rolled his eyes and stood up. "Is there anything about my life that Aspen Springs doesn't know?"

"Not much, and that's a fact." Tilting his head back, Wes studied the flinty sky. "If I was you—and I'm not helping out, you understand—I'd take a look at the Hathaways' shop over there across the square. Might suit your purpose just fine, and the price is right."

A sigh lifted John's shoulders. "I had this crazy idea that no one but me knew my plans."

Grinning, Wes looked up at him. "Not hard to figure them out, son. I can't recall the last time this town witnessed a genuine market study. What did you think? That no one would notice all those questions and requests for information?" He paused. "If you don't mind my asking, you haven't told Penny about this, have you? Does this mean you two are dumb enough to let that divorce go ahead?"

John made an exasperated sound. "Remember our deal? Live and let live?"

"Just trying to help out, that's all."

"Wes, I don't want any help from anyone, okay? Not now, and not in the future."

Frowning, he remembered Wes's philosophy about accepting help.

"John?" Wes called, stopping him as he was about to open the door of the Porsche. "Thank you for the baked goods." Wes studied him with a thoughtful expression. "Someone said that a lot of cellophane packages just like this one showed up on the doorstep of Reverend Cowper's church. You wouldn't know anything about that, would you? No, I didn't think so. Too bad. Reverend Cowper is awful anxious to know who to thank. A lot of folks are going to be real happy to get these cellophane packages."

A flush of embarrassed pleasure climbed from John's collar as he backed his car out of the post office parking lot.

AS USUAL it was after ten o'clock when Penny arrived home on Monday. The kids were asleep. Alice was dozing in front of the channel-nine news, and John was cleaning the kitchen.

"You know, I'm starting to think you look cute in a ruffled apron," Penny commented as John poured them each a cup of coffee and slid one across the counter to her.

He laughed. "I'm hoping Santa will bring me something more tailored. Maybe a nice masculine tweed with a leather belt." His dark eyes softened. "It's been a long day. How are you feeling?"

"Baby Whosit has been trying out for the Kiddie Olympics today," Penny said, gently rubbing her stomach. She shifted sideways so that she could lean an elbow on the counter top. "What have you been up to, or need I ask?" The kitchen table was hidden beneath stacks of cellophane packages tied with red Christmas ribbon.

"The first batch were mostly mailouts. I sent packages to our friends in L.A. This batch is for Aspen Springs. I have Alice's list, and I'll need yours by the day after tomorrow at the latest."

"It's really thoughtful of you to do all this, John, but *why* are you doing it? Are you that bored?"

He leaned against the kitchen sink, studying her across the counter. "It's not boredom. I like to bake. Always have. I know," he said, smiling and raising a hand, "there hasn't been much evidence of it in recent years. But I haven't had the time before. Now I do and I'm enjoying it. Plus, I have an idea, something I'm working on."

"Do you want to talk about it?"

He hesitated. "I'd love to talk about it. But this isn't the right time," he said glancing at the clock. "I know you're tired. And I still have some things to check out. Besides, I know you have a lot to deal with already."

Penny frowned. "That makes it sound like your idea is something I'll be upset about..."

"That's possible," he said after a minute. It had occurred to him that Penny might not welcome having her ex-husband in the same town. She had wanted him here once, but now that she had decided there was no possibility of a reconciliation, she might feel very differently.

"Then you're right to delay telling me," she said after a minute. "Right now I don't think I could cope with one more thing. Not to change the subject, but before you arrived I'd convinced myself I couldn't tell freshly ground coffee beans from canned coffee. But I have to admit, since you've taken over the coffee-making detail the coffee has been especially good. What's this I'm drinking?"

"I'm experimenting with blends. Do you like it?"

"Yes." She tilted her head and returned his look of examination. "You know, there are sides to you I never suspected."

"Is that good?"

"Yes, I think it is. But it's confusing."

"I suppose there are sides to everyone that just need the right time and the right circumstances to emerge."

"Are you suggesting you've noticed sides to me you didn't suspect?"

"Everyone has hidden aspects."

She sensed he was being tactful, guessed if she had asked if her emerging sides were good ones he would have switched the direction of the conversation. The suspicion made her bristle.

"Well, it's late," she said, sliding off the counter stool. "I'll leave you to finish whatever you're doing and take myself off to figure out next week's personnel schedule."

It didn't make sense to wish John was staying at a hotel, she decided as she prepared for bed, because every hotel room was booked through the holidays, he saw more of the kids by staying here, and his visit would end in a couple of weeks. All good reasons for remaining here. But, oh, how she wished he was staying in a hotel. Seeing him every day was doing strange, confusing things to her nervous system. She thought of him first thing in the morning, and she thought about him while she was driving home from work. At odd times during the day, she wondered what he was doing. Considering the circumstances, it struck her that she was thinking about him much more than she should.

It was going to be extremely painful to say goodbye again after the baby was born. She dreaded the moment and felt a little angry about it. She'd thought the worst was behind her and the children; they had made the final break. Now, after John's lengthy stay, they would have to endure the pain and upset again.

Unless…

But love wasn't enough.

This thought ran through her mind long after she had turned her light out. Tossing, then turning, trying to find that elusive comfortable position, she finally decided sleep was impossible. She kept remembering Lydie's speech about love, and love being the only thing that mattered. The conversation continued to disturb her.

What if Lydie was right?

When she heard the noise, she sat bolt upright in bed, straining to hear. What she heard was the stealthy approach of a car, rolling almost, but not quite, soundlessly over the frost-brittle snow in the driveway.

Throwing back the blankets, Penny swung her legs over the bed and pushed her feet into her slippers. As she knew the pattern, she knew there wouldn't be time to run down to the basement and fetch John. But she could wake Alice and prove once and for all that Alice was wrong, that she was not imagining someone in their driveway.

Quickly she duck-walked down the corridor and rapped on Alice's door. There was no answer.

"Alice?" she called, trying the handle to Alice's bedroom door. The door swung open and she peered inside.

The first thing she noticed was how frosty cold it was in Alice's bedroom. And no wonder. Alice's window was open about three inches, the draperies billowing slightly in the frigid night breeze. A tiny red glow beside Alice's bed indicated the electric blanket was on. Penny decided the electric blanket was the only thing that allowed Alice a hope of sleeping in this cold, cold room.

Except Alice was not sleeping in this room, Penny noticed with a jolt. The coverlet was still in place, neatly tucked over the pillows. Immediately her gaze swung to the luminous dial on the bedside clock. It was three o'clock in the morning. And her mother was missing! Kidnap headlines flashed through Penny's mind.

Before she could spin around to run for help, she heard the familiar bump against the side of the house, louder in Alice's room than she had heard it before. Frozen in place, Penny stared at the window.

Mittened fingers appeared in the crack between the sill and the edge of the opened window. A scream stuck in Penny's throat. The trellis was directly beneath the window; obviously someone had climbed the trellis and was now creeping inside. Every instinct shouted at her to get out of here, to run for John and let him handle the intruder while she telephoned the police.

But she couldn't move. It was as if her slippers had taken root in the floor. Helplessly, her throat working, she watched the window slide silently up. A dark-clad figure climbed over the sill, stepped inside, then bent to close the window.

As the figure started to turn, Penny's paralysis thawed. She screamed.

Chapter Ten

"Mother!"

"Oh, dear." With a sheepish smile, Alice pulled the dark ski cap from her head and shook out her springy tumble of white curls.

Penny dropped to the edge of the bed; her mouth fell open. "I...I don't understand. You're the person driving into the yard in the middle of the night?"

Her mind raced. No wonder there was no evidence of a stranger's car when she or John had checked outside. The only car in the yard was Alice's. And if Alice was embarking on midnight jaunts, it was also no wonder that she insisted Penny and John take the spaces in the garage.

"I suppose you want an explanation," Alice murmured, dropping her parka on the chair beside the window.

"You suppose... I feel like I'm dreaming! If you discovered *your* mother climbing a trellis and sneaking into her bedroom in the middle of the night, wouldn't you want to know why?" Penny stared at her mother, incredulous.

"I guess I knew I'd get caught eventually." Alice bent to peer at Penny. "Darling, why are you still awake? Couldn't you sleep?"

"Alice, for heaven's sake. Here you are, dressed like a ninja, climbing in windows in the middle of the night, and you want to discuss why I can't sleep?" Penny rubbed her fingertips against her temples.

The door burst open and John rushed into the room.

"I heard a scream. Are you all right? Is anyone hurt?" The kids were behind him, their sleepy eyes wide.

"Oh, dear," Alice repeated. "This is all my fault."

"We're fine." Penny brushed back her hair and released a sigh as Amy and Flash jumped on the bed beside her.

"It's freezing in here," Amy said, pulling down Alice's coverlet. She and Flash climbed under the blankets.

"You know the sounds we've heard in the middle of the night?" Penny asked John. "It was Alice coming home from God knows where. And…and you won't believe this, but I discovered her climbing up the trellis and through the bedroom window."

They all stared at Alice, watching a furious blush heat her cheeks.

"Wow! Grandma Alice climbed in the window?" Flash's shout was loud with admiration. "Cool!"

"That's neat, Grandma Alice. Can we watch you do it?"

John blinked at Alice's trim black slacks and sweater. "I don't get it," he said slowly. "Why didn't you come in the door?"

"Well," Alice said, rolling a pointed glance toward Amy and Flash, "it's very late. Perhaps we should wait until morning—"

"Oh, no," Penny said, shaking her head. "I want to hear about this right now. Kids, the excitement is over, back to bed you go." She lifted Flash out of Alice's blankets and set him on his feet. "Come on, Amy."

"Aw, we always miss the good stuff."

"Give Mommy and Grandma Alice a kiss," John said, "then I'll tuck you in. Don't start without me," he called over his shoulder as he led the children into the corridor.

Penny and Alice looked at each other, then Alice smiled. A hint of pride twinkled in her eyes. "You really didn't guess?"

"It never entered my mind that it was you. Not once. In fact—"

"No," Alice interrupted, anticipating what Penny was about to say. "I didn't lie about it. If you'll remember, I always tried to change the subject." Walking toward the door, she gestured to Penny to follow. "It's cold in here. I could use a cup of hot decaf, couldn't you?"

John appeared in the kitchen as Alice was pouring three cups of coffee. He grinned as he slid onto one of the counter stools and raised his cup in a salute. "Alice, I have to say there is more to you than meets the eye."

"You sound like you know what this is all about," Penny said, turning to look at him.

"I think I've guessed."

"Oh?"

Smiling, he looked at Alice and raised an eyebrow. "I think it's possible that Alice is having an affair."

"What?" Penny spun on the stool to stare. Alice's cheeks flamed bright crimson. "Mother? You're suggesting my mother is having an affair?" She studied the color on Alice's face and her mouth formed a tiny circle.

"You needn't look so astonished, dear," Alice said in a mild voice. "One has to keep up with the times."

Penny swallowed and pressed the collar of her robe to her throat. "It's true then? You're having an affair?" She couldn't believe it. After glancing at her coffee, she pushed it away. "Forget this, I need a drink. John, is there any wine?"

No one ever quite viewed their parents as sexual creatures, Penny thought. Naturally it could be assumed one's parents had done "it" however many times it required to produce the number of children they had, but beyond that... Few people ever thought about their parents' jumping into bed for fun. Certainly one seldom thought of one's mother—a grandmother, for heaven's sake—as being hot to trot.

"I mean I just..." Penny spread her hands. "I never thought about..."

"Well, I wouldn't exactly call it 'hot to trot,'", Alice said after Penny explained some of her difficulty in accepting what she was hearing. "It's more like giving a long-term affection a chance to blossom into something more." She sucked in her cheeks and contemplated the kitchen ceiling. "On second thought, maybe it is being a bit hot to trot." She smiled. "The younger generations don't have a corner on the market, you know. Just because my hair is white doesn't mean I'm too old to love or be loved."

"I didn't mean that," Penny murmured hastily, her cheeks burning. "I just...I meant..."

"I know what you meant," Alice said, leaning to pat her hand. "It's a shock, that's all. You're accustomed to thinking of me as being alone."

"I've been very shortsighted. But I don't remember there being anyone else since Daddy died."

"For a long time there wasn't." Alice took a seat at the kitchen table. "Frankly life was pretty lonely."

"You never said a word," Penny whispered. "I feel terrible that I didn't realize..."

John spoke into the silence. "Alice, I love the idea of your climbing the trellis and crawling in the window. I wish I had been there to see it. But why didn't you just use the door?"

"Then you and Penny would have known."

"Would that have been so terrible?" Penny asked. "All these months...why didn't you just tell me?" The minute the question left her lips, she guessed the answer.

"The timing seemed wrong," Alice explained gently. "Your life was falling apart. You were devastated, talking to a lawyer about a divorce... It didn't seem right to parade my happiness when you were so dreadfully unhappy. Bill and I decided to delay any announcement until you were feeling better and were more settled about your future."

"Bill... Do you mean Dr. Adler?"

Alice's face lifted in a glorious smile and she nodded confirmation. Then she laughed at John's expression. "You look like one of those cartoon characters with a light bulb flashing over his head. What on earth are you thinking?"

"Now I understand why everyone in Aspen Springs is so eager to push Penny and me together. It's because of you and Bill Adler, isn't it?"

"I'm afraid there aren't many secrets in a small town."

"Everyone figures the quickest way to get you and Dr. Adler together is to get Penny and me together."

"Oh, Mother. Didn't you think I could handle the idea of you remarrying?"

"I knew you could handle it, darling. I just didn't want you to have to. Not yet. I believed it would be hard for you to be happy for me when your own situation is so up in the air."

"I haven't jumped to a conclusion, have I?" Penny asked uncomfortably. "I mean you are planning to marry Dr. Adler, aren't you? Or is this just..." She couldn't say it.

Alice smiled. "I think it's fair to say Bill intends to make an honest woman of me." Now that the cat was out of the bag, she seemed to be enjoying the conversation. "Although there's a lot to be said in favor of an affair."

"Well ladies, I have an idea the two of you have a lot to discuss." Standing, John finished his cup of decaf, then yawned, pressed Penny's arm and started toward the basement stairs. "I'll see you in a couple of hours."

"Tell me honestly, Penny," Alice said, after John had left. "Are you upset?"

"I'm more upset that you didn't tell me than I am about anything else."

"I didn't know how you would feel about my seeing someone. I know it's been a lot of years since your father died, but still, I didn't know if you would accept the idea of someone taking your father's place."

"I think the world of Bill Adler," Penny said honestly. "And I...I'm glad for you." She summoned a smile. "So. Let's have another cup of coffee while you tell me everything. When did you start dating and when is the wedding and will you live here or move to Bill's house? I want to know all."

It was as if a dam had burst. Face glowing, Alice spoke until pink streaks spread across the mountain peaks. Penny heard Alice's happiness and was genuinely glad. She felt guilty to realize that Alice had been right. Watching and listening to her mother's happiness and her plans for the future underscored the chaos and uncertainty in her own life. Alice was beginning a satisfying new relationship; Penny was ending one.

"Will you have a problem with Bill being on twenty-four-hour call?'' she asked when Alice paused to cover a yawn. ''Babies aren't always born between nine and five.''

''No relationship is perfect,'' Alice answered with a sleepy smile. ''When balanced against everything else, I think I can cope with a telephone ringing in the middle of the night.''

Before they went upstairs to prepare for work, they embraced each other tightly.

Alice brushed a lock of Penny's hair back behind her ear. ''I hope things work out for you and John,'' she said softly. ''He's a good man, Penny. And he loves you.''

''There are just too many problems. Maybe you can cope with a man who's at the beck and call of everyone except you, but I don't seem to be able to.'' A sad smile touched her lips. ''Particularly if I have to do it in Los Angeles.''

''You always were a stubborn child,'' Alice said, shaking her head.

''I don't remember that it hurt this much.''

''It doesn't have to, Penny. I know you love John.''

Penny bit her lip. ''Love isn't enough.''

''Good heavens,'' Alice said, her eyebrows rising. ''If love isn't enough, then what is?''

The words rang in her ears while she performed a quickie set of exercises before she dressed for work.

Amy ran into her room, ready for school, and jumped on Penny's bed. ''Don't forget, Mommy. The party is after school. Don't worry about the fudge, we're making that. And Daddy is going to drop by a plate of cookies.''

''What party, honey?'' Rolling from her side onto her back, Penny fought to catch her breath. Right now, she would rather have crawled through a blizzard than face a day at Santa's Village. What she wanted was to climb into bed and sleep for twenty-four hours.

Dismay pinched Amy's face. ''The Brownie party, remember? You promised you would come.''

Oh, Lord. She had forgotten. If she recalled correctly, her schedule was jammed today. After a minute, she rolled back onto her side and looked up at Amy's face leaning over the side of the bed.

"Honey, is this party really important to you?" Of course it was. At age eight every party was important.

Amy hid her face beneath the ends of her braids. "You promised," she whispered, fighting tears. "You said you would come!"

"I know, honey. And I would if I could." Sitting up, Penny stretched out a hand, but Amy drew back. "Sometimes things don't work out like we plan..."

But Amy was gone, slamming the bedroom door behind her.

Some Christmas this was turning out to be. What had happened to the joy? To the magic?

What had happened to the love?

Sighing, pulling herself to her feet, Penny went into the bathroom to put on her makeup. But it wasn't her face she saw in the mirror. It was Amy's, filled with the pain of disappointment.

BAKING SATISFIED a creative need John had almost forgotten he possessed. There had been a time not too long ago when he had begun each morning with knots tying his stomach as he reviewed the day ahead. No more. Now he awoke eager for the day, his thoughts filled with variations of this recipe or that blend.

Maybe this was what magazine writers meant by male midlife crisis, this sudden shift of ambitions and priorities. But what he was doing felt right. He felt as if he were awakening from a long period of slumber. On some unrecognized level he had been marking time, waiting for this period in his life, accumulating the wherewithal to pursue dreams he had believed long dead.

Now the dreams had resurfaced with renewed vigor. And to his surprise, he found himself in the perfect place to achieve them.

The real-estate agent unlocked the door to the Hathaways' gift shop and followed John inside.

"It's been vacant for quite a while, as you can see," Lon Thompson said, waving a hand around the dusty interior. "But the size seems right for what you have in mind. The location is good, and the traffic statistics support the town-square exposure.''

Slowly John walked the perimeters of the shop imagining how it would be. He could place the pastry cases just there, and a coffee bar would be perfect across the back wall. There was floor space for a dozen four-tops, plus wall space for shelves to display tinned bakery goods and prepackaged coffee blends. Plenty of kitchen space.

Thrusting his hands into his pockets, he returned to the center of the room to stand in a bar of sunlight falling through the front windows. The tall sunny windows begged for hanging plants. Already he could imagine the fragrance of freshly brewed coffee filling the room, and the yeasty scent of bread hot from the oven. The chatter of customer's voices rising from the tables. The cases would overflow with cakes and pies and cookies the size of saucers. He would sell them by the item or by the slice. Eat here or take home.

During the past weeks of thorough research, he had concluded there was a strong potential market; a quality pastry and coffee shop could be successful. The demand existed. The challenge of launching a new business, a new career, stimulated his competitive nature, stirred his business acumen.

''Do you want to discuss this with Penny before you commit to anything?'' Lon Thompson asked as they stepped outside and he bent to lock the empty shop.

John hesitated. He had been waiting for the right moment to discuss his plans with Penny, the changes he had made in his life and the changes he intended to make. But the right moment never seemed to arrive. They saw each other in passing or in the company of Alice and the kids. He suspected Penny preferred it that way.

Moreover, he couldn't guess how she would respond to learning he planned to make a life in Aspen Springs. He suspected she would believe he was doing this for her, when in truth he really wasn't. Somewhere deep inside he had begun to accept defeat. He and Penny weren't going to be able to put things back together. It wasn't what she wanted.

But being in Aspen Springs was what he wanted. The realization still had the power to amuse and astonish him. At some point during the past weeks, Aspen Springs had seduced him with its charm, pace and, yes, its people. There was opportunity here. And most important, his children were here.

"No," he said finally. "I'm ready to make an offer now."

Lon Thompson's face brightened. "Excellent. I don't think you'll regret this decision, John." He walked toward his car. "If you'll follow me back to the office, we'll draw up a contract."

Knowing Aspen Springs, the news would be all over town before supper. That part of small-town living he doubted he would ever like. Frowning, John eased the Porsche onto Main Street. He had to find a private moment with Penny. He preferred that she learn about this from him.

PENNY WAS NOT HAVING a good day.

First, she arrived late to work, sliding into the staff meeting with a look of guilt and frustration, trying to hide her yawns behind her note pad. Second, no one had shoveled the snow off the ice rink because she had forgotten to leave instructions for the crew. Ian Allenby was not happy to discover the rink would open late. Third, she had let the letters to Santa pile up unread, and the editor of the Village newspaper was calling every fifteen minutes pleading for copy. Fourth, her mind kept straying back to that incredible moment when she realized it was Alice sneaking in the window. And finally, Baby Whosit was kicking up a storm, dancing to the Christmas music blaring over her office speaker. She leaned over her desk and closed her eyes.

"We wish you a merry Christmas," kick, kick, punch. "We wish you a merry Christmas," punch, punch, somersault. "And a happy new year." Deep bow, back flip, double kick to mommy's bladder.

Stroking a hand over her stomach, Penny stifled a yawn, sighed, then lifted the top Santa letter and tried to concentrate.

Dear Santa,

Please make Stinky Bolen look at me in science class.

He should want to marry me. I also want a kitty, a white fluffy one and a Barbie doll and twirling lessons. And world peace.

Love,
Jeanne Ann

Stinky Bolen—the hunk of tomorrow? Penny smiled. The mating dance began at a younger age every year. She wondered how old Jeanne Ann was. Amy's age? She placed the letter in her undecided pile.

Dear Santa,
I want a color TV for my room and a VCR. Don't bring me any clothes. I want a bionic arm and a cape that makes me invisible. Don't tell Bruce Evans about the invisible cape. And don't give an invisible cape to anybody else. I also want a Nintendo and all A's from Miss Gladden. I'll leave you a glass of milk and cookies so don't eat too much at Bruce Evans's house. Is your beard real? See you next year.

Your friend,
Al Frye

She wouldn't mind having an invisible cape herself, Penny thought, her mind drifting. Leaning back from her desk, she tapped a pencil eraser against her teeth and studied the snow floating past the window. She kept thinking about what Alice had said.

If love isn't enough, then what is? What indeed?

Was a promise of next time enough for Amy? Did a promise soothe the hurt of knowing her friends' mothers would be at the Brownie party but her own mother wouldn't? Was a quick kiss on the way out the door enough for Flash? Or did he wish she was there to pick him up after school? How much was enough?

Was John satisfied with a terrific challenging job and a view of the ocean? Was that enough for him?

Were midnight trysts enough for Alice?

And what of herself? What was enough for Penny Martin?

A stimulating job in a town she loved? Which she pursued at the expense of the people who loved her?

Guilt deepened the furrow across her brow and she bit down on the pencil eraser.

"Face it," she whispered. "No one's happy. Your mother is sneaking in and out of windows. Your children are becoming strangers and you're disappointing them. You're divorcing the best man you ever knew. You're three years pregnant and running yourself ragged to win a promotion you don't want and won't accept. You're so exhausted, you'll probably sleep through your baby's delivery and miss the whole event. You don't have time for any of the things you used to think were important. And this is the worst Christmas you've ever had."

All because of some stupid idea that love wasn't enough.

If love wasn't enough, then what was? Alice was right. What on earth could be more important than love?

This job? With stunning clarity Penny suddenly comprehended that she had not changed her life-style. She had merely changed location. Ambition in Aspen Springs was still ambition. And she was as much a victim to ambition as John had ever been, she saw that now. She could promise herself from now until judgment day that her schedule was only temporary, but in her heart she knew it was not.

True, the pace at Santa's Village would slow somewhat after the holidays, but her responsibilities were never going to be nine to five. Management positions didn't work that way. There would still be nights when she had to close, weekends that required her presence. The conflicts between her personal and professional life were not going to magically disappear.

That type of conflict was exactly what she had hoped to escape by moving to Aspen Springs. Instead, she had thoughtlessly recreated the same situation she had objected to in Los Angeles. Except she had put herself in the lead role instead of

John. And Flash and Amy were relegated to minor supporting roles, a situation she had never wanted.

"Oh, you really fixed things, didn't you?" she muttered, flinging down her pencil. Leaning forward, she buried her face in her hands. "How could you be so dumb?" She had made a mess of every area of her life.

After a moment she realized she was staring down at the next letter in her Santa pile.

Dear Santa,

Please make Mommy and Daddy love each other again. Don't send Daddy back to Los Angeles. And please let Mommy be home more. That's all we want. And a baby sister. Please, please.

Amy and Flash Martin

Penny stared at the smeared page. The word *sister* had been crossed out and *brotter* printed beside it. *Brotter* had been crossed out also and *sister* reinserted. The writing was unmistakably Amy's.

"Oh, God," Penny groaned, rubbing at her eyes.

When she regained her composure, she stood and adjusted her skirt and smock. Then, lips pressed together, she walked down the candy-cane corridor to Ian Allenby's office, feeling her spirits rise with each step. Oddly her decision was not impulsive although she understood it would appear that way. For the moment she understood what she was about to do, she also understood she had been planning it in the back of her mind for at least a week.

"Ian," she said, after knocking at his door. "Can we talk a minute."

"Come in. Sit down."

Show me, John had said. *If you honestly don't want the promotion, take your name out of the running.* But she wasn't doing this for John. Or for Lydie. She was doing it for herself. And it felt good. It felt very, very good.

"You are withdrawing yourself as a candidate for the promotion?" Ian Allenby repeated, his eyebrows rising toward his hairline.

"Yes." She drew a long breath. "My plans have changed. After the baby is born, I...I'll be returning to Los Angeles." If John still wanted her. Please God, let him still want her.

A weight shifted near her heart and lifted.

"I'm sorry to hear that," Allenby said, staring at her. "You had a future with Santa's Village."

"I appreciate your saying so, Ian." As the weight floated off her heart, it pulled up the corners of her mouth. Her smile stretched from one pearl earring to the other, a silly happy smile that felt wonderful. "May I ask a favor?"

"Early leave?" he guessed, eyeing her stomach.

"Don't tell Lydie I withdrew my candidacy. Would you do that, Ian? Please?" When he said nothing, she hurried on. "I know this sounds arrogant and I honestly don't mean it that way. But I want Lydie to believe she was first choice. Not the only choice."

Ian Allenby's fingertips touched an envelope lying on his desk blotter. "As a matter of fact, the corporation's decision arrived this morning." His eyebrow lifted. "Do you want to know who they chose?"

She hesitated, then straightened her shoulders. "No. If Lydie was the corporation's choice, I'll feel like a fool for saying these things. If I was the choice, I'll feel...well, I'd prefer not to know." It didn't matter anymore. She drew a breath. "What's important is that Lydie has the promotion." As she reached for the door latch, she asked, "When will you tell her?"

"There's no reason to delay," Ian said, reaching for his desk phone. As Penny left his office, she heard him say, "Miss Evans, please ask Mrs. Severin to come to my office immediately."

For a moment, Penny stood in the corridor, looking at the red-and-green candy-cane wallpaper. A prick of moisture stung her eyes. But the dampness behind her lashes was not from regret, but from happiness.

"What's up?" Lydie asked, walking toward her. "Why does Allenby want to see us?"

"Not us, you." Penny pressed Lydie's arm. "Stop by my office when you're finished with Allenby, will you?"

When Lydie returned to Penny's office, she looked stunned. "Did Allenby tell you?" she asked, dropping into the chair facing Penny's desk.

"Congratulations." Smiling, Penny poured champagne into two paper cups.

"You are magic," Lydie marveled. "Where did you find a split of champagne in a children's park?"

"Ah. My secret. To the new manager of Santa's Village!" Penny raised her bubbling paper cup. "You deserve it."

"You're really being terrific about this, Penny," Lydie said uncomfortably. "Look, are you sure you're okay with the way this worked out?"

"Don't I look okay?"

Lydie narrowed her gaze above the cup of champagne. "As a matter of fact, you look better than you've looked in several days. Which doesn't make sense. Didn't you tell me you didn't sleep last night?"

"I feel great! Lydie, I'm so glad you got the promotion."

"Thank you. I was absolutely certain they would chose you."

"Now—" Penny grinned "—I hate to tell you this, but your first problem on your new job is me."

"I knew it," Lydie groaned. "No one is this good a sport."

"I'm quitting. I'm not coming back to work after the baby is born."

"Oh, Penny. Please don't take it like—"

"No, no. It isn't sour grapes. Lydie, this is good news. The champagne is a celebration for both of us. I'm going back to Los Angeles. If John will have me."

"That *is* good news!" Jumping up, Lydie ran around the desk to embrace her. "I'll bet John is delighted!"

"I haven't told him yet. Things have been so hectic." She spread her hands and smiled. "I thought I'd tell him Christmas Eve after everyone else is in bed."

"Very romantic," Lydie said, beaming approval.

"There's more." Penny glanced at the clock. "I'm leaving early today."

Lydie straightened in her chair and frowned. "Quitting I can handle. You being terrific about losing the promotion I can handle. Your leaving early I can't handle. Penny, we're buried. They're shorthanded in the toy shop, Helga is having a nervous breakdown, the new Santa is having an affair with one of the chestnut vendors, two cases of broken nutcrackers have to be packed for shipment, there's no heat in the ice rink and the movie projector is broken again. I need you."

She didn't waver. "I'm sorry, I really am. But I'm leaving here in twenty minutes. It's important, Lydie."

"What could possibly be more important than the items I've listed?" Lydie raked a hand through her hair and leaned forward.

"A party."

"Tell me you're kidding!"

"Nope." Taking the Santa letter from Amy and Flash off her desk, she folded it into her pocket. "This party is the event of the season. I'll hate myself if I miss it." She grinned. "I understand there will be homemade fudge and gallons of Kool-Aid. And a rousing game of musical chairs."

"The Brownie Scout party. I saw it on your calendar."

"Right. And tomorrow is Flash's class party. Another season spectacular I can't miss." She smiled in Lydie's direction, but the smile was directed inward. "You were right, Lydie. Christmas is love. I don't plan to lose sight of that ever again."

"Well," Lydie said after a minute. She leaned back in her chair. "I guess we'll manage somehow. We always do."

"No one is indispensable." For a time Penny had forgotten that. She wouldn't again.

"MOMMY! YOU CAME!"

Amy bounded across the hall and flung her arms around Penny, tears shining in her eyes.

Penny hugged her tightly, moisture glistening on her own

lashes. Kneeling, she smoothed back Amy's bangs. "I told them I had to have some time off. I couldn't miss my daughter's party. It was too important."

"I helped hang the crepe paper."

"It looks terrific!"

For the first time in months she didn't think of Santa's Village once. Although she was too heavily pregnant for musical chairs, she took second prize in Pin the Tail on the Donkey, and she and Amy won first prize in the mother-daughter charades.

"Thank you for coming to my party, Mommy," Amy said sleepily when Penny tucked her into bed that night. "I love you."

"I love you, too, honey."

When she thought how close Amy had come to sitting out the mother-daughter charades, Penny felt a tightness in her throat. It would never happen again, she promised, looking down at her sleeping daughter.

But life didn't make things easy.

Her earlier elation at quitting her position at Santa's Village had begun to fade. She didn't regret the decision, and she knew she wouldn't regret it in the future. But at the same time she felt a little bereft, as if she had lost something important.

She had let her job responsibilities get out of hand, she recognized now. She had let ambition and pride in a job well done run away with her, which was exactly what she had accused John of doing. And that was wrong.

Yet she also knew she would miss working. She would miss the contact with people, the decision making, the sense of accomplishment at the end of the day.

A sigh dropped her shoulders as she tiptoed from Amy's bedroom. She knew she couldn't have it both ways.

Suddenly she wished there really was a Santa Claus.

Chapter Eleven

The next few days were unbelievably hectic. On a constant run, Penny attended Flash's class party, arranged a small dinner party for Alice and Dr. Adler, scribbled her Christmas cards, rushed through her duties at Santa's Village, swept through the shops in a frenzy of last-minute shopping, and attended two holiday parties.

"You look dead on your feet," Susan Galloway noticed, pausing beside Penny with a tray of fancy canapés.

"Thanks. You look terrific, too."

Susan laughed. "Sorry. I guess I could have phrased that better. Seriously, how are you feeling?"

"Like a very large tennis ball that's lost its bounce. I must be the only mother-to-be in Aspen Springs who is looking forward to a new baby as a period of rest." They smiled at each other.

"Before I dash off to play hostess, tell me what you think of John's new venture. I'm dying to know."

"His baking binge?" Penny smiled. She supposed everyone in town knew by now that John had gone berserk in Alice's kitchen and was turning out bakery delicacies as if he had a mission to bury the valley in cookies, cakes and pies. She had no idea what happened to all the pans and sheets of baked goods, although Alice hinted that Reverend Cowper had come into a baked windfall and it would be a happier Christmas for his parishioners because of it. It was both amusing and a little worrisome that John seemed obsessed with making the Great American Cookie.

She saw him across Susan's living room talking to Lon Thompson, the realtor, and Dan Driver, president of the Optimists Club. John had always been able to talk to strangers, but he usually maintained a reserve that wasn't always evident to those he was speaking to but that had always been obvious to Penny. Oddly, she didn't notice that reserve now. He seemed genuinely relaxed, talking and laughing with an ease that surprised her. Then she remembered with a little shock that he had been in Aspen Springs long enough to meet people and build relationships of his own, even if the relationships were temporary.

"I wasn't referring to his baking binge," Susan said, then stopped. "Oh, dear, I hope I didn't let the cat out of the bag. I guess it's supposed to be a surprise." After a quick glance at John, she murmured something about needing to refill the canapé tray and eased through the crowd toward the kitchen.

What was that all about? Penny wondered. A frown crossed her face. Sometimes small towns could be exasperating. Small-town residents made secrets out of nothing and everything. Or they protected secrets better made public. Or they revealed secrets better left private.

Shifting slightly, she located Alice and Dr. Adler in the holiday crowd, laughing at something Wes Pierce had said. They were standing close together, fingers touching, both looking ten years younger than Penny knew them to be. That was a secret Aspen Springs had kept well. Penny smiled, genuinely happy for her mother.

As she turned to look again toward John, her smile became a sigh. The past few days had been difficult for them. She supposed they were both wondering if this was the last Christmas they would spend together as a family. She knew she was. Now that she had quit Santa's Village and made a commitment to herself to return to Los Angeles, she felt less and less sure that John would welcome her back.

Something had changed in the past couple of weeks. He wasn't as tentative as he had seemed when he first arrived. An air of confidence had returned, and with it an excitement she recognized as an indication he was thinking about a deal and eager to get on with it. More and more frequently she had seen a look of distraction in his eyes, and she assumed it meant he was thinking about leaving them and returning to Los Angeles. He had said nothing more about her returning with him.

She pressed her lips together. Maybe this time together had convinced him a divorce was actually the best thing. Her chest constricted and Baby Whosit vaulted through a series of somersaults.

What if she had waited too long? She bit her lip.

If John wanted her back, wouldn't he have said something more about Los Angeles? Pressured her a little? Concentrating, she tried to remember when they had last talked, really talked. They had both been so busy....

At that moment, he lifted his golden head and their eyes met and held. After excusing himself, he crossed the room to her side.

"Penny, are you all right?" Touching her elbow, he studied her expression with a frown of concern.

"I...yes, of course." Reaching deep, she summoned a smile. "I must look awful. Everyone keeps asking if I feel all right."

"You look beautiful," he said softly, his gaze sweeping the green ribbon in her hair, her holiday dress.

It was nice of him to tell her what she needed to hear, even if she didn't believe him. "John—" she drew a breath "—I need to talk to you. There's something I want to tell you."

"There's something I want to tell you, too."

She saw the leap of excitement flash in his eyes and her spirits sank. He was thinking about work. She had seen that look too many times not to recognize it.

But what had she expected? Of course he was eager to return to Los Angeles and work. John wasn't the kind of man to adjust easily to small-town boredom. Witness the peculiar binge of oven madness. If she returned with him to L.A., she had to accept everything that went with that decision. Anything less than total surrender just wouldn't work. They had to do it his way.

For an instant resentment flared in her. Then she relaxed. She loved this man. And that meant accepting him the way he was—ambition, long hours and all. In the end, she knew she would rather live with John in a smog pit and see him on the run than live on a quiet mountaintop with anyone else.

John saw a flicker of resentment in her eyes and immediately dropped her arm. An ache tightened his stomach. He knew what she wanted to tell him. She wanted to tell him that she had learned of his plans for the coffee and bake shop, and it made no difference that he would be living in Aspen Springs. The divorce was still on.

When he dropped her arm, she wanted to weep. It was true then, she had waited too long.

"When would you like to have this talk?" he asked, looking away from her.

"I thought tomorrow night, but if you don't think Christmas Eve...?"

"No, that's fine. Why not?"

They stood together looking toward Alice and Dr. Adler, both aware that, in one of the few times in their life together, they had nothing to say to one another.

IT WAS SNOWING HEAVILY when Penny awoke after sleeping late. After doing her morning exercises, she pulled back the bedroom drapes and studied the blizzard swirling past the windowpanes, glad Lydie had insisted she stay home today.

"You're running on empty, Penny," Lydie had informed her briskly. "You need some rest. Besides, Christmas Eve day should be a light day at the park."

"Liar," Penny had responded, but with a smile of gratitude. "Sundays are our busiest days."

"Not this one. The weatherman predicts the storm of the season. If he's right the highway patrol will close the tunnel and stop all traffic. We'll be lucky to see three people all day. You can sleep in guilt-free and enjoy the day at home."

For once the weatherman was right on target. A heavy white

curtain blew past the window, so thick Penny could not see the road looping through the subdivision. Snowdrifts, mounded across the yard like waves, were formed into exotic shapes. The branches of the pine near her window drooped, bowed by the weight of the snow.

They were snowed in for Christmas. The thought delighted her now as it had when she was a child. Penny pressed her face to the glass, watching the blizzard with pleasure.

When she came downstairs Alice was sipping a cup of coffee in front of the windows, watching the snow pile up on the balcony. "This one is a real corker," she said to Penny. "We've got about four inches so far and there's no sign the storm is slowing down."

"Are you worried about Bill?" Penny asked, looking out the windows.

Alice nodded. "He planned to leave for Denver early. I hope he got down the mountain before the worst of this hit. The radio said they've closed the tunnel and traffic is backed up on both sides."

"Why don't you call? You'll feel better. He may not know you're worried. You know how different the weather can be between here and the other side of the mountains." Dr. Adler was spending Christmas with his son and his son's family in Denver.

"You were right," Alice said, beaming with relief after completing her phone call. Color had returned to her cheeks. "It's only starting to snow in Denver. Bill didn't realize it was so bad up here." This time when she looked out at the blizzard, she did so with contentment. "We have plenty of coffee and snacks, the shopping is finished, there's lots of firewood and Christmas dinner is in the fridge, so...let it snow, let it snow, let it snow."

"'Oh, the weather outside is frightful,'" John sang, appearing in the living room with an armful of firewood. "'But in here, it's so delightful.'" After building and lighting the fire, he joined them in the kitchen for freshly ground Brazilian coffee. "Which one of you ordered the perfect traditional Christmas weather?" he asked with a grin. "Those of us more accustomed to Christmas smog and balmy temperatures thank you."

His smile wrapped around Penny's heart and her throat tightened. The words *too late* rang in her mind. To drown them she turned on the radio and let carols fill the room.

"Perfect," John said, nodding. "I used to imagine Christmases like this."

"You did?" Penny looked at him in surprise. Then the telephone rang.

It was Lydie. "With Ian back East for the holidays, you and I are in charge," she began. "Our new Santa is stuck in a snowdrift somewhere between Frisco and Santa's Village. He called in on his CB and the state patrol is looking for him now. I can't get out of my driveway—it's a sheet of ice. I'm calling to see if you agree that we should forget it for today. According to the radio the plows can't keep up with the snow. The roads are drifting over faster than the plows can clear them. I'm in favor of not opening."

"Lydie, you're the boss, remember?" Penny said into the telephone. She spoke in a low voice so John wouldn't overhear.

"Not until the end of January. Until then, we're both in charge. So what do you think?"

"I think a person would have to be insane to go out in this storm. Don't give it another thought. Do you need some help calling everyone to tell them not to go in?"

"Are you joking? They're calling me! Telling me they can't get out of their garages. Just about everyone is accounted for except Helga and Sims Delacorte. Their lines are busy. I'm guessing they're phoning their people and telling them not to go in."

"So all we have to worry about is Santa."

Lydie laughed. "According to the state patrol, Santa is marooned with the chestnut vendor I mentioned. He told the patrol not to hurry."

"It sounds like you've taken care of everything."

"Unless you can think of something I've missed. Before I

say Merry Christmas and get off the line, I want to wish you good luck tonight.''

Biting her lip, Penny gazed out the windows at the storm. She lowered her voice again. ''I don't know, Lydie. I'm having second thoughts about saying anything to John. It's been so long since he's mentioned anything about—''

''Listen to a friend, Penny Martin. Don't be an idiot. Tonight is Christmas Eve, remember? It's magic, the night all wishes come true.'' Penny could imagine Lydie's smile. ''Besides, I know what you're getting for Christmas. And you're going to like it.''

''How could you possibly know what I'm getting for Christmas?''

''The whole town knows. Everyone is waiting with bated breath to see what you'll do.''

''Do? I have to do something with this mysterious gift?''

''I know what you'll do, but I'm not telling.''

''Lydie Severin, I am so sick of secrets!''

''Then you're living in the wrong place,'' Lydie said, laughing. ''I have to get off the phone and try Helga and Sims again. Have a wonderful Christmas, and I'll see you the day after tomorrow.''

''You, too. Have a merry, merry Christmas.'' After hanging up the receiver, she carried her coffee into the living room and sipped it while she examined the gifts under the tree, wondering which was the one everyone in Aspen Springs knew about. Several of the gifts were lumpy and strange-looking, wrapped with love and yards of tape. Penny smiled. Next year she would have homemade gifts for everyone, too. This year she had broken the agreement. There hadn't been time to make anything.

From the shape of the packages, she guessed Flash had made her a pencil box or a penny bank. At Amy's Brownie party, she had overheard hints of embroidered place mats. She had surprised Alice making mosaics out of rice, beans, dyed macaroni and seeds. That left John's gift. She studied the shape of the container. It looked suspiciously like the containers he had wrapped in red cellophane. Maybe a special rum cake?

None of the gifts impressed her as meriting a town secret. They were precious to her, but not what she would consider as ranking in the "bated breath" category. And she couldn't imagine what she might have to "do" with or about any of them.

"I'm sorry I didn't have time to make anything for you guys," she said as John came up from the basement, the kids behind him. "I promise, next year will be different."

"We understand," John said lightly. Before she could say anything more, he winked at the kids, then looked back at her. "We have been challenged to a game of Go Fish. What do you think? Can we beat this pair of cardsharps?"

"It's a tough job, but I think we can do it," she said, watching the kids' faces light with delight. "Girls against the boys?"

"Oh, no," Amy said, suddenly anxious. She and Flash exchanged a conspiratorial look. "We're a team, and you and Daddy are a team."

"You guys just don't quit. Well, if it's okay with Daddy, it's okay with me," she said, not looking at John.

"I don't know." Teasing her, he pretended to hesitate. "As I remember it, your mother is hopeless at cards. You guys are saddling me with a severe handicap."

For the kids' sakes, she went along with him. "What? I'm a handicap? I'll show you! We'll beat these two so bad they'll plead for mercy."

Laughing, loving it, Amy and Flash informed them they had to sit close together on the same side of the kitchen table.

"Closer," Flash insisted, pushing them. "Partners have to sit close!" When Penny and John were self-consciously arranged to suit their children, Flash looked out the windows at the storm. He tried not to look worried. "Can Santa come in a storm?"

"Hey, this is the best Santa weather there could be," Penny said, shuffling the cards.

"Mommy's right. Santa loves storms like this. Don't

worry,'' John assured them. ''Santa's on his way right now, it's a long flight from the North Pole.'' Neither he nor Penny looked at each other at mention of the North Pole. ''And I'll bet he brings you everything you asked for.''

Startled, Penny looked up from the cards. John didn't know what he was saying. But then, he hadn't read Amy's and Flash's letter to Santa Claus.

''I'm sure you'll like whatever Santa brings you,'' she amended, managing a smile. ''Okay, the cards are ready. Who goes first?''

She didn't have to glance at the clock over the stove to feel the minutes ticking toward evening. Suddenly she decided it was a bad idea for her and John to try to settle things tonight, of all nights. They should have given themselves one last perfect Christmas.

''Think positively,'' John said as her hand hovered above the Go Fish pile. ''Picture a match in your mind.''

She studied him a moment, trying to read his thoughts. ''Yes,'' she said finally. ''That's the only thing to do. Think positively.''

SNOW CONTINUED TO FALL throughout the day. The intensity of the storm deepened. The radio crackled with road closings and travel warnings. By late afternoon more than twelve inches of snow had accumulated on Alice's balcony. The windows were laced by lovely fernlike tracings of frost.

Inside it was cosy and warm, the air filled with carols and the scent of freshly baked sugar cookies. Penny read and dozed before the fire, smiling at the sounds of cowboys and cowgirls emanating from the basement as two wound-up kids tried to work off a little of the excitement. John and Alice visited companionably in the kitchen as they prepared Christmas Eve dinner.

It had been a perfect restful day, Penny thought, disturbed only by an occasional cramp. The first cramp had occurred about three o'clock and Penny sat up abruptly, letting her book fall to the floor as she placed her hands on her stomach and made herself go still inside. When nothing further happened, she relaxed and reminded herself that she had a history of false labor.

Another cramp arrived after dinner, passing so quickly she told herself she might have imagined it.

"The baby isn't due for another two weeks," she said, cupping her hands over her stomach.

Alice looked up from the pie she was slicing. "We know, dear. Now, who's ready for cherry pie?"

After dinner they watched a Christmas Eve special on television, then Flash and Amy argued over what to leave Santa, cookies or a piece of cherry pie, and where to place it so that Santa would be certain to see.

Then John donned a red Santa's hat and, as he and Penny had agreed, they allowed Flash and Amy to open one present before bedtime, having chosen the presents in advance to make certain they weren't gifts that would excite the children too much and keep them awake. Flash received a color-and-paste set; Amy opened a new Nancy Drew book. Eventually it was time for baths and bedtime.

When Flash ran upstairs fresh from his bath, his face scrubbed and shining, he rubbed his palms over his pajama top and cast a worried look at the fireplace. "You'll put the fire out before you go to bed, won't you, Daddy?"

"Absolutely," John promised solemnly. "We wouldn't dream of singeing ole Santa's beard."

"And you're sure he'll see the pie and milk?" Amy asked doubtfully. "Maybe we should put the tray under the tree..."

"Santa will see the tray on the coffee table the minute he steps out of the chimney," Penny promised, giving her a hug.

"Did you hear that?" Flash gasped, his eyes widening. "Jingle bells!"

Alice laughed. "It's too early, big fella. What you heard was the wind chime on the balcony. Santa doesn't come until all little boys and girls are sound asleep."

Penny took Amy's hand and started toward the basement stairs. Behind her came John and Flash. "Silent Night" played on Alice's stereo; the lights twinkled on the tree. Outside, the driving snow drifted through the night, wrapping the house in a blanket of white. Inside it was warm and lovely with the sights and sounds of Christmas. Tears of happiness glistened in Penny's eyes. She wished she could capture this moment and keep it with her always.

After the children had been tucked in for the third time, the adults returned to the living room for hot spiced wine and a slice of John's Christmas fruitcake.

"This is excellent," Alice enthused. "Usually I don't care for fruitcake."

Penny grinned. "Remember the theory you used to have? That there were only ten fruitcakes in the world, and they were being mailed back and forth to people who kept them in a closet for a year then mailed them to someone else. You were positive no one ever ate them." Baby Whosit apparently enjoyed the story. He chose the moment to perform some spectacular acrobatics.

Alice's smile turned to concern. "Penny? You have such a peculiar look on your face. Is everything all right?"

"I can't seem to find a comfortable position tonight." If she hadn't known she was prone to false labor, she would have thought she was beginning real labor. She'd had several cramps since dinner.

"Would you like a pillow for your back?" John asked.

"Thank you."

Alice studied her thoughtfully while John slipped one of the decorator pillows between Penny and the sofa back. Her gaze turned to the snowy blackness against the windows. The outside lights decorating the balcony rail, a few feet from the windowpane, were a dim shine of color, blurred by the thickly falling snow. "I don't think we've had a storm this bad in years," Alice commented absently, tapping a red fingernail against her throat. "I'd hate to try to go out in this."

"Thank goodness we don't have to," John said, poking up the fire. He was still wearing the red Santa cap, humming with the carols drifting from the stereo.

"The wind comes down the gully behind the house and pushes drifts all down the driveway," Alice continued, looking at Penny.

"I used to love that," Penny said, smiling at the memory. "It meant I didn't have to go to school." She explained to John. "The driveway is about a quarter of a mile long, and with all the drifts we couldn't get the car out until the plow came to dig out the subdivision. The plow usually didn't get to us before noon."

"I wonder how soon they'll have the plows out tomorrow," Alice said, her eyes still on Penny.

"According to the radio, the plows and sand trucks are out now," John told them. "They just aren't doing much good. The snow's too heavy and coming down too fast. They're concentrating on the major highways."

"Which means the loop road is buried under at least twelve inches of snow. Probably more by now. And drifts."

"Alice, what are you worrying about? Are you planning to go somewhere?" Penny asked. Then her stomach tightened beneath her smock and she concealed a wince of discomfort.

Alice continued to study her daughter. "I wish Bill were here instead of in Denver," she said quietly.

John's head snapped up and the ball on the end of his Santa's cap bounced against his shoulder. "Is something going on here that I should know about?"

"Yes, Penny, is there?"

"I've been experiencing some discomfort off and on throughout the day." She dismissed the cramps with a shrug. "It's nothing to worry about. You both know I've had false labor before."

"As I recall, it happened in your seventh month," Alice said into the silence. "Not this close to your due date."

"Penny?" Sitting beside her on the sofa, John tilted her face up to him.

"Honestly, if there was anything to worry about, I'd tell you." She gestured toward the windows. "I'd be insisting we start for the clinic if I really thought this was the real thing."

"I hope you're right," Alice said slowly, staring at her. "Because I doubt we could get the car out of the garage tonight, let alone down the driveway and out of the subdivision."

Penny smiled at them. "Will you two stop worrying? It's nothing."

"You're absolutely certain?" Alice demanded.

"Absolutely." Penny's gaze darted toward the clock. It was almost eleven. If she and John were going to talk…

Alice noticed the direction of her glance, then stood and smothered an exaggerated yawn. "Well, I imagine Flash and Amy will be up at dawn. I think I'll call it a night."

John stood, too. "Shall I get more firewood from the garage?"

Penny nodded, realizing too late he was actually asking if she still wanted to talk. For an instant she hesitated, thinking to call him back. Then she bit her lip. Maybe it was best to get it over with. Either he wanted her back or he didn't. She didn't want to spend another night not knowing.

"Before you go, help me up, will you?" she asked Alice, indicating that the sofa had trapped her. After hugging Alice and wishing her a merry Christmas, Penny went into the kitchen to pour fresh cups of hot spiced wine for herself and John.

A hard cramp bit into her stomach and she gasped, grabbing the kitchen counter for support until the clamping sensation passed. When her stomach softened again, she stood beneath the kitchen light staring down at herself.

That had been a contraction.

Not a cramp, not a moment of discomfort. What she had just experienced had been an authentic contraction. This was not false labor; it was the beginning of the real thing. Automatically she glanced at the clock, then let her eyes travel slowly toward the black snowy windows.

"Oh, my God," she whispered.

At that moment John reappeared, his arms filled with firewood, the red Santa cap pushed back at a jaunty angle. He dropped the wood on the raised hearth, then walked toward her, rubbing his hands together.

"It's cold out there."

A warm gush of water spilled down the inside of Penny's white wool slacks. For a moment she thought she had lost control of her bladder and was suffering the ultimate embarrassment. Then she understood what had happened, and stood helplessly as the water ran out her pant legs and puddled around her feet.

"John, this is crazy, but my water just broke."

His mouth dropped. His expression froze. "Oh, God." They both looked at the snow hissing softly against the windowpanes. Then John came around the counter and held her in his arms, stroked her hair back from her face. "Don't worry, honey. I'll get you to the clinic."

She looked deep into his eyes, telling herself not to panic, then she nodded. "I'll have to change clothes." She looked down at her wet pants and the water spreading across the kitchen tiles. "I made a real mess, didn't I?"

"Don't worry about it. I'll clean up while you're changing." Arm around her waist, John led her toward the stairs. "Tell Alice we'll be leaving in a few minutes, will you?"

Alice flew down the stairs and took the mop from John's hands. "I'll do this. You get on the phone." She gave him the number to call for road conditions. For a long moment she and John looked at each other, then Alice bent over the mop and John reached for the telephone.

A recorded message listed a lengthy number of road closings. The person who had made the recording sounded tired and frazzled. The recording ended with a strongly worded warning to stay indoors and off the roads. Slowly John replaced the receiver.

"Not even emergency vehicles are getting through," he said to Alice.

"The news said this is the worst storm in a decade. John—"

But he didn't wait to hear. He dashed for the stairs and opened the foyer door to the garage, flipping on the yard light as he hurried toward the windows on the garage door. The snow was too thick for the yard light to penetrate more than a few feet into the swirling darkness. But it was enough to see that a four-foot drift lay against the garage door. A series of snowdrifts, like waves tossed up by a violent white sea, ran down the driveway and flowed into the blackness.

"You can't see where the driveway ends and the side ditches begin," Alice said from behind him. Anxiously, she wrung her hands. "The loop road will be impassable."

John looked at the Porsche, cursing himself that he hadn't yet traded it for a jeep. At least he'd installed snow tires. But at this moment, he would have given everything he owned to see a four-wheel drive sitting where the Porsche was.

"I'll dig out the driveway."

"You can't," Penny said quietly.

They spun to see her standing behind them, holding her overnight bag, dressed to leave. She looked out the garage windows at the blowing snow.

"Even if it wasn't still snowing, digging out would require hours," Penny said. Alice nodded. "And the loop road will be drifted over, too."

Alice threw out a hand and steadied herself against the trunk of the Porsche. "We're stuck here." Her eyes rounded and she spoke in a whisper. "What on earth are we going to do?"

Penny and John looked at each other in the snowy light.

"I guess we're going to have a baby," John said softly. He touched the red cap he was still wearing. "It looks like Santa is going to deliver this one."

"I'm a little frightened," Penny said simply.

John came to her and held her gently in his arms. Then he framed her face between his large capable hands and looked into her eyes.

"Almost two thousand years ago tonight, another baby was born without a hospital and without a doctor present. And look how well he turned out."

As little as three months ago he had been so big-city uptight that the present situation would have shaken him badly. He would have been frantic, thinking they could not possibly have a baby without the safety and comfort of a modern hospital. Right now, he was uneasy, yes, but he was not frightened. He felt sure enough of himself and of Penny to give her the support she needed.

"Once upon a time you and I believed we could lick any problem if we faced it together, remember?" he asked, still framing her face between his hands, looking into those lovely large eyes.

"I remember," she said softly. "We forgot that, didn't we?"

"I think we forgot a lot of important things along the way."

A contraction bit down hard and she gripped his arms until it was over.

"We've both been stubborn idiots," she gasped when the contraction released her.

"Darling Penny—"

Alice flung out her hands. "You two are turning me into a nervous wreck! Will you stop talking and go inside? We need to figure out what we're going to do!"

They looked at her in surprise.

"We're going to have a baby," Penny said, laughing.

"That's what we're going to do," John confirmed.

"We used to be a pretty good team," Penny said, smiling up at him. "Think we can pull this off successfully, Santa?"

"When you and I are pulling on the same team, Ms. Claus, there is no stopping us."

They looked into one another's eyes.

"It's going to be all right," John said gently.

"I know." She was still holding onto his arms. "There may be some scary moments—"

"This is one of them!" Alice said, pushing at them. "Will you please go inside so I can have a breakdown where it's warm?"

Chapter Twelve

After John helped her inside and upstairs, Penny warmed her hands in front of the fireplace and drew a breath to steady her nerves. It was going to be all right, she told herself, silently repeating John's words. This baby, her little Whosit, this baby about whom she had felt such ambivalence, had suddenly become very, very precious.

Smothering a gasp, she sat abruptly on the ottoman before the fire and wrapped her arms around her stomach as another contraction gripped her. "We'll be fine," she whispered when the tightening eased and the tug on her lower back loosened.

"Okay," John said briskly. He sounded a hundred percent more confident than he felt. If the birth was normal, he knew he and Penny could handle it. There would be a few shaky moments, and this was a situation neither of them would have chosen, but they could make it work. But if anything went wrong... "Here's what we're going to do." Alice and Penny looked at him expectantly, and he hoped something sensible would fall out of his mouth.

"Yes?" Alice prompted. She spoke in a calm tone but he read the anxiety in her eyes.

"Okay. This is the plan." He exhaled slowly. "Alice, take Penny upstairs and help her change into something more comfortable. Get her into bed. I'll phone Dr. Adler in Denver and find out if we should be boiling water or something."

"Boiling water? I've always wondered what the boiling water is for," Alice said, raising an eyebrow. "Does anyone know?"

"Maybe it's to make coffee and spaghetti afterward to celebrate. We'll find out." John made a shooing motion with his hands. "Scoot. I need to get on the telephone."

Because he didn't want to worry either of them more than necessary, he waited until Penny and Alice had disappeared up the stairs before he turned to the kitchen, poured himself a shot of brandy, then phoned Bill Adler in Denver.

"You said her water's broken?" Bill Adler asked after John had explained the situation. During the long silence that followed, John could hear his heart thudding against his rib cage.

"What does that mean?" he asked when he couldn't bear the silence another second.

"I'd be happier if her water hadn't broken yet."

"What does *that* mean?"

"It could mean things are going to happen pretty fast, especially if the contractions are as close together as you indicated."

"Or?"

"I'll level with you John." There was another pause. "A dry birth can be dangerous."

"Oh, God," John whispered. All the moisture vanished from his mouth and he sat down hard on the kitchen chair.

"For the moment we'll assume we're dealing with the first circumstance. John? Are you still there?"

"Yes."

"Your situation is unfortunate—we all wish it could be otherwise. But Penny is healthy, and she's delivered twice before. According to her records, her previous deliveries were comparatively swift and without complication. There's no reason to assume this delivery will be any different."

"If it's a dry birth—"

"You have plenty of time before that becomes a possible problem. I probably shouldn't have mentioned it."

"No, I'm glad you did. I assume you'll give me signs to watch for and—"

"We'll get into everything. We'll walk you though this,

John. The main thing right now is for you to remain calm. Okay?"

He stared at his reflection in the snowy black window. "I was present during the birth of our first two children, if that means anything."

He sensed Dr. Adler's smile. "It means you probably aren't going to faint on us."

"So." John inhaled deeply, watching the snow fly out of the blackness and melt down the windows. "What happens next?"

"Probably nothing except a lot of waiting. Things aren't going to get interesting for a while yet. Meanwhile, I'm going to give you a list of what you'll require and remind you that everything will have to be sterilized."

"The infamous boiling water."

Dr. Adler laughed. "Right. Have you got a pencil?" After he dictated the list, he continued. "I'll phone Dr. James Harrington at St. Anthony's Hospital and tell him what's happening. We'll make sure you have an open line to St. Anthony's. When the time comes, I'd suggest you put Alice on the phone and she can relay any questions or information."

"Where will you be? I think Penny would be more comfortable if she knew you were on the phone. No disrespect to Dr. Harrington, but—"

"I'll leave for Aspen Springs as soon as I get off the phone with Dr. Harrington."

"Bill, wait a minute. The roads are too dangerous. And it'll take you three hours to travel what's usually a forty-five-minute drive to the tunnel. Then, if you manage to get that far, the state patrol won't let you through. The tunnel is closed. If somehow you convince them to let you pass, you're facing another dangerous situation on the other side. And that's before you get to the loop road, which is impassable."

"I can't guarantee I'll get there in time, John, but I promise you I will get there."

John's throat tightened. "Thank you," he said quietly, the words inadequate for what he felt. "I appreciate it."

"As it's likely I won't arrive in time, let's review what you'll need to do. Have you still got that pencil?"

He took it slowly, wrote down every word. "Sounds easy enough," he said in a weak voice when he had copied Dr. Adler's instructions.

Dr. Adler laughed again, his cheerfulness raising John's spirits. "That the right attitude. Now, before I get off the line let's find out how far along we are." He told John what to do.

John placed the telephone on the kitchen counter, stared at it a moment, then he squared his shoulders and walked across the living room to the bedroom stairs.

Penny was in bed, resting against a pile of mounded pillows. Alice had brushed her hair into a ponytail and tied it with a length of red Christmas ribbon. She looked more relaxed than he could believe, considering the circumstances and considering that he was all they had by way of medical assistance.

He swallowed and looked at her, pushing his hands into his pockets, feeling the set of rubber gloves Alice had found for him earlier. "I have Dr. Adler on the phone. He, ah, asked me to..."

Penny and Alice looked at him expectantly.

"Dr. Adler suggested that I...it seems that it's normal procedure to, ah..." He looked at Penny's hands folded on top of the blankets and wondered how she could be so damned calm. "The thing is, he'd like to know how far along..."

A blush tinted Penny's cheeks as she began to understand, then a small smile formed under twinkling eyes. "Alice, if you'll excuse us a moment..."

"Of course," Alice said. "Yes, yes, I see." She gave John a wicked smile, then chuckling, she ducked into the bathroom and closed the door as Penny lowered the blankets and raised the hem of her nightgown.

Blushing furiously, John checked as he had been instructed, then he hastily pulled Penny's nightgown back into place and tucked the blankets around her.

"Who does that in the hospital?" he asked.

"Nurses, the doctor." Penny shrugged and grinned. "The

last time we had a baby, I was positive the staff was pulling people in off the street to come up and have a look at me." She laced her fingers together on top of the coverlet and grinned at the red Santa cap he had forgotten to remove. "Well, Santa. Now that you've had a peek, how are we doing?"

He grinned back. "As far as I can tell, Baby Whosit is positioned exactly as Dr. Adler said he should be." In an exaggerated parody of a doctor, he said, "We seem to dilating nicely, Mrs. Martin."

"We do, do we?"

"I've got Dr. Adler waiting on the telephone. I'll be back in a few minutes."

The moment he stepped outside Penny's room, relief overwhelmed him. He sagged against the wall and offered a silent prayer of gratitude. The baby was positioned properly for a normal delivery. Penny's body seemed to be doing everything it was supposed to be doing.

"Good," Dr. Adler said when John had completed his report. He, too, sounded relieved.

After John had been issued a few more suggestions, he hung up. For several minutes he stood beside the telephone, watching the reflection of the Christmas tree lights blinking on and off against the windowpane. Then he found the telephone book and dialed.

"Hullo?" A sleepy voice answered on the fifth ring.

"Wes? This is John Martin." Even a few days ago he would have sworn there could be no circumstance under which he would telephone Wes Pierce and ask for help.

"Wha' time is it?"

"Midnight. I apologize for phoning so—"

Instantly Wes came awake. "What's wrong?"

Quickly John explained their situation. "I know all the state and county plows are in service, trying to keep the major roads clear for emergency vehicles."

"That's right, son. Even privately owned plows are out helping tonight."

John drew a breath. "Wes, if you have any influence, if you

know anyone with a plow—I don't care what it costs—we need—''

"You need a way into the subdivision and a path to your door."

"I'm sorry to disturb you on Christmas Eve and especially this late, but if you could make a few phone calls, I'd—''

"Consider it done. You say Bill is coming up from Denver?''

"He's going to try. Frankly I don't have much faith that he'll make it."

"You gotta have faith, son. Remember the Indian and his snow dance? Remember what tonight and tomorrow is all about? Faith. That's all, just faith."

"So simple. And so hard." That wasn't all that was hard. Placing the phone call to ask Wes's help had been equally hard. And Wes would know it. When this was over, John had an apology to make. He had been a fool to think other people might need help, but not him. Covering his eyes, John leaned away from the storm blowing against the windows.

After a moment he went into the kitchen and made a few preparations. He collected some crushed ice, which he put into a bowl, then carried it and a spoon up to the bedroom.

"How are we doing?" he asked Penny, taking a seat beside the bed and placing the bowl on the bedside table.

"Pretty good, I think. I'm doing my breathing exercises, trying to remember everything else I'm supposed to do."

She lay on her side, one leg almost straight, the other bent at the knee. Another contraction came as he watched, and he fell silent, not wanting to interrupt her concentration as she focused on minimizing the discomfort. When the contraction passed, she gave him a weak smile.

"Are you frightened?" he asked softly, taking her hand.

"A little," she admitted. "Are you?"

"A little."

They smiled at each other, speaking softly so they wouldn't wake Alice who dozed in the rocking chair near the window.

"Do you feel like pushing yet?" John asked, pulling his chair closer.

"Not really." She glanced at the bedside clock, measuring the time before the next contraction. "I think it's going to be a while yet."

"Is there anything I can get you?"

"No. But thanks for the ice. I'll appreciate it when I get the nervous nibbles. As I always do."

They didn't say anything for the next few minutes, but it was not an uncomfortable silence. They listened to the sounds of the storm and to the Christmas carols drifting from the living room.

"Lousy timing, huh?" Penny commented after she had caught her breath following the next contraction. "The good news is the kids will get what they wanted for Christmas. They asked for a baby sister—though, if it's a boy, I'm sure they'll be just as happy." She thought of what else Amy and Flash had asked of Santa. "I'm sorry we didn't get to talk, John," she added softly.

"I realize you're a bit busy," he said. "But I'm just hanging around. Would you like to talk now?"

"Now?"

"It might take your mind off...things."

She closed her eyes and breathed. When the clamping sensation passed, she nodded. "All right. You said you had something to tell me."

"So did you. You go first."

"No, you go first."

"No, you."

"I quit my job," they said in unison. They stared at each other.

"You quit Blackman Brothers?" Penny asked incredulously.

"You quit Santa's Village?" John blinked. "Why? What about the promotion?" Slowly comprehension dawned in his eyes. "Oh, Penny, are you saying what I think you're saying?"

She looked at him from shining eyes, and he thought she was more beautiful than he had ever seen her, wearing a white flannel nightgown and a red ribbon in her hair. She was more beautiful, more precious to him now than on their wedding day. He held his breath, loving her so much he ached, praying he had not misjudged her meaning.

A look of sudden shyness came into her eyes as if she was unsure of his reaction. "I'd like to go back to Los Angeles with you, John. If...if you still want me."

Joy burst inside his chest, paralyzing him with happiness. He wanted to scoop her into his arms and dance her around the room. Instead he leaned forward and gently placed his hand on her cheek, tracing the curve of her lips with his thumb.

"No," he said. Then realizing how that sounded, he smiled and added hastily, "We're not going back to Los Angeles, darling." Then, between contractions, he told her about buying the space facing the town square and his plans for a coffee and bake shop.

When he finished Penny said, "So that's my mysterious Christmas gift." She repeated what Lydie had told her and how Susan Galloway had given her a hint.

"For once I'm glad this town can keep a secret. I wanted to tell you myself." Catching her hand, he covered her fingertips with kisses. "So...what do you think?"

"John—" she stroked his beloved face "—is this really what you want? A coffee and bake shop in a small town?"

"Are you kidding?" His eyes twinkled. Everything was going to work out. He told her all his plans. "It's the opportunity of a lifetime! And Penny, I promise you—our shop is going to be open from nine to five *only*."

"Maybe until seven during tourist season," Penny teased gently. He was a workaholic; he always would be. But if he could turn his life upside down and move to Aspen Springs, surely she could accept the late nights and an occasional working weekend.

"It's probably too soon to mention this..."

"But?" she asked. She was gripping his hand, and gazing lovingly up at him. She had been wrong to think total surrender was the only course. If two people loved each other a compromise could be found. It meant giving in here and there, but good marriages were built on compromise. It was one of the things they had both forgotten.

"But think about this. If the shop is successful, maybe we can consider franchising. Not immediately, of course," he added hastily. "I mean in a few years, like after the kids leave for college."

Penny's laugh changed to a groan as another contraction wrapped around her stomach. When it passed, she was panting, and a light sheen of perspiration had appeared on her brow. "This is hard work," she explained. "That's why it's called labor. It's almost as exhausting as being an assistant manager at Santa's Village."

"I love you, Penny. God, I love you. I can't stand to think how close I came to spending a life without you!"

"I love you, too, John Martin. I love you with all my heart. I'm sorry I was so foolish and stubborn."

He placed a finger across her lips. "Shhh. It's all worked out for the best. And maybe we learned something. One thing is certain. Our lives are going to be better for it."

"Love is enough, isn't it? If you really love someone, the answers eventually come."

The contractions were arriving faster now, the spaces between them shorter and shorter. Penny looked toward the bedroom window where Alice was dozing beneath an afghan. The blackness outside the window had begun to fade toward gray. The storm was easing.

"Are you—" she ground her teeth and tried to remember her breathing exercises "—going to need..." The contractions seemed almost constant now.

"An extra employee?" John had been right. He wasn't the only workaholic in the family. But compromise was possible in this area, too. She could work part-time until the children were old enough not to need her as much as they did now.

"Because if you do—" she was panting, knew it was time to push "—I'm unemployed at the moment. And I've always—" breathe, in and out, slowly "—wanted to work in a coffee and pastry shop."

"Right. But if this is an application for part-time employment, you're hired,'' John said, laughing. Then he stood quickly as he recognized the signs. Moving across the room, he gently shook Alice's shoulder. ''I think it's time,'' he said softly. ''Would you mind bringing the tray I prepared? It's in the kitchen. Don't touch anything. It's sterilized. And Alice, please phone Dr. Harrington at St. Anthony's. He's prepared to stay on the line as long as we need him.''

''Part-time only,'' Penny gasped. She managed a wink at Alice when Alice paused beside the bed to stare at her. ''We're working out...the terms of our employment.''

Alice rolled her eyes toward the ceiling, then shaking her head, she hurried toward the stairs.

''I think we'd better have a look,'' John said. Leaning, he kissed her perspiring forehead, then gently pulled up her nightgown. She had kicked the blankets off some time ago.

''Good heavens!'' Awe transformed his expression. ''Penny, we're about to have a baby!''

''Darling, I know that. It's time to push. I need to push!''

''Okay.'' Mind racing, he returned to her side. ''Okay. Now here's what you're supposed to do. Remember? Put your knees under your arms....''

She stared up at him. ''You're kidding! Maybe you haven't noticed, but I have this stomach in the way.''

''I'll help. Don't push yet. Wait a minute.''

''Wait a minute?'' Panting, she looked at the ceiling. ''Just once, one time only, I wish you could be pregnant!''

Sweat appeared on his own forehead as he lifted her knee and pushed it back where she could grab hold. She yelped, but she grabbed. Then he raced around the bed and pressed her other knee upward.

Penny released a long breath and relaxed a bit as the space between contractions lengthened again now that delivery was imminent.

''There is no dignity in this process, is there?'' she asked the ceiling, holding her knees as near her armpits as she could. Then she closed her eyes, gripped her legs and bore down.

''I think it's going to happen,'' John said as Alice set the tray on the table he had placed at the end of the bed.

"Rubber gloves, Santa?" Alice said solemnly. She spoke to John, but her eyes were on Penny, urging her on.

"Thank you, nurse." After pulling on the gloves, he drew a long breath and bowed his head briefly in silent prayer. "Is Dr. Harrington on the telephone?" At Alice's nod, he said, "Okay, tell him what's going on now. And tell him, for God's sake, to tell me what I need to know." When Alice hurried out of the room, he glanced at Penny. "Keep pushing, sweetheart. Remember your breathing."

"I'll work...the front counter...and do the books... Can you see the baby yet?"

"This baby's got a head of hair you're going to love!" He was watching a miracle! A thrill of joy brought a flood of moisture to his eyes. He blinked rapidly, trying to clear his vision. "If you work the front counter, then I can do the baking exclusively. We'll be a hell of a team, darling. Push!"

"Martin and Martin...franchises all over...the country!" Her face reddened with effort. "But only after...the kids start college."

At the time it seemed to happen very fast. Later they would both remember Alice running in and out of the room relaying messages and questions as the sky gradually lightened outside the windows. Then Penny gave a tired triumphant cry and suddenly John was holding a wiggling infant. Behind him Alice leaned against the bureau and wept with joy. A lusty cry rose from a set of tiny lungs.

Quickly John finished as he had been instructed, while Alice cleaned the baby and wrapped it in a small warm blanket before she kissed Penny and quietly tiptoed from the room. Then John, his eyes brimming with tears, carried the bundle to Penny.

"My dearest Mrs. Martin," he whispered. "Your daughter wishes you a merry Christmas."

Stretching out beside Penny on the bed, he placed the baby against her breast, then enclosed them both in his arms.

PENNY AND THE BABY were dozing and dawn had broken against the frosted windowpanes when John heard a sound outside. Careful not to wake them, he eased from the bed and hurried downstairs, noticing as he passed through the living room that the radio was still playing carols and the Christmas tree lights were still on.

He looked through the window next to the front door and saw that the storm had blown itself out. The wind had finally died, leaving enormous drifts across a sea of white. A few lazy flakes still floated down, but a pale yellow glow stretching up the eastern sky signaled a clear day to come. Then his heart moved in his chest as he saw the blade of a big orange plow swing around the bend in the road and cut up the driveway. It was one of the most welcome sights he had ever seen. Sitting in the cab beside the plow driver were Dr. Adler and Wes Pierce. They waved when they saw him at the window.

John threw open the door as Dr. Adler climbed down from the plow and waded through knee-deep snow toward the porch, holding his bag in front of him.

"How is she?" the doctor called as he hurried up the porch steps, pausing only long enough to stamp the snow and ice from his boots.

"Mother and daughter are doing fine," John said, smiling and clasping Bill's hand. "But I can't tell you how glad I am to see you!"

The weariness vanished from Bill Adler's eyes. "Terrific, John! That good news makes a very long night worth every minute." Talking while he peeled off his coat, hat, muffler and gloves, he quickly sketched how he'd fought the blizzard up the mountain, talked the state patrol into allowing him through the tunnel, and then had found Wes Pierce waiting on the other side with the plow. "It took us almost three hours to get here from the tunnel. The roads are impossible. I couldn't have made it in my car. If Wes hadn't been there with the plow..." Dr. Adler moved past John and started up the stairs where Alice was waiting to lead him to Penny. "After I have a look at Penny and our newcomer, I'd sure like a cup of John's hottest coffee. Wes and I exhausted the thermos hours ago."

John stepped off the porch, his throat working, and he

clasped Wes Pierce's hand in a bone-crushing grip. For a moment neither man spoke.

"I don't know what to say," John began, "except that I've been a damned idiot. You spent Christmas Eve sitting in a plow. You didn't have to..." Unashamed tears glistened in John's eyes. His voice thickened around a lump of emotion and he spoke with difficulty. "How can I ever thank you for what you've done for us?"

Wes clapped him on the back and gave him a tired grin. "You can start with a cup of hot coffee. And I'd like to use your phone to call Edith and let her know we arrived safe and sound."

"Wes, I..." He was still gripping the older man's hand, needing to say more, but unable to find adequate words. Nothing seemed strong enough. "I've said some pretty stupid things. You must have thought I was an arrogant fool. And I was."

"Seems to me the key word there is *was*." Wes returned his handclasp, then stepped up on the porch. "You know, John, I've been thinking. Edith says I'm too set in my ways, too much a creature of habit. So I've been thinking about getting a summer place." His eyes twinkled. "How would you feel about setting me up a park bench in front of your new shop? Next to the aspens?"

John laughed, liking this man and the solid values he stood for. "I'd be honored. And I can promise you a steady supply of the best free coffee you ever tasted." He met Wes's gaze. "Your presence would help launch our new business. I'd be grateful."

Accepting help was never going to be easy. But maybe each time he let himself take as well as give, it would feel a little more comfortable.

Wes smiled and dropped an arm around John's shoulders. "Welcome to the family, son. And welcome to Aspen Springs. Wouldn't surprise me if one day you ran for mayor. Hell, I might even campaign for you."

"Mayor John Martin. It has a kind of ring, doesn't it?"

Laughing, knowing they were beginning a lifelong friendship, they went inside to inspect the new arrival.

AN HOUR LATER, Wes and the plow driver had wished everyone a Merry Christmas and left. When Amy and Flash came running upstairs at seven, horrified to discover they had overslept, Penny was lying on the sofa in front of the twinkling Christmas lights, her face tired but radiant in the light of the fire John had built in the grate.

"Santa came!"

"Oh, Mommy, look! Santa brought me an Elizabeth doll!"

Penny smiled. "Santa brought everything you asked for," she said, her eyes shining as she nodded toward the stairs leading to her bedroom.

John stepped into the living room, wearing his red Santa cap, and holding a red-and-green blanket in his arms. "Look what Santa brought us," he said smiling. Kneeling, he drew back the blanket so Flash and Amy could see a tiny red face and a cap of golden hair. "This is your sister, Holly Noel."

"Wow," Flash said. "She came down the chimney?"

John laughed. "Something like that." He winked at Penny.

"Can I hold her?" Amy asked, her eyes round.

"I think we should let Mommy hold her now. After you've unwrapped your presents you can hold her."

Later in the morning, Penny adjusted the folds of a slim new robe and lay back on the sofa in John's arms. Tears of joy filled her eyes as she listened to Alice and Bill talking together in the kitchen as Alice prepared Christmas dinner. Amy and Flash played with their new toys on the floor in front of the fire. Holly Noel dozed in a bassinet.

Penny gazed around her, radiant with happiness. Everyone she loved was here with her. And nothing else mattered but that. Love. Love would always be enough.

"I just remembered," she said, shifting in John's arms to gaze into his eyes. "I didn't have time to mail this." Reaching into the pocket of her robe, she removed a folded sheet of paper she had placed there earlier.

He raised an eyebrow, then opened the page and read aloud.

"'Dear Santa, if you can tear yourself away from the North Pole, Mrs. Claus loves you and wants you to come home.'" John grinned. "Does this mean I can sleep upstairs?" Tenderly he caressed her glowing face with his fingertips before he covered her temples, her eyelids, her parted lips with a dozen eager kisses that left her laughing and breathless.

"Wowee," Flash said, nudging Amy and giggling. "Look at Mommy and Daddy—they're necking. This is the best Christmas ever!"

"The best Christmas ever," Penny agreed, smiling against Santa's lips.

Two stubborn adults.
Three matchmaking kids.
The adults don't stand a chance!

THREE WAIFS AND A DADDY

Margot Dalton

CHAPTER ONE

DECEMBER SUNLIGHT spilled through the trees, thin and pale as spun gold, creating pools of violet shadow across the drifted trail and weaving a sparkling web of mist between the dark, snow-shrouded pines. The air was keen and vibrant, singing with cold and freshness, so crisp that the tiniest sounds hung suspended in the air like brittle snowflakes.

The double grooves of a cross-country skiing trail curled out through a small clearing and disappeared among the trees, the freshly groomed parallel tracks sharp and inviting in the winter afternoon. Light and shade played across the trail, highlighting each subtle curve and ridge, creating dark pools of mystery in the overgrown areas just beyond the smooth track with its lacy edging of pole marks.

On this weekday afternoon few people were using the skiing trails. The silent forest beyond the clearing seemed to close in upon itself, wrapped in an ageless, ancient sense of privacy and self-sufficiency, excluding outsiders and presenting a cold, impenetrable face to the world. The trail lay still and deserted, going nowhere, washed by the cold, pale light and the eerie, hushed music of the wind in the swaying pines.

Suddenly the spell of silence and mystery was broken. A man appeared around a distant curve, skiing swiftly and expertly into the little clearing. He wore navy blue ski tights that showed to fine advantage the superb muscle structure of his long legs, and a heavy white-and-blue patterned Nordic sweater over a white turtleneck. The rich wool of the sweater rested with casual ease across his broad, flat shoulders and chest, its bright color matching to perfection the deep blue of his eyes.

He was a tall man, with a beautifully formed masculine body and sculpted blond good looks that gave him an almost godlike appearance, mystically accentuated by the silence of the winter afternoon and the graceful swiftness of his effortless flight. He could have been a visitor from another galaxy, a vastly superior being dropped somehow through time and space into this quiet golden winter afternoon in the Canadian west.

But when he paused, leaning back on his ski poles to breathe deeply, and then grinned up at a small black squirrel chattering in a tree high above him, he suddenly looked completely human. His dark blue eyes sparkled with fun, a warm dimple popped into one flat, tanned cheek, and his wide mouth curved upward with sunny good humor. He threw back his head with its smooth, shining cap of thick golden hair and waved one pole at the noisy squirrel.

"Hey!" he called. "Why all the noise, kid? And," he added as an afterthought, "what are you doing up there, anyhow? Aren't you supposed to be hibernating or something? It's almost Christmastime, you know."

The squirrel peeped down at him, bright-eyed and alert, and made no response.

The tall man reached behind his body, fumbling with the fastenings on the small pack he carried around his waist. He withdrew a cardboard carton of apple juice, opened it and drained it while he continued to watch the squirrel, and carefully restored the empty carton to the pack. Then he checked the bindings on his ski boots, flexed his muscular arms and shoulders a couple of times, gripped his poles and bent down to fly away once more along the trail.

Before long he reached the summit of the trickiest portion on this section of the run, his blue eyes shining with anticipation as he checked to make sure there were no stragglers or groups of children blocking the trail.

But, in fact, there was only one person in evidence on the

snowy landscape. She rested awkwardly on her skis at the top of the hill, peering down at the steep, twisting trail with forlorn concentration. As he passed the woman, Jim had a quick impression of bulging flesh in bright turquoise jogging pants, of a white sweater straining over an ample stomach and an anxious, grandmotherly face framed by gray curls under a turquoise knitted cap.

Jim nodded, sidestepped past the solitary woman, and dropped into a tuck to negotiate the downhill, edging into a sharp snowplow with the snow hissing beyond his skis. At the curve he swerved perfectly to execute a rapid, graceful step turn, and then dropped into racer position to ride the downhill, his lips parted joyously over his white teeth, his golden hair lifting and stirring as the wind sang in his ears and the trees spun dizzily past him.

The trail finally flattened and smoothed, leveling out and then climbing up into the trees again. Jim skied to a stop, laughing, still exhilarated by the speed and smoothness of his flight. Suddenly he paused, his face clouding briefly, and cast a glance over his shoulder at the double grooves behind him in the snow. He hesitated, looking once more at the empty trail. Finally he frowned, stepped over into the other track and began the long, slow climb back up the hill in the direction he had come.

When he reached the bend in the trail and gazed up the sharp incline, the plump woman was still there at the top, a lonely, silent figure among the immensity of the dark, towering pines.

Jim watched her thoughtfully for a moment and then began a rapid ascent of the hill, setting his skis in a swift, skillful running herringbone that carried him upward with astonishing speed. At the summit he paused, resting on his poles and breathing deeply, and looked over at the plump woman.

She stared back at him, her brown eyes full of sadness, her sweet, wrinkled face puckered with anxiety.

"It's really not so bad, ma'am," Jim said gently. "You just

need to snowplow a little at the start, that's all. The part around the bend isn't nearly so steep."

"But I don't *know* how to snowplow!" the woman wailed. "I've only been on skis once before in my life. I can hardly stand up, let alone snowplow!"

Jim stifled a grin. There was something so lovable about her, something touching and childlike in the way she stood there teetering on her shiny new skis, her plump face desolate as she gazed down the hill.

Sternly he composed his features and regarded her. "If you're just a beginner," he said, "you really shouldn't be on this trail, you know. This is rated 'expert,' mostly because of this one downhill."

"Oh," the woman said blankly. "Is it? Isn't this the Chipmunk Trail?"

This time Jim couldn't help grinning. His deep blue eyes sparkled, and his wide mouth lifted to reveal the engaging dimple in his left cheek. "Hardly," he told the woman cheerfully. "This is the Timberwolf Trail."

"Oh," she said in alarm, and then seeing his dimpled smile, her eyes widened suddenly with the look of dazzled recognition that he knew so well. "My goodness! You're—what's his name, aren't you? The football player?"

"Jim Fleming," he said briefly. Then, as the woman hesitated, flushing with embarrassment, he added cheerfully, "Are you a football fan, too?"

The plump woman chuckled warmly. "Hardly. In fact, I personally think it's just about the most senseless game ever invented. The reason I know you," she added, reaching down to pull up one of her heavy woolen socks, "is because my two grandsons have that poster of you…you know, the one where you're standing with your helmet under your arm, smiling just like that…?"

Jim nodded. "I know the poster," he said without enthusiasm.

"Well, they've had that picture hanging between their beds

for ages. In fact, you've watched me read a lot of bedtime stories over the years. How could I not recognize you?"

He laughed, beginning to enjoy his conversation with this pleasant matron. "You know my name and everything, and I don't know anything about you."

"Maude Willett," she said, smiling and extending a damp, mittened hand.

"Hello, Maude," Jim said, shaking her hand and smiling back at her. "How do you happen to be on the Timberwolf Trail all by yourself?"

"It's a long story," she said mournfully, and extended one plump turquoise leg. "You see these terrific skis, all shiny new?"

Jim nodded again, trying to keep his face sober.

"Well, my son and his wife bought these for me last year for Christmas. Everyone else in my family is just a fiend on skis, and they wanted me to learn, too."

"But you didn't."

"I went out once last year, during the holidays, tripped and rolled down the hill the little kids were practicing on, wound up at the bottom looking like the world's largest snowball and decided this wasn't my thing. My favorite athletic event is double canasta, actually."

"You bet," Jim said solemnly. "It takes a lot of conditioning to play a whole game of double canasta. The deck is so heavy with all those extra cards."

She giggled and continued. "So I decided that my Christmas gift to *them* this year would be that I'd surprise them by learning how to ski. We're all going on a winter family holiday to British Columbia after Christmas, and I was going to dazzle them all by being able to swoop down hills like a bird and fly across the countryside like a speeding bullet."

Jim found himself growing more and more fond of this plump lady.

Apparently this opinion was mutual, because she examined him thoughtfully for a moment and then said, "You know, for a world-famous football pinup, you're not such a bad type, actually."

"I'm not just another pretty face," Jim told her solemnly. "I'm really a very sensitive guy."

She guffawed loudly and shifted awkwardly on her expensive skis. "So," she went on, continuing her story, "my granddaughters brought me out here today, and the idea was that they were going to teach me everything I needed to know to become a world-class athlete in one easy lesson. At least that's the way they made it sound."

A light began to dawn in Jim's mind. "But after you got here..."

"After we got here, they ran into a couple of boys they know from school, and they all wanted to ski together, so the girls took me to the beginning of the Chipmunk Trail and told me to practice, that the only way to learn is just to do it...."

Jim was careful to hide his sudden, quick surge of irritation with this nice woman's selfish and thoughtless grandchildren. Instead, he smiled at her pleasantly and said, "Well, I guess you took a wrong turning. Several trails converge up there by the warming hut, and you got onto a much more advanced one."

"Oh, good," she said with relief. "So it's not just me, right? I've been so scared by some of these hills that I wanted to lie down and slither along on my tummy." She was silent for a moment. "Several times that's what I *have* done, actually," she confessed. "But not voluntarily."

Jim grinned again. "Well, all you need is to master a little basic snowplow and you can handle any downhill. Just watch and I'll teach you."

Her plump face brightened and then fell again. "Look, you shouldn't be spending all this time with me. Don't you have...you know...people waiting for you, or anything?"

"Not a soul," Jim said cheerfully. "I'm all alone up here."

"You're retired, right?" she asked curiously. "You don't play football anymore?"

"Not anymore. Knee surgery," Jim explained laconically.

"The same thing that ends most professional football careers eventually."

"Oh, I see," she said. "You know, when my husband was alive, he was a great admirer of your father, the senator. Me, too, as a matter of fact, but then he's so handsome, isn't he? Just like you, actually. I just finished reading your father's book," she added with a warm, ingenuous smile, "and I thought it was just wonderful."

Jim's pleasant mouth tightened a little. To forestall further conversation he launched immediately into a demonstration of downhill technique. "Now what you do, Mrs. Willett," he explained, "is slide your skis out like this, so the edges catch..."

He suited actions to words while Maude Willett watched gloomily.

"Then you drop your bottom like this..."

As he spoke, Jim tucked in that muscular and extremely attractive portion of his own anatomy, lowering himself into an easy, relaxed crouch, and turned to look over his shoulder at the matronly woman behind him.

"What you want to do," he explained, "is pretend you're riding a horse and keep your hands low on the reins like this..."

He began to slip down the hill, his long, narrow skis skillfully held in their inverted V, riding the incline with perfect control. At the curve he paused and smiled encouragement up at the plump, lonely figure on the top.

"Your turn," he called cheerfully. "Give it a try."

The woman in turquoise gripped her poles, spread her skis, brought the tips together, dropped into a crouch and then, dismayingly, just kept on dropping, sinking onto the snow and rolling frantically over into the soft powder at the edge of the trail.

Maude swore quietly and fervently, got up, dusted herself off grimly and tried again. This time she got halfway down the hill before her ski tips crossed and she once again became, in her own words, "the world's largest human snowball."

Jim continued to give instruction and encouragement, helping her to brush the snow from her clothing and position her skis correctly. On her fourth attempt she snowplowed slowly and awkwardly all the way down the incline, arriving upright beside him, her round pink face blazing with triumph.

"I did it!" she shouted to Jim, overcome with joy. "I did it. Just wait till I show the kids! They'll never believe it, never. Oh, thank you so much!"

Jim grinned, delighted by her pleasure with herself.

"Look," Maude said finally, puffing and bending to examine her skis with enormous satisfaction, "I'm going to stay here and go up and down this hill till I can do it perfectly. You just carry on, all right? I feel guilty already about taking up so much of your time."

"It was a pleasure," Jim said sincerely. "Are you sure you'll be all right on your own?"

"Absolutely," his new friend said. "After all," she added smugly, "I know how to snowplow, don't I?"

"Yes," Jim agreed solemnly, "you certainly do."

She chuckled and then watched with affection as he prepared to depart down the winding trail. "Mr. Fleming…Jim!" she called suddenly.

"Yes?" He paused and looked back over his shoulder, his burnished hair shining warmly in the afternoon sunlight.

"Would you…would you like to come to dinner with us tonight? I'm feeding all the grandkids at my apartment. It's not much…just meat loaf, but my meat loaf is pretty fantastic, you know. And the girls would be so thrilled to have you, to say nothing of their brothers.… I have two grandsons, too, just old enough to be really interested in football.…"

"It's very nice of you to invite me," Jim said sincerely, "but I'm afraid I can't. I'm a creature of habit, you see, and every Monday in the winter I watch the Monday night football game with some friends of mine. Otherwise I'd really like to come."

"Well," Maude said cheerfully, "some other time then,

okay? I'm in the phone book, the only M. Willett, and I'm all alone. I'd love a visit from a handsome football star."

"*Ex*-football star," Jim said with a grin.

Maude grinned back, nodded and began toiling back up the hill, setting her skis with new confidence, her plump body fired with determination.

Jim smiled and watched her for a moment longer, then turned, kicked once and surged powerfully off down the trail again, settling rapidly into his easy, rhythmic stride.

But, as he stroked and poled, he was thinking about meat loaf in Maude Willett's household, visualizing the warmth and chatter and uproar of her big, happy family. His feeling, he realized with surprise, was one that he hadn't consciously experienced for a long time—a troubling sense of oppressive loneliness and a deep, wistful yearning.

AT APPROXIMATELY the same time that Maude Willett was rejoicing in her very first successful snowplow attempt, another small victory was being celebrated about thirty miles away in the same prairie city of Calgary, Alberta, that was home to both her and Jim Fleming.

This triumph, though, was being observed under very different conditions in a botanical laboratory where the heat hovered near thirty degrees Celsius and the air was warm and humid, heavy with the earthy fragrance of green and growing things.

The laboratory was part of a huge, sprawling complex of greenhouses, atriums, clinically sterile research facilities and warrens of offices all occupied by swarms of white-coated research scientists and staff assistants. In this particular portion of the complex vast banks of plants were germinating under moisture-beaded plastic hoods, all of them carefully monitored as to soil heat, air temperature, moisture conditions and mineral balance.

Near one of the banks a woman and a man stood together, staring down at the neat rows of tiny seedlings. The woman smiled, turning aside to make a series of notations on the clipboard she carried.

She wore gray fitted slacks and a pink turtleneck of soft angora wool, but her body was concealed by a crisp white loose-fitting lab coat that fell almost to her knees. Her long hair was dark, pulled back severely into a ponytail and then neatly braided, and her appearance was further concealed by a big pair of dark, heavy-rimmed glasses that looked far too large for the delicate structure of her face.

The elderly man beside her was small and roly-poly, with a rosy face that radiated enthusiasm, and a gingery fringe of hair encircling his shiny bald head.

"Look at that, Sarah!" he exulted. "*Ninety-one percent!* That's the best germination rate we've ever had on this genetic structure."

The woman smiled, and even the heavy glasses were unable at that moment to disguise the exquisite warmth and classic beauty of her face.

"It's wonderful, Carl," she said in a voice that was gentle and musical, strangely appropriate in this room filled with fresh and flowering greenery. "Now," she added, her tone suddenly rueful, "if they can just survive drought, blight, genetic insufficiencies we don't know about, the tendency to root too shallowly, a weakness in propagation and so on, we might just have a viable new structure."

Carl shook his head. "What a pessimist. Sarah, I've been working for you...how long has it been?"

"Seven years," she said, looking at him in surprise. "Since I first came here. You were assigned to me right at the start, and you've been helping me ever since. Why?"

"Well, in all that time I've never known you to get excited over any of your accomplishments. Everybody else in the field is getting excited over them, but you're always just looking for flaws in your work. You're so hard on yourself."

She grinned and reached out to touch his chubby shoulder fondly. Her face, behind the heavy glasses, was pink with the humid warmth of the greenhouse and glowing with pleasure at the successful germination rate of her experimental plants, and she was, all at once, almost incredibly lovely. The elderly little man beside her, accustomed though he was to her appearance through all the days and seasons of their working lives, nevertheless was briefly astounded, gazing at her with wordless pleasure.

"People don't succeed by standing around patting themselves on the back, Carl," she said cheerfully. "You know that. Looking for the flaws in my work keeps me honest and humble."

He smiled back at her with undisguised affection. "Honest and humble!" he jeered gently. "If you ask me, Sarah, it wouldn't hurt you to toot your own horn a little just occasionally."

"You just wait. When I have a horn to toot, old friend, I'll make more noise than anybody. I just want—"

She was interrupted by a voice calling loudly from the doorway at the end of the corridor.

"Dr. Burnard! Hey, is there a Dr. Burnard in here?"

"Here I am," Sarah called, peering around a bank of tall, leafy oat plants, heavy with seed, to the doorway where a young man leaned in, his face pink with cold.

"Supplies," he said briefly. "Where do you want 'em?"

"Supplies?" Sarah echoed blankly. She turned to Carl, still at her elbow. "How can it be time for supplies? They always come on Monday."

"It *is* Monday, Sarah," he said gently.

She stared at him, her lovely face puzzled, her big gray eyes full of alarm. "But...how can it be Monday?" she asked again. "We didn't have a weekend."

Her assistant stifled a chuckle. "Everybody else had a weekend, Sarah. You spent both days in here doing moisture graphs. Didn't you notice there weren't a lot of people around the past couple of days?"

Sarah continued to gaze at him, wide-eyed, struggling with her own thoughts. "Oh, my goodness," she breathed finally. "*Monday!* You mean today is *Monday*, Carl?"

"All day, my girl. What's so special about Monday?"

"It's just...oh, my goodness," Sarah repeated helplessly with a touch of panic in her voice. "It's just that Monday is..."

She shifted on her feet, her face reflecting a growing alarm while the others watched her in surprise. Finally she turned to leave, heading off down the wide, steamy corridor at a rapid pace.

"Show him the right shelves in the storeroom, Carl," she called back over her shoulder. "And if he has the new shipment of culture dishes, leave a box of them out for me, okay? I'll be right back."

She hurried out of sight, moving swiftly on her long legs, her white coat swinging, while her lab assistant and the delivery boy stood side by side watching her.

Sarah left the greenhouse and entered the office complex, relieved by the feeling of the cooler air on her hot face and body. She almost ran through the wide, gleaming wood-paneled corridors, arriving soon at her own door and shutting herself gratefully inside the neat, austere confines of her office.

She leaned against her polished oak door for a moment, reaching up to remove her glasses, closing her eyes and rubbing her forehead. Her face, without the heavy glasses, looked vulnerable and lovely, with a delicate, fine-boned structure, alluring high cheekbones and smoky gray eyes set in a sooty fringe of eyelashes, with dark, strongly defined eyebrows. Her mouth was rich and curving, surprisingly sensual in a face so disciplined and intellectual.

After a moment, she replaced the glasses, composed her features and instantly became once more a scientist, clinical, efficient and impersonal in appearance. She drew a deep breath and crossed the room to her broad teak desk, opening a small upper drawer and taking out a chart and a thermometer.

Sarah popped the thermometer into her own mouth, glancing over the chart while she waited for her body temperature to register. After a few minutes, she removed the thermometer, examined it and made a couple of tiny, neat notations on the chart. She sat for a moment, tense and still, studying the figures while her face grew pale and her eyes darkened with emotion.

"Okay," she murmured aloud finally in a small, shaking voice. "That's it, then. I guess tonight's the night."

With trembling hands she restored the thermometer and chart to their place and drew out a file folder from a concealed compartment in the lower part of the drawer.

She placed the folder on her desk unopened, her hands hovering just above it as she stared at it with a sort of fascinated reluctance. There was a small, neat tag on the edge of the folder, labeled with Sarah's own meticulous printing. The tag read simply, "Jameson Kirkland Fleming IV."

Sarah studied the folder for a moment longer, drew a deep, shuddering breath and slowly opened the cover. The first thing exposed was a large color photograph of a smiling blond man holding a football helmet under his arm. It was, in fact, a smaller print of the same picture the plump woman on the ski hill had mentioned to Jim Fleming.

This picture, though, wasn't nearly so interesting to Sarah as it apparently was to other women. She gave it a quick, cursory glance, pausing only to observe the fine, clean lines of the man's handsome face, the breadth between his eyes and the height of his forehead, all positive genetic features. Then she moved on to items of greater interest.

There was a surprising amount of material in the manila folder: newspaper clippings about Jim Fleming's marvelous career as one of the few Canadian athletes ever to succeed in American pro ball, about his final damaging injury, the painful surgery he had undergone and his eventual decision to retire and attend to his business interests.

Sarah skimmed over these as well, barely pausing to concentrate. Jim Fleming's football career, though colorful and impressive, was hardly even of passing interest to her. But she paused and began to read with careful attention when she reached the documents at the back of the folder.

These included a variety of items. There was a clipping

about Fleming's graduation from the University of Alberta, where, while launching his football career, he had also managed to earn a law degree with highest academic honors. And there were news clippings and stories about his father, Senator Jameson Kirkland Fleming III, with a couple of good pictures of the craggy old man, which Sarah studied with approval.

Jim Fleming bore a remarkable resemblance to his father—the same intelligent, alert facial expression, the same tall, erect, wide-shouldered body, the same clean, muscular lines and planes of bodily structure. This genetic dominance of positive traits was, as Sarah well knew, an extremely favorable indicator.

She set aside the pictures of Senator Fleming and picked up a neat, exquisitely documented genetic chart, drawn by Sarah herself, setting forth as much of Jim Fleming's family tree as she had been able to ascertain in the course of her meticulous research. This information was also highly favorable, showing strong, hardy bloodlines, vigorous character traits, no intrusive genetic illnesses and an inherent tendency to be healthy and long-lived.

For the family name they had, apparently, only counted back four generations to the last Fleming to live on the ancestral estate in Scotland. But, as far as Sarah could tell, there had been Flemings around—rich, vigorous, intelligent and combative—since long before records were even kept.

She grinned suddenly, thinking that she wouldn't be at all surprised to learn that when the first Romans arrived to work on Hadrian's Wall, they were met by a Jameson Kirkland Fleming, riding up in a swirl of hoofbeats and tartan to inform them arrogantly that they were trespassing on private land....

Her smile faded and her hands trembled a little as she set aside the genetic chart and picked up the final documents in the file.

These were more real and immediate, with information considerably more troubling and unnerving to her than the cool, impersonal data of the other material. They consisted of notes, neatly typed and chronologically ordered, tracking what she had been able to learn in the past year of Jim Fleming's daily activities and social habits.

And there wasn't much.

For a handsome, desirable and famous man he seemed, in fact, to lead a very quiet existence. There was a restaurant he favored on the rare occasions he dined out, a badminton club he belonged to but attended only sporadically and, surprisingly, an art class were he had studied watercolors during the previous spring session on Tuesday afternoons. But now there was only one regular appointment he kept, and Sarah had only learned of it by accident, through a friend who had worked briefly at a downtown pub until her student loan came through.

"He never fails," Wendy had said. "Jim Fleming, the ball player, you know? He comes into the pub every single Monday night, rain or shine, to watch the football game with a couple of other guys. And, Sarah, he's just the most delicious man you ever saw. Absolutely gorgeous. I mean, he's just so incredibly..."

"Alone?" Sarah had interrupted, careful not to look too interested. "Does he come alone, or does he bring a date?"

"Oh, alone," Wendy had said. "He's always alone. And women try all the time to pick him up, but he's just so good at getting away from them without being rude. It's really an art form. I know he dates sometimes, but he's terribly selective. He's got to be careful, you know, because there's *millions* of girls who'd love to get their hands on him, and believe me, I should know, because I'm one of 'em...."

Sarah remembered her effusive friend's chatter, staring moodily down at the chart of Jim Fleming's habits and activities. Her face grew pale, and her hands still shook a little as she idly traced the outline of the molding on the edge of her desk, her gray eyes dark and preoccupied.

For such a long time this had all seemed safe and distant, just a game of research she was playing, something that would never turn out to be real. But, like many scientific endeavors, Sarah's project had carried itself of its own momentum to a conclusion that she now faced with nervous reluctance.

All she knew definitely was that the moment had arrived. Monday was the day, because that was the only time when she knew for certain where Jim Fleming would be in the evening. And this was the Monday she had been waiting for, because today her body temperature indicated that her cycle was precisely at midpoint, and she was ovulating today.

And tonight, though he would never, ever know it, Jameson Kirkland Fleming IV was going to father Dr. Sarah Burnard's baby.

CHAPTER TWO

SARAH RETURNED to the research lab behind the greenhouse and went through the rest of the day wrapped in an intense preoccupation, her mind far away from the routine chores that her hands performed. While she stained and mounted slides of wheat kernel cross sections, her thoughts circled and whirled with a kind of panic-stricken excitement.

Part of the problem, of course, was that although she had chosen Jameson Kirkland Fleming IV as the ideal male to father the child she wanted so desperately, she hadn't actually laid eyes on the man for almost twelve years.

Sarah paused in her work with her hands poised above the tray of tiny glass plates, her pale face distant and withdrawn, her eyes far away.

She had been just twenty when she first saw him, already into her third year of university, academically brilliant but shy and withdrawn in her plain, drab clothes and thick, heavy glasses. And that year Jim Fleming, who was a year older and finishing his second term of pre-law, had been in her English literature class. She could still recall the fine golden splendor of him, with his sunny, handsome face, his tall, fine body and the easy grace of his movements, and the horde of adoring fans, both male and female, who seemed to follow him everywhere.

And as clearly as if it were yesterday, she could remember the warm autumn day when he sat across from her, listening intently to the lecturer, his intelligent, handsome features alert with interest, his big athletic body relaxed and confident in the wooden desk.

Sarah, concealed behind her dark-rimmed glasses, neat and studious in a gray pullover and skirt, had stolen a glance at him, and the thought had popped unbidden into her mind.

If I ever have a baby, that's the man I'd want to be its father....

At the time she had dismissed the thought as idle foolishness, even been irritated with herself for jumping on the bandwagon, ready to fall all over herself and make herself look silly over this man, just like all those other poor moonstruck girls who constantly dogged his footsteps. Afterward, she had carefully avoided even looking at him. During the course of the semester, they had never even exchanged a word of conversation.

In the years afterward, of course, Jim Fleming had faded from her mind, to be recalled only when his picture was in the paper, or his famous father did something newsworthy. But after her own father's death, when Sarah had earned her doctorate and embarked on her distinguished career, she was haunted more and more by the aching sense of something lacking, of something she didn't have and desperately wanted.

Finally she realized the truth. What she wanted more than anything else in the world was a child of her own. She was over thirty, time was flying by with alarming swiftness, and if she was to have the experience of pregnancy and motherhood, she couldn't afford to delay much longer. But now she was so deeply into her study and work in genetic research, so conscious of the crucial role that heredity played in the development of all living things, that choosing the right father for her child was a matter of paramount importance.

Alone in the big gleaming lab, Sarah shook her head and returned to her chore, meticulously staining the slides, holding them to the light to check then, labeling and filing them for future use. Her beautiful face was pale and calm under the broad banks of fluorescent lights that illuminated the worktables, but her mind still wrestled with memories and the anxious, panic-stricken doubts that had tormented her ever since she had read the thermometer and realized the significance of this particular Monday.

Her career these past ten years had allowed no time to build any kind of serious relationship, and Sarah understood that few men had any desire to compete with her beloved cereal grains. In fact, her patient, obsessive search for a drought-resistant strain of wheat had always seemed far more important to her than the need to find a man. As a result, at the age of thirty-two, Sarah didn't know any man she wanted to share much of anything with, let alone something as wondrously important as her own baby.

And artificial insemination wasn't an option, either, although the concept had initially been interesting to her trained, scientific mind. But after Sarah researched the process, she rejected it outright. The only information they were willing to give you about the prospective donor was his hair and eye color and, if you were lucky, his occupation. For someone who spent her whole life studying genetics and the importance of inherited properties, this was far too little data on which to base something so monumentally important as the birth of a human baby.

So eventually, almost against her will, Sarah had found her thoughts turning once more to Jim Fleming, who possessed all the physical and mental attributes she considered genetically critical, whose family tree was impeccable, whose gene pool complemented her own perfectly—Jim Fleming, who was now retired from his football career and back in his home city....

As she worked, frowning intently over her tray of slides and trying not to think about the evening ahead of her, the winter sky darkened beyond the laboratory windows and the lights began to flicker all over the compound. Carl popped his head in to say good-night, receiving only an absent smile and a nod from Sarah, who didn't see him leave, bundled like a dumpling in his heavy winter overcoat, his kindly round face puckered with concern.

As so often happened the building began to empty while Sarah worked, but she was hardly aware of the deepening silence, the dimmed corridors and the hushed stillness of the parking lot beyond the windows where her own car finally stood all alone, plugged in against the winter cold, covered with a ghostly dusting of fresh snow.

At last she paused and leaned back in the hard metal chair, arching her back wearily and rubbing a hand over her forehead. She glanced out at the deserted, moonlit parking lot, suddenly becoming aware of her lonely little car huddled in its blanket of white.

It's snowing, Sarah thought with a wild surge of hope. *It's probably too cold to go out tonight anyhow. Maybe I'll wait till next time....*

Then she shook her head, her gray eyes bleak and troubled.

She knew all too well she couldn't wait till next time. It might take a long, long time for her cycle to coincide again, to fall on a Monday night when she knew the man would be accessible. He might even move away, or go on an extended holiday after Christmas—anything could happen. If she wanted to get pregnant, and she wanted this particular genetic pool for her future child, then it had to be tonight.

And, Sarah thought wearily, *I'd better get busy, because it takes time to stage a seduction scene, especially if you've had as little practice at the whole business as I have.*

She shuddered with distaste, tidied up her equipment and left the laboratory, walking briskly through the darkened corridors to her office. Finally, muffled in her heavy tan duffel coat, she let herself out of the complex and waded through the fresh snow to her car.

On the way home Sarah was bemused, as frequently happened in the winter, by the intense contrast between the humid green warmth of the research facility and the wintry, moonlit bleakness of the snow-shrouded world beyond her car windows. On any other evening she would have been enchanted by the journey from one world to another, by the austere beauty of the winter moon shining on the silvered snow and the buildings etched with Christmas lights like gingerbread houses, flinging jeweled bands of light across a black velvet sky.

But tonight she found no pleasure in the magical scenes all around her. She could think of nothing but the evening ahead, and of her own extreme reluctance to do what she knew was necessary.

Because, of course, Jim Fleming must never know that he had fathered her child. She couldn't bear the idea of that kind of involvement. He had to be convinced absolutely that what happened on this night was nothing more than a casual sexual encounter, a one-night stand with a total stranger.

For Sarah, who had never in her life had a one-night stand, it wasn't going to be easy....

Still preoccupied with her thoughts and concerns, she pulled into her garage, plugged her car in and slipped through the connecting door into the house. Sarah shrugged out of her overcoat, hung it up in the entry closet and switched on the lights, walking slowly into the bright yellow kitchen.

"Amos?" she called. "Where are you?"

Amos padded into the room, a huge marmalade tomcat with an awesomely impressive air of personal dignity. He rubbed politely against Sarah's legs, allowed himself with a long-suffering sigh to be picked up and tickled beneath the chin and then commented that his dish was empty and somebody had better attend to the matter immediately.

"In a minute, okay?" Sarah said, setting him gently on the floor. "I really need a cup of hot coffee, Amos. It's freezing out there."

Amos gave her a reproving frown and marched from the room, head high, tail waving ominously.

"All right, all right," Sarah said meekly, padding along behind him. "First I'll fill your dish, *then* I'll make a cup of coffee."

Satisfied, Amos watched as his food was carefully measured out, then expressed his appreciation by allowing Sarah to pick him up again and bury her face in his warm fur, smelling deliciously as it always did of sunshine and catnip.

"Oh, Amos," Sarah murmured, "I love you, you big fat tyrant...."

He wriggled impatiently, and she set him down hastily by his dish, then went back into the kitchen to place a mug of water in the microwave. After it boiled and she stirred in a judicious amount of instant coffee, Sarah wandered down into the sunken living room, curled up in a big, padded armchair and looked around wistfully.

It's so cozy and nice, she thought with painful longing. *I wish I could just stay home tonight, forget the whole thing, not have to go out and...*

Forcibly she quelled her treacherous thoughts and sipped her coffee, still gazing absently at the room.

Sarah had inherited this house when her father died. Carlton Burnard, also a scientist, had loved his only child deeply, and had invested all his hopes and dreams in her when his lovely Spanish-born wife had died just a few years after their little girl was born.

Sarah had never lived in any other house, but familiar though her home was to her, it still looked vastly different than it had when she lived here with her father. Carlton Burnard hadn't lived to see his daughter earn her doctorate and become a distinguished scientist, nor had he been around to enjoy the fruits of Sarah's success—the research grants and fellowships and salary increases that went along with her growing importance in the world of botanical genetics.

These days Sarah could afford to make her home the way she wanted it to be, and its appearance would have surprised many of her co-workers who didn't know her well and sometimes thought of her as cold, mechanical and passionless.

The room around her glowed with color and richness, with deep, warm earth tones and vivid splashes of crimson and gold and turquoise. Sarah loved the American Southwest, traveling there whenever she managed to drag herself away from her work, and the square sunken living room bore evidence of her wanderings—woven Navaho rugs, throws and murals, heavy, rough-hewn furnishings and small, bright paintings that sparkled like jewels on the white plastered walls.

And everywhere there were horses, Sarah's favorite animal. Dainty china horses pranced and postured in glass-fronted display cases, rough, textured clay horses marched across the deep, plant-filled windowsills, and whimsical straw horses stood casually in the shadowed corners. The focal point of the room was a full-sized wooden carousel horse mounted on an oaken stand near the hearth on the shining hardwood floor, his sorrel mane flying, his black eyes gleaming, his pale blue saddle and bridle exquisitely detailed and outlined in gold and silver.

Sarah sipped her coffee, gazing moodily at the beautiful little horse, crafted so lovingly by some long-ago artisan. But, for once, even the carousel horse brought her no pleasure.

She finished her coffee in preoccupied silence, debated briefly whether to toss a frozen dinner into the microwave and decided she wouldn't be able to eat, anyway. Reluctantly, with dragging steps, she climbed the stairs to her loft bedroom, followed by Amos, and began the difficult and unappealing task of transforming herself into the kind of woman who would be able to entice a man like Jim Fleming into going to bed with her....

Sarah's bedroom, like the rest of her house, was surprising and delightful. The room was homey and comfortably old-fashioned, with heavy antique maple furniture, ornate picture frames holding faded sepia photographs of long-deceased family members, rich lace curtains against dark-papered walls and a handmade patchwork quilt on the massive bed.

And, of course, more horses.

Also in the loft of her house were Sarah's bathroom, as well as a tiny alcove equipped with a personal computer system, and another little dormer just large enough to hold a crib and dresser.

The other small bedroom down on the main floor was where the nanny would have to live after the baby was born....

Sarah paused, frowning with sudden concern as she thought

about the rooms in her house. This was a familiar worry, the knowledge that this house, much as she loved it, was far too small and impractical to stay in once her baby became a reality. The rooms were just too tiny, and there wasn't enough space for live-in help, and no yard to speak of—the empty lot next door that Sarah had played in as a child was now occupied by a huge fourplex that dominated the whole block.

She had been planning and saving for years, and there was enough money in the bank now, added to the proceeds from the sale of this house, to buy a bigger place after she had the baby. Probably next summer, much as she hated the idea, she'd have to start looking at real estate. She frowned again, her face reflecting the pain of this decision. Then she thought about the baby she longed for, about a bright, sunny nursery and a cosy eating nook with a yellow high chair, and a big, shady yard with a swing set....

Sarah felt a sudden surge of immediacy, of vibrant, stirring excitement. She ran across the rough braided rug in her bedroom, stripped rapidly from her working clothes and pulled on a long, heavy terry-cloth robe, navy blue with crisp white trim, and a pair of fluffy white mules.

Amos leaped onto the foot of the bed and marched up its length, sinking down on the big pillow next to a pair of whimsical white fabric horses with manes and tails of blue yarn. He slitted his eyes rudely and began to knead the patterned surface of the quilt with his paws.

"You can stay there while I get ready," Sarah told him darkly, "if you don't say a single word. *And* you'd better have your claws in while you're doing that, buster."

Unperturbed by her tone, Amos shouldered the fabric horses aside, turned around twice and subsided into a warm furry ball on the pillows, resting his chin on his paws and watching her lazily through narrowed lids.

Sarah hurried into her bathroom, leaped in and out of a quick hot shower and set her hair on hot rollers. Then, working with unusual care and trying not to feel silly, she applied her makeup in the manner she had practiced in preparation for this night, using a good deal more than her customary touch of mascara and dash of lipstick.

When she finished, she carefully inserted her seldom-used contact lenses, combed out her hair and regarded her face critically in the mirror.

"Okay," she said aloud. "So far you look all right."

In fact, she looked very good indeed. Her dark chestnut hair tumbled in soft curls around her shoulders, full of bronze highlights, and her naturally lovely features, artfully enhanced by the subtle but dramatic makeup, were both glamorous and alluring.

Sarah gave herself one more careful examination, added a touch more blush to accentuate her high, beautiful cheekbones and hurried back across her bedroom to the closet.

She had spent a long time deciding on just the right dress for the seduction of Jameson Kirkland Fleming. Her first inclination had been to buy something frankly suggestive, something bright and vulgarly loaded with sequins that would fit tightly over her hips and show a lot of cleavage.

But, after listening to Wendy's ingenuous chatter about the fascinating and famous man who came regularly to the bar on Monday nights, Sarah had changed her mind.

"You should just see all the gorgeous, sexy women who come on to him," Wendy had said, "and it's like he doesn't even notice them, you know? Like, the only time he ever shows any interest at all, it's gotta be someone kinda classy, you know? He seems to have a built-in radar, like he only responds to classy women, not sexpot types."

So, armed with this information, Sarah had gone in search of a dress that would look both seductive and "classy," and finally she had found it. The dress was deceptively simple, a soft smoky black silk with a high, demure neckline and a bodice and skirt that slid with casual suggestiveness over her breasts and thighs, clinging gently in places and swaying deliciously as she moved.

Sarah was only medium height but appeared taller because she was unusually slim, and because she held herself so proudly erect. Her figure, sculpted and firmed by miles of walking in all kinds of weather, was trim and slender, with full, high breasts, a taut, flat abdomen and long, shapely legs. When the black dress slipped over her head and fell with a soft, silky whisper around her body, she was transformed instantly into a woman so alluring that no man could fail to give her at least a second glance.

Sarah tugged on a pair of black snakeskin sandals with high spike heels and moved across the room to her dresser, opening a gleaming mahogany jewel case and taking out an exquisitely fashioned necklace and earring set of heavy antique silver, one of her few legacies from her beautiful Spanish mother. She fastened the jewelry carefully in place, then stepped aside to regard herself critically in the long cheval mirror, holding the black silk skirt a little away from her body and pirouetting slowly.

"So, Amos," she asked the big cat, who lay watching her in sleepy silence, "what do you think? Will he approve?"

Amos parted his mouth in a huge, toothy yawn and twitched his whiskers with drowsy insolence.

"Well, he'd better," Sarah said. "Because we've waited a long time for our baby, haven't we, Amos? We want to buy a crib, and wallpaper with bunnies on it, and little dancing mobiles, and stacks and stacks of snowy white cotton diapers...."

Overcome with sudden joyous excitement Sarah whirled across the room in her high heels, picked up the big cat and hugged him fervently while he glared out beneath her chin in baleful silence. Then she tossed him back onto the bed, watched with affection as he rolled himself into a fuzzy orange ball of insult, and slipped into her little white fox jacket. Her beautiful face glowed vividly above the soft fur of the collar, and her gray eyes shone like stars in the shaded lamplight.

"I'll be back by midnight, Amos," she said softly from the doorway. "And when I come home, I'm going to be pregnant."

Then she was gone, slipping the shoes from her feet to run

lightly down the stairs while the house closed in upon itself, warm and silent, to await her return.

SARAH HAD BEEN inside the pub briefly one fall day in the interests of research after she first formulated her plan. But she knew all too well that a rehearsal, even a dress rehearsal, was never the same as the real thing, and she was filled now with terror and a disconcerting sense of not belonging, of being in absolutely the wrong place at the wrong time.

She sat alone at the bar, nursing a weak mixed drink, trying hard not to panic. Everybody here seemed to know everybody else, to have a kind of easy kidding relationship that made her feel isolated and excluded. But when a couple of men approached her with clumsy attempts at friendliness, she felt even greater panic.

What if someone moved in on her and she wasn't able to shake him, so that when Jim Fleming arrived he would think she was already taken and lose interest?

Coldly Sarah resisted their advances and left them feeling chilled and shaken by her beauty and aloofness.

By the time she started her third watered drink, the football game was well advanced, being watched with lusty cheers and comments by a group of men on wooden chairs and stools drawn up near the big-screen television, but there was still no sign of Jim Fleming.

Tonight of all nights he chooses to be undependable, Sarah thought gloomily. *Every other Monday night he's here in his place by seven o'clock. Tonight he won't even show up.*

Just as she framed this thought the door opened and the man himself entered in a gust of chill night air, pausing to brush the snow from his wide shoulders and smiling at the roar of greeting that went up from the rowdy circle of football fans.

Turning casually on her stool at the bar, Sarah stared across the room at him, feeling her throat suddenly tighten and her palms begin to grow moist.

He was just so…so…

She floundered, trying to absorb the reality of the man without losing her resolve, all at once terribly unnerved by the fact that she hadn't seen him face-to-face since those long-ago college days. All of her information about him had been gleaned from three sources: the press, the very discreet and highly expensive services of a private investigator she had hired for a couple of weeks earlier in the year, and Wendy's idle chatter.

Now, despite all her careful research, Sarah found herself totally unprepared for his sheer physical impact, his big, graceful maleness and his overwhelming personal presence. She swallowed hard, trying not to appear obvious as she watched him brush the snow from his shining blond hair, hang his jacket on the coatrack near the door and cross the bar to his circle of noisy friends.

Jim Fleming wore blue jeans, casual suede shoes and a tan crewneck sweater over a blue plaid shirt that made his eyes look even bluer, and he still moved with the easy athletic prowl that Sarah remembered so well, his big shoulders relaxed and easy, his stride lithe and powerful.

Sarah heard the loud chorus of affection that greeted him, and his deep voice explaining cheerfully, amid much delighted male laughter, how he had driven into a snowdrift coming down from the ski hill that afternoon and been forced to wait over an hour for a tow truck.

Sarah's heart began to hammer painfully in her chest. As she gazed across the room, Fleming swiveled idly in his chair, glancing around at the occupants of the bar, calling greetings to others in the room. His eye caught hers and he fell abruptly silent, staring at her in startled admiration for a moment. Sarah returned his look, cool and unsmiling, deliberately keeping her face calm and impassive.

She was the first to turn away, returning to her drink and the polite attentions of the bartender, but she could feel the way his glance lingered on her before he turned back to the television screen.

So far so good, Sarah told herself nervously. *He's shown some interest at least. Now, if I can just keep from making any really dumb mistakes...*

She sipped her drink in silence, facing the long, glistening rows of glasses and colorful decanters that lined the back of the bar and listening to the bartender with an occasional absent smile as he talked about his children. He was, apparently, an ardent family man, with a growing brood who participated in a bewildering variety of sports and cultural activities, all observed and recounted with enormous pride by their doting father.

I'll probably be just as bad with my own child, Sarah thought wistfully. *Bragging to anybody who'll listen about how smart she is, how fast she learns, her rare and incredible talents...*

She smiled suddenly, her lovely, delicate face glowing, her huge gray eyes shining, almost incandescent with pleasure. The bartender stared at her, transfixed, then turned aside hastily to take another order, his cheerful, blunt features still awed and amazed.

Unaware of his reaction, Sarah drank her warm tomato juice and brooded on the mysteries of male and female attraction. Grimly she wondered how she could have been so foolish and presumptuous as to think *she* could capture the attention of a man like Jim Fleming just by dressing up and sitting in the same room. After all, a lot of women who were sexier and prettier had tried to attract him with little success. Why should Sarah be any different?

But then there was Wendy's theory about attracting men.

"Any woman who's reasonably presentable," Wendy had once said, "can attract any man she chooses, just by being near him and concentrating hard enough. Like, we give off...a scent or hormone or something, like insects, or moths, you know, and they feel it and can't resist? Like, a male moth will fly miles and miles to get to a female who wants him. It's, like, nature, you know?"

Sarah, whose scientific training included an encyclopedic knowledge of the processes by which smaller creatures managed to reproduce, had merely smiled with amusement, enjoying Wendy's chatter. For somebody working toward an advanced degree in economics, she often thought, Wendy had retained a great deal of childlike naiveté.

But now, in desperation, she recalled the conversation and wondered if there really was any truth to it. Could she actually draw Jim Fleming to her side just by wanting him badly enough?

She swiveled slightly on the bar stool and stole a look across the room at the back of his head with its smooth cap of golden hair, and his broad, flat shoulders beneath the soft, creamy wool of his sweater. Then she turned back to the bar, concentrating on him, narrowing her thoughts so that the only thing in her mind was this one man and the passionate depths of her need to be with him, to draw from his body the magic spark that would ignite her own waiting cells, form a new human being, bring her precious little baby to life and start its wondrous cycle of growth.

I want you, she thought fiercely, staring into her drink. *I want you and nobody else to do this thing for me, and I'm going to have you. Right now, tonight, within a couple of hours, it's going to happen, because I'm* willing *it to happen, with all my energies.*

"Could I buy you another drink? That one's looking pretty low," a voice said at her elbow.

Still deep in concentration, Sarah was about to make a cool, dismissive response when something in the man's tone caught her attention. She turned and stifled a gasp of astonishment.

Jim Fleming sat on the stool next to her, smiling, his big, lean body almost touching hers.

Sarah had never been this close to him before, and she was stunned by his physical magnetism, his pure masculine appeal. His face, with the fine, arrogant bone structure that she admired so much, was tanned by the sun and wind, glowing with good health, his blue eyes clear and vivid. His features were alight with friendliness and good humor, and a kind of easygoing, considerate warmth that would probably be irresistible to most women.

Sarah, however, wasn't at all concerned about this man's personality, because she was convinced that such qualities weren't genetically transmitted. She was greatly interested in his physical structure, his background and heredity, but she wasn't in the least impressed by his charm.

"Thank you," she said calmly. "One more drink would be nice. I'm leaving soon and it's a cold night."

Jim Fleming signaled the bartender and turned back to Sarah with increasing interest. "You know, you have a beautiful voice," he said. "Really beautiful."

"Thank you," Sarah said, wondering if she was going to be able to go through with this whole thing. She just felt so silly....

"Pardon me for the line, but do you come here often?" he went on with an easy grin. "I mean, I keep having the feeling we've met before, but I can't remember where."

Sarah felt a quick stirring of alarm that clutched briefly at her stomach and made her feel a little sick. Then she reminded herself sternly that those college days had been twelve years ago; he couldn't possibly remember her from then.

"That sounds like yet another line, doesn't it?" she asked lightly. "The old 'haven't we met before?' routine."

Jim Fleming chuckled. "I guess it does at that. But I'm serious, except I just can't seem to place..."

"Probably," Sarah said, accepting her new drink with a smile for the bartender, "it was just somebody who looked like me."

"I doubt it," the tall blond man said abruptly. "I don't think I've ever met anyone who looked like you."

Sarah stared at him, wide-eyed, and found him regarding her with a steady, intent look, all the laughter and teasing stilled.

She was dismayed to feel a little flush mount on her cheeks, and turned aside quickly, biting her lip, painfully aware that women accomplished in the art of seduction weren't supposed to blush at compliments.

"*Another* line," she said with a small, brittle laugh, trying to keep her voice from shaking. "You're just a walking guidebook to singles repartee, aren't you?"

"Hardly," he said. "In fact, I'm really not very good at this sort of thing at all. My problem," he added, swirling his rich amber rum in its tall glass and gazing thoughtfully into the golden depths, "is that I'm not good enough at being insincere. I tend to say what I think, and it costs me every time."

Sarah, who often did just the same thing, felt a warm surge of empathy and stifled it instantly. She had no intention of establishing any sympathetic human communication with this man. She didn't want to be friends with him, and she certainly had no wish to see him again, ever, after he served his biological purpose. In fact, she couldn't allow herself to respond to him at all. She had to remain within the character she had shaped for herself and carry it through to the end so that he could be successfully seduced and then discarded.

"Sincerity," she said lightly, sipping her drink, "is highly overrated."

"Why do you say that?" he asked with interest.

"Well, because people run around being sincere, helping each other, getting all involved in things that don't really concern them, and in the long run everybody winds up taking advantage of each other and getting hurt. A nice, comfortable hedge of insincerity is absolutely necessary for protection in the modern world, I think."

"Lord, what a cynical outlook," Jim Fleming said with awe. "I couldn't live if I felt that way about other people."

Neither could I, Sarah thought. *But I'm not about to tell you all the secrets of my soul, Jameson Kirkland Fleming IV.*

"Do you know anything about me?" he asked abruptly. "My name, for instance?"

"How would I?" Sarah asked idly. "Is it embroidered on your mittens, or something?"

He grinned. "No, I just wondered. Most people seem..."

He fell silent again while Sarah struggled to keep her expression light and casual, with the cool, mocking tone she had adopted to suit the character she was portraying.

"All I know about you," she said, "is that you appear to be a fairly presentable physical specimen, maybe a little too given to honesty and sincerity, but with definite possibilities."

"Possibilities for what?"

"For the capacity to be highly entertaining."

"I see," her companion said lightly. "And what exactly do you find entertaining, my pretty lady?"

Sarah turned and met his eyes steadily, gazing fully at him, desperately aware of the crucial importance of this one moment—probably the most vital and pivotal moment of her life.

"I'm entertained," she said in her low, beautiful voice, "by the music of the universe, the conjunctions of celestial bodies, the fact that when two entities coincide with perfect precision, the earth moves...."

A small, amused Sarah somewhere inside her head, who was watching this whole scene with detached merriment, chuckled and hooted at the trite, hackneyed words.

Corny, she thought in despair. *Just so ridiculously corny. What's wrong with me? Why can't I do this a little better?*

But Jim Fleming stared back at her, mesmerized by her words and the stunning, hypnotic beauty of her face and form.

"I think," he said slowly, "that you might be bad news, pretty lady."

Sarah's heart began to pound, and she bit her lip, hoping frantically that it wasn't audible, knowing with her rational, scientific mind that, of course, it couldn't be, but still afraid of betrayal by her body.

"I just might be really good news, too, you know," she whispered. "And there's only one way to find out, isn't there?"

Jim Fleming leaned toward her, so close that she could smell the soft fabric of his sweater mingled with a faintly spicy after-shave, a clean, fresh scent of outdoor cold and warm, healthy maleness.

"What's your name?" he asked.

"Whatever you want it to be," she murmured. "Pick something that pleases you."

He settled back, studying her thoughtfully. "That's the way it is? No names exchanged?"

Sarah nodded. "That's the way it is," she said quietly.

"And where do we go? Your place or mine?"

Sarah made a conscious effort to hide the overwhelming surge of relief that suddenly flooded through her.

It's going to work, she exulted. *Oh, my God, it's actually going to work!*

"Neither," she said aloud. "You don't want me in your life after tonight, and I certainly don't want you in mine. So we just go somewhere neutral, like the hotel down the street."

"The Kingston Arms, you mean?"

Sarah nodded, sipping her drink calmly.

"Maybe you're overestimating me," Jim said with a sudden grin. "Maybe I can't afford the Kingston Arms, you know."

Sarah slid from the stool, reached for her fur jacket and gave him a calm, level glance. "That doesn't really matter," she said quietly. "I can."

CHAPTER THREE

JIM FLEMING STOOD in the small white-and-gold bathroom adjoining the luxurious room at the Kingston Arms, which despite his companion's quiet objections, he had insisted on putting on his own charge card.

He splashed cold water on his tanned face, buried himself in the depths of a big soft yellow towel and then examined his reflection thoughtfully in the mirror, thinking about the woman waiting in the other room.

There was something about her...something so strange.

Jim frowned and shook his head, still disturbed by his own behavior. This particular episode was completely out of character for him, something he hadn't done for as long as he could remember. For one thing, sex with strangers was distasteful to his naturally fastidious nature. And then men in his position had to be so careful, pursued as they were by publicity seekers, neurotics, cunning manipulators and others who just wanted to ride their coattails to a bit of the limelight.

That was the problem, he thought, running a hand moodily over his shining blond hair. Life for men like Jim Fleming could be surprisingly lonely. Come to think of it, his sex life hadn't been exactly terrific lately. In fact, if the truth were told, it had been an uncomfortably long time, which had probably helped to make him vulnerable to this particular encounter.

But there were other influences, too: the sad brittle gaiety of the big city all dressed up for Christmas, the glowing warmth of lighted windows that sheltered families in their little houses all cozy with togetherness, even the thought of the plump woman he had met skiing that afternoon who was now having meat loaf with her grandchildren.

Jim shook his head, fighting off the gray sadness that sometimes crept into his soul these days and threatened to upset the careful structure of his life.

Besides, he thought briskly, hanging the towel away on the rack and stripping off his shirt and sweater, it wasn't just the holiday surroundings, or even his uncharacteristic blue mood that caused him to be here. The main reason for this liaison was the woman herself.

He tugged off his socks, stepped out of his jeans and folded his clothes carefully on a shelf opposite the basin. Then he stood for a moment, naked except for his shorts, his tall, splendid body filling the little bathroom with golden hard-muscled male beauty.

But he wasn't even looking at his reflection in the long, gilt-edged mirror. He was still musing about the woman who waited for him in the other room.

She was such a woman of contradictions, a fascinating, quicksilver kind of person. In the bar her incredibly alluring beauty had attracted him at first, given him the urge to hear what her voice would sound like and see how her face looked when she smiled, just the way anyone would want to get a closer look at a lovely work of art. Then, after he began to talk with her, he had been powerfully aroused by her smoldering, evident sensuality, her subtle suggestiveness, the obvious indicators that she was passionately interested in him as a sexual partner.

All of this, though, was no new experience to Jim Fleming. He had met many, many beautiful women and heard all kinds of sexy come-ons. What he found most enchanting about this particular woman were the mysterious nuances of her personality, the things that didn't quite mesh. For instance, she had seduced him with quiet authority and raw sex appeal, and yet on the brief walk to the hotel she had seemed to relax, as if at a task accomplished, and had pretty much ignored him altogether. Instead, he had noticed that she gazed about with childlike pleasure at the Christmas lights and decorations on the snowy downtown streets.

And at the hotel desk she had smiled shyly at the desk clerk and then withdrawn hastily and stood muffled in her soft fur, looking around at the elegant lobby and seeming, all at once, like a little girl embarking on some scary adventure.

Either she was playing some kind of really weird game, or else she was an actress so accomplished that she could create the impression of a deep, multilayered personality.

Probably it was *all* playacting, Jim thought. Most likely she was just another adventuress, out for a thrill, living her own complex fantasy.

But she was undeniably classy, and she was so incredibly beautiful.

He switched off the bathroom light, opened the door and walked out into the other room, pausing in the semidarkness to give the woman in the bed a level, challenging look as he faced her and slowly, deliberately, stripped off his undershorts.

He stood naked before her, all taut, flat muscles and hard, arrogant maleness, looking carefully into her face. She rested against the crisp, soft pillows, her wings of dark hair flowing behind her, the sheets drawn up to her creamy, bare shoulders, and returned his gaze with apparent calm. But again there was something about her, a flicker of alarm when he stripped in front of her, a brief unreadable expression, that made him suspect, implausible though it seemed, that she wasn't really as used to this sort of thing as she pretended.

Anyway, who the hell cares? Jim thought with sudden weariness. *A one-night stand is a one-night stand, and nothing more.*

He reached down with an abrupt gesture and drew the sheet away from her body, surprised by her quick reflex move to cover her nakedness. Then, as if making a conscious effort, she relaxed and stretched languidly in the bed, displaying herself to him.

Jim stared down at her in silent, stunned amazement, feeling the first urgent stirring of strong physical desire and the resulting thrust of maleness.

She was so absolutely exquisite—the most beautiful woman he'd ever seen. Her breasts were full and high, pink-tipped and virginal-looking, although he calculated that she had to be close to his own age. Her pale skin was silken smooth, and her figure was both slender and lush, with firm, shapely curving lines connecting breast to abdomen to hip and thigh in a symphony of richly delicate womanly beauty that enraptured him.

"Lord, you're beautiful," he whispered in spite of himself. "You're just so unbelievably beautiful..."

"You're not so bad yourself," she said in a low, husky voice, gazing up at him as he stood over her. "Come here," she whispered.

And yet as he climbed into bed beside her, shuddering with desire, his sense of puzzled surprise mounted. There was something really strange going on here...something that was so hard to figure out....

The way she moved against him, and the warmth of her lips as she kissed him, were provocative and enticing, arousing him to a fever pitch of need that was painful in its intensity. But her hands didn't seem to match. They were awkward, hesitant, almost as if she were inexperienced in the art of touching a man. Far from being a turnoff, Jim found this the most exciting thing of all, the sense that she was somehow innocent and new to the arts of love, needing his guidance and instruction.

God, she's good, he thought in some part of his mind that was able, even in the throes of passion, to remain detached and objective. Not many women would be able to create an impression of innocence in the midst of all this heat.

Deliberately he slowed and paused, lost in pleasure, caressing the length of her body with slow-sensual hands. He wanted to go on forever, just touching her and holding himself in check to prolong the experience, to spend the rest of his life in this warm bed with this woman's lovely, rich curving body, fondling her sweetness....

But the urgent rush of his desire was too strong. At last he surrendered to his pounding need and moved to enter her, groaning with passion, his body arching and plunging as he lost himself in the silken depths of her, breathing hard, moaning out loud with joy.

And she responded to him like no other woman he had ever known. It was as if she wanted all of him, every ounce of maleness he could give her, as if she wanted to draw the very essence of himself into her body and make it her own.

The intensity and excitement of her passionate, silent response was more than he could bear. He reached his climax and felt her slender body shudder beneath him in her own private release. Then, abruptly, he relaxed, drawing gently apart from her and taking her tenderly in his arms, so overcome with sleepy satisfaction that he could hardly think.

They lay for a long time in drowsy silence while the warm-air register hummed softly near the bed and passing traffic in the streets below threw ghostly fingers of light over the walls and ceiling. Finally Jim leaned up on one elbow and looked at the woman beside him.

She lay with her eyes closed and an intent, wondering look on her face, curled up in a little ball as if she were protecting something precious within the curve of her body. In the dim light and the aftermath of passion her delicate face looked vulnerable and childlike, not at all the seductive, sophisticated woman she had been in the bar.

Jim remembered the marvelous, fiery passion of her body's response and the strangely inexperienced, almost shy movements of her hands, and wondered again....

"Hey," he whispered huskily. "Hey, pretty lady. You're really something, you know that? You're just incredible. That was awesome."

She made no response, her body still curled carefully in upon itself, her face quiet. Jim watched her for a moment in silence, then eased himself carefully out of the bed and padded into the bathroom to collect his clothes. He carried them back into the bedroom, along with one of the big yellow towels, which he placed gently over her shapely body.

"Here," he murmured, "Your bathrobe, my lady. You can use the bathroom, and I'll get dressed out here. Unless," he added hopefully, struck by a sudden thought as he looked down at her, "you were perhaps interested in seconds?"

She shuddered delicately and sat up, avoiding his eyes, wrapping the towel securely around her. Then, still silent, she gathered her clothes and vanished into the bathroom.

Jim switched on the bedside lamp and dressed rapidly, savoring the rich warm glow of sexual contentment that still flooded him, but realizing with a small tug of alarm that it wasn't going to be very long before he wanted her again.

She was bad news, after all, just as he had suspected. She was one of those alluring, bewitching women who somehow possessed the ability to ensnare a man, to captivate him and make him drunk on her charms, hopelessly, insatiably addicted to the sweetness of her rich womanly body.

Well, whatever she wants, he thought helplessly, *I'm willing to go along with it. I'm hooked. I just have to see her again, be with her.*

As he framed this thought, the bathroom door opened and she emerged, fully dressed even to her shoes, looking quiet and self-contained. She was as lovely as ever in the simple black dress, but there was no longer anything provocative or alluring about her movements at all, no flirtation or suggestiveness. Her step was brisk and businesslike as she crossed the room, still not looking at him, picked up her handbag and fur jacket and started toward the door.

"Hey!" Jim said abruptly. "Not so fast, all right? Can't we...just relax a bit, and talk?"

"What about?" she asked, pausing with her fur coat over her arm.

"I don't know," he began helplessly. "Just about...the kind of things people talk about." He paused, his eyes widening in surprise as she hesitated nervously near the door.

She looked back at him, obviously waiting for him to finish speaking so that she could leave.

"You mean," he began slowly, "this is it? Nothing to say to each other, no names exchanged, no plans to meet again?"

"That was our understanding right at the beginning," she said.

"And what if I've changed my mind? What if I've decided I'd like very much to see you again? What then, pretty lady?"

He caught the brief flicker of panic in her eyes and his heart sank.

She's married, he thought. *Probably to some rich guy that she hates, but she doesn't want to lose him because of the money, so she sneaks around looking for adventures just to make life bearable.*

But Jim Fleming wasn't a man to be dismayed by obstacles. He had held this woman in his arms once, and he fully intended to have her again, regardless of the consequences.

"In that case," he heard her say quietly, "I suppose you would have to find me."

"And you think that's going to be really difficult?"

"Very difficult," she said.

He nodded, reached for his jacket and stepped up beside her. "Then I guess I'll just have to give up," he said cheerfully. "Won't I?"

She looked up at him suspiciously and then nodded, clearly relieved. "That would be best," she agreed with quiet seriousness.

"Can I at least see you into your car, or put you into a taxi or something? It's late for a pretty lady to be on the street alone."

"Thank you," she said, "but I'm fully able to look after myself."

"You know something?" Jim said, staring down at her intently. "An hour ago I would have agreed with that. Now I'm not so sure."

SARAH WALKED down the frosty midnight sidewalk beside her tall blond companion, still brooding over his last words. He seemed to have suspicions about her, and some kind of insight into her personality that was surprising and unsettling.

In fact, Sarah thought, the whole experience had been surprising and unsettling. She had expected the man beside her to be arrogant and self-absorbed, narcissistic and dull, and he had turned out to be quite the opposite. He was funny, witty and tender, deeply intelligent and gently considerate, with an endearing boyish side to his nature that made him extremely appealing.

And, Sarah mused, striding along with her hands thrust deep into her pockets and her breath gusting in the chill blackness, the sex act itself had been amazing, too.

Completely absorbed in her work, reserved and distant as she always was, Sarah's relationships were few and far between. She could hardly remember the last time she'd made love, and she could never recall an experience so exciting, so erotic and fulfilling and deeply, richly satisfying.

She smiled grimly. All the books said there was a better chance of conceiving if the woman had an orgasm, and considering the shattering intensity of the one Jim Fleming had given her, it had to be practically a sure thing.

"Would you like me to go back to the hotel and call a cab? There should be one coming along here soon, but I can..."

His voice interrupted her thoughts, and she forced herself to concentrate. She had been reluctant to have him call a cab from the hotel, thinking that it would make her too easy to remember and trace if he should actually set out later to find her. Her own car, of course, was parked just a couple of blocks away, but she had no intention of letting him get a look at the make, model and license plate.

If she could get into a cab, have the driver take her a few blocks and drop her off, then she could just circle back to her car on foot, drive home, have a hot bath and relax.

Oh, God, she thought plaintively, *I hope I'm pregnant, because I can't go through all this again.*

Jim hunched his broad shoulders against the chill night air, peered around the deserted streets and looked down at the woman beside him. "Look," he began with concern, "I think we should..."

Sarah glanced up at him, trying to keep her tired mind clear, desperately anxious to get away from him. By now, all that she wanted was to be safely home with the precious burden she carried so that she could concentrate on nurturing and protecting it. If she had really conceived, or was about to, then the wondrous new cells within her body were like a tiny, pale flame that needed to be guarded, shielded, coaxed gently to life.

Suddenly, as she stood gazing up into his tanned, sculpted face, a great many things seemed to happen all at once, leaving her shuddering and limp with terror.

She felt something pressing harshly into her ribs beneath the soft leather of her little jacket, saw Jim's jaw muscles tense with startled alarm, heard a rough, deep voice in her ear.

"Anybody makes a move," the voice said behind her, "and I cut the lady to pieces. And I ain't kidding."

The words sounded like a line from some low-grade movie. Sarah almost laughed hysterically, but the look on Jim's cold, set face told her that this was no joke.

This was the real thing.

Sarah felt hollow and sick, nearly on the verge of fainting, and struggled frantically to maintain control, to think clearly, to keep herself upright and rational.

"Get that thing away from her," Jim said harshly to the unseen presence just behind her.

"Shut up. I'm the one giving the orders here. Now, first, you take off your watch, nice and slow, and give it to me. And then I want what you got in your wallet, and no tricks, okay, 'cause I'd hate to hurt this nice lady."

Sarah couldn't see him, but she could hear the rough voice grating on her ear, the breath hot and ragged, and judged that their assailant wasn't a tall man, perhaps not even her own height. She could feel his nearness, smell the musty, unwashed human scent of him, sense the terrible dank coldness of his fear.

He's more scared than I am, Sarah thought, but the idea wasn't at all comforting. She knew enough of human psychology to understand that with a knife in his hands, their attacker was even more volatile and dangerous because of his fear.

Jim seemed to realize the same thing, because he quietly did as he was told, removing his slim, expensive gold watch and handing it over, carefully emptying his wallet of bills. His brown hands trembled with fury, his big shoulders were tense and his handsome face was so grim that Sarah grew even more terrified.

Something was going to happen, something dreadful and inevitable, and she was powerless to do anything about it, caught as she was between two violent, angry men, with a knife jammed against her ribs....

"Now, you," the voice grated. "Give me your money and your jewelry."

Sarah swayed on her feet, and Jim looked down at her with grim concern. He reached toward her, but the knife point jabbed painfully, making her wince. Then there was a quick, threatening gesture, and Jim drew back, his blue eyes smoldering dangerously.

"You heard me, lady," her attacker repeated. "Get a move on."

"I don't have...all I have in my bag is a twenty-dollar bill. Just for cab fare."

"Give it to me."

Sarah fumbled in her bag, her hands shaking, and took out the bill, handing it blindly behind her, feeling it grabbed from her fingers.

"Now the jewelry."

"But..." Sarah's voice rose in panic. "But...this was my mother's! It's all I have of hers. It's not valuable. It's just silver. Please don't make me give you my mother's—"

"Shut up!" the voice said again, low and furious. "Don't give me all that crap. Just take it off and hand it over."

Tears trickled down her cheeks, warm and salty in the cold night air. With a great, aching sense of sorrow and loss Sarah unfastened her necklace and earrings and handed them back to be snatched greedily.

"Okay," the voice said. "Now I'm gonna leave. But I'm taking the lady with me for a ways, just so *you* don't get any ideas, mister. C'mon, broad. Nice and easy. Just walk along in front of me here."

Suddenly, as he spoke these last words, the mugger's voice rose a couple of registers, ending on a high, fluting note that contrasted oddly with his earlier course, grating tone. After a brief instant of stunned silence, Jim launched himself forward, his athletic body moving with incredible swiftness, and threw himself onto the other man.

Sarah turned, shaking in terror, her eyes wide, her hand covering her mouth, and watched as the big knife clattered to the pavement and Jim wrestled with their assailant. For the first time she could see the man—a small skinny figure in ragged jeans and a tattered, dirty ski jacket with a black stocking mask over his face.

Though he was wiry and agile, he was no match for Jim Fleming. Silent and frantic, he struggled vainly in the bigger man's grasp, as slippery as a fish. While Sarah stood looking on Jim held him firmly in the crook of his arm, ripped off the stocking mask and then gasped in astonishment.

The face that stared out at them defiantly was that of a boy, barely into his adolescence, with smooth, childlike cheeks and a liberal dusting of freckles across his nose.

The boy glared at them furiously, blinking back tears of angry frustration. Jim shifted his position to get a better grip, and quick as a cat the child seized the opportunity. He ducked under the big man's arm, wrenched himself free and was gone, flying off down the street in his dirty sneakers with Jim pounding along behind him.

Sarah watched them vanish around a corner, still stunned

by everything that had happened to her within the space of a couple of hours.

"Hey!" she suddenly shouted out loud to the deserted street. "He's got my mother's jewelry!"

She bent, slipped off her high heels and jammed them into her pocket, then began to sprint along the sidewalk in the direction the other two had disappeared, barely conscious of the rough, frozen pavement that burned harshly against the soles of her feet.

As she ran along narrow streets and through garbage-filled alleys, trying frantically to keep Jim's distant running figure in her sight, Sarah was only dimly aware of the neighborhood she passed through. They were in one of those dismal downtown slums situated so incongruously near the tall, gleaming office complexes and elegant little boutiques—pockets of sad squalor and poverty side by side with areas of great wealth. In these smoke-blackened, crumbling old brick buildings people actually lived out their lives in cramped, airless rooms that sometimes lacked even the most basic amenities.

But she didn't have the time to ponder the social contradictions all around her. Her breath was coming in huge, ragged gasps, her side ached and there were sharp pains in her feet. Worst of all, Jim, far ahead of her, seemed to be on the verge of disappearing forever.

But just as she was about to abandon her pursuit, she saw him pause at a narrow doorway and then plunge inside, and she forced herself to run faster. Sarah entered the dim, musty building soon after he did and peered up the sagging, dirty stairs to see him hesitating by a scarred wooden door on the rickety landing.

Sarah shuddered. The whole building was so dank and depressing, full of smells that she didn't even dare to analyze.

And who knew what was behind that door.

But before she could call a warning to him, or even let him know she was in the building, he had set his big shoulder against the door and begun to push. The flimsy lock gave way immediately under his strength, and the door swung inward on a square of sickly light. Cautious and catlike, he peered into the room and then stepped slowly through the open door, disappearing from her sight.

Sarah watched in horror, her eyes wide, her chest heaving, expecting at any moment to see him stagger and reel back out into the hallway under a rain of gunfire.

Nothing happened. It was silent in the smelly foyer, silent on the grimy wooden stairs, silent out in the littered, moonlit alley. Sarah cast a frantic glance outside, looked up the stairs again and gathered all her courage. Then she climbed slowly upward, pushed the door aside, slipped into the room and stopped in astonishment.

Jim stood in the center of a tiny, dingy space that contained almost nothing except a narrow metal cot, a heap of blankets in another corner and a shabby little crib half concealed behind a tattered old curtain hanging in front of a doorless closet. Besides these basic furnishings, there were just a few scraps of household equipment, an old hot plate sitting on a battered cupboard and a couple of cardboard boxes apparently used for storage. The boy who had stolen Sarah's necklace stood defiantly in front of the cot, trying to shield it from their view. Behind him another child peered up at them from the nest of rumpled, musty blankets, its wide eyes and pinched face giving it the look of a sleepy, frightened owl.

The boy's eyes flicked over Sarah as she came in, and Jim turned in brief alarm. "You shouldn't be here," he muttered.

"He has my necklace," Sarah said doggedly.

The boy tensed and appeared to be on the verge of flight. Jim leaped suddenly across the room and grabbed their small attacker once again in a firm bear hug. Skilfully, without relinquishing his hold, Jim reached into the boy's dirty jacket and took out their money and belongings, slipped them safely into his own pocket while the boy struggled in furious silence and the child on the cot began to whimper with terror.

Sarah hurried across the room, pushed past Jim and the boy and knelt by the cot, gazing down at the contorted, pale face. It was, she judged, a girl about ten, with fine, straight blond hair cut raggedly around her ears and big blue eyes swimming with tears. Sarah stroked the matted, silky hair back from the child's forehead, almost unbearably moved by the little girl's fragile thinness, her wide, imploring eyes and her painful fear.

"It's all right, dear," Sarah whispered. "Nobody's going to hurt you. What's your name?"

"It's..." the child gulped and swallowed, then began again in a low, husky voice. "My name's Ellie."

"And is he your brother?" Sarah asked, indicating the wiry figure that still struggled frantically in Jim's iron grasp.

"Yes," the little girl whispered. "His name is..."

"Shut up, Ellie!" the boy said, stopping his futile wriggling long enough to glare furiously at the little girl on the cot. "Don't tell them anything!"

The thin blond girl bit her lip, and her eyes filled with tears once more.

"Look, kid," Jim said to the boy, "I don't think you have this whole situation completely figured out, do you? Now stay still for a minute and listen to me, okay?"

He emphasized his words with a gentle pressure of his restraining arms that made the boy wince a little with discomfort, then stand meekly silent.

"Now we know where you live, and we know what you did, you understand? And if we decide to press charges, you could be in big trouble. So you're not really in a position to be giving orders, are you?"

The boy stood glaring at the scarred wooden floor and didn't answer.

"*Are* you?" Jim repeated softly with another gentle pressure of his muscular arms.

"No," the boy muttered sullenly. "I guess I ain't."

"Good. Now what's your name?"

"Billy."

"Fine. Now, Billy, who looks after you kids? Who's the adult in this household?"

"I am," the boy said proudly, lifting his freckled face to glare up at the big man who held him.

Jim stared back at him silently and began to tighten his grip once more. "Tell me the truth, Billy," he warned. "I don't want to hear any lies."

"It *is* the truth," Billy said. "Let me go, okay? I won't run away."

"How can I be sure of that?"

"Because," the skinny boy said, as if amazed at his captor's stupidity, "I ain't likely to run off and leave you alone here to take the kids away, am I, now?"

"Kids?" Jim said blankly. "Is there another one besides the little girl there?"

As if in response to his words, a small furor suddenly erupted from behind the dirty, ragged curtain. The crib began to creak and rock, and a tiny figure heaved itself erect, grasping at the curtain with chubby hands and beginning to roar in a surprisingly lusty voice. All four people stared at the little indignant person balanced precariously on dimpled pink legs, the round red face screwed up with indignation.

"I think he's getting another tooth," Ellie explained, as concerned and apologetic as any young mother. "He has five already," she added proudly while Sarah smiled at her.

Ellie slid from the cot, exposing a pathetically thin little figure in a limp yellow T-shirt and ragged jogging pants, and lifted the plump baby from the crib, sagging under his weight. He continued to howl, squirming in her grasp.

"Here," Sarah murmured, "let me take him."

After a moment's hesitation, Ellie handed the baby over, and Sarah took him, cuddling him on her shoulder, resting her cheek against his downy fair head. He was about ten months old, healthy and sweet-smelling in his little cotton shirt and diapers, the only clean and beautiful thing in this whole squalid place.

Ellie and Billy were both silent, watching anxiously. Sarah smiled reassurance at them, patting the baby's small back tenderly while he hiccuped, quieted and nestled warmly against her.

"What's his name?" she asked Ellie, who came bustling

toward her with a soft blue blanket to cover the little bare pink legs.

"Arthur."

"That's a nice name. And he's a lovely baby," Sarah said gently to the two older children. "You're taking very good care of him."

"That's why...that's why I tried to rip you off," Billy said. His voice was low and abashed, all the toughness gone, and he sounded for the first time like the child he really was. "Like Ellie says, Arthur's getting more teeth, and there's all this flu going round, and he needs lots of milk and orange juice and expensive stuff, and he's almost walking already, so he needs shoes, 'cause the floor is cold and there's slivers..."

Sarah shuddered a little and held the baby's soft, warm body closer to her.

Jim was staring at the two children, his open, handsome face drawn with concern, his blue eyes full of disbelieving horror. "You mean..." he began slowly, and hesitated. "You mean, you weren't kidding? There's no one looking after you kids? You're all alone here with this baby?"

"Yeah," Billy said.

"I don't believe it," Jim said flatly. "It's not possible."

"Why not?" Billy asked. "I'm thirteen, and Ellie's almost eleven. I guess we're old enough to look after one little kid. Matter of fact, Arthur gets looked after better than most kids around here."

"For how long?" Jim asked, still stunned by the boy's words. "How long have you three been alone here?"

"Since summer. Our Mom died in the summer. She drank," Billy added by way of explanation.

"She was nice sometimes when she wasn't drinking," Ellie said loyally. "For a long time before Arthur was born she didn't drink at all, and she even had a job working nights cleaning buildings and stuff, and she brought us apples and chocolate bars and things sometimes."

Ellie sighed in bliss, her wide blue eyes reflecting the joy of those long-ago remembered treats.

"But after Arthur came she started drinking again," Billy said. "She was too drunk most of the time to look after him, and she wanted to give us all to the Welfare, but she said they'd split us up and send us to different places."

"What then?" Jim asked.

"I told her I'd run away and take the kids if she tried to give us to the Welfare," Billy said calmly. "And I told her I'd look after us all, so she didn't need to worry about it. And I have."

"By stealing from people," Jim said.

"Hey, man, I *never* did that before. This was the very first time. Usually I find papers and sell them downtown, run errands for people, lots of things. It's just that, like I said, we were scared Arthur was gonna get sick, and he needs so much stuff...."

Sarah still clung to the warm, yielding softness of the baby's little body, feeling faint and sick hearing this story.

"When your mother died," she said softly to Billy, "how did you manage to stay on your own? Didn't the authorities realize then that you were alone and..."

Billy shook his head. "Nobody knew. She died..." He glanced at Ellie, who stood pale and tense beside the crib, clutching a baby bottle in her small, thin hands, and then continued. "She died in an alley quite a ways from here, and nobody there knew anything about her. I was watching," he added without emotion, "when they took her away in the ambulance. They called her Jane Doe."

"But...the other people in the building," Sarah began, "don't they...?"

"The other people don't even know she's gone. They think somebody's looking after us, and they ain't the kind who care much what happens to anybody else. I just cash the Family Allowance and give the man the rent money every month, and nobody ever bothers us here, not a bit. They're all busy looking out for themselves. That's just the way it is," he said, concluding his little speech with a touch of defiance, glancing up at the two well-dressed adults.

"We have to...we have to call somebody," Jim began helplessly. "You can't go on living like—"

"If you do," Billy interrupted calmly, "I'll just take the kids and run away, and then they probably won't even be in as good a place as they are now."

"But why?" Jim asked. "Why would you resist getting help for all of you, and food and decent clothing and school—Do either of you go to school?" he asked suddenly, glancing from Ellie to Billy.

The boy shook his head. "Not this year. Not since Mom died. Schools are too nosy," he said briefly. "I got some books, and I teach Ellie lots of stuff, and we have some book about how to take care of Arthur, too. You see," he went on, "we can't go to Welfare. Right away somebody will adopt Arthur and take him away, 'cause he's a real nice baby and everybody wants babies. But they don't want me and Ellie."

The little girl's eyes filled with anguished tears that welled up suddenly and flowed unchecked down her wan, pale cheeks.

Sarah looked at her with concern, then turned to Jim. "Don't," she said softly. "Don't do anything just now. Let's give them some money for the things they need, and tomorrow we can come back and make sure they're—"

As if suddenly remembering her existence, he shot her a quick, keen glance, his face registering a strange mixture of emotions at the sight of her standing flushed and lovely in her stockinged feet, her elegant fur jacket and black silk dress, tenderly cradling the sleepy baby against her breast.

"Tomorrow, pretty lady?" he asked softly. "That sounds great. Should I pick you up at your place or meet you somewhere or what?"

Sarah suddenly came crashing back to reality, remembering the purpose of the evening, the precious seed she guarded within her body, the absolute necessity to maintain this charade of hers and keep Jim Fleming from ever finding out who she was or what she had done.

"On second thought," she murmured coolly, "I'm sure you

can handle it on your own. You'll have to fix their lock before you leave, of course, and make sure they're safe, so don't think about leaving them alone and trying to follow me. Could I just have my necklace, please? And then I'll be on my way."

I'll come back, she told herself. *As soon as I can be certain he's not around, I'll come back and bring them a whole lot of things—food and clothes and some warm things for the baby and books and toys....*

With a painful surge of regret, carefully concealed, she handed the drowsy, sweet warmth of Arthur back to his anxious sister and moved over beside Jim. Silently gazing into her eyes, he handed her the silver necklace and earrings along with her crumpled twenty-dollar bill.

Sarah pocketed the jewelry, gave the money to Billy, and bent to slip her shoes on, moving gracefully toward the door.

In the dank, musty hallway she hesitated, ignoring Jim altogether and smiling at the two older children, who stood watching her in silence.

"He really is a beautiful baby," she told them softly, and then ran swiftly down the creaking stairs and out into the silent, moon-washed night.

CHAPTER FOUR

JIM GLANCED HELPLESSLY at the three children, looked around the shabby little room and then clattered down the stairs to peer frantically out at the receding figure of his beautiful mystery woman. He watched as she neared the corner, walking swiftly, her dark head high, her slender, elegant legs flashing beneath the swinging silky fabric of her skirt.

"Damn!" Jim muttered aloud, pausing in the doorway, torn by powerful and conflicting emotions. Part of him wanted to run after her, seize her in his arms, demand that she tell him her name and where she was going. He was haunted by a desperate certainty that if he let her vanish tonight, he would never, ever be able to find her again.

And yet the three children were upstairs, alone and unprotected in this dreadful neighborhood, and he had broken the lock on their door.

As he continued to hesitate, the woman rounded the corner and disappeared from sight, swallowed up in the rumbling late-night stillness of the big city. Jim stood for a few moments longer, gazing at the emptiness of the frosty streets. Finally he shrugged his shoulders in despair, turned back into the dingy building and trudged up the stairs.

He stepped through the sagging door and into a scene of considerable noise and activity. Arthur sat in the middle of his crib, howling lustily and gnawing on his fist, his little red face screwed up alarmingly. Ellie and Billy were moving quickly around the room, gathering things up and throwing them into the cardboard boxes. They appeared to be having an argument in furious whispers, and it was obvious by the dispirited set of Ellie's shoulders and the tears on her thin cheeks that Billy was winning the dispute.

Both of them looked up guiltily when Jim came into the room. Ellie dropped the pile of tattered baby clothes in her arms as if they had burned her, while Billy gazed defiantly at the tall man, his freckled face pale and set.

Jim looked from one young face to the other, wincing as Arthur's howls increased in volume and the crib began to rock violently. One of the corners, Jim noticed, was heavily reinforced with masking tape, and the whole structure looked dangerously unstable.

"Is he all right?" he asked Ellie. "Shouldn't you pick him up or something?"

She opened her mouth to answer, but Billy silenced her with an abrupt gesture and turned to face Jim. "Look, mister," he said wearily, "just give it a rest, okay? Go home and leave us alone. I'm real sorry I tried to rip you off, and now you got your stuff back, so there's no problem, okay? Just leave us alone."

"Sure," Jim said, returning the boy's gaze steadily. "Leave you alone, and two minutes after I'm gone you'll have these poor kids out on the street in the cold, running away."

"We've done it before," Billy said flatly. "I've always looked after them before. I guess I can do it now."

"Look..." Jim began helplessly, and then broke off to look over at Ellie, who had lifted Arthur from his crib and was attempting to silence his roars of misery.

She glanced at her older brother, her little white face pinched with worry. "He's hungry, Billy, I think. He needs a bottle."

"So give him one."

"But...we don't have anything. We used the last milk at bedtime, and you said you'd get some money tonight and bring some home, but you—"

"Shut up!" Billy hissed at her, casting a quick, warning glance in Jim's direction. "Look, Ellie," he went on in a gentler tone, "the lady gave me that twenty. I'll go out right now and buy some milk at the store. Give him a bread crust or something to chew on. Maybe that'll hold him till I can—"

The boy paused, looking up at Jim as if just remembering his presence. "Please," he said wearily, "can you just go away and let us be, mister? I'll look after the kids. You don't have to worry about us."

Something in the boy's voice caught Jim's attention, not the tough-guy bravado or the raw defiance, but a tired undertone that spoke of a weariness almost too great to be borne.

The poor kid, Jim thought suddenly, forgetting all his earlier anger. *Thirteen years old, and he's got all the responsibility of the world on his shoulders.*

"Listen," he said with sudden decision. "This has gone on long enough. I'm taking you kids home with me, okay? And I don't want any arguments. I'll give you a place to sleep, and we'll feed the baby, and tomorrow we'll think about what to do with you. Now come on. Get some coats on and dress the baby."

Ellie's face turned even whiter. Her wide blue eyes filled with panic as she clutched her tiny brother in her thin arms.

Billy glanced at her, then turned back to Jim. "No way," he said grimly. "As soon as we get there, you'll be on the phone to Social Services, and within a week they'll have me and Ellie in two different foster homes and Arthur put up for adoption. No way! I'll kill you first."

Jim looked at the boy, chilled and dismayed by the cold anger in Billy's voice and the furious glint in those young eyes. But he faced him steadily with a calm, level glance until Billy finally dropped his eyes and kicked at the rotten floorboards, his thin cheeks flushed.

"Maybe you can push your little sister around and scare her with threats like that, kid," Jim said quietly, "but you can't scare me. I have no intention of calling Social Services, and I give you my word that I won't allow you three to be split up. I just want to see these two little kids warm and fed and safe, and I intend to take them home and make sure they are, with or without your cooperation. Now, are you coming with us or not?''

Billy glanced up sullenly, his eyes dark and cold with suspicion. But he said nothing, just gave a weary shrug and another of his harsh gestures to Ellie. She handed the baby to Jim, giving him one sad and desperate glance of appeal, and then returned to her task, stuffing baby clothes into the cardboard box.

Jim held the baby awkwardly, surprised by Arthur's wriggling strength and the startling volume of his screams at close range. Automatically he shifted the baby's firm little body to the crook of his left arm and began to rock him. Arthur, who had never been held in a grasp so large and muscular, paused in midbellow, looked up at Jim with startled blue eyes swimming in tears and then suddenly smiled.

Jim gazed down, enchanted by the smile and by Arthur's little pearly teeth. ''Hi,'' he murmured, smiling back foolishly. ''Hi, there, big fella. Are you hungry? Should we take you home and give you some milk? Yes, we should. Oh, yes, we should.''

Ellie looked over at them, the ghost of a smile on her anxious face, and lifted the big cardboard box, staggering a little under its weight. Billy, still grim and silent, carried another box, and the two of them paused in the doorway.

''Okay,'' Billy said sullenly. ''We're ready. Let's go if we have to go.''

Jim held the baby while Ellie wrapped him in a big torn blanket. Then he looked with dismay at the ragged cardboard boxes and the thin jackets of the two older children. ''What about the rest of your stuff?'' he asked. ''There's no lock on the door. Won't somebody steal it?''

''This is all our stuff,'' Billy said. ''Everything we own, except the furniture, and that ain't worth nothing.''

''What about your coats? Doesn't Ellie have something warmer? It's really cold out, and my car's a few blocks away....''

"Ellie's used to cold," Billy said grimly. "Come on, let's get going before Arthur starts yelling again."

Hesitantly, still holding the bundled weight of the baby in his arms, Jim guided the two children out of the building and through the wintry streets to his car. They trudged silently beside him, each carrying a cardboard box. Ellie cast an occasional anxious look at the silent, wriggling cocoon in Jim's arms. Billy, though, stared straight ahead, his expression cold and unreadable.

Jim glanced sidelong at him, realizing the boy was planning to take the two smaller children and make a break for freedom just as soon as he found an opportunity.

Oh, God, Jim thought wearily, *I'm going to have to watch them every minute. How can I go to work in the morning? How can I take care of them? What in hell am I getting myself into?*

They reached his car and dumped the two cardboard boxes into the back seat with Billy. Ellie sat beside Jim in the front, clutching Arthur in her arms, gazing in wondering silence at the Christmas lights decorating the rows of houses.

"Oh, my, but they're pretty," she said so softly that Jim could hardly hear her.

"What's pretty, Ellie?"

"The lights. I never seen anything so pretty."

Jim glanced at her in surprise. "Haven't you seen Christmas lights before, Ellie?"

She shook her head, setting her fine blond hair swinging. "I don't think so. Just on the stores and stuff. We never had a car, you see. And Mom, she was always out at night, so Billy looked after me, and he never took me anywhere after dark. We were always just at home." She gazed out at the multicolored display that spangled the winter darkness and gave a little sigh of bliss. "This is just so pretty," she repeated, holding Arthur's body tightly. "It's like fairyland, or something all magic. I love it."

Jim swallowed hard and pulled up into his own parking spot beneath his massive high-rise apartment building.

"Will the lady be here?" Ellie asked suddenly as they were walking through the parkade.

"The lady? Who do you mean?" Jim asked.

"The beautiful lady who was at our place. Will she be here?"

"No," Jim said, glancing down at the little girl's anxious features. "She won't be here."

Ellie's face fell, but she persisted despite her shyness. Obviously this was important to her. "Will she be here tomorrow?"

"Why do you ask, Ellie?"

"She was so beautiful. Just like a princess," the little girl breathed. "And she was so nice to me. I'd just...I'd like to see her again."

"So would I," Jim said softly, while Ellie gazed up at him in surprise. "So would I, Ellie."

Awed by the size of the building and the splendor of the lobby with its uniformed doorman, both children stood silent and nervous in the elevator, clutching their cardboard boxes while Jim once more held Arthur, who seemed, mercifully, to have fallen asleep during the car ride.

Jim shifted the sleeping baby gently into the crook of his arm and unlocked his apartment, standing aside to let the two thin, shabby children precede him into the living room.

Ellie stood gazing around with shining eyes and parted lips, as if she had been suddenly ushered into paradise. "Oh, Billy," she whispered in rapture as amazement overcame her fear. "Look how beautiful it is! Look at them pretty pictures and stuff, and that big rug. That's real fur, isn't it, Billy? And look at them big couches and all the plants, just like on TV!"

Startled by the little girl's reaction, Jim examined his warm, comfortable apartment, trying to see it through her eyes. The rooms were well-proportioned and tastefully finished with the earth tones and rough, natural fabrics he favored. The rug that had enchanted Ellie was a huge white goatskin spread in front of the fireplace, and the plants that Jim loved were everywhere, some of them the size of small trees.

But the apartment was really quite modest, particularly by the standards of many of Jim's friends. Knowing his background and the vast wealth of his family, they often wondered, sometimes aloud, why Jim refused to move into something "a little more appropriate." What none of them knew was that Jim had sunk all of his own money into his business and hadn't taken a penny from his father since his school days. Many of those same friends, Jim thought grimly, would have been amazed if they knew what a struggle he had sometimes just to pay the rent on this place, let alone something larger and more lavish.

"Don't get all excited, Ellie," Billy said coldly. "This ain't the place for people like us, and we sure won't be here long."

Once again Jim hesitated in dismay, wondering just what he thought he was doing.

Billy was right, he realized. It was cruelty, not kindness, to give these poor children a taste of comfort and security if it was just going to be snatched away again immediately. But how could he look after these three waifs in a one-bedroom apartment? What would they do all day? How could he look after their needs, get them to school, get medical attention for the baby…and a baby-sitter for Arthur, too, he realized suddenly, if Ellie were to attend school.

Suddenly he became uncomfortably aware of Billy's eyes resting on him with a knowing and sardonic expression as if the boy were reading his mind, seeing all his fears and panic.

Jim's tanned cheeks flushed a little and he squared his shoulders, turning to Ellie with forced heartiness. "It's okay, Ellie," he said with considerably more confidence than he felt. "You're going to be here for a while, and if you do leave, it'll be to go somewhere just as nice. And both your brothers will be with you. I promise. Now let's find places for everybody to sleep, okay? This couch here makes out into a bed, and there's a corner back here that I think would be safe for Arthur."

While Jim and Ellie bustled around, making up beds and barricading off a comfortable space to deposit the sleeping baby, Billy slouched in a corner and followed their movements with his eyes. The boy said nothing, but his face was cold, his expression grim and watchful.

"THE LENGTH of the shot blade stem on the sample group has increased an average of 2.6 millimeters," Sarah dictated into her small microphone, "while the ancillary leaves are now—"

She broke off suddenly and whirled around in her chair, gazing absently out the window at the snowy landscape as she toyed with the cord on the little tape recorder. Her face softened, and she lifted her big glasses off, rubbing her temples and smiling faintly.

"It is now three days..." She paused to check her watch and then continued speaking into the microphone, her voice gentle, almost dreamy. "Approximately sixty-two hours since conception. The zygote has advanced through orderly mitotic process to the blastocyst stage and is now preparing for implantation in the wall of the uterus."

As she spoke the words, she felt a strange flutter inside her, a mysterious little thrill deep in her core, and smiled once more at her own foolishness. Even if she had conceived on Monday night, Sarah was fully aware that it was far too soon for her to feel anything resulting from the pregnancy. And the chances that she had conceived were really not good, considering all the ensuing trauma...the shock of the "mugging" immediately afterward, her breathless sprint through icy streets and her upset and alarm over the plight of the three children. The odds for a successful conception under such adverse conditions were, scientifically speaking, almost nil.

And yet there was this mysterious little tug within her, this awesome, mysterious sense of something wonderful happening.

"Soon," she murmured ruefully into the little tape recorder, "I'll be having morning sickness and food cravings, and some poor doctor will be forced to tell me that it's all in my mind."

She switched off the microphone, ran the machine backward

to erase the tape and then gazed out the window once more, her lovely face withdrawn and troubled.

Once again the image of the three children invaded her thoughts, urgent and distressing. In the few days since her encounter with them Sarah had quelled all impulses to go back and see how they were, determined to leave that entire evening behind her.

She was haunted by the irrational fear that Jim Fleming would somehow use the children as bait, that he would be in hiding somewhere, waiting for her to go back to their dreadful little room so he could pounce on her.

Her fears weren't based on the fact that she considered herself particularly desirable or unforgettable, but simply because she might be pregnant. Now that the possibility of pregnancy actually existed, Sarah was constantly tormented with the possibility that Jim Fleming might somehow find her, learn who she was and lay claim to her child.

After all, she reasoned, the Flemings were a wealthy and powerful family. Jim was the only child of Senator Jameson Kirkland Fleming III, and Jim had never married. And they kept giving the boys in the family these numbers. What if Sarah had a little boy and they found out about him and wanted to make him Jameson Kirkland Fleming V?

The thought of the powerful Fleming family making a claim to her child, possibly going to court to argue their rights to him, interfering with Sarah's careful plans for his upbringing, was almost more than she could bear. More than anything, what Sarah wanted now was to forget about Jim Fleming and his part in her life, put it all behind her and carry on.

At this point she refused to consider what she would do if she hadn't conceived, whether she would seduce Jim Fleming another time or look for some other man to father her child.

Wearily Sarah shook her head, put her glasses back on and turned back to the pile of computer sheets and folders on her desk. But she couldn't erase the image of Billy's stubborn freckled face, of the sweet, drowsy weight of the baby in her arms, of Ellie's pinched and terrified little features.

Abruptly Sarah flipped the lid on her tape recorder and stored it away in her desk. As she did so, there was a brief knock and the door popped open to admit Carl, her assistant, who was brimming with holiday spirits.

Literally as well as figuratively, Sarah thought, grinning privately. There had been a small but lively staff Christmas party in full swing down the corridor over the lunch hour.

"Well, I'm off, Sarah," Carl said. "Merry Christmas. See you next week."

"Next week?" she asked in alarm. "But this is only Thursday, isn't it?"

"Sarah," he said patiently, "Christmas is on Sunday. Most of the staff is taking tomorrow off, as well. The facility is going to be closed down for four days except for maintenance. Remember?"

She gazed at him blankly for a moment, her lovely, delicate face clearing as she absorbed this information. "Right," she said briskly, getting to her feet and shrugging out of her lab coat. "Christmas is on Sunday. I'd better get going."

Carl watched as she folded the big glasses away, crossed her office and took her long tan duffel coat from the closet.

"Sarah..." he began hesitantly, "where are you going?"

"Christmas shopping," she said cheerfully. "I have to buy some Christmas presents."

Carl continued to watch her in troubled silence. "But I thought you said you weren't going to bother with Christmas this year," he began cautiously. "You said you didn't know anyone to celebrate the holiday with, and you were just going to use the long weekend to get a lot of extra work done."

"I am," Sarah said. "But there are some children I know, you see, and I want to buy presents for them."

"Sarah...Sarah, dear, you know that Melanie and I would love to have you at our place. You know we've always said you're absolutely welcome, and the kids would love to have you with us."

"I know you have, Carl." Sarah smiled at him as she wound her heavy plaid scarf over her shoulders. "I know you have. But Christmas is no big deal, especially if you have no family, and I don't want to be part of another family's holiday. I really do intend to get a lot of work done while I have the place to myself. I just happen to know these children who could use a little touch of Christmas, that's all."

She patted his shoulder, smiled and gathered up her big leather shoulder bag. Carl stood watching in silence, bemused as always by the classic, exquisite lines of her face without the heavy glasses, and the sudden glow that lit her huge gray eyes when she smiled.

"GREEN WOOLLY WORMS," Sarah said to the clerk in the department store. "I want a couple of green woolly worms. They're the best thing for lake trout."

"If you say so, ma'am," the harried young clerk said. "It's just that, you see, fishing items aren't really seasonal right now, and I don't know if..."

"Please," Sarah said, smiling shyly at the tired young man. "I know it's an inconvenience, and I'm so sorry. But I'm buying a fishing outfit for a boy who's probably never gone fishing in his life, and I'd really like him to have a couple of green woolly worms in his tackle box."

At the sight of her glowing, incandescent smile the clerk was as enchanted as Carl had been a few hours earlier. He swallowed hard, forgetting all his tiredness and irritation with the floods of last-minute Christmas shoppers. "Sure thing ," he murmured, his face warm with admiration. "I'll just...I'll just check the back and see what we've got."

Sarah watched him vanish, still smiling to herself as she recalled long-ago summer days with her father, idling on the cool, shaded banks of the creek while they trailed their fishing lines in the water and he lectured her serenely about the botanical properties of the plant life growing all around them.

Had Billy ever known an afternoon like that?

Suddenly she frowned, her eyes almost brimming with tears at the thought of the dingy, horrible little room where the three children lived and the pinched, undernourished look of their faces.

I'll take him this summer, she told herself, forgetting for the moment how completely irrational this plan was. *The first nice day of spring I'll bundle them all up and we'll take a picnic lunch and spend the whole day fishing.*

The clerk returned with some gaudy lime-green bits of fluff and plastic in his hand. "Just two left," he said apologetically, "and they're four dollars each, I'm afraid. We had a real heavy run on green woolly worms over the summer."

"Oh, I'm glad you found some! They're the only thing for lake trout," Sarah said gratefully. "Thank you so much for your trouble. I'll pay for them at the front, because I have a lot more things to pick up yet."

With another shy, luminous smile she took the lures and the other equipment she'd selected, put them into her shopping cart along with a leather baseball glove and a yellow plastic radio, then vanished into the depths of the store, leaving the young clerk grinning after her foolishly and smiling to himself as he turned to serve his next customer.

Shopping for Arthur wasn't difficult. Recalling the cold, bare room with its splintery, wooden floor, Sarah picked out a pile of warm blanket sleepers, sweaters, fuzzy little socks and overalls, as well as several pairs of sturdy shoes and slippers. She agonized briefly over the sizes and then, remembering Arthur's weight and substance, opted for generously large shoes and garments.

After selecting the clothes, she gave some careful thought to toys, picking things designed to emit interesting squeals and impressive bursts of music when the proper buttons and levers were manipulated.

The older children seemed to be taking good care of Arthur's physical needs, but Sarah wasn't as confident that his intellectual development was being guided properly.

At last, with the boys taken care of, Sarah turned her attention to gifts for Ellie. She had deliberately saved Ellie for last, because shopping for the little girl was going to be so much fun. Sarah had the scientist's gift for full recall of detail, and she vividly remembered what it was like to be ten. She had a pretty good idea what would appeal to the child.

Not dolls, of course, since Ellie had Arthur and any facsimile would seem pretty pale in comparison with the real thing.

But clothes... Sarah frowned, thinking about Ellie's torn jogging pants. She browsed through the girls' clothing section, selecting warm sweaters, skirts, slacks and tights in the pale pastel colors that would suit the little girl's delicate complexion and her prim, endearing old-fashioned manner.

At last Sarah turned her attention to the really fun things—a complete set of "Anne books" by L. M. Montgomery, a beautiful little leather-bound diary with gold lock and key and a shellcraft set. Sarah beamed with delight when she discovered the hobby kit, remembering the one she'd owned and what fun it had been to construct delicate little pieces of jewelry and ornaments from the array of dainty seashells. Still smiling to herself, she bought extra packets of shells and adhesive just to be sure Ellie would have all the materials she'd need.

Finally she wheeled her loaded shopping cart through a front checkout, not even blinking at the staggering total of all her purchases. Sarah was usually so preoccupied with her work that she had very few opportunities to spend money. Buying gifts for these unfortunate children wasn't a sacrifice at all, just a pleasure to her.

Humming along with the canned Christmas music that echoed through the downtown streets, Sarah stashed her mountains of gaily wrapped boxes into her car and drove through the crowded afternoon traffic to where the children lived. As she neared the familiar area and passed the pub where she had seduced Jim Fleming, Sarah felt a brief stab of alarm and a cold little shiver of fear. She glanced around nervously, almost as if people in other cars were watching her and remarking her presence, and then shook her head, distressed by her own foolishness.

Still, she felt frightened and conspicuous when she parked

in front of the shabby tenement that was home to Billy, Ellie and their baby brother. Casting a quick anxious glance over her shoulder, she locked her car securely, kicked aside a couple of bulging black plastic garbage bags that crowded the doorway and hurried up the rickety flight of steps, holding her breath in the fetid dampness of the old building.

Sarah hesitated on the landing, staring at the broken lock on the door. Tentatively she swung the door open and peered into the room. It was empty except for a few scraps of paper, the sagging old crib, the dirty cot and the pile of blankets in the corner. The room already had a musty, unused smell, and it was obvious that nobody had been there for several days.

Sarah gazed around, her gray eyes wide and strained, her mind racing.

They've run away again, she decided. *After we left, Billy must have taken the little ones and run away so we couldn't come back for them.*

She thought of the snowy, bitter streets, of Arthur's soft, sweet-scented pink skin and Ellie's pinched and frightened little face, and felt tears stinging behind her eyelids once again.

"Oh, no," she murmured aloud. "Oh, no..."

Then, suddenly, she recalled Jim Fleming as he had looked on Monday night in this room. She remembered his sunny features drawn with alarm and disbelief when he realized the three children were alone here, and the warm, confident way he had responded to all of them and their situation.

Sarah felt a sudden surge of hope. Maybe Fleming had done something for the children, found a decent place for them to live and taken them away from this dreadful room to something more suitable. He had seemed like the kind of man who would do the right thing...had seemed, in fact, like a really warm and caring person—much to Sarah's surprise.

But it wasn't enough for her to speculate. She had to know if he'd taken care of the children or if they were, even now, roaming the frozen streets in search of a place to stay. And that meant, Sarah realized with a sinking heart, that she really had no other option.

Much as she hated the idea, she was going to have to call Jim Fleming and ask him.

CHAPTER FIVE

THE BOTANICAL laboratories were almost deserted by late afternoon, with only a few stragglers in the halls exchanging cheerful greetings as they prepared to dash off for last-minute Christmas shopping or holiday preparations.

Sarah hurried to her office, tossed her coat over a chair and seated herself at the big teak desk, taking Jim Fleming's file from its place in her top drawer. She glanced through it rapidly, confirming what she had suspected.

Fleming's home phone was unlisted, and even the dogged private detective she'd hired last spring hadn't been able to get hold of the number. So she couldn't just call his home and hope to find anything out from a housekeeper or maid. She'd have to call Fleming at his office.

Sarah frowned, her face drawn with anxious reluctance. Jim Fleming was executive director for a company that managed a small chain of sporting goods shops, and also marketed an independent line of athletic clothing and footwear. And he was no figurehead boss, chosen for the position just on the strength of his colorful and successful football career. According to all indications Jim Fleming took his job seriously, spending long days at the office and only taking occasional breaks for his regular hobbies and activities, like the badminton club and the watercolor classes.

Today, on a Thursday afternoon, it was likely that Jim Fleming would be in his office. And the office number was printed clearly on a sheet of paper right in front of Sarah's eyes. She stared at the number gloomily, fighting a growing sense of reluctance. Then, thinking about the fishing tackle, and the little fuzzy socks for Arthur, and Ellie's shellcraft set, she drew a deep breath and dialed the number.

"Could I speak with Mr. Fleming, please?" Sarah asked the receptionist, hoping crazily that he wouldn't be in, that he'd already left for his Christmas holiday, that she could just hang up...

"May I say who's calling?"

Sarah hesitated in panic.

"Just say...say it's a friend of Billy and Ellie's, please. Tell him it's...it's the lady in black," she added, feeling hot and foolish.

Jim's receptionist, who had to be superbly trained, gave no reaction to this apart from a polite, murmured response, and a moment later Jim's voice came on the line.

"Hello?" he said. "Is it really you? Is it you, pretty lady?"

At the sound of his warm, masculine voice memories washed over Sarah with a sudden and astonishing flood of feeling. She remembered with vivid clarity the feel of his hands and his lips, the strength and gentleness of his big, lean body, the incredible, fulfilling sweetness of his lovemaking....

"Hello? Are you there?" he asked, a note of anxiety in his voice.

"I'm...I'm here," Sarah whispered. "I just...I wanted to ask you about...about the children."

"What about them? And how did you know how to get hold of me, by the way? I thought you said you didn't know my name."

"I never said I didn't know it," Sarah told him calmly, beginning to regain a little of her poise. "I just allowed you to assume I didn't, that's all."

"I think," he said cheerfully, "that you allowed me to assume quite a few things, didn't you, my lady? I wonder why."

"Well," Sarah said firmly, "I didn't call you to argue or to discuss our evening together. I just wanted to ask about the children."

"Go ahead," he said. "Ask about them."

"They're not in that room anymore," Sarah said. "I wondered if you knew where they'd gone."

"How do you know they're not in the room? Did you actually go to see them?"

"I bought them some Christmas presents," Sarah said, her voice deliberately cool, "and when I went to deliver the gifts this afternoon, I realized that nobody's lived in the room for several days. I was afraid..."

"That Billy took them and made a run for it," he finished cheerfully.

"Yes," Sarah said. "The thought crossed my mind. Billy seemed pretty defensive."

"No kidding," Jim said, his voice suddenly gloomy. "That was really nice," he added, "buying gifts for them, I mean. Ellie's going to be so happy."

"So you *do* know where they are," Sarah said, surprised by her sudden flood of relief and happiness.

"Oh, yes, I know where they are," Jim said. "Ellie talks about you all the time," he added. "She calls you the 'Princess Lady,' like somebody from a fairy tale, and she keeps asking when you're coming back. She just refuses to accept the fact that I don't know."

"Oh." Sarah smiled helplessly, her cheeks suddenly warm. "That's...that's nice."

"So," Jim went on, "what can I tell her? When are you coming back?"

Sarah hesitated, feeling edgy and frightened. "Are they... do you mean the children are with *you?*"

"Yes," he said briefly. "They are. Four of us in a one-bedroom apartment. Five, counting Maude, but she goes back to her own place at night."

"Maude?" Sarah asked, feeling a sudden, inexplicable stab of pain.

"Maude Willett," Jim explained. "She's a terrific grandmotherly type that I met on the ski hill. Just on Monday, in fact, the day you and I—"

"Yes," Sarah said hastily, her face pink with embarrassment. "I understand. Go on, please."

"Anyhow, I made friends with her when we were skiing, taught her to snowplow, actually, and she gave me her name and invited me over for meat loaf. I didn't go, but next day when I found myself with these three kids on my hands, I called Maude and she came right over and made order out of chaos. She's a marvel, Maude is. One of the seven wonders of the modern world."

Sarah grinned, tempted to ask him about the other six and then pulled her thoughts firmly back into line. There was something so diverting and entertaining about Jim Fleming, something that made him so enjoyable and easy to talk to.

"So," she asked briskly, "what are your plans? Are you going to keep them with you now, or what?"

"Oh, Lord," Jim said, his voice suddenly strained and weary. "It's not so simple, pretty lady. You see..."

A woman, probably the secretary, interrupted him in the background, and he paused to say, "Not for a while, Shelley, thanks. And hold my calls, okay? This is important. Whoever it is, tell them I'll get back to them later."

Sarah waited, and then heard his voice come back on the line, strong and warm. "Hello? Still there?"

"Of course," Sarah said. "You were telling me about the children?"

"Right. I don't know *what* to do. I'm in a real mess. Have you ever noticed," he added surprisingly, "that when you set out to help people, even with the best intentions in the world, how often you just wind up making a big mess?"

Sarah heard the note of pain and bewilderment in his voice and felt a powerful surge of sympathy, which she repressed firmly. "What's the problem?" she asked. "Aren't they adjusting to life in the lap of luxury?"

"Oh, they're adjusting, all right. It's amazing how fast kids can adjust. They already know how to program the VCR and run the remote control, and how the microwave works, and how to adjust the room temperature and all kinds of exotic technical stuff.''

Sarah began to understand. ''And the problem,'' she said softly, ''is that they're adjusting *too* well, right? After just a few days of warmth and comfort, they're not going to be able to go back to their old life.''

''Billy knew it,'' Jim said helplessly. ''He understood better than I did, that first night when I took them home with me. He just looked at me as if to say, 'Okay, mister. Here we are. *Now* what?' And he was right.''

''You can't...'' Sarah began cautiously, and then continued. ''You can't just...keep them with you? I mean, is it impossible for...'' Her voice trailed off.

''Not impossible,'' Jim said grimly, ''but damn difficult. Billy's mad at me all the time for what I've done to the kids by giving them a taste of comfort and luxury. He's a cold, cynical, streetwise kid, and he just doesn't trust me to keep on providing for them. He'd grab them and run in a minute if somebody wasn't watching him all the time. And there's no room at my place for all these people, and besides, other tenants already know they're there, and the super's warned me, ever so tactfully, that they have to be gone as soon as possible.''

''It's an adults-only building?''

''Yes. It is.''

''Oh, my.'' Sarah was silent for a moment, thinking. ''What about Social Services? Have you checked with them?''

''Yes, I have. And Billy was absolutely right. They're overburdened, understaffed and underfunded. There's no way they can guarantee a foster home that would keep the kids together. The caseworker I talked to told me frankly that in all probability Arthur would be put up for adoption while the other two went into some kind of interim-care facility.''

Sarah shuddered, picturing shy and gentle little Ellie in an ''interim-care'' facility.

''I suppose,'' she began cautiously, ''that government care

would still be better than…than where they were when you found them. Wouldn't it?"

"Not for those kids," Jim said. "You just can't believe how much they both love that baby. It's heartrending. Ellie's just ten years old, but if she lost Arthur, I truly believe she'd never recover from the anguish of it."

Sarah hesitated, looking around her office at the piles of folders, the neat rows of books and technical abstracts, the framed prints on the walls along with complex charts of cereal grains.

"So," she said finally, "what can you do?"

"I don't know. Maude's going to help as much as she can, but she's leaving soon for a winter holiday with her family, and I'll be on my own. I guess I'll have to take time off work to stay with them. And I'll have to look for somewhere else to live, maybe buy a house, though God knows how I'll come up with that much money on short notice."

He sounded weary and overburdened, and Sarah's heart ached for him. She was tempted to offer her own house, but resisted firmly, knowing how many complications *that* would create. She would become involved with Jim Fleming's life, he would know where she lived and how to get to her, and if it should happen that she was really pregnant, she would soon have a baby of her own to provide for. Besides, her house was so small that she probably didn't have much more room for the three children than he did.

"Anyhow," he said, his voice cheerful again, "this is my problem, right? I'm the one who took them home with me, and I'm the one who has to deal with the consequences. I'll figure something out. Meanwhile we have to decide what to do about you."

"Me?" Sarah asked, startled. "What about me?"

"Well, you have these presents for the kids, right? And you want to deliver them?"

"I'd…yes," Sarah said, feeling shy all at once. "Yes, I would, if that's possible."

"Of course. How about tonight? You could just stop by for

a Christmas drink, and we'll put your presents under the tree. It's the first time," Jim added ruefully, "that I've ever had a Christmas tree in my apartment. Ellie wanted one so badly. We bought lights and a star and everything."

"Oh," Sarah said softly. "It must be lovely."

"When we finished decorating, we dimmed the room lights and switched on the tree. Ellie burst into tears, crawled into the pantry and cried for an hour. It was all I could do to coax her to come out and settle down."

"Why?"

"According to Ellie, it was just too beautiful. It made her hurt inside, she said, because it was just too beautiful."

"Oh," Sarah said again, feeling her own eyes stinging with hot tears of sympathy.

"You see what a position I'm in," Jim said. "After a few experiences like that, it'd be damn hard to put those kids back out onto the street or into some kind of institutional care."

"Yes," Sarah whispered. "Yes, I can see that it would."

"But," Jim added cheerfully, "the tree isn't quite as beautiful now. It's looking a little ragged these days. Between Arthur and Lancelot the lower branches are getting far too much attention."

"Lancelot?"

"Maude's puppy. He doesn't like to stay alone, so Maude brings him with her every morning. He and Arthur play their own version of 'demolition derby' in my front room."

"Poor Jim!" Sarah said, laughing helplessly.

"Oh, pretty lady, it's nice to hear you laugh," he said, his voice gentle and husky with emotion. "You just don't know how much I've wanted to see you again."

"Please," Sarah whispered helplessly, shivering a little at the intimate tone of his voice. "Please don't..."

"Okay," Jim said briskly, all business once more. "I get the message. No pressure. Now, about those presents. Is tonight okay?"

Sarah paused, twisting the phone cord anxiously.

"I understand," Jim said. "You don't want to see me, right?"

"I'm...I'm sorry," Sarah whispered. "It's just that—"

"No problem," he interrupted. "How about tomorrow? After lunch, maybe? I'll be at the office all day, and I'll give you my address so you can stop by with their gifts and stay as long as you like."

"That would be best, I think."

"I promise I'll be out of the way, and nobody will spy on you or try to follow you. Word of honor. Not that I wouldn't like to," he said frankly, "but it would mean a lot to the kids if they can see you again, so I won't do anything to spoil it. Do you trust me?"

"Yes," Sarah said, surprising herself. "Yes, I do."

"Okay. Here's my address. Got a pen?"

Sarah knew the address off by heart...had, in fact, driven by the building several times while planning the seduction of Jim Fleming. Actually, he lived in an elegant residential area not too many blocks from the laboratory where she was sitting right now. But she just muttered something in reply, pretending to write down the directions as he dictated them.

"Good," Jim said briskly. "I'll tell the kids you're coming sometime after lunch, okay? Little Ellie will be out of her mind with excitement. When she's excited," he added, his voice softening, "she just gets quieter and quieter and paler than ever and her eyes get as big and round as saucers."

"Thank you," Sarah murmured, smiling into the phone. "Thank you very much."

"That's okay. Just remember," he said softly, "that if you ever change your mind and want to see me, after all, *I'd* be pretty excited, too. Will you remember that?"

"Yes," Sarah whispered, feeling warm and shaky. "Yes, I'll remember."

"Goodbye, pretty lady. Thanks for calling," he said, and then hung up, leaving Sarah wide-eyed and thoughtful, gazing at the telephone receiver.

JIM, TOO, SAT for a long time after he hung up, staring at his own telephone. His mind was a confused blur of thoughts and impressions, foremost among them a kind of boyish delight that she had actually remembered him and called him.

Not that she was particularly interested in *him.* She'd made it clear that she was only concerned about the children. But still, she'd taken the trouble to learn his name and find out his office number.

Jim frowned, staring with narrowed eyes at a glass-fronted display case on the opposite wall filled with football trophies.

Something nagged at his mind, the ghost of a memory…the echo of her voice, the way she'd laughed when she said, "Poor Jim!"

Somewhere, sometime in the distant past, he'd heard that voice before. Jim's recall for voices was almost uncanny in its keenness, and he knew he wasn't mistaken this time. More and more he was growing convinced that his meeting with his lady in black hadn't been the casual encounter it had seemed. She knew him, in spite of her denials, and she'd sought him out for some reason, some motivation of her own beyond the casual gratification of a one-night stand.

I'd give anything to know what it was, he thought. *Damn! If I could only remember where I've seen her before…where I've heard that voice….*

"Jim? Are you free now?"

He looked up to see his secretary's cheerful young face in the doorway, and nodded. "Yes, Shelley, I'm free. Who've you got out there who's so important?"

"It's the senator," Shelley said with a cautious, sidelong glance at her employer.

Jim's thoughtful, bemused smile faded and his handsome features grew tense. He glanced at his watch, swiveled to gaze briefly out the window while he composed himself and then turned back to his secretary. "Okay, Shelley," he said tonelessly, "show him in, please."

He picked up a small jade paperweight and gripped it in his hands, holding it so tightly that his knuckles were white. Apart from this, he displayed no emotion as the door opened and his father entered the room.

"Hello, Jim," Senator Fleming said, seating himself casually in a leather armchair across from his son. "Merry Christmas."

"Merry Christmas, Dad," Jim said, giving the older man a cold, level gaze. Jameson Kirkland Fleming III, at sixty-three, was a powerfully handsome and attractive man. For Jim, looking at his father was like looking into a mirror that reflected the future, because he knew that this was exactly how he himself would look in thirty years.

Jim's father had thick iron-gray hair, bright blue eyes in a tanned, weathered face and a tall firm body that still retained much of the athletic strength and trimness of his youth. He wore shining gray riding boots made of fine, soft leather, charcoal dress slacks with a knife-edge crease, and an expensive tweed blazer in a western cut that sat beautifully on his wide shoulders. His dress shirt, as always, was snowy white, his tie crisp and perfectly coordinated.

The old man took good care of himself, Jim admitted grudgingly. No matter what you thought of him, you had to acknowledge that he created a good impression....

"How've you been, son?" Senator Fleming asked as casually as if they spoke to each other every day instead of once a year.

"I've been fine, Dad," Jim said briefly. "Just fine."

"Business good?" the older man asked, glancing around Jim's well-appointed office. His voice was still easy and casual. If you didn't notice how firmly he gripped the arms of the chair and how taut his body was, you'd assume the old man was perfectly relaxed and comfortable, Jim thought.

"Yes," Jim said noncommittally. "It's pretty good. The high interest rates are costing us, just like everybody else, but we can weather it."

The senator nodded thoughtfully, cleared his throat and looked at his son with a sudden expression of appeal in his blue eyes. "We were wondering..." he began, and paused.

Jim watched him calmly, offering no help, and his father finally went on, his voice carefully composed once more. "Your Aunt Maureen and I…we were wondering if you'd like to come out to the ranch for Christmas. There'll just be the two of us and some of the staff members, and Mo thought it would be nice if you'd…I mean, she'd like to cook all your favorite things and give you a family Christmas for once."

Jim's blue eyes, so like those of the man opposite him, hardened with sudden anger. "Look, why do you *do* this every year?" he asked, his voice low and furious. "When will you ever get the message? You and I have nothing to say to each other. I told you long ago what I think of you, and you've done the same for me. We've got nothing to talk about, Dad. Why don't you just give it a rest?"

The senator looked steadily across the broad desk at his son. "Maybe it's not as cut-and-dried as all that, son. It's been almost seventeen years since your mother died, more than ten years since you left home. Times change. People change. Maybe I'm a different man than you thought I was back then."

"I doubt it," Jim said coldly. "You're like a force of nature. You'll never change."

"Nor will you if you don't give things a chance. Life needs tending, son, and so do relationships. They don't just happen by accident."

Jim stared at his father in disbelief. "I wonder if you have any idea how completely ironic that sounds," he said softly. "The fact that *you,* of all people, should be lecturing me about relationships. My God."

Jameson Fleming returned his son's cold gaze in silence. "Look, Jim," he said finally, "I know you don't like me, and I know why, and in some ways you're probably justified. But could you consider calling a brief truce for your aunt's sake? Mo would love to see you this Christmas."

"I see Aunt Maureen occasionally," Jim said. "I don't have to go to your house to see her. She understands that."

Senator Fleming shook his handsome gray head. "You're a bitter man, son," he said finally. "Terribly bitter. I'm sorry." The older man got slowly to his feet and started for the door, then paused.

Jim watched, his face expressionless, waiting for his father to leave.

"Someday, Jim," his father said, pausing by the door, "I hope someone will come into your life that you really care about. And when that happens I truly do hope for your sake that you'll be able to be warm and accepting. I hope you won't be so cold and uncompromising that you lose her and all your chances for happiness along with her."

Jim's blue eyes kindled dangerously, but he restrained himself, merely giving his father a curt nod, watching as the heavy oak door closed behind the older man's departing figure.

Alone in the office, he clenched his hands tightly together to stop their trembling and gazed blindly out the window. Part of him regretted his own brusqueness and cold response to the older man's plea. He genuinely wished, sometimes, that he could be more forgiving, more accepting, more able to provide what his father and his aunt wanted of him.

But another part of him, an urgent, angry part, could never forget his mother's suffering. As if it were yesterday, Jim remembered her tears, her pain, her anguished longing for the kind of love and warmth that her powerful, wealthy husband selfishly refused to give her.

He killed her, Jim thought. *As surely as if he'd taken a gun and held it to her temple, he killed her. And how am I supposed to forget that? How do they expect me to laugh and be sociable, to pretend we're just one big happy family, when I* know *what happened between my parents?*

With a small, grim smile he recalled his father's parting words and shook his head at the incredible gall of the old man.

If there ever was a woman in Jim Fleming's life, he thought, it was certain she would be better treated, more warmly loved and cherished than his father's wife had been.

Restlessly he got up and prowled around his office, touching objects here and there, straightening chairs and pictures, closing file drawers and rearranging the little nativity set that Shelley had set up on the gleaming wooden console along one wall.

At last he took his leather jacket from the closet, shrugged it on and opened the door, pausing in the outer office to look at his secretary.

"I'll be out for the rest of the day, Shelley, all right? If there's anything really important, you can reach me at home later on. Otherwise just hold things till tomorrow."

"Okay." Shelley hesitated, fingers poised over her computer keyboard. "About tomorrow," she began, flushing a little, "I mean, I promised my boyfriend I'd go with him tomorrow to his parents' place, and you said last week that I could have the day off, but if you'd rather I came in for the morning, well, I guess I could."

"No, no," Jim said hastily. "Take your holiday. I'd forgotten all about it. I'm going to be here all day, but I doubt that anything much will be happening. Merry Christmas, Shelley."

"Merry Christmas," she said, brightening and smiling at her employer. "Jim," she added cautiously, "is everything all right?"

"What do you mean?" Jim asked, standing in the doorway and glancing back at his secretary.

"Oh, I don't know. Lately you've just been looking kind of tired, you know?"

Jim smiled wanly. "Family troubles," he said briefly. "I've got family troubles, Shelley."

His secretary knew nothing about Jim's new responsibilities. In fact, partly due to Billy's dark warnings, Jim was so nervous about the powers of Social Services that he had told nobody about the three children he sheltered in his apartment, except for Maude, of course, who was sworn to secrecy.

Shelley obviously assumed that her boss, when he spoke of "family troubles," was referring to the visit from Senator Fleming, who arrived every year about this time in a vain attempt to coax his son into coming home for Christmas.

"It's hard," she agreed, nodding her young, curly head with

great wisdom. "Family stuff, it can really eat you up. Believe me, I know."

Jim grinned at the girl's knowing tone, smiled at her again and let himself quietly out the door.

"YOU MEAN you've never seen her before? *Never?*" Jim asked the bartender in disbelief.

"Just that one night," the bartender said, polishing another glass and hanging it carefully away in the ceiling rack.

"But she seemed...I mean, I assumed she came here frequently."

"So how come *you* never saw her before, then?"

"I only come to this bar on Monday nights," Jim said. "I thought maybe she came on...weekends or something."

"Never," the bartender said emphatically. "Never been here before. Just the one night."

Jim felt a rising tide of hopelessness and quashed it firmly. "Are you absolutely sure? It isn't possible that you're mistaken?"

The bartender paused with another glass in his hand and looked directly at Jim. "Look, son," he said cheerfully, "I may be middle-aged and potbellied and married, but I'm still human, you know. Now, you saw that woman. You really think a woman who looked like that could be at my bar without me *noticing* her?"

Jim smiled. "I see what you mean. Okay, I guess I'll just have to ask around at some other bars, that's all."

He set down his empty glass, pulled his jacket on and started for the door. There were just a few other people in the place—a solitary executive, some weary Christmas shoppers and a couple incongruously attired in formal wear who seemed to be arguing bitterly in low tones. Jim glanced idly at the other drinkers, his sense of loneliness and depression growing deeper.

"Hey, mister!" the bartender called as Jim reached the door.

"Merry Christmas," the little man said. "And I hope you find her."

"Thanks," Jim said. "So do I."

But his sense of futility deepened as he tramped the snowy streets, working his way in and out of all the bars on the grimy strip of theaters and night spots. Nobody had ever seen a woman who looked like his description of the mysterious lady in black.

Maybe, Jim thought gloomily, she patronized other, classier bars in more elegant neighborhoods and just made an occasional brief visit to this part of town. If so, how was he ever supposed to find her? He could hardly go to every drinking place in the city. Besides, it was a waste of time when he didn't even have a picture to show people, just a description of an incredibly alluring woman, a beautiful dark-haired woman with shining gray eyes and a serene, ladylike manner.

He began to regret the promise he'd made to her earlier that day. The woman he was searching for, the woman he longed more than anything to see one more time, was actually coming to his own house tomorrow. She would be there in the flesh, walking up to his apartment and ringing the bell, and he had promised he wouldn't be around. He had even given his word that nobody would try to follow her or search her out in any way.

And Jim was a man of integrity, a man who took promises very seriously.

Frantically he considered his options, trying to think of some way to find out who she was and where she lived without breaking his word not to follow her.

At last he decided that his only choice was to write her a letter. He would leave it with Maude to deliver to the mystery woman when she paid her visit to the children, and in it he would tell her how much he wanted to see her again, stress that it could all be on her terms, invite her to take the initiative and arrange the meeting place.

Feeling a little more optimistic now that he had a plan, Jim circled back across the wintry streets to his car. He drove home through rushed and crowded early-evening traffic, tapping the wheel idly and whistling along with the Christmas music on the radio, composing the letter in his mind.

But, as he drove, he was haunted once more by that old nagging sense that he knew this woman, that at some time in his life he had encountered her before under different circumstances. He had seen her face and heard her voice, and if he could somehow force his mind to make the connection, then he would have it all. He would know her name, who she was, everything about her.

Jim frowned, his handsome face taut with frustration, and then forced himself to relax, diverting himself by thinking about the children who were waiting eagerly for him at home, and the superb meal Maude would have on the table.

Almost voluntarily he smiled. The dimple popped into view in one flat, tanned cheek, and he began to sing softly as the traffic rumbled and snarled around him.

CHAPTER SIX

SENATOR JAMESON FLEMING drove his white Lincoln up the curving drive to the long garage, pausing in front of one of the doors and waiting for it to flow upward. Inside the garage he heaved his tall body from the car and made his way carefully along the row of shining parked vehicles to a small lighted room at the rear of the big building.

In this room a little man of indeterminate age, wearing navy blue coveralls, crouched beside a large cardboard box lined with sacking. As the senator entered the room and pulled off his leather driving gloves, the little man looked up, his wrinkled face breaking into a vast, toothless smile of adoration.

"Hello, Manny," the senator said. "How's she doing?"

"Verr' good, sir," Manny said happily. "She's-a doin' verr' good. Six puppies, sir. All beauties."

"Well!" the senator exclaimed, pleased. "You were right after all then, Manny. I didn't think she was ready."

He squatted by the box, still smiling, and fondled the silky ears of the big golden spaniel who lay exhausted and triumphant with her new brood of puppies.

Jameson examined the puppies, touching them gently with his broad, finely shaped hands while their mother watched in loving pride.

At last he stood erect, shaking out the creases in his crisp trousers, and turned to leave. "Thanks, Manny," he said in the doorway. "Anything else?"

Manny frowned. "The new fence posts, they're not delivered yet, sir. Me and the boys, we can't do that job without the posts."

"Right. I'll call them as soon as I get into the house. If we don't get the posts today, we'll have to wait till after Christmas, I guess."

"And the new bull, he's-a look a little down, you know?"

"Down? What do you mean?"

Manny waved one hand in an eloquent Latin gesture. "Just...not so good, sir. Maybe a little sick, needs some vi-t'mins, you know?"

"I'll have a look at him and call the vet if we need him. Has my sister seen the puppies?"

Manny's grin widened, threatening to split his seamed, leathery face.

"Miss Mo, she been out here most the afternoon. She already got names for all of them."

Jameson smiled suddenly, nodded to his foreman and left the garage by the side door. Outside, he took a deep breath of the crisp afternoon air, marveling at how much fresher and cleaner it seemed out here than just a few miles away in the city. He glanced around at the rolling acres of his ranch. The house and grounds were bleak and sere in the winter chill, but they were still well groomed and impeccable, the hedges neatly trimmed, the curving fieldstone ledges and walks swept clean of snow.

The senator paused, looking with pleasure at his property. Since his career in politics had become so absorbing, he had sold off much of the holding, and the ranch was now more of a hobby than a living, just a few hundred acres where he ran a small herd of purebred Galloway cattle and a few beautiful horses. But the setting was lovely, and Jameson never came back here, even after the shortest of absences, without an overwhelming sense of peace and homecoming.

He hesitated briefly, looking over at the cattle sheds and thinking about Manny's concern about the new bull, which had cost just over forty thousand dollars at a recent auction. Finally, deciding that the bull could wait an hour or two, Jameson turned and strode along the curving flagstone path to the big house. As he walked, he remembered every word and detail of the interview with his son. His handsome, creased face was grim, his blue eyes bleak.

He entered the foyer, hung his long fur-trimmed suede coat away in the front closet and then paused, looking around. Somewhere deep in the house Handel's *Messiah* was playing loudly in stereo. The majestic chords of music flowed over the gracious curving staircase, the gleaming rich oak paneling and wainscoting, the leaded glass and fine old crystal and priceless jewel-colored Turkish carpets.

The house smelled richly of flowers, furniture polish and spicy baking, and Jameson took a deep, appreciative sniff before he went in search of his sister.

He paused in the archway leading to the dining room, grinning. A pair of sneakered feet protruded from beneath the big oak table while a muffled thumping noise emanated from the same general area.

"Mo!" Jameson said, bending to peer under the table. "What on *earth* are you doing?"

The sneakers slid along the carpet, followed by slim, denim-clad legs and a small, active body in a pink sweatshirt. Maureen Fleming ducked her head out from beneath the table and stood erect, clutching a battered red oil can with a long spout.

"The damn thing sticks," she said with dignity. "I was just giving it a drop of oil, that's all."

Jameson smiled at his sister, whom he still thought of as "the kid," although she was now fifty-three years old.

Maureen Fleming was indeed a pleasure to behold, even in the casual clothes she wore for her active daytime life at the ranch. She was small and brisk, with the trim, athletic figure of a young girl. Her face, too, was youthful despite the creases and laugh lines around her eyes and mouth, and always warmly tanned from hours spent outside on the cross-country ski trails behind the ranch house. Maureen had the dark flower-blue eyes so common in the Fleming family, and a bright mass of red-gold curls that were fading now and lightly streaked with gray.

When Jameson's wife died, leaving him alone with a big

house and a fifteen-year-old son, Maureen had come to the ranch for a few weeks to help out. At that time Maureen was thirty-five, and she had already lost one husband to divorce and a second, a few years later, to cancer. She faced a bleak and lonely future, and she was happy to be absorbed into her brother's household, where she soon became indispensable. Her visit stretched into months, and then years, and now Jameson sometimes wondered how he would have managed without her.

He stood in the dining room and examined her gravely, troubled by the taut energy of her small body and the look of contained excitement in those beautiful blue eyes.

"Why are you fixing the table, Maureen?" he asked quietly.

"I told you, it sticks. You can't pull it open to put the leaves in, and I thought—"

"Mo, we won't be opening the table out for Christmas. We won't need to. There'll just be you and me, Manny and Tom, Clarice and Eloise. Just the six of us."

Maureen hesitated, clutching her oil can and staring down at the carpet while her brother gazed unhappily at her bent head.

"He's not coming, Mo. I tried, but he still feels exactly the same. He'll never come back here as long as he lives."

"Oh, Jamie..." Maureen gazed up at her brother, her blue eyes eloquent with sympathy and unhappiness.

"I wish I could do it all over, Mo," Jameson said abruptly, staring at the lavish Christmas centerpiece on the gleaming oak table. "If we could only get second chances in life, we'd do so much better, wouldn't we?"

"We *do* get second chances, Jamie," Maureen said firmly. "We always do. And yours will come. Jim won't be this way forever. Someday, somehow, he's going to realize there's two sides to every story, and that your side is worth listening to as well as his. Just wait and see, Jamie. He'll come back someday."

Jameson shook his head, giving her a bleak smile. "I wish I had your optimistic outlook, kid. But I'm the one who goes and talks to him every year, and he's as cold as ice. Not a flicker of warmth or forgiveness, not ever."

"Just every bit as stubborn as his old man," Maureen said, trying to smile back at her brother. "A real chip off the old block."

Jameson nodded, bending to take the oil can from his sister's hands. "And now we won't talk about it anymore, Mo. We'll enjoy our Christmas with the staff members and not mention Jim again, all right? And I'll take this back to the garage for you. I have to go out later to check on the new bull. Manny says he looks 'a leetul down,' whatever that means."

Maureen brightened. "Did you see the puppies? Aren't they lovely?"

"Absolutely lovely. You were right. That dog of Willoughby's was the perfect sire. We'll have to use him again. By the way, did the lumber yard call about the posts? Manny says..."

Still talking cheerfully, Jameson took his sister's arm and escorted her firmly out into the foyer. In the archway he paused, casting a wistful glance back at the big dining table with its warm centerpiece of holly and juniper. Then, abruptly, he flicked off the switch for the sparkling chandelier overhead, plunging the room into darkness.

SARAH HESITATED in the lobby of Jim Fleming's apartment building, her arms piled high with brightly wrapped Christmas gifts, and glanced around nervously. There was nobody in sight near the doorway, but she still had an irrational fear that people were hiding in every alcove and behind every marble column, ready to jump out and grab her.

She was so terrified of having Jim Fleming learn her identity that she had even come by cab this afternoon rather than use her own car. The cabdriver stood just behind her, also laden with parcels.

"Okay, ma'am?" he asked. "You look kind of funny. Is something the matter?"

"No," Sarah said, touched by his evident concern. She glanced once more around the lobby, quiet and deserted except for the sturdy gray-haired doorman in his little cubicle who watched them with polite detachment.

"So, do you need help to get this stuff upstairs? You want I should hang around?" the driver asked.

"No, thank you," Sarah murmured again, glancing nervously over her shoulder at the street beyond the plate glass windows. "No, that's fine. Thank you so much for all your help."

She set her pile of gifts down on a velvet love seat near the entry doors, rummaged in her handbag and handed the cabby a bill, smiling shyly. He gazed at her, dazzled both by the smile and by the size of the bill. Then he set his mountain of packages down next to hers, tipped his hat respectfully and backed out the door, still gazing at her with warm admiration. Sarah returned his smile gratefully and crossed the lobby to speak to the doorman.

"Excuse me," she began tentatively, "but I have some parcels to deliver…to Mr. Fleming's suite. I wonder if I could…?"

"Certainly, miss," the older man said politely. "Mr. Fleming told me to expect you. I'll help you carry the things up."

"That would be nice of you," Sarah said. "There's quite a pile here."

She followed the doorman into the elevator, her heart pounding thunderously in her chest as the door slid shut and enclosed them.

"Still cold," he observed politely as the elevator glided soundlessly upward. "But then it's nice to have snow for Christmas, isn't it?"

"Yes," Sarah murmured. "Yes, it is."

She was gripped by sudden panic, by a shattering, breathless certainty that Jim Fleming had deceived her, and that even now he was waiting in his apartment, ready to seize her as soon as she rang the doorbell, to force her inside and make her reveal her identity, to tell him her deep, precious secret about the baby she longed for, and then he would—

"Here we are, ma'am. Are you sure you can manage all those parcels? You look a little pale."

"I'm fine, thanks," Sarah said, taking a deep breath and stepping out into the carpeted hallway. Suddenly, with overwhelming stunning clarity, she remembered the way Jim Fleming had looked when he stood naked and arrogant in front of her, and how his hands and lips had felt on her skin, and the wild, sweet magic he had wrought in her own body.

She shivered, bit her lip and tried to smile at the anxious man beside her. Then, with a carefully neutral expression, she followed him to a door marked J. K. Fleming on a discreet brass plate.

The door was answered by a plump, smiling woman in an orange velour jogging suit, whose gray curls framed a soft pink face of great sweetness.

"You must...you must be Maude," Sarah whispered. "I have some things for the children."

"Yes, of course. Jim hoped you'd be coming," Maude said cheerfully, beaming at the doorman who gazed back at her with silent adoration. "He's at the office, but the kids are here. Even Billy's here."

The doorman retreated back along the corridor, with obvious reluctance and one last abject look at Maude, who took charge of the packages, deposited them on a table in the foyer and drew Sarah inside, taking her coat and scarf while she continued to talk. Finally Maude directed Sarah toward the living room and then disappeared tactfully into the depths of the kitchen, murmuring something about coffee.

Trembling and feeling breathless, Sarah stepped into the big, plant-filled living room. Despite its size the room seemed crowded and cluttered, jammed full of children's clothes, toys, and a big white crib and changing table that dominated the long wall by the windows. A huge, bushy Christmas tree filled one corner, sparkling with shiny new ornaments of all kinds. Near the tree Arthur sat on the soft white goatskin, banging a wooden spoon against an aluminum cake pan with noisy satisfaction. A fat black puppy crouched beside him, worrying one edge of the rug, gripping it between his sharp little teeth and flinging himself about in a fury of flapping ears and puppy growls.

Ellie and Billy sat side by side on a creamy leather couch near their baby brother, silent and tense. They both seemed warmer, cleaner and less pinched and hungry than they had been on the memorable night of that first meeting, but their expressions were still the same. Billy looked guarded and watchful, almost sullen, as he examined Sarah. Ellie was wide-eyed and breathless, her features pale and taut, her thin hands gripped tightly on a small cushion in her lap.

All thoughts of Jim Fleming left Sarah's mind as she smiled at the three children. She crossed the room hesitantly and crouched near Arthur, who looked up at her with a sparkling, damp grin and pounded lustily on his cake tin in greeting.

Sarah laughed and picked him up. He felt even heavier than she remembered and comfortably cozy in a pair of warm denim overalls and a tiny hockey sweater.

"Hello, Arthur," Sarah murmured. "How are you? How's our great big baby?" She nuzzled against his sweet, fat neck, and Arthur chuckled deep in his throat, making Sarah laugh with him.

She held the merry baby in one arm and moved over to stroke Ellie's hair softly while the little girl gazed up at her, blue eyes round with adoring wonder.

"Hello, Ellie," Sarah said softly. "You look so pretty in that blouse. The color suits you perfectly."

Ellie blushed as pink as the ruffled shirt that she wore. "Maude brought it," she whispered. "It used to belong to one of her granddaughters."

"Well, it looks like it was made just for you."

Ellie clutched her pillow more tightly and moved over to let Sarah sit between her and Billy, giving Arthur a reproving frown as he clutched at Sarah's dark plait and tugged it.

Sarah gently disentangled her hair from Arthur's damp pink

fist and gave him back his wooden spoon, which he examined with deep satisfaction. He began to wriggle and whimper, looking around for the cake tin, and Sarah set him back on the white rug. Immediately he crawled briskly back to the center and set up his noisy drum chorus once more.

"How are you, Billy?" Sarah asked, holding Ellie's small hand and looking at the tense, silent boy on her other side.

"Fine," he said briefly, avoiding her gaze.

Sarah studied him thoughtfully. Unlike the other children, Billy still wore his ragged jeans and sneakers, and Sarah suspected he had resisted attempts to attire him in anything better.

"Is something the matter, Billy?" she asked gently. "What is it that's bothering you?"

His face turned so pale that the freckles stood out on his strong young cheekbones in stark relief. "This!" he burst out, waving his hand at the warm, luxurious room, the big Christmas tree, the chuckling, well-dressed baby. "This is bothering me, if you want to know."

Ellie gripped her hand convulsively, and Sarah winced at the strength of the little girl's grasp. But she went on holding Ellie's hand tenderly and looked at Billy again.

"What about it, Billy? Why does it bother you?"

"Well, it can't last, can it? And then what happens to us?"

"What do you mean?"

"Oh, come on," Billy said roughly. "I'm not stupid. I mean, he brought us home like a sackful of kittens or something. But he can't keep us. They're already mad at him for having us here. And if he turns us over to Social Services, they'll split us up and give Arthur away. And after this—" Billy waved his hand in fury at the luxury all around them "—after all *this,* how can I take them back where they were before? Huh? How can I?"

Sarah regarded him in silence and then put an arm around Ellie, who had begun, in utter silence, to cry. Big shining tears rolled down the little girl's thin cheeks and dripped onto the pink ruffled collar of her new blouse.

"Billy..." Sarah began. "Billy, don't you trust anybody?

Can't you believe that Mr. Fleming means what he says, and that we're all going to look after you and see that the three of you are kept together?"

"How?" the boy asked bluntly. "Maude can't help. She lives in a tiny little apartment even smaller than this one, and anyway, she's going away next week for a holiday. We can't stay here because they don't allow kids in the building. And how can you help? Jim doesn't even know your name. He told me so."

"That may be true," Sarah said, "but it doesn't mean I can't help you. I wish you'd trust us a bit, Billy."

"I don't trust anybody," the boy said darkly. "Trust anybody and they'll wind up messing you around. That's what I believe."

Sarah was saved from answering by Maude, who came bustling into the room with a purposeful gleam in her eye. "Well, mister," she said to Billy, "that may be what you believe, but *I* believe that our guest is probably cold and hungry, and she'd like a cup of coffee and some of those Christmas cookies Ellie and I baked this morning. Am I right?"

Sarah smiled up at her gratefully. "You're right, Maude," she said. "That sounds wonderful."

"Good," Maude said briskly. "Ellie, you come and help me get a tray ready. Billy, you get the lady's presents from the hall and put them under the tree, and give Lancelot a good swat if he tries to rip them open. And *you,*" she said, lifting Arthur and tucking him under her arm like a loaf of bread, "you need a new diaper, my little man. And not a moment too soon."

She carried Arthur, still beaming and wriggling, over to the changing table. Ellie slipped from the couch, reluctantly letting go of Sarah's hand, but Sarah got up and followed her. "I'll come with you, Ellie," she said, "and help get the coffee things ready."

As they went toward the kitchen, Arthur cooed and gurgled, waving his bare pink legs on the changing table while Maude tickled him. Billy knelt to arrange Sarah's pile of gifts under the tree and gently cuffed Lancelot, who crowded close enough to seize one of the trailing ribbon ends in his tiny teeth.

Lancelot howled and retreated, glaring balefully. Maude laughed, Arthur crowed, and Sarah and Ellie giggled together in the doorway. All at once Sarah forgot her fear and nervousness. She felt wonderful, contented, warm and at home, and happier than she could remember being in a long time.

JIM HESITATED outside his door, his heart beating fast. He knew he was being irrational, that there was no chance his mystery woman might still be in the apartment. In fact, it was most likely that she hadn't come at all. But still his mouth felt dry, and his heart hammered as wildly as if he were a boy ringing the doorbell for his first date.

He walked through the foyer, shrugging out of his jacket, and glanced into the living room. A new pile of colorful gifts glowed beneath the tree, but there was no other sign of company. Ellie was curled quietly in a corner of the leather sofa, reading, while Billy was nowhere to be seen.

Arthur lay on the rug at Ellie's feet, flat on his back, squinting thoughtfully up at his interlaced fingers and murmuring unintelligible phrases. When he saw Jim, he rolled promptly onto his stomach and began to crawl across the floor with astonishing speed, arriving at Jim's feet and grasping a handful of trousers to haul himself upright.

Jim grinned as the plump baby swarmed up his leg. Then he bent, swooped the little boy aloft and held him high in the air, hands encircling the plump midsection while Arthur beamed down at him with sparkling brown eyes, gurgling in delight.

"Hi, Ellie," Jim said, settling the baby comfortably in the crook of his arm and cuddling him. "I see you have some more presents under the tree. Did Santa come, or what?"

Ellie smiled at him, her pale, shy face translucent with pleasure. "The lady came," she said. "The Princess Lady. She was even prettier than I remembered, Jim. She's just so beautiful and *so* nice.'' Ellie sighed in bliss, thinking about the lady who had enchanted her right from their first meeting.

But Jim's concerns were more practical and urgent.

''What did she look like? What was she wearing?'' he asked, settling himself beside Ellie and mounting Arthur on one of his outstretched legs. The baby grasped Jim's long, tanned fingers in his dimpled hands and shouted with delight as the big man jogged him gently up and down.

''Gray slacks,'' Ellie said eagerly. ''And a white shirt, kind of plain and soft, and a little vest made of wool or something, kind of bumpy and all soft gray and blue, sort of…'' Words failed her, and she trailed off into silence for a moment. ''And,'' the little girl added dreamily, ''she smelled just wonderful. Like…like flowers in the sun.''

Jim was silent, absorbing this information and wistfully recalling the scent of that particular sunny floral perfume. Ellie snuggled close to him, and he rested one arm around her thin little body.

''I don't suppose you happened to look out the window when she left and see what she was driving?'' he asked casually, feeling traitorous.

Ellie shook her head, setting her pale blond hair swinging. ''She went away in a taxi.''

''I see,'' Jim said, swallowing his disappointment. ''And I guess she didn't tell you her name, either?''

Again Ellie shook her head. ''She said she couldn't. But she said she'll come back again and visit us sometime really soon.''

Jim felt a surge of optimism and jogged Arthur higher until the plump baby was red-faced and gasping with excitement.

Maude bustled in, wearing her coat and carrying a box under one arm. Lancelot's blunt nose protruded from a hole at the front of the box, whiskers quivering. Clearly Lancelot could tell that Arthur was having a lot of fun, which he strongly desired to join.

But Maude clutched the box firmly and smiled at Jim. ''I

heard you come in," she said. "And I'd better be off. I still have Christmas shopping to do."

"Thanks for everything, Maude," Jim said fervently. "I mean it. I never could have managed without you."

"Oh, pooh," Maude said with a dismissive wave of her free hand. "It's been a pleasure." She paused and gave Jim a keen glance. "You're sure you'll be okay here, Jim? It's not easy, you know. And," she added hesitantly, "I could always beg off from this holiday. I don't really need to go out there and spend a couple of weeks falling down all those ski hills."

"Don't be ridiculous," Jim said firmly, setting the breathless, chuckling baby down carefully on the white rug and getting to his feet. "You've been planning this holiday for ages. And I won't have any problems here. I've got my office all organized so that they can get along without me for a while, and I've got Ellie here to help me look after Arthur. If anyone knows how to look after Arthur," he added, smiling down at the little girl, "it's Ellie."

Maude, too, smiled fondly at Ellie. "That's certainly true," she said, reaching out to stroke the child's smooth blond hair. "She's ten going on thirty-two, this one is. What a marvelous kid."

Ellie turned pink and smiled shyly.

"And there's Billy," Jim began. He paused, looking around. "Speaking of Billy, where is he, by the way?"

Maude's mouth tightened. "Who knows? *I* certainly don't know where that child goes all day. He managed to be here for the lady's visit, though. I will say that for him."

Jim hesitated, looking cautiously at the plump, grandmotherly woman who had in such a short time become one of his best friends.

"She really is lovely, Jim," Maude said softly, reading his expression. "Absolutely lovely. What a sweet woman. And so shy and nice."

"Shy?" Jim asked, remembering the elegant creature who had seduced him so skillfully. "Did you get the impression she was *shy*, Maude?"

"Oh, absolutely," Maude said, nodding with confident wisdom. "And terrified, too. Scared to death that you might pop in and catch her, I think. And yet when we settled in the kitchen with our cookies and coffee, she relaxed and had as much fun as the kids, didn't she, Ellie?"

Ellie nodded vigorously while the two adults smiled down at her.

Maude looked at Jim again, her eyes questioning. "Where did you meet her, Jim? How did you happen to be together the night you found the kids if you don't even know her name? I wish you'd tell me the whole story. She's such a darling."

Jim shook his head. "That part of it is kind of private. Just between the lady and me." He paused, struck by a sudden thought. "Maude, did you give her my letter?"

Maude nodded sadly. "But she wouldn't take it with her, Jim. She said she didn't want to have it or answer it or anything."

His heart sank. "Didn't she even read it?"

"Oh, she read it all right." Maude grinned suddenly, remembering. "It was so cute, Jim. I gave her the letter just before she left, and she said what I told you, you know, that she didn't want to take it, but she did agree to read it. So then she took these big, heavy-rimmed glasses out of her purse and put them on, and just kind of disappeared behind them. It was so cute, seeing her in those big glasses. And after she finished she smiled, handed the letter back to me and said to tell Mr. Fleming thank you."

"That's all?" he asked, aching with disappointment. "Just 'Tell Mr. Fleming thank you'? Nothing else?"

"Sorry, Jim." Maude patted his arm. "If it's any comfort," she added briskly, "I'm sure she'll be back. She seems to be crazy about these kids."

Jim smiled absently, helping Maude to gather her belongings and watching as she bade a loving, lingering farewell to Ellie and the baby.

"Well," she said finally in the doorway, still gripping Lancelot's box, "goodbye, all. Merry Christmas, and I'll see you in a couple of weeks. Jim, are you *sure* you can manage?"

Jim grinned at her with considerably more confidence than he felt, wondering uneasily where Billy was and if Arthur might be planning to cut any more molars in the near future and what could possibly be said to divert the building supervisor the next time he asked about the children....

"I'm sure," he said firmly. "You have a good holiday, and don't you dare disgrace me by forgetting how to snowplow, you hear?"

Maude beamed, her pink face dimpling, and suddenly looked about sixteen. She waved, gave them a last loving smile and departed for the lobby where her new conquest, the doorman, was waiting patiently at the end of his shift to give her a ride home.

When she was gone, Jim settled back on the couch and opened the evening paper. Ellie snuggled close to him, picking her book up again, while Arthur crawled busily across the rug, dumped a big plastic rabbit in Jim's lap and then climbed up after it in a businesslike fashion. Jim cuddled him awkwardly with one arm, turning the pages of the paper with the other.

"Ellie," he asked presently, "did you remember to slip that envelope into Maude's purse like I told you?"

Ellie nodded. "I was really careful," she reported. "I tucked it way down so she won't find it till she gets out her keys to open her apartment."

"Good girl." Jim grinned. "She'll be mad at us, Ellie. She keeps saying she doesn't want to be paid for this, but she certainly deserves something for all she's done, don't you think?"

Ellie nodded gravely and turned a page in her book.

"Did she leave anything for supper?" Jim asked hopefully.

"Baked ham and something else with a funny name. I think Maude called it scalped potatoes," Ellie said. "They're in the oven."

Jim grinned at the idea of "scalped potatoes," and then sighed blissfully as he visualized the meal that awaited them.

Beside him Ellie echoed the sigh, her thin little face alight with pleasure.

"How about Billy?" Jim asked. "Will he be home, do you think?"

Ellie shook her head. "Not for a while. But he'll come later. Don't worry. Billy says he doesn't like it here," she added with one of her surprising flashes of shrewdness. "But I think he likes it a lot better than out there on the street. He just doesn't want us to know."

Jim nodded, his face briefly troubled. He returned to his paper, wincing a little as Arthur gnawed with sudden, startling intensity on his index finger.

But the printed letters swam in front of his eyes to be replaced by a puzzling, persistent image.

He pictured the mystery woman reading his letter, saw her in his mind's eye as Maude had described her, and it jogged something deep in his memory. Somehow, somewhere, he was certain he had seen this woman *wearing big, heavy-rimmed glasses.*

The image hovered at the edge of his consciousness, maddening and tantalizing, just out of reach. He was sitting somewhere in a room where he could smell a scent of warm pine and freshly mown grass through an open window, and this woman was somewhere nearby, wearing heavy glasses.

But where? And when? *When* had he seen her before?

He moaned softly in frustration. Ellie glanced up at him in concern and snuggled closer to him while Arthur, surprised by the moan, registered an expression of gratified satisfaction before biting down harder on the big man's finger.

CHRISTMAS CAME AND WENT, filled with laughter and fun, and Jim's apartment echoed with sounds never heard before within those quiet, luxurious walls. The three abandoned children adapted with astonishing ease and swiftness to a life of pleasure and plenty, especially Arthur, who crawled through Jim's life with the cheerful, buoyant confidence of a baby born to luxury.

"This is Arthur's first Christmas," Ellie said shyly to Jim, "and it's so wonderful. Maybe he'll never, ever have a Christmas like—"

She broke off abruptly. Jim looked down at her pale face, his heart aching. "Like what, Ellie?" he asked softly. "What did Christmas used to be like for you?"

Ellie shuddered and looked away, her shining golden hair falling forward to hide her face. "I don't want to talk about it," she whispered. "Usually," she added reluctantly, "Mom used to drink a lot more at Christmas time. Sometimes she didn't come home for days, and if Billy couldn't find anything for us to eat, we'd get so hungry. When I think of Christmas," she concluded simply, "I just think of being so awful hungry that I felt like crying all the time."

"Oh, God," Jim muttered, pausing by her chair to stroke her shining head. "Oh, Ellie, I'm so sorry."

"It's okay," she said, looking up at him with a smile. "We're happy now, and you're looking after us, and Maude, and the Princess Lady, and I'm not hungry anymore. Actually, I'm so full of chocolates and stuff I can hardly move," she added with a grin. "And look at Arthur."

They both examined the cheerful baby, who was sitting on the furry white rug, busy with his favorite toy. Arthur adored the big activity board that Sarah had given him, and had already shown considerable intelligence by mastering the intricacies of making bells toot, whistles shriek, balls fall through transparent tubes, and small shiny windows click open and shut. Every time he succeeded at a specific task he whooped aloud and drummed his little boots on the floor, adding to the general din.

Ellie smiled at the fat baby and then turned back to her careful work on her shellcraft set. She was ensconced at the dining room table, which had been liberally padded with newspaper, and she would sit there for hours gluing the dainty multicolored shells into position, arranging intricate designs on small glass squares and discs.

Jim watched her, smiling at the look of concentrated intensity on her delicate face. The "Princess Lady," he mused, had certainly known what to buy for these children. Even Billy had been obviously pleased by the fishing rod and tackle and frequently sorted through it, wistfully fingering the shining spoons and lures, studying his instruction book to learn the techniques of threading line onto the reel and how to attach hooks and leaders.

"Ellie," Jim asked absently, "do you think you could look after Arthur by yourself some afternoon?"

Ellie looked up at him in surprise. "I used to look after Arthur all by myself all day long," she said quietly. "Even when he was a lot smaller than this."

Jim smiled, a little abashed. "I guess you did, didn't you, sweetie? I just keep forgetting how capable you are."

"Are you going away somewhere?" Ellie asked, absorbed once more in her work.

"No, but I wondered if Billy might want to go ice-fishing with me some afternoon and try out his new equipment."

Ellie's face shone with happiness. "Oh, Jim," she breathed, "that'd be so nice. Billy would love it."

"I don't know," Jim said gloomily. "Billy doesn't seem to like me very much, you know. He might not want to go with me."

"Of course he likes you," Ellie said calmly. "You're the nicest man in the whole world, and Billy knows it. He's just worried, that's all."

"About what's going to happen to all of you?"

Ellie nodded. "Billy says we have to leave here in a month. The man told him so one day when he took the garbage down. We have to be gone by the end of January, he said."

"Well, that's not entirely true," Jim said. "I'm sure Mr. Clement would give me an extra month if I really needed it before he'd turn us out in the street."

"But we can't stay here," Ellie said. "And we can't go to Maude's, and we don't even know the Princess Lady's name. That's why Billy's worried. He doesn't know where he can take us, that's all."

Jim looked at her curiously as she selected a tiny pink shell no bigger than one of Arthur's fingernails and fitted it with a group of others that were forming a delicate rosebud.

"What about you, Ellie?" he asked. "Aren't you worried? You know about all these problems, but they don't seem to bother you."

Ellie shook her head and then lay down her tweezers to give Jim a long, thoughtful glance. "I'd be worried," she said finally, "if I thought we were going to Social Services and they were going to take Arthur away. I'd be out of my mind with worry. But I know Billy won't let that happen. If that happens, we'll just run away like before, and Billy will look after us."

She returned to her work while Jim studied her, appalled by her words. "But, Ellie," he began finally, "how could you stand that? Living in a room like you had before, and being cold and hungry all the time. Could you live that way again, Ellie?"

"If I had to," the child said calmly. "See," she added, "it would be different now. Whenever it was hard or awful, I could think about all the nice things here, and then it would be easier. Like," she went on earnestly, "one day I'd think about Maude and Lancelot, and one day I'd think about how you took us out to that fancy restaurant for Christmas dinner, and how wonderful it was, and sometimes I'd think about when the Princess Lady came and brought our presents. There'd be so many nice things to remember," she concluded. "It'd be lots easier now."

Jim swallowed hard and dashed a hand across his eyes, turning aside to busy himself with Arthur for a moment while he regained his composure. Then he looked up at the older child.

"Well, Ellie," he said calmly, "that's not going to happen. You're not going to go back to some hole and live on memories. You'll be looked after, and you won't lose Arthur, and you can tell Billy that, too. If I have to," he added, "I'll find some way to sublet this apartment and buy a house, so nobody can tell us you can't live with me."

Ellie looked up at him. "Or maybe," she said wistfully,

"the Princess Lady will come back and take us to her castle. I bet she lives in a castle, don't you think, Jim? Like in the book you gave me, with a moat and a tower, and her bed would be all made of gold, with silk curtains hanging around it. Don't you think so?"

Jim grinned at this picture. "Maybe," he said cheerfully. "And maybe not."

They were both silent, watching Arthur who had suddenly discovered a knob that made a jack-in-the-box pop up with an insane grin. Arthur was holding his breath, a fist in his mouth, eyes wide with amazement. Puffing, he touched the jack-in-the-box, then stared in wonder and distress as it disappeared slowly into the box again. He screwed his face up and prepared to howl until Jim hastily lowered himself to the carpet and showed the baby how to find the magic knob again.

When Arthur was contentedly making the puppet figure appear and disappear, Jim returned to his conversation with Ellie. "Did you see the lady when she put the glasses on?" he asked idly.

Ellie nodded, searching through a pile of tinted shells for some flat ones to use as leaves.

"What did she look like, Ellie? With the glasses on, I mean," Jim asked.

After all this time he still had the feeling that if he could just picture the woman in those glasses, get a clear mental image of how she had looked, he could somehow capture the elusive memory of where he'd seen her before.

Ellie bit her lip thoughtfully, setting a green shell into position on a tiny drop of glue.

"Like a doctor," Ellie said. "That's what she looked like. Or a scientist or something. You know how they look on TV, those really smart ladies who...?"

But Jim was no longer listening. He was staring unseeing into the distance, his blue eyes wide with shock, his face pale and startled.

He knew, at last, where he had seen the woman before.

CHAPTER SEVEN

SARAH SAT WAITING for the doctor to return. Her face was pale and tense, and she stared fixedly at a big chart on the opposite wall. The chart was arranged like a giant wheel covered with calendar dates and was designed to tell a pregnant woman precisely when her baby was due.

Sarah bit her lip and fought back a sudden flood of emotion. Lately she kept having these erratic, weepy moods for no reason at all, it seemed. Her rational, scientific mind was alarmed by the sudden bouts of depression and anxiety, of sadness and intermittent euphoria.

She knew, of course, what was wrong. By now, even though she hadn't menstruated on schedule after her encounter with Jim Fleming, she was convinced she wasn't pregnant. She felt nothing happening inside her, no sense that a fetus was developing, and she was certain that if a baby were there, she'd feel *something*. She had failed to conceive, and as a result she either had to forget the whole thing or go through it all again.

Sarah sighed and fingered the soft straps of her leather handbag. The disappointment was crushing. She had been so sure the timing was right, that she'd chosen the absolutely optimum time to have intercourse. But how could she control all the variables? There was nothing she could have done about the terrible, unexpected shock of Billy's attack on her and Jim Fleming, her frantic run through icy streets, the trauma of seeing those poor abandoned children.

Sarah shifted in the chair, gazing unseeingly at her own reflection in the steel-framed mirror across the room.

She felt weary and hopeless, crushed with doubts and uncertainties. Should she go through it all again, call Jim Fleming up at the right time of the month and pretend she'd just experienced an uncontrollable urge for another night of sex? Would he believe that?

Sarah frowned at her reflection. Jim Fleming, she realized, was much more than just a handsome, empty-headed athlete. He was a clever, perceptive man, and any time she spent with him was dangerous. There was a real possibility that he might figure out what she was doing, even find some way of discovering her identity.

And yet the thought of choosing another man upset her immensely.

Her gloomy thoughts were interrupted by a swift knock on the door. The doctor popped his curly gray head into the room, beamed at Sarah and said, "Okay? All dressed and decent?"

Sarah smiled wanly. "If I weren't, we'd both be embarrassed by now, wouldn't we?"

He grinned. "No, dear, likely just you. Now let's see what we've got."

He flipped out the tails of his lab coat, seated himself at the desk and moved aside a large framed photo of his grandchildren, one of many which filled the little office.

"Great kids," he said, smiling at the bright faces with absentminded fondness. "The joy of my life. Now, Sarah, I'm not sure I know exactly what you want to hear from me."

"Yes, you do, Dr. McLellan," Sarah said. "I just told you. I want to know if I'm pregnant or not."

The doctor glanced up quickly at her lovely, withdrawn features, then looked down at the file again, sorting through the papers in the folder.

"I know that, Sarah. What I mean is that I'm not sure which of those two answers is the one you really want to hear."

"I just want to know," Sarah repeated, her eyes remote, her face expressionless.

"All right, my dear. According to my manual examination, coupled with the test results, I would estimate that you're approximately four weeks pregnant. If you're confident of the accuracy of the dates you've given me, you can probably expect to give birth on or about September 10.''

Sarah stared at him. Her hands trembled, and her face went white with shock.

The doctor looked back at her gravely, guarding his expression as he waited for her to speak.

All at once Sarah's huge gray eyes lighted with wondering happiness, and her delicate features flushed pink. Tears shimmered in her eyes as she gazed at him, smiling mistily, still searching for words.

''Well,'' the doctor said dryly, looking at her joyous, shining face, ''I guess that answers *that* question, doesn't it?''

''I...I beg your pardon?'' Sarah asked, her voice hesitant and faltering.

''I take it you want this baby, Sarah,'' the doctor said gently.

''Oh, yes,'' she whispered. ''Oh, yes, I do, Dr. McLellan. Very much.''

''Right. That's what I assumed from your reaction. Well, there shouldn't be any problem. You're a very healthy girl, and you've always taken intelligent care of yourself. I'll just give you some reading material to look over.''

Sarah sat in a daze of happiness, hardly able to concentrate on the things the doctor was telling her, the pamphlets he handed over, the diet sheets and other information.

She wanted only to be out of this place, alone in a quiet room where she could think about the miracle that had happened. She wanted to brood over the wonder of her own baby, alive and sheltered within her, her very own, growing and developing this very moment within the nurturing, enclosing safety of her body.

''Four weeks,'' Sarah said aloud, interrupting Dr. McLellan who was lecturing her earnestly on the dangers of excessive sodium consumption. ''At four weeks she already has a full three-part brain starting to form, and eyes and ears have begun to develop, and arms and legs...''

The doctor smiled. ''It's a girl, is it, Sarah?''

"Oh, yes," Sarah said, blushing again. "I think so."

The doctor nodded. "Well, be that as it may, you're absolutely right about the development, my dear. It's a vitally important time to watch what you eat and drink, what kind of medication you ingest, all that sort of thing."

"I would never, never do anything to hurt my baby," Sarah said simply.

The doctor nodded. "Good. Your baby will never be as vulnerable in her whole life as she is right now. What you do in these next few months can have lifelong effects for her."

"Nothing in the world matters as much as her," Sarah said. "Don't worry, Dr. McLellan. I'll take good care of her."

He grinned cheerfully, gave Sarah a few more instructions and handed over a sheaf of information, telling her to stop at the desk on her way out to make her next monthly appointment.

At last Sarah was alone in her car, driving through the snow-covered streets wrapped in January cold. She could still hardly believe the wonder of what she had just been told. Sarah had always been so certain, despite what the doctors and scientists said, that she would be able to *feel* the early process of cell divisions and fetal development, that such a momentous thing couldn't possibly be happening in her own body without her knowledge.

And right after her night with Jim Fleming she had actually felt little stirrings, whispers of something, but she had dismissed them as wishful thinking. When she finally kept her appointment with her doctor on this bitter January afternoon, she had been absolutely convinced she wasn't pregnant, and that the delay in her cycle this month was due to nothing more than stress and overwrought nerves.

"I'm *pregnant,*" she whispered aloud. "I'm going to have a baby. On or about September 10 I'm going to have a *baby.*"

Even hearing the words spoken aloud in her own voice didn't make them seem real. It was too wonderful...just too wonderful.

Sarah parked in the lot at the laboratory, plugged her car in and entered the building, pausing at the reception desk to check for messages.

Joelle, the receptionist, glanced up at her with a smile and Sarah wondered if her marvelous news was somehow visible on her face, if it was even remotely possible that people could look at her and not read the truth blazing from her eyes.

But Joelle merely nodded cheerfully and reached for the message pad at her elbow. "Hi, Sarah. Still cold out there?"

"Freezing," Sarah said, gripping her handbag in trembling fingers and unwinding her big plaid scarf. "Joelle, did Apex Industries call about the microscope? I've been expecting all this week to hear something from them."

Joelle shook a pencil at her and consulted her message list. "They said yes, the lens is still under warranty," she reported. "They said you can either get it fixed here and bill them, or pack it up and send it to them and they'll look after it."

"Oh, good. Anything else?"

"Let's see. Your accountant called about half an hour ago," Joelle went on. "He wants you to get your receipts and stuff into his office so he can start on last year's income tax."

Sarah made a face. "Right. I guess I can't keep putting that off forever, can I?"

"None of us can," Joelle said sadly. "Oh, by the way," she added, "there's a man in your office."

Sarah, who had been on her way down the hall, paused and cast an inquiring glance over her shoulder. "A man? Who? What does he want?"

"I didn't get his name. Carl came out and talked to him. But he's a *very* acceptable item. I can tell you that much. Absolutely gorgeous, actually."

Sarah looked alarmed. "What do you mean?"

"Never mind, Sarah," Joelle said fondly. "The man will be completely wasted on you, anyway. I swear, I never met a woman with more potential and less interest in the finer things."

Sarah grinned at her friend's teasing, tossed her dark plait of hair back over her shoulder and rummaged in her handbag for her heavy glasses, which she fitted onto the bridge of her nose.

"There," she said cheerfully. "That's about as glamorous as I can manage on such short notice. Now what did you say this man wants?"

"I don't know," Joelle said patiently. "Like I told you, it was Carl who talked to him. I think he was asking Carl something about your college days and your early training, stuff like that."

"Oh," Sarah said, her face clearing. "He'll be from the committee for the new fellowship, then. They've been exploring my educational history all the way back to kindergarten, it seems. I hope he doesn't take too long," she added half to herself. "There are so many things I need to—"

She paused abruptly, stared into space for a minute and then flashed a warm, distracted smile at Joelle and hurried off down the hallway.

Outside the closed door of her own office Sarah hesitated, then knocked briskly and entered, shrugging out of her heavy camel hair coat as she closed the door behind her.

A tall, golden-haired man stood near her bookshelves, examining the titles, and he turned as she entered to smile at her. Sarah stared back at him, thunderstruck, the color draining from her face.

The man in her office was Jim Fleming.

"Well, hi, there, pretty lady," he said softly, smiling at the look of speechless shock on her face. "Wearing those big glasses again, I see."

Sarah struggled for words while Jim stepped forward calmly, took her coat and hung it away in the closet, still smiling.

She felt terribly vulnerable and exposed under his gaze, as if those vivid blue eyes could see into the very core of her and read her precious secret. Sarah felt an urgent terror, a need to protect her baby from him, to keep him from ever, ever finding out about the treasure she now carried in her body. She snatched her long white lab coat from its hanger and pulled it on over her slacks and sweater, wrapped it around her with trembling hands.

"Too late, I'm afraid," Jim said, still grinning. "I've already noticed how terrific you look in that sweater, Dr. Burnard."

His handsome face was warm with amusement, the dimple very evident in one flat, tanned cheek. Sarah avoided his eyes, moving nervously over behind her desk and pretended to busy herself with a sheaf of papers on a clipboard. "How did you find me?" she murmured.

"Not easily, that's for sure. May I?" Jim asked, giving her another brilliant blue glance and walking casually across to one of the leather chairs opposite Sarah's desk.

"Yes...yes, of course," she murmured distractedly. "Have a seat."

Jim Fleming seated himself and extended his long legs comfortably. He wore casual gray slacks and a black cashmere pullover with his shirt and tie, and looked heartbreakingly handsome even to Sarah, who didn't usually notice such things.

He smiled at her cheerfully and rested his firm, tanned hands on the arms of the chair. "Now," he went on, "you were asking about how I found you?"

"Yes," Sarah murmured, settling her glasses more firmly on the bridge of her nose and pretending to be absorbed in the papers in front of her. "I'm really quite curious about that."

"Well, as I said, it wasn't easy. I went back and made the rounds of all the bars and pubs in that neighborhood quite a few times, but nobody could remember seeing you. And I kept having the feeling," he added, "that I'd met you before, but it didn't register until Maude told me how you put those big, heavy-rimmed glasses on to read my letter—remember?"

He paused and gave Sarah an inquiring glance. She nodded without looking up. "I remember," she murmured. "Please go on."

"Well, a few days ago I happened to ask Ellie how you looked in the glasses, and she said you looked 'really smart, like a scientist or something,' and then it hit me like a ton of bricks."

Sarah flushed and stirred uneasily in her chair while he watched her.

"A science major," Jim went on, regarding her carefully. "That's what you were, Sarah Burnard. You were in one of my English classes in college, an absolute knockout of a girl hiding behind those big glasses, and you never said a single word to me. It was quite a blow to my youthful ego, as I recall, the way you studiously ignored me all through term."

Sarah was so startled by his words that she looked up in spite of herself, meeting his amused gaze. "You're kidding," she said flatly. "You were such a big man on campus, and I was just a drab little bookworm. You never even knew I was alive."

"You might be surprised," Jim said quietly. "It's possible that you don't know as much about me as you think you do, Miss Burnard."

Sarah remembered the hours she had spent studying this man, and the masses of meticulous research that were still filed away in a desk drawer right under her hands. She dropped her eyes quickly, hoping none of those thoughts were evident on her face.

"So, anyway," Jim went on, "as soon as I remembered that English class, it was easy. I went through my old yearbooks, found your picture and your name and then called Howie Meyer to ask if he knew where you were working these days."

"You know Howie?" Sarah asked in surprise.

"Sure. We play racquetball together sometimes. Howie still plays a pretty mean game of racquetball," Jim added with a grin. "And since he was always a shining light in the chemistry lab, I figured he might have some idea what happened to all the other science types from our college days. He told me you were working over here, so here I am."

"Here you are," Sarah echoed uneasily.

"Howie also said," Jim added casually, "that you were still single. Never been married, he said, except to your work."

Sarah flushed and bit her lip nervously. "What does that have to do with anything? Whether I've ever been married?"

"Well, I was certain you must be married and that was why you were being so elusive. You know, a married woman just out for a little night of fun and games, not wanting to get caught."

Sarah made an expression of distaste. "If I were married," she said finally with quiet conviction, "I wouldn't be out for 'a night of fun and games,' believe me. Cheating is definitely not my style."

Jim nodded. "I know. Even though that was my first impression, it never seemed to ring true." He smiled at her. "And *that,*" he added, "made me even more determined to find you, no matter what it took."

Sarah looked up at Jim directly for the first time, forcing herself to meet his warm, intent gaze. "But why, Jim? Why did you go to all this trouble to find me?"

"Isn't that funny?" he asked, raising his dark brows. "You know, I was just going to ask you the same thing."

"What do you mean?"

"Come on, Sarah," he said impatiently. "That night in the bar was no random encounter, was it? Nobody could ever remember seeing you there before. Why did you happen to be out cruising the downtown bars just on that particular night?"

Sarah felt a chill of fear and fought it down, forcing herself to think rapidly enough to come up with some kind of convincing story. "Do you remember..." she began, faltering a little, and then her voice steadied as she gained confidence. "Do you remember Wendy? She worked in that bar for a while as a bartender's helper last fall."

"Small girl?" Jim asked, frowning as he searched his memory. "Frizzy reddish hair and big freckles, talks all the time without saying much?"

Sarah nodded, trying not to smile at this unflattering but accurate description of Wendy. "That's her. Well, I've known

Wendy for years, and she always told me what a fun place the bar was, and that night I was feeling so lonely with Christmas coming and all that, and I decided to go down there just to have a couple of drinks. And when I saw you, I remembered you right away from college, even though I could tell you didn't know who I was. And I was so lonely," Sarah went on, her words tumbling over one another in her haste, "and I *did* know you. You weren't a complete stranger, so when it looked like...like something might be going to happen between us, I thought, why not?"

Jim sat across the desk, watching her thoughtfully. "It's a plausible story, Sarah," he said finally, "but I'm not sure I believe you."

"Why would I lie?" Sarah asked, taking a deep breath and forcing herself to meet his eyes with a calm, level gaze. "Do you think there's something sinister going on here, Jim? Do you really think I sought you out specifically for some dark, evil purpose of my own?"

Jim sat quietly in the padded chair, his big body relaxed and still as he regarded the beautiful woman across the desk. Finally he shook his head. "I guess not. It all just seems a little strange. Something kind of...doesn't quite mesh, you know?"

"People get lonely," Sarah said briskly. "Even scientists," she added with a small smile. "And when people are lonely, they quite often do some really strange things. Now forgive me for changing the subject, but how are the children?"

The austere lines of his face softened, and his blue eyes sparkled. "As if you have to ask," he teased. "You've been there what—three times since Maude got back from her ski trip? Sneaking in when I'm away at work to see them?"

Sarah blushed and avoided his eyes. "I know, but it's been...I've been busy the past few days," she confessed, "and I haven't been there to see then since early this week. I just wondered how they are," she added wistfully.

"Okay, you asked for it. Well, first of all, Ellie still loves that shellcraft set you gave her. Oh, I almost forgot. She made you a present." Jim went over to his jacket, which hung on a brass coatrack near the door. He took a small wrapped package from one pocket, crossed the room with his lithe, easy prowl and smiled as he handed the gift to Sarah.

She looked down at it and laughed. "To the Princess Lady from Ellie with lots of love," the tag read in careful, tiny lettering.

"You haven't told them my name?" Sarah murmured, feeling absurdly warm and pleased.

Jim shook his head. "That's your business, Sarah. You can tell them if you choose. They're all just crazy about you," he added. "Including Maude. You've really made some conquests in that group."

Sarah unwraped the tiny package to reveal a square little box lined with cotton. She lifted away the top layer of cotton and caught her breath. Nestled in the soft cloud of white was a dainty pair of earrings constructed of tiny, delicate shells glued with painstaking care onto little plastic disks.

"Why, they're *beautiful,*" Sarah murmured, examining them in awe. "Just beautiful. I had no idea she'd be so talented. This work looks almost professional."

"She's really good with her hands," Jim said, sounding as indulgent and proud as any young parent. "And she spends hours sitting there working at that stuff, not saying a word. I was amazed," he added, "that you managed to pick such a perfect gift. She loves it."

Sarah took off her glasses and looked up at him, her cheeks pink, her big gray eyes shining. All at once she was so lovely that he caught his breath and stared back at her in silent awe.

"I had a shellcraft set at her age," Sarah said softly, "and I've never forgotten how much I loved it. But," she added, laughing a little, "I'm sure I was never as talented as Ellie."

Jim recovered his equilibrium and laughed with her, then went on to report Billy's appreciation of the fishing tackle and Arthur's lusty absorption in his activity board.

Sarah forgot her reserve, even forgot briefly her fear of Jim Fleming's presence and what it could mean to the future of herself and her child. She pictured the scenes in his apartment as he described them and laughed merrily while Jim joined in, his blue eyes sparkling with fun.

Finally she sobered and looked at the little earrings on her desk. "Jim," she asked softly, "what are you going to do with them? These kids, I mean. Can you really keep them with you, all three of them?"

"Oh, God, Sarah," he muttered, shifting in his chair and gazing out the window with a bleak expression. "I don't know. There's just so much to consider."

"Ellie told me you can't keep them much longer in that building," Sarah ventured. "They're going to enforce the adults-only policy, aren't they?"

Jim nodded. "I'm supposed to have them out by the end of the month, with maybe a couple of weeks' grace if I really beg."

Sarah looked at him, appalled. "That's not enough time to make other plans, is it?"

"It sure isn't. Worst of all, I've just signed a three-year lease. I can't get released from it, so if I can't find someone to sublet, I'll have to pay rent on that place as well as mortgage payments on a house. I doubt if I could even qualify for a mortgage under those conditions."

Sarah gazed at him across the desk, her face soft with sympathy and concern. "Jim…what are you going to do?"

"I don't know," he said grimly. "I definitely can't keep them where I am. I've looked at houses, but just now, with the amount of money I've sunk into my business, I can hardly qualify for enough mortgage money even if I do get out of the lease. Up until now," he added, trying to smile, "a house wasn't really way up there on my priority list."

"And Maude can't…"

Jim shook his head. "Maude's whole apartment isn't much bigger than your office here. She likes it that way, says it's easy to clean and leaves her time for all the activities she's involved in. Maude's a busy girl," he added with a distant grin.

Sarah nodded, still gazing at him in concern.

"One of Maude's kids might take them for a while...in a pinch," Jim went on. "But they all have kids of their own, so it'd just have to be temporary, and I hate that idea."

Sarah nodded, understanding exactly what he meant. "They've had so much disruption and instability in their lives already. They should be able to move into a place that's going to be a permanent home, somewhere they can settle in and not have to leave again."

"Exactly," Jim said, giving Sarah a gratified look. "That's just how I feel about it."

Sarah thought for a moment, her delicate black brows drawn in concentration. "Jim," she said finally, "do you really want to keep them with you? I mean, is it important for you to have them living with you?"

He met her eyes honestly. "Not in that sense," he said finally. "I mean, I've never thought of myself as much of a family man, you know? Adopting a ready-made family was another thing that wasn't really high on my priority list. It's just that I feel so damn responsible."

"Because of what Billy says? That after giving them a taste of warmth and comfort, it's cruel to snatch it away again?"

Jim nodded, his blue eyes troubled. "Yes. He's right, you know. I brought them home with me on an impulse, without giving a thought to the consequences. And it's one of those things that takes a second to do but changes your whole life from then on."

Sarah looked with quiet sympathy at his tense features. "But," she persisted, "what you're saying is that you wouldn't mind parting with them as long as you knew they'd be kept together and properly cared for?"

"That's right. I don't need to have them in my house every single day to make me happy. Actually, I'm a man who likes my own privacy, and a quiet, uneventful kind of life. But you're right. I'd need to know they were happy and well before I could let them go. I love those kids," he added with a sudden burst of emotion. "It's amazing how quickly they can get close to your heart, little kids like that. I could get along without having them in my house, but I'd still want to see them all the time, visit them whenever I could.''

Sarah twirled a pencil thoughtfully in her fingers, her brows still drawn in concentration.

''Why, Sarah?'' Jim asked, looking up at her hopefully. ''Can you think of somewhere they could live?'' he paused, struck by a sudden thought. ''Do *you* have room for them? Where do you live, anyhow?''

''I inherited a house from my father. It's on the west side near the university,'' Sarah said automatically, and then instantly regretted her words. Jim was sitting bolt upright, gripping the arms of his chair and staring at her intently, his eyes alight.

''You live in a *house?* And you're not married? You're all alone there?''

Sarah looked back at him, caught his meaning at once and felt a deep chill of unease. ''Jim,'' she began hastily, ''I don't really have room for—''

''But you do live in a house,'' he interrupted. ''Isn't that right? With a yard, and a fence, and all that stuff? More than one bedroom?''

''No yard,'' Sarah said. ''None at all. And only two bedrooms. Actually, my place isn't much bigger than yours. I wish I could—''

''Look, Sarah, I know I started this. I know I'm responsible. I wouldn't expect you to take over my burden for me. I'd pay whatever it cost for you to keep the kids, and also pay Maude or another baby-sitter to look after Arthur so you wouldn't have any interruptions in your work. Please, Sarah,'' Jim went on passionately, ''just consider it. All these kids need is some space and a place to live where they won't be split up or turned out on the street. They're really good kids, Sarah. Please, just think it over for a minute.''

Sarah gazed into his brilliant blue eyes, her soul shrinking away from his words. She pictured her house, so small and self-contained, thinking of how completely inadequate it was as a home for three active children. There would barely be room in her house for her own baby when it arrived, let alone three others.

But she wanted to desperately to help, to see the children safely and permanently settled somewhere. Maybe she could move her plans up by a year or so and start shopping right away for the new house. Still, she couldn't afford another house until she got hers sold, and the housing market was slow now, caught in the usual midwinter slump. By the time she found a buyer, it might already be too late for Jim and the three children....

She drew in a deep, ragged breath, struggling to compose herself and think clearly. "Look," she began, "I don't really have room for them, Jim. I'd like to take them, believe me. I love those kids, too, and I feel just as responsible as you do. But I have...I have other obligations, things in my life you don't know about. And I honestly don't have any more room for them than you do. If I took them, they'd just have to move again soon, anyhow. I'm sorry, Jim, truly I am. I would if I could, in a minute. But I can't."

He nodded and settled back in the chair, still giving her a quiet, level gaze, his disappointment showing clearly in his eyes.

Suddenly she had a thought and hastened to blurt it out before she could think it over and change her mind. "There *is* one thing we could consider," she said.

"And what's that, Sarah?"

"Well," Sarah began awkwardly, studying a pile of folders stacked on the corner of her desk, "from what you're telling me, I gather the main problem is money, right? I mean, you've got everything tied up in your business, and not enough ready cash right now to make a big purchase like a house. Isn't that right?"

"Pretty much," Jim said grimly. "Don't get me wrong. Things are going well and I'm a competent manager. I expect my business to be really profitable in the future. But right now things are tight. I don't have a lot of cash reserves, and even my credit at the bank is stretched to the limit these days so that I can retain an adequate inventory.''

Sarah hesitated, gripping her letter knife tightly in her hands to control their trembling. ''Maybe I could help, then,'' she said slowly. ''I've been saving for a long time to buy a bigger house, Jim. I could postpone my own plans and loan you what I've got, and I'm sure it would be enough for a down payment. And you could pay me back over the years as your business improves.''

Even as she spoke the words Sarah felt a deep stab of pain and sadness, thinking miserably about all her visions of a big, sunny nursery for her baby, a yard to play in and a spacious, comfortable suite for the live-in nanny. It was so hard to see those cherished dreams evaporate before her eyes. Still, she had to think about the three children she had come to love, whose needs were so much more immediate.

But when she looked up at Jim Fleming he was shaking his head, his blue eyes dark with emotion. ''It's great of you to make an offer like that, Sarah, but you must know I could never accept it. I'd sell my business and work at three jobs before I'd clean out your nest egg.''

Sarah nodded, realizing from the taut expression on his face that argument was useless. Suddenly she had another thought, and she glanced up again hopefully. ''Jim...how about your family? Your father, the senator?'' she asked shyly. ''I mean, everybody knows how wealthy he is. It would be a big struggle and sacrifice for either of us to buy a house right now on our own, but surely your father could advance you enough to—''

''Forget it,'' Jim said curtly.

Sarah gazed at him, startled by the sudden chill in his voice and the tense set of his jaw.

''I wouldn't take a cent from him if I was starving to death,'' Jim went on in that same tight, emotionless voice. ''I never have, and I won't start now. Not even for three kids that I love.''

Sarah stared at the handsome blond man across from her.

"Why? I mean, all the papers always describe him as being such a warm, wonderful person. The media seems to adore him."

"Sure," Jim said bitterly. "The media adores him, all right. They never had to live with him."

"I'm just dumbfounded," Sarah said finally, shaking her head. "I had no idea there was such a deep rift in the Fleming family. How long have you been angry with him?"

"All my life, Sarah. Leave it alone. It has nothing to do with any of this."

"But do you see him?" Sarah persisted. "Do you talk with him?"

"Not if I can help it. I haven't talked to him of my own accord since I was seventeen years old."

Sarah gazed at him, her face drawn with concern. "When did you last see him, Jim?"

"Just before Christmas. He came to my office, like he does every year, trying to pressure me into coming out to the ranch for Christmas."

"And you refused him?" Sarah asked. "He came to make peace and you turned him away? Is that what happened, Jim?"

Jim's blue eyes glinted dangerously. "Look, Sarah, I told you. This is none of your business, and it has nothing to do with anything. How I feel about my father is my own concern. Leave it alone."

"I loved my father so much," Sarah murmured, gazing past Jim without really seeing him. "I just adored him. I'd give anything to see him one more time, just talk to him for an hour. But I never will. And *you*—" she turned to Jim, her gray eyes stormy with emotion "—you have a father who comes to seek you out, begs you to make things right between you, and you turn him away."

"There are a lot of things you don't know about my situation and my life."

"Oh, certainly. Everybody's life is like that. But there are things I *do* know about, too, like compromise and forgiveness and compassion."

They stared at each other for a long moment, eyes locked in charged intensity. Finally Jim forced himself to smile.

"Okay," he muttered. "I'm sorry if I upset you, Sarah. You're right, I came here partly for your help and advice, and I shouldn't be angry with you for offering it when you don't understand the whole situation. The fact is, I just can't go to my father, and I don't want any help from him. I'll work this out somehow without causing the kids any more anxiety or disruption than I can help."

Sarah nodded, feeling awkward and uncomfortable under his frank, steady gaze.

"Actually," Jim went on, "I also came here for another reason. Maude and the kids and I are going cross-country skiing next Sunday, and we wondered if you'd like to come along."

"Me?" Sarah asked blankly.

"Sure. Why not? Do you have a pair of skis? You can rent some if you don't, and it's really easy to learn."

"I know. Actually," Sarah confessed, "I was a competitive skier when I was a teenager."

Jim stared at her. "No kidding? Cross-country?"

"Silver medalist in the Alberta Winter Games about fifteen years ago," Sarah told him with a shy smile.

"Wow! What a lady this is!" Jim looked at her with warm approval, as if their recent emotional exchange had never happened, and Sarah felt herself relaxing a little.

"So," he said, "how about it? Want to come with us? Come on, Sarah, it'll do you good. Howie says you work about twenty-eight hours a day over here."

"I have a project I'm working on," Sarah murmured. "We're trying to develop a drought-resistant strain of wheat. It's very time-consuming."

"Sure, but you can give yourself the occasional weekend off, can't you?"

Sarah's mind whirled. She felt an urgent panic at the thought of developing a relationship with Jim Fleming, knowing that before too long her body would begin to betray her secret. And if he counted back the months, he could easily put two and two together and realize that the child she carried was his own.

Sarah shuddered, thinking about how instantly and firmly this man had bonded with three children the first time he ever saw then. What might he be like where his own flesh and blood was involved? And what would be the legal ramifications of some kind of custody battle with him over the care and upbringing of the child nestled in her womb? At that thought Sarah's throat tightened and she felt herself curl protectively around her child, ready to do battle for her absolute right to her own baby.

"Sarah?" Jim asked, watching her face with a touch of anxiety. "Are you all right?"

Sarah gazed at him blankly, her mind still surging with thoughts and emotions. Sternly she forced herself to deal with all this logically.

First, Jim Fleming knew her name and where she worked. He could find her anytime he wanted, and he probably would, so there was no real way to avoid him. Second, he had no knowledge of her real reason for going to the bar that night. He probably still thought she was an attractive but lonely woman who picked men up occasionally when she felt the urge. If she did nothing to correct this impression, then when her pregnancy started to show, she could argue that the father might be any number of men, and he would have no way to disprove it, certainly no right to lay claim to the child.

In fact, avoiding his company, especially when they all knew how much she cared about the three children, would actually look more suspicious than a casual acceptance of his invitation, wouldn't it?

"All right," she said at last. "Did you say everybody's going? Doesn't Maude have to stay home and look after Arthur?"

"Arthur's going, too. My secretary at the office has a baby ski sled, and I'm going to pull it."

"Oh, my goodness," Sarah said. "We'll have to make sure he's bundled up."

"You should see his snowsuit," Jim said cheerfully. "He looks like an astronaut. Arthur could crawl around on the moon in complete safety in that snowsuit."

Sarah laughed. Suddenly, in spite of all her misgivings, she felt a surge of pleasurable anticipation. "It's been so long since I've been up to the ski hill," she said wistfully. "Years, I guess. I used to love it so much."

"Well," Jim said, his eyes sparkling, "I have to warn you that we won't be functioning at silver medalist level, my girl. It'll be the first time on skis for Ellie and Billy, and Maude's improving, but she's still no ball of fire, she says."

"How about you?" Sarah asked, giving him a teasing glance. "As a skier, are you a pretty good football player, Jim Fleming?"

Jim drew himself up with mock outrage. "I'm a pretty good skier, you arrogant woman. Although," he added with a grin, "I've never pulled a baby sled before. That could slow me down a little."

He got to his feet and moved toward the door, reaching for his jacket while Sarah pushed her chair back and followed him. "We'll be leaving about noon," Jim said, smiling down at her. "Do you want me to pick you up?"

"No, I'll come to your place. You'll be loaded down with skis and poles, to say nothing of the baby sled. We should go out to the ski hill in two cars, anyhow, just to have room enough for everybody."

"Okay," Jim said. He gave her an intent, meaningful gaze. "It's going to be so good having you with us, Sarah. I can hardly wait."

Sarah gazed up at him, shivering all at once in the grip of another distressing flood of emotion. She was standing casually beside him in her office, but her mind was reliving the night of their passionate lovemaking, the warmth and silken fire of their naked bodies together, the glorious, sweet abandon of her own response.

Horrified at her lack of control, she stared into his blue eyes, helpless in the grip of this flood of feeling, remembering the sweetness of those sculpted lips on hers, the feel of his hands caressing her body, the rich sensation of him moving and surging within her.

Sarah turned aside hastily, murmuring something incoherent. Jim regarded her thoughtfully for a moment, smiled, patted her cheek gently, then turned to leave.

Long after he was gone the room seemed to retain the golden aura of his tall, handsome body and his sunny, vibrant personality. Sarah wandered back to sit behind her desk, her mind still whirling as she stared in bemused silence at the door through which he had vanished.

CHAPTER EIGHT

ARTHUR RODE SMOOTHLY along the snow-covered track in his padded sled, warmly bundled in a silvery gray snowsuit with fur trim and a voluminous red woolen scarf. Only his eyes were visible, round and bright with astonishment as he surveyed the unfamiliar and wondrous things that skimmed past him.

By the side of the trail, fir trees stood draped and bowed in soft white snow, glittering shapes against the deep blue of the sky. Shrubbery etched with lacy shawls of frost lined the edge of the path, and rock faces shone with frozen waterfalls.

Other skiers passed them on the trail, smiling at the little family group and beaming on Arthur, who waved back at them solemnly with tiny red-mittened hands. One group had a dog with them that looked like a collie crossed with a shepherd. To Arthur's delight, the dog paused to snuffle at his face before racing ahead to its master.

Jim paused frequently to check the baby in the sled. Every time he did Arthur registered intense impatience with the cessation of movement and made imperious demands for Jim to get back to work at once. The big man skied easily along the trail, with the sled snugly belted to his waist harness. His powerful stroke was hardly affected by the extra weight, and he had to hold himself in check, even with his added burden, to match the pace of the rest of the group. Maude skied beside Jim, also keeping a cautious eye on Arthur who chuckled and wriggled with delight every time he caught sight of her plump, smiling face.

Billy, however, had shown an instant affinity for the sport

and already scorned their slower pace. The boy had vanished somewhere up ahead, but dropped back every few minutes to scoff at them mercilessly for their lack of speed.

Just ahead of Jim and Maude, Ellie floundered valiantly along, falling often, laughing and shaking snow out of her hair, her face rosy with cold and happiness. Sarah was with her, patiently helping her back to her feet, teaching the child how to hold her poles and balance on her skis, how to glide and stroke and establish smooth forward momentum.

Jim idled comfortably along beside Maude, half listening to her cheerful comments while his eyes rested thoughtfully on the bright figures of the dark-haired woman and the little blond girl in front of him.

Sarah wore a one-piece fitted ski suit, bright pink trimmed with white, the dainty shell earrings that Ellie had made for her and a wide pink knitted headband that fitted smoothly under her long, dark plait of hair. The vibrant color accentuated the loveliness of her complexion, while the ski suit hugged her shapely body, showing to perfection her narrow waist, her slender, rounded hips and long legs.

She was so beautiful, Jim thought, that no man could take his eyes off her. In fact, every man who passed them on the trail turned to give Sarah a second and even a third glance, although she was so absorbed in Ellie that she didn't even notice.

And her body was so graceful and elegant on skis—it wasn't surprising that she had at one time in her life been a championship-level athlete in this sport. Even now, after years away from it, she had relaxed instinctively into the rhythm and strength of a smooth, easy diagonal stride, and her slow pace and preoccupation with Ellie couldn't hide her skill.

Jim fretted suddenly at all the conventions and responsibilities that bound them. He wished passionately that he and Sarah could just be alone, skimming shoulder to shoulder down the trail and through the woods, free to fly and soar, to talk together and laugh and learn about each other, to kiss in the sunshine and fall in love.

Suddenly he caught himself and forced his wandering mind back into check, distressed by the turn his thoughts were taking. For one thing, all the responsibilities that now burdened him had been his own choice, and he certainly wouldn't be much of a man if he decided to back away from them as soon as they became a little oppressive. And besides, Sarah had never given him the slightest indication, apart from that one passionate night of lovemaking, that she had any kind of romantic interest in him at all. They had the children in common and nothing else, that was her clear message.

But she was so beautiful, and so completely, adorably desirable, and Jim knew he was venturing more and more onto dangerous ground here, especially since he had discovered her identity and learned she wasn't just another bored, rich housewife who sometimes went out pub-crawling in search of adventure. This was a fascinating, brilliant, complex and highly intellectual woman, with strong opinions accompanied by a puzzling and inexplicable shyness that made her even lovelier and more mysterious.

And the night he had held her naked body in his arms she had filled his whole world with sweet, shimmering wonder that shook him to the core every time he thought of it....

"Jim," she called suddenly, pulling him abruptly back to reality, "can you come up here a minute?"

"What's the problem?" he asked, a little abashed by what he had just been recalling. He skied up beside Sarah and Ellie and paused, causing Arthur to hammer on the arms of the baby sled and begin to make muffled noises of outrage beneath his red scarf.

"Arthur!" Sarah said, glancing down at the small, squirming bundle on the sled. "What's the matter?"

"He hates it when I stop," Jim explained. "Lucky for me the kid doesn't have a whip. He'd just lay it on without mercy. Arthur likes speed."

Sarah giggled and Jim smiled at her, delighting in the glow on her beautiful face, the way her eyes shone, the vibrant happiness of her whole shapely body in the bright ski suit.

"You look like you're having a good time," he observed solemnly.

"Oh, Jim," Sarah murmured, closing her eyes in bliss, "this is just heaven. I'd forgotten how much I loved it out here, you know. It's been so long since I've done anything like this."

"Far too long, I'll bet," he said critically. "From now on, Dr. Sarah Burnard, we're going to supervise your social life and see that you get out more for your own good. Right, Ellie?"

Ellie bobbed her head vigorously, but Sarah's smile faded and she looked away in sudden alarm. Jim watched her for a moment, troubled by her expression. Every time he mentioned the future, or made any kind of plans, she got this cautious, guarded look that worried him, as if she was afraid of him for some reason and searching for a way to escape.

Maybe she was just afraid of commitment, Jim thought, although she was certainly deeply committed to her work. Actually, it seemed more as if she was specifically nervous about *him,* for some reason, but he couldn't imagine why. He'd never done anything to threaten her.

"What's the problem, Sarah?" he asked aloud. "Didn't you call me up here for something?"

"I think the binding is loose on Ellie's left ski," Sarah said. "Her boot keeps slipping, and the man at the rental shop showed you how to tighten them, didn't he?"

Jim nodded, bending to examine Ellie's boot while the little girl stood patiently, looking down with interest as he fiddled with the metal bindings. Sarah, meanwhile, knelt by the sled and began to tickle and distract Arthur, who was still complaining bitterly about the delay.

Maude was just down the trail, resting on her poles and chatting with a paunchy man in a sweater and black tights who had approached her from the opposite direction.

"Who was that?" Ellie asked over Jim's shoulder as Maude detached herself from her admirer and rejoined the group.

"Oh, just somebody I know from swimming lessons," Maude said airily.

"Clarence will be jealous," Ellie said with a teasing smile, referring to the smitten doorman in their apartment building.

"Oh, pooh," Maude said, dismissing Clarence's agony with a cheerful wave of her hand. "Arthur, what on earth is all this fuss about? Give poor Jim a minute to rest, you awful baby."

Billy reappeared, skiing back to them on the opposite trail, his thin face alight with excitement. Jim glanced up at him, thinking that he couldn't recall seeing Billy look so relaxed and involved in the family, so much like a normal thirteen-year-old boy. Billy had scorned any type of formal ski wear for this outing, and was still clad in his tattered jeans and jacket. But then, Jim thought with a private grin, most of the other teenagers on the trail were dressed exactly the same, so Billy certainly wasn't conspicuous in his shabbiness.

"Hey, hurry *up,* you guys!" the boy shouted. "There's a totally awesome hill just ahead! I was going about fifty miles an hour by the time I hit the bottom."

"Oh, *great,*" Maude muttered. "Just what I need."

"Now, Maude," Jim said sternly, "you know how much you love to snowplow." Setting Ellie's binding firmly in place, he stood up on his skis, paused to smile down at the little girl and ruffled her hair gently before he pulled his gloves back on. He felt Sarah's eyes resting anxiously on his face and raised an inquiring eyebrow at her.

"The hill, Jim," she said. "Aren't you concerned, with Arthur on the sled? What if you fall or something?"

He smiled. "It's not a bad hill, Sarah. I won't fall. As a matter of fact," he added with a rueful glance over his shoulder, "Arthur will love it. We'll finally be going fast enough for him. Come on, gang!" he added. "Lunch at the warming shed in half an hour."

Jim bent to set his poles, kicked off and watched with satisfaction as his little group spread out beside him, moving off down the trail in the bright winter sunlight.

When you came right down to it, Jim thought with considerable contentment, life wasn't really such a bad deal for a family man. Not such a bad deal at all.

LATER THAT EVENING, when the children were asleep and Maude and Sarah had gone home after a merry take-out dinner of pizza and milk shakes, Jim sat alone in his living room, sipping a glass of white wine and gazing thoughtfully at the dying fire.

He got up to dim the lights, set another log on the glowing embers and moved over to his stereo to select a soft tape of Chopin waltzes, adjusting the rippling strains of music low enough that they wouldn't disturb Arthur in his crib. Glass in hand, Jim paused by the crib to look down at the sleeping baby.

The tall man smiled, his fine, sculpted features softening with affection, his hair glowing dull bronze in the muted light. Asleep, he mused, Arthur was a joy to behold. The baby's plump cheeks were pink, and his thumb, as usual, was firmly tucked into his mouth. He held a soft, woolly rabbit close to his face, its long ears lying softly against his cheek. The baby lay on his stomach, his little rounded posterior raised high into the air, his tiny feet braced to hold him in position.

Jim bent to kiss Arthur's fat neck, sniffing the delightful scent of powder and warm, milky sweetness, then tucked the soft blanket gently up around the little sleeping face and tiptoed back to his chair by the fire.

Still thoughtful, he gazed around the room at the chaos of his apartment. Ellie had been moved into Jim's room and was the only one of them to have complete privacy. Arthur slept in his crib in the corner of the living room while Jim opened out the sofa bed each night. Billy bunked in the kitchen, cramped but uncomplaining in a sleeping bag tossed onto an air mattress on the floor near the sink.

They were managing well enough, but Jim was growing more and more uncomfortable. Particularly on quiet nights like this he found himself longing wistfully for his old life, for the peace and serenity of his solitary tidy home. The crowded apartment always seemed so full of people, of noise and clutter and uproar, and Jim sometimes could hardly remember a time when he'd had his home all to himself.

At least he could get away in the daytime, go to his office where life proceeded in a quiet, orderly fashion just as it always had. Thank God for Maude Willett, Jim thought fervently. Without Maude he'd probably be a nervous wreck by now.

Jim sipped his drink and listened to the music, thinking about the ten days Maude had been away on her skiing holiday, when he was forced to stay all day long in the apartment with the three children. He shuddered, staring gloomily at the fire.

No woman's face, as long as he could remember, had ever looked as beautiful to him as Maude's plump features the morning she had finally reappeared in his doorway with Lancelot in the box under her arm, full of cheerful stories about her vacation.

It wasn't that they were bad kids, Jim thought. And it wouldn't have been necessary to stay with them all that time, either, if he hadn't chosen to. After all, the two older children were both mature and self-sufficient beyond their years and certainly able to care for their baby brother.

But Jim had an uneasy feeling whenever he caught a certain expression on Billy's face that the boy was still poised to escape. Billy didn't trust any of the adults he met, and Jim was certain that at the first opportunity he would pack up the two little ones and flee to a hiding place where he could be sure of keeping them together.

By this time the thought of Ellie and Arthur returning to the kind of setting where he'd first seen them was more than Jim could bear. And yet, in moments of deep honesty, he was able to understand Billy's point of view.

Jim felt himself growing more and more trapped in a desperate and hopeless situation, and he knew Billy was aware of his feelings. Sometimes he sensed the boy staring at him, sizing up Jim's state of mind, trying to judge how much longer it would be before the big man gave in, admitted defeat and turned to the authorities for help.

Jim shifted restlessly in the chair, drained his glass and set it down on the coffee table. Then he leaned back, still frowning, thinking wearily about the problems of providing housing and care for three children, wondering for the thousandth time just what he'd gotten himself into, and what he was going to do about it, and most of all, how he was ever going to find the money he needed to buy a house so the children would be safe and secure.

Despite himself Jim's thoughts turned to Sarah. He remembered her saying that she lived in a house, and that she was alone, and firmly quelled the little glow of speculation that flamed in his mind every time he thought about this. After all, she'd made it very clear that she didn't want the three children living in her house with her, even if Jim shouldered most of the expense.

He was still a little puzzled by her reaction, because she seemed truly fond of the children, and Howie Meyer, who knew her quite well, stated unequivocally that she had few involvements in her life. In fact, Sarah Burnard apparently had no social life at all that anyone knew about.

Maybe, Jim thought, looking ruefully around at the shambles of his living room, she just liked peace and tidiness and wasn't willing to sacrifice her own privacy for a mess like this. And who could blame her? After all, she was a scientist, involved in complex and time-consuming research. No wonder she didn't want to add a lot of complication to her life.

And yet, no matter how often he ran through this line of reasoning, it didn't quite ring true. After all, she had chosen to seek him out after their first encounter, just out of concern for the children. She had bought them gifts, come to see them, expressed a genuine interest in their welfare. In fact, she had even offered her own carefully saved nest egg to help him with his financial problems and give him enough money for a down payment on a house to shelter the three children. That certainly wasn't the act of a self-absorbed and uncaring person.

And when she was with the children, she was loving, warm, tender and deeply involved, especially with Ellie, who adored her.

Jim frowned, his blue eyes narrowing thoughtfully, the firelight glinting on his fine cheekbones.

She was such an enigma, this strange woman called Sarah Burnard.

His thoughts roamed on, wandering through all his mental pictures of her, recalling how appealing she'd looked earlier that day in her bright ski suit, and how elegant she'd been the night they met in her black silk and fur. Jim contrasted those images with the way she'd been when he went to her office, reserved and businesslike in her white lab coat and her heavy glasses. And over all, like a haunting stain of remembered music, was the incredible loveliness of her in his arms, the passion and fire and warmth that still melted his heart and turned his body to jelly even after all this time.

He was assailed by an abrupt longing to hear her voice and looked thoughtfully at the telephone. He had her home number now, extracted from her so that he could call her if he had a problem with the children and needed emergency help when Maude wasn't available. Sarah had been clearly reluctant to give it, but once again her concern for the children had overcome her obvious desire to keep Jim at arm's length.

Jim reached for the phone, wondering what she was doing, picturing her in a dainty lace nightgown, maybe reading in bed with her dark hair in a loose cloud over her bare shoulders the way it had been that night in the hotel bed.

He swallowed hard, feeling weak and shaky with desire, and set down the telephone receiver again. It wasn't fair to take advantage of her by calling the very first night after she gave him the number, especially when he had no problem with the children, no real excuse to bother her.

He'd give it a while.

But, as he stared at the fire and listened to the soft, cascading strains of piano music, he wondered how long he would be able to keep himself away from her.

SARAH SAT CROSS-LEGGED on the braided rug near her hearth, leaning back against the painted carousel horse with Amos in her lap. She wore old gray jogging pants with a heavy pink sweatshirt and socks, and she was brushing the big cat, working delicately on the snarls and tangles that always developed in his long, silky fur, murmuring softly to him to keep him from marching off in a fury of indignation.

"Just relax, you big baby. Look at the mess you're in. If I didn't comb out these tangles, you'd look like a mop. Besides, it doesn't hurt that much. You're just such a..."

She stopped abruptly, her beautiful face pale and drawn. Then she dumped Amos in a heap on the rug, scrambled to her feet and ran for the bathroom. Amos slitted his eyes in outrage and watched when she returned, halting and shaky, pausing in the kitchen to run herself a glass of water and take a couple of soda crackers from a box on the counter.

"I don't know why they call it morning sickness, Amos," she muttered, picking the big cat up again and smiling as he settled himself on her lap with a long-suffering sigh. "I seem to get it worse in the evening, actually. But it's the funniest thing, Amos, you know? I mean, I feel so sick I could die, and then I throw up, and then a few minutes later I'm just fine. Totally spry and chipper again, like nothing ever happened. I've never experienced anything like it."

Amos stretched and luxuriated in her lap, eyes half-closed, kneading his paws against her leg.

Sarah looked down at him and felt a sudden desolate wave of loneliness. She had such a longing these days to talk to somebody about all the wondrous things that were happening to her. She wanted to share the miracle and mystery of birth, but there was nobody in her life to act as confidant. In fact, nobody but her doctor even knew she was pregnant.

Two weeks had passed since the day on the ski hill with Jim and Maude and the children, and in that time Sarah had been back to the apartment twice in the daytime to visit the little ones, but had carefully avoided any further encounter with Jim Fleming.

She realized with gratitude that he was continuing to respect her privacy, and had refrained from calling her even though he'd coaxed her into giving him her phone number. Sarah told herself she was glad he was leaving her alone. After all, if he should become deeply involved in her life now, it would lead to all kinds of complications.

But still, sometimes, she felt so lonely....

In spite of herself Sarah gave a wistful look at the telephone. Just as she did so, it rang, startling her so much that she jumped and dislodged Amos, who gave her a bitter look and stalked away into the kitchen.

"Hello?" she said.

"Hi, Sarah. What are you doing on this snowy night?"

"Jim!" Sarah hesitated, dismayed by the warm glow that crept through her whole body at the sound of his voice. Then she felt a flicker of alarm. "Is something the matter, Jim? Are the kids—?"

"No problem," he said. "Everybody's fine."

Sarah winced as a sudden burst of noise and merriment erupted in the background, sounding clearly along the telephone wire.

"In fact," Jim went on, "there's a bit of a party going on here. Clarence...that's the doorman, remember?"

"The one who has a crush on Maude?"

"Right," he said, chuckling. "Well, he organized a canasta tournament with another couple, just to get close to Maude, I think. They're having it up here at my place."

"I see," Sarah murmured, still distracted by the sweet, wild surge of excitement that tinted her cheeks and made her heart race.

"So," Jim went on casually, "I have a baby-sitter for the evening. Four of them, in fact. They're going to be here for hours."

"I...I see," Sarah whispered again, feeling helpless in the grip of her tumultuous emotions.

"And I wondered if I could come over to see you for a

little while. There's something I'd like to talk over with you, about the kids, actually."

Sarah felt another twinge of alarm, and a sudden, panicky feeling, but suppressed it firmly. "All right," she said after a moment's hesitation. "All right, that's fine. Are you coming right away?"

"If I may? I mean, I'm not interrupting some kind of vital scientific endeavor, am I?"

"I'm combing my cat," Sarah said, and then smiled at his hearty burst of laughter.

"Well, that's interesting. I always wondered what scientists did in their free time," he said. "I'll be right over, okay, Sarah?"

"Okay," she said, and hung up slowly, letting her hand rest gently on the telephone receiver for a long time before she suddenly turned pale and raced for the bathroom again.

Sarah was so preoccupied with recovering her poise and hiding all traces of sickness that she had no time to change her clothes or tidy her hair before the doorbell rang. She hurried to open it and stood gazing mutely up at Jim Fleming, who stood tall and smiling in the porch light, his broad shoulders dusted with snow.

As always, the reality of the man was almost overwhelming, even though Sarah spent a good deal of her time thinking about him. She forced herself to smile, held the door open and murmured, "Hello, Jim. Please come in. It's so cold out, isn't it?"

He grinned and walked past her, shaking out his jacket, smiling at her sweatpants and socks and her long, casual braid. Then he paused, gazing with delight at her living room. The sunken space was cozy and inviting, dimly illuminated by the warm glow of the fire, filled with soft strains of music.

"This," Jim said with a blissful sigh, "is beautiful, Sarah. Just beautiful. I take it you like horses," he added with another warm grin, eyeing her collection.

"My favorite animal," Sarah said, hanging his jacket away. "Would you like coffee or something? Hot chocolate?" she added, trying not to think about food or drink very much and hoping fervently that he would refuse her offer.

"No thanks. This is great. And so quiet and peaceful," he added, seating himself comfortably in one of the padded leather chairs near the fire. "But you're right, after all," he added, looking around.

"About what?" Sarah asked.

"About it being too small for the kids. It's just like a little doll's house, this place. I can see the whole house right from where I'm sitting, can't I?"

"Pretty well," Sarah said, smiling. "And what you see is all there is. No yard, no basement, just this little main floor and a loft."

"What's in the loft?"

"My bedroom," Sarah said, and then flushed warmly as his bright blue eyes met hers. "You said…you said you wanted to talk about the kids?" she ventured, sitting down opposite him and tucking her stockinged feet under her. Amos appeared from the kitchen, gave Jim a slit-eyed look of hatred and leapt into Sarah's lap with an arrogant, proprietorial air.

"Same to you, buddy," Jim told him cheerfully.

"He's a very rude cat," Sarah said. "He's just awful to me, but then he gets jealous if anybody else is even talking to me."

"Well," Jim said, gazing at her lovely, shadowed features, "I can't say I blame him, Sarah."

She flushed and looked down at the cat, toying with his silky fur. Her eyelashes cast dark fans of shadow on her warm cheeks, and her face was delicately tinted by the glow of the fire.

Jim watched her for a moment in silence, drew himself together and said, "I'm in real trouble, Sarah. I don't know what to do."

"About the children, you mean?"

He nodded, gazing into the fire with a brooding expression. "It's the same old story. This is the end of January, Sarah. At best I can only keep them at my place for another few weeks.

I can't find anyone to sublet the place, so I can't get out of my lease, and I can't get a mortgage with those payments to make. If I don't find somewhere for them to live, and find it soon, I don't know what's going to happen."

"But you don't want them to go somewhere temporary and then have to move again, do you?"

"Not if I can help it. God, I wish there was some place...."

Sarah hesitated, still toying idly with Amos's velvety ears.

She wanted passionately to offer her house, but her rational mind knew it was impossible. Her pregnancy seemed much more of a reality to her now that she was suffering from morning sickness. The life within her was a real entity, a living, growing, developing human being that would soon need its own space. It was Sarah's responsibility to protect that space, to provide a comfortable, secure home for her child.

And part of protecting this child involved keeping its existence a secret from the man by the fire. No matter how genial and attractive he might be, he was a threat to her baby. He could turn on Sarah at any moment, lay claim to the baby, demand the right to be a full-time father, to interfere with Sarah's decisions about the child's upbringing, even to sue for custody.

Sarah shivered in the warmth of the small room and felt a familiar, dismaying wave of nausea.

"Ex-excuse me," she muttered in panic, dumped Amos on the floor again and raced for the bathroom.

When she returned, pale and trembling, Jim was watching her in alarm.

"Sarah! Are you all right? What's the matter?"

"Nothing," she said, trying to smile. "Just a touch of the flu that's going around. It's really awful."

"I know," he said, still concerned. "Half my staff has it, and I keep worrying that I'll take it home to the kids, but so far they're just fine."

"Jim," Sarah said after a moment's silence, "may I ask you something?"

"Sure."

"It's about your father," Sarah said, avoiding his eyes, trying to keep her voice casual. "I mean, I know you two are at odds, but I wonder if you'd mind telling me why."

Jim gazed at her, his face cold and grim in the dim light. "He killed my mother," he said abruptly.

Sarah's eyes widened.

"Not like that," Jim said. "I mean, not with a gun or something. But he still killed her, as surely as if he'd taken a weapon to her. He killed her by the way he treated her. She died of a broken heart."

"And how old were you?"

"Thirteen when she died. God," he added softly, "how I hated the old man for that. I'll never stop hating him."

Sarah nodded, chilled by the bitter depths in his blue eyes. "Did you ever talk to him about it? Tell him how you felt, or anything?"

"I have nothing to say to him, Sarah. Please don't talk about him anymore, all right? He has nothing to do with me. Let's change the subject."

Sarah nodded again, falling lightly in with his animated conversation about her collection of horses. But a tiny seed of an idea was growing in her mind, and she determined to examine it more carefully after he was gone.

They spent a long time in front of the fire, talking and laughing, discussing thoughts and dreams and ideas. Sarah, normally so private and withdrawn, was amazed at how easy it was to talk with this man, and how readily she was able to confide in him. He seemed to understand her instantly, almost without words.

But her deepest, sweetest secret she held close to her heart, determined that he would never know. Even if she had to run away for a few months, no matter what she had to do, Sarah was going to keep Jim Fleming from realizing that she carried his child. It was the only way she could guarantee safety and independence for herself and her baby. She still wasn't taken in by his pleasantness and understanding, because her primitive mother instincts kept telling her that he could rapidly become an enemy, a threat to her child, and Sarah wasn't going to allow that to happen. Not ever.

Still, when he finally got up to leave, she felt a tug of regret. She moved over to the door beside him, handed him his jacket and watched in silence as he put it on.

He paused, his hand on the doorknob, looking down at her. Then he reached out, put his hands on her shoulders and drew her close to him. Sarah shivered as his strong arms went around her, and she felt his body straining against hers, felt the warmth of his breath on her skin, felt his lips searching for hers.

She melted into his embrace, helpless and weak, loving the feeling of his nearness, the strength of his hands moving over her body, the warmth as he lifted her shirt and explored her silky naked skin. His hands moved gently around and up her sides, cupping her breasts while his lips roamed over her face, kissing her cheeks, her eyelids, her earlobes, the hollow of her neck.

Sarah felt herself burning, melting, drifting on a warm, rich sea of desire. Her body remembered their union, the sweet thrill of his lovemaking, the wonderful, satisfying fulfillment of him, and she wanted him again, more than anything.

Suddenly another wave of nausea clutched at her. She barely had time to tear herself from his arms and make it down the hall to the bathroom.

When she returned, he was standing by the door with a rueful grin. "I guess that's not so good, right? Are you saying I make you sick, Sarah Burnard?"

Sarah gave him a shaky smile. "Not really," she whispered, unable to meet his eyes.

He watched her in concerned silence for a moment, then reluctantly took his leave, striding down the snowy path under the street lamps.

Sarah stood gazing after him through a crack in the door, her heart pounding, her body gripped with a longing so sudden and intense that she had to bite her lip to keep from crying out.

CHAPTER NINE

IN MID-FEBRUARY a warm chinook wind came howling down out of the mighty Canadian Rockies and danced across the icy plains, melting the snow and warming the sky to sapphire, teasing moisture and freshness from the frozen prairie. Sparkling streams of water flowed though deep coulees into shallow, sunlit lakes, and small snowbound animals appeared miraculously from nowhere, playing and frisking through the tall, damp grass as joyously as if springtime had arrived.

Sarah's mood changed with the weather, becoming buoyant and optimistic, full of hope and delight at the new life within her. Even her morning sickness grew more tolerable. The discomfort didn't actually go away, but it settled into a regular, first-thing-in-the morning kind of occurrence that no longer interfered much with all the activities of her busy day.

On a balmy, breezy Saturday afternoon she drove into the country outside Calgary, delighting at the space and vistas all around her, the land rolling off to the distant mountains and the blue sky soaring into infinity. She felt free and young, so light and joyous that if she were to leave her car and run across the prairie, she might just lift and glide on the warm air currents like an eagle.

But when she turned down a long, tree-lined drive toward a mansion that stood at the end partly obscured by a screen of bare, blackened poplar branches, her mood changed again. She felt tense and breathless, even frightened by what she was about to do.

"Nerves," she muttered aloud, gripping the wheel so tightly that her knuckles whitened. "Pregnant-lady nerves, that's all."

She parked in the curving front drive, trying not to feel intimidated by the looming bulk of the big stone house in front of her, standing silent and withdrawn in the winter sunlight, its glittering leaded-glass windows sheltered by discreet, expensive draperies.

Somewhere in the distance beyond the sprawl of well-kept outbuildings she heard the muffled sound of a dog barking followed by the low, outraged bellow of some large animal, probably a bull. The homely noises were somehow reassuring. Sarah took a deep breath, laced her fingers nervously through the leather strap of her handbag and rang the bell.

After what seemed like a long time, the door was answered and Sarah stood gazing at the beautiful woman on the threshold. She was small and brisk, wearing a faded denim jumpsuit with a large patch on one knee, her vivid graying hair caught up in a careless knot on top of her head. In her arms she held a fluffy golden puppy, which looked up at Sarah with the same expression of cheerful curiosity.

The woman's blue eyes were so much like Jim Fleming's that Sarah was struck speechless, her throat dry and tight. She hesitated awkwardly in the doorway, searching for words.

"Hello?" the woman said politely in a sweet, husky voice. "May I help you?"

"Yes, please," Sarah murmured. "My name is Sarah Burnard, and I'm a...a friend of Jim's. Jim Fleming, I mean. I'd like to...to speak for a moment with Senator Fleming, if I may."

The small woman's beautiful blue eyes widened, and she stood aside, frowning at the puppy that squirmed suddenly in her arms, trying in vain to lick her ear.

"Samson, you *stop* that," she whispered furiously, and then smiled apologetically at Sarah. "He was the runt of the litter," she explained, "and I babied him a lot. I'm afraid he's completely spoiled. I'm Maureen Fleming," she added, extending a small, calloused hand from beneath the puppy. "I'm Jim's aunt."

"I know," Sarah murmured. "He talks about you a lot. He really loves you."

Maureen Fleming's fine features softened, and she smiled. "Please," she said, "come with me to the library. I'll call my brother."

Sarah followed her hostess, still feeling hot and tense, hoping desperately that she wasn't going to be sick. Maureen led her into a comfortable square room lined with books and warmed by a flickering wood fire on the hearth. Sarah sank gratefully into one of the big worn leather chairs and shook her head hastily at the other woman's offer of coffee.

"Oh, no, thank you," she murmured. "I won't be staying long. I just wanted a brief word with Senator Fleming, if he's not too busy."

"Certainly. He's just outside talking with the foreman. He'll be in directly."

After the other woman left, Sarah waited nervously, looking around at the richness of the room in which she found herself. Old polished oak gleamed around the hearth and on the mantel, and small pieces of bronze statuary stood carelessly about. Some of them were horses, and Sarah studied them with a keen collector's eye, knowing that each of them must be worth a small fortune. Many of the books were calf-bound and looked much read. One paneled wall was empty of books, and the small framed paintings that hung there appeared incredibly old and valuable.

There was no doubt, she thought, that Jim Fleming had grown up in great beauty and luxury. She thought of his apartment as she had last seen it—crowded with baby equipment, messy and cluttered with children's toys and piles of clothing. Involuntarily her throat tightened with sympathy.

Just then the door opened and a man entered.

Sarah gripped the arms of the chair and gazed up at him, wide-eyed and startled. She had known about his appearance, of course, from seeing him in pictures, but the reality of the man was so much more impressive. And Senator Jameson Fleming was the image of his son. He not only looked like

Jim, he *was* Jim, miraculously recaptured from some time in the future. He had the same wide shoulders and tall, sturdy build, the same fine, aquiline features and astonishing blue eyes, the same firm jaw softened by that charming, incongruous dimple.

Sarah was assailed by a sudden almost suffocating sense of family, of dynasties and legacies and physical continuity. She realized that this was precisely what she had most feared, the sense of powerful connectedness between father and son and the child in her womb. She had been terrified of the wealth and influence of these people, their sense of family, their possible and quite legitimate claim to her own child.

And yet now here she was in the man's home, having sought him out of her own free will. The whole thing made no sense. Why was she here? Sarah shook her head, trying to clear her thoughts, trying to organize her scattered impressions.

She realized in dismay that the man who looked so much like Jim was still standing near his desk, regarding her with a look of courteous inquiry. Sarah forced herself to meet those piercing blue eyes, feeling faint and confused. Jameson Fleming brought with him an aura of freshness and outdoors, a clean scent of hay and animals. He wore high polished riding boots, worn to a silky sheen, and soft faded denims, and looked every inch the gentleman farmer. Arching one dark eyebrow, he extended a finely shaped brown hand and smiled politely.

"Miss Burnard? My sister tells me you're acquainted with my son, but I doubt that he's aware of your visit here."

"No," Sarah murmured, watching as the senator moved around the desk to seat himself in a high-backed oaken chair. "No, Jim doesn't know I've come to see you. He'd be…very upset if he knew."

Jameson Fleming smiled dryly, but when he met her eyes Sarah was struck by the bleak pain in those vivid blue depths.

The older man's glance was so revealing, so eloquent in its

unspoken suffering, that Sarah began to recover her poise and concern herself more with the man opposite the desk.

"Jim's in trouble," she said briefly, and wasn't surprised to see an expression of instant alarm on the senator's craggy features. His eyes widened, and Sarah hastened to reassure him.

"Not like that," she said. "I mean, he's not sick or in trouble with the police or anything. But he has a real problem, and none of us has any idea how to deal with it."

Senator Fleming listened in silence, toying with a paperweight made of a huge gold nugget set in black onyx, while Sarah told him about the three children, about Jim's impulsive acquisition of them and his subsequent struggle to keep them together and provide a home for them.

The man across the desk looked so intelligent and sympathetic, so full of humor and understanding, that Sarah found herself telling him a good deal more than she had intended, although, of course, she carefully omitted any mention of the reason she had been with Jim Fleming on that particular evening. After she finished her story, she waited in silence, looking awkwardly at the polished expanse of wood between them.

Finally she glanced up at Jameson, who shook his head and gave her a rueful grin. "I must say I'm completely amazed by what you're saying," he told her slowly. "I just can't believe it's my son you're talking about. The boy I remember was much too self-absorbed to inconvenience himself by becoming involved in the problems of a trio of abandoned children."

"That's just it," Sarah said earnestly, leaning forward. "He's not the boy you remember any longer, Senator Fleming. He's a man well past thirty, and he's probably changed in a lot of ways over the years. And," she added, shocked by her own boldness, "I wouldn't be surprised to learn that you've changed a good deal, too. I think it's likely that both of you have."

She paused, holding her breath while the man's face tightened and looked grim, his blue eyes turning to ice. Then, surprisingly, he smiled.

"You think so, do you? Well, you may be right. You're an interesting young lady, Miss Burnard. I certainly applaud my son's taste in women."

Sarah flushed painfully. "I'm not…it's not like that," she said. "There's nothing romantic between Jim and me, Senator Fleming. We're just friends, and even that is entirely because of the children. And I came to see you today because I wanted…to understand the situation a little better, that's all."

"Does my son want my help with these children?" the senator asked bluntly, his gaze direct and disconcerting. "Is that what this is all about? Does he want me to give him the money to provide them with adequate housing?"

Sarah looked back at him, once again a little intimidated by the man's overwhelming air of power and command, the instinctive authority of his manner.

"No," she said. "To be honest, that was my suggestion, but Jim rejects it absolutely."

Once more she saw that flare of pain, that deep, deep hurt in the man's surprising blue eyes. Sarah drew a long breath.

"What happened, sir?" she asked softly. "What really happened between you and your son all those years ago?"

The senator raked her with a sharp glance and then turned his chair a little to look out the window at the rolling acres of his small holding.

"What answer does Jim give to that question?" he asked.

"He says you made his mother very unhappy," Sarah answered quietly. "He says he can never forgive you for the way you treated her."

The older man turned back to look steadily at Sarah, his tanned face silent and drawn beneath the shock of silver hair. He nodded silently, and Sarah watched him, waiting for him to speak.

"Cecile was certainly an unhappy woman," Jameson said finally, gazing moodily out the window once more, his eyes dark with memories. "When I was younger, I felt guilty over it, felt that I had failed her somehow, and if I'd been a better man, she would have been happy with me. In later years," he added with a small, bitter smile, "I came to realize that nothing and nobody in the world could have made her happy. But by then, of course, it was much too late."

Sarah stared at him, stunned by the pain on his face, unable to find any words of response.

"I could have forgiven her the scenes and the tantrums, the many, many times she hurt me and embarrassed me in public," Jameson went on. "What I could never forgive was the way she used the boy in her battles with me and turned my own son against me out of spite and selfishness."

"Is that the way it happened?" Sarah asked, her mouth dry. "Is Jim really so mistaken, sir, about what actually happened?"

Jameson Fleming regarded her directly, his face intent and thoughtful. "We all have our own versions of the truth, Miss Burnard, and we see things through our own eyes, usually to our own advantage. As a result, truth is often a very difficult thing to determine. But as far as I am able to understand, and believe me, I've given it many years of thought, what I'm telling you is the truth."

He hesitated, toying with the costly paperweight once more, and then looked up at Sarah as if coming to some kind of decision.

She met his eyes silently, her face white with tension, waiting for him to go on.

"Cecile was beautiful," he said finally, "and a woman of rare charm when she chose to be. She was the kind of woman who knew how to arouse all the protective instincts in any male, including her own son. Jim adored her, and she encouraged him, urged him to side with her, appealed to all the gallantry and idealism of a young adolescent boy, convincing him that he was her only friend and I was an enemy to both of them. He had to bear all the burden of her pain and unhappiness—far too great a burden for a sensitive and impressionable young boy."

Sarah stared at the man opposite her. "Was there...was there nothing you could do?" she whispered finally.

He shook his silver head regretfully. "God knows, I tried. I argued with her, pleaded with her, tried to talk with him, get him away into a more wholesome setting, but the damage was too deep. I was the villain as far as he was concerned, and he came to hate even being in the same room with me."

He fell silent abruptly.

Sarah waited, gazing cautiously at his patrician profile as he stared out the broad windows.

"What happened in the end?" she asked finally.

"She killed herself when Jim was thirteen," the senator said tonelessly. "She took a razor and opened her wrists, making sure that Jim would be the one to find her and the note she left in which she blamed me for everything."

Sarah stared at him, appalled. "But..." she whispered. "But she must have known how awful that would be for a young boy. How could...?"

"How could any normal loving mother do such a thing to her child?" Jameson Fleming echoed bitterly. "Is that what you're asking me, Miss Burnard? Well, believe me, I don't know. I could forgive her everything else, because she really was a terribly troubled and unhappy woman. But I've never been able to forgive that final monstrous act of selfishness and cruelty."

He was silent again, his brown, veined hands trembling slightly against the polished surface of his desk. At last he glanced back up at Sarah, trying to smile. "Once again," he said, "I must try to be fair. I don't believe I'm the villain of the piece, but I'm not totally without blame, Miss Burnard. Much of what Jim says *is* true. I was selfish, I was wrapped up in my career, I neglected my family, I was addicted to my work and I didn't spend as much time with him as I should have when he was small. Those things are absolutely true."

Sarah looked back at him, her gray eyes calm and level. "Those are mistakes, Senator Fleming, that many men make. But in my opinion they're not such terrible crimes that you should be cut out of your son's life for the rest of your days because of them.''

He returned her gaze in startled silence for a moment, and then his face twisted with sudden pain and he looked away abruptly. ''My sister tells me the same thing,'' he murmured, his voice unsteady. ''But you have no idea how good it feels to hear those particular words coming from a woman like you, Miss Burnard, who is also a friend of my son.''

Sarah was silent for a moment, looking down and toying with the strap of her handbag to allow him time to regain his composure.

''You really love him, don't you?'' she said finally, her voice soft. ''I wish he could understand that.''

Jameson Fleming sighed. ''There's never a day goes by that I don't think of him, wonder what my son is doing and if he's well,'' he said simply. ''The most precious, vitally important thing in my life is gone, and I'll never get it back.''

The sadness in his voice, the weary slump to those broad shoulders and the anguish in his blue eyes, so like Jim's, were suddenly more than Sarah could bear.

''There's something I'd like to tell you, Senator Fleming,'' she said, aghast at herself, unable to believe what she was doing. But she knew she couldn't stop herself.

He gave her a questioning glance, clearly struck by the sudden, taut seriousness of her voice.

Sarah drew a deep breath, sat erect clutching her handbag tightly in her lap and looked directly at the older man. ''I'm two months pregnant, Senator. The child I'm carrying is Jim's. It's your grandchild.''

He stared at her, thunderstruck, hope and disbelief both showing plainly on his aristocratic face. But when he spoke his voice was harsh. ''Why have you come here, young lady? What do you want, exactly? Is it money?''

Understanding the emotions that racked him, Sarah was unable to be angry at his words. Quietly she explained what had happened, how she had decided to have a child, chosen Jim

Fleming as the father and managed to get herself pregnant without his knowledge.

Jameson stared at her, astounded. "And he still doesn't know?"

Sarah shook her head.

"But...but why?" he asked, still bewildered. "Why such a calculated, cold-blooded approach? And why my son in particular?"

"I'm a botanical geneticist, Mr. Fleming. I have a doctorate, in fact, and I'm deeply involved in research at the moment. Genetics and heredity are extremely important to me."

His weathered face sparkled with sudden humor and understanding. "And you chose the Flemings as likely genetic specimens. Is that the idea? Good hardy Scots stock?"

"Exactly," Sarah said, smiling back at him.

Jameson Fleming appeared to set aside all of his earlier emotion, throwing his head back and laughing heartily. "Miss Burnard," he said finally, wiping his eyes and chuckling, "you are a rare treat. You are certainly a bright spot in a dull world today."

"I think you'd better call me Sarah," she said calmly. "After all, I'm going to be the mother of your grandchild, aren't I?"

The old man's vivid blue eyes kindled with sudden fire, and he gazed at her, his face taut with feeling once more. "Yes," he whispered finally. "Yes, it seems that you are. Why haven't you told Jim about this, Sarah? Why all the secrecy?"

"I was afraid," she said simply. "I want a baby, more than anything, and I wanted this particular genetic pool for a variety of reasons. But I didn't want Jim or his family to know because I can't bear the thought of anyone making claims on my baby. It's *my* baby," she concluded fiercely, staring at him, her gray eyes blazing. "Nobody else's, just mine. I can't bear the thought of custody battles or joint visitation or that sort of thing. And especially after I saw how involved Jim got with these three children, just after one meeting, I've been so afraid that he might—"

She broke off abruptly, biting her lip and staring down at her hands.

Jameson Fleming gazed thoughtfully at her bent head. "Then, Sarah," he asked softly, "why have you told me? Aren't you afraid of me, too?"

"Yes," she said honestly, looking up to meet his gaze again. "Of course I am. I know how much power and influence you have, and I know I'm taking a big risk by telling you. But I feel—" Her voice broke and then steadied. "I feel so sad for you, Senator Fleming, because of the choice Jim has made, and the way it makes you feel. I just wanted you to know about your grandchild and to make a sort of... agreement with you, I guess."

"What sort of agreement?"

Sarah drew a deep breath. "If you'll promise," she began, "absolutely *promise* not to interfere or ever make any kind of legal claim on my baby or anything like that..."

She paused and cast a questioning glance at the powerful man across the desk. He nodded quietly, waiting for her to go on.

"Under those conditions," Sarah said, "then I would agree to give you regular access to the baby, allow you to be a part of her life. I don't want money from you," she added hastily. "I have a good job, and I'm very secure financially. I can afford to provide comfortably for my child and hire live-in care while I'm working. I guess what I'm saying," she concluded lamely, "is that I just think you deserve the chance to be a grandfather, Senator Fleming."

When she looked up at him, she was deeply moved to see the expression on his rugged face and the tears that gathered in his eyes. He brushed at them impatiently with his hand and struggled to compose himself.

"Sarah Burnard," he murmured finally, "you've made an old man very happy today. I'm afraid you'll never know just how much this means to me."

Sarah swallowed hard, feeling her own eyes begin to sting warmly. She smiled at him in gentle silence, and then remembered something. "Senator," she said warningly, "I still don't want Jim to know about this."

"About what? About your visit to see us or about the baby or what?"

"About anything," Sarah said firmly.

The senator gave her a shrewd glance. "You're a slender, elegant woman, Sarah Burnard. You aren't going to be able to conceal a pregnancy indefinitely. And I understand that you see my son regularly."

Sarah flushed, but met his eyes steadily. "It was just a...a casual sexual encounter that we had," she murmured awkwardly. "What's known as a one-night-stand. He thinks...he believes that I do that sort of thing all the time. There'll be no reason for him to conclude absolutely that this is his child, if I don't tell him."

"Well," Jameson said with a sudden edge of bitterness to his voice, "there's not much likelihood that I'll be telling him, Sarah. I don't even see him from one year to the next."

Sarah got to her feet, looking steadily at the man opposite her. "Then it'll be our secret?"

"Well..." Jameson hesitated. "I *would* like your permission to tell my sister Maureen. She's very discreet," he said with a fond smile, "and this news is going to delight her more than anything in the world."

Sarah paused and then nodded. "Of course, if she promises not to tell Jim. You sister seems like a real darling," she added impulsively.

"She is. She certainly is. This baby of yours," Jameson said with another shining smile, "will have the fondest, most indulgent grandpa and auntie in all the world, Sarah. I can promise you that."

Sarah's eyes misted again, and she smiled back at him. She still felt frightened, apprehensive, deeply shocked by what she had done. She could foresee all kinds of problems and complications in the future, all kinds of repercussions that would inevitably arise from her actions this day.

But, gazing into the joyous depths of the old man's wise

blue eyes, she still knew absolutely that telling him about her baby had been the right thing to do.

NEAR THE END of the following week the weather changed again. The mercury plunged to the bottom of the thermometer and stuck there until well into March, so bitterly cold that the very air seemed to freeze and crack in the blue-white stillness. At night houses stood silent and withdrawn, glowing faintly behind frost-painted windows like fragile shells protecting their occupants from the icy fury of the elements.

Sarah cuddled in an easy chair by her fireplace, frowning through her heavy-rimmed glasses at the enigmatic symbols of the knitting pattern on her lap, trying to remember if "pss" meant "purl second stitch," or "pass slip stitch."

"I think," she said aloud to Amos, who lay spread-eagled in front of the fireplace like a small furry rug, "that it has to refer to the slip stitch, doesn't it? Otherwise how could—"

The doorbell rang and she glanced up blankly, wondering who could possibly be out soliciting on this bitter night. Then, hastily, she jammed the tiny white jacket she was knitting into her bag, folded the pattern book beside it and padded across to answer the door.

Jim Fleming stood there, holding a couple of laden grocery bags, his blond hair gleaming in the light, his big, solid body filling the doorway while the breath came from his mouth in frosty white clouds.

"Jim!" Sarah said, gazing up at him wide-eyed. "What on earth—?"

"God, you look cute in those glasses," he said, smiling down at her fondly. "Have you had your supper yet?"

"Well, not exactly, just a slice of toast a while ago, but I'm not really—"

"Aha! Just as I suspected," he said cheerfully. "You've been looking awfully thin and pale these days, Dr. Burnard, and I've been fairly certain you're working too hard and not getting enough to eat. Let me in, why don't you, before the wine freezes?"

"Does wine freeze?" Sarah asked, standing aside to let him in and watching while he set the bags carefully on the floor, stamped the snow from his boots and stripped off his heavy down-filled jacket.

"I don't know. I would assume that it does. You're the scientist," he said, picking up his bags again. "Where's the kitchen?"

Sarah gazed at him, still confused by his sudden arrival and the way his big body and his golden masculinity filled her whole house with light and warmth. Her heart began to pound, and she struggled to sound cool and collected.

"May I ask," she said dryly, "just what you think you're doing?"

"You may," he said equably, following her toward the kitchen. "I'm visiting for the evening, and I propose to make you the best omelet you've ever tasted and force you to eat every bite of it. I hope you have a microwave."

"Why?" Sarah asked, still a little stunned by his presence and his cheery air of command.

"Because, dummy," Jim said, setting his bags carefully on the shining kitchen counter, "a microwave is the best thing that's happened to the omelet since the egg. You don't have to flip it, you see. It just cooks through smoothly and perfectly, top to bottom, and makes the chef look extremely professional. I trust you have basic tools like whisks and spatulas? Or is this place just equipped with Bunsen burners and petri dishes?"

Sarah chuckled in spite of herself, showing him her well-stocked cutlery drawer and then watching with interest while he unpacked brown eggs, fresh mushrooms, cheddar cheese, romaine lettuce, a thick loaf of fragrant garlic bread.

Her mouth began to water, and she realized with a little shock of surprise that she hadn't experienced any morning sickness for several days now, and that she was, in fact, ravenously hungry.

"That all looks so good, Jim," she said with a little sigh.

"You're right. I haven't been eating much lately, and I'm just starved all of a sudden."

Jim smiled down at her and bent casually to kiss her cheek. Sarah's face flamed at the warmth and spontaneity of his unexpected gesture. She seated herself awkwardly on one of the kitchen stools, looking at the assortment of groceries.

"Just give me a few minutes, my pretty lady," he said cheerfully, "and I'll serve you a repast worthy of the princess that you are."

"You're so corny," she said automatically, feeling absurdly pleased by his words and suddenly deeply happy to be with him. "How did you get away?"

"You mean," he asked, glancing up from where he knelt before an open cupboard, "why am I not baby-sitting tonight and tending to my responsibilities? Do you have a metal mixing bowl, by the way?"

"Next door over, lower shelf. Yes, that's what I mean. I thought you said last week that Billy was getting rather edgy and you were afraid to leave the kids alone for a minute these days."

Jim found the bowl, placed it on the counter and began to break eggs into it, his handsome face darkening with concern.

"He is. He's getting really tense and nervous, knowing how much hassle I'm having finding a place to live in, and I'm scared what he might do." Jim paused in his vigorous whisking of the eggs, added some seasoning salt and looked up at Sarah, his blue eyes troubled. "That place didn't work out," he told her. "The one I was hoping for, remember? There were no schools nearby, and I hated the thought of Ellie riding for an hour on some damn bus. Besides, it was just as cramped and ugly as all the others."

"Oh, Jim," Sarah murmured. "I'm sorry to hear that. I know how much you were counting on it."

She watched as he took a heavy cast-iron skillet from the drawer under the stove, set it on the burner, tossed in a pat of butter and began to slice mushrooms with casual expertise.

"What now?" she asked finally. "What will you do?"

He shrugged. "Not much choice. No place that's halfway decent will take kids, and if they do, there's a six-month waiting list. As soon as I get back, we're moving into a motel with a kitchen and we'll just wait until something comes up."

Sarah absorbed this information in silence and then looked up, startled. "Get back? Are you going away? Where are you going?"

Once again his face glowed with fondness and he reached out to pat her cheek. "For a bright girl," he observed, "you're really quite slow sometimes, you know that? Yes," he added, slicing green onions in with his mushrooms, "I'm going away. To Europe, as a matter of fact. I hope you like onions."

"Love them," Sarah said absently, still watching his skillful brown hands. "Why are you going to Europe?"

"On a buying trip," he said briskly. "You wouldn't believe it, kid. Athletic clothing these days is as haute couture as evening wear. I have to buy running shoes at fashion houses as fancy as Dior, where they serve little canapés and chilled champagne in crystal goblets."

Sarah giggled at the image, then sobered. "How long will you be gone? When are you leaving?"

"About ten days, and first thing tomorrow morning. That's why I'm able to be here. Maude is staying with the kids, and she moved in today since I'll be up and gone early in the morning. Why do you look so troubled, pretty lady? Don't tell me you're actually going to *miss* me?"

"Of course not," Sarah said firmly. "It's just that all this is going on... I mean, you're moving into a motel, Billy's all upset, you're going away for ten days, and nobody ever tells me anything."

"It's hard to tell somebody anything," Jim said calmly, "when they shut themselves up in a laboratory for eighteen hours a day and refuse to return calls."

Sarah blushed. "I'm sorry, Jim. It's just that we're on the edge of a real breakthrough. We've developed this incredibly hardy strain, with all the right indicators, but we can't seem to get it to—oh," she added, interrupting herself, "that smells just heavenly! I'm so hungry!"

He paused, holding a spatula and looking thoughtfully at her shining face, her huge gray eyes alight with happiness, her slender, shapely body in a casual sweater and slacks. With a visible effort he collected himself and grinned.

"Then why don't you help a bit?" he said with forced lightness. "Make yourself useful, woman. Set the table, and put out some wineglasses. And salad dressing."

Sarah smiled, hurrying to obey, watching hungrily as he slid the fragrant omelet onto a serving dish and carried it to the table along with warmed slices of garlic bread and a hastily tossed salad.

"Do the kids know you're here?" she asked over her shoulder.

"Are you kidding? If they knew I was coming here, nothing on earth would have kept Ellie from coming along. And I wanted to be selfish just this once. I wanted you all to myself for a little while."

Sarah smiled nervously at this, uncertain how to respond, while Jim paused by the table to admire his handiwork.

"I told them I was working late at the office, getting ready for my trip. A harmless lie, right? Now sit down and eat before this omelet caves in and makes me look bad."

Sarah seated herself opposite him, eating the delicious meal with enormous appetite while he looked over at her placidly. Once again she was struck by the ease and pleasure of his company, the way their conversation sparkled and flowed, the comforting manner in which he seemed to understand her instantly and the way he laughed so heartily at all her jokes.

"Come on," he said, lifting his wineglass as they finished their meal. "You haven't touched your wine yet, Dr. Burnard. Doesn't Riesling go with a mushroom omelet? Did I make a bad choice?"

"Oh, no," Sarah said, suddenly nervous. "It's just that I..." She hesitated, casting about for excuses. "It's just that I...I don't drink," she concluded desperately.

"Not at all?"

"No," she said. "Not much at all."

Not when I'm pregnant and entering the second trimester, she added silently. *Not for anything in the world.*

Jim was frowning, his blue eyes thoughtful. "But..." he began, and paused. "But the night I first met you in the bar, weren't you drinking then? I was sure you were nursing a drink most of the evening."

Sarah gazed at him, wide-eyed, searching frantically for a response. Suddenly she felt an almost overwhelming urge to tell him the truth, to tell him all about the baby. "Jim..." she began.

"Yes?"

This was crazy, Sarah thought firmly. All her efforts, ever since that fateful night, had been directed toward keeping her secret, holding him at arm's length. And now, after one pleasant evening, she was considering upsetting months of careful, meticulous planning.

"Thank you for the lovely meal," she said aloud, holding her wineglass up and taking a valiant sip. "Here's to the chef."

He smiled and toasted her silently, then turned to fetch the coffeepot from the counter. While his back was turned Sarah quickly poured the rest of her drink into the potted rubber tree by the table.

Her eyes shone and her cheeks glowed. She was warmed by the fun of their impromptu meal and pleased by the way he deliberately kept things light, tried to keep that disturbing, hard gleam of longing from tightening his face when he looked across the room at her.

They did the dishes together, still easy and companionable, talking about her work and his trip, about the children and the weather and their co-workers, laughing and interrupting each other while they tidied the kitchen.

Sarah found herself growing more and more conscious of him, with a warm, rising excitement and a deep, aching hunger that surprised her. She was sharply aware of his lean, muscular body, his finely molded lips, his firm brown hands. In troubled astonishment she realized that she wanted, more than anything, to feel his arms around her and his lips on hers, craved his touch and the feel of his naked skin burning against hers.

She looked up as they stood in the middle of the kitchen, her lips parted, her eyes full of the emotion she could no longer conceal, and he gazed down at her in wonder.

"Sarah," he whispered. "Oh, Sarah..."

Wordlessly she moved into his arms and clung to him, responding with fiery passion when he lifted her face and sought her lips with his. She didn't seem able to control herself, couldn't keep a check on her emotions, couldn't stop herself from burrowing into him, straining into the core of him, yearning with all her being toward the delicious fire and fulfillment she remembered, and knew that only he could give.

Swept away by her passion, he held her, murmuring broken endearments in her ear, kissing her eyelids, her earlobes, her mouth and neck, pulling her sweater aside to kiss the fragrant hollow of her throat.

Still without words, she drew him gently toward the stairs and began to climb silently up to her room while Jim followed her. His hands still caressed her slender, rounded hips as she mounted the stairs in front of him, and his handsome golden face was taut with passion and desire.

CHAPTER TEN

AT ABOUT THE SAME TIME that Jim and Sarah were finishing their mushroom omelet, Senator Jameson Fleming stood in the doorway of his luxurious living room, smiling at his sister. He was dressed with casual distinction in a tweed sport jacket, slacks and polished boots, topped by a leather coat with a wide silver fox collar. His gray hair shone like dull pewter in the firelight, and his tanned, handsome features were cheerful and composed.

He carried a black leather briefcase in one gloved hand and a giraffe under the other arm. The giraffe was enormous, at least four feet tall, beautifully constructed in a patchwork pattern of soft tan suede and white calfskin, with shining blue eyes, a benign, alert expression and long, flirtatious eyelashes.

"Well, I'm off, Mo," the senator said. "I'm meeting Jock and a couple of others at the Cattlemen's Club. One of them," he added, shifting the giraffe into a more comfortable position, "is apparently interested in supplying some party funding. Jock feels that he could potentially be a big contributor if we handle him just right."

Maureen glanced up from the creamy baby shawl she was working on, crochet hook poised, eyeing him thoughtfully over the gold rims of her granny glasses. "I'm sure," she said dryly, "that they'll all be *very* impressed by the giraffe, Jamie. He's quite lovely."

Jameson shifted nervously on his feet and looked a little defensive. "I'm stopping off at Sarah's on the way to the club," he said. "The other day, when I dropped by the lab to see her, she mentioned that she was ready to begin decorating the nursery soon, and I spotted this fellow yesterday at Abercrombie and Fitch when I was in Edmonton. I just couldn't resist him, Mo. He's handmade, you know, imported from Guatemala.''

Maureen continued to eye her brother thoughtfully, trying to control the little grin that tugged at the corners of her mouth. ''Jamie,'' she said at last, ''don't you think it would be more practical to give her...I don't know...a crib, or something?''

''To *Sarah?* You think she isn't already busy researching the various crib designs, comparing consumer reports, organizing all the scientific data to determine which crib is the safest and most effective? Believe me, Mo, this is a girl who wants to make that kind of decision for herself.''

Maureen nodded, looking down at the soft length of wool on her knees, smoothing it thoughtfully with her calloused fingers. ''I guess you're right,'' she said at last. ''I just...''

''What, Mo?'' her brother asked. ''What's bothering you?''

''I don't know. I just think maybe it's risky, Jamie, you going to her house. What if Jim's there or something? We promised not to give away her secret, and I think we should be very careful to keep that promise as long as she wants us to.''

''I agree. You're absolutely right. But I happen to know that he's not there.''

''How do you know?'' Maureen asked, leaning forward to poke at a blackened, smoldering log that was threatening to roll off the grate.

''I called his apartment, ready with some pretense if he was home. But one of those children answered the phone and said he was working late at the office tonight.''

''Which one?'' Maureen asked wistfully.

''I believe he only has one office, Mo. Do you really like the giraffe?''

''Jamie, that is absolutely without a doubt the most elegant and expensive giraffe that any baby ever received. I *meant,*'' she added, ''which child answered the phone?''

Jameson stared at his sister in surprise. "I don't know which one, Mo. It sounded like a girl."

"Then it would be Ellie," Maureen said with a fond, private smile. "Billy's voice is already changing, getting quite deep."

Jameson continued to regard the small red-haired woman in astonishment while she shifted a little awkwardly under his gaze. "I've gone over to Jim's place a couple of times lately," she said, "just by chance, you know, and the children are always there, at least Ellie and the baby are. Billy comes and goes. You should see them, Jamie," she added, smiling fondly. "They're all such darlings. That fat little baby, so bright and happy, he's just learning to stand alone and reach for things. And Ellie is a lovely child, so sweet and quiet, and she looks after the baby like a real little mother."

Something in her voice, a subtle, hidden note of pain and yearning, made Jameson give her another sharp, thoughtful glance. But when he spoke, his voice was gentle. "You know that you can go there any time you want, Mo. You could get to know those kids, take them places, even bring them here, be a real auntie to them."

Maureen looked up, her blue eyes dark with emotion. "How could I bring them here, Jamie? Jim would never allow it. And as long as he's going to be that way, I know what side I'm going to be on. I don't approve of his attitude, Jamie, and he knows it. We've discussed it many times. And while he persists in treating you as he does, I don't like to involve myself in his life or go to his home when *you're* not welcome. There's such a thing as loyalty, after all."

Jameson looked at her with affection, deeply moved by her words. "There's also such a thing as divided loyalties, Mo," he said. "I know you suffer from this whole situation as much as I do. Believe me, if it brings you pleasure, I'd be happy for you to involve yourself with these little waifs of Jim's. I wouldn't mind at all."

Maureen shook her head sadly. "Not unless he brings them here to see us. But seeing those children, even for a little while, make me realize how terribly much I've missed, Jamie.

I wish I'd been able to have little ones of my own. Sometimes I feel so..."

She choked and looked down, gripping her yarn tightly while she fought to calm herself.

Jameson stood in the doorway, watching her quivering shoulders with helpless concern.

"Anyway," Maureen said, looking up finally and trying to smile as she smoothed her length of crochet work, "we're going to have a baby to play with soon, Jamie. And Jim has no say in the matter at all."

"None at all," Jameson agreed, smiling at her. He turned to go, and Maureen got up to wander over to the window, watching as he backed his big car out of the garage and into the floodlit yard. The giraffe sat in the passenger seat, looking out the window with cheerful alertness, its long, curly eyelashes silhouetted against the frosty moonlight.

The lines of pain and loneliness smoothed from Maureen's face, and she laughed, watching with a fond grin as the elegant, heavy car with its two unlikely occupants circled in front of the house and drove off through the moonlight. Then, still smiling, she returned to her crocheting.

THROUGHOUT THE CITY the same moonlight shone down with impartial radiance on frozen streets and alleys, on snow-covered yards and delicate, frosted shrubbery.

Soft silvery beams filtered through the heavy lace at Sarah's bedroom windows, casting a dappled, shifting glow over the two people on the bed. The room was still and washed with silver, silent except for their breathing and their occasional broken whispers.

Sarah moved above Jim's body, kissing his face and shoulders, lying across him in total abandonment as she felt him move within her, felt his hands caress her body with slow, languorous movements.

She marveled at his iron self-control, almost overcome by his deep, caring tenderness, by his overwhelming concern for her pleasure.

"Jim..." she whispered, eyes closed, face raised toward him.

"Shh," he murmured, holding her, stroking her rounded silken hips. "It's all right, Sarah. It's all right."

"But you're—" Then suddenly she fell silent. Overcome with pleasure she felt herself rising and falling, drowning and gasping in rippling waves of delight, felt herself soaring up to touch the sun and falling back to earth, warmed and sated and rich with joy. Beneath her, Jim, too, shuddered as he finally allowed himself the release he'd held back so long.

"Oh, God," she muttered when she was able to find her voice again. "Oh, my God," she repeated helplessly.

Jim laughed beneath her, still holding her and stroking her gently. With great tenderness he rolled her onto her back and cuddled her beside him, burying his face in her hair and holding her close in his big, hard-muscled arms.

"Do I understand you to say, pretty lady, that you found that a somewhat enjoyable experience?"

"Oh, God," Sarah repeated, still at a loss for words.

Jim chuckled again and raised himself on one elbow, gently tracing the line of her cheek and lips in the moonlight with his finger.

"Maybe you should do this more often, pretty lady," he whispered huskily.

Sarah smiled up at him. "Maybe I should," she whispered back. She regarded him with fondness, overcome by warm emotion. He was so tender, so considerate, such a generous and thoughtful lover, such an altogether loveable man.

"Jim," she whispered suddenly, "I want to talk."

"Sure," he said at once, pulling the bedclothes up and tucking them snugly over her shoulders, then his own. "Go ahead."

"Jim, about the kids... I don't want you to have to take them to a motel. I want you to bring them here."

"But, Sarah..." he began, his eyes widening in surprise.

Sarah reached up tenderly and covered his lips with her fingers. "No, Jim. Don't argue with me about this, because I mean it. You've made so many sacrifices already, and it's time you had some help. I don't want you to be forced to leave your apartment and go live in some shabby, crowded motel just so that they have a place to stay. It's not fair, that's all."

He stared down at her, his eyes dark in the moonlight, his face thoughtful.

"They can come here," Sarah went on, "and Maude can come over during the day to watch them, just like she does at your place, and you can stay in your apartment and have some peace and privacy for a change. And later on when—" Sarah fell abruptly silent, realizing with a little shock of alarm that she had been on the verge of telling him about the baby.

But Jim didn't notice the break in her conversation. He was considering her words, his face dubious. "There's no doubt," he began slowly, "that it would be kind of wonderful to have some peace and privacy at home for a change. I certainly can't deny that. But, Sarah, I don't think you really know what you're giving up. It's a full-time job, kid, and it can be pretty wearing when you come home from work to that kind of chaos. You haven't actually experienced it, you know."

"But you have. That's just what I mean, Jim. You've done your part, and now I think it's my turn for a while. It's only fair. Tell them I'll come over tomorrow," she added, "in the morning after you leave to pick them up. Clarence can help us move their stuff and get them settled in here. He'll do anything if it involves getting to spend a couple of hours with Maude."

Jim was still leaning on one elbow, absently stroking her hair while he thought about what she was saying. "God knows, it's tempting," he said wistfully. "But," he added with a sudden grin, "after a few days of that kind of that kind of uproar, you may not even be speaking to me by the time I get back, Sarah. That's a big risk for me to take. Especially now."

The tender significance in his tone made Sarah flush with sudden warmth and happiness. "I'll still be speaking to you," she whispered, pulling him down toward her and kissing his lips gently. "I promise."

He drew back, smiling, and looked at her, still thoughtful. "Why, Sarah?" he asked suddenly. "Why, just now, do you make this offer? You always resisted any idea of the kids living with you, even though anyone can see how much you love them. It was like...like something was holding you back, something you didn't want to tell me. Why have you suddenly changed your mind?"

Sarah gazed into his eyes, considering, torn by a deep longing to tell him about the child she carried. He was so good, so kind and generous. She knew, with deep, instinctive confidence, that she had been wrong about him. This man wasn't going to cause any problems to her or to her baby. He would just be overjoyed at her news, full of sympathy and eager to help. And once he knew, once he understood about the baby, then they would be able to make more intelligent long-term plans for the care of the other children while considering the needs of their own child, as well.

But, with the stark honesty of her orderly, scientific mind, Sarah knew that rationality and reasoning actually had little to do with her conflict. She yearned to tell him about the baby simply because she wanted him to know, and to share her happiness.

She loved him.

When Sarah finally realized this, fully and completely, it wasn't a blinding revelation like a lightning flash. It was more like a sunrise, creeping with silent radiance above the horizon and flooding her world with light and warmth. She laughed, almost crying with the sheer joy of the moment, her body trembling with happiness.

"Jim," she whispered. "Jim, darling, there's something I have to tell you."

He heard the depths of tenderness in her voice, and his face softened and glowed. He drew her into his arms again, cradling her, kissing her cheeks and hair. "What is it, Sarah?"

he murmured gently. "What did you want to tell me? Because, sweetheart, there's something I want to tell you, too."

Sarah smiled against his chest, thinking how surprised he was going to be, savoring the sweet, rich delight of this special, precious moment.

But before she could say anything the doorbell rang, echoing through the silent lower floor of the house.

They drew apart and looked at each other, their eyes wide and startled.

"Were you expecting anybody?" Jim asked.

"Not a soul," Sarah said. "Not even you, in fact," she added with a smile. She sat up, swinging her legs over the edge of the bed and reaching for her robe as the bell shrilled once more.

"Don't go," Jim protested, grasping the trailing end of her belt. "Just let them go away, darling, and come back to bed. Come on. This is my last night before I have to leave for ten days."

Sarah hesitated, looking down at him, and then shook her head. "I can't, Jim. It might be someone from the lab. We have student assistants on an all-night shift this week, tracking germination rates, and Carl might..." As she spoke, she was tying the belt on her robe, rummaging under the bed for her slippers, running a distracted hand through her hair.

Acknowledging defeat, Jim swung his long body out of bed, stepped hastily into his shorts and jeans and grabbed his shirt, following her down the stairs.

Sarah went to the front door as the bell rang a third time. Jim stood barefoot behind her in the dimness of the foyer, tugging his sweatshirt over his head.

His head emerged and he looked out, grinning cheerfully at the man standing in the pool of light on the threshold.

It was his father.

Jim's smile faded. His chest tightened with amazement and some other emotion, something halfway between shock and outrage, as he stared wordlessly at the other man. His father looked as smug and expensive as ever in his five-hundred-dollar boots and his fur-trimmed leather topcoat. But he was carrying... Jim blinked in utter disbelief.

The old man was carrying a *giraffe!*

Jim frowned, peering at the object under this father's arm as if it just might be an incendiary device or a weapon of some kind. The giraffe smiled blandly back at him, its long, thick eyelashes fluttering in the chill night wind.

"Come in, Senator," Sarah was saying calmly. "We might as well discuss this inside where it's warm. Jim, move over and let your father in."

Blindly Jim obeyed, standing aside while his father passed him in the foyer, maddened even more than usual by the distinctive scent of expensive leather and after-shave that was so uniquely the old man's.

At least, he observed, if it was any satisfaction, his father appeared to be just as dazed and shell-shocked as Jim felt, and was clearly uncomfortable. Besides, he looked completely ridiculous clutching that damn giraffe, which he seemed to have altogether forgotten.

Sarah led them into the living room, switched on a couple of lamps and put a fresh log on the smoldering embers, turning it gently until it burst into a cheery little blaze. Jim sank into a chair opposite his father and watched the calm efficiency of her movements, dazzled in spite of himself by her beauty even in the old terry-cloth robe with her hair tumbled around her face.

His mind whirled with questions, struggling to absorb the crushing impact of his father's unexpected appearance. Wildly he tried to devise scenarios, tried to impose some kind of order on what was happening.

His father had been passing and recognized his car out front, stopped to tell him something, he improvised frantically. Maybe there was something important going on in the family that just couldn't wait, and his father had— He shook his head, holding his bare feet awkwardly toward the warmth of the fire and trying not to look at the man sitting quietly opposite him.

Jim realized what he was attempting to do. He was struggling to arrange things so that it wasn't the way it looked, so that his father and Sarah didn't already know each other. He realized that he couldn't bear the idea of Sarah having some kind of relationship with his father. His mind just refused to absorb the possibility, and he was searching desperately for some other explanation.

But this hope was dashed when Jameson said quietly, "I'm sorry about this, Sarah, believe me. I called Jim's home, and the children told me he was working late at the office tonight. I had no idea he'd be here."

"Well, then," Sarah said with a bleak little smile, sinking down on the couch and tucking her feet nervously beneath her, "this is just what he gets for telling lies to children, I guess."

"Look," Jim burst out abruptly, addressing himself to Sarah because he was still unable to look at his father. "Look, just quit talking about me as if I'm not here, or as if I'm six years old, okay? And tell me what's going on, please."

"Jim," the senator began, his deep voice low and concerned. "Son, please don't—"

"Not you!" Jim said harshly, casting a brief, bitter glance at the older man. "I want Sarah to tell me what's going on. I don't have anything to say to you."

His father's hand tightened on the plump leather body of the giraffe.

"It's all right, Jameson," Sarah said quietly. "I'll talk to him. He had to find out soon, anyway. In fact, I was about to tell him."

"Tell me *what?*" Jim shouted. "Goddamn it, tell me *what?*"

He was almost beside himself with outrage and frustration. But even in his agitation he was able to realize that what tormented him the most was the easy air of understanding between Sarah and his father, the way they spoke to each other with the casual warmth of old friends.

Jim felt confused, betrayed and nakedly exposed. But most of all he felt concerned for Sarah. The man across the room from him was dangerous and unreliable, a man who had caused untold suffering and damage to another woman Jim had loved. He just couldn't bear to think that Jameson Fleming had somehow gotten close to Sarah, as well, wormed his way into her confidence, made her believe that he was...

"Would you like me to leave, Sarah?" Jameson asked quietly, ignoring Jim's outburst.

"I think it might be best," Sarah said. "I'll talk to Jim." She got up, following the senator's large, sturdy figure to the door. "And I'll call you tomorrow," she promised. "Thank you for stopping by," she added with a bleak smile.

Jameson hesitated awkwardly in the doorway as if about to speak, then nodded and reached for the knob.

"Aren't you forgetting something, Senator?" Jim asked bitterly from his chair near the fire. "You seem to have left your toy behind," he added with cold sarcasm, indicating the big giraffe that stood on the floor near the other chair, gazing at the fire on the hearth with gentle interest, its blue eyes wide and cheerful.

"That's for Sarah, son," Jameson said in the doorway.

"For *Sarah?*" Jim asked. "What does Sarah want with a goddamn toy giraffe? It's horses that Sarah likes, isn't it?"

Jameson looked thoughtfully for a long moment at his son's puzzled, angry expression, then smiled sadly at Sarah, squeezed her hand and let himself silently out the door into the bitter night. Sarah gazed at the closed door, drew a deep breath and came slowly back into the room to stand in front of Jim's chair.

"Jim," she began, "I'm truly sorry that things had to happen this way. Please believe me. And believe, too, that I was about to tell you, I truly was, just before your father arrived."

"Tell me what?" he asked, staring up at her, his blue eyes cold and wary. "For God's sake, Sarah, what is going on here?"

Sarah sank down to kneel beside the chair, her hands folded on his leg, her eyes searching his face with a pleading expression. ''I'm pregnant, Jim,'' she said softly. ''I'm almost into my fourth month. And it's your baby.''

He stared down at her in disbelief, his mind whirling, realizing that of all the things she might have said, these words were absolutely the most shocking and unexpected.

''What did you say?'' he asked numbly. ''What did you just tell me?''

''I told you that I'm pregnant,'' Sarah repeated patiently. ''I got pregnant that night we first slept together, way back before Christmas, at the Kingston Arms.''

He gripped the arms of the chair, his mind still numb with shock, feeling dull and stupid. ''Pregnant,'' he repeated slowly. ''You're pregnant. And you say it's my baby.''

''Yes,'' Sarah murmured. ''Yes, Jim that's right. I didn't want to tell you at first because...''

Jim caught sight of the giraffe, still gazing blandly into the flickering flames. Suddenly the full significance of the expensive child's toy came crashing into his dazed thoughts. ''And—'' he interrupted her, not listening at all, still struggling to get his mind to work properly ''—and the old man knows about it. You told him before you told me. You told my father about the baby.''

He glanced down at her sharply, his eyes flashing cold blue fire while she watched him in silence, still kneeling beside him.

''Right?'' he asked, his voice harsh. ''That's right, isn't it?''

Sarah nodded.

Jim's handsome golden face twisted with pain, but he kept his voice calm and level. ''How long?'' he asked grimly. ''How long has the old man known about this, Sarah?''

''Jim, please, don't—''

''How long?'' he shouted.

''Almost a month,'' Sarah said quietly. ''I went out to the ranch about mid-February, just to meet him and...and hear his side of the story, I guess. I hadn't intended to tell him about the baby—it was the last thing on my mind, actually—but I found that I couldn't stop myself. After I met him, I discovered that I really wanted him to know."

"What are you, Sarah?" Jim asked, his voice dangerously quiet. "Are you a fortune hunter, or what? All this 'I'm just an absentminded scientist,' is that all just a front for the devious, plotting mind of a big-time gold digger? Do you want to get into the old man's bank account? It's big enough, God knows," he added bitterly. "It'd certainly be worth your while, although this really seems like a lot of trouble for anyone to be going to."

Sarah looked up at him sadly, too concerned for him to be angered by his words. "Jim," she began, "things aren't always the way they seem, you know."

He ignored her, staring fixedly at the tall leather giraffe still poised so elegantly beside the chair that his father had recently occupied.

"That night in December," he said slowly, "I was right about that, wasn't I, Sarah? You did seek me out for a purpose. It wasn't any kind of casual pickup, was it? You *intended* to get pregnant."

"Yes," Sarah said quietly. She stood up gracefully, crossed the room and sat down opposite him, leaning forward, her voice low and earnest. "Yes, Jim, it was deliberate."

"And you're enough of a scientist," he continued doggedly, "to have it all planned precisely, right? You knew that was an optimum time for you to get pregnant, so you used me for your purpose."

Sarah nodded again, her face composed.

"Why, Sarah?" he asked quietly. "Why me?"

"I remembered you from college," she began, "and I'd followed your career a little in the press. I knew quite a lot about your family background and your father and all, and I—"

She looked up, startled by the cold intensity of his gaze, and faltered briefly, then went on. "I liked the genetic indicators," she concluded finally. "I wanted to have a baby, and there was nobody in my life that I cared about, and I just wanted to ensure the best possible hereditary factors, since I was in a position to choose."

"In a position to choose," he echoed. "So you picked me," he went on, still staring at her with cold disbelief. "You selected me like a goddamn bull in a pen and said, 'I want that one over there. Bring him into the barn.'"

At the pain in his voice Sarah's composure weakened, and she shifted awkwardly in her chair, her face bleak with unhappiness. "It didn't seem like that," she whispered. "Not at the time."

"Sure it didn't," he said bitterly. "Not to *you,* right? Because you're so wrapped up in numbers and figures and genetic charts that you never think about people's feelings, right, Sarah? To you they're all just statistics."

"That's not true!" she burst out, staring at him, her gray eyes huge and dark.

"I'm not just talking about being selected to stand at stud for you, Sarah," he went on, his voice dangerously soft. "Although God knows that's bad enough. But if you cared about me, cared even a tiny bit about my feelings, you would have told me before you told *him.* That was just monstrous of you, Sarah. It was unforgivable."

Sarah bit her lip nervously and gazed at him, her eyes full of appeal. "Jim," she pleaded, "try to look at it from my point of view. I was afraid to tell you about the baby. I didn't want to get involved with you at all, and you know how hard I tried from the very beginning to avoid any kind of further contact."

"So your intention was to just go ahead, have this baby that's half mine and never, ever allow me to know about its existence?"

"Yes," Sarah said. "That's what I intended. I didn't know what you were like," she went on earnestly, "and I didn't want to put you in a position where you could make claims on the baby, try to seize custody or have some input into the child's upbringing. I just wanted to be completely free of you after I conceived, all alone with my baby."

He nodded thoughtfully. "So what went wrong, Sarah? What happened to all these careful plans?"

"Oh, lots of things," Sarah told him with a sad little smile. "The three kids to begin with. I could have turned my back on you at that time, Jim, just as I'd intended, but it was awfully hard to walk away from them. And then there were your father and your Aunt Maureen. I hadn't expected to feel the way I did about them, either, but I've visited them several times since that first weekend, and your father has come to the lab and taken me out to lunch a couple of times, and I find that I'm growing very close to both of them. And," she concluded simply, "I never expected to feel the way I do about you."

"And just how's that?" he murmured, gazing at her fixedly. "How do you feel about me, Sarah?"

I love you, she wanted to shout. *I love you with all my heart and soul the way I never dreamed I could love a man, and just looking at you, my darling, makes me feel all weak and shivery and melting inside, makes me want to—*

"Sarah?" he prompted, still in that same low, dangerous tone. "You haven't answered my question."

She gazed at his bitter face, knowing she couldn't say it, knowing that now wasn't the time to speak of love to him, not while he was so angry.

Instead, she lowered her head and murmured, "I care very deeply about you, Jim. You're a good, kind, generous person, and also a very good friend. I was going to tell you about the baby tonight just because I believe that you deserve to know."

"But I didn't deserve to be the first to know, right?" he asked coldly. "The old man got *that* honor, didn't he, Sarah?"

Sarah stared at him, wide-eyed, appalled by the depths of bitterness in his voice.

"Jim," she whispered, "why do you hate him so much? Tell me why."

"Because he's a monster," Jim said coldly. "A selfish, egotistical, destructive monster."

"How do you know that?" Sarah asked, forcing her voice to stay calm, knowing all too well the crucial importance of this conversation, and the absolute necessity to proceed with caution, to choose her words with extreme care. "Do you know it through your own observations or just because of all the things your mother told you about him?"

"Leave my mother out of this!" he burst out in sudden anguish. "I don't want to talk about my mother!"

"Maybe it's time you did, Jim," Sarah said gently. "She's been dead for over seventeen years, but she's still at the heart of all this, isn't she? Your mother was always the cause of the estrangement between you and your father, right?"

Jim gazed at Sarah's face for a long time, not seeing her, his blue eyes shadowed with thoughts and memories.

"She was so beautiful," he said finally in a low, choked voice. "So beautiful and so sweet when she was happy, laughing and playing with me as if she were just another kid, telling me all kinds of stories and singing to me."

"You said, 'so sweet when she was happy,'" Sarah persisted gently, treading as gingerly as a person picking her way through a swamp full of quicksand pools. "But don't you think there might, just *might* have been another side to her, too, Jim? A different person that she didn't necessarily show to a young son, but that her husband might be aware of? Did you ever think that things might have been a little more complicated than you always thought, that maybe she wasn't entirely the victim or your father completely the villain?"

Jim looked at the earnest face of the woman across the room, hearing her words but not wanting to consider them, not wanting to deal with what she was suggesting.

"Think of it from your father's point of view, Jim," Sarah urged, leaning forward again. "Think of yourself at Billy's age. That's exactly how old you were when she died, Jim, just about the age Billy is now. I want you to visualize it."

Sarah paused and drew a deep breath while Jim watched her in tense silence.

"Imagine that you and I were married, Jim," she went on, "and Billy was our son. Imagine me telling him the kind of things your mother told you, terrible things about you and about our marriage, burdening him with all that information. As a father, think how you might feel. Think how angry you might be about what I was doing to the boy, and how, from an adult point of view, you might fight with me over it and question my motives."

Jim stared at her, his blue eyes wide and strained. Sarah realized that he had never thought of his parents' relationship this way before.

"And the way she died," Sarah hurried on, pressing her advantage when she saw him waver. "Think of that, Jim. Think how selfish an act it really was, to do that to you when you were—"

But, looking into his taut, passionate face, Sarah realized with a little shock of dread that she had gone too far.

"Damn!" he burst out finally, his voice shaking with fury. "You two really had a cozy little chat, didn't you? Talked about everything under the sun, right? Even talked about—" his voice broke, and he dropped his head into his hands, muffling his words "—about how she died."

Sarah looked at his heaving shoulders, her throat tight, aching with love and concern as she thought of the horrors that her words must have unleashed in his mind. But when he raised his face, there was no visible emotion there at all, just a cold, bitter stillness that frightened her. He got to his feet, walked over to the closet and began, slowly and methodically, to put on his jacket and boots.

Sarah watched him in helpless silence, not knowing what to say, bruised by the terrible pain she could feel emanating from him.

"Look," he said slowly, his hand on the doorknob, "I'm going away tomorrow. When I come back, I want it to be over. I know that I can't stop you from having this baby or spending every day with my father if you want to, but I don't want any part of it. I never want to see you again, if that's the choice you're going to make. Do you understand me?"

Sarah nodded, her mind numb with anguish, staring at him with wide, strained eyes.

"And," he continued tonelessly, "I don't want you having anything to do with the kids, either. I certainly don't want you to bring them over here to live the way you were planning."

He gave her a questioning look, and she nodded.

"That's not enough, Sarah," Jim said quietly. "I do have the right, after all, to make certain stipulations regarding the kids. I want you to swear to me that you won't bring them here to live."

"I swear, Jim," Sarah said quietly. "I swear that I won't bring the kids here to live."

Jim watched her face for a moment, then bent his head in acknowledgment, turned and let himself out the door into the night. Sarah wandered to the window, lifted aside the heavy drape and watched him go, her whole body aching with a sorrow so vast that she could scarcely contain all the sadness.

When his car left the curb and he'd driven slowly off into the moonlight, Sarah let the curtain drop, picked up the big giraffe and sank down into an armchair, curling up as if to shield her pain from the world. She hugged the plump, soft body of the giraffe, resting her chin on its back while she gazed with brooding, unseeing eyes at the dying flames on the hearth.

CHAPTER ELEVEN

MAUDE WILLETT STOOD uncertainly in the foyer of Jim's cluttered apartment, looking with some misgivings at the two older children.

"Come on, Maude," Clarence said from the doorway. "Let's go if we're going. I have to go on shift at four, so we'll hardly have time to get down there and get all those groceries back here, especially when the streets are so icy."

Maude nodded absently, barely hearing him. Her gaze turned to Arthur, who stood clinging to the edge of an end table with one chubby fist, stretching his small body toward the inviting lower fronds of a tall, bushy palm in the corner. His other hand just barely missed grasping the trailing greenery, and his small fat face was red with effort and frustration.

"When the baby finally starts walking," Maude said darkly to nobody in particular, "there's going to be hell to pay, let me tell you. Jim's going to have to hire more help full-time just to follow Arthur around and clean up after him."

Neither Ellie nor Billy responded. Ellie was busy at the table, a pencil clutched in her thin hand, writing with great concentration. At Sarah's urging, Jim had enrolled both the children in correspondence school so that they could catch up with their respective age groups before the next school term, and Ellie took her work very seriously, handing in neat, exquisitely detailed assignments.

Billy, on the other hand, disdained the lessons and dashed them off sketchily, if at all. Now, slouched casually in an armchair, he smiled blandly at the two adults over the top of a fishing magazine and then returned to the article he was reading.

Maude glanced at him suspiciously. There was something about Billy today, ever since Jim had left, in fact, something that disturbed her a little, though she couldn't actually put her finger on it.

Maybe, Maude mused, it was just that the boy was being a little *too* cheerful and cooperative, although that idea certainly sounded ridiculous when she thought about it.

Or maybe, she decided, trying to be optimistic, he was just finally coming around, realizing that these really were people who could be trusted and he might as well relax.

"Come *on*, Maude," Clarence urged, interrupting her troubled thoughts. "I'm a busy man, you know. I don't have all day."

"Yeah, right," Maude said with a grin, gathering herself together and starting toward the door. "I know how busy you are, sitting down there all day long playing solitaire and looking so important in your fancy uniform."

Clarence grinned back at her, holding the door open with a flourish.

"We won't be gone more than an hour or so," Maude told the two older children. "Remember now—don't let anybody in, and don't touch the stove, because I've got the oven set to come on automatically. And *watch that baby*," she concluded, glaring at Arthur who was oblivious to everybody else, still thoughtfully measuring the distance between himself and the tall plant. "He's going to get into that thing before long, you know," Maude predicted with deep gloom, "and then there'll be such a mess." Shaking her head, she disappeared through the outer door, and silence fell.

Billy and Ellie looked at each other, and then at the closed door. Billy tossed the magazine aside with contained excitement, walked over and gazed down at the street, watching until Clarence's car pulled away from the curb. The little car with its two gray-haired occupants eased off down the street, fishtailing slightly on the ice, and vanished around the corner. He kept watching, forcing himself to count slowly to one hundred. Finally he turned back to Ellie, his face blazing with purpose.

"Okay, they're gone. Hurry up, El, we only got a little time!"

Ellie sat behind the table and stared at him, her eyes round and full of pain. "Oh, Billy," she whispered, "do we *have* to? Billy, it's so cold...."

The boy's face darkened angrily. "Come *on,* Ellie!" he shouted. "Don't give me all that crap. You know we gotta do this. You know we got no choice. Now come on! You get your stuff and Arthur's, and I'll get the boxes from the storage room."

Ellie's pale face set with quiet stubbornness. "I won't," she said, gripping her pencil and avoiding her brother's eyes. "I don't want to go, Billy. It's so mean to just run off like this."

"Mean?" Billy echoed in disbelief. "You call it *mean* for us to go off and look after ourselves the way we always did before? What's mean about it?"

"Jim will be so sad," Ellie whispered. "When he gets home and we're gone, he'll feel just awful. You know he will."

Billy's eyes flickered momentarily and then hardened again. "Jim won't be mad," the boy said firmly. "He may worry a little, but we'll call him and tell him we're all right after I find us a place to live. I promise you we'll phone him, Ellie. And then, believe me, El, he'll just be glad. All this mess will be gone, and he won't have to go to some little motel with us, and he can have his life just like it used to be before we came along. He'll be glad, Ellie. And you know it."

"I don't think so," Ellie said staunchly. "I think Jim loves us, Billy."

"Oh, sure," Billy said scornfully. "And how much do you think he's going to love us when he has to move away from here next week and live in a motel? He's going to get sick of it pretty fast, Ellie, and then he'll call in the Welfare, and then you know what'll happen. Goodbye Arthur, that's what'll happen."

At this familiar threat Ellie's blue eyes filled with tears, but she continued to shake her head defiantly. "No he won't. Jim would never, ever do that. He cares about us. All of us."

"Ellie," Billy said in the slow, patient tones of an adult dealing with a backward child, "that may be true, but things are getting too hard for Jim. He can't take much more, and when he cracks, we'll be the ones to suffer. Just wait and see."

He crossed the room to stare at his sister, his face passionate with conviction. Ellie stared back at him, wide-eyed and unhappy.

"You know what happened the night just before he left, El," Billy said softly. "That was just the icing on the cake as far as I'm concerned. We gotta get out of here fast."

"I don't think it was so bad that night," Ellie began loyally. "I think maybe he was just sad about having to go away on this trip, that's all."

"Ellie, don't be such a *feeb*, okay? Jim was mad, and you know it. You stayed up on purpose to give him that dumb going-away card you made, and he barely looked at it. He was so mad he could hardly talk to us. Believe me, Ellie, he's getting sick of us. I can tell."

Ellie thought about Billy's words, remembering how cold and distant Jim had been the night before he'd left on his trip, how he'd almost ignored the card she'd spent so much time making.

He'd gone down to work late at the office, catching up before he left on his trip. That was what he'd said. And he'd seemed really happy when he left right after supper, hugging all three of them, joking with Maude and Clarence, kissing Arthur twice on his way out the door. But when he came home, he was tight-lipped and angry, and even though he tried not to show anything, it was easy to see that he felt like yelling at everybody.

Maybe Billy was right. Maybe Jim *was* getting tired of all of them and ready to get rid of them.

She hesitated, still gazing at her brother while a couple of sorrowful tears slipped unheeded down her pale cheeks.

Seeing her waver, Billy pressed his advantage. "The only way we can be safe, El, is to be on our own where they can't find us. And I know just the place. I talked to a guy at the arcade who knows another guy who says— *Jeez! Arthur!*"

This last shout was occasioned by a sudden crashing noise that echoed through the apartment. Both children turned to gaze in horror at the plump baby in his denim overalls, who had succeeded at last in grasping the lower fronds of the palm and pulling the whole tall plant over onto the floor.

The mess was awe-inspiring. There was broken greenery everywhere. Bushels of dirt spilled over the carpet and the goatskin rug, intermingled with the shattered crockery of the big planter. Arthur stood wide-eyed and silent in the midst of it all, amazed and a little frightened by the havoc he had created.

"Well, that does it for sure," Billy muttered. "We gotta get out of here, fast. These people can't stand no more of this crap, Ellie. Believe me, we gotta get *out* of here."

Galvanized by his panic and by the dreadful sight of the huge plant lying flat and broken on the floor, Ellie nodded sadly. She got to her feet and began to move around the room in a troubled, distracted manner, picking up articles and setting them down again.

Billy followed her, barking out instructions. "No toys and stuff, Ellie. Just what we can carry. Just some clothes and things, a few diapers for Arthur, something for him to eat later on today, that's all. Now hurry up while I get the boxes."

Blinking back the tears that stung in her eyes, Ellie put together a little pile of clothes for herself and Arthur, tossed in the baby's soft plastic rabbit and then hesitated in agony between Arthur's beloved activity board and her own shell-craft kit.

"Don't even *think* about it, El," Billy said, returning with a couple of cardboard boxes in his arms. "You gotta carry Arthur, so I have to carry both boxes. We can't take much."

"But, Billy—"

"Just hurry up, will you?" Billy said wearily. "Before

Maude gets back? For God's sake, Ellie, you'd think you *wanted* us to get sent to the Welfare and have Arthur taken away and all."

At his words, something snapped in Ellie. Her face hardened with sudden decision, and she moved rapidly around the room, a cold, distant look about her while she sorted clothes with quiet efficiency.

A few minutes later they were down on the street, the bitter wind tugging at their clothes and stinging their cheeks as they struggled toward the bus stop.

Arthur seemed to have gained a ton in the months they'd lived with Jim. Ellie staggered a little under his weight. He was slippery and hard to hold in his bulky, metallic snowsuit, and he kept wriggling and whimpering, trying to get down.

Beside her Billy plodded along, shivering in his thin jacket and sneakers, his head lowered into the wind, clutching the two heavy boxes. They waited in the little glass shelter at the bus stop where Arthur stood solemnly beside Ellie on the bench, gripping the back with his red-mittened hands and staring at passersby, his eyes round above his scarf.

An older lady with a sweet, wrinkled face looked dubiously at the shabby teenager and well-dressed little girl, the two big cardboard boxes, the solemn baby.

Billy smiled at her blandly. "Our mom's sure gonna be surprised," he observed in an easy, casual tone.

Ellie stared at him while the woman continued to eye them with quiet concern.

"She's doing some volunteer work down at the Goodwill," Billy went on with that same air of cheerful, informative politeness, "and we decided to surprise her. We're taking a bunch of our old toys and clothes and stuff down there to give to the poor kids. She doesn't even know we're coming."

"You're sure she's there right now?" the woman asked. "It's really awfully cold for that baby to be out, you know."

Billy nodded. "She just called," he said smoothly. "She checks on us all the time. She said she'd be coming home around five, so we thought we'd just go down on the bus, surprise her with our stuff and then get a ride home with her later on.''

The woman's face cleared, and she smiled as the bus ground to the curb, its exhaust sending out great clouds of frosty steam into the stillness of the winter afternoon.

''Well,'' she said, ''that's fine, then. It's very sweet of you children to want to share your things with others who are less fortunate.''

Still smiling, she followed them onto the bus, carrying one of the boxes for Billy, who thanked her courteously as he sat down beside Ellie and his baby brother.

Ellie gazed blindly out the big side window of the bus, biting her lip and trying not to cry. She knew all too well what kind of world they were returning to, and she wondered how long it was going to be before any grown-up ever again showed them any trace of kindness or interest.

She lowered Arthur's scarf and kissed his cheek, burying her face briefly in his warmth and sweetness, her eyes bleak. It was starting all over again, the lonely nightmare time that Ellie most dreaded. And knowing what she faced, she didn't really feel frightened or worried or even sad anymore.

She just felt tired…so terribly, awfully tired.

THE MEADOW WAS wide and green, silent and washed in early-morning freshness, starred sweetly with drifts of wildflowers that glowed like rainbows. Jim floated over the fragrant grass, his feet barely touching the ground, his eyes fixed on a little glade in the distance where he could hear the soft ripple of running water and see a silvery glimmer through the trees.

He knew that he was dreaming because the place that he moved through was so ethereal and lovely, pure and far removed from anything of real life. And yet the experience was so vivid, so rich in color and texture that he seemed to be completely inside this magic world, living it with all his consciousness.

His heart began to beat faster as he neared the sheltered glade, knowing who waited for him there. He brushed aside the long, trailing fronds of fern that enclosed the green and secret sun-dappled space, peered through and caught his breath in wonder.

Sarah lay on the grass beside the silver stream of water, smiling up at him, wearing a long, diaphanous gown that seemed to be spun from moonbeams. Through the delicate transparent fabric he could see the beautiful, alluring lines of her body, the radiant, pearl-like glow of her skin and the delicate buds of pink that tipped her breasts.

He knelt beside her, suspended in time and space as dreamers often are, and passed an endless age just caressing her, lifting the silky clinging fabric away to reveal all of her loveliness, gazing down at her in rapt stillness.

Slowly, languidly, he stroked the long, curving lines of her body, cupped and touched her soft, full breasts, bent to kiss her lips, her neck and shoulders, intoxicated by the perfumed fragrance of her skin and the gentle, loving promise in her wide, starry eyes.

At last, somehow, his own clothes seemed to melt away, as well. He lowered himself into her arms and felt himself sinking, falling, drowning endlessly in the silken warmth and sweetness of her, groaning and murmuring her name, knowing that he was lost and rejoicing, wanting to stay forever with her, in her, surrounded by her....

Jim was awakened by his own voice muttering her name brokenly as he thrashed and stirred on the lumpy, unyielding hotel mattress. He groaned again and rolled his aching head on the pillow to gaze blearily at his little bedside clock.

Three o'clock.

Still groggy, Jim lifted himself on one elbow and stared at the clock, trying to remember if it was afternoon or early morning. The deep, dark stillness of the room convinced him that it was still the first hours of the day, and he sank back on the pillows, shivering a little, longing wistfully to close his eyes and lose himself once more in the delicious sweetness of his dream.

But sleep eluded him. He rolled over again on the pillow,

hands behind his head, staring moodily at the shifting patterns of shadow and darkness that washed softly through the heavy drapes muffling the window.

He was still exhausted and disoriented, suffering the effects of jet lag and the need to compress a month of business into a one-week trip. But when he was completely honest with himself, he knew he was suffering most of all not from this trip, but from the events that had happened at home just before he'd left.

Jim winced, recalling his last evening with Sarah, thinking about the things he'd said to her and the way she'd responded.

He remembered the cheerful, casual intimacy of their impromptu dinner, and then the incredible richness of their lovemaking. That night in her bed had been the first time he'd sensed himself really getting close to her. Somehow he'd managed to penetrate her armor of aloofness and reserve. He'd felt her drawing near to him, finally beginning after all those months to trust him and respond to him.

We were just on the verge of a real breakthrough, he thought in anguish. *She was ready to turn to me, to open up a little, even to love me. And I had to ruin everything.*

He turned over again, restless with pain, and buried his head in his arms, trying to block out the memory of how brutally shocked he had been to see his father standing there on Sarah's doorstep, and the things he had said to Sarah afterward.

But his mind worked as efficiently as a movie projector, playing back the whole scene on the backdrop of his memory in steady, relentless sequence.

Jim remembered every expression and nuance, every word his father had said before he left. And then, still shuddering with pain, he went through all the details of his own conversation with Sarah.

The same memory had been haunting him ever since he'd boarded the plane, gritty and restless with lack of sleep, vaguely aware that Maude and the children were distressed by his behavior. He'd been unable to respond to them at all.

But at last, in the chill black silence of the Parisian night, the murky fog of pain and emotion began to dissipate and things became clearer to him. He could see now how unfair he had been to Sarah, and how hard she had tried to show him the truth.

"You were the same age Billy is now, Jim," she'd said earnestly. "I want you to visualize it."

And he could.

He'd never thought of it that way before, never once questioned what his mother had done or whether she might have been wrong in her actions. He had always just loved her so much, believed that he was her only friend, bitterly hated his father for his cruelty to this poor, helpless woman. And yet now, when Sarah insisted that he look at the past from a different point of view, he wasn't so sure about anything.

Jim frowned thoughtfully against the pillow, his golden handsome face drawn and taut in the dim stillness of the little hotel room.

He thought about Billy, about the boy's touching air of bravado, his sturdy attempt to be a man and shoulder all the responsibility of his little family while he was still only a child himself, with a child's terrors and uncertainties.

The memory aroused a tenderness and hurt in Jim that was almost unbearable. He thought of the way he cared so deeply for this proud and touchy boy, longed to lift all those crushing responsibilities from Billy so that the boy would be free to enjoy his own precious and fleeting childhood.

Then, as Sarah had urged, he tried to place himself in his father's position, watching in helpless outrage as a self-absorbed and thoughtless woman heaped a load of terrible pain and pressure on a young boy's frail shoulders, a burden that he was too young to bear and too gallant to refuse.

What his mother had done, including the manner of her death, had been wrong and selfish. Jim knew at last that this was the truth, and that he had realized it as soon as Sarah pointed it out, but refused to accept the fact.

Now he found that he could face it, and the realization no longer caused him the same kind of agony. In fact, it made him feel washed clean, empty and even a little frightened, stripped at last of the bitter anger that had enclosed him and defined his life for so many years.

Sarah was right, after all. There were two sides to every story.

Jim's father had undoubtedly been far from perfect, but he had probably also not been the complete villain Jim had always accused him of being. Jameson Fleming had merely been a troubled man trying to deal with a woman whose insecurity and discontentment had made her spiteful and unhappy, a woman who had managed, even in death, to take from her husband something of great value.

Jim rolled over again and sat up in the rumpled bed, hugging his knees, racked with a painful, visceral need for Sarah's warmth and sweetness, for her laughter and wisdom and the rich beauty of her womanly body in his arms.

He loved her so much. And he wanted her with him right now, today, this morning as the sun rose over Paris. He wanted to stroll with her through the crowded, snowy streets, enjoying the winter sunlight in her hair and the glow of cold on her cheeks. He wanted to take her into exquisite little shops and buy the kind of beautiful jewelry for her that matched her rare and classic loveliness. He wanted to stop at a street vendor's, buy her a hot baked potato, steaming in the frosted air, and laugh as she ate it, her gray eyes sparkling at him over the fluted edge of the paper dish.

Jim moaned softly, aching with need and yearning, and finally allowed himself to explore the last, sweetest, most painful memory of all.

Sarah was pregnant. She was carrying his baby.

The wondrous strangeness of this was almost more than he could bear to contemplate. He thought of her grave, lovely face, her awesome, soaring intelligence that contrasted so delightfully with a sort of childlike simplicity, and the adorable sweetness of her in his arms. He remembered, smiling, the matter-of-fact way she had told him of her plans, of her desire for a child and the way she had set out, all on her own, to achieve her goal.

"I liked the genetic indicators," she had said calmly.

Oh, Sarah. Sarah, my love, my darling...

Still smiling, he thought of the generosity that had prompted Sarah to share her secret with his father and his aunt, despite her own fears for her child. It had been the sweetest, most unselfish thing she could have done, and yet, learning of it, he had made all those wild, bitter accusations.

Jim's smile faded. He was almost crushed by a sudden, urgent need for her, by his overpowering longing to tell her how he adored her, to shield and protect her, to surround her and their child with love and safety and endless security. He glanced at the telephone, yearning to call her, and struggled to remember what time it was back in Alberta.

But at last he shook his head and stretched out on the hard mattress again, pulling the blankets back up to his chin.

He had a lot of fences to mend, and Jim knew that he couldn't do any of it over the telephone. It wasn't just Sarah. There was also the memory of Ellie's sad, crumpled little face when he brushed off the goodbye card she'd made so carefully to show her love....

Jim winced at the memory of the little girl's disappointed expression, which she'd tried so hard to hide, and at the wary, angry look in Billy's eyes. Even Maude had seemed quietly disapproving as she stood and watched him leave in silence.

He needed time to make a proper apology to all of them, not just to Sarah. He needed to stand face-to-face with the people he loved and explain how foolish he'd been, too wrapped up in himself and his own angry memories to think very much about anyone else.

Less than a week, he thought. In just a few more days his plane would touch down in Calgary, and he'd be home, back where he could start undoing all the wrong he'd done. Until then all he could do was wait, try to drown himself in work, to push aside all the thoughts and memories that stabbed him with their sweetness and their pain.

He closed his eyes and felt himself slipping back into sleep. Sarah's sweet gray eyes glowed in the darkness, and he drew close to her, yearning passionately to fall back into his dream, to find once again the green sun-warmed glade where she lay smiling, waiting for him.

SARAH WAS in a green sun-warmed place, but it was a botanical laboratory, not an enchanted glade. The greenery was supplied by endless rows and banks of seedlings sprouting in orderly fashion in trays and wide plastic flats, and the warmth came from a fading winter sun filtering through acres of greenhouse glass.

Sarah leaned over one of the flats, frowning in concentration as she studied a row of little wheat plants. Carl was at her elbow, listening for her murmured observations and noting them carefully on a chart attached to a clipboard.

Sarah finally straightened and turned to her assistant with a little teasing smile. He gazed at her with anxious expectancy.

"Maybe," she said finally, still smiling. "A definite maybe, Carl. That's all I'll give you."

"But, Sarah," he protested. "Look at the numbers, Sarah. Look at the test results. There's no doubt. We've got it this time. We've got it, girl!"

"Maybe," Sarah repeated firmly. "But I want to see a lot more test results first."

Carl's round, freckled face registered extreme agitation. He opened his mouth to speak and then fell silent, looking in surprise at Joelle, the pretty front-desk receptionist, who was approaching hesitantly along one of the damp, leafy aisles.

"Sarah?" she murmured. "I'm sorry to bother you in here while you're working, but there's a phone call for you. It seems really important."

Sarah wiped the sleeve of her lab coat across her damp forehead and smiled at the girl. "It *must* be important, Joelle," she said cheerfully, "for you to come all the way in here. I know how much you hate being in the greenhouse."

Joelle shivered, gazing around her with distaste. "It's all so hot and icky and…and *green*," she muttered. "Who knows what kind of horrible things you scientist types are growing under there? Pods developing into monsters, and all that stuff."

Sarah chuckled. "You watch far too many of those awful science fiction movies on television. Who's calling, Joelle?"

"Oh," Joelle said, turning away from her gloomy examination of the botanical laboratory with its verdant banks of lush and steaming growth. "A woman named Maude. She said you'd know. She said it was an emergency," Joelle added cautiously, glancing at Sarah. "I think maybe she was crying, Sarah."

Sarah stiffened and stared at the girl, her gray eyes wide, her face suddenly white with shock and fear.

"Sarah?" Carl queried, moving hastily toward her, but Sarah wasn't even aware of him.

Jim, she thought wildly. *It's Jim. Something's happened to him. Oh, God, how can I live if something's happened to him?*

Nightmare images beat like dark wings within her mind. She saw his plane banking and slipping, plunging from the sky toward the cold, enclosing waves of the ocean, heard the muffled screams of the people trapped inside the little silver capsule, saw the golden warmth that was Jim Fleming swallowed up in icy, unforgiving blackness, gone forever.

In the searing anguish of the moment Sarah realized at last just how deeply she loved this man. He was the one, the only man for her, now and always. As long as she lived, she would love him. And if she had lost him now, then her love was gone, everything was gone, and she'd never even had the chance to tell him.

She found herself moving along the aisle toward the front office, walking blindly, unaware of the whispers and anxious glances of the laboratory staff workers. All she could think of was the moment when she would pick up the telephone and Maude would tell her what she dreaded to hear.

Joelle punched the call through to one of the executive offices behind the front desk and then closed the door quietly, leaving Sarah alone.

"Maude," she whispered, clutching the telephone receiver so tightly that her fingers ached. "Maude, what is it? Is it Jim? Has he been hurt?"

"No," Maude said, sounding briefly startled. "No, as far as I know, Jim's fine. It's the kids, Sarah."

The relief was so enormous that Sarah couldn't speak at first. She sagged against the desk, her head spinning, feeling weak and giddy with the floods of joy that washed through her.

"Sarah?" Maude said anxiously. "Sarah, are you still there? Have we been cut off?"

Sarah heard the note of panic in Maude's normally cheery voice, and realized that the woman was, as Joelle had said, close to tears.

Instantly contrite, she pulled herself together and forced her voice to sound as normal as possible. "Sorry, Maude," she murmured. "It's just that when they told me you were calling, I was so sure that...that Jim had been hurt or something."

"No, it's the kids," Maude repeated miserably. Sarah finally began to grasp the situation.

"What about them, Maude?" she asked sharply. "What's happened?"

"Oh, Sarah," Maude said, no longer able to control the quaver in her voice. "They're gone, Sarah. I thought there was something strange about Billy today, I truly did, but he's been so nice lately, and Clarence just had a few minutes to take me down for some groceries. It's so much easier when he has the car, and I never dreamed that anything would happen when I was only going to be gone for—"

"Okay, Maude," Sarah said soothingly. "Steady now. Just relax, slow down and tell me what's happened. Nobody's blaming you, dear. You've given so much time, so unselfishly, to help Jim with these kids. Nobody could ever have done more. Now just take a deep breath and tell me where they've gone."

"We don't *know,*" Maude wailed. "Clarence is out now asking around the building to see if anybody's seen them, but I know Billy's too smart for that. He must have had this all planned, and he just took them and ducked out of sight somewhere the first chance he got, and now we'll never, ever find them."

Sarah was silent, listening as Maude sniffled and blew her nose firmly on the other end of the line.

"My poor baby," Maude quavered, coming back on the phone after a moment. "Out there in this awful cold. And poor little Ellie, the darling. She was so happy here, Sarah, reading and doing all her hobbies, having good food to eat and all those nice clothes to wear, looking forward so much to going back to school next term. Sarah, just *think* where they probably are right now. I can't bear it, Sarah."

"We'll find them, Maude," Sarah said automatically, glancing with growing concern at the evening sky, already darkening from a livid sunset glow to black and frosty stillness. "Don't worry. We'll find them right away. Maude," she added, "why do you think this happened just now? What made Billy decide to take off today? Maybe if we knew that, it might give us some clues where to look for them."

"I doubt it," Maude said gloomily. "I think he just decided it was too risky staying here because Jim might be losing interest in them and getting ready to turn them over to the authorities or something."

"But," Sarah began, puzzled, "I don't understand. Why would Billy especially be worrying about that just now? I thought things have been going pretty well between them lately."

"The other night, you know, the night just before Jim left?" Maude began. "Well, he told us he was working late at the office, and Ellie waited up to give him this big going-away card she made for him. She worked on it all day, cutting pictures from magazines of airplanes, the Eiffel Tower, all the things he was going to see, you know?"

Sarah nodded miserably. She knew what Maude's next words were going to be and dreaded hearing them.

"And then when he came home," Maude went on, "it was like he was mad at everybody, you know? He hardly paid any attention to Ellie's card at all, and he snapped at Billy. I could see right then that Billy was starting to think about things."

"What, Maude?" Sarah asked, her mouth dry with fear. "What was Billy thinking?"

"Oh, you know, that Jim was getting tired of them all, upset about having to move out of this place, maybe ready to dump them, just get rid of them. Billy's never had much reason to trust adults, Sarah," Maude added. "I guess it was too much to expect that he could change that quickly."

Sarah nodded again, gazing with growing anxiety at the swirling darkness that gathered beyond the window and the thin columns of frost rising straight up from the chimneys into the icy, brittle night air. It was a brutal night for anyone to be out on the streets, let alone three helpless children, one of them a baby.

And it was mostly her fault, Sarah thought. If she'd just offered her home earlier...if she hadn't let Jim go away angry that night...

"What should we do?" Maude asked, interrupting Sarah's scattered thoughts. "Should I try to call Jim? Should we contact the police, give them a description of the kids?"

Sarah thought rapidly, forcing herself to put aside her emotions and deal logically with the problem at hand. "No, don't do that. I don't think it makes any sense to bother Jim, because there's nothing he can do and chances are we'll find them by tomorrow, anyhow. And I don't want the police involved, either, not at first, anyway. Not till we've had a chance to try on our own."

"But, Sarah," Maude protested, "the police would be able to—"

"Think about it, Maude," Sarah said firmly. "If we notify the police, then they'll know about the kids and their situation. Jim's not even a legal guardian, and besides, he's out of the country. We don't have any assurance that the authorities might not just decide to keep them in their custody when they find them. After all, we can't just lay claim to a group of kids because we happen to like them, as if they were puppies in the pound or something."

Maude began to sniffle again, possibly picturing her beloved Arthur and Ellie trapped in a cage, gazing wistfully through the bars like a pair of homeless little puppies.

"You're right, I guess," she said slowly. "And if that happens, then all Billy's worst fears will have come true, right?"

"Right," Sarah said firmly. "I think you should just stay right there in case they come back, and then we'll have somebody central so we can contact each other. Get Clarence to find anybody he can and start looking downtown, anywhere Billy might be likely to take them, and I'll do the same."

After a few more hasty words of encouragement, Sarah hung up and stood gazing for a moment in bleak unhappiness at the darkened square of window rimmed with frost.

At last, her face pale and tense with misery, she gathered herself together, hurried out of the room and ran down the hall toward her own office to get her coat and her car keys.

FOR THE THIRD TIME in her life Sarah trudged up the stairs to the room that had once been home to Billy, Ellie and Arthur. Again she shuddered at the dismal poverty of the place, the unkempt squalor, the mingled smell of dirt and hopelessness that hung over everything.

The cold was vicious, knifing through the thin, tacky walls of the building, creeping in around poorly fitted doors and broken windows. Even inside on the upper landing Sarah could feel it. She shivered within the enclosing warmth of her heavy duffel coat, pulling her scarf closer around her face.

There was a new lock fitted on the door, a few tattered bits of paper lying outside, other signs of recent occupation. Sarah's heart leaped and began to pound wildly when she heard footsteps shuffling across the floor in answer to her knock. But the door was opened by a thin woman of indeterminate age with ragged, unwashed hair and a pinched, frightened expression.

"Who are you?" the woman whispered in panic, staring at Sarah's expensive coat and boots, her dark hair that shone softly in the glow of the naked light bulb overhead. "What do you want?"

"I'm looking for some children who've run away," Sarah murmured gently, trying not to frighten the woman who stood poised on the splintered threshold like some timid woodland animal.

"Children?" the woman asked blankly. "No kids here 'cept my own," she said. A sudden scream of anger split the musty air inside the room, followed by a heavy thud and a high, fretful wail. "An' God knows," the woman added wearily, "there's times I'd just give them kids away to anybody who asked. I'm sick of 'em tonight, believe me."

At the note of ineffable, hopeless despair in the poor woman's voice Sarah's throat tightened painfully in sympathy. She was about to speak when a man appeared behind the woman, wearing nothing but faded dirty jeans that hung low on his skinny hips. He looked very young, and as weary and desperate as the woman.

"Is she from the Welfare?" he whispered, as if Sarah couldn't hear him. "Does she have the check?"

The woman glanced at him pityingly. "The check don't come for two weeks yet," she said. "An' it's bread an' water for them kids till then, no matter how hungry they get."

Sarah peeped into the room and saw the children in question, a sad little trio ranging in age from six months to about six years, inadequately clothed against the chill and fretful with hunger.

"The children I'm looking for," she said, clearing her throat nervously, "are a boy of thirteen, his sister who's ten, and a baby about a year old. They used to live here in this room," she added by way of explanation. "That's why I came here first. I thought they might have come back."

"They won't likely come back here," the woman said matter-of-factly. ''Not if they know you're lookin' for 'em. Street kids, they know how to stay away from the Welfare if they have to.''

''I'm not from the Welfare,'' Sarah said. ''I'm just an ordinary person who's a friend of these children. I...I love them, and I'd like to find them before they get hurt or something.''

The skinny woman on the threshold examined Sarah's face in thoughtful silence and then smiled wanly, showing small white teeth and a sudden, startling glimmer of the delicate prettiness she must have had just a few years earlier.

''Okay,'' she said. ''If I see them around here, maybe I could call you or something?''

''That would be just wonderful of you,'' Sarah said fervently. She rummaged in her purse and took out a small business card with her phone number. On impulse she opened her wallet, noted with relief that she had recently been to the bank and pressed two hundred dollars into the woman's thin hand.

''Some cash for the telephone,'' she whispered.

''Oh,'' the woman breathed, holding the money up in her shaking fingers so that the man behind her could see it, too. They both gazed in awe as Sarah smiled awkwardly, backed away and started to descend the steps.

All the way down to the street she could feel their eyes burning into her back. The memory of their rapt and wondering faces made her feel like crying.

Sarah stumbled back to her car, unlocked it, climbed behind the wheel and sat silently, trying to control her trembling, trying to think.

She glanced up at the dismal, battered buildings that surrounded her. Shutters banged desolately in the bitter wind, and lights blinked dimly behind torn curtains and window shades. Dark shadows lurked and slithered in the alleys, probably just dogs and cats, Sarah hoped, because it was far too cold, now that night had fallen, for people to be on the streets.

She wondered if Billy and Ellie were huddled in an alley somewhere with Arthur, bent over a little flickering fire in a trash can. Would they know enough to protect Arthur's small cheeks and fingers from frostbite? She thought of Arthur's chubby little hands, his beautiful, tiny, shell-tipped fingers and the dimples at his wrists, and her eyes stung with hot tears.

Surely Billy wouldn't have taken them away in cold weather like this without a place to shelter them. Surely he would be more responsible. And yet Billy was only thirteen and frightened. What if he had just assumed that he would be able to find...?

The endless weary speculations and dark, creeping fears were almost too much to bear. Sarah dropped her head briefly onto the steering wheel, closing her eyes and struggling to block it all out, trying to think logically about nothing but what she had to do next.

After a long time, when the freezing night air began to creep into the little car and chill her body, she raised her head, her eyes enormous and dark with purpose. She put her car into gear, pulled away from the curb and drove slowly along the dirty, deserted street, staring intently into every alley, every doorway, every side street that stretched away beyond her sight, black and forbidding in the chill darkness.

CHAPTER TWELVE

JIM GAZED DOWN through the window of the plane at the dazzling whiteness of the prairie carpeted in snow. He smiled, realizing he was startled by the chill, wintry look of the wide plains beneath him. Accustomed as he was to the changeable extremes of prairie weather, he had half expected, after little more than a week's absence, to find Calgary sunning itself in balmy breezes, lush and warm under a cloudless blue sky amid the first flowers of spring.

But this wasn't the case, not at all. As soon as Jim stepped from the plane, the cold bit into him, seeming even more icy and penetrating than when he had left. And there was an ominous edge to the wind, a threatening, rising whine as it snarled around the buildings and rows of grounded planes on the broad airport grounds. Jim hurried through the terminal, casting a glance through the wide bank of windows at a mass of gray clouds brooding low and dark along the ridge of mountains.

Something terrible was coming, he thought, probably one of the vicious spring blizzards that could strike so suddenly and harshly on the Canadian plains. He thought longingly of his own comfortable little apartment, cozy and warm with its cheery clutter of children and toys. Even their clutter seemed appealing today, after more than a week away from them.

He retrieved his luggage and bundled it into a waiting cab, still thinking longingly about all the people who waited for him in this city, people who had in such a short time grown incredibly dear to him. He gave the cab driver his address and rested his head briefly against the back of the seat, allowing himself, now that he was so close to her, to dream a little about Sarah. He pictured her home with its beautiful sunken living room, the fire glowing on the hearth, the dainty carousel horse poised elegantly nearby, and Sarah warm and sweet in his arms, smiling and kissing him while the storm raged outside.

"Here we are," the cabbie said. "Looks like this weather is getting ugly," he added cheerfully as Jim wrestled his luggage out onto the sidewalk and peeled off a couple of bills.

"I don't care," Jim told him with a grin. "I'd still rather be here than anywhere else in the world."

"Well, you must be crazy, man," the cabbie observed, still cheerful. "Me, I'd rather be anywhere else *but* here."

Still grinning, Jim hurried across the lobby and up to his own floor, fitting the key into the lock with a hand so anxious that his fingers shook a little.

When he stepped inside, the absolute stillness assaulted him like a physical blow and made him almost unsteady on his feet for a second. He felt a clutch of apprehension and fought against it, moving cautiously through the foyer, pausing to hang his tweed topcoat away in the closet.

The silence wasn't just that of a place temporarily unoccupied. It was the deep, settled quietness of a place where nobody had lived for a long time.

Jim stood in the entrance to the living room, staring around, his face white with shock.

The room looked exactly as it had back before Christmas, before Sarah and the three children had ever entered his life. There was no trace of them anywhere, not even a discarded toy or a stray sock. The room was gleaming clean, freshly dusted and almost clinically neat.

Jim moved hesitantly across the living room and into the kitchen, holding his breath, and then edged back out into the other room again.

Everything that had anything to do with the children had been removed. The crib, the changing table, the box where Ellie kept her lessons and her shellcraft kit, Billy's fishing gear and magazines—everything was gone.

Jim's heart began to beat heavily with growing alarm. He looked desperately around the room for something, anything, that would give him a clue about what had happened to them. But all he noticed was a tiny difference in the big palm in the corner, something vaguely strange and puzzling.

Jim moved closer to examine the plant, certain that it was new. The old palm had been taller, the leaves a paler green with less prominent veins. He stared intently at the planter. This was unfamiliar, too, a rough terra-cotta with a frieze of stylized horses painted around its wide lip.

Still gazing at the planter, Jim smiled wistfully, thinking that it looked like something Sarah would like. Suddenly the smile froze on his lips, and he bent closer to examine the big piece of pottery. He was certain, now that he thought of it, that he had seen this same planter at Sarah's house, sitting with a couple of other pots on the tiles at the entry to her living room.

He knelt and ran an absent hand over the little painted row of horses, trying to force his tired mind to work, to sort out this situation and determine what must have happened.

Maybe one of the kids had done something really out of line and the patience of the other tenants had finally snapped. Maybe Maude and Sarah had been told to move the children out of the building immediately and they had packed them up in a hurry and taken them, along with all their things, over to Sarah's house.

Jim nodded in relief and stood up, still gazing thoughtfully at the beautiful rounded lines of the earthenware planter. He remembered forcing Sarah to promise that she wouldn't take the children to her house, and shook his head angrily, cursing himself for being such a blind and arrogant fool.

Taut with anxiety, he went over to the telephone and dialed Sarah's home number. The phone shrilled again and again before he finally gave up and replaced the receiver.

All right, he told himself silently, trying to be calm. Steady now.

He struggled to develop a likely scenario. Maybe the kids

weren't at Sarah's. After all, before he'd left on his trip he had required her to swear that she wouldn't take them to her house, and Sarah was a woman who was likely to honor her word no matter who extracted the promise or under what circumstances.

Once more Jim shook his head at his own obtuse foolishness. He picked up the telephone again, this time calling Sarah's office number. But the receptionist told him with her usual dispassionate courtesy that Dr. Burnard was out of the facility for the day delivering a guest lecture at a nearby college, couldn't possibly be located until much later in the afternoon and would return his call as soon as she was back.

Jim responded with a polite murmur, smiling bitterly at the phone as he hung up.

"Oh, sure," he muttered aloud. "*Sure* she will. We all know when Dr. Burnard is going to start returning her calls, don't we? When wheat grows on the moon, that's when."

It was heartening to hear a human voice, even his own, disrupting the heavy, enclosing stillness. Jim looked around, wishing he had something that was alive, even a hamster or a bird to talk to. He had never been so lonely.

He sank wearily down on the couch, drew the telephone into his lap and dialed Maude's home number. Again the phone shrilled hopelessly in some far-off silence, but this time Jim felt a little cheered by the lack of response.

"Okay," he said aloud once more, just to hear his own voice again. "Okay, now we're getting somewhere. The kids aren't at Sarah's, but wherever they are we can assume Maude's with them. That's good, right?"

But there was nobody in the deserted apartment to answer his question.

He opened his address book, frowning thoughtfully, and looked up the name of the only other contact he had for Maude, which was her son.

This time, miraculously, a woman answered, sounding warm and cheerful against the gathering violence of the storm outside.

"Mrs. Willett?" Jim said. "This is Jim Fleming. I wonder if you could tell me how to locate your mother-in-law?"

There was a brief silence. "I'm sorry," the woman said cautiously. "Maude's not in the city just now. She's gone to Seattle for a few weeks to visit her daughter, my sister-in-law, that is, who just had a baby."

"Seattle?" Jim repeated numbly. "But...what about the kids?"

There was another brief, charged silence, and Jim hastened to explain himself.

"Look, I'm not sure if you know who I am," he began. "Maude's been helping me to look after these three children, and I've been away in Europe for the past week. I got home just a few minutes ago, and there's no sign of the kids or Maude here at my place. Nothing at all. I just wondered if you might—"

"I'm sorry," the woman interrupted firmly, although Jim thought he could hear, deep in her voice, a note of sympathy. "I really can't say anything about that, Mr. Fleming. Maude just told us that she didn't have the baby-sitting job anymore and she was feeling a little lonely, so she thought she'd fly down to Seattle and spend a few weeks with Bonnie. Her baby was cesarean," the woman's comfortable voice added, "and she's having a real hard time getting back on her feet. Poor Bonnie. I just know she'll be so happy to have her mother there for a while."

Most of these medical and family details went completely over Jim's head. All he knew for certain was that Maude was gone from the city, Sarah was unavailable and the children had disappeared.

He murmured something polite and hung up slowly, staring at the new palm tree in the corner.

"She doesn't have the baby-sitting job anymore," the woman had said.

On a sudden inspiration he grabbed the phone again and called the front desk, but Clarence wasn't on duty. It was one of the newly hired younger men, courteous and anxious to be helpful.

"Children?" the young man said blankly. "I don't think so, sir. I mean, it's an adults-only building. There are no children living here."

"But..." Jim began, and then hesitated. "When will Clarence be on shift?" he asked.

"Clarence is on holidays," the young doorman responded. "I think he's gone to Seattle for a few weeks."

Jim silently acknowledged defeat and hung up, troubled by a mounting tide of fear and tension. Something had clearly happened, possibly something terrible. But there was nothing at all that he could do about it now. He could hardly go out and run around in a blizzard, calling their names. All he could do was wait until Sarah got back to the lab and he was able to find out from her just what was going on.

Feeling hungry all at once, Jim wandered into the kitchen, opened the fridge and rummaged inside, looking for something to make himself a sandwich.

He sat at the table, eating, feeling waves of weariness roll over him. All the euphoria of homecoming had evaporated, leaving him numb with fatigue. He wanted to crawl into bed, pull the covers over his head and sleep the day away until he could see Sarah, get some kind of handle on this situation, figure out what to do. He got up to put his dish in the sink and something caught his eye, a tiny ragged corner of pink behind the big refrigerator.

Jim bent to retrieve it, pulling a square of folded construction paper from where it had lodged between the fridge and the gleaming chrome of the trash can. Suddenly the significance of what he held in his hand dawned on him with harsh clarity.

It was the going-away card that Ellie had made for him.

Jim looked down at the careful printing, the little pictures cut out so meticulously, with so much thought and care. "Have a good time and hurry home, Jim," Ellie had written in her tiny, precise lettering, "because we all love you lots."

His eyes flooded with tears, and he wiped at them unashamedly with the back of his hand, smoothing the crumpled paper between his fingers.

Light-headed and weak with exhaustion, he wandered through the living room again, still carrying his little square of pink paper. He undressed in his bedroom, drew the drapes to muffle the howling of the wind, set the card carefully on the night table where he could see it in the glow of the clock radio and crawled into his bed, dropping like a stone into a dark, bottomless pool of sleep.

SARAH NESTLED on the couch of her living room, an open book beside her, a cup of hot chocolate on the end table next to her, and Amos purring lustily at her feet. She took a little sip of chocolate, lifted out a scoop of melted marshmallow with the spoon, savored it, then picked up her book again. But the print swam in front of her eyes and she set the book aside, drew her knees up and rested her chin on them, gazing at the fire with brooding eyes.

She knew that Jim was back in town, because he had left a couple of messages at her office earlier in the day. But she hadn't returned his calls, simply because she dreaded having to talk to him and still didn't have a clear idea of what she was going to tell him about the children.

Now it was late in the evening, almost time to go to bed, and he hadn't called again. She dreaded the moment when the phone would ring and she would have to pick it up, hear his voice, try to think of something to tell him.

Maybe, she thought hopefully, the storm had gotten so fierce that it already knocked the telephone service out, and she would have a few hours' reprieve.

With this thought, Sarah got off the couch, stepped into her fluffy slippers and wandered over to pull one of the drapes aside and peer out.

The wind shrieked around the eaves of the house, driving gusts of snow that whispered and spattered against the windowpanes and piled in huge, billowing drifts along the roadways and sidewalks. The neighboring houses looked distant and isolated in the storm, looming mistily through the shifting screen of white. Snow was piled around the foundations up to the windows in places so that the houses reminded Sarah of Arthur with his scarf pulled over his face and just his bright eyes peeping out.

The memory made her feel sad and a little lost. She turned away abruptly, let the drape fall and went to pick up her mug, carrying it into the kitchen and rinsing it out carefully before hanging it away in the cupboard. Just as she did so, a bell shrilled through the house, and Sarah jumped a little, thinking it was the telephone, bracing herself for the ordeal to come.

But it wasn't the telephone, she realized almost instantly. It was the doorbell.

Sarah belted her robe tightly around her waist and ran to answer the door, recoiling from the icy blast and the fierce shrieking of the wind around the veranda columns.

Jim shouldered his way into the foyer and took off his sheepskin jacket, handing it to Sarah, who hung it away silently in the closet.

"How did you ever manage to get over here in this storm?" she asked, trying hard to keep her voice casual and conversational.

"With more luck than brains, I'm afraid," Jim said quietly, his handsome face still vivid with cold. "It didn't look so bad at my place when I started out, but the traffic's hardly moving. There are abandoned cars everywhere, some of them blocking the streets. I just kind of slid in here on a wing and a prayer."

"You shouldn't have driven over," Sarah told him severely, terrified as she always was by the thought of something happening to him. "You should have just stayed home and telephoned."

"I didn't want to telephone," Jim said, sitting down by the fire. "I wanted to see you."

Amos roused himself, cast Jim a bitter glance and moved over with an elaborate air of injured dignity to resettle himself near the hearth.

Sarah came hastily across the room and sat down opposite her visitor, drinking in the sight of him. He was so tall and golden and splendid, so masculine and powerful-looking in his jeans and a casual navy blue woolen pullover that accentuated the dull blond gleam of his smooth hair. She studied his face, enjoying all the things she loved the most—the straight aristocratic line of his nose, the startling blue of his eyes, the strong but sensual curve of his lower lip....

"How are you, Sarah?" he asked abruptly. "How have you been?"

"Oh...fine," she began. "Just the same as always, I guess."

"Sarah, where are the kids?"

Sarah trembled a little and looked down, pleating the soft fabric of her belt with nervous fingers. Then she met his eyes, looking at him silently.

"Sarah?" he prompted. "I want to know where they are. You *do* know, don't you?" he added, his face suddenly anxious.

Sarah nodded, her eyes wide and strained.

Jim looked at her in growing surprise, his blue eyes flashing with a sudden, quick flare of impatience.

"What's all this about, Sarah? Are you waiting for me to apologize for my behavior the other night? Well, I apologize. I came here prepared to tell you that you were right and I was wrong. And now I want you to tell me where the kids are so I can go see them, please."

"About what?" Sarah asked, her voice low. "What was I right about?"

"About my father," Jim told her wearily. "I know I behaved badly the other night, and the only excuse I can make for myself is that it was just such a terrible shock to see him here unexpectedly like that, you know?"

He gave her a quick, questioning glance, and she nodded, her gray eyes troubled. "Jim..." she began.

"It's all right, Sarah. Let me finish my apology. I had a lot of time to think while I was away, lying around in those lonely hotel rooms. I know I've been way out of line, and lots of things I've said and done have been wrong. I want you to know that, Sarah,'' he went on earnestly, looking up and meeting her eyes.

Sarah nodded. ''It doesn't matter who's right and who's wrong,'' she began in a low voice. ''All that matters is getting things sorted out in the end so everyone can be happy.''

''I know. And I think I'm well on my way, Sarah. I want you to understand that. I'm getting my mind straightened out, and starting to look at the past from a more adult point of view, thanks to you. I love you, Sarah,'' he added, his voice suddenly low and husky with emotion.

''Oh, Jim...'' Sarah gazed at him, her lips parted, her eyes luminous. ''Then you'll go to your father?'' she asked. ''You'll go and see him and talk things over with him?''

Jim moved restlessly in his chair and looked away again, staring at the fire. ''No,'' he began slowly. ''I don't think so. I mean, there's been too much said and done between us for my father and I ever to be friends, Sarah. I don't actually hate him anymore, but I don't want to be friends with him, either.''

Sarah tensed and sat up straighter, her eyes shadowing. ''He wants to be friends with you, Jim. He wants it more than anything.''

Jim leaned forward, his handsome face taut with emotion. ''Look, Sarah,'' he began, ''don't push me so hard, okay? Don't ask more of me than I can give. I'm willing to admit that he wasn't a complete monster. I'll even admit that my mother wronged him in some ways. But I still remember a lot of things from the past, Sarah, and I can't just set them aside and be pals with him. Maybe I'll go there for Christmas dinner next time he asks, and for Aunt Maureen's birthday—that sort of thing. But I don't want to be drawn back into the fold and play all my father's games again. I just don't.''

''What do you mean, play all his games? Maybe there aren't any games, Jim. Maybe there's just a man who loves his son and wants to be close to him.''

''He was never that simple,'' Jim said stubbornly. ''I'm

trying to be fair, but I still happen to believe, Sarah, that he's never done a single unselfish thing in his life. There's always something in it for him, and I just don't want to get drawn into that world again."

"Oh, Jim." Sarah looked at him sadly, shaking her head. "For a minute there I really thought you were making some progress. And I know that if you'd give him a chance, just go and see him and talk with him, you'd change your point of view, because you're too fair and intelligent not to. But you refuse to bend an inch, don't you?"

"I've already bent enough," Jim said stubbornly. "I've told you I don't blame him altogether, and that sometime in the distant future I might even consider going to his house for a visit. But not right away, and not for any heart-to-heart chats. Forget it, Sarah. It isn't going to happen."

Sarah looked over at him, and their eyes locked in a long moment of silent challenge while the wind shrieked outside and the fire crackled cheerily on the hearth.

"Now for our other business," Jim said, moving restlessly under her level gaze. "Where are the kids, Sarah?"

Sarah continued to look at him, emboldened by the anger she felt at his stubborn refusal to give his father a chance.

"The kids are gone, Jim," she said steadily, "and they won't be coming back."

Jim stared at her, stunned and disbelieving. "What are you saying?"

"They ran away," Sarah said. "Right after you left on your trip, Billy seized the first opportunity he could. Maude went out to get some groceries, and he took the kids and a few clothes and headed back to the streets with them."

Jim continued to gaze at her, his face white with shock. "My God," he whispered. "In this cold?"

Sarah nodded grimly. "It took us two days to find them. They were in a horrible little deserted tenement that was slated for demolition, trying to keep warm with an old hibachi they'd found somewhere."

Jim's face twisted and he searched for words. "Were they...were they all right?"

"They were all starving hungry, and Ellie had a bad cold, just on the edge of pneumonia, but it's better now, and Arthur had a terrible diaper rash. Billy was the worst, with some frostbitten fingers and toes, but he's going to be all right."

"Sarah...why did they run away? Why did Billy do it?"

Sarah looked at him, weighing and measuring his state of mind, wondering how much he could bear. "They were afraid, Jim," she said finally. "The night you left here and went home, and you were so angry, you remember?"

He nodded, numb with sorrow.

"Well," Sarah went on calmly, "they were sure you were upset because of them, getting tired of them and ready to turn to the authorities for help, and Billy felt he just couldn't risk that, so he ran."

"Oh, God." Jim dropped his head into his hands and sat slumped on the couch, his face hidden, while Sarah looked over at him sadly.

"How did you find them?" he asked finally, looking up at the quiet woman opposite him, his face haggard.

Sarah smiled grimly. "It certainly wasn't easy. We didn't want to call the police in, because we didn't want the authorities to know about them if we could help it."

She cast Jim a questioning glance, and he nodded quietly, waiting for her to continue.

"So," Sarah went on, "we had everyone we could think of wandering around those seamy downtown streets in the bitter cold. Maude's entire family, my lab assistants, Clarence's brother, all looking everywhere for two kids with a baby and a couple of cardboard boxes."

"And?" Jim asked tensely when she paused, staring at the fire.

"We were almost ready to give up and call the police for help when I got a phone call from some people I met the first night the kids disappeared."

Sarah went on to tell him about the couple living in the old room the children had once occupied. Jim listened intently, his face unreadable.

"The woman called," she said, "to tell me that her husband had been out looking for the kids all that night and the next day, and he'd heard about a couple of kids seen going into this certain building. Clarence took Maude and me down, and there they were."

"Thank God," Jim murmured fervently. "Thank God, Sarah." He looked up. "I should give them something," he said. "That couple, I should give them some money, Sarah. You say they live in the room where we first found the kids?"

"Not for long," Sarah said with another fleeting smile. "I got them a job, Jim. We needed a night janitor team at the facility, and I asked if they'd be interested. They've been working several nights already, and you should see the job they do. Everything is just shining when they finish. They bring their babies with them and put them to sleep in the waiting room while they work so they don't have to pay child care, and I got them a month's advance on their salary so that they could move to a better place."

Jim looked at her, his eyes full of emotion. "You're a remarkable woman, Sarah," he said quietly. "You seem to have a profound effect on every life you touch."

Sarah shifted awkwardly under his gaze. "Hardly, Jim," she said. "Lots of times I just make mistakes and cause all kinds of problems."

They were both silent for a moment.

"So," Jim said finally, clearing his throat, "where are they now?"

Sarah braced herself, looked up and met his gaze steadily. "I can't tell you, Jim."

His blue eyes widened in disbelief.

"I can't tell you," Sarah repeated quietly. "They're with friends of mine, a professional couple who have no children of their own and live in comfortable circumstances. The kids are happy there. That's all I can tell you."

"But...Sarah, I don't understand. You mean you're not going to let me see them?"

"Not just now," Sarah said. "Not until you've decided to have a talk with your father and give him a chance to tell you his side of the story."

Jim stared at her, his face tightening. "That's blackmail, Sarah. Pure blackmail. My relationship with my father is none of your business, and certainly nothing to do with the kids."

"In a way it is." Sarah took a deep breath and went on with the speech she had been rehearsing all day. "I told you, Jim, that the kids are with friends of mine. I go to see them all the time and have regular contact with them. I want to keep on doing that, but I'm afraid I don't want to have any more contact with *you* until you've repaired the hurts you've caused and restored your own family situation. So I prefer that you don't know where the children are just now. Otherwise you'll go to see them, too, and our paths will be crossing all the time and it'll just be really awkward for everybody concerned."

She stopped, out of breath, and looked away, stung by the hot flare of blue anger in his eyes. "So that's the way it's going to be, is it?" he asked, his voice low and furious. "Either I shape up and do things your way, or I'm cut off from everybody, right? No kids, no Sarah, no baby—nothing."

Sarah nodded, trying to look calm despite the turmoil within her. "That's the way it is, Jim. But I'd prefer to word it differently."

"I see. And how would you word it, Sarah?"

Sarah looked up and met his eyes bravely. "I'd say that the choice is entirely yours. You can do the generous and loving thing, and everything will be fine. Or you can go on being stubborn and selfish, but you'll have to do it all alone."

He stared at her, his glance hardening into dangerous blue fire. "I'm not going to accept this, Sarah. It's been me, not you, who's had full responsibility for those kids for months now, and I intend to go on taking care of them. You can't just step in and push me out like this, because I won't allow it. Tell me where they are, Sarah, right now."

Sarah gazed at him quietly. "The kids are happy and comfortable, Jim. If you truly cared about them, you'd leave them alone for a while to adjust. Besides," she added, "I don't really see what choice you have. Maude is gone, and there's nobody else who can tell you where they are except me. And," she concluded simply, "I certainly don't intend to tell you while you're being like this. You'll just go storming around and cause problems for everybody."

"God, you're a hard woman, Sarah," he murmured, gazing at her. "I just told you a few minutes ago that I'm in love with you. I've been thinking about you ever since I left, longing to see you again, and now I find that unless I do everything just the way you want, you'll go ahead and freeze me out, rob me of everything that matters to me. I just can't believe this."

Sarah was silent, aching at the bitterness in his tone, knowing that if she tried to speak, there was a good chance she wouldn't be able to control her own voice.

"Sarah," Jim went on, leaning forward, his face tight with pain and anger, "do you care about me at all? Do you love me even a little bit? Or is everything just a scientific equation to you?"

Sarah returned his gaze, thinking about the melting sweetness of their lovemaking, of the rich and endless depths of her adoration for this man, of the hungry yearning for him that permeated her whole being through all her waking hours.

"Everything is just a scientific equation to me, Jim," she said.

She stayed on the couch, watched quietly while he got up, crossed the room, pulled on his coat and boots and let himself out into the storm, not even looking back at her as he left.

CHAPTER THIRTEEN

JIM CROUCHED OVER the steering wheel of his car, peering ahead through the screen of white that swirled in a dizzying, wild dance just beyond his windshield. His tires slipped and caught in the hard, rounded drifts banked across the street, and the car was flung sideways occasionally by its own momentum, even though he was barely crawling along through the storm.

The snow was so thick that it took a moment for him to realize that he was no longer moving at all. He got out, hunched deep into his upturned sheepskin collar and waded around by the front fender, seeing the problem at once. Two cars had been abandoned in the middle of the street after a collision. They stood humped and silent under mounds of drifted snow, blocking the whole roadway, with Jim's car wedged solidly up against the rear bumper of the nearest one.

Jim gazed at the scene gloomily for a moment, blinked against the stinging wind and hesitated. Then he locked his car, turned reluctantly and began plowing his way back through the heavy, sculpted drifts toward Sarah's house.

He had come only a few blocks, but by the time he had retraced his steps he was almost frozen, even in his heavy coat. He paused by a street sign, scraped the snow from it and studied the numbers to make sure he wasn't lost, then started trudging wearily up the last block to her house.

While he struggled on into the wind, Jim thought about the recent scene with Sarah, and the fact that he seemed, every time he met her, to go stamping out of her house in a rage. She must think him so childish. No wonder she treated him like that, trying patiently to teach him his manners and manipulating him into doing the right thing, as if he were no older than Billy.

And it *was* the right thing.

He knew that, recognized even through his anger that Sarah was entirely correct in what she said. His father deserved a chance, at least, and Jim was being harsh and unfair by not giving it. But it was just so hard. After all those years of bitterness, all the things he'd said and done, it would almost be impossible to swallow his pride and go hat in hand to make peace, pretending that nothing had ever happened.

Maybe, Jim brooded as he slogged along through the drifted snow, he just wasn't the man for Sarah. Maybe he wasn't good enough, strong enough, forgiving enough. No wonder she didn't love him the way he loved her. No wonder she looked at him all the time with that cool, scientific appraisal instead of the loving, melting warmth and passion that he craved from her.

Like the icy wind that tore at his face, Jim's mood slowly chilled and hardened. He thought of Sarah's refusal to tell him where the children were, her cool assumption that she could force him to do as she wished by withholding that vital information. And his feelings shifted. It was time for him to have it out with her, quit being so easygoing and present her with a few hard facts. He had a case to argue, and he intended to force her to listen to him, no matter what he had to do.

His face tightened with resolve, and his pace quickened as he stumbled forward through the drifted snow.

Soon he was at her door, growing angrier all the time, still without any real idea what he was going to say to her when she answered. Nobody came, and he rang again, wondering if she had gone to bed, if she was asleep already and couldn't hear the bell.

He felt the knob, realizing with a quick twinge of alarm that the door was unlocked. He was almost certain that he'd locked it behind him as he'd left.

Stamping the snow from his boots, he stepped inside into a pool of light in the foyer.

"Sarah!" he shouted furiously, hearing some muffled footsteps from the direction of the kitchen. "Listen, my girl, there's a few things we have to—"

He broke off and stared, his mouth suddenly dry.

Sarah had appeared in the entry to the kitchen. She was as pale as sculpted marble, trembling, clutching her robe around her in shaking hands. Her eyes were wide and vague with anguished depths of emotion.

"Sarah!" Jim said, forgetting all his anger and hurt in a flood of concern. "Sarah, darling, what is it? What's the matter?"

He gathered her into his arms, and she began to sob against his chest, increasing his alarm.

"Sarah," he whispered against her hair. "Sarah, it's all right. It's just me. Did I frighten you?"

She shook her head and leaned back in his arms, looking up at him through her tears with an expression of such abject childlike desolation that he wondered how he could ever have thought her clinical and devoid of feeling.

"Jim," she whispered, "I'm having a miscarriage. I'm losing the baby."

He gripped her shoulders and stared down at her, numb with shock.

"I was going upstairs to bed," she went on tonelessly, "and Amos was with me. He wedged in front of me the way he does, rubbing against my ankles, and I tripped over him and fell sideways on the stairwell. I caught myself on the railing before I went very far, but I twisted my back as I fell, and a few minutes later I realized I was bleeding. Oh, Jim—"

Her voice broke, and she burrowed into his arms again, hiding her face against his chest. Jim held her tenderly, cradling her, feeling the tears burn in his own eyes.

"I'll call the doctor, sweetheart," he murmured. "What's his number?"

Sarah shook her head, sniffling. "I already called. I just

hung up a second ago. His service said he was on the way home from the hospital, and I should try him there, but his wife said he hadn't made it home yet. You know what it's like out, Jim. I went to look out a minute ago, and it's so—"

"Did she have any ideas? Did she mention anybody else we could call?"

Sarah shook her head. "She just said...she said I should lie down, elevate my hips and feet and try to relax, and that she'd have him call or come over as soon as he got home. Oh, Jim," Sarah finished in sudden agony, "I can't bear to lose this baby. I just can't *bear* it!"

"Shh," he whispered, patting her back, kissing her hair and her wet cheeks, tasting the warm, salty tears and aching with sorrow. "First, we're not going to lose this baby, Sarah. We're going to do just what the doctor's wife said. Where do you want to lie down? Should I carry you up to your room?"

Sarah shook her head. "No, I'd rather...I think this is fine," she murmured, looking up at him piteously. "You won't leave again, will you?"

"Oh, darling..." He gazed down at her, aching with sympathy, marveling again that he could ever have thought her cold and unemotional. "No," he whispered. "I'm not leaving again, sweetheart. Not ever. Come on, now."

He lifted her and carried her into the living room, settling her on the couch, covering her with a blanket from the big wooden chest in one corner, and a warm knitted afghan. Finally he hurried into the bathroom, folded up a couple of big bath towels and slipped them under her slender hips, then carefully positioned a cushion beneath her feet.

"Is that comfortable?" he asked, frowning as he studied the position of her body. "Not elevated too much?"

"It's fine," Sarah murmured, trying to smile, her face bleak and full of misery.

Jim knelt beside her, stroking her hair tenderly. "Do you have any pain?"

"Some," she admitted. "Just little crampy pains, nothing major. They come and go."

Jim looked away from her through one of the narrow leaded glass windows by the front door, measuring the strength and fury of the storm. He would have been completely willing to carry her in his arms through the blizzard, all the way to the hospital if necessary. But he knew that it wasn't possible. They were stranded here, and she had nobody else but him. It was up to him, whatever happened, to look after her. His face tightened, and he had to force his jaw muscles to relax before he turned back to her.

"Okay," he said cheerfully. "Now listen up, you stubborn woman. The doctor's wife said you were supposed to take it easy, and that's exactly what I want you to do. Just relax."

He settled himself on the floor beside her, holding her, whispering and murmuring to her as he stroked her hair and gently kneaded her arms and shoulders.

"Sarah," he whispered, "you're so tense. Try to relax. Try to fall asleep."

"Jim, how can I relax? I'm so scared. I'm just so scared."

The telephone rang, muffled and distant through the howling noise of the storm.

Jim ran to answer it, his heart beating crazily in his chest.

"Dr. Ian McLellan here. Who is this?" a hearty male voice asked on the other end.

"Thank God," Jim said fervently. "Dr. McLellan, this is Jim Fleming. I'm here with Sarah. I'm...I'm the baby's father," he said, feeling a little flare of pride at speaking these words for the first time. Then, remembering, he was almost overcome by a terrible, desolate wave of sorrow.

"Well, well," Dr. McLellan said thoughtfully. "I really had no idea *you* were on the scene at all, young man, but I'm certainly glad you're there now. Describe the situation for me."

Jim obeyed, carefully repeating the story Sarah had told him, describing her condition and what he had done for her.

"And you say the bleeding hasn't increased?"

"I don't think so. Not since I came, anyway," Jim said.

"Any pain?"

"Little cramps, she says."

"Hmm," Dr. McLellan said. There was a long pause while Jim gripped the receiver anxiously, staring at the archway leading into the living room.

"Listen, son," the doctor said finally, "there's nothing at all I can do. Even the emergency vehicles aren't getting through tonight, so I'm afraid you're on your own. Now this is what I want you to do. Just keep her warm and try to get her to sleep. Either she's going to miscarry or she isn't, and by morning we should know the score. Give her a couple of drinks," he added. "Good stiff ones."

"Drinks?" Jim echoed blankly. "But...she's pregnant. She won't ever take a drink at all. Not even a sip of wine."

"Good for her," the doctor said approvingly. "Sarah's a smart girl, and she knows what careless alcohol consumption can do to an unborn child, but this is an exceptional circumstance. In cases of premature labor, where there's no other medication available, we often find that a few ounces of alcohol can relax the muscles surrounding the uterus, and sometimes even stop the contractions."

Jim hesitated and the doctor chuckled wryly, a warm, cheerful sound above the howling fury of the blizzard outside.

"Trust me, son," he said. "I'm a doctor."

"MORE ORANGE JUICE?" Sarah asked in dismay, propping herself unsteadily on one elbow. "But, Jim...I just finished a whole glass of orange juice. And half of this one."

"Try to drink another glass," Jim urged, kneeling beside her and holding the glass to her lips.

"But I'm not thirsty," she said piteously, glancing up at him with childlike confusion.

"Come on, Sarah," Jim said. "The doctor said liquids were good for you."

Well, he told himself, that wasn't entirely a lie. The doctor had definitely said *something* like that.

Jim grinned wanly, thinking how lucky he was, just the same, that he'd found that half bottle of vodka in Sarah's cupboard. He was sure, doctor or no doctor, that Sarah would never have taken the orange juice if she could smell or taste what was in it.

"Why?" she was asking, regarding him owlishly with what he recognized as her "scientist look."

"Why what? Here, have another sip."

She gave up and leaned forward to sip obediently at the foaming glass of juice, then looked up at him again with wide-eyed bewilderment. "Why are liquids good for me, Jim?"

Jim floundered, casting about for a plausible answer, remembering how much she knew and how difficult it always was to mislead her. But she wasn't listening anymore. Instead, she was frowning intently at some thought of her own as she traced one hand in the air in slow, dreamy circles.

Dr. Burnard, Jim realized, was getting a little inebriated.

He felt a small stirring of concern, wondering if he might be making the drinks too strong. But the doctor had said "a few ounces," and she hadn't had more than that—just one stiff drink, and now this one.

"Sarah," he said, "did you have any supper?"

She pondered, her eyes narrowing as she tried to remember. "Maybe not," she said finally, and hiccuped.

"What do you mean, maybe not? Either you did or you didn't."

"Can't remember," Sarah said, her voice a little slurred. "Don' think so. Too…" She hiccuped again, then tried to smile at him. "Too scared," she said apologetically.

"Scared? What were you scared of?"

"You," she said simply. "Scared you'd be mad about the kids. And," she added with another sad, smiling glance at him, "sure enough, you were."

Jim forced himself to smile back at her and held the glass for her to sip again. That explained it, he thought. On an empty stomach, and not accustomed to alcohol, it wasn't surprising that she was reacting like this.

She reached out an unsteady hand to stroke his hair. He smiled down at her tenderly, acknowledging to himself that perhaps Dr. Mclellan had been right. At least she seemed much more relaxed now, her cheeks pink, her body limp and flexible.

"Pure gold," she murmured. "Jason's fleece."

"What's that, Sarah?"

"You hair. Pure gold. A treasure beyond price."

She looked at him in silence for a moment, her eyes wide and luminous.

Jim met her gaze in startled silence, thinking that nobody could accuse Dr. Sarah Burnard of being a belligerent drunk. In fact, he was finding her absolutely adorable.

"I'm a cheat, you know," she announced solemnly. "Jus' a big cheat. Even…even cheated myself."

"How, Sarah?" he asked gently. "What do you mean?"

"Pretended I picked you out to be…baby's father…jus' because of genetics." She shook her head vigorously on the pillow. "Not true."

"Then why, Sarah?" he asked, his heart beating fast as he held the glass to her lips again. "Why did you pick me?"

"Loved you," she said simply. "Loved you since the…since the firs' time I ever saw you, way back in school. Didn't even admit it to…to myself. But it's true."

He drew away and gazed down at her, astonished. "What do you mean, dear?"

She peered up at him, looking confused, and then smiled. "There was nobody like…nobody like Jim Fleming," she murmured. "Never. Made my heart stand still whenever I saw you, right from the very first time. Pretended not to care, because there were always so many pretty girls crowding around you."

"Sarah, I never knew that you…"

"Found your timetable on the floor in English class one day," she confessed with a little giggle, her voice growing more slurred. "Kept it forever. I still have it," she told him solemnly. "In my desk at work."

Jim stared down at her lovely, flushed face against the dark fan of her hair, struggling to absorb all this. "And you're saying that you…you felt this way all these years? That's why you wanted me to be your baby's father?"

Sarah nodded solemnly. "That's the truth," she said, and hiccuped. "Pretended to myself that it was all scientific, because of genetics and stuff, but it wasn't. It was just all about…about loving you, that's all."

"Oh, Sarah—" His voice broke, and he gathered her into his arms, humbled by the tremendous depths of his love, and the knowledge of how badly he had misjudged her. She was shy and reserved and intellectual, and she clung fiercely to her own convictions of right and wrong, but she wasn't cold. There were depths of sweetness and emotion to this woman that he could spend a lifetime exploring and never fully discover.

"Sarah," he whispered against her hair, "will you marry me?"

She pulled away and gazed up at him in childlike surprise. "But," she whispered, her face crumpling, "there's no need, Jim. We're not…there's not going to be a baby. No need to marry me."

"There's every need to marry you, darling," he said, smiling down at her, his face alight with tenderness. "I can't live without you, for one thing. And we'll have more babies. Tell me you'll marry me, sweetheart. I need to hear you say it."

She lay on the pillows, her hair like dark wings around her face, her gray eyes shining as she continued to regard him with that same solemn, owlish look. Then she shook her head. "After," she said.

"After what, dear?" Jim asked, puzzled.

"After you've gone and talked to your father," Sarah said firmly, and closed her eyes, falling asleep almost at once.

Jim looked down at her peaceful, flushed face and laughed in spite of himself. Sarah Burnard had to be the most stubborn woman in the world. And he adored her. He put a hand to his face and was surprised to find his cheeks wet with tears.

THE FIERCE WIND finally began to die in the small hours of the night. By morning the world was still and silent, muffled in white and bathed in sunshine, crowned by a wide, arching prairie sky of serene and cloudless sapphire.

Jim stood at the kitchen window in Sarah's house, sipping a cup of coffee and staring moodily out at the massive snowdrifts, sculpted by the wind into fantasy shapes that curved around the houses and across the streets. Here and there he could see the soft, lumpy mound that indicated a parked car was concealed somewhere beneath the snow.

Snowplow drivers and sanding crews were already at work, their big vehicles rumbling through the white sun-sparkled stillness of the morning. A few cars were beginning to labor down the streets, moving slowly in the wake of the emergency vehicles.

Jim thought of his own car, nosed into the other two and blocking the roadway a few blocks over. He knew that he had to walk down there soon and get it moved out of the way, but he couldn't go yet. He was taut with fear, unable to think about anything but what was happening just now in the other room.

Over the dull, muted roar of the passing trucks Jim could hear another sound, softer but closer to him. It was the muffled conversation between Sarah and her doctor, who had arrived a few minutes earlier and was examining her in the living room.

His jaw clenched with anxiety. Restlessly he moved across the kitchen to pour himself another cup of coffee, his movements stiff and jerky, his eyes darkly shadowed. Jim hadn't slept at all the night before, haunted by a terrible, hollow fear that if he fell asleep something would happen to Sarah. He had sat for hours on the floor by the couch, watching the gentle rise and fall of her breathing, and for hours longer in the opposite chair, just studying the clear, classic beauty of her profile as she slept.

And during all those hours of silent vigil, he had been thinking about what he had found, and what he had come close to losing, a loss that he could hardly bear to contemplate.

"Jim," the doctor's voice called from the other room, "could you come in now, please?"

Hesitantly, dreading what he was about to hear and to see in Sarah's face, Jim walked through the archway into the living room where the morning sun lay in soft rectangles on the floor and burnished the rich jewel tones of the little carousel horse.

Sarah lay on the couch with her hair spread all around her in glorious disarray, her eyes huge and dark in her pale, tired face.

"How do you feel, sweetheart?" Jim asked, walking slowly over to her.

"I have a terrible headache," she said. "Just terrible."

Jim turned with alarm to the doctor, who was packing his bag. Dr. McLellan looked up, blue eyes twinkling. "Nothing to worry about, son," he said cheerfully. "I already told her that the headache is just because she's such a lush."

Jim turned back to Sarah, who was trying to smile at him. "You got me drunk last night," she said. "What a dirty trick."

"Now, Sarah," the doctor said, "don't you be so hard on him. He was only following the doctor's orders. I've known you a long time, my girl. I was pretty sure that the only way to get you to relax, apart from a couple of drinks, would have been a firm blow on the head with a blunt instrument, and all in all this was probably the easiest."

"And you're *sure* it won't do any harm?" Sarah asked, her eyes beseeching, her face anxious.

Dr. McLellan smiled down at her. "Sarah," he said gently, "if you'd gone to the hospital, you'd probably have been given drugs in an attempt to stop the contractions. I don't think a few ounces of alcohol are going to present that much danger under the circumstances."

Sarah nodded uncertainly. The doctor grinned, his face creasing with good humor. "Just don't make a practice of it for the next few months, okay?" he said, winking at Jim as he reached for his coat.

Jim handed the heavy topcoat to the other man automatically, his blue eyes wide and startled. "Then she's..." he began, almost afraid to frame the words.

Dr. McLellan smiled. "I think she is, son. I think you two are still in the baby business. I've got an ambulance coming," he added, "and I'll want to keep her in the hospital for a few days just for tests and safekeeping, but things look fine to me."

"What happened?" Jim asked. "Why did the miscarriage start and then stop like that?"

The little silver-haired doctor plunged an arm into the sleeve of his topcoat, shrugged it on and looked up thoughtfully.

"Could have been any number of things, all of them too complicated and technical to explain easily," he said. "Most likely things just shifted a little in there when she fell, maybe a little tear that triggered the premature contractions, but still minor enough that it was able to repair itself and reverse the process when she relaxed and fell asleep."

Jim and Sarah listened to him in silence, unable to speak, both preoccupied with the amazing wonder of what they still possessed.

Dr. McLellan met Jim's eyes in silence for a moment. He reached out to pat the younger man's arm. "I must say, Jim," he began gently, "that I'm certainly glad you were here last night. I don't want to be an alarmist after the fact, but these are the kinds of situations that can sometimes lead to internal hemorrhage if they're not stopped in time, and even be life-threatening. And we wouldn't want our little Sarah to be facing something like that all at home alone in a blizzard, would we now?"

Jim's face paled beneath the tan, and his mouth went dry with shock. He stared unseeingly at the doctor's weathered, kindly face, thinking again about his own relentless stubbornness, his refusal to compromise and yield, and what it might so easily have cost him. He marveled at the wonderful, precious gift that life had given him, a gift that he had come so dangerously close to squandering just because of his blindness and foolish pride.

There was a muffled sound of voices and stamping feet on the veranda. The outside door opened to admit a gust of fresh morning air and two ambulance attendants carrying a heavy canvas stretcher.

"She has a list of things she needs," Dr. McLellan said to Jim as the two men lifted Sarah carefully into position, "but I don't want her climbing any stairs for a while. Maybe you can pack them up and bring them over to the hospital later."

"Of course," Jim said. He smiled at Sarah, who lay on the high-wheeled stretcher, pale and beautiful against the coarse linen pillow. "I'll be there right away, darling," he told her. "As soon as I can get my car back on the road."

She reached up and placed one hand on his cheek, her eyes soft with love. "Thank you," she murmured. "I love you so much, Jim."

He took her hand and held it, glancing over at the doctor, who was waiting nearby with the two burly young ambulance attendants.

"Dr. McLellan," Jim said abruptly, "how soon do you think she'll be able to travel?"

"Travel?" the doctor asked. "You're planning to go on a trip?"

"Just a little drive in the country," Jim said. "Just to pay a family visit."

He heard Sarah catch her breath beside him, but kept his eyes on the doctor's face.

Sensing from their tension that the question was far more important than it seemed, Dr. McLellan frowned, considering. "Well, let's see now. A few days in the hospital to do some tests, and a few more days' bed rest at home… I think," he concluded with a smile, "that by about the end of next week you should be able to take her for a little drive in the country."

The doctor turned aside for a brief conference with the other two uniformed men. Jim looked down at Sarah, who was gazing up at him, her gray eyes shining.

"Jim...?" she whispered.

"Shh," he murmured, tucking the blankets up around her face and smoothing back her hair. "Just rest now, Sarah."

"But why...what made you...?"

"I had a lot of hours to think last night," he told her, his blue eyes serious and intent. "I began to get just a little glimmering, Sarah, of what love really is while I was sitting there watching you sleep. It's going to take the rest of our lives for me to learn everything I need to know about loving you, but I think I've finally made a pretty good start."

She smiled at him drowsily, squeezing his hand, unable to speak.

"And," he went on slowly, "all that time, thinking about everything that's happened and what was going on just then, I think I started to realize just what it is to be a father, too. And you can't come to that kind of realization without beginning to reorganize your life a little bit."

"Oh, Jim," she whispered. "I hope you know how much I love you."

He bent forward, kissed her lips gently and then followed as the ambulance men wheeled her out and lifted her carefully into the big van, its sides dark with sand and road salt.

Long after the vehicle pulled away from the curb and ground slowly off down the street, followed by the doctor's Cadillac, Jim stood bareheaded in the winter sunlight, gazing after them. His eyes were dark and thoughtful, his face white and tense with emotion.

CHAPTER FOURTEEN

BY THE TIME Sarah's term of enforced bed rest was over and Dr. McLellan finally allowed her back on her feet, winter had turned to spring.

The prairie beyond the city was dotted with melting patches of snow fringed all around the edges with lacy, delicate crystals of ice. Here and there sloughs of meltwater sparkled and shimmered in the hollows, miniature lakes that caught and reflected the endless blue of the sky. Above the shining expanses of water, occasional pairs of waterfowl circled, chattering raucously to one another, as if they might already be discussing the search for a perfect nesting place.

The air was crisp and sunny, though it still carried a keen, bracing edge of frost in the morning, and the breeze caressed the waving carpet of dried grass that was beginning to show a touch of green near its roots. The whole world smelled damp and rich, fresh and full of promise.

Jim glanced over at Sarah, who was gazing out the window of his car, her lips parted, her cheeks flushed with happiness. Her dark, beautiful hair was loose around her face, and she was wearing maternity clothes for the first time—a pair of soft faded jeans, a white turtleneck and a roomy pale blue denim smock that made her gray eyes look smoky and luminous.

She turned to smile at him gently, and Jim's heart turned over as it always did these days whenever he saw her face. His love for her was growing all the time, developing into something so deep and powerful that it almost frightened him. He felt incomplete when he was away from her, as if he couldn't even talk or walk or breathe properly. He needed her presence like food and water, needed her warmth and her smile and the gentleness of her voice or he couldn't exist.

"I got a letter from Maude yesterday," she said suddenly, interrupting his thoughts. "Did I tell you?"

"You mentioned it, but then the phone rang and you didn't get a chance to tell me what she said."

"Well," Sarah said, turning toward him with another smile, "she said she's having a lovely time in Seattle and she's staying another week, then going to Vancouver Island for a couple of weeks."

"Clarence, too?"

"Certainly," Sarah said with a grin. "I think it's generally understood by now that Clarence goes where Maude goes."

Jim grinned back at her, then returned his attention to his driving. "What about his job?"

Sarah waved her hand in dismissal. "Clarence has a pension from his old job. He never really needed to work. He just had that job in your building to keep from getting bored. And nobody can be bored if they follow Maude around."

"Are they living in sin?" Jim asked cheerfully.

"Certainly not," Sarah said with dignity. "Maude's living at her daughter's place, and Clarence is staying with his brother." She paused, recalling the letter. "Maude says," she added, "that Clarence wants to get married and she might consider it later on, but she just doesn't have time right now."

Jim grinned again. "Sounds a lot like a girl I know," he said innocently. Sensing Sarah's sudden tension, he retreated immediately to safer ground. "What are they going to do on Vancouver Island?"

Sarah chuckled. "It's an Elderhostel thing, just for seniors. A survival course. Maude says you have to go rock climbing and traverse a big, deep canyon, hanging on to a rope strung thirty feet above the ground—that sort of thing."

Jim laughed. "*Maude* and *Clarence?*" he asked. "You're kidding. Let's go and do it with them. It sounds like fun."

"We can't. You have to be over sixty to join."

Jim shook his head in awe. "These are great days to be

alive, you know that?'' He was silent for a moment. ''So,'' he said finally, treading carefully, ''Maude won't be coming back for a long time? She won't be looking after the kids anymore?''

Sarah gave him a quick, sidelong glance and then looked straight ahead at the lacy drifts of cloud along the mountains. ''I told you, Jim. The kids are staying where they are. They're quite happy there.''

''Look, I might have something to say about that, you know,'' Jim began abruptly. ''After all, those kids are—'' But then, seeing the sudden nervous movement of her hands and the way she quickly averted her face, he caught himself and went on in a gentler tone. ''I just miss them so much. I want you to tell me where they're living. I need to see them, Sarah.''

''I know,'' she said evasively. ''They're anxious to see you, too, Jim. They talk about you all the time, especially Ellie. But I wanted to be with you the first time you went, so we've had to wait until the doctor allowed me up again.''

''But we'll go right away?'' he persisted. ''Tomorrow maybe?''

''Right away,'' Sarah promised. ''As soon as we can.'' She looked at him, hesitating, as if about to say more, and then gave a little jump. ''Oh!'' she said, pressing her hand to her abdomen. ''Oh, Jim!''

He ground the car to a halt, pulling hastily over onto the shoulder and turning to her, his face white. ''What is it, Sarah?'' he asked urgently. ''What is it, dear? More pain?''

She looked up at him with shining eyes, her lips trembling. ''The baby,'' she whispered. ''I felt the baby move. Oh, Jim, this is the very first time.''

He stared at her, breaking slowly into a delighted grin. ''No kidding? He really moved? What did it feel like?''

Sarah smiled, closing her eyes with a blissful little sigh. ''Like...butterfly wings. Just the most delicate, gentle little— Oh, there, it's happening again,'' she said breathlessly. ''Feel it, Jim.''

She took his hand and held it against the small swelling beneath her smock. He leaned forward intently and then shook his head. "Can't feel a thing."

Sarah smiled. "You will. Just wait a few months till he's big enough to play football in there."

Jim smiled, lifting away a shining strand of her hair and bending to kiss her ear. "Are you sorry that we let them tell us?"

"That he's a boy?" Sarah shook her head. "I'm glad to know in advance. I always sort of assumed it was a girl, so this way I have time to adjust."

Jim grinned. "It doesn't take any adjustment for me. I'm just going to love him."

Sarah glanced thoughtfully over at him as he moved back behind the wheel and pulled out into the driving lane again. "You mean you wouldn't want to have a girl?"

"Sure," Jim said. "I'd love to have a little girl. Especially one that looked like you," he added, smiling at Sarah. "It's just that men are so much easier to understand. When I'm just an amateur, learning all this for the first time, I think I'd rather start out with a guy."

Sarah laughed. "And," she teased, "I suppose you're going to insist on calling the poor child Jameson Kirkland Fleming the Fifth?"

Jim's smile faded, and his mouth tightened involuntarily. "Not likely," he said tersely. "I'd much rather call him Butch, to be honest with you."

Sarah looked at him, troubled by the pain in his voice, and he turned to meet her eyes briefly.

"Jim," she murmured, "this is really hard for you, isn't it? Going to see your father, I mean."

"Sure it's hard," Jim said, staring straight ahead once more. "It's the hardest thing I've ever done. I'm scared, Sarah."

"Scared? Why would you be scared? What can he do to you?"

"It's not what he can do," Jim said, his handsome, sculpted face taut with concern. "It's just that...Sarah, what if I can't stand him? What if I honestly try, but the old feelings are just too strong and I find I can't bear to be in the same room with the man despite my best intentions?"

"What do you mean, Jim?"

"I mean, what happens then, Sarah? Do I lose you, after all, if I find that I'm just not able to make peace with him?"

Sarah looked steadily at his fine, aristocratic profile, then turned away. "We'll cross that bridge when we come to it," she said. "Here we are," she added as they swung into the long, tree-lined drive leading up to the big stone ranch house.

Jim gripped the wheel in white-knuckled hands, stunned by the experience of driving for the first time in more than a decade down this stretch of road that was so familiar and yet so deeply strange, like something from another life.

He parked by the garage, got out and walked around to open Sarah's door, amazed by the smells of the ranch, of wet soil and animals and rich alfalfa bales damp beneath a warm spring sun. The old remembered scents brought back his boyhood with startling vividness. He felt confused and disoriented, like a time traveler moving too swiftly between different ages.

Sarah gripped his hand. Jim squeezed her fingers gratefully, walking beside her up the curving flagstone path to the wide front door.

She pushed the door open with an easy familiarity that surprised him, and they stepped into the foyer. Jim blinked and gazed around, lost in the wonder of returning to this house that he had loved so much, where he had spent all the early years of his life. The rooms seemed crowded with memories and ghosts, and the impression was suddenly heightened by a far-off remembered burst of childish voices and laughter.

Jim started and lifted his head, his blue eyes puzzled. It was so strange to hear the ghostly sounds of childlike voices in this silent, luxurious house. He knew that it was just a trick of his overwrought imagination, a recollection of his own childhood days with his friends. Nevertheless, the distant, muted sounds had seemed so eerily real that he glanced down quickly to see if Sarah had heard anything.

But she was gazing straight ahead, her delicate face pale and tense with emotion. Jim knew how much this visit meant to her, and how vitally important it was, for her sake, that he keep a firm grip on himself. He took a deep breath, squared his shoulders and turned toward the hallway.

A woman appeared in the entrance to the living room. She was a full-blooded Blackfoot Indian, wearing a vivid orange tent dress, her thick graying braids lying on her shoulders. Her body was immensely tall and broad, and she had a slow-moving, massive dignity and an ageless, bronzed face that radiated wisdom and kindness.

"Hi, Clarice," Jim said softly.

The woman regarded him steadily, a light shining deep in her black eyes. But when she spoke, her voice was as brusque and matter-of-fact as if she had seen him only the day before.

"Well, you've certainly turned into a good-looking boy, Jimmy," she said. "Come in. They're expecting you. And mind you wipe your feet before you step on that hardwood."

"How's Eloise?" Jim asked, turning obediently to the mat and scrubbing his feet as vigorously as if he were ten years old again.

Eloise was Clarice's sister, as small and thin and nervous as Clarice was broad and placid. The two of them had been working in Jameson Fleming's household since they were teenagers, and they were a warm, rich part of Jim's earliest childhood memories.

"Eloise is just fine. She's in the kitchen," Clarice said. "With you-know-who," she added to Sarah, rolling her dark eyes eloquently.

Sarah nodded back at her, smiling. Jim cast both of them another puzzled glance and then fell into step behind Sarah, following Clarice's massive orange form down the hallway.

Part of him was busy with surface impressions: how light and graceful Clarice still was on her feet, despite her bulk, how the house still carried that old tantalizing aroma of cookies and furniture polish, how much he had missed the objects and places of his childhood, like the big painted leather globe on its wooden claw feet, and the secret curtained window seat in the morning room....

Bur on a deeper level he was suffering a powerful, wrenching crisis of emotion. He was drawn relentlessly down the hall toward his father's library, pulled along by the power of his love for the woman beside him. Inside, though, part of him was resisting, longing to escape, yearning to run back through the foyer and out the door into the fresh air, far away from this gracious, quiet house with all its painful memories and unbearable conflicts.

Sarah took his arm and squeezed it gently, letting her head rest against his shoulder for a brief moment of reassurance before she smiled at Clarice and walked past her through the open door of the library. Jim drew a deep breath, paused to still the wild beating of his heart and followed Sarah into the room, then stopped abruptly in confusion.

Jameson Fleming sat casually in a big oak chair at the side of the room, wearing slacks and a cardigan, his silver hair carefully brushed. He was leaning back in his chair, smiling as he explained something to Billy, who sat beside him, frowning intently at the figures on a computer screen.

Jim continued to stare at the two of them, his blue eyes wide with disbelief, his face stunned.

"Hello, Sarah," Jameson said, his voice gentle with affection. "It's so good to see you back on your feet, dear." Then he turned to Jim. "Hello, son," he said as casually as if Jim was in the habit of dropping in every day for lunch.

Jim was saved from having to respond by Billy, who glanced over his shoulder with a cheerful grin, his thin, freckled face alight with happiness. "Hi, Sarah," he said. "Hi, Jim. Good to see you."

Jim gazed back at him, his throat tight with emotion. Billy looked so different, so easy and relaxed. Jim realized in amazement that this was the first time he had ever seen the boy give him a real smile instead of that customary streetwise, sardonic grin. He grappled with his own feelings, beginning to understand at last the tremendous strain that Billy must have been under during all those months.

Billy was finally wearing some new clothes, too—jeans faded almost white, a tooled leather belt with a big shiny buckle, a clean, soft white shirt and fine suede moccasins. Jim realized that somebody had at last gotten Billy into a new wardrobe, and they had managed it simply by taking the trouble to find out what kind of clothes the boy really wanted to wear.

One of his hands was still lightly bandaged, and he kept it in his lap. The other played idly over the keyboard of the computer.

"This boy's a marvel, you know," Jameson was saying proudly to Sarah. "A genuine mathematical genius. A few basic accounting courses, and I could probably turn my entire business over to him."

Jim still felt a little dizzy, staggered by everything that had happened, by the strangeness of actually being in this room again and the incredible implications of Billy's presence. He cleared his throat and tried to smile at the boy.

"I thought you weren't all that interested in school, Billy," he said.

"Not *school,*" Billy said. "Not dumb essays and stuff. But this..." He waved his hand at the figures on the screen, his eyes shining. "This stuff is just so *neat.*"

Jim turned to Sarah, still groping to understand. She watched him quietly, her gray eyes gentle with love and concern.

"Sarah," he began, "why didn't you tell me they were here?"

"I couldn't, Jim," she said, returning his gaze steadily. "We were all afraid that if we told you when you first got home, you'd come charging out here and insist on taking them away. And that would have been terrible."

He was silent, thinking. "You're probably right," he said, giving her a wan, mirthless smile. "That's probably exactly what I would have done, considering the way I was feeling back then. How long have they been here?"

"Ever since we found them," Sarah said quietly. "They were in pretty rough shape, Jim, and we knew they were going to need full-time care for a while. And we were all too worn out to take it on, so we just brought them out here and turned them over to Clarice."

Jim grinned faintly at Billy. "I remember Clarice's medical remedies," he said. "Did she burn bits of rabbit fur over your bed and dance around in a circle?"

Billy laughed, a sound that Jim had never heard, warm and infectious in the quiet, book-lined room. "Not exactly," he said, "but she ground up some kind of root into paste and put it on my hands and feet, and it took the pain away just like magic."

He smiled at the memory, and the adults in the room smiled with him, forgetting the tension of the moment in his easy, boyish spontaneity.

"Arthur, too," Billy added as an afterthought. "She put the same stuff on his diaper rash, and he quit screaming right away. Poor little guy," he added, his face shadowing briefly.

As if in response to the mention of his own name, Arthur appeared in the doorway in the arms of Maureen. Both of them beamed at the assembled group.

If the baby had suffered recently, he showed no signs of it now. He looked clean and plump, grown-up and splendid in emerald-green corduroy overalls and a dark green plaid shirt, and his round face was blazing with excitement.

"Da!" he shouted, catching sight of Jim. "Da da! Da!"

"Listen to that," Jim said, grinning foolishly. "Arthur's calling me Daddy."

"No, he isn't," Billy said. "It's the only word he knows, the dummy. He calls everything Daddy."

Arthur struggled in Maureen's arms and demanded to be put down, but she held him firmly, covering his face and neck with kisses.

Jim, who was studying the baby with fond attention, suddenly gave a little start of surprise. "I'll be damned," he murmured in awe. "Arthur's wearing the Fleming clan tartan."

"Indeed he is," Maureen said serenely. "We had a small bolt of fabric left, and Eloise made up a few things for our baby. Three shirts and a kilt," she added with satisfaction.

"A *kilt?*" Jim asked, choking a little. "Arthur has a *kilt?*"

"Aye, he does," Maureen said, overdoing the Scottish accent and grinning at Sarah, "and a fine wee mannie he looks in it, too."

Arthur twisted to pat her cheeks and plant a damp kiss near her eye, then began to squirm once more, clamoring to be released.

"Watch this," Maureen said proudly, setting him down on the floor and holding him briefly to steady him.

She lifted her hands away carefully. Arthur took three wobbling steps across the floor, his eyes wide with awe at his own daring. He lurched forward into Jim's hands, and Jim swept him aloft, laughing and kissing him while Arthur patted the big man's cheeks with a complacent smile.

Jim held the baby and turned to his father, his face growing taut and serious. The others in the room fell silent, watching.

"How long are they staying?" he asked Jameson, his voice rough with emotion.

"What do you mean, son?" Jameson said.

"Just what I said. What do you plan to do with them? How long are you going to let them stay here?"

"This is their home, son," Jameson said quietly. "They live here."

While Jim stared at him in amazement, Jameson turned to Sarah with a gentle smile. "I did what you advised, Sarah, and used my political leverage shamelessly to expedite things. The papers for legal guardianship arrived yesterday by courier. Now we can begin adoption proceedings."

Jim held Arthur, his eyes wide, his face pale with shock. "You're going to *adopt* these kids?" he asked his father. "All three of them?"

"Well, we certainly hope so," Jameson said while Maureen

smiled mistily and reached over to place a gentle hand on Billy's shoulder. "Except...well, son, I was hoping to talk it over with you first."

Jim looked at his father in amazement. It *sounded* as if he was asking for Jim's blessing. Jim stood speechless, then turned aside, briefly distracted by Arthur, who was burrowing energetically under his sweater, searching for his shirt pocket and the soft felt pen that Jim always carried.

"The other pocket, Arthur," he murmured. "Try the other pocket."

He glanced into the hallway behind Maureen, his face reflecting a sudden, wistful anxiety. "Where's Ellie?" he asked.

"Where she loves to be best of all—in the kitchen with Eloise," Maureen said. "That child prepared the entire main course for our luncheon today all by herself. And anybody who doesn't praise it to the skies," she added sternly, "will have *me* to answer to, let me tell you."

Maureen's red hair sparked fire, and her blue eyes looked so fierce that the others in the room were startled, then amused.

Maureen moved across the room, pausing to give Sarah a fond little hug and exchange a few murmured words before she stopped beside Jim and gazed up at Arthur, who was clutching the pen triumphantly in his hand. Smears of color already marked his face, and a number of experimental strokes trailed over his fat fists and onto his shirt cuffs.

"It's washable, Aunt Mo," Jim said humbly.

Maureen ignored him, still glaring at Arthur, hands on hips. "Look at you," she said with mock outrage. "All bathed and dressed not twenty minutes ago, and now we need to do it all over."

Arthur beamed, holding the pen out to her. Maureen's face softened, and she smiled at Jim, her flower-blue eyes shining with rich depths of happiness and contentment that he had never seen in her before. She lifted the chuckling baby from his arms.

"I'll just tend to this little man," she said, moving briskly from the room, "and then we'll eat. Billy, come help me for a minute, would you dear?"

Billy smiled at her with warm affection and followed her from the room, murmuring something in an undertone that made her throw her bright head back and laugh heartily.

The laughter lingered in the air when they were gone and Jim stood alone with Sarah and his father in the quiet room.

Jim's mind whirled. Part of him was outraged by everything that had happened, by the way circumstances had somehow slipped so far beyond his control. They had taken charge of everything, these people around him.

But even in the midst of his anger he recalled that rich look of sweet fulfillment in his aunt's blue eyes—Maureen, whom he had always loved, and who had never looked as contented as she did today. He thought of the aura of security and happiness that shone in Billy's eyes and brightened Arthur's plump baby face, and the wonderful life that the three children could have growing up in this big comfortable house in the country.

Most of all, he thought of his father standing quietly opposite him, of the kind of family love and warmth that had been denied the older man through all these years and that was now, incredibly, in Jim's power to give back to him.

It was too much to ask of any man, Jim thought in anguish. He knew in his rational mind that leaving the children here was the best solution for everybody else, but it was wrenching for him. He still didn't know if he had any feelings at all for his father, if he could even bear to have anything to do with him. What if he walked out of this house, leaving the children behind, and then wasn't able to come back again? How much did he have to sacrifice to make amends for the past?

His chest tightened with nervousness. He gripped the edge of the desk to steady himself while the other two watched him silently. At last he turned to Sarah.

"Could you leave us alone for a minute, please, Sarah?" he said. "I'd like to talk with my father."

SARAH SAT with the others in the morning room, smiling automatically at the warm chatter all around her. But she felt tense and awkward, and her eyes kept turning anxiously to the closed door of the library. She knew, without really framing the thought, that whatever was happening behind that broad oak door was of vital important to her. Not until the door opened and she saw Jim's face would she really know what her future was going to be.

She couldn't live with a man who nursed the kind of bitterness Jim had carried around with him all these years. Sarah understood too well that people who nourished that kind of unforgiving anger tended sooner or later to sour the lives of everybody close to them. And yet the thought of a life without this man had become intolerable, almost unthinkable.

She sighed involuntarily and put an arm around Ellie, who was nestled beside her on the couch, cuddling the little girl warmly. Across the room from them Maureen and Billy sat opposite each other over a chessboard on a big drum table, their faces alight with fierce competitiveness.

"That game's been going on for three days," Ellie whispered to Sarah. "They both take forever to decide what they're going to do next."

Sarah smiled down at her. Of all the children, Ellie had changed most dramatically, Sarah thought. Ellie had always been the mother in her little family, the one who worried about everyone's welfare and wanted them to be happy and safe. Back in Jim's apartment her concerns about the future had often shadowed her thin little face, giving her a wan, pinched expression even in the midst of happiness.

Now, though, in a spacious, warm house surrounded by people she loved, secure at last in the knowledge that she was loved in return and never had to leave, Ellie had blossomed. Her face was pink with happiness, her eyes sparkling with a new confidence and a shy, sweet joy that brought a lump to Sarah's throat.

But as she gazed down at the little girl, Sarah saw a look of sudden tension appear on Ellie's face. Ellie was gazing through the broad archway into the dining room where Eloise moved silently around, putting the finishing touches on a festive, beautifully decorated luncheon table.

Sarah followed Ellie's eyes, seeing at once the source of the child's concern. Arthur had crawled up onto one of the chairs near the dining table and was standing on it, one fat hand gripping the chair back as he studied the big centerpiece of spring flowers that Ellie had just arranged with such care.

"He's going to try to get into those flowers," Ellie muttered darkly. "I just know he is."

Sarah glanced at Arthur, recognizing the look of thoughtful sweetness that invariably appeared on the baby's face just before he did something especially terrible.

"I think you're right, Ellie," she murmured. "He's about to make his move."

Ellie got up swiftly and crossed the shining hardwood floor to grasp Arthur by his plump corduroy middle and lift him down. He shouted in protest and began to drum his heels on the floor, causing the chess players to look up in surprise.

But before anyone could speak the library door opened and the two men emerged, their faces still and silent. Father and son paused in the hallway and stood a little apart from each other while the others glanced up at them nervously.

Only Arthur failed to recognize the tension in the room. He crowed when he saw Jameson, turned over to brace his hands on the floor and raise his small posterior into the air, then pushed himself erect. With cautious, wavering steps he crossed the floor, grasped the older man's trouser leg and tugged, raising his arms to be picked up.

Jameson smiled and lifted the baby into his arms, reaching into one pocket to give him a red jelly bean. Arthur chuckled and examined the bright candy for a moment with deep satisfaction before popping it into his mouth.

Ellie came over behind her little brother, smiling shyly up at Jim and leaning with total lack of self-consciousness against Jameson's side. The senator gazed tenderly down at the little girl, stroking her shining hair with his brown, veined hand.

Sarah felt a lump in her throat at the sight of the tall, dignified statesman with those two bright-haired children. She was still afraid to look at Jim, but she glanced anxiously into Jameson's blue eyes, hoping to read something there about what had happened between them.

Jameson smiled at her, his craggy face warm and tender. "Sarah," he said, clearing his throat awkwardly and reaching out to touch Jim's arm with a gentle hand, "I believe my son has something to say to you."

Sarah looked over at Jim then, realizing as soon as she saw his face that she was probably never going to learn exactly what had happened behind that closed door. But it didn't matter anymore.

Jim looked washed clean and completely at peace, his handsome face almost transparent with relief and a new, gentle strength that had never been there in the past. Sarah caught her breath as she gazed at him, thinking that he looked both younger and more mature than he had just a few hours earlier.

He met her eyes, his blue gaze steady and unwavering. "I love you, Sarah," he said quietly. "Will you marry me?"

Sarah got slowly to her feet, awed by the way he looked. Jim Fleming had always been larger than life to her, a wonderfully handsome golden man, but just now he seemed rimmed and suffused with gold, burnished with a glowing aura that touched his face and hair with fire and set him somehow apart.

Maybe it was a trick of the spring sunlight pouring through the tall windows of the morning room, but Sarah had the feeling that he was standing just beyond her at the edge of a wondrous, enchanted world where the air was richer and warmer and the rivers flowed with happiness, and he was inviting her to come and join him there.

She smiled, her eyes misty, and crossed the room toward him, oblivious to everyone else. Jim took her in his arms, and she could feel the warmth that flowed between them, feel his body rejoice in the tides of rich, womanly love that she didn't have to hold back any longer.

His lips finally found hers. They clung together, wrapped in stillness, bathed in sunshine. The warm, sweet fire of their kiss filled Sarah with overwhelming joy, and a deep, rich certainty that all the lost and wandering years were finally over.

Her family man had found his way home at last.

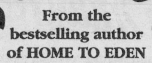

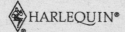

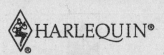

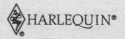